TEXAS ANGEL

Praise for
JUDITH PELLA'S
Texas Angel* and *Heaven's Road

Judith Pella in *Texas Angel* shows how two extreme lifestyles come together and are drastically touched by God's love.

—*Christian Library Journal*

" "

Historical fiction fans will love this offering from Pella.

—*Church Libraries,* about *Texas Angel*

" "

You'll be riveted by this remarkable tale of adventure and romance that brings life to the courageous pioneers and the magnificence of God's plan.

—*Crossings,* about *Texas Angel*

" "

Judith Pella's *Texas Angel* sweeps you back to the Old West where romance and adventure await you.

—*Christianbook.com*

" "

As one would expect, Ms. Pella's skillful pen has given us another memorable story. Never one to disappoint, she always creates characters with such depth, you believe they really lived.

—*Rendezvous,* about *Heaven's Road*

TWO BESTSELLING NOVELS
IN One Volume

TEXAS ANGEL

Also includes
HEAVEN'S ROAD

JUDITH PELLA

BETHANYHOUSE
MINNEAPOLIS, MINNESOTA

Texas Angel

Published previously in two separate volumes:
Texas Angel © 1999
Heaven's Road © 2000

Cover illustration by William Graf/Paul Higdon
Cover design by Paul Higdon

Unless otherwise identified, Scripture quotations are from the King James Version of the Bible.

Published by Bethany House Publishers
11400 Hampshire Avenue South
Bloomington, Minnesota 55438

Bethany House Publishers is a division of
Baker Publishing Group, Grand Rapids, Michigan.

Printed in the United States of America

Library of Congress Cataloging-in-Publication Data is available for this title.

ISBN 978-0-7642-0565-1

JUDITH PELLA is the author of several historical fiction series, both on her own and in collaboration with Michael Phillips and Tracie Peterson. The extraordinary seven-book series, THE RUSSIANS, the first three written with Phillips, showcases her creativity and skill as a historian as well as a fiction writer. A Bachelor of Arts degree in social studies, along with a career in nursing and teaching, lend depth to her storytelling abilities, providing readers with memorable novels in a variety of genres. She and her family make their home in northern California.

Books by
Judith Pella

Beloved Stranger

*The Stonewycke Trilogy**

Texas Angel

Mark of the Cross

Daughters of Fortune

Written on the Wind

Somewhere a Song

Toward the Sunrise

Homeward My Heart

Patchwork Circle

Bachelor's Puzzle

Sister's Choice

***with Michael Phillips**

TEXAS ANGEL

PART ONE

APRIL 1834

CHAPTER 1

THE TERRIBLE SECRET WAS OUT. Elise Toussaint Hearne had hoped for more than merely a year of wedded bliss before her happy life shattered. In fact, even now she sat alone in her room, still hoping somehow there would be a way to salvage it. Maybe she would not be summoned to answer for her awful lie. Perhaps her husband, Kendell, would show mercy on her for the sake of his love and for the child she had borne him.

When he had confronted her an hour ago with the incriminating documents, which she so poorly denied, he had been in complete shock. As he shambled from her room, shoulders hunched forward like a broken man, she had not been able to venture even a guess at what he would do next. She had simply hovered silently in her room, now nearly pitch dark since the sun had set behind the woods dominating the west side of the Hearne plantation. Perhaps Kendell had gone into town to get drunk. When he sobered up in the morning, he'd have a better perspective.

But Elise feared her husband had gone instead to where he always went when he had problems: to his parents—his mother specifically.

Was it possible they would discount the papers as mere slander, lies that were so apt to surface at election time? And if they believed the papers, would they show mercy on their daughter-in-law, for whom they had developed some fondness in the time she had been married to their son and living in their home?

Not likely.

William Hearne cared only about becoming governor of South Carolina. He liked Elise, but his ambitions came first. Nevertheless, it was not he who worried Elise as much as her mother-in-law did. Daphne

Hearne had little love for Elise, for no one was good enough for her only son. Lately Mother Hearne had become more tolerant because Elise had proven herself of some worth by bearing a sweet granddaughter. Elise shuddered at how quickly that toleration would cease when she learned of the horrible deception Elise had carried into her marriage.

The clock on the mantel struck nine, and Elise gasped at the intrusive sound that sent her heart racing like a panicked horse. Kendell had been gone over an hour. What was he doing? Where had he gone? And what of her plight? How could she face the terrible consequences of what she had done?

Elise shivered as a breeze lifted the lace curtain on the window. But it wasn't the cold of the spring night that made her tremble so. Her terror arose from the dreadful reality that her sweet life was about to change forever. She must face the possibility that she could lose everything. The man she loved, her child—oh, dear God, not my child!

"I mustn't think that way," she muttered, pulling a quilt over her icy cold body as she lay on her bed, knees curled up against her chest, as if for protection. But she found no comfort. The warmth of the covers could not penetrate the bone-deep chill of her fear.

A knock at the door startled Elise again. She groaned inwardly but said nothing. Maybe whoever it was would think her asleep and go away. But the dreaded sound came again.

"Miz Elise, the massa wants to see you," called Carrie, Elise's maid.

Still Elise remained silent. How odd to feel so vulnerable in her own home, her own bedroom. She had come to love the Hearne plantation, located just outside of Charleston. She had never known a real home, and in spite of Daphne's contentious nature, she had come to think of this place as such. The Hearnes were a real family. They cared about each other. Kendell's sisters, two of them, came often to visit. Even the slaves seemed happy and content.

Elise's hope of reprieve plummeted again when the door opened. Like a coward, she squeezed her eyes shut as if that would block out reality, but she knew the slave had come into the room and was walking toward the bed.

"Miz Elise, he says it don't matter if you are asleep. You gots to come."

Elise groaned out loud this time. "I . . . am not feeling well."

"He says it don't matter. He will come after you if he must. He's right distraught."

Elise debated on further resistance. Let him come up and drag her from her bed. What did it matter? Her life was over anyway. But an image sprang to her mind of such a scene—her flailing and screaming, his sweating and cursing, the whole house privy to her disgrace.

No, if she must fall, she would do so with dignity. There was still a small chance of reprieve.

"All right, Carrie. I will be down in a minute."

"Can I help you with anything, ma'am?"

"No, I can manage. You may leave now." When the slave hesitated, Elise added with as reassuring a tone as she could feign, "I will come. Don't worry."

Carrie left, and Elise crawled from her bed feeling as if she were leaving the only safe haven she would ever know. She went to her dressing table and lit a candle. The reflection that greeted her in the oval mirror was dim and shadowed. How very appropriate, she thought. But even the shadows could not hide the pallor of her skin nor the dark circles under her eyes. She pinched her cheeks in a useless attempt to give the appearance of health. She also tried to put her rumpled hair into some order by gathering the mass of thick dark curls—Much too dark! Much too curly!—and twisting them into a knot, which she fixed to the back of her head with a comb. The effect was severe, emphasizing her present ashen look, but perhaps that would work to her advantage. Finally, she straightened her navy blue linen day dress. It had been a mistake to take to her bed fully clothed.

Then, taking a deep, determined breath, she headed for the door and the fate that awaited her.

CHAPTER 2

THEY WERE WAITING FOR HER in the drawing room. Mother Hearne was seated on the satin divan, dressed in matronly brown taffeta. She looked the picture of southern virtue and womanhood. She was an attractive woman with light brown hair, a long aristocratic nose, and cold blue eyes. Elise tried to avoid those eyes as she entered the room but felt them fixed firmly upon her, laden with reproach.

Kendell was standing by the hearth. His eyes, blue like his mother's but not cold at all, were now purposefully averted from his wife. Elise, too, avoided looking at him, not wanting to witness again the tortured pain she was certain still resided there. He was a genteel man, and it had been that quality more than his rather plain and nondescript looks that had won Elise's heart. Some interpreted his soft-spoken, kindly nature as weakness. Indeed, he was not an aggressive, forceful man. But Elise refused to believe he was truly weak. Still, she had been barely eighteen when they had married, so in love and blind to reality. Now she feared that particular reality was about to be her undoing.

It was William Hearne who spoke first. "Elise, please be seated." His tone was stern but not harsh.

Elise didn't want to sit, but neither did she want to begin this interview by disobeying her father-in-law. She thus sat on the very edge of a ladder-back chair, positioned so that she had a direct view of William when she looked straight ahead, but little of her husband or mother-in-law. Father Hearne seemed the safest refuge for the moment. He was seated by a small table that held a decanter and glasses. In his hand he held a glass of bourbon, his drink of preference.

With his free hand, Hearne held up the envelope Elise had seen earlier. "You are familiar with this?"

She nodded.

"What have you to say for yourself?"

"It is a lie," she replied, silently cursing the fact that she could not make her voice sound convincing.

"I do not deny the malicious intent of these papers," Hearne said. "They could well damage my political aspirations. I do not want to believe them."

"Then don't," Elise answered desperately. "Burn them, and the entire matter will soon be forgotten. Why give place to those who would deal in dirty politics?"

"This goes far beyond politics," Daphne said. "We cannot blithely ignore this thing. The very name of our family could be blackened forever."

That was a poor choice of words, and everyone knew it. A heavy silence fell upon the little group. Elise stared at her hands folded primly in her lap.

Finally William spoke. "Do you know of the painting mentioned in the letter?"

"No. There are no paintings of my mother. My parents were never so wealthy that they could afford such extravagances."

"Yet the painting was in your father's possession before it was forfeited in a game of chance."

Ah, Papa! Elise had always known her father's gambling habit would come to no good. The letter in William's hand told how Dorian Toussaint had paid off a debt with the deed to his modest property in New Orleans. Somehow the painting had been left behind in the house, which was careless even for Papa. It was, in the words of the letter, "A very touching family portrait" of Dorian Toussaint and a woman of tan complexion holding a very young infant. Elise herself had never seen it and, until the arrival of the letter, had not known of its existence. Papa had been so careful to keep his wife's true identity a secret. But he was old now, and his mind was often muddled by strong spirits.

William went on as if his daughter-in-law had not read the letter herself. "The house and its contents came into the possession of Maurice Thomson. Your father's likeness in the painting is easily identifiable and undeniable. But Mr. Thomson also recognized the woman seated in front of your father. She was obviously his wife."

Even in her present distress, Elise found herself wondering about the woman in the painting and longed for a chance to see it. Her mother had died when she was only a few months old, so Elise had never known her. What did she look like? Was she as beautiful as her father always said? She must have been for him to have risked so much to marry her.

Suddenly an inspiration struck Elise. "Who is to say the woman in the painting is my mother?"

"Your mother's name was Claire, was it not? That name is inscribed with your father's name on the back of the portrait. But Mr. Thomson is sending it to us that we may judge for ourselves."

"That is most kind of him," Elise replied dryly.

"Thomson makes a strong claim," William continued, pointedly ignoring her words. "He says the woman named Claire Toussaint was once named Jewel and was his property. He claims your mother was a runaway slave."

It was the first time anyone had dared to speak the word *slave* out loud. It had the force of a blow, and Elise winced at the sound of it. Her reserve, which she had been clutching as desperately as a drowning person grasps a floating log, began to crumble.

How much longer could she deny it? The letter was true! All of it. Her mother had been a quadroon woman and a slave. Papa had told Elise the entire story but had waited until her wedding day to do so. She had known nothing until that day. She had been raised a white female among the gentry, though her father was bankrupt more often than not. He had fallen in love with Claire in New Orleans and had helped her escape to Pennsylvania, where they married and where Elise was born. Papa said Claire could pass for white by claiming to be of French extraction, and she did so until her untimely death. It had then been an easy matter for him to continue the ruse. Elise looked as white as Mother Hearne herself except for her hair, which was the color of a lump of coal, and her rich chocolate brown eyes. Papa said her eyes were just like her mother's. And if so, the portrait would surely reveal that the woman in it was indeed Elise's mother.

"It's true, isn't it?" Mother Hearne said, full of accusation. Her eyes were narrow and incisive, showing no hint of a willingness to forgive. "Don't deny it, girl! I see it in your face. You have deceived us—you . . . you nigger!"

"Mother!" exclaimed Kendell, rousing as if from a stupor. Poor Kendell. His face was ashen, his lips trembling as he fought to hold his composure.

Elise's own emotion broke at last, and tears spilled from her eyes. "Please . . ." Denials were no use now, not after seeing her husband's agony. She owed him the truth. "Forgive me. . . ." Her sobs made further speech difficult.

"No . . . it can't be. . . ." Kendell murmured.

"You must let me explain," Elise managed to say.

"There can be no acceptable explanation," Daphne said. "You have disgraced this family. We will never be able to hold up our heads in society again. Our son has married the child of a slave—she is a slave herself for that matter. Our granddaughter is—" But as Daphne spoke, the full import of what she was saying hit her, and she was stricken momentarily to silence. "I . . . I think I shall faint. . . ."

"I didn't know," Elise blurted through her tears. "That is"—she focused imploring eyes upon her husband—"my father told me the morning of our wedding. I was confused and afraid."

"And you think that is reason enough to have deceived us?" William challenged.

"I didn't know what to do. . . ."

"We will never believe another word you say!" cried Daphne, who had not fainted and in fact had never fainted in her life. "You knew what shame such a thing would bring upon your husband and his family. That is why you kept it a secret."

"I thought love would be enough—"

"Don't speak that word. It is a foul obscenity from your lips. You know nothing of it. I doubt you are capable of love. I feared when you married—and I am certain of it now—that you married Kendell for money and security only."

"It's not true!"

"You lying wench."

"Kendell, you know I love you."

Kendell looked away from Elise, and she knew in that dreadful moment she would find no mercy, no forgiveness from him. If her husband turned away from her, all was hopeless. What would happen now? The question echoed in her mind, but she could not voice it. She was not surprised that it was the level-headed, shrewd William who broached the subject.

"Before we called you," he said, "Kendell, Mrs. Hearne, and I discussed what we ought to do if these allegations were true. This is not easy for any of us. In the last year we have accepted you as part of our family. Indeed, we have grown fond of you—" A loud harrumph from Daphne clearly indicated what she thought of that statement. Casting his wife a quick glance before giving a lame shrug, William went on. "Well, anyway, you have taken on our name and given birth to our blood. We have accepted you and lavished upon you all the finest comforts, yet you have repaid us with the most heinous of deceptions. There can be no way for life to continue as it was. There is no way our son can continue in a marriage to one such as you."

A sob escaped Elise's lips before she could rein it back.

"The state of South Carolina," William continued, ignoring Elise's display of emotion, "does not recognize divorce. At twenty-two, our son's life is ruined because of you. He can never marry again. . . ."

"Please!" Elise begged. "We can go far away from here where no one knows us. We can have a life together. We could be happy—"

"Do you think our son wants to spend his life with a nigger, raising little pickaninnies?" Daphne scoffed. "You foolish woman!"

"Mrs. Hearne," William said, "I don't believe Elise yet fully understands the implications of her plight. Even if we were to permit Kendell to stay with you, even if he wanted to do so, it is not our decision to make. Your mother was the property of Maurice Thomson. She was never a free woman but always a fugitive slave. That means she and her offspring are Thomson's property. You are Thomson's slave."

"No!" screamed Elise.

"If Kendell would help you run away, he would be a felon himself. But he would never do that because he has too much respect for the system in which he was nurtured." William gulped down the bourbon he had ignored until now. "Thomson's lawyer will be here in a few days to verify his claims and to collect his . . . property."

"You can't do this!" Elise jumped from her seat and threw herself at her father-in-law's feet. "I beg you. Think of your granddaughter . . . for her sake, please don't do this!"

"You belong with your own kind," William said coldly.

Elise then went to her husband and fell on her knees before him. "Kendell! You could not be so cruel. Our baby . . . what will become of her . . . of me? Has your love grown cold so quickly? I know you must still care. Have mercy on us!"

He turned his back on her. And in that moment, there on her knees before a rich white planter, she truly felt who she was—a despised slave, and nothing more.

CHAPTER 3

A BILLOWING CLOUD OF DUST ENVELOPED the wagon, blurring the eyes of the passengers, choking their throats, and dampening their spirits. Benjamin Sinclair, seated next to the driver of the wagon, was thirty-three years old, tall, lean, and, despite his well-muscled body, appeared unsuited to travel upon a trail in the wilds of America. His handsome, clean-shaven face, though covered with grit now, had an intelligent, scholarly look that fit more with his gentlemanly garb of corduroy trousers, black serge coat, waistcoat, and silk cravat than with his surroundings. His blond, baby-fine hair further softened the initial impressions his physique might lead one to form of this man. Only his eyes, a vibrant blue, almost turquoise, hinted of a fire, an inner grit matching that of the wilderness trail.

At the moment, however, even that fire was dimmed. He longed for the sights and sounds of civilization after so many weeks of travel through the wilderness. Then he silently scolded himself for dwelling too much upon temporal comforts, placing them above that of his holy calling.

He had known from the beginning that his mission to the wasteland of Texas would not be easy.

Unfortunately, the endless days upon the trail—the hardships, the fear of molestation by Indians, wild animals, or highwaymen—had dimmed his vision. Moreover, it had been difficult watching his family suffer. Benjamin had not the funds to purchase steamboat fare, so they made their way on the hard trail. The trip had taken its toll on his wife, Rebekah, who was several months advanced with child. She had eaten little food and was now so weak she could barely sit upright in the back of the wagon where she was wedged in with the children, their belongings, and a load of supplies their guide had brought.

Benjamin wondered many times during the long days of travel if he had made the right decision, if he truly had heard the voice of God calling him to minister to the heathen wilds of Texas. When he wasn't occupied with the labors of survival, he was on his knees beseeching God's reaffirmation of his call.

"Are we almost there?" a whining voice called out.

Benjamin turned in his seat next to the driver to meet the questioning gaze of his twelve-year-old son. "Be still, Micah," Benjamin said. "Your complaints will not hurry this wagon along."

"Another hour or so will get us to Natchez," interjected the driver.

Benjamin shot the man a cross glance. Tom Fife, their guide, had been an unsavory companion for the last week, but Benjamin tried to be patient. After all, the man had rescued them when their previous guide had left them stranded on the banks of a swollen river far from their destination. The scoundrel had stolen their horses, leaving them only a wagon with a broken axle. Fife, driving a wagon drawn by two huge mules and loaded with furs and other trade goods, happened along and showed them a better crossing. He then offered them passage and agreed to guide them to Natchez. It had been a hard blow to leave his costly wagon behind, but Benjamin thanked God that at least their belongings could fit onto Fife's conveyance.

Now Benjamin's forbearance of the man was wearing thin. Fife's foul tongue, his crude manners, and his constant interference in matters involving Benjamin's family were trying even Benjamin's vast reserve of Christian tolerance. After two days on the road, he had forbidden his family to have any contact with Fife. Micah had taken a liking to the trapper and spent the days after Benjamin's edict sulking. It didn't help that Fife constantly defied Benjamin by continuing to socialize with the children, telling them stories, giving them treats, or performing other indulgent acts.

No, it had not been easy following God's will in uprooting his family and transporting them hundreds of miles from their civilized home in Boston to this wild, godless land. Some had called Benjamin crazy or even heartless to impose such a fate upon a genteel woman and two helpless children. But God must always come first, and His will must always supersede the desires of the flesh.

Nevertheless, Benjamin would never reveal to another human, not even his wife, that he often feared what lay ahead and was sickened at the thought of what he had left behind—a comfortable frame house, a pastorate in a small but fine church, his ailing parents, whom he knew he would never see again. And yes, in the privacy of his prayer closet, he even at times doubted the very calling of God.

Benjamin glanced covertly back at his family huddled together on the hard wagon boards with only a few blankets to pad them against the bouncing and jolting. The children, even Micah, were clinging to their mother. Five-year-old Isabel looked especially helpless, but she had always been a frail child.

Rebekah, thank God, was asleep, but her eyes fluttered beneath the thin, pale lids. It was almost impossible now to see through her weariness the lovely woman she was. Creamy skin with a small smattering of freckles across her nose was the inevitable legacy of her voluminous auburn hair. It had always given her such a vibrant appearance, but now it only emphasized frailty. She had never supported her husband's caprice, as she often called it. She tried to tell him that one did not have to go to the wilderness to serve God. There were sufficient sinners in Boston to keep a man of God occupied honorably. She had wept every day for two weeks before their departure. She had several sisters with whom she was quite close and a younger brother whom she adored, not to mention parents she loved. Then there were scores of friends and a pleasant life filled with social gatherings, ministrations to the needy, sewing circles, and the like. She had been a minister's wife to be proud of, happily active in the church, submissive to her husband, and beloved by her children.

Benjamin knew more than ever that because of her sacrifices, he must never allow his fleshly doubts to surface. He had to ignore them and stand firm in his convictions. She must never know that he wavered at times.

In that spirit, he turned his face forward again, setting his jaw, gathering his resolve around him like a shield. He had always lived by the strength of his convictions, so why should now be any different? He was wearing the mantle of God, and that mantle was large enough to cover his family as well.

Natchez, located on the Mississippi River, on the border of the states of Louisiana and Mississippi, was a thriving port town of several thousand inhabitants. Here the Sinclair family would take passage on a riverboat, which would transport them to New Orleans. From there it was but a five- or six-day sea voyage to Texas. With the end of the long journey finally within sight, Benjamin was feeling hopeful once more.

"Rebekah," he called to the back of the wagon, "we have come to a city at last. We shall rest a night here in a hotel on a real bed."

Rebekah wearily pulled herself up so as to peer over the sideboards of the wagon. She nodded her head without enthusiasm. "As you say, Benjamin."

Benjamin was silent. He did not wish to rebuke his wife in front of the children or their heathen driver, but he would speak to her privately later regarding her attitude. Her negativity was affecting the children and making it difficult for him to hold to his vision. It was difficult enough for him to present an optimistic front, especially as he began to observe the town of Natchez more closely.

It hardly warranted much enthusiasm. Nearing the docks, he viewed a squalid and unsavory expanse of saloons, crowded even in early afternoon. Dirty, foul-mouthed dock workers and disreputable women roamed the streets, as did characters who looked like the very highwaymen Benjamin had feared on the trail.

"This ain't no city," Micah piped up sourly. "The slums of home looked better'n this."

"Hold your tongue, Micah." Even if Benjamin agreed with his son, he would not abide such insolence and had no qualms about rebuking his son in public when it was deserving. How else would the boy learn humility?

"Are we gonna live in a slum, Papa?" Isabel asked in a tremorous voice.

"I will tolerate no more impudence from either of you children. Say no more until I give you permission to speak."

"I reckon the young'un asked a fair question," Fife said.

"No one asked you, sir," Benjamin barked.

"Well, I don't need no permission to talk, Reverend," Fife sneered, his curling lip revealing yellow and rotten teeth. "And I says 'tis a fair question, especially from someone who's only knowed the likes of civilized Boston. But this is a long way from Texas, Issy," Fife added pointedly to Isabel in a more tender tone. "And you can be thankful this ain't your final abode."

Benjamin was perturbed that he had to agree with Fife. "That is true, Mr. Fife, but it is the very sin and immorality here that confirm the urgency of my calling."

Fife shrugged but said nothing. Benjamin knew the man was avoiding a discussion of spiritual matters. They had already engaged in several such discourses while on the road. Benjamin had made faithful attempts to convert the driver's godless soul, but to no avail. Knowing such a debate would be useless, Benjamin fell silent also. No use wasting his breath. If Fife burned in eternal damnation, it could not be laid to Benjamin's account.

Five silent minutes later, Fife said, "I reckon I'll take you to one of the steamship company offices where you can find out 'bout buying tickets."

"Thank you, Mr. Fife. That is most kind of you." Benjamin spoke stiffly but politely, for he had yet another request to make of the driver. "Could I impose upon you to take me and my family from the office to a suitable hotel?" At Fife's momentary hesitation, Benjamin added, "I know you are anxious to take your leave from us, but it should only mean another half hour of your time. I would not ask, but in a place like this it is difficult to know whom to trust."

"I'll do it for the lady and the young'uns, but if'n it were just you, Reverend, nothing would get me to go another mile with you! I would've deserted you like the last man if'n it weren't for your family. When I first heard what that feller done I was steamed, but I know now he just couldn't take another minute of your uppity holy attitude, not to mention your durned—"

"Please, Mr. Fife, watch your language in the presence of a woman and children!"

"You drive me to it, Reverend! I been a patient man because I had no choice, but now I'll tell you what I really think. You treat them sweet children like they was criminals. I ain't seen you smile at them since we started. And that poor sufferin' woman! What would possess a man to drag her away from home and hearth?"

"Stop this wagon immediately!" Benjamin shouted. "I'll hear no more of your abuse. You have no idea of what you speak. You are a godless fool and have no right to judge a true man of God."

"I said I was gonna take you to the steamship office and then to the hotel—and that's what I'm gonna do! But before I do, I'll say one last thing. I may be ignorant and no highfalutin eastern-educated minister. And I may be ten kinds of fool, but I ain't godless, and I'll not be accused of being so by anyone!" Fife took a sharp breath, then snapped his mouth firmly closed, jerking his gaze forward and urging the horses on at a faster pace.

Benjamin focused his eyes stubbornly forward also. The man had incredible nerve. If he were a Christian man as he claimed, he would not treat a servant of God in such a manner.

A few minutes later the wagon came to a stop before a building with a sign over its door reading *St. Louis Steamship Company.*

"Here we are," Fife announced tightly.

Benjamin went inside and made arrangements for passage on a riverboat, which would be departing in two days. Benjamin was disappointed at the delay, but he supposed Rebekah could use the extra rest. He returned to the wagon and unloaded the goods that would be stored at the office until departure. Then Fife drove them to an inexpensive but respectable-looking hotel.

After a room was reserved, Benjamin returned to the wagon and reached into his coat pocket, withdrawing his wallet and counting out ten dollars, the amount he and Fife had agreed upon at the beginning of their journey together.

Fife looked at the money Benjamin held out but made no move to take it. "Never mind that," he said instead.

"We agreed—" Benjamin protested.

"I only agreed because I figured you'd be too pigheaded to accept my assistance otherwise."

"But—"

"Listen, Reverend, I ain't never yet taken no money from a servant of God, and I sure don't intend to start with you, even if you did make me earn it more than most folk. Keep your money, Reverend. I don't want it."

"As you said, you earned it." Benjamin didn't know what else to say. He didn't know what to make of this man he had traveled with for over a week.

Fife shook his head, then jumped from the wagon. "Come on, young'uns." He turned his attention to his other passengers. "Let ole Tom help you out of this hard wagon." Setting each one upon the street, he gave them a warm smile, so incongruent with his grimy, unkempt countenance. "I'm gonna miss you kids."

"We'll miss you, too, Tom," Micah said with a fleeting glance toward his father. Benjamin chose to ignore the defiance in that glance.

"Well," Fife said, "I might take myself to Texas one of these days, so I reckon our paths could cross again."

Isabel reached up and gave him a hug. Fife picked up the child and planted a kiss on her forehead. Benjamin pretended not to see as he helped his wife from the wagon, then busied himself with unloading their carpetbags and other belongings. Finally, however, he could avoid the driver no longer. Decency demanded he bid the man a proper farewell.

"Mr. Fife, thank you again for your generous assistance. We couldn't have made it without you."

"I doubt that, Reverend. Whatever else you may be, you are tough. You ain't one to give up easily."

"Nevertheless . . ." Benjamin paused, then added hesitantly, "And about what I said before . . . perhaps I spoke harshly. God bless you, Mr. Fife."

"And you, too, sir."

CHAPTER 4

ONE BY ONE THE WOMEN shuffled out of the low-ceilinged, dimly lit room and followed a big male slave carrying a cast-iron pot of greens and ham.

Elise shrank back into the shadows, clutching her baby, little three-month-old Hannah, tightly to her breast, feeling no comfort from the contented sucking of the child. She had no appetite herself. The filth and smell of the slave quarters were only part of the reason, but that was nothing compared to the humiliation Elise felt at her circumstance. An outcast in the only world she had known, she might have hoped this new world would at least open up to her. But many of the slaves resented and despised her almost as much as did the Hearne family. She had shown her disdain for her Negro blood by trying to hide it, and thus the Negro community shunned her as well.

"At least dat baby do eat good" came a woman's voice from the doorway of the hut. She entered, closing the door behind her. She came up and held out a bowl of greens. "Here you go. I don't want no niggers dyin' in my hut."

"I'm not hungry," Elise said.

Hattie was a kindly woman, middle-aged with graying hair and a soft, intense voice. She worked in the sewing hut. Unlike many of the others, she had been less hostile toward Elise. It still made Elise shudder when she thought of the last three nights. Since she had not been put to work, she spent her days mostly alone, caring for Hannah and preparing the evening meal for the slaves. She dreaded the nights most, when all the slaves returned from their work. Not that they mistreated her—if it were only that! The cold silence was far more disturbing. Even Carrie, who had been her maid for a year, had changed. Elise had always been kind and considerate to the girl, but now Carrie acted as though Elise had whipped and abused her.

Elise almost wished Thomson's lawyer would arrive quickly and rescue her from this existence. Not that she could hope for anything better from Thomson.

"Lookee here, girl," Hattie scolded, "your milk is gonna be weak if'n you don't eat. Den what of de chile?"

"What do you care?"

"I know we ain't be welcoming of you, girl. You ain't one of us, even if de massa says so. But I been thinkin' it ain't your fault neither. . . ."

"How do you know of these things?"

"You think folks don't talk?" She chuckled, a low sound that barely broke through her lips. "Why, der ain't nothin' dat happens in de big house dat we darkies don't know 'bout."

"What have you heard?"

"Your mama was a quadroon dat passed for white. You didn't know till jes' before you married wid de massa's boy. I guess anybody would of done what you did."

"That's not the impression everyone here has given me. They act as if I have betrayed my race by trying to pass as white."

Hattie shrugged. "Dey gots to say dat. But I'll wager der ain't a person here who don't wish every day dere skin was white as snow. A person's got to do what a person's got to do, dat's all."

"What do you want, Hattie? Why are you talking to me now?"

"I got da conviction, dat's all. Jesus done tole me to show you Christian kindness. So I'm obeying." She pushed the bowl toward Elise.

"I don't believe in God. . . ."

"Everybody believes in God!" Hattie's tone rose from its calm, deep timber, expressing surprise at such a terrible admission.

"Well, I suppose I believe. He just has never been that important to me." Elise didn't want to offend this woman who might be her only friend.

"Mebbe dat's why He's finally turning His back on you."

"Why not? Everyone else has." Elise heard the bitterness in her voice and hated it. "Is that what you really wanted, Hattie, to preach at me?"

"I wanted to give you some greens. I ain't gonna preach no more at you. What's betwix you and God ain't none of my business."

"I'm sorry I snapped at you."

"Now eat so's you stay alive for de chile." Hattie laid a dark brown hand on Elise's arm.

"I suppose you're right. I'm all she has now. I only wish things could be different . . . for my baby's sake." Elise wanted to weep whenever she thought of Hannah's bleak future and that her father had so rejected her.

"I was born a slave," Hattie said. "I ain't knowed nothing else. It's different for you. Dis life is gonna go a lot harder on you. It ain't right."

"Well, I've not much choice in the matter. I keep hoping my father will come and help me somehow. I'm sure he has no money if he lost his house. But he might be able to raise some so that he could buy me from Thomson. . . ." Elise sighed hopelessly. "Hattie, how much do you think a strong young woman such as myself, with a baby, would go for on the auction block?"

"A lot, girl."

"Yes, that's what I thought. More than my father could ever raise."

"Mebbe der's another way. . . ."

"What do you mean?"

"I heard dat the overseer's wife came by the big house to ask after you."

"Rowena?"

Elise had met Rowena Cowley when she first came to the plantation. They were both about the same age, and though Rowena had been at that time far below Elise's social station, Elise had liked her and found her better company than Kendell's snooty sisters. Once, when Daphne had learned Elise had visited Rowena at her house, she had given Elise a severe reprimand for mixing with white trash.

Yes, she and Rowena had been friendly at one time, but who could say what her attitude would be now? It could be risky for Rowena to show sympathy for the outcast daughter-in-law of her husband's employer.

"Mebbe she could help you," Hattie suggested.

"It might bring trouble on her."

"Mo' trouble than you being shipped off as a slave?" Hattie's dark eyebrow arched, but no more was said because at that moment the door opened again.

Kendell Hearne stood framed in the opening, the last rays of the setting sun illuminating him eerily. Nevertheless, the sight of him brought a lump to Elise's throat. She couldn't help that she still loved him, although the love was liberally mixed with hatred, too.

Yet even as she felt that ire toward him, a spark of hope rose up in her. Had he come to rescue her at last?

"Leave us," Kendell said to Hattie.

"Yessir, massa." Hattie gave Elise a reassuring pat and stood to exit the hut.

Elise smiled tentatively. Then she laid Hannah in the box that was her cradle, and she, too, rose and faced her husband. "Kendell, have you come for me?" How she hated herself for her pleading tone, especially when it was met with a blank expression, cool and devoid of emotion, just like his father's. Even some of Daphne's fire would have been welcome just then.

"I wanted to let you know we have been officially granted a legal separation. My father saw to it that the matter was expedited. Neither of us are free to remarry, of course."

"I don't want to marry another, Kendell. I love—"

"Stop!" His voice was sharp but a little desperate, too. "Our marriage is over."

"But you said yourself it isn't—"

"There is still the possibility of an annulment. I am certain the courts will side with me in this matter."

"I love you!" Sobbing, Elise threw her arms around Kendell, not caring about her pride. He had come to her; it must mean something. She had to do everything in her power to make him take her back. She clung to him and kissed him, and for a moment she was certain he responded, holding her as he used to, kissing her thick hair. Then suddenly he stiffened and pulled away.

"You deceived me. You ruined me." His voice shook with accusation, and Elise realized that his love, too, was mixed with hatred.

"Must I suffer the rest of my life for one mistake? Should our child suffer?" she implored.

"I don't want to see you suffer." His voice softened. "But it is out of my hands. You are Thomson's property."

"You could buy me from him."

"And then what?"

"We could be together. You wouldn't be the first white man to marry a . . . Negro." The word still caught in her throat. Her stomach knotted each time she realized who and what she was.

"That would mean losing everything, Elise. I've already lost my place in society, but at least I will still inherit the plantation. Maybe in time people will forget my mistake."

"Isn't love worth it?" But even to Elise the words sounded trite.

Kendell turned away from her. "I would have to live my life as an outcast because I could never perpetuate the lie as your father did. I would never pass my child off as white to some poor unsuspecting man. And they say if we had more children, one could come along that was black as night. I couldn't live with these things."

"Why?" she pleaded.

"Because . . ." Still he could not look directly at her. "I am not strong enough."

"Oh, Kendell . . ."

"Forgive me, Elise." He walked away, leaving the hut without a second look at her or their child.

What made her most angry was that she felt sorry for him. As she crumpled down upon the dirt floor, she heaped a load of recriminations upon herself. She had ruined him, and she had no right to expect him to give up what little he now had for her.

It was time for her to accept her lot. She was a slave, a piece of property of less value than a thoroughbred horse. Her skin may as well be as black as Hattie's. But acceptance made the truth no easier to bear. She lay down on the thin pallet that was her bed and wept. Hattie returned and tried to comfort her, to no avail. Elise cried the whole night through.

CHAPTER 5

THE SOUND OF CHIRRUPING CRICKETS had no soothing quality this night. Elise's taut nerves jumped with every musical note. When her foot snapped a twig, her heart nearly stopped. She clutched Hannah tighter in her arms with each step. She had every reason to be afraid. She was breaking the law, committing a dastardly crime. She was seeking her freedom.

Five days had passed since that final discussion with Kendell in the slave quarters. In the meantime, Hattie, acting as a go-between, had arranged with Rowena Cowley a plan to help Elise escape. Rowena's brother, an abolitionist, was willing to help her. Elise wasn't sure what an "abolitionist" was, nor was Hattie certain, but the slave said it sounded like a good thing.

Elise was to meet him after sundown in a specified place in the thick woods on the west side of the plantation. There was a big tree stump where she and Rowena had once picnicked after picking berries. The brother and Rowena would be waiting there. Elise had only her baby and a small rucksack slung over her shoulder, which contained her only possessions—the few baby things Mother Hearne had allowed her to take from the big house. For herself, she had not been allowed to take anything. When she had donned one of the slave's castoffs, she had been required to return to Daphne the stylish day dress she had been wearing. She now wore an ill-fitting homespun dress that was old and ragged and had been passed around among many slave women. Elise's beautiful gowns and jewelry no longer belonged to her. They belonged to the Hearnes, as she also did—until Maurice Thomson claimed ownership.

The night was chilly, for it was still early in the month of May. There was no moon and Elise had difficulty finding her way, but this night had been chosen specifically for that reason. The darkness was her ally. If anyone did come after her, she hoped they would have as difficult a time in the woods as she.

Just as she began to fear she had taken a wrong turn, the dark mass of the large stump appeared before her. Her sigh of relief was only momentary, for she immediately noted there was no one there to greet her. Not liking to stand exposed in the clearing surrounding the stump, she crouched down behind it, her heart thumping wildly.

Then Hannah began to cry.

"Hush! Hush, my baby," Elise cooed softly. But it was feeding time, and the child did not heed her mother's entreaty.

Suddenly the sound of footsteps crunched and crackled into the clearing. Elise prayed the sound came from Rowena and her brother.

"Miz Elise!" came Rowena's welcome voice.

Elise scrambled from her hiding place.

"Don't do no good to hide if you got a wailing baby waking up the entire countryside," said the man standing next to Rowena.

"Hold your tongue, Wade!" Rowena hissed. "She can't help it."

"I've got to feed her," Elise tried to explain. "It'll be the only way to keep her quiet." Elise looked from Rowena to Wade. Even in the darkness she could see sympathy emanating from Rowena, a pretty girl with a round face and plump figure. Wade, on the other hand, was tall and gangly, and his eyes were two sharp scowling bits of white in the night.

"Get on with it, then!" Wade said.

"Turn yourself around," Rowena snapped at her brother. "The poor girl don't want the whole world to gawk, you know."

Wade obeyed. Elise squatted down by the stump and took the thin blanket she'd used in the slave quarters. Then tucking it discreetly around the baby, she quickly began feeding the hungry child. With his back still turned, Wade started to talk.

"Soon as you're finished there," he said, "we're gonna head north. I can get you to the border. That's about a hundred miles."

"What will I do then? That's still in the South, isn't it?"

"I'm taking a mighty big risk doing that much." Somehow Wade did not seem as enthusiastic as Elise had hoped.

"But how will I know the way?" Elise was beginning to despair before she even began her perilous escape.

"Honey," interjected Rowena's kindly voice, "there's folks along the way who'll help you. Wade has a couple names. It's risky, but wouldn't you rather do that than end up a . . . well, you know?" Dear Rowena had no more accepted Elise's fate than she had herself.

"I suppose so. It wouldn't be so fearsome if it wasn't for Hannah."

"You can do it, Miz Elise." Rowena sat beside Elise and put her arm around her thin shoulders. This was the only friend Elise had in the world. Then Rowena said something that truly surprised her. "You know, Miz Elise, I always knew you were a strong woman. That's what I admired about you."

"Me?" Elise could not believe she had heard right. "I've been pampered and cared for all my life. I really never had to do anything for myself. Even when my father was flat broke, I had a maid. Rowena, I've never done a brave or courageous thing in my entire life."

"Well, now you got to be brave—for Hannah. I know you can, too."

"You are a good friend, Rowena. Mere thanks aren't good enough."

"You was decent to me when everyone at the big house treated me like trash, Miz Elise. You don't need to say nothing about thanks. We're even."

Wade was pacing about anxiously. "Ain't that kid done yet?"

"Just another couple of minutes."

Wade rambled on about their journey, what towns they should avoid, good places to find food, and what difficulties they might encounter. The things he said were very sketchy, and Elise wondered how often he had made the trip. From the way he paced so skittishly, it appeared possible he had never done it. Perhaps he had never aided a runaway slave either. But Elise didn't have the courage to ask him. At least he was willing. No sense ruining that with too much scrutiny.

Finally Hannah stopped sucking and dozed off. Elise stood. "We're ready."

Rowena held out a bulging flour sack. "It ain't much, just enough food for a couple days. It's all I could spare. There's a dollar in there, too, from my egg money."

Overcome by sudden emotion, Elise threw her free arm around her friend. She couldn't speak.

"Now get on with you." Rowena kissed Elise's cheek.

"I'll . . . never see you again," Elise finally managed to say through her tears.

"I hope not!" Rowena's voice was choked as well. Smiling, she added, "We'll see each other in the Hereafter."

Elise shrugged and tried to return the smile. Then she gave Rowena a squeeze with her arm and brushed her cheek with a kiss before hiking from the clearing with Wade.

Elise started awake, but the bright light of day made her clamp her eyes shut again. Lying in the damp grass with only the single blanket to cover her and the baby, her body felt stiff and cold. Wade was snoring about four feet away. They were nestled in among thick bushes. A faint scent of jasmine wafted rather discordantly in the air.

She wondered what time it was. She was hardly adept at reading the sun, but it must be nine or ten in the morning. She and Wade had hiked nearly all night—six or seven hours at least—before halting, exhausted, just before daybreak. Wade said they shouldn't travel by day, but Elise wondered what they would do all day. She didn't think she would be able to go back to sleep on the hard ground. Even in seven hours they couldn't be more than ten miles from the plantation. She wouldn't feel safe until she'd put at least a hundred miles between herself and the Hearnes, perhaps not even then.

Rubbing the sleep from her eyes, she looked about, wondering what could have disturbed her sleep. When she had fallen into slumber a few hours ago, she had been so tired she thought nothing would wake her. Then she remembered her dream. She had been crawling in the mud, covered head to toe with the oozing brown mess. But when she found a stream and jumped in to wash, she discovered the mud would not wash away. Her skin was stained permanently!

That was not the worst of the dream. She had become panicked at the sight of the dark skin and had begun to run. She ran until she thought her lungs would burst. Her heart was beating so fast it made her head throb, but she couldn't stop. They were after her. The sound of baying bloodhounds kept coming closer and closer. That's what must have finally awakened her. That horrible sound!

Thank God it was but a dream.

She started to lift the blanket to check on Hannah, who was snuggled close to her. All at once Elise froze and her heart skipped a beat. Was it her imagination? Could her dream be coming true? Or had reality imposed, in fact, upon her dreams? The sound was becoming distinct now, and she was certain it was no longer her imagination. Now it was a waking nightmare.

Bloodhounds!

The sharp, persistent baying was clear. Panic seized Elise. She threw aside the blanket and grabbed the baby, waking her roughly. Then she sprang to her feet. But something made her pause. It was madness to take off in blind flight. She must think first. But Hannah started to cry, making rational thought nearly impossible.

Wade. She needed him now more than ever. She ran to where he still lay snoring. How could he sleep at a time like this? Shaking him hard, she bit back the strong urge to scream his name, to simply scream anything.

"What the—?" He mumbled in a sleep-thickened voice.

"Wade, there's bloodhounds! We've got to get away."

"Huh?"

"Listen!" She did scream now. Hannah was crying so hard, Elise had to make herself heard over the din.

Even over the sound of the crying baby the hounds could be heard. They were getting closer.

"They found us. I gotta get out of here," Wade cried.

"Where can we go?"

"We? No, I can't help you no more." He jumped up, his eyes wild with fear.

"You can't leave me now," Elise pleaded.

"I'm truly sorry. . . ." But he said no more and took off at a dead run in the opposite direction from the sound of the dogs.

Elise couldn't blame him. He could get into as much trouble as she for helping her escape. And he had a far better chance of getting away. Quickly she gathered her belongings. She would have left them, but if she did get away, she would need the food and the blanket. Besides, there was no sense leaving evidence of her presence. It amazed her, however, that she could think so clearly with her head throbbing and her knees shaking so badly she could barely stand. But she had to do more than stand. She had to run.

Dashing off in generally the same direction as Wade, she veered slightly to the left of the path he had taken to give him a better chance. She did not want him to get into trouble—not only for his own sake but also because it would implicate Rowena. Already she had lost sight of him and could barely hear his mad race through the woods. He undoubtedly could hear her, and so could her pursuers. Hannah would not quiet, and Elise could not stop to give her the one thing that would satisfy her.

Elise ran and ran, just like in her dream. But she could not get away from the loathsome sound of the dogs. At times she seemed to be surrounded by them, the sounds coming from several directions at once. Still she kept running, up hills and down, through thickets with briars that cut her painfully. Sloshing across a muddy creek, she slipped and nearly lost her hold on Hannah.

In a matter of minutes, she lost all sense of direction. She could be racing right back to the Hearne plantation, but she knew she could not stop, no matter where she ended up. She had to run. She had to make it. She had to be free again.

Groaning inwardly, she faced yet another hill. Where would she find the stamina to climb it? Her feet were like bricks, but she did not slow until halfway up the hill she tripped over a root and fell sprawling to the ground. Hannah tumbled from her arms, screaming. Elise frantically gathered the baby back into her arms, and with the child secured, she tried to stand, but a shooting pain forced her back down. She had turned her ankle in the fall.

The baying came closer. Shouts of men also ripped through the morning air.

"We've caught you! Give it up!"

Holding Hannah in one arm and clawing at grass and roots with her other hand, Elise crawled to the top of the hill, her eyes filling with debris and tears on the way up. Spitting grass and knuckling dirt from her eyes, she waited for her vision to clear. What met her sight made her drop her head to the ground in despair. The dogs were coming straight toward her, less than a hundred yards away.

CHAPTER

I DON'T BELIEVE YOU NEED THOSE." William Hearne nodded toward the ropes that bound Elise's wrists. "You won't run away again, will you?" He eyed Elise with that patronizing superiority he wore so well.

She shook her head. "Just make them give Hannah back."

She and her captors were standing in the middle of the yard of the plantation house where the slave hunters had brought her after finding her on that hillside. One of them had taken Hannah and another had tied Elise's hands and put her on a spare horse. It had taken less than an hour to ride to the plantation. She had been only five miles away when they had discovered her. What a pathetic escape she had attempted!

One of the men unbound her wrists and gave her the baby, who had not stopped crying since the chase. The poor child was red-faced and gasping for air. If the erstwhile escape had been harrowing for Elise, it had been torture for the innocent babe. She had not only been wrenched from her mother's arms but had not had anything to eat all morning. Her captors had refused to allow time for that. Hannah calmed a little when she realized she was with her mother, but still she sobbed and hiccuped.

"I must feed her," Elise said.

"There will be time for that in a few minutes," Hearne replied.

"But she hasn't—"

"Don't sass the master!" one of her captors ordered, giving her a painful swat on the side of her head.

"That'll be all," Hearne said to the man. "Go by the overseer's, and he will pay you for your services."

The men left. It was nothing to them what Hearne did with his runaways, though Elise sensed they would just as soon have given her the whip in order to remind her of her place. But the Hearnes took great pride in the fact that they never whipped a slave. Elise hoped their intense animosity toward her did not encourage them to break that noble trend.

"Elise," Hearne said, "this is Mr. Carter, your new owner's lawyer."

She had noticed the stranger standing in the yard with Mr. Hearne. She had also noticed that Kendell was nowhere to be seen.

"Since it is still early, I'd like to take my leave with the girl as soon as possible." Mr. Carter glanced distastefully toward Elise. "I don't want to risk her running off again."

"Yes, I suppose that would be best." Hearne's lips twitched in an insincere smile.

Just then Daphne Hearne stepped from the house. She made her way down the porch steps to join the group in the yard.

"I heard she was found." Mother Hearne averted her eyes from Elise.

It was just as well, for Elise had defiantly opened her dress front and pressed Hannah to her breast. She no longer had a blanket to cover her with, but with the pathetic cries of her baby filling her ears, Elise cared little about propriety. If she was nothing more than a lowly slave, no one should care. If they did . . . well, it gave Elise a certain satisfaction to shock the lot of them.

Much to Elise's surprise, when Mrs. Hearne did note the scene, she slipped off her shawl, marched up to Elise, and laid it across the baby. Elise lifted her eyes and met those of her mother-in-law.

"They wouldn't let me feed her." Elise's words were tight, far from an apology.

Without a word, Mrs. Hearne returned to her husband's side. Only then did Elise note that the men had stopped talking and were gaping at the scene. She restrained a self-satisfied smile.

"Mr. Carter," said Daphne Hearne, "she will be well taken care of, won't she?"

This comment was even more surprising than the offering of the shawl.

"Mr. Thomson knows the value of his property and treats it accordingly," Carter answered rather evasively.

"It is just that . . . well, we have a certain fondness for the girl."

Now Elise was more than surprised. She was dumbfounded. Was Mother Hearne having a change of heart? Was revenge not as sweet as she had hoped? Or was she merely trying to salve a seared conscience with a show of Christian concern?

"If you have doubts about parting with her," Carter said, "Mr. Thomson might be induced into selling her—at a fair price. She is obviously valuable stock."

"No . . . no." Daphne's previous words appeared to have been just for show after all. The last thing she wanted around was a constant reminder of her family's shameful mistake. "Much to our regret"—Daphne's syrupy tone could not have fooled the most naïve simpleton—"we feel it is best for all concerned to put some distance between the girl and us. It will be as much to her benefit as ours. She can start a new life. Perhaps Mr. Thomson has a nice young buck for her. And we can try to move ahead with our lives as well." She then turned to Elise. "In that vein, you might wish to know Mr. Hearne has practically sealed the matter of an annulment. Our son will be free to marry properly and bear us *white* heirs."

And that was all that mattered to Daphne. Elise's freedom was of no consequence to her.

"You can be assured," the lawyer was saying, "that Mr. Thomson has fine plans for the girl. She will be treated well, and I can assure you she will be a . . . house servant. She will have some decent clothes and be well fed, as will the child. Oh yes, a slave like this is merchandise to be well cared for."

They spoke of her as if she were a breed mare. Not that women in general weren't often spoken of in such a manner, but Elise felt deep inside that the words were true. This morning she had been hunted like an animal. Now she would be herded off and taken to a place not of her choosing to be fed and clothed and cared for . . . just like a beast. If she were lucky, it would be as a pampered kitten rather than a cow. She was no longer a person. Her only value now was in dollars and cents. It was useless to fight it. Escape was impossible.

"Then," Carter was saying, "you have no objections to our leaving posthaste? I believe all the paper work is in order."

"No objections at all. The sooner the better." Hearne was cool, detached.

Elise wondered fleetingly about Kendell. What had he thought about his wife—*his wife!*—being hunted down like wild game? Quickly she banished such thoughts from her mind. She must forget about Kendell.

"Wilbur!" Hearne called to the stable slave. "Have Mr. Carter's carriage hitched immediately."

These words, the sheer immediacy of them, stirred Elise from her dumbness. "Please!" she appealed to her father-in-law, though she didn't know why. Perhaps it was harder than she thought to completely crush the free human spirit within her. "Mr. Hearne, sir, would you do but one thing for me?"

"Well . . ."

"It isn't much." She turned pleading eyes upon him. "I want to get word to my father about my whereabouts. That isn't asking too much, is it?"

"I suppose it couldn't hurt."

"I doubt that would be possible," Carter put in. "You see, after your father lost the house, I heard he left the country for Europe."

"But how could he?" Elise's despair mounted. "He had no money."

"Dorian Toussaint is nothing if not resourceful. I could not divulge any details in mixed company of his means, but let us just say he did not depart alone."

No, Papa was never alone. There were always women flitting in and out of his life. He had married again several years ago to the daughter of a rich northern banker, but when he gambled away her fortune, she left him. He didn't marry again after that because the banker's daughter refused to suffer the shame of a divorce. But that would not stop him from forming less permanent relationships with women.

It was futile to count on him for help. He loved her, she knew, but it was more than he could do to keep his own life in order. Even when Elise was a child, he had often gone off on his adventures, leaving her behind in the care of her nurse. If only Barbara were still alive, the free black woman who had cared for Elise since her birth. She would have found a way to rescue Elise. At least she would have been there to comfort her in her misery. But Barbara died last summer during a yellow fever epidemic.

Elise had no one but herself to count on, and it was clear what little power she had. Disheartened, she let the stranger take her away. At least she still had Hannah.

CHAPTER 7

Rebekah Sinclair began her labor the morning she and her family were to depart Natchez. The child was not due for another month, and

Benjamin had prayed the child would wait until they had arrived in Texas.

That prayer was not to be answered, or at least God's answer was otherwise. For some reason, He intended that the new Sinclair baby would enter the world in this dirty, squalid town. The hotel clerk was not pleased with the circumstance. A hotel was not for birthing babies. Benjamin heartily agreed. But what choice was there? He only hoped he would not be called upon to deliver the child himself. In Boston, of course, there had always been a doctor, or at the very least a midwife. But Benjamin pushed these thoughts from his mind, for they only encouraged those nagging doubts he worked so hard to suppress.

Instead, he left the hotel room, against Rebekah's protests, to search for a doctor or a midwife. His search proved fruitless on both counts. But God in His mercy did not abandon Benjamin. As always, He provided a ray of hope in a desperate situation.

Unable to find the town doctor, Benjamin stopped at the steamship office to inform them that he and his family would not be on the morning ship. By God's grace, the clerk, however unhappily, refunded Benjamin's ticket money. Benjamin left the office absorbed in his worries, not watching where he was going. He nearly knocked over a man entering the doorway.

"I'm terribly sorry!" Benjamin reached out a hand to steady the fellow.

The man recovered quickly from his initial surprise. "Think nothing of it." He smiled pleasantly.

"I was not watching my step. My mind was elsewhere."

"No harm done." The man proceeded to the desk and addressed the clerk. "I'm here to see if a shipment has arrived for me. Reverend Ezra Bancroft."

Benjamin had not yet exited, and when he heard the man's name, he stopped short and turned back.

"Excuse me, sir," he said boldly. "Did you say *Reverend* Bancroft?"

"I did, sir."

"My name is Benjamin Sinclair, *Reverend* Sinclair." He thrust out his hand and was relieved when Bancroft took it warmly.

"A fellow man of the cloth! What a blessing!" Bancroft had a large mouth, so when his lips parted in a grin, it very nearly went from ear to ear. He was an older man, at least past fifty, with thin, graying hair, pink skin, and pale gray eyes covered with a pair of wire spectacles.

"I wondered if this town had a church," Benjamin said.

"I wouldn't exactly call it a church. I have been here only a few months, and there has been neither time nor money to build. We meet on Sunday in a saloon."

"How terrible!"

"I am grateful to God that at least one day a week such a place can be washed with His presence."

"Yes, yes. I suppose that is a way to look at it." Benjamin didn't know what more to say. He thought of Rebekah and wondered if this man had a wife. That would truly be a godsend. But even if the man was a minister, he was still a stranger, and Benjamin was reluctant to foist his troubles upon him.

Yet, if not this man, who? Benjamin swallowed his pride. "Sir, that is, Reverend Bancroft, I . . . I have a problem. . . ."

"Please, Reverend Sinclair, we have only just met, but we are brothers in Christ. If I can be of any assistance to you, I will gladly do so."

"I . . . I don't know what to say. . . ."

"Tell me your problem."

Benjamin would never cease to marvel at the wondrous provision of God. Reverend Bancroft did indeed have a wife, and eight hours after meeting Bancroft at the steamship office, Martha Bancroft delivered of Rebekah a small but healthy baby daughter. Rebekah wanted to name the child Leah. Benjamin knew the name meant "weary" and thus wanted to protest in favor of something more hopeful, but his wife looked so pale and weak that he did not have the heart to argue. Perhaps, too, that name would always be a reminder of the sacrifices made for the cause of Christ.

Then, as if the Bancrofts had not been generous enough, these people whom the Sinclairs hardly knew invited them to stay in their own home while Rebekah recovered.

"A hotel is not the place for a newborn babe and mother," Martha Bancroft said cheerily. She was a plump, rosy-cheeked woman whose only fault Benjamin could find was that she talked a great deal.

"I insist you bide in our home as long as need be." Bancroft winked at his wife. "Mrs. Bancroft has longed for new folks to talk to, haven't you, dear? And another woman! There are so few respectable women in town that this is truly a gift of God."

"I am anxious to complete my journey." Benjamin had told the minister of his call to Texas.

"Commendable indeed! But you will do the work of God no good if you succumb to exhaustion."

"Your wife should have at least a week, if not two, for proper recovery, especially with an arduous journey still ahead of her." Mrs. Bancroft's words were not a suggestion, they were practically an order.

In any case, Benjamin knew Rebekah would need some rest. When Martha Bancroft had extended the invitation, he had glanced at Rebekah, and she had actually been smiling. He hadn't seen her smile since leaving Boston.

The town of Natchez was divided into two distinct regions. The respectable part of town lay up on a hill. Below this, mostly centered on the waterfront, the more disreputable area flourished. The Bancrofts had a four-room frame house between these two places. Ezra explained that he did not wish to be too far removed from the people who most needed his ministry. He came from Maryland and, like Benjamin, had set out to minister in Texas. But when he came to Natchez, he had seen such great need that he and his wife had decided to tarry there for a time.

"So you will not go to Texas?" Benjamin asked.

"I will see what comes. I expect God will let me know in the fullness of time."

"Yes, I am sure He will." Benjamin found Ezra to be a solid Christian man even though he was not a Methodist like Benjamin. As long as they avoided doctrinal discussions, he believed they would get along well.

That first night, Mrs. Bancroft put out a fine meal. Though her children were grown and married with homes of their own back East, she said she could not break the habit of cooking for a full family. However, nothing was wasted because there always seemed to be guests at their table. Benjamin was impressed with the Bancrofts' hospitality.

The Sinclairs had not eaten so well in weeks, and Benjamin had to caution Micah twice at the table about greed and gluttony. The boy would have eaten more than both grown men combined if allowed. When pie and coffee were served, Micah dug in as though still starved.

"Micah," Benjamin rebuked, "you have had enough to eat."

"But I'm not finished."

"Yes, you are. Leave the table. In fact, you may go outside and reflect upon proper deportment when dining with civilized people."

"But—"

"Now!"

With a fleeting look at the slab of apple pie on his plate, Micah skulked away.

"He's a growing boy," Ezra said.

"Grown enough to learn how to behave." Benjamin waited until Micah had left and closed the door behind him to add, "I suppose it is not entirely his fault. We have spent too long on the road, living in barely human conditions. You can see why I am anxious to reach Texas and get settled in a proper manner."

"Surely you don't think you will find much civilization in Texas." Ezra leaned back contentedly in his chair and sipped his coffee. His wife fixed a tray of food for Rebekah, who was resting in the guest bedroom, and took it to her, leaving the men alone for a time.

"Do you know much of the region, Ezra?" Benjamin tasted the coffee. It was the best he'd had since leaving Boston. The pie was delicious also.

"Only what I hear. But I am in a fairly good position to gain information. Few come or go from Texas without passing through Natchez. Why, I have even met Stephen Austin himself."

"Indeed! What can you tell me about him?"

"He's a good man, entirely dedicated to his colony in San Felipe. The last I heard, however, he had been imprisoned by the Mexican government."

"I did not hear of this. Do you know why?"

"Apparently he went to Mexico to lobby for the statehood for Texas, which has been part of the state of Coahuila. But the Texians have grown weary with the distance they must travel in order to accomplish official business. At any rate, it appears as if an official believed Austin was attempting to foment revolution."

"I didn't know this." Benjamin fell silent, wondering what kind of situation he was about to step into.

"May I ask, Benjamin, how you came to choose Texas as your destination?"

Benjamin welcomed this question, especially with his brief moment of doubt. It would be good to recall his initial vision.

"I had hardly even heard of the place two years ago," he began. "That was when my younger brother, Haden, decided to travel there. He returned to Boston a year later to put his affairs in order with the intent of going to Texas permanently. He tried to encourage me to join him. His stories of a vast, wide open land were enticing, I admit. I'm afraid both my brother and I inherited a bit of the wanderlust from a seafaring grandsire. I was far more successful in repressing it than my brother, who has been traveling all about the country since he came of age."

Ezra smiled indulgently. "But there is indeed something alluring about a new land where miles upon miles have never been seen or touched by mankind."

"I would not be swayed by such a frivolous notion," Benjamin stated, but he often wondered if he had been so influenced. It served no good to admit to it anyway. "I had a wife and young family to consider, as well as a thriving parish."

"But you did set out for Texas. . . ." Ezra prompted, surprisingly with more curiosity than ire.

"I did, but not of my own will."

"I do not think it would be such a terrible thing for a man to seek adventure. That certainly would not negate the call of God. Where would the world be if some of God's people were not given an adventurous spirit?"

Benjamin cocked an eyebrow at this unorthodox thinking. "Of course that may be, but I assure you I received a true call from God."

"I don't doubt it, my boy."

Uncomfortable with the direction of the conversation, Benjamin steered it to a more desirable topic. "Ezra, I have learned many things about the land of Texas, but because my brother is not a God-fearing man, he had little to say about the spiritual state of things. Do you know anything of the Mexican attitude toward the Protestant church? I have heard they have begun to show more tolerance."

"Officially that is not the case. Some Mexican officials turn a blind eye toward the activities of Protestant missionaries. But the Catholic Church is the sanctioned religion of Texas and will remain so as long as Texas is part of Mexico. Protestant ministers continue to operate secretly. And I must be honest with you, Benjamin. The Mexicans are especially intolerant of you Methodists. You . . . uh . . . it is their impression that Methodists tend to be a bit more emotional than some of the other faiths, and thus are perceived to be more threatening to the Mexican government. There are also more Methodists in Texas than other Protestants."

Benjamin's bishop had informed him about the situation with the Mexican government, but he now could see there was probably a great deal he had *not* been told. The call for missionaries, coupled with Haden's enthusiasm about Texas, had worked Benjamin's zeal into an almost feverish pitch. He had asked very few questions, believing God would cover and bless him no matter what. Of course the Methodist missions board had not wanted to lose a zealous missionary by burdening him overmuch with the facts.

Now he could see the error in that judgment. Too much information could never hurt, and it certainly was not going to dampen his resolve. This seemed as good a time as any to broaden his knowledge and appease his curiosity.

"Is it true that Americans in Texas have had to convert to Catholicism?" he asked.

"It is the only way for them to own land."

"How appalling! Certainly they don't *practice* that . . . faith?"

"When the risks of practicing Protestantism are so great—"

"That is no excuse!" Benjamin cut in fervently. "To deny their faith over a few grains of dirt! Why, the first-century Christians risked their very lives to follow Christ."

"Well, even if they were willing to take such a risk, most must wait months before they see any minister, whether it be Catholic or Protestant."

"It seems to me all these people need is to be reminded of the expediency, indeed the utter urgency, of professing Christ. They have forgotten that their very souls hang in the balance."

"Perhaps . . ." Ezra sipped his coffee thoughtfully. "There are those who might argue that Catholics also profess Christ."

"It is a dangerous apostasy," Benjamin countered with conviction. "Dangerous because, like that other vile apostasy, Mormonism, it mingles evil doctrine with enough truth to fool many. I cannot abide the worshiping of more than one deity as Papists do. I believe one of my main missions in Texas will be to break the pope's bondage of the people. If it means ending up in chains, then so be it."

"The only way to free Texas of Catholicism, I believe," Ezra put in rather blandly, "would be to break free of Mexico altogether."

"I believe you are right, Ezra. Texas independence should be the top priority of all God-fearing men!" Benjamin surprised even himself with his impassioned response.

"But, Benjamin, you'll do neither God nor the independence movement any good if you end up in a Mexican prison. I say, tread lightly around the Mexican government. The slim chance that you might convert one is not worth it. You would win a small victory only to lose the entire war."

"I will try to proceed in the wisdom of God."

Ezra nodded but did not appear to be convinced. Benjamin suspected that the man, well-meaning though he might be, had had his convictions dulled by the godless surroundings of the frontier. It certainly had been known to happen in some cases. Benjamin vowed such would not happen to him.

CHAPTER 8

BENJAMIN TOOK HIS LEAVE FROM Ezra and went to see to his wife's well-being. She was lying comfortably on the bed, Isabel snuggled up next to her asleep, and the new baby in her arms. Rebekah was awake, and Benjamin leaned down, kissed her lightly on her forehead, then peeked under the infant's blanket.

"She is a beautiful child," he said gently.

"Yes, she is." A smile twitched upon Rebekah's pale lips.

"You were very brave," he said, "not only in your time of travail but during the whole trip. I know it wasn't easy."

"God strengthened me."

Benjamin pulled a chair up to the bed and sat down. "He strengthens us both as we seek His will."

"Indeed . . ."

He ignored the lack of conviction in her voice. She was tired. She had been through a lot. "We are on a mighty mission, Rebekah. I have just spoken to Reverend Bancroft about Texas. He has some knowledge in this matter, and he has convinced me more than ever that there is enormous need where we are going."

She only nodded.

He went on. "The field is ripe and ready for harvest. Remember my dream, Rebekah? It is surely coming to pass. I am the workman sent to the field."

"You need not waste your breath trying to convince me," she said dully.

He had ceased expecting fire in her eyes, but if only there were a mere spark.

She added, "I have come this far. You don't think I will leave, do you?"

"I only want—" He stopped. This was neither the time nor the place to beat a tender subject. How many times had they had this very discussion? She was here at his side. Perhaps it was simply too much to expect more.

"Where is Micah?" she asked, opening another touchy subject. "I thought he would come see the baby after dinner."

"He . . . there was a bit of a problem at dinner." Sometimes Benjamin felt so alone. Wasn't it bad enough that the world was against him at times, did his family have to be also?

"Oh, Benjamin, what happened?"

"The boy has such a rebellious spirit."

She sighed. "This move has been very difficult for him. Must you be so hard on him?"

"I am trying to bring him up in the wisdom of God."

"Sometimes he just needs love."

"I do love him!" Benjamin did not want to think how many times they had had this conversation. The baby stirred as his voice rose. Benjamin stood abruptly. "I best go before the child wakes. I'll see you in a bit."

Benjamin left the bedroom. In the front room Mrs. Bancroft was cleaning up after dinner while Reverend Bancroft was seated reading a book—not the Bible, though Benjamin could not make out the title. Still feeling tense from the exchange with his wife, he would have gone outside to be alone, but Micah was still there serving his punishment. He sat in an empty chair. Bancroft glanced up and smiled.

"I don't mean to disturb you," Benjamin said.

"Do you wish to talk some more?"

"No. Please continue with your reading." Benjamin got to his feet. "Perhaps I shall read also." He took his Bible from his carpetbag, then sat again and opened the covers. But he couldn't concentrate on the words before him. He felt a deep disquiet inside and knew it had to do with his son.

Rebekah wanted him to be more lenient with the boy. Yet the Word of God clearly instructed, "Spare the rod, spoil the child." His own upbringing had mirrored such a philosophy, though his father had no concept of the spiritual basis of such. Richard Sinclair had ruled his home with a heavy hand, using the kind of unbending discipline he had learned from his years as an officer in the army. Col. Sinclair's sons were but soldiers under his command.

Yes, when he was young Benjamin had resented his father for the constant drilling of instruction, for the complete lack of mercy, and especially for the many beatings given when orders were not carried out with due military precision. By comparison, Benjamin was moderate with his own son, but still he could not ignore the teachings of the Scriptures. He sincerely believed that applying spiritual truths would make the difference in disciplined child rearing. If his own son resented him, it was because of the boy's rebellious nature, not due to any flaw in the handing out of God's truths.

Yet in this present situation regarding his son, he was forced to admit that Rebekah might be right. It had not been easy for the boy to leave friends and family. And the struggles upon the trail had only magnified his bitterness about the move. Perhaps it would not harm Micah if Benjamin dealt a lighter hand while the boy adjusted. Benjamin set aside his Bible, rose to his feet, and headed outside.

Micah was sitting on the front porch whittling a small tree branch he had no doubt found lying under the oak planted near the house. The sun had set behind that oak, leaving the sky a dusky orange and the grounds in partial shadow. Benjamin saw Micah's face in dark silhouette, and the boy did not look up in response to his father's approach.

"Micah." Benjamin walked around to where he could get a clearer view of the boy.

"Yeah."

Benjamin bit back a sharp retort at his son's disrespectful response. He had sought out the boy in order to reason with him calmly and peacefully. Why did the boy always make that so difficult?

"Son, we have been traveling for a very long time." Benjamin stood awkwardly before the boy. He considered sitting next to him on the step, but Micah had planted himself directly in the middle, thus Benjamin would have had to ask to sit there. He felt that would undermine his authority just when he needed it most. Clearing his throat, he began again. "In deference to the hardships of our journey, I have been amiss in maintaining proper discipline these last several weeks. For that reason, I will not blame you entirely for your crude behavior earlier. In this instance I believe mercy is called for. It is natural for a person, be he man or child, to revert to his sinful nature when there is no discipline to restrain him. But from now on I will not permit further breech of those things you know to be right and proper. We will soon be in our new home, and I will expect you to behave in a way that honors your home and those who live in it. Do you understand?"

"Yeah—I mean, yes, sir. At least I understand most of it."

"What is it you don't understand?"

"That part about home. My home is in Boston, with my grandparents and my cousins and my friends. Texas will never be my home."

"It will come to be. Wait and see."

"No! It won't!" Micah looked up, his eyes burning.

"Don't talk back to me!" Benjamin replied with as much fire, then regretted the rebuke. This was not how he had planned this discussion to progress. More softly he added, "Give it time, boy."

Micah shook his head.

"Mrs. Bancroft saved your pie," Benjamin offered. "You may go in and finish it if you wish."

Micah said nothing more but rose, sheathed his knife, laid aside the branch, and strode into the house.

Benjamin walked several paces away from the house to a place behind the oak where he was somewhat shielded from view. He dropped to his knees in the dirt and clasped his hands together.

"Almighty God, I come before you a contrite and needy man. Each minute since I have left Boston I have seen more and more my need for you. I am nothing without your grace and mercy. I am weak and vulnerable without your covering. Only in you can I be the authority my family and my church desperately need. Only in you can I bear the burden of responsibility that rests upon me. My flesh would have me be as those who have shirked their duties as men, like my brother, Haden. My flesh longs after the so-called freedom of worldly ways. Subdue my flesh, O God! Bring it into submission to your righteousness.

"And now, God, I lift up my family. Thank you for the blessing of a new child and for sending her healthy and whole. Thank you for preserving my wife's health through her birthing. Dear God, Rebekah's delicate condition has made these recent changes much more difficult for her. Help her to put her faith in you, and give her the strength to submit to her husband as a godly wife should. Only then will she find true fulfillment. Let her be a shining example of godly virtue to our daughters, who will one day have to submit to husbands of their own.

"And Micah . . . Almighty God, break his rebellious nature, bring his sinful heart into submission to both his heavenly and his earthly fathers. He is nearly at the age of accountability. Let him not be lost to sin and perdition. I have striven to set an example of righteousness for him, but for some reason he has blinded himself to it. Open his eyes, God. Make him see clearly the path to holiness. . . ."

An hour and a half later, Benjamin rose from his knees. The sun had set long ago, but he had hardly noticed the gathering darkness, so absorbed was he in his petitions to the Most High God. He had spent longer than his usual hour in his evening prayers. Not only had he prayed for his immediate family, but he had also lifted up his family in Boston, lingering longer than usual over Haden. He prayed for the new land to which he was bound and decided that in the future, especially as more new needs arose, he might have to extend his prayer time to two hours. This was such a needy land. Nevertheless, he was regaining confidence that he was truly God's chosen vessel to minister in this place and to these wayward people.

When he returned to the house, only a small candle burned on a table for his benefit. No doubt Rebekah had informed their hosts of his prayer routine, and they had left him to himself. He was saddened that there were loud snores coming from Bancroft's room. Apparently the man had finished his evening prayers long ago, if he had offered them at all. Benjamin tried not to judge the minister, but with so much need in this frontier land, it seemed an unwise thing to forego prayer.

CHAPTER 9

ELISE WAS TAKEN TO A hotel in the French Quarter in New Orleans. For the middle of the afternoon, it was quite dim inside, made even more so by the dark mahogany paneling and the black-and-red flocked wallpaper on the walls. Heavy red velvet drapes kept out light as well, and the ornate lamps were turned down low. A cloying odor of cheap perfume mingled with whiskey hung in the stuffy air.

Elise wondered what work she would do here. She supposed she could learn to clean if she must. But before she could worry too much about this, Carter took her upstairs. Here she glimpsed several women in the corridor who were young, and by their skin color she guessed they were quadroons, or octoroons, like herself. They were dressed in fancy clothes that seemed quite inappropriate for the afternoon, and some wore only wrappers in bright colors. Something about them indicated they were not hotel guests, but they did not appear to be servants, either. Two other women and one man, all three very dark-skinned and obviously servants, were sweeping and dusting in the corridor.

Mr. Carter took Elise to an office where he told her to wait, then he himself exited without even so much as a farewell. She took a seat on a silk brocade chair.

Elise had always wanted to come to New Orleans, because this was where her parents were from. She had seen little of it when she rode through in the closed carriage. Perhaps she would have a chance, on a day off perhaps, to see a bit of the picturesque town. But for now her thoughts focused on where she was at this moment and upon her new life that lay ahead. Carter had said nothing to her on the journey from South Carolina, treating her like mere baggage.

"Hannah," she murmured to the child in her arms, "maybe it won't be so bad. This place is a lot nicer than the slave quarters at the Hearne place."

After about five minutes a man entered the office. He was thick and muscular and over six feet tall, without much of a neck to support his large head. His muttonchop whiskers made his round face seem even broader, but his small, narrow-set eyes balanced the effect. He wasn't entirely unhandsome, but his eyes were cold and his thin lips were taut, detracting from the pleasant qualities. When he spoke his voice held neither warmth nor tone, but was flat. His manner of speech pegged him as a man of low quality trying to mold himself to a higher level of society.

"I am Maurice Thomson, your new master."

"Sir." She nodded but did not rise.

His chilly eyes roved over her in a long, intense scrutiny. She felt oddly violated by his look, and a chill ran down her back.

"You are as beautiful as your mother," he said, opening a gilded box on the desk and removing a cigar.

"You knew her?" She couldn't help the eager entreaty in her tone.

"Oh yes, I knew her. I owned her, as you must know."

"And now you think you own me—"

"I *do* own you." His lip twisted in a superior sneer. "Surely you don't plan on being difficult about this. The law is on my side. You have no recourse."

"But why?" Even now Elise could not quell her natural tendency to question her destiny. "Is a little financial loss so important that you would ruin two lives for it?"

"I simply do not like to lose." He casually took a lighter stick from a container near the hearth and lit the tip from the fire. This he applied to the end of his cigar, puffing heartily as he did so. "Your father's first mistake was in stealing your mother away from me twenty years ago. His second mistake was engaging me in a game of cards a month ago. He can't be blamed for that entirely though. I have changed much in twenty years, and he simply did not recognize me. Actually, word had circulated several years ago that I had died, so he felt himself quite safe in returning to his old haunts. Losing your mother was a rather personal blow to me. Nevertheless, I feel I am now vindicated and recompensed. I have little doubt you shall bring in twice the revenues she did even in her prime."

"What do you mean?"

The chill of his eyes flared momentarily in a kind of evil relish. Elise shivered again.

He reached out a hand and ran a thick finger along the line of her jaw. "So innocent, so pure. Even though you are not technically a virgin, I think at first you shall appeal as such. But I will see for myself soon enough."

She flinched away from his touch. Hannah stirred and whimpered.

"The baby is a difficulty I hadn't counted on." He grimaced at the child. "Until she is old enough to earn her keep, she shall be an encumbrance, but I suppose we shall simply have to make the best of it for now."

"I assure you Hannah will not get in the way of my work." The haughty defiance in her eyes was that of a southern lady, not a slave.

"I hope I don't have to break entirely that little bit of fire you display. It, too, can have an appeal." His lips smiled as his eyes bore like ice into her. "I would like you to get situated immediately. Please wait here until someone comes to fetch you."

After he departed, Elise waited about ten minutes before someone else came in. This time it was a quadroon woman several years older than Elise's nineteen years. The woman was attractive, despite rotting teeth and a scar under her right eye. Her skin was the color of chocolate mixed with a liberal amount of cream.

"My name is Mae." Her voice was husky with a foreign accent, probably French. "You are to come with me."

"I'm Elise Hea—" Elise started to say her married name but decided against it. Daphne Hearne said she should start a new life. This would be her first step in that direction.

"How about if I just call you Liz—seems more fitting than a fancy name like Elise."

Elise nodded. She saw no reason to begin a relationship by being contrary.

"Well, then, Liz, come on." Mae did not smile, but there was a warmth in her brown eyes, offsetting the hardness of her tone. It was a warmth that Elise clung to hopefully.

Elise followed Mae down the main corridor, around a turn, and into a narrow hallway with guest rooms on either side. Two women were conversing outside one of the doors.

"So Maurry's got himself a new girl," one of them said. " 'Bout time. I been working way too hard lately."

Elise directed a tentative smile at the woman who appeared to be about her age. It seemed wise to be friendly. Who knew? These women might well become her only friends.

Mae paused before a door at the end of the hall with the number ten painted on the wood surface. "This is the smallest room." Mae opened the door. "It's only proper that the new girl get the worst room."

"I understand."

"Do you?" Mae eyed her curiously then led the way inside. "It's right on the street, so it's noisy with street sounds, but you'll get used to it."

"I'm sure I will." Actually Elise was pleasantly surprised at the accommodations. This room was almost as nice as her room on the plantation when she was wife of the heir. Yes, it was small and cramped, but the bed was roomy and made of solid oak, and there was a matching dresser. It seemed to lack but one thing. "I was wondering," Elise ventured, "if there is a crib available for my baby?"

"You can't have the kid right out in the open, you know. But this ought to suit it—"

"She," Elise put in. "Her name is Hannah."

"Well . . . yeah . . . sure." Mae opened a door to a small closet. "This room was the servant's quarters at one time, and this was the broom closet. A crate for the kid . . . ah . . . Hannah ought to fit inside. That's another reason for giving you this room."

"I suppose it will have to do." Elise didn't like the idea of her baby sleeping in a broom closet, but in the last couple of weeks, Hannah had slept in worse quarters. Elise set her small satchel on the bed and walked to the window, pulling aside the curtain of old yellowed lace. The street below was bustling with activity. She turned back to Mae. "Will I have time to rest before I begin my work?"

"It won't get busy here for a couple of hours."

"What exactly will my duties be?"

"You don't know?" When Elise shook her head, Mae rubbed her chin and grimaced. "You mean Maurry didn't tell you anything?" Again

Elise replied in the negative. "That coward! Naturally, he left it to me. You have no idea what kind of business goes on here?"

"A hotel . . . ?"

"That's a nice way of putting it. There are other names more fitting. Maybe you've heard of a bordello, or a bawdy house?"

Elise gasped.

"That's right, dearie. But this is a special place. We are all quadroons or, like yourself, light enough to pass for white. Maurry serves a broader clientele that way. And since he owns all of us, you can guess what his profit margin is."

"I . . . I don't care!" Clutching Hannah tighter than ever, she cast wildly about as if she could find a way of escape. "I won't—"

"Liz, you don't have no choice now, do you?"

"I'll run away!"

Mae nodded indulgently. "Come with me."

Elise hesitated, her mind in disarray, then dumbly she followed. They went to another room and Mae knocked. A dark-skinned girl answered. She could not have been more than fourteen or fifteen. Dressed only in a red silk wrapper over a ruffled chemise, she was quite lovely, even though she had not yet developed all her womanly attributes.

"This is Gina," Mae said. Then to Gina she explained, "This is a new girl. She has the idea she can avoid working for Maurry. I thought you could set her straight."

Gina shrugged. "I had the same idea once," she said to Elise.

"Show her what changed your mind," Mae said.

Gina turned her back toward Elise then lowered the shoulders of her dressing gown. Her back was crisscrossed with several scars, which, though mostly healed, were still red and angry looking. After rearranging the gown, Gina turned back and said, "I tried to run away. It didn't take very long for Maurry to find me. I won't do it again. What use is it? We're only slaves, a fact best not to forget." Then she shrugged resignedly. "Anyway, there's lots of white women that don't have it as good as us."

The girl's words were true enough, yet at the same time horrifying in her tone of glib practicality. Elise gaped, stunned both at the words and at the sight of Gina's back.

In a moment the numbness subsided, and Elise cried, "I'll never accept it!" Tears and fear clogged her voice. "He can't make me! I'll die first!" She spun around. She would flee this place. She didn't care how hopeless it was. Let them kill her. She could not live like this. Death was preferable.

But as she started blindly forward, she crashed up against a towering solid obstacle. Maurice Thomson.

"What's this?" His tone was mocking. "Do I detect resistance? This simply won't do. I have customers arriving soon."

The collision had started Hannah crying, but Elise hardly noticed through her own tears of rage and terror.

"You can't make me!"

Before she perceived her danger, certainly before she was able to guess anyone could be so heartless, Thomson whisked Hannah from Elise's arms.

"No!" she screamed.

Her sudden lunge for the baby was anticipated, and Thomson quickly jerked out of her reach, causing Elise to stumble forward, her flailing arms only reaching for air. Mae caught her before she went sprawling on the floor.

"You will not see the baby again until you prove complete submission to my will." Thomson's cool voice rose to a growl. "And just remember, your own death will not protect the baby."

"How can you be so heartless?" Elise sobbed.

"This is business. You are my property, as is the infant. If you are not obedient, I will sell the baby for whatever I can get and have done with it. Now return to your room. I'll be there shortly to ensure you are in the proper frame of mind for work. If you behave and my clients depart contented, you may see the infant in the morning."

PART TWO

JUNE 1834

CHAPTER 10

EARLY AFTERNOON WAS USUALLY QUIET at the hotel. The women didn't wake until late morning, and because they had few chores, the time until the evening activities was spent lounging about, gossiping, and taking care of personal needs like laundry, mending, and such. Elise had the additional task of caring for Hannah.

The baby had been returned to her after two days. It had been a harrowing separation for both the mother and the three-month-old child. The child had been placed in the care of a maid who knew nothing about children. She had tried to wean Hannah, and Elise had helplessly listened to the baby's cries of protest echoing through the house. Mae eased Elise's worries somewhat by telling her a wet nurse had been found. Maurice traded one of his maids straight across for the wet nurse, who could also perform maid's duties. Elise's encounters with Thomson thus far told her this act was more for the protection of his investment than for charitable reasons.

Only thoughts of Hannah kept Elise going. Determined to get her daughter back, Elise performed her duties to the satisfaction of her new master. It had sickened her so that she had literally vomited after her first encounter, though she had waited until she was alone so as not to displease the customer.

Once Hannah was returned to her, Elise tried to perform her loathsome duties in a way that would appease Maurry, but she could not shake her visceral sense of revulsion each time she led a customer to her bed. She tried to smile in a beguiling, tempting manner as the other women did. Perhaps if she indulged in alcohol as they did, she might be able to pretend more easily, but she refused that temptation because she wanted to have a clear head for Hannah. Thus, even she could sense the wooden, stiff result of her attempts at merriment. How could one smile and laugh when each time her insides twisted and trembled, writhing like an animal half-dead, half-alive?

The copious amounts of strong drink consumed by the men certainly did not keep them from complaining and refusing her company. But Maurry was furious with her. His threats became more and more ominous, and finally he came to her bed himself to teach her how to behave. He arrived drunk, as he often was, and executed his "lessons" in such a vile and violent manner that she was left physically bruised and emotionally shattered. Instead of turning into a saucy strumpet, she cowered in terror.

Elise thought frequently about taking her life but knew she would never do that and leave Hannah to the bereft mercies of her owner. She must escape. It was her only hope. So early one morning after her last customer had departed, Elise made a desperate attempt to flee. She had not even as viable a plan as she had had with her hapless flight back at the Hearne plantation; she simply gathered Hannah into her arms and slipped out of the house. But having been in New Orleans only one week, she had yet to venture out into the city, so she had no idea where to go once she left the house. It was too late to ask directions or to find a hack. Even if she could do so, she had no money to pay for passage from this town, her prison. She wandered the streets for hours, fear gnawing at her. Hannah's cries echoed that fear.

Maurry found her eventually and dragged her back to the house. After wrenching Hannah from her arms, he took her into her room and beat her, not with a whip and in no place where the marks would readily show, for he was conscious of not damaging prime property, as he called her.

When he was done with her, she asked, like the fool she was, "Where is Hannah?"

"Forget about the brat. You ain't never going to see her again."

"No!" she screamed.

For the next three days she was allowed to believe the worst, that Maurry had sold Hannah. In a fit of despair, she found a knife and would have used it on herself, but Mae, fearing such an action, had been keeping a close watch on Elise and stopped her in time.

Later Maurry came to her room. "You ungrateful little tart!" he railed. "I give you a roof over your head, food, everything a body could want, and you repay me like this."

She could almost have laughed at the gall of the man. He now thought *she* owed *him* something! Yes, it was laughable, but all it did was bring tears to Elise's eyes.

"Without my baby, I don't care if I live or die," she sobbed.

"Well, I don't like hearing that."

Suddenly Elise realized she had her own weapon, though she was painfully aware that it was a weapon with a double edge, just as lethal to her as it was to Maurry. Only her desperation made her use it.

"Maurry, I'll do anything if you get Hannah back to me."

"How can I get her back if I sold her?"

"You can do it. I know you can." She crawled from her bed where she had been lying and dropped to her knees in front of Maurry. "Please! I'll give you what you want. I'll do all you ask. Just get me Hannah!"

Maurry rubbed his chin, his beady little eyes narrow with thought. She knew he was thinking of his investment. She no longer cared. All that mattered was getting Hannah back.

"No more shenanigans?" he said.

"I'll be good. I'll be obedient."

"How can I believe you?"

"I . . . I give you my word."

"You know what the word of a nigger is worth?" His eyes glittered with cutting amusement.

"It's all I have," she replied lamely.

"That ain't exactly the case. . . ." His smile made her skin crawl. "Okay, I'll put you on . . . I think it's called 'probation.' You prove to me I can trust you, and I'll see what can be done about the brat. But I swear, you cross me again, and I will do more than sell her!"

Thus, after a week, Elise had learned to be a very obedient prostitute. And for her good behavior she was allowed to *visit* Hannah. It was several more weeks before Elise was given permission to have her child whenever she wished.

Mae taught Elise their nefarious trade well. Her first lesson being, "Think of something else, dearie. I think of all the fine dresses in the latest *Godey's Lady's Book*, which ones I would like and in what colors."

Clothing was one of the few pleasant aspects of Elise's plight. Maurice Thomson prided himself in operating a high-class bordello and wanted his women to look accordingly. Elise was given a few hand-me-downs at first, but after two weeks of obedience, Mae was given permission to take her to a dressmaker to be fitted for several outfits of her own. These were hardly of the style worn by a plantation lady, especially a matron, who was encouraged to wear sedate navys, browns, grays, and such. A genteel southern lady most often wore her hair confined to a conservative chignon, and face painting was considered absolutely scandalous. Sometimes, for a ball, Elise had been able to get away with a bit of pale rouge on her lips, but little more. Not so for the women of Maurice Thomson's employ. He insisted on gowns of bright, saucy colors, usually with a plethora of lace and the lowest cut décolletage possible.

Elise accepted this not only as a distraction, which she indeed learned to cling to, but also as another vital way to cope with her circumstance. The bawdy clothes and the liberal face painting provided a way in which Elise could further distance her inner self from what she had become. When she was outfitted in such a manner, she could hide her true self. In a small way this seemed to protect the core of who she was. It helped that when she looked in a mirror, she did indeed look like another person. Mother Hearne, or even Kendell himself, probably would not have readily recognized her.

In this way Elise managed to live from day to day. She survived, but it was a survival built on the shabbiest of foundations, much like the set of a stage play—very showy on the outside, but behind the glitter, nothing but scaffolding and sandbags. Elise had become an actress, playing the part of a fancy lady. Thus her world, such as it was, took on a semblance of security.

All this was to change drastically.

Elise had assumed Thomson was an established element in New Orleans. If he had used her mother in the same business twenty years ago, it seemed logical that he had been operating his shady "hotel" for that long. Elise learned otherwise one afternoon.

Mae came into her room as she was bathing Hannah. The older woman was carrying a carpetbag, which she laid on the bed. "Get yourself packed up, Liz."

"Why?" Panic surging through her, Elise dropped the sponge.

"We gotta vacate this place, that's why."

"We?"

"Everyone, Liz, not just you, so don't worry." Mae took on a motherly tone. She was only thirty years old, but her position of authority over the girls and the fact that she was the oldest lent her a certain air. Often she was kind, especially to Elise, but she could be hard as well. If a girl got out of line, her discipline was firm and sometimes harsh. She was like a berry patch—full of sweet fruit but surrounded by thorns.

"Where are we going?"

"You do ask a lot of questions, Liz."

"I suppose it is a difficult habit to break," Elise replied with a wry grin.

Mae allowed her taut lips to curve up at the corners. She didn't often let more of a smile than that escape because she was vain about the condition of her teeth.

"Well, Maurry is in trouble, and he is moving us out—lock, stock, and barrel. Well, probably not the barrel, maybe not even the locks. He's in a hurry. He was in a duel last night and killed the son of a high government official."

"Maybe they'll hang him." Elise felt no compunction at all for the hopefulness in her tone.

"It was all on the up-and-up. But the father of the victim holds some loan markers of Maurry's. He says he will call in the debts unless Maurry leaves town fast."

"That wasn't very bright of Maurry, was it?" Elise said with relish.

"You know men. Sometimes they think with their trigger fingers and not their heads." Mae shrugged. After fifteen years as Maurry's slave, she had been around him too long to be shocked by anything. "I never did think Maurry would be able to hang on to this place. Two years in one place is a long time for him."

"He's only been here two years?"

"He had a place here when he bought me fifteen years ago. Then he took off—I'm not sure why. Had a place in Natchez for a while, then Baton Rouge, and a half dozen places in between."

Elise tried not to think of the irony of her father's coming to New Orleans when he did. If he had waited two months . . . Elise shook those thoughts from her mind. They didn't help.

Instead, she said, "Mae, you've been with him all this time?"

"Do I have a choice?"

The matter of choice was something else best not to think about. Elise grabbed a towel from next to the tub, where she was bathing a contented Hannah. This was all she must think about—that Hannah should always be content like this.

"I'll finish with Hannah, then start packing." It made no difference to Elise if she did what she had to do in New Orleans or in some other place. In fact, she didn't even pursue the subject of their destination. She'd find out soon enough.

Saul, the house servant, came up a half hour later with a big trunk. Elise was to stow her possessions—except for immediate necessities—in the chest along with the belongings of the other girls.

The next morning the trunks and packing crates were taken down to the docks in a wagon. Six of Thomson's girls and the three slaves he kept as servants piled into two buggies and were transported to the docks on the river several miles south of New Orleans. He had sold off four of his remaining girls to finance the journey. Maurice met them at the dock, looking quite dapper in one of his expensively tailored broadcloth suits. He hardly looked like a man who was on the run. He certainly showed little worry about his future.

"Well, ladies, we are about to embark on an adventure!" He rubbed his hands together with an eagerness that almost dispelled the cruelty Elise had come to associate with the man.

"Where we goin', Maurry?" asked Gina, the young girl who had been whipped for attempting to escape.

"We are heading for Texas. I have a brother there who has been wanting me to go into business with him. Don't you know? I own a commodity much in demand in a frontier like Texas. I shall be a wealthy man. Don't know why I didn't think of doing it sooner."

"We gotta take a boat?" asked Sheila, an octoroon with blue eyes, tan skin, and hair dyed red. "I'm not fond of the water, Maurry."

"We will be sailing on the *RaeAnn*, a sound vessel. And it's only a five-day voyage." He turned to Mae. "Were you able to procure some stomach remedies?"

"I got tea and some powders." Mae did not seem enthusiastic about this.

Elise had never been to sea, but she had heard about seasickness. It could not be worse than the soul-deep sickness she had experienced in the last month. She would go where she must, do what she must so that she and her daughter might survive. Only once was she roused from her detachment. The stevedores were loading the ship, and one carried a peculiar-looking crate. It was rectangular and about three feet by four feet and fairly flat. She had once seen a similar parcel when the Hearnes had received a painting from a friend in London.

Elise nudged Mae. "Are they loading Maurry's belongings now?"

"I think so."

"Do you know what that is?" Elise nodded toward the parcel.

"No, but it must be something special for him to crate it up so careful-like."

Elise thought the same. She also determined to have a look at it at the first opportunity. She had not yet had a chance to see the painting of her mother. Maurice either did not want to hang it out in the open or simply hadn't had a chance to display it since its return from South Carolina—if he had intended to hang it at all. She'd thought about simply asking to see it but refrained because it galled her to ask anything of Thomson.

Benjamin arrived at the New Orleans dock about an hour before their ship, the *RaeAnn*, was to set sail. The luggage had gone ahead of them the night before, so he had only his family to deal with. That was responsibility enough. After many weeks on the trail and the short riverboat journey from Natchez, one would think the family would have mastered the art of travel. It was amazing how one tiny baby could so upset the order of things. He supposed with all the chaos that morning, he should be thankful they had not missed their ship entirely.

He could hardly believe they were less than a week from their destination, Texas. For so long it had been only an image in his mind, a sentence in his prayers, but soon it would become reality. The three-week delay in Natchez had been difficult for him, but it had worked wonders upon Rebekah. She was almost her old self. True, her smile was still halfhearted, but at least in a physical sense she was stronger.

"Come along, children," he said enthusiastically, "it is time we boarded our vessel."

"Will we be truly sailing on the sea?" Micah also was showing some enthusiasm.

"The Gulf of Mexico," Benjamin explained. "Not exactly the open sea, but close enough."

"Will we get wet, Papa?" Isabel asked tremulously.

"Of course not, child. This will be great fun."

Isabel looked up at her father, and he could not tell if it was doubt in her large blue eyes or merely incredulity at his speaking of fun. He wanted to defend himself, telling her he had nothing against fun, not really. It was only that the work of God was so serious and consuming that it often seemed frivolous to take time for amusements. But he said nothing. She was too young to understand deep matters of the spirit.

There was a large crowd on the dock, all either waiting to board the ship or waiting to bid farewell to passengers. Benjamin kept his family in a tight knot around him. He knew there would be all manner of unsavory sorts mingling with this crowd. For that reason he was keeping a sharp eye about him, and because of his watchfulness he saw a pickpocket ply his art upon a nearby woman—a woman holding a baby, no less!

"You there!" he called. "Stop this instant!"

The lad—he could not have been older than thirteen or fourteen—dropped the reticule, which had been dangling from the woman's arm by a string. He spun around as Benjamin took a step toward him. Their eyes met briefly before the boy sprinted away and made an expert dash through the crowd. Even if Benjamin had been of a mind to chase after him, he would not have succeeded because the lad disappeared so quickly.

The woman, now aware of the situation, glanced at Benjamin. She was dressed as a lady and quite beautiful despite much too liberal face paint. Her abundant hair was black, and thick lashes framed dark eyes, but her gaze was hard and bitter.

"It was a pickpocket," Benjamin explained, lest she think he might have committed some offense.

"Thank you for chasing him away. But I have no valuables." Her eyes flicked toward the child in her arms then back to Benjamin. "It was kind of you." She spoke in a genteel manner, belying the hard edges of her appearance.

An older woman came up to her and took her arm, nudging her forward. "Come on, Liz, it's time to board." This woman was also dressed like a lady, but unlike the younger woman, she did not look the part in any other way. Her skin was also of a shade to peg her as a mulatto.

"Good day," Benjamin said to be polite.

"Thank you again." Then the woman was bustled forward toward the ship.

Benjamin turned his attention back to his family, and soon they, too, were boarding the vessel *RaeAnn*.

CHAPTER 11

POINTING ENTHUSIASTICALLY TOWARD THE SHORE, Micah looked over the rail of the ship. They were still in the Mississippi but quickly approaching the mouth of the river. Benjamin knew this trip was an adventure for the boy, despite the deep resentment he usually showed over having been taken from his friends and family.

"What do you see, Micah?"

"Over there. What are those creatures? They are monsters, to be sure."

Lying upon a rock near the bank of the river were three or four alligators sunning themselves as if they had not a care in the world. The largest was a good ten feet in length.

"They are alligators, reptilian creatures. Don't you remember Uncle Haden telling about them? They are common in these parts."

"They look dangerous."

"I am certain they are."

Suddenly one rose up on its tiny legs, seeming to stretch, and opened its huge mouth revealing a frightening array of teeth. Micah gasped. Benjamin chuckled, then immediately forced himself to be sober. It was important that he maintain a stern demeanor so that his son would grow to be self-controlled and godly. Regardless of what men like Tom Fife or even Ezra Bancroft might say, Benjamin was certain that cavorting about with his children would cause a complete breakdown of his authority. As a father, he simply did not have the luxury to act as a friend to his children.

Benjamin added more seriously, "I'm sure it would not harm you unless you tried to harm it. That is the way with wild animals."

"I'd like to shoot me one and have it stuffed to hang over my bed like Uncle Haden did once with that big buck he shot."

"That is a frivolous endeavor. Animals should be killed for practical use, not merely for trophies and sport."

Micah shrugged. "I'm gonna see if the captain ever killed himself one."

With that, the boy skipped off, leaving Benjamin alone at the rail and wondering what it would be like if his son enjoyed his company as much as he did that of men like Haden or Fife or the captain. But that was the sacrifice he as a parent must make if he desired to raise godly children. He thought again of his own father and the fact that his stern rearing had produced godliness in Benjamin. He glossed over the evidence that his father's strict parenting had brought about a completely different result in Haden.

He was about to go seek out a quiet place to conduct his evening prayers when two passengers strode up to the rail near him and began conversing with each other.

"We chose an excellent time to come to Texas, I should say." The man who spoke was tall and dressed in buckskin, with a bushy brown beard on his weathered face.

The other man snickered. "I'll say!" He was shorter and thinner than the first man and wore an ill-fitting, frayed black broadcloth suit. "The place is looking better by the minute."

"Pardon me," Benjamin said, drawing closer to the men. "I couldn't help overhearing your conversation. It is encouraging to hear of positive elements in what will soon be my new home. Might I inquire of what you are speaking?"

"The . . . ah . . . special cargo aboard this ship," answered the man in buckskin.

"Cargo? Farm equipment and such?" Not a farmer himself, Benjamin found enthusiasm over such matters perplexing.

The broadcloth-clad man chuckled. "Females, sir."

Benjamin shook his head, still confused. "There are less than a dozen females aboard ship. Three or four are children, and the rest, I assumed, are attached."

"Not Maurry Thomson's girls."

"His daughters?"

Now both men laughed outright. "Ain't you never heard of Thomson?" asked the buckskinned fellow. When Benjamin shook his head, the fellow continued. "I heard Thomson was run out of New Orleans, and he's making for Texas with his girls." Still Benjamin responded with a blank stare. The man grinned slyly. "You ain't no man of the world, are you?"

"I am a minister of Christ."

"Oh . . ." The two men looked at each other and nodded knowingly.

"Well, sir," added the man in buckskin, "I'm sure it won't interest you."

"I couldn't say," Benjamin was growing impatient, "since I still have no idea of what you are talking."

"I think the minister's got a right to know," said the man in broadcloth. When his companion shrugged, he went on, a glint of amusement lighting his eyes, "Well, Reverend, Maurry's girls are . . . well, ever hear of women who entertain men for a living?"

First the blood drained from Benjamin's face, then he felt it return in a rush of heat.

"Aboard this ship?" he managed to say through his shock.

"That's right, Reverend. I'm surprised you didn't know of it, 'cause I saw you conversing with one of 'em on the docks yesterday before we set sail."

"You are quite mistaken. I would never!"

"Maybe you didn't know at the time, but you chased a pickpocket away from her."

"No!" He felt himself flush even deeper. "But she . . . that is . . . I . . . can't—"

"You think they gonna have horns in their heads or something, Reverend?" The amusement on the man's face was as distressing as his dismaying revelation.

"This is outrageous!" Benjamin hid his embarrassment in righteous indignation. "I cannot believe Mr. Austin would allow such immorality into his colony."

"Well, I reckon even Mr. Austin's got to turn a blind eye to some things. And in a country where men outnumber the women ten to one—"

"That's enough!" Benjamin huffed. "I'll not listen to lame excuses and glib defenses. There is no just argument for such wanton immorality. I see I am needed in the colony of Texas more than I ever dreamed." Then it occurred to him that the very ship in which he now traveled might be assailed with immorality. "Does the captain know?"

"It's hard to say. He might not have given them passage if he did."

"Well, I'm going to speak to him immediately."

As Benjamin spun around, one of the men called, "Too late to put them off the ship now."

Filled with a sense of outrage, Benjamin continued on his way. It took him fifteen minutes to locate the captain because one of the crew mistakenly sent him to the man's cabin, which was empty. He finally found him on the bridge, but by the time Benjamin reached it, his rage had calmed somewhat. He realized there was little to be done now that they were already en route. But he would at least register his protest.

However, when he reached the bridge and found his son there with the captain, Benjamin was torn in yet another direction. The boy's eyes were glowing with excitement.

"Papa! The captain let me steer the ship!" This was not the same boy Benjamin had been traveling with the last several weeks.

"Reverend Sinclair, you have a fine boy," the captain put in.

"I hope he has not been a bother to you, Captain Wakefield," Benjamin said.

"Not in the least. Haven't had such an enthusiastic pupil in years." The captain had eyes that glittered with sincerity and nearly as much enthusiasm as Micah's.

"Captain Wakefield said if I come up tonight, he will show me how to steer by the stars," Micah said.

"That's very kind of him." Benjamin could not make himself take that moment to browbeat the man who appeared to be his son's hero. "Perhaps we should go now, Micah, and leave Captain Wakefield to his work."

"He's welcome to stay," the captain said. "He's no trouble."

"Please, may I, Papa?"

Benjamin hesitated. As much as he hated to admit it, it stung knowing his son would rather be with this stranger than with his father. But he was too proud to force the issue.

"All right, but only for a few minutes. The captain does have work to do."

"You are welcome to stay also, Reverend Sinclair," put in Captain Wakefield.

"No, thank you. I have . . . uh . . . some errands to see to." He turned and left the bridge. He had forgotten all about *RaeAnn*'s heinous "cargo."

To distract himself from weighty thoughts of his son and the delicacies of fatherhood, Benjamin set out upon his former mission of trying to find a quiet place for his evening prayers. He wouldn't need the retreat until after dinner, but there was no sense wasting time then to find it. Besides, the exercise required by the search would do him good.

His venture took him from one end of the ship to the other without success. There was constant activity on the decks, so no nook or alcove there was suitable. He encountered two or three passengers at the rails looking decidedly green from seasickness. He thanked God he apparently was immune to that weakness. Micah and Isabel, too, had not been affected, but Rebekah was somewhat ill, though, thank God, not nearly as much as he noted in many other passengers. Benjamin once again felt God's hand upon his family.

Finding no proper retreat above deck, Benjamin made his way below decks. He was getting into areas that were no doubt near the cargo holds when he decided he would have to speak to the captain or first mate and have them suggest a place. There might be a vacant cabin. His own cabin of one small room was cramped, housing his entire family and offering very little quiet.

It was then he heard the peculiar noise. A crashing sound followed by a sharp cry that was not quite so serious as a scream but distressful nonetheless and definitely female. What would a female passenger be doing in these parts? He thought fleetingly of the "cargo" the two men had spoken of, but even as such, they would not literally be kept in the cargo hold.

He went toward the sound and soon came to a hatch that was open a crack. Pushing it open further, he stepped inside. The only light in the room came from a single candle at the far end. In the shadowed light he saw a figure, definitely female by the shape of the skirts surrounding it.

"Are you all right?" he called.

"Oh!" was the startled response. "Yes. I . . . I was trying to find something, and a crate nearly fell on me."

"Can I be of assistance?" Benjamin strode toward the candlelight.

He stopped short when the woman turned and the light caught her full in the face. It was the very woman he had assisted on the dock. Recognition dawned upon her face at the same moment.

"It seems you have come to my rescue once again, sir," she said lightly.

His mouth hung ajar, but no sound came out. This was *that* kind of woman. A fallen woman, a harlot. He gaped, as if she did indeed have horns growing from her head. But to his further amazement, she looked quite normal, even refined. Like a proper lady. She was even beautiful, but he quickly banished that particular observation from his mind. Instead, he thought how Satan often appeared as an angel of light. He also thought that he had never, to his knowledge, actually seen such a person and definitely never spoken to one. Yet twice within two days he had rescued her, speaking to her as if she were deserving of conversation with decent folk.

"Sir, is something wrong?" Her brow wrinkled in perplexity, and she glanced down at her feet as if expecting to find a rat sitting there.

"No." The word merely squeaked from Benjamin's lips.

"Well, then, I am quite all right. I do appreciate your concern."

She smiled, and that single gesture seemed to shake Benjamin from his numb shock. Though her lips merely twitched, it appeared to Benjamin to be the wanton grin of a temptress. And he realized that he was alone with her in the darkened hold of the ship, fair game for her dastardly designs.

"You . . . you should be ashamed!" he sputtered, then spun around and fled from the place as if running from the very fires of hell.

He did not stop until he was on the upper deck and breathing in the fresh, clean air of the sea.

CHAPTER 12

ELISE WATCHED THE MAN'S RETREAT, momentarily stunned. It took her a full minute before she realized what it was all about. Obviously between the encounter on the dock when he had rescued her from the pickpocket and this moment, he had learned of her nefarious occupation. Naturally, a respectable man would find himself nonplussed to come face-to-face with her kind of woman—not that Elise hadn't received many seemingly respectable men in her quarters in the last month.

But this particular man was probably *truly* respectable. He no doubt had never laid eyes upon a "fallen woman" before this moment. The idea of a man of his maturity exhibiting such innocence made her want to laugh and cry all at once. In a mere month she had almost forgotten such innocence existed. She had certainly forgotten her own. Survival meant constructing hardened walls about herself and eschewing memories of who and what she once had been. She *was* fallen. She was a woman from whom decent folk should flee.

Forcing these thoughts from her mind, Elise returned her attention to the task that had drawn her to the cargo hold of the ship. She was determined to have a look at the parcel she had seen carried aboard, which she was almost certain contained the portrait of her mother. Though Maurice's lawyer had brought the portrait to the Hearne plantation when he had come for Elise, she had not been given a chance to view it. After arriving in New Orleans, she had taken several opportunities to search about the hotel for it, but unsuccessfully. Perhaps it was silly to think Maurice would carry the painting with him in his flight from

New Orleans, especially in view of the fact that he had not exhibited it to the public at the hotel. But Elise was determined to find it.

Unfortunately, her quest was still unsuccessful. A crate had nearly fallen upon her head as she rooted about the cargo. She had avoided a serious mishap, but her shoulder still hurt where the crate had struck her. It must have been that which had alerted the man to her presence.

It occurred to her that he might tell the captain of her invasion of this part of the ship, obviously an off limits area to passengers. Well, what could they do to her? Put her off the ship? Then she thought of Hannah and realized afresh that her enemies, whoever they might be, would always have leverage over her.

Well, she was having no luck finding the painting anyway. It was probably stowed in some far corner and buried beneath other baggage. Perhaps she would just boldly ask Maurry to see it after they arrived in Texas.

She exited the cargo area and climbed the companionway up to the next deck where the cabins were located. Maurry had been able to afford only three cabins. One for himself and Saul, his butler, and two others in which his six girls and the two maids were evenly divided. With four women in one tiny cabin, it was cramped, to say the least. The fact that three of those women were suffering terrible seasickness made it worse. The odor in the room was foul and nearly did to Elise what the sea had been unable to do—turn her stomach.

As she approached the cabin, she could hear Hannah crying. She hurried down the corridor and stepped inside. Elise's three roommates were sprawled on their beds, oblivious to the crying child. Elise picked up Hannah.

"I'm sorry, sweetheart," she cooed, kissing the baby's downy soft hair. She noted absently that the child's hair was a medium brown, very much like her father's. Hannah could pass for white with even less difficulty than Elise.

Hannah was becoming quite a fussy child, but certainly not without cause. The last month had been extremely traumatic for the now four-month-old baby. Elise simply could not be the attentive mother she had once been. She could no longer even suckle the child. At least the nurse was a kindly woman who, having lost her baby within hours of its birth, was happy to have another child to fill her own void.

Still, Elise supposed she might, in a small sense, be withdrawing from her daughter. Maybe both of them would be better off if she didn't care so intensely for the child. Elise knew it was flawed reasoning, yet she feared it might still be so. And not once, but several times, Elise had entertained the idea of sneaking the baby out and abandoning her on the steps of some church. Surely Hannah would find a better life that way than in a brothel. But Elise could not let herself do it. It was pure selfishness, she knew, but she had lost so much in the last weeks that she could not bear to lose her daughter as well. She was almost glad that when they arrived in Texas the prospects of abandoning Hannah would be pretty slim. There were too few women in that country to entrust her daughter to.

Elise closely observed Hannah and could tell it was not merely fussiness that was causing her to cry. Laying her cheek against the child's head, she felt Hannah's skin and found it to be much warmer than normal. The child was also flushed, and her breathing, despite the crying, was rough.

Elise tried to wake Fannie, the nurse, but the young woman just moaned and begged to be left to die. One thing Elise had learned about the nurse was that the woman knew less about the care of children than did Elise—and Elise knew precious little. She could not expect the nurse to be of much use.

Over the next three hours, Hannah grew worse, and Elise's panic rose. She tried to think back to the plantation and things she had heard about caring for sick children. One of Kendell's sisters had spoken of her child once having croup. The symptoms were similar. But for the life of her, Elise could not recall what had been done for her nephew. He had survived the illness but had been sick for a long time.

When Hannah's breathing became so labored that her lips actually turned bluish, Elise left the cabin, clutching Hannah to her breast. Perhaps there was a doctor aboard. First she went to Maurice's cabin.

Any doctor or crew member would be more likely to assist her if the request came from Thomson rather than a mere slave. But Maurice was also prostrate with seasickness and none too civil.

"That brat's more trouble than she's worth!" His words were accompanied by a stream of curses. "Get that cryin' little chit outta here before I toss her into the cursed sea!"

Elise went to Mae's cabin. A couple of the girls there were well but had no idea what to do. Mae was feeling poorly but told her to leave the child with her and try to seek the help of the captain.

Captain Wakefield received Elise in his cabin. Though he must have known of her position as a slave if not a woman of ill repute, he was very polite and understanding.

"I'm afraid I have no medical personnel aboard." He rubbed his hand over his graying whiskers. "My first mate has some medical knowledge, but I know for a fact that he has no experience with children. I suppose that would be better than nothing—" He stopped short, and a light brightened his expression. "There is a woman aboard with three children. Perhaps she might know what to do."

"Who is it? I'll speak to her."

But the captain hesitated, seemingly flustered. "Well . . . I . . . uh . . . that might not be . . . you see, she is a minister's wife."

Ah yes. Again, Elise had forgotten who she was and the great impropriety it would be for a genteel woman to associate with her. But she wasn't about to back down, not when Hannah's life was at risk. She had already sacrificed much for the sake of this child.

"Captain Wakefield, could you speak to this woman? Perhaps she will relay any information she might have through you."

"That's an excellent idea! I'll do that very thing. You go wait in your cabin, and I will be there directly."

Rebekah opened her cabin door to find Captain Wakefield standing before her.

"Good evening, ma'am." He was a soft-spoken man with a gentleness about him one did not expect from a sea captain.

"Good evening, Captain. I'm afraid my husband is not here." She could think of no other reason for this man's visit. Benjamin was off somewhere at his evening prayers.

"Actually, ma'am, it is you I wish to see." He quickly and somewhat awkwardly explained his mission. "The young woman feels she is too far beneath your station to expect you to come to her, but I will gladly impart to her any wisdom you might have."

"Well, that's nonsense, Captain. I see no reason why I shouldn't go to her."

"Ah . . . it's just that . . . well . . . your husband might not approve."

Rebekah knew her husband had many quirks, but snobbery wasn't one of them. He had often visited the poor in their Boston neighborhood and ministered to them.

"I'm sure you are wrong. My husband has encouraged me to serve the poor."

"It's more than that, ma'am. I mean, there's more to it, but it just isn't proper for me to say more."

"Captain, you are not making sense. And as we stand here mincing words, a child lies ill. My husband isn't here, so I must make the judgment. And I say I need to see this child for myself before I can help it. Now please wait a moment while I gather up a few things."

Before the captain had arrived, Rebekah had been feeling sick herself with a queasy stomach from the rock of the boat, but suddenly she forgot about that. She had always been a person eager to serve others, but more than that, it was exhilarating to make her own judgment in this particular matter without having to seek her husband's wisdom.

"Micah," she said as she gathered a few items into a satchel, "please mind your sisters while I go on an errand."

Feeling a lightness in her step she had not felt in weeks, Rebekah followed the captain down the corridor.

CHAPTER 13

Rebekah was shocked to find four women sharing a tiny cabin half again as small as the one she shared with her family. It was stuffy inside and reeking with the stench of seasickness. Had Rebekah not been so intent upon her mission, she might have wondered at the peculiarity of four women, two obviously women of color, traveling together.

But upon entering the cabin, the crying baby immediately absorbed her attention. It was all the more pathetic in that the poor child was having quite a difficult time breathing. The young woman holding the baby was in nearly as much distress.

"Thank you so much for coming," she said. "But you didn't have to come here. . . ."

"Nonsense." Rebekah laid her hand on the infant's forehead. "How could I know what to do for the baby without seeing it? Is your baby a girl or a boy? I hate to keep referring to it as *it*."

"A girl. Her name is Hannah. I'm Liz."

"I'm happy to make your acquaintance, though I wish it were under better circumstances. I'm Rebekah Sinclair. Now, let's see what we can do for little Hannah. She seems to have a bit of a fever, but her breathing concerns me most." She set her satchel on a table, then looked about the cabin. "Do you have a kettle?"

"No, but I can find one."

"I would go myself, but I am afraid I am not tolerating the tossing of the ship very well."

"You really shouldn't have come if you are ill."

Rebekah smiled. "This will take my mind off my own woes. Now please fetch a kettle of water, and we will heat it on your stove here. I can hold Hannah if she doesn't protest too strenuously."

Within a fifteen minutes the kettle was boiling nicely. Rebekah added some eucalyptus leaves, then instructed Liz to place the baby's bed near the stove.

"Normally I would take a blanket and fix a tent over Hannah, but this cabin is so small the steam should build nicely without the tent. You'll be able to hold her. If only there was a rocker for you."

Liz set a chair by the stove and settled there with Hannah in her arms. "This will be fine. How long will it take for the medicine to take effect?"

"A few hours, I should think." Rebekah began packing up her satchel.

"The captain said you have children of your own. Is that how you know what to do?"

"I've just had my third child. I've learned through their illnesses and also from my mother."

Liz shifted uncomfortably in her chair. "I have neither of those benefits. I know next to nothing about children."

"You'll learn."

"You said you just had a baby?"

"She is nearly a month old." Rebekah smiled tenderly. She thought how she had resented Leah for so long while she carried the babe in her womb, but now that she was here, she thanked God for the joy the child brought. "My husband had hoped she would wait to be born in Texas, but I'm rather glad she came when she did. I'm afraid in Texas we will be even more in the wilds than we were on our journey from Boston."

"What brings you all this way from Boston?"

Rebekah restrained a bitter sigh. "My husband is a minister, and he has been called to Texas to spread the Gospel. What brings you to Texas, Liz?"

Liz's eyes flickered away from Rebekah, and she was silent for so long that Rebekah began to think she had unwittingly tread upon forbidden ground.

Finally Liz replied, "My master decided to settle there."

"Your master . . . ?"

"I thought the captain had told you . . ."

"No, he didn't."

"I should have said something, then. But I was so afraid you might not help if you knew."

Rebekah now understood about the women in the room. They were slaves. But this young woman before her looked nothing like a normal slave. Her skin was completely white, just like Rebekah's. Oh, perhaps it had a bit of a tan, but hardly enough for her to be a Negro. It completely baffled Rebekah. But what baffled her more, and even distressed her, was that Liz would think that might have influenced Rebekah's decision to help.

"It wouldn't have mattered, Liz." Rebekah's tone was filled with quiet intensity.

"There's more—"

"It would make no difference." She was firm in her conviction. In her inner, often unspoken, opposition to her husband, Rebekah sometimes doubted her faith, or at least doubted that she was a very good Christian. But even if she wasn't worthy of Christ, she did love Him and desire to serve Him. The fact that she didn't desire to share her husband's choice of service proved most confusing to her. "I know Jesus himself would not have refused you, no matter your race. How could I then do so? I would be no Christian if I saw need, especially the need of a little child, and turned away from it."

Liz's sad lips twitched into an uncertain smile. "Maybe I wouldn't have turned away from God if I had known more people like you, Mrs. Sinclair."

"Oh, but Liz, surely it is a mistake to base your personal faith on others. People can be so fallible."

"What other way is there?"

"The Bible shows God's true nature. You could not read the New Testament without meeting a God of love. May I tell you a little secret?" Rebekah actually glanced about as if she expected Benjamin to be standing over her with disapproval. She didn't know why she was speaking so candidly to this woman. Perhaps it was just because it had been such a long time since she had spoken with a woman near her own age and one, despite her situation, of obvious intelligence. "My husband preaches much about sin and retribution. His God is so wrathful at times it truly frightens me. I suppose he's right because he is a man of God, but . . . sometimes I think he has forgotten about God loving us so much He allowed His Son to die in our place. I suppose I am just being a sentimental female, but that is the God I cling to." She stopped suddenly and gave an awkward titter. "But I do go on! And I thought my husband was the preacher!"

"Thank you so much for coming, Mrs. Sinclair." Liz reached up a hand, which Rebekah took and gently squeezed. "I'll think about what you've said. I don't know how I will ever repay you for your help."

"I have been paid already." Rebekah flashed a conspiratorial smile. "I haven't felt this good in weeks. Now, I will hear no more of payment. But I do insist that you inform me if Hannah isn't better by morning. And if she worsens at all during the night, send for me immediately. I'm also going to have the steward keep you supplied with water through the night, so you won't have to fetch it. And I have left you some spare eucalyptus leaves."

CHAPTER 14

THE NEXT MORNING REBEKAH WAS anxious to see her patient again. After breakfast, which she and her family took in their cabin, she asked Benjamin if they could take some air on the deck.

"Of course, my dear!" He laid aside his napkin and studied her closely. "I'm so pleased to see you in better spirits. Even your color has returned."

"Yes, I do feel better. It truly lifted me to help that woman I told you about." She drank the last of her tea.

"I'm glad of that, but I still think you should have awaited my return before going. I should have accompanied you. I would have offered a prayer."

Rebekah felt a twinge of guilt that she had forgotten completely to pray for Liz and Hannah.

"I'm sure we can still pray for them. We can right now," she suggested.

"Yes, a very good idea."

It wasn't often—and it happened far less lately—that Rebekah felt such approval from Benjamin.

They bowed their heads as they sat at the small table. Benjamin prayed for ten minutes, touching upon several other topics besides Liz and the baby. When they finished, he helped Rebekah into her cloak, and they went up to the deck, leaving Micah to mind the girls.

The sky was clear, but a steady wind out of the southeast greeted them. Though chilly, the fresh air felt good after the closeness of the cabin. Rebekah leaned against the ship's rail, closed her eyes, and let the wind waft over her face. Benjamin stood beside her, and when she opened her eyes, she was surprised to see him smiling at her. He looked almost as he had when they first met, before he had been called to the pulpit, before the heavy mantle of God had been laid upon his shoulders.

"Have I done something to amuse you, Benjamin?"

He shook his head. "I was only thinking of the saying about seeing a light at the end of the tunnel. We have been in a long tunnel these last months, Rebekah, but I believe I finally see a light—the light of God himself. It makes me quite joyful."

"I am glad to see you joyful. There are times . . ." She paused, looking out at the expanse of sea, blue capped with frothy white. "I feared the joy had gone completely from our lives."

"Not as long as we keep focused upon our Lord." Benjamin patted his wife's hand, then was distracted as his eyes wandered from hers. When she turned, she saw the captain down at the other end of the deck conversing with a group of men. "Rebekah, I must speak with the captain. Do you mind if I leave you momentarily?"

"Not at all."

"I have been wanting to volunteer to hold Sunday services the day after tomorrow."

"Go on ahead. I'll wait here and enjoy the view."

She watched him depart, and when she began to turn back to the rail, she saw Liz approach from the opposite direction. She smiled a welcome, noting that though the young woman was not holding Hannah, she did not seem in any distress.

"I was going to come see you after I took some air," Rebekah said.

"There is no need, Mrs. Sinclair. Hannah is much better today. I left her sleeping better than she has in days."

"I'm so glad!"

Liz glanced toward the group of men. "Was that your husband?"

"Yes. I shall introduce you when he returns."

"I . . . I really can't stay." She suddenly looked like a scared rabbit. "I should go check on Hannah."

"Wait, Liz!" Rebekah laid a hand on Liz's arm just as she was about to retreat. "I have something for you."

"I don't think I will need more medicine—"

"It's not that." Rebekah opened her reticule and withdrew a book. "It's my New Testament. I would like you to have it."

"Thank you, but I couldn't take it."

"Please. It would make me so happy if you would. Let's just call it a loan. We will both be in Texas, so it is likely we will see each other again. You can return it after you have read it."

"It is I who should be giving you a gift for what you did for Hannah. But I have nothing to give."

"Someday you may be able to give me something. We won't worry about it until then. Now take this"—she pressed it into Liz's hand—"as a loan."

Liz looked at the book, sudden tears welling into her umber eyes. Her lips trembled with emotion as she tried to speak. "You are so kind—"

"Rebekah!"

Both women jerked their heads in the direction of the sharp tone. Benjamin was approaching, his eyes filled with stern displeasure.

"Benjamin, I would like you to meet Liz, the mother whose child I helped yesterday." Rebekah simply could not fathom the look in her husband's eyes.

"*This* is the woman you helped?"

"Y-yes, of course. . . ."

Rebekah's husband and Liz locked eyes as Rebekah looked on, astonished. Did Benjamin know the woman was a slave? Though he was a hard man at times, Rebekah knew he intensely opposed slavery and would never despise a person simply on the ground of their ancestry or station in life.

"Come with me, Rebekah," Benjamin said tightly.

"That won't be necessary." Liz fairly spun around on the heel of her shoe and swept away.

Rebekah secretly applauded the woman for her hauteur. "Benjamin, that was terribly rude of you," Rebekah said boldly.

"I will give you the benefit of ignorance. You simply cannot understand about that woman."

"I understand that she is a decent woman in need."

"Decent!" He clamped his hand around her elbow and began to propel her away. "This is not the place to discuss such a matter."

Rebekah noted that several more passengers had ventured onto the deck and were in close proximity. She let Benjamin lead her to a private alcove near the dining hall where there was a small table and two upholstered chairs.

"Sit down," he ordered, scolding her as if she were one of the children.

She hesitated stubbornly but could tell by the glint in his eyes, like ice shaved from a pond, and by the adamant way in which his arms were crossed that she could not win a battle of wills with him. She seldom could. She sat on the very edge of the chair. If he was going to treat her like an errant child, she would behave as one. She faced him silently while he took the adjacent chair.

"Rebekah, it is my duty as your husband to protect you from the evils of this world." His tone remained stern, but the rebuke was gone. "You are of a genteel, well-meaning nature, but your weakness is to place these above good sense. However, even that cannot be placed to your account in this particular matter."

"I don't understand what you are getting at." She was more confused than ever.

"Rebekah . . ." he sighed her name in a more benevolent way. "You simply must be more careful in your associations. That is why you have a husband to determine these things for you."

Ignoring the last part of his statement, which grated on her in its own right, she said, "Benjamin, you have never been a snob, nor have you looked down on others for their stations. You have your faults, Benjamin, but that is not one of them. You are a fair man."

"You should know I would never tolerate sin!"

"What has sin to do with this? Slavery is a sin. And I feel it is my God-given duty to reach out a hand of kindness to those who have been so abused." He could not possibly fault her argument.

"Slavery? That has nothing to do with this." He shifted in his chair, suddenly looking very uncomfortable himself. "I shudder at having to discuss such a delicate matter with you, and that alone makes me furious at the woman for forcing me to do it. You should not have to be confronted with such things." He paused, glancing around as if seeking rescue. Finding none, he continued. "The woman you helped, Rebekah, is a . . . a . . . a woman of . . . well . . . ill repute."

"I don't understand."

"Surely even you are not so naïve. That woman . . . entertains men!"

Rebekah's brow knit, revealing her perplexion. Then suddenly understanding dawned upon her. With a gasp, her hand shot to her mouth in shock.

"No!"

Letting out a relieved sigh that he would not have to give a more detailed explanation, Benjamin nodded. "Now you can understand why I was so upset that you socialized with her in any manner."

"But, Benjamin, if she is a slave, does she have any choice in the matter?"

"There are women in Boston, free women, of whom the same could be said. Whether willful or not, what they are doing is sin. If they had a true heart for God, if they cared for their immortal souls, they would do anything to avoid committing this terrible sin."

"But—" Rebekah stopped. She wanted to argue that there were ways in which women could be forced into such behavior, which she thought even God might forgive. She wanted to say that men held such a dominance over women she could fully understand how one could fall into, or be forced into, such behavior. But she held her tongue, for the words smacked too much of rebellion, which she knew would enrage her husband. Best not to antagonize him.

She decided upon a different tack. "Benjamin, if they are sinners, isn't it our duty as Christians to minister to them?" She spoke sweetly, smiling innocently.

"There are those who are called to minister to such people. *You* are not one of them."

"What if I felt God were calling me—"

"I'll tell you what God is calling you to!"

"But—"

"Don't argue with me, Rebekah. Your only duty is to do as I say. And I am telling you I do not want you to associate with that woman or any like her."

"Her child was sick. I could not refuse."

Relenting slightly, he said, "Then I will act as a go-between. If I am not present, you must refuse."

Sighing helplessly, Rebekah nodded. Just as there were ways a man could dominate a woman, there were ways a woman could find around them. Subtlety was one of them. It might not always work for women like Liz, but Rebekah found it served her in some instances. She would agree with her husband, then do what she wished, accepting the inevitability of a tongue-lashing later.

"I best see to the children," she said, rising.

He stood also. "I am glad we have come to an understanding, Rebekah. I will remember to pray that God gives you strength in these things."

"Thank you, Benjamin." As they reached the companionway to the lower deck, she paused. "Benjamin, are you certain she is really that kind of woman?"

"Yes, of course I am."

"Oh my!" She continued down the stairway. She could not help being in just a little awe. She had been raised to think of such women as next to Satan himself. To have actually spoken to one, to have touched one—she didn't know what to think. Liz seemed like such a sweet, gentle girl. She was no monster bent on driving decent men into perdition. Maybe she was a sinner, but the Bible said that all have sinned.

Even I am a sinner, she thought. She wondered if the sin Liz committed was worse than the sin of bitterness and anger Rebekah held in her heart. She dare not ask her husband. She also dare not tell him she had given that woman the New Testament he gave her for their engagement.

Elise rose in response to the knock on her cabin door. She supposed it must be the steward with water, though she thought she had told him his services would no longer be necessary. She could barely hide her shock when she opened the door and saw Rev. Sinclair. On their three previous encounters, she had been too flustered to really take note of this man who was becoming rather a nuisance, if not a thorn in her flesh.

She had to admit he had a handsome appearance that could have been rather disarming if he would allow his taut lips and disapproving scowl to relax. Since seeing him on the deck with his wife, she had wondered how such a sweet, gentle-natured woman like Rebekah could have fallen in love with such a man. She decided the marriage must have been arranged and poor Rebekah had had no say in it.

However, a closer look made Elise think there might have been a time when Rev. Sinclair was a young man of humor, perhaps even a romantic. If he chose to smile, even laugh, he could well have won the heart of a young lady. Too bad that whatever inclination he might have had toward humor was gone now. Too bad, especially because Elise felt certain that dour bearing was about to be leveled upon her.

"Reverend Sinclair, may I help you?"

"I feel led to speak with you." His gaze flicked briefly over her shoulder then back to her face. He was obviously nervous, his hands twisting the book he held. But his voice was full of hauteur.

"Would you care to come in?" Though she knew it was cruel of her, his tone made her relish the slight lilt in her voice and the very subtle innuendo to the invitation.

This time he refused to be flustered. "I think it would be best to talk here in the corridor."

"As you wish. One moment, please." She went back into the room and securely tucked a blanket around Hannah, who lay sleeping on Elise's bunk. Then, closing the door behind her, she stepped out into the hall. "To what do I owe the pleasure of this visit?" Her lips slanted into a lopsided smile.

"I see this visit is more expedient than I thought."

If it were possible, his mouth seemed to become even more taut and thin. Elise had an almost overwhelming urge to find a way to crack the ice of his demeanor. The last person she had seen so proud and arrogant had been Daphne Hearne. "What do you want, Reverend?" she asked more soberly, resisting the urge to goad him, to knock him down a notch, to vent on him what she had been too cowardly to do upon Mrs. Hearne.

"My wife, foolishly, perhaps, but with a sincere heart, ministered to the physical needs of your child."

He licked his lips, and for the first time Elise realized that he might not *like* doing or saying what he felt he must.

"The Word of God clearly indicates that as the physical needs are met, so must the spiritual needs be ministered unto. My wife failed to do this."

"You are wrong there, sir. Mrs. Sinclair very kindly spoke of God's love and care."

His eyebrow twitched with disdain. "My wife has a rather simplistic view of matters of the Spirit." He lifted his hands, opened the book he held, and began to speak. "Hear the Word of God: 'And fear not them which kill the body, but are not able to kill the soul: but rather fear him'—God, our Father—'which is able to destroy both soul and body in hell.' "

Pausing, he turned several pages. Elise wondered why he even bothered, since it was apparent he knew the words he read by heart.

" 'For the wages of sin is death; but the gift of God is eternal life through Jesus Christ our Lord.' Have you heard these words before, ma'am?"

"Would it matter if I had?" she countered defensively.

"It would matter if you cared for your soul. Do not deal lightly with the things of God. Your very soul lies in jeopardy. As the prophet Isaiah has written, 'Your iniquities have separated between you and your God, and your sins have hid his face from you, that he will not hear.' "

"Thank you for informing me of this, Reverend," she said coldly. "But I don't need you to tell me of my failings."

"Apparently you do. I have yet to see a repentant spirit in you."

"And it will be a cold day in that place of which you speak so eloquently before I'd repent to you!"

"You have no right to take offense. I speak but the message of God, and I do so because I despair for your soul. Do you not care that you will burn in eternal damnation?" His face reddened with his zeal, and she actually thought he truly did care about her.

Too bad he did so with such self-righteousness, such pretension. If he did care, it was only as a god cares for the lowly minions groveling at his feet. Well, maybe she had to grovel to Maurry Thomson, but she'd never do so to this pinch-faced, vainglorious buffoon!

Glaring with all the disdain she could muster, she spit out her reply. "I never expected to do anything else but burn in hell, Reverend. Now I must see to my daughter."

She spun on her heel to make a grand exit from their conversation, but the door latch would not respond quickly enough to her hand. Muttering a curse, she gave it a shove with her shoulder, to no avail.

Sinclair stepped forward and, without actually touching her, nudged her aside. "My door does this also." He gave the latch a couple of tugs and jiggles and got the door to open.

"Thank you," she said out of mere instinct, cursing herself for the words the minute they were spoken. So much for her grand exit.

"You are welcome."

His words were spoken deliberately. Maybe he thought she was taking the opportunity of the stuck door to thank him for his sermon.

Perish the thought!

"Thank you for opening the door." Following her pointed words, she swung inside the cabin and shut the door with what she hoped was a firm motion.

But once inside, Elise leaned against the closed door, her heart pounding as if she had just been chased by slave hunters, or worse. She heard the click of his shoes as he retreated down the hall.

"I don't want to burn in hell or anywhere else," she murmured.

But she supposed she would, just like he said. Surely God made no allowances for extenuating circumstances. Sin was sin whether one did it willfully or not. She was a sinner—no doubt about that. And the wages of sin is death, according to the reverend's Bible. Then her gaze fell upon Rebekah Sinclair's New Testament. The woman had said she should judge God by His words, not by the words of others. She wondered if Rebekah had been thinking of her husband when she'd said that.

In that case, she thought, I will read her book . . . next chance I get. Tomorrow, perhaps.

CHAPTER 15

San Felipe de Austing, formally established in 1824, just a little more than ten years ago, was situated on a pretty bluff surrounded by good land, plentiful timber, and, as evidenced by many patches of green, sufficient water. The town near the banks of the Brazos River had a population of some two or three hundred, and there were well over fifty houses. True, they were coarse buildings of unhewn logs and clapboard roofs. But it had very much the feel of an American frontier town. The residents of both San Felipe and Texas were overwhelmingly American, exemplified in the act of dropping the Mexican name of *Tejas* for the more American name of *Texas.* They even called themselves *Texians,* showing further disdain for their Mexican overlords.

Benjamin felt certain he could be content in this land. Their final destination, however, was some distance northeast of this town. But after debarking the ship in Galveston and taking a coach to San Felipe, he had deemed it prudent to rest for a couple days before undertaking the final leg of their journey.

Being so close to their destination, the two days' wait had been excruciating for him. But Rebekah was so weary after the boat trip that she had begun to fall back into the melancholy that had lifted a bit after the birth of Leah.

Rebekah came up to him as he stood on the porch of the hotel.

"We are all packed." The absence of even a hint of excitement in her voice made him wince.

"Rebekah, we have come to a fine land. Truly a promised land."

"As you say, Benjamin."

He hated to rebuke her yet again, but her attitude was once again affecting the children. "Rebekah . . ."

Just then the man they had hired to guide them to their destination of Cooksburg approached.

"Morning, Reverend Sinclair." His name was Walt Ramsey, and he was a seasoned frontiersman, dressed in worn buckskin with a beaver hat perched over long, unkempt hair. "Got the horses and mules all ready down at the stable."

"Thank you, Mr. Ramsey. I'll get my family together and meet you there."

Fifteen minutes later the Sinclair entourage was gathered in the stable. Benjamin had purchased two horses, a dapple-gray mare, which was young and sturdy, and a bay gelding that was a bit older. These he would need for use on his circuit as well as for his family. He and Rebekah and Leah would ride these on the journey. He had also hired another horse and four mules to carry Micah and Isabel and all their belongings. He had been told when he arrived that wagons were out of the question because the roads, where there were roads, were little more than dirt tracks through rough terrain. In addition to these animals, he had also made the purchase of a milch cow. He felt certain they would want for nothing in their new home.

"We're getting a good early start," Ramsey said when they were all mounted up. "I'll bet we can get to Cooksburg by tomorrow afternoon."

"I don't bet, Mr. Ramsey. I trust God," Benjamin replied.

"Well, then. God willing"—Ramsey's tone held a hint of a sneer—"we'll make good time."

Benjamin groaned inwardly at the prospect of traveling two days with another uncouth specimen. He was disappointed his brother had not been in San Felipe to greet them. But then, Haden knew nothing of Benjamin's decision to come to Texas. After asking around town, Benjamin learned that Haden was off somewhere exploring the country. Benjamin had left a message with the storekeeper, so he hoped that in due course Haden would catch up to him. True, Haden could be as uncouth as both Ramsey and Fife together, but he was family.

Benjamin reminded himself, as he had been doing frequently since their journey began, that each unsaved soul he met was just further proof of the great need here for his ministry. And this urged him forward. For the next two days, he was constantly several lengths ahead of the group. It took all his restraint to keep from charging forward at a full gallop.

The last leg of the long journey from Boston had just the opposite effect upon Rebekah. Two days of jostling on the back of a horse made her wonder how she would bear another minute, much less a lifetime, of this wilderness. Even in San Felipe there had been other women and social activities. The day after they left there was to be a ball, not that Benjamin would approve of dancing. The wife of the storekeeper had invited her to join the few women in town for their weekly sewing circle. But she had had to refuse because they would not be staying.

Rebekah's misery was compounded by their arrival at the settlement of Cooksburg. It seemed euphemistic to even bother attaching a name to a place that consisted of nothing more than a tavern and a trading post. Albert Petty, the proprietor of both establishments, extended to them a rather stilted welcome. He seemed a dour, introverted man, and Rebekah sensed he felt awkward having a man of the cloth invade his premises, where the odor of ardent spirits was quite strong. He did offer directions to the cabin that had been occupied by Benjamin's predecessor, Rev. Meredith. Presumably this would be the Sinclairs' new home. It was seven or eight miles northeast of Cooksburg.

Mr. Petty also had some disturbing news. "Hope you have better luck in these parts than Meredith."

Ignoring the frivolous reference to *luck*, Benjamin inquired, "What happened to him?"

"He was arrested about a year ago. The fool started preaching to the alcade himself. Made a right nuisance of himself, as I heard tell. Well, he was no young man, and he died in prison down in Saltillo."

Benjamin's eyes skittered toward Rebekah. Had he known this all along and withheld it from her? A closer look at her husband showed he was just as shocked at the news as she. The bishop, no doubt out of Christian kindness, had been the one to withhold this information. Rebekah felt bitterness wrap itself more firmly than ever around her heart.

They arrived at the cabin after dark. Benjamin managed to find a candle upon entering the log structure, but Rebekah was almost sorry he had, for the small flame justified her worst fears. The crudely built cabin consisted of only one room. And that room was not even as large as the typical Texas dwelling, which usually contained two rooms with an open-air corridor, often called a dog run, between them. Rebekah did not even want to think of how it compared to her cozy little home in Boston!

Rev. Meredith had been a widower, a fact quite apparent in the shadowed view of the place. There were no furnishings to speak of save for a coarse table, crudely built, with two matching benches on either side. There was not even a stove. A blackened kettle hanging in the hearth indicated where Meredith had done his cooking. Rebekah's lip quivered as she thought about cooking for a family of five over an open fire.

The sleeping arrangements brought a lump to her throat. The one bed in the cabin was nothing more than a pile of weeds covered with a filthy blanket. It looked as if wild animals had recently enjoyed its use. The cabin was not just untidy—it was downright dirty. The women in San Felipe had jokingly referred to Texas dust, but this place seemed to be the source of it all. Benjamin had to chase out a family of raccoons that had taken up residence since Meredith's absence. The animal odors were horrendous.

Rebekah burst into tears.

"By adversity we are made strong," Benjamin said.

She did not respond, knowing if she uttered a single word, it would be to scream things at her husband that were unfit for the tender ears of their children—not that she even knew such words. Silently she began chastising her worldly innocence.

Benjamin continued in an annoyingly buoyant tone. "You have a wonderful, God-given talent for housekeeping, Rebekah. You shall have this place transformed into a cozy abode in no time. Think how blessed we are to have a house already built."

Still silent, she opened one of her carpetbags and took out a quilt her mother had made for her wedding. With as few words as possible she instructed the children to lie on the weed bed, then she covered them with the quilt. Isabel had begun to weep also, but Micah was stony. She knew she should comfort them, but she simply had nothing to give.

"You have given the children the only bed in the place," Benjamin pointed out.

Ignoring him, she forced her attention to the sleeping Leah, whom Ramsey had taken from Rebekah's arms when she had dismounted her horse.

Silently, but with tears still flowing from her eyes, she found an empty wooden box no doubt used for firewood that she deemed would be a suitable cradle. Into this she placed a second quilt, the only other one she possessed, then took the sleeping baby and laid her in the box. Sitting down on the rickety bench by the table, Rebekah blew her nose into her handkerchief, avoiding her husband's eyes.

"Rebekah, I demand that you answer me!" He moved around to face her, but she kept her eyes fixed upon her hands folded in her lap.

Sniffing back a fresh flow of tears, she dabbed her eyes. Maybe she would never speak to him again. That would serve him right for dragging her to this nightmarish place.

"All right, wife! I will bring in the bedding from the trip. Perhaps by the time I return you will have come to your senses. I suggest you seek God for wisdom and strength to accept the lot He has bestowed upon you."

She wanted to yell that she would never accept it, but she said nothing as he exited. Neither did she pray. Stubbornly she refrained from all thoughts of God and faith. She loved God as much as anyone, but for the moment it galled her to obey her husband, even if it kept her from doing the one thing that really might help.

Instead, she nursed her anger and self-pity. When Benjamin returned and spread out the bedding they had used on the trail, she silently lay down and closed her eyes.

Benjamin wisely made his bed across the room from her.

CHAPTER 16

Benjamin awoke while it was still dark. Quietly he pulled on his boots, then made his way outside. Walt Ramsey had bedded down outside and was still asleep. Benjamin was glad to slip away without having to socialize.

He walked about fifty yards into the woods surrounding the cabin and knelt to pray in a small clearing. He did not lift his bowed head until the sun had fully risen. It did not concern him that Rebekah would be worried over his absence. Morning and evening prayers had been his habit since he had entered the ministry. But this time when he finished he did not return directly to the cabin. Instead, he took a few minutes to walk around in the woods and assess their new surroundings by the light of day.

Whoever had built this cabin had chosen a pretty spot. He could hear the sounds of a creek not far away. Standing on a little knoll, he could see scattered groves of trees—oak, pine, hickory, magnolia—in a sea of undulating grass. The sky overhead was clear and a vivid blue.

A rider approached from the west, and Benjamin waved vigorously. The fellow waved back and soon reined his mount before him.

"Good morning, sir," Benjamin greeted.

"Morning!" The rider looked Benjamin over carefully. "You wouldn't be the new preacher, would you?"

Benjamin hesitated before answering, taking a moment to scrutinize the rider first. After all, if this man was an agent of the Mexicans, it could cause no small amount of trouble to disclose his calling. Yet he could not have much of a ministry in this new land if he cowered in fear with every stranger he met. Luckily, or rather by the grace of God, the man spoke up again.

"You don't need to be a-feared of me if'n you're the preacher, though I sure can understand if you are, seeing as how I'm a stranger."

"I fear none but the Lord God, sir." Benjamin held the man's gaze steadily. "But for the sake of His mission, I feel prudence is required."

The man grinned. "I reckon you don't need to say more, Preacher."

Benjamin shrugged. He had already decided not to lie to anyone. "Does mere chance bring you this way, sir?"

"No, as a matter of fact, it don't. I came to the trading post last night to trade some furs, and Al Petty said you was here. There's a mighty lot of folks in these parts that'll be right glad to know you're here."

"I'm pleased to hear that."

"Well, anyhow, I got me a couple hours sleep at Petty's, then rode on up here as fast as I could in order to find you." The man paused, dismounted, then thrust out his hand. "Name's John Hunter."

Hunter was a man of about Benjamin's age; short but powerfully built, with a broad, beardless face and heavy freckles. The addition of red hair gave him the look of an Irish leprechaun. His dress was suitable to the frontier—worn denim trousers, a coarsely woven brown shirt, and a leather vest.

"I'm Reverend Benjamin Sinclair." Benjamin shook Hunter's hand. The man had a strong, firm grip that impressed Benjamin. He often used this means to make initial judgments of a man. "Can I be of service to you?" he asked.

"That you can, Reverend. You see, my mother's been ailing for a couple of months now, and I honestly think the only reason she's hanging on is in hopes of seeing a man of the cloth so's she can make her peace with God. When I heard you was here, I knew I better not go home unless I had you with me. Not that I'm anxious to see my ma die, but if she's got to go, then I reckon it better be with a contented heart."

"That would be preferable. Is she not a Christian?"

"She's as God-fearing as they come. It's just that . . . it ain't never set well with her what she done when she came to Texas. She only did it for my pa. He was set on having land and—"

"And he converted to Papism in order to do so?" Benjamin's words were far more an accusation than a question. Logically, he could understand the difficult position of the settlers, but in his heart he could not abide the choice they had made in rejecting their born faith for material gain. Perhaps these people had little choice, yet he saw them as weaker for it.

"In our hearts we're still Methodists, Reverend." Hunter's tone was understandably defensive. "It's just on paper that we are Catholic."

"You minimize both faiths by your actions."

"We had to have land. What else could we do?"

"Whatever you did in the past, Mr. Hunter, you must now turn from those things. Humble yourself before God and implore His mercy."

"That's just what my ma wants to do, Reverend. That's not to say I oughtn't to do it, too, but right now she's my main concern. Will you come to my place and speak to her? It's been a powerful long time since we seen a preacher. There ain't even been a priest through here since . . . I can't remember when."

"I will come, Mr. Hunter. Where do you live?"

"Northeast of here a mite. If we leave now and ride hard, we'll get there late this afternoon."

For the first time Benjamin hesitated. He could not forget, though he almost had, what awaited him at his own home. "I don't know how soon I can leave," he said, desiring to do the right thing. "We only just arrived last night, and I don't like leaving my family alone in this strange place so soon."

"I hate to be pushy, Reverend, but I just don't know how long my ma'll hang on."

Benjamin chewed on his lip in thought. "Come back to my cabin with me."

By the time they arrived at the cabin, everyone was awake. Isabel was playing outside in the front yard, and Micah had passed them on the path carrying a bucket in order to fetch water from the creek. Ramsey had gathered a load of firewood and was carrying it to the cabin. Benjamin relieved him of the wood and, asking both men to wait outside, headed toward the cabin. He deemed it wise to confront his wife outside the earshot of strangers.

Upon entering the cabin, Benjamin saw Rebekah bent over the low hearth of the stone fireplace attempting to place a cast-iron kettle on a hook. Benjamin strode up to his wife, laid his burden of wood down near the hearth, then reached for the kettle.

"Let me do that," he said gently. He knew he had to make up for her anger last night and for the decision he had made as he approached the cabin with Mr. Hunter.

Rebekah stood aside, giving him a cold glance, unsmiling, unwelcoming.

"Rebekah, I must speak to you." He fastened the kettle into place, then reached for a handful of the smaller branches of wood to use for kindling. "Please get me my tinderbox." He arranged the branches under the kettle.

She found the tinderbox in his knapsack and gave it to him. In a few minutes he had a nice blaze going.

Straightening his back, Benjamin looked around the cabin. "It is amazing how much a fire does to warm a home and make it cozy."

She replied only with a sour look.

He rubbed his hands together over the flames. "Rebekah, God has confirmed to me how vital is my mission to Texas. I have been here less than a day and already there is an urgent call for my ministrations. Isn't that wonderful? A man has come seeking for me to visit his dying mother. I doubt they have seen a minister in at least a year. Imagine that! No spiritual guidance for that long! This place is truly ripe and ready for harvest. Haden might have been jesting when he said Texas needed men like me, but it was God's truth nonetheless." He paused and looked at his wife, hoping for some break in her icy demeanor. There was nothing. He almost preferred her tears to this. He forged ahead. "I must be gone about three days—"

"What?" A crack now appeared in the ice.

"The Hunter place is a day's ride away."

"How could you, Benjamin!"

"Why can't you support my ministry?" he retorted, forgetting his desire to be conciliatory. "You did when we were first married.

You basked in being a minister's wife! Now you behave like a heathen." He grabbed a chunk of wood and tossed it into the fire. Sparks sprayed everywhere, and he had to step aside to avoid them singeing his boots.

"I can't believe you would consider leaving me—leaving your helpless family in this Godforsaken wilderness. We don't even know where we are. Our nearest neighbor is more than five miles away. I haven't even a—" She stopped as her voice broke in emotion, and her ice melted altogether. New tears sprang to her eyes. "There's not even a stove to cook on."

Her voice shook, and Benjamin could not tell if it was with anger or misery.

"We don't even know where to get water. Micah could be lost forever trying to find it. And what about Indians—"

"There are no hostiles in these parts."

"How do you know that? Because the mission board told you? The same people who forgot to tell you your predecessor had been arrested?"

The truth of the words stung, but Benjamin focused only on the tone and attitude in which they had been spoken. "Rebekah, bridle your tongue before you say something you will regret."

"My only regret is that I came here in the first place."

"Please, Rebekah, I don't want to leave like this."

"Oh, you want my blessing? Is that it?" Her sarcasm was especially ugly coming from her usually soft-spoken voice.

"I will speak to Mr. Ramsey. I'm sure he will agree to remain here a few days to help out."

"I don't want Mr. Ramsey. I want my husband!"

"You cannot always have what you want. I belong to God. You know He comes first."

"Go then!" she yelled in a most ungodly way. "Good riddance, too! We will manage just fine without you. It will be nothing new for us."

"Rebekah . . ."

He came to her and put his arms around her, but her body stiffened in his embrace. He tried to remember when it had been different, when she had responded to his affection. But those early years of their marriage when it had been so were dim in his memory now. He held her anyway and kissed her forehead, taking a very small comfort in the fact that she did not pull away. Perhaps a few days apart was just what they needed after all. It would cause her to appreciate him more. They both had known from the beginning that his job as a Texas circuit rider would take him away from her for long periods, though he did conveniently forget that he had never asked her if it was what she wanted.

He felt bad that his job had to take him away so soon, but he could not ignore God's call. He never had in the past, and he never would.

CHAPTER 17

LIZ WIPED BACK A COIL of hair from her eyes, smearing a swath of soapsuds across her nose as she did so. She brushed a damp sleeve over her nose, then continued washing the shirt in the big wooden tub.

Texas was not New Orleans. Here a small aura of respectability was needed to cover Maurice Thomson's business, so he had put his girls to work doing laundry for the many single men in the settlement. Of course, most folks knew what really went on but were apparently quite willing to overlook the hidden activities. There weren't enough women around to make a loud protest, and the men, well, they certainly weren't going to protest, now, were they?

Thomson had settled his entourage on his brother's land about five miles west of San Felipe. Lyle Thomson was more than happy to welcome them. He was a bachelor with the same moral fiber as his brother. He had only a two-room cabin, but he and Maurry set about immediately to add on a couple of rooms for what they hoped would become a burgeoning business. Even when the rooms were finished, the girls would only have cubicles separated by thin walls. Privacy was almost completely obliterated by expediency.

Liz rubbed the shirt against a board to get out the sweaty dirt. The thing hadn't seen the benefit of water for years, nor had its owner. He was with Gina now, poor thing—Gina, not the oaf who owned the shirt.

Sighing, Liz dropped the shirt in the tub filled with clear water. In an hour, Gina, or one of the other girls, would be doing the laundry for one of Liz's customers. That was the usual routine.

Routine.

Yes, it had become so. Liz had come to accept her life. Struggle was not only futile, it was upsetting. Acceptance seemed the only way to obtain for herself and Hannah a life of relative peace. She had given up any serious thoughts of running away or of being rescued. The only one who might possibly rescue her was her father, and . . . well, it had always been futile to count on him for much of anything. She had even dismissed from her mind the mysterious painting of her mother. She'd asked Maurry about it, but he had been vague in his answer. It certainly was nowhere in the cabin. And what good would seeing the painting do anyway? Just give her another impossible fantasy to long for.

Another outward sign of Liz's surrender was her acceptance of the name Mae had dubbed her with that first day. She ceased being Elise. She was now a slave and a "soiled dove" named Liz. It far better suited what she had become. The more she thought of herself in those terms and the less she remembered the genteel lady named Elise, the more peace she had.

And Hannah, far more than she, needed that desperately. Though Hannah had recovered from the illness on the ship, she was becoming what Mae called a "sickly child." She almost always seemed to have a runny nose and a bit of congestion. She was not growing as Liz believed a child should. Liz recalled her sister-in-law saying her baby had sat up on his own at six months. At five months, Hannah had not even rolled over on her own power. She rarely smiled. Mostly she cried. Even now Liz imagined she could hear the baby's pathetic whimpers. And that was reason enough for Liz to do whatever she had to do to get a normal life, at least one free of strife for the child.

"Liz!" Mae called from the cabin.

Liz looked up. The woman's voice was full of frustration. She had left Hannah in Mae's care while she did the wash.

"What is it?" she asked with no small trepidation.

"This kid woke up crying, and I can't get her to quiet down."

So she hadn't been imagining it at all. "I'll be right there, Mae." Liz wrung out the shirt, laid it across a line Lyle had built in the yard, then trod back to the cabin.

No wonder Hannah was crying, Liz thought, entering the room in the cabin where the girls lived. Not only were the six of them cramped into the small room, but customers were also entertained there. However, until the new rooms were built, Maurry agreed that only two customers, privated behind two curtained cubicles, could be handled at a time. There was now noise from both cubicles, not to mention conversations among the other girls.

"I tell you that's my blouse you're wearing!" Ruby hovered over Belinda as if she would rip the garment from the girl's body.

"It is not! Mae, tell her. You was with me when I bought it."

Mae was holding the crying baby and could not be bothered with the petty argument. "Liz, do something with this baby!"

"Yeah!" came a male voice from behind one of the curtains.

Liz took Hannah. She was a bit warm, no doubt from having just woken from her nap, but her nose was crusted with secretions, and her cries sounded like rattles.

"Oh, babe . . ." Liz's tone was gentle but revealed her frustration. "What's wrong now? Maybe you're just hungry."

"I'm warming some milk for her," Mae said.

Liz gave her a grateful smile. "Thank you, Mae."

Except for Sheila, who wanted nothing to do with Hannah and constantly complained about the child's noise, the other girls were fairly fond of the baby. At least they played with her and fed her when Liz was busy.

Liz held Hannah against her shoulder, bouncing her gently as she liked when she was crying. Mae poured the warm milk into a bottle and gave it to Liz, who first tested the temperature, then gave it to Hannah.

But the baby wasn't much interested because it was hard for her to breathe when she sucked the liquid. Liz turned questioning eyes on Mae.

"You got more of them leaves that woman on the ship gave you?"

Liz shook her head dismally. "Used them up last week."

"When I was croupy like that," offered Ruby, distracted momentarily from the dispute over the blouse, "my ma would rub bear grease on my neck and make me drink it, too."

"Camphor is what you need," countered Belinda. "Mix it with a little spirits and hartshorn. Rub that on her throat and it'll fix her right up."

"Suddenly everyone is an expert on child care," Mae observed. "Wasn't long ago you didn't know one end from the other."

"Well, we been trying to put some thought to it seeing as how Hannah is one of the girls now—" Belinda stopped, lifting apologetic eyes to Liz. "I'm sorry, Liz, I didn't mean . . ."

"That's all right," Liz didn't make her finish. She knew it had been an innocent *faux pas*, though the words still stung. But it was an issue Liz could not—would not—let herself think of. She could only think of the here and now. If she worried about the future, she would go insane. "Anyway, I appreciate all of you. Ruby, I don't think I'm going to put bear grease on my child, but next time I get to town I'll see if I can find camphor."

"That still don't help the problem now," Mae said practically.

"Maybe just plain steam would help," Liz said. "I'll get a kettle from the kitchen."

"I'll do it, Liz. You just sit and rock that child." Mae headed for the room across the dog run where the kitchen was located and where Maurice and Lyle lived.

Liz sat in the rocking chair with Hannah. Humming a little tune, she tried to block out her surroundings—the bickering of the girls, the sounds behind the curtains, the smell of sweat and cheap perfume. She thought it would help if she could think of something pleasant, but there wasn't much. Thinking of her previous life was out of the question, and her present life simply did not fit the bill. All that came to her mind was the kind lady she had met aboard the ship.

Rebekah Sinclair had seen Liz for the person she was inside, not for what she did. It was really quite incredible. The respectable women Liz had thus far encountered in the settlement had not been nearly so accepting. Of course, it got around quickly what Liz was and what she did, and probably these women had every right to avoid her. She represented a threat to them and also a reminder of what could so easily become of any of them if they lost the security of a husband or a father. Thus, it was no surprise to her that conversations became hushed when she entered a store. Or that she was given a wide berth whenever she passed a lady on the street.

Not so with Mrs. Sinclair. Could it have had something to do with her being a minister's wife? Liz didn't think so, because the Rev. Sinclair had been full of rebuke and judgment. She knew that most of the ladies in the settlement claimed to be Christians. But Rebekah Sinclair had said that Jesus wouldn't have turned away from her and that Rebekah would be no Christian if she saw a need and ignored it. Obviously she had a different idea of Christianity than these others—than even her own husband.

Rebekah had said something else, too. What was it . . . ? That she shouldn't base her personal faith on others because people can be so fallible. That was why she had given Liz her New Testament.

Liz felt bad that she hadn't read it yet. There was so little time—no, that wasn't the real reason. It simply felt sacrilegious to read holy writings in her present situation. She supposed she could walk a ways into the woods.

"Yes, Hannah, I think I will do just that." She smiled at the baby, who had quieted a bit.

Liz reasoned that she had nothing else good in her life besides Hannah. Perhaps if she could find something else, she could survive. She had never thought of Christianity as more than attending church on Sundays and the occasional social where the ladies gossiped and the men argued politics. Actually, as she had once told the slave Hattie at the Hearne plantation, God and religion had never been important to her. She had never given such matters any thought at all.

Hattie had said God might be punishing her for her lack of interest, but Rebekah, instead, had told her of a God of love. She said it was that God—the God of love—she herself clung to. Perhaps, too, it was that God who gave Rebekah her loving spirit. Liz thought of the way Rebekah had spoken the words "*That is the God I cling to.*" She'd meant it in the most passionate sense, as if God were a lifeline. Liz had been so wrapped up in her own problems at the time that she hadn't noticed just what Rebekah had meant. That kind and compassionate woman did not have a life in perfect order. Now Liz could see the undertones of dissension Rebekah probably had with her husband and certainly her unhappiness in making the move to Texas.

Rebekah Sinclair was not a happy woman. Yet she found contentment in her loving God. Perhaps Rebekah's God could offer the same to Liz.

"Soon as I get you settled, Hannah, I'm going to get that Bible and find a quiet place in the woods. I'm going to find out for myself about this man Jesus."

CHAPTER 18

After that first call on John Hunter's mother, heavy rains from a hurricane in the gulf kept Benjamin at the cabin longer than he had planned. Rebekah, of course, was pleased about the delay. And in truth, Benjamin felt better about beginning his work after he had laid in a good supply of wood and meat for the winter. John Hunter, as payment for Benjamin's services, offered his help around the cabin for two days. He went hunting with Benjamin and bagged a deer and a couple of turkeys. Benjamin had shot nothing, or at least he didn't hit anything at which he fired.

With the help of Hunter and still using brush and weeds as mattresses, Benjamin had made more suitable beds. Two small ones for Micah and Isabel and a larger one for himself and Rebekah. He'd also built a cradle for Leah. True, he was no carpenter, and the thing was a bit lopsided, but it was better than the woodbox his wife had been using.

They had also made a few repairs on the cabin and patched the leaky roof. He blessed God that the job was completed before the heaviest of the rain had begun.

The second morning after the last day of rain, John Hunter, who had by then returned to his home, reappeared on Benjamin's doorstep. He had volunteered to show Benjamin around the circuit, and they had previously arranged that when the weather cleared they would start. Benjamin had prepared Rebekah for this moment, but when it came, she behaved as if it were a surprise.

"I can't stay here alone," she complained.

"We have talked about this already, wife. It is the way of things in the wilderness. Even if it were not for my circuit, I, like most men, would have to leave for long periods to hunt and trap and make a living."

"Please don't go, Benjamin!" Her tone was imploring rather than contentious.

He hated to refuse her, but what else could he do?

"You know this is why I came to Texas." He drew her to him in an embrace. "You'll have the company of the children. And Micah will help. I have taught you how to shoot. You will manage wonderfully, I am certain."

He tried to ignore her silence as he bid her and the children good-bye. It would take a month for him to ride the circuit, which covered several hundred miles. If it hadn't been for the weight he bore of his wife's discontent, he would have been in ecstasy during the next days.

Six months ago when Benjamin had answered the call to Texas, he had little idea of what the life of a circuit rider would be like. At thirty-three years old, he had been an ordained minister for only ten years, all of which he spent in a pastorate: two years in a small church thirty miles west of Boston, four years as an assistant pastor in a large Boston church, and finally four years with his own congregation in a smaller church just outside of Boston. Thus, the life of an itinerate preacher was completely foreign to him. He dressed in much the same manner as he had in Boston, feeling that the formality of his black frock coat, waistcoat, and cravat were necessary here on the frontier, where men had given up so many of the niceties of civilization along with the proper Christian faith.

The mission board had tried to prepare him and his wife, but few of those men had any real experience in that capacity. So it was with some surprise that Benjamin came to realize he loved his new calling.

He stayed no more than one or two nights in any single place. There were no churches or meeting halls, of course, so the assemblies were held in the cabins of individual settlers. Usually the news of his arrival to an area spread quickly, and several families would trek to a central location for the meeting. But often settlers were in such remote places that Benjamin ministered to a single family at a time. It was not unusual for neighbors to live fifteen or twenty miles apart.

Each day was different. He never knew what situation he might be walking into. Once he was waved away from a cabin because there was fever present. Another time he was intercepted and taken to a new location other than the one his predecessor usually used because three Mexican soldiers had stopped for the night in the old location. It made Benjamin realize he was technically a law breaker, a secret agent in the enemy's land. He justified his actions with the reminder that he worked for the cause of Christ.

More disturbing yet were the immoral practices he discovered among the settlers themselves, specifically in regards to marriage. Several couples were living together without the benefit of having said vows before a clergyman. Some had even borne children in that state. They defended themselves by saying they had no choice since they could not know when a minister might come. Benjamin brooked no defense. They had placed lusts of the flesh over their moral duty to God. He enjoined them to seek forgiveness and marry immediately. He performed a half dozen marriages in that first month.

One man, Amos Hawke, refused to marry his woman. Taking Benjamin aside, he confided, "I can't marry with her, Reverend, 'cause I got a wife back in the States."

If he expected absolution, he received none from Benjamin. "Then you place not only yourself but the woman you profess to love in danger of eternal damnation. The sin of the others is nothing compared to what you are doing. They have fornicated, but you are an adulterer and have made her one also. You must leave her immediately and cease living in sin."

"I can't do that, Reverend. I love her. What will become of her without me?"

"Your temporal comforts mean nothing compared to your eternal souls."

"I just can't leave her."

Benjamin shook the dust of the Hawke cabin off his coat and left. He had a great work to do in this country. His predecessor had failed in many respects because some of the situations, including that of Hawke's, had been in existence before Rev. Meredith had been arrested. Benjamin vowed to make it his priority to reach every resident on the circuit and reclaim them for Christ.

One day as he and John Hunter were riding to visit one of Benjamin's flock, they came to a swollen river.

"Usually, at least this time of year, you can walk across this stream." Shielding his eyes from the sun, Hunter gazed down the stream's length. "That rain made it swell up good."

"What do we do now?" Benjamin, too, was studying the waterway. It was a daunting torrent.

"There's three families of settlers across it, but usually Meredith would turn back when it was like this. There's been talk of building a ferry, but nothing's ever come of it."

"I want to cover the entire circuit." No wonder the lives of so many of his people were in such shambles if Meredith gave up so easily. Benjamin knew he was made of better fiber.

"Well, I've crossed worse, but . . ." Hunter slanted a dubious glance at Benjamin. "I've had some experience, and so has my horse. You ever . . . ?"

"Let's do it."

Hunter's brows arched and he wore a look that said, *Are you sure?* Benjamin's response was to nod and grip his reins firmly in hand. He was not a frontiersman by any means, but he was determined to learn even if it meant jumping literally into the water, sink or swim.

The rushing river was awesome. Even Benjamin lost some of his enthusiasm as he urged his horse forward. But the dapple-gray mare tensed beneath him and pranced skittishly on the bank.

"Come on, girl," Benjamin encouraged, trying to steady his own shaky voice.

"Maybe that animal's got more brains than us," observed Hunter. But defying his own words, John dug his heels into his mount's flanks and spurred it into the water. "Seeing my horse might give your gray some courage."

Bejamin had to give Hunter credit for not calling into question the green minister's own courage. With a little more encouragement, the gray did indeed take the plunge. Both animal and rider kept their eyes on the man ahead. Benjamin had to keep such a firm rein on the gray that his shoulders and arms began to ache. Yet he hardly noticed that in the exhilaration of the roaring, rushing water. To be in the center of such a powerful maelstrom! He simply could not describe the strange pulsing sensations coursing through him just then.

He squelched the urge to whoop, reminding himself of the danger. The gray seemed far more cognizant of the perils, for the animal twitched and whinnied. Then with a suddenness that no one could have anticipated, especially a greenhorn, the gray reared. Benjamin clutched at the gray's flanks with his knees, but it did not prove enough. The beast thrashed, jerking its head violently so that Benjamin lost his grip on the reins. In that same moment, the gray went down, spilling its rider into the angry torrent of water.

Benjamin went under but fought mightily with his feet and legs and managed to break the surface and gulp in a breath of air. Before he went under again, he caught a glimpse of the gray, which had found its footing and made a mad run for the shore. Benjamin also saw John reach the shore. Then Benjamin went under again.

Although he was a fair swimmer and a strong, broad-shouldered man, Benjamin was caught in the current and was carried many feet before he could force his head above the surface and cry for help. John would never be able to hear him over the noise of the river, but surely he would know what had happened when he saw the riderless gray.

But Benjamin despaired if even that would help when he saw a rapid straight ahead that made the place where they had crossed seem tame. He fought harder than ever to swim to the shore. His arms were numb with cold and shaking with his efforts. The few feet to the shore could have been a thousand miles.

"Oh, God . . . help me!" But it had been foolish to utter a verbal prayer. The attempt got him a gut full of water.

Then he saw it—an outcropping of rock and brush several feet ahead. It jutted far enough into the water so he might just be able to reach it. But the rapids came first, buffeting him about as if he were a helpless twig. He rode the waters with an odd mixture of fear and elation, almost forgetting that he was probably going to die. But before he was assailed with despair, he saw John crawling out on hands and knees toward the same outcropping.

The sight injected Benjamin with renewed strength, and he pushed and struggled agains the tumult engulfing him until he came near the rock and thrust out his hand toward it. John was reaching out also, his own body hanging precariously over the rushing rapids.

"Just a little more!" John yelled.

Another mighty stretch. Then the hands met and gripped. John instantly grasped Benjamin's sleeve, which would not be as slippery as bare skin. Then Benjamin managed to get an arm around a sturdy branch, providing some traction as John pulled. And in the next instant, Benjamin's soaking body was dragged up on the rocks.

"Whew!" Benjamin exclaimed, and it was a moment before he realized that his coughing and sputtering was mingled with eruptions of laughter.

"What're you laughing about, Reverend?"

Benjamin simply could not keep from laughing outright. "I have never had such an exhilarating experience."

"You plumb near killed yourself—and me, too—and you're laughing?" groused Hunter.

"Oh . . . yes . . ." Benjamin instantly sobered. "I am so sorry. I wasn't thinking. I . . ."

Hunter grinned. "I was just funning you, Reverend. It was quite an experience. I guess even a preacher is allowed a pleasure or two, eh?"

"That was a worldly pleasure, Mr. Hunter. My joy should be in Christ alone."

"Well, God made the river, didn't He? For our enjoyment, right?"

"That, Mr. Hunter, is the kind of thinking that leads a man to perdition."

"I wouldn't know about that." Hunter shook his head, sending a spray of water everywhere. "But I do know we better dry off or we'll catch our deaths."

With that he climbed up the bank and proceeded to gather wood and build a fire. Benjamin took care of the horses, which had made the crossing unscathed, then joined him at the fire where they stripped down to their long underwear, laying their outer garments in the sun to dry. Sitting before the fire, Benjamin continued to think about the river crossing and the conversation that had followed. His reaction to the experience troubled him. He did not completely frown upon certain amusements. He took great satisfaction from a walk in the woods; he enjoyed a good meal; he was even known to take pleasure in his children's antics at times, though fear of spoiling them kept that at a minimum. He found great delight in preaching and in reading the Word of God. Indeed, God often said in His Word that He wanted His children happy.

Yet there were so many areas where pleasure was far too close to the lusts of the flesh. Succumbing too easily to such pleasure, one took a great chance of falling into sin. Benjamin believed for himself it was best to curb pleasure. He was a man of God and simply could not allow himself the luxury of such risks.

But there was more to what had happened on the river. When he had come to his senses after laughing, he realized that his laughing self resembled not Rev. Benjamin Sinclair, but rather his devil-may-care brother, Haden Sinclair. He'd always known there was some of Haden in him, but it frightened him when that side broke free of his carefully reined person. Haden's whole life was spent seeking one wild adventure after another. He was a prime example of how living for pleasure could lead to sin and eventually to spiritual death. Thus Benjamin had to work harder than most men to keep his own natural wildness in check. The journey to Texas was a concession Benjamin tried not to think about.

"Reverend?" Hunter broke into his thoughts. "You want something to eat? It's gonna take a while to get everything dry."

"Yes, that's a good idea. We won't need to bother with a stop later."

Hunter retrieved a packet of biscuits and jerky from the saddlebags. The food had been wrapped carefully and was only a little damp. He handed a portion to Benjamin.

"You know, Reverend," Hunter said around a mouthful of biscuit, "I gotta ask you about what you were saying before. You know, about pleasure. Don't God want us to have fun? It just don't seem right that all fun is bad."

"Of course it is not, Mr. Hunter. But given our limited human understanding, a man should approach such things cautiously. There is an old saying, 'When in doubt, don't.' "

"Maybe that's why folks have such a hard time with religion. There's just too many *don'ts*."

"You would not view it in such a negative light, Mr. Hunter, if your whole being were set upon God. I do not see my faith in terms of the sacrifices I make but rather in the ultimate sacrifice God made in giving His son to die on the cross for the abject sinner that I am. Does giving up some temporal pleasure compare with that in magnitude? You should fall on your knees and praise God for His mercy instead of complaining that you can't have as much *fun* as you'd like."

"I reckon if you put it that way . . ." Hunter scratched the stubble of a beard on his face. He didn't appear completely convinced. "I'm a Christian man, Reverend, and yet I just can't let myself be so sober about life."

"Perhaps as a man of God I am expected to hold to a higher standard."

"Seems an awful heavy burden to be carrying around." Hunter held his hands over the fire, warming them.

"I am equal to it, Mr. Hunter. By the grace of God."

Hunter looked at Benjamin and shook his head, not in disagreement, but more with a sense of wonder or confusion, as if he could not understand anything about the burdens a man of God carried. Even Benjamin had difficulty understanding at times. And at the moment he couldn't understand why he felt such a loss that he had nearly forgotten what that moment of laughter and enjoyment of the river crossing had felt like. In truth, he had forgotten—though not entirely—how very *good* it had felt.

CHAPTER 19

AFTER COMPLETING THE CIRCUIT, Benjamin returned home and stayed for two weeks before commencing the circuit once again. Rebekah, of course, complained, but her laments were becoming so much the norm in their marriage that he found it easy to ignore her. She was growing so morose and withdrawn that he feared she would bring him and his entire ministry down with her if he let her.

With each day Benjamin felt the weight of the burden for his parish grow heavier, and he knew he must minister unrelentingly until he had well established the spirit of God in his assigned region. But the needs he encountered were so great that he was certain he would never come to the end of them.

The members of his circuit parish always welcomed him and had never ending requests for his services—marriages, funerals, baptisms. Yet he never ceased to have the sense that they wanted only the form of faith, the means to comply with the social standards of the times.

A few, of course, were eager to hear the Word of God and to talk of spiritual matters. But many more than that received such matters politely, as if they knew religious instruction must be tolerated in order to have the service they desired. Seldom did he find a Bible in a home. Yes, many in his parish couldn't read, but that was no excuse for the absence of the Word of God. He was certain they didn't speak of spiritual matters when he wasn't around. Once when he was invited to dinner at a home, one of the children was so nonplussed as Benjamin delivered grace that he stared openmouthed at the reverend. Later, the boy asked why the minister was talking to his plate!

Conversions were so few that he was going to be embarrassed to send his six-month report to the mission board. Thus, as he set out on his circuit on a cold autumn day, upon what would be his third ride of the circuit, he determined to bring about a revival among his flock. He had prayed and fasted for five days before setting out, beseeching God to bring a true spiritual awakening upon the lost souls entrusted to him. He had sent word ahead throughout the circuit that he would have a two-day meeting at one of the central homes in his area.

He was gratified when he reached the Butler home to find about fifty people waiting for him. Tents dotted the meadow around the house, and there was a charged atmosphere over the company. Benjamin wanted to think this was due to an anticipation of the descent of the Holy Spirit, but it was plain many of the folks were using the gathering for social interaction as well.

He complained to John Hunter, who had accompanied him to the meeting. "They are more interested in visiting than in hearing the Word of God."

"Well, Reverend, most of these folk, especially the women, go for weeks and even months without seeing another soul besides their families."

Benjamin thought of Rebekah and how she so often groused about that very thing. However, he had asked her to come to this meeting with him, but she had declined because Isabel was feeling poorly. He wondered if that was a mere excuse, but it was true the child did have a bit of a cough. At least Micah had come, though Benjamin had had to force the boy with threats of eternal damnation.

The first day of the meetings Benjamin preached two services, both with rousing sermons on repentance, exhorting the people to give up their evil ways and come to God. He felt at times as if he were speaking to a wall. Faces stared stonily back at him, appearing to have no concept of their precarious position on the edge of eternity. The only excitement roused that day was when five Indians showed up.

Several women screamed, and one fainted. The men were obviously regretful they had not been allowed to carry their guns into the service. Benjamin had seen only a few Indians during his travels, and those from a distance. What he knew of the Indian population of Texas was that the two tribes thought to be the most dangerous—Apache and Comanche—were far to the west in regions largely unsettled. The tribes here in the eastern settled regions were for the most part peaceful.

John Hunter sidled up to Benjamin. "They ain't Tonkawas." Benjamin knew the Tonkawas were a rather docile tribe who did little more mischief than steal and drink whiskey. "I think they're Karankawas, though they are a mite far from their usual habitat along the coast. But they sure smell like Karankawas."

Benjamin had noted a sickening odor emanating from the new arrivals. "What *is* that smell?"

"They rub their bodies with fish oil as protection from mosquitoes."

The smell, of course, was the least of Benjamin's concerns even if it was the most pungent. "Are they dangerous?"

"They ain't as hostile as the Apache, but they ain't the most friendly, either. It's said they are cannibals." But in response to Benjamin's shocked expression, Hunter added quickly, "They won't do nothing in a crowd like this."

Because of his place of leadership—and also because he knew he had the most to lose if the meeting broke up—Benjamin strode boldly up to the Indians.

"Do you speak English?" he asked.

"Speak white man's tongue," said one, a tall, stately man, though all the Indians were quite tall.

"You are welcome to join us."

"You have party?"

"This is a church service." Benjamin had never felt a calling to minister to the Indians in Texas. For the most part, his hands were so full with the needs of the whites that he simply had no time to consider the dark-skinned residents. But he certainly was not opposed to converting a few natives. Perhaps they would be more receptive to the Word of God than the lackadaisical settlers. He added, "Sit down and hear the Word of God."

The Indian said something to his companions in their language, then the group sat on the ground, keeping at the edge of the gathering. Several of those nearest the Indians scooted discreetly away from the visitors.

After assuring everyone that there was no need for alarm, Benjamin continued with his program, pausing in his sermon to lead the group in a few hymns before getting back to preaching.

Whether it was the disruption and distraction of the Indians or simply the ambivalence of his audience, he felt the day was a complete disappointment. He had only two converts.

Benjamin prayed and fasted all that night, and when the gathering came together the next day, he felt in top form. The Indians had returned, but by now the people had grown accustomed to them and no longer feared them. Nevertheless, Benjamin made sure his audience had more to capture their attention than a few Indians. That day he delivered what he believed was the most inspired sermon of his life.

" 'O generation of vipers, who hath warned you to flee from the wrath to come?' " Benjamin waved his worn black Bible in the air as he quoted from memory the Scripture. " 'Bring forth therefore fruits meet for repentance. And think not to say within yourselves, We have

Abraham to our father: for I say unto you, that God is able of these stones to raise up children unto Abraham.

" 'And now also the ax is laid unto the root of the trees: therefore every tree which bringeth not forth good fruit is hewn down, and cast into the *fire*.' " He laid great emphasis on the word *fire*, and his voice shook.

He spent the next two hours in that vein, expounding on the fires of hell, the wrath of God, and the prospects of eternal damnation. He went on delivering Scriptures and impassioned speech until his voice became raw. Only then did he let the people have a break, but they were called back after the briefest of midday meals, and he continued his harangue for another two hours.

He was trembling with exhaustion by the time night fell, but when he delivered the altar call, twenty people came forward. Many were weeping; two were slain in the Spirit; even the Indians seemed excited, though none came forward. It was the kind of day Benjamin and every preacher dreamed of. He felt he stood at the very threshold of eternity. These people had come face-to-face with the wrath of God in the person of Benjamin Sinclair and had turned from their wicked ways.

CHAPTER 20

NO ONE CAME RUNNING OUT into the yard to greet Benjamin when he rode up to his cabin. He was alone, having sent Micah home with John Hunter after the revival so that Benjamin could continue his circuit and visit those who had failed to attend the meetings.

A stream of smoke belched from the cabin chimney, so he knew they must be home. He would have thought at least someone might have come to the door to see who was approaching. Perhaps something was wrong.

Quickly dismounting and tethering his horse, he hurried to the cabin and threw open the door. He was greeted by a scene of quiet tranquility. Rebekah was bent over the hearth stirring a kettle. Isabel was playing with her doll in a corner, and Leah was lying peacefully in her cradle. Only Micah was missing.

Rebekah straightened her back. "Oh, you are home." There was no smile, no warmth, hardly even a greeting in the statement of pure fact.

"Yes." He bit back any words about his welcome, or lack thereof. He put his rifle up in the rack under the one he had left for his family, then he strode to Isabel, bent down, and kissed her cheek. "Your papa is home."

Her brow knit, as if she wasn't quite certain what kind of response was expected, then said quietly, "Hello, Papa."

He did the same with Leah and was pleased to note that she appeared to be thriving. Then he approached his wife, secretly and somewhat bitterly hoping she noted her place in the succession of his greetings.

"That smells good." He leaned over the kettle, inhaling. "What is it?"

"Stew."

"After days of hardtack and jerky, it will be welcome."

"Your parishioners didn't feed you?" Finally she was making conversation, albeit stiff and stilted.

"Yes, occasionally, but no one's cooking compares to yours, Rebekah." He made his tone gentle, hoping somehow to break through the barriers between them.

"It will be ready soon. You have time to wash the dust of the trail off first."

"Where's Micah?" He poured water from a pail into a basin and, after stripping off his coat and waistcoat, began to wash.

"He found a grove of pecans and has been checking daily to see when they will ripen."

"Very industrious of him." Benjamin took a towel and wiped his hands and face.

"How good that you approve." Her tone was still cool.

Ten silent minutes later, Micah returned. His greeting mirrored his mother's, respectful, reserved, distant. Benjamin tried to bridge the gap between them by telling stories of his experiences on the circuit, but he stopped when there was little response from his listeners. There was not even enthusiasm over his successful camp meeting. Micah acted as if he hadn't been there.

Benjamin ached inside. He could hardly eat the meal set before him but forced it down so as not to offend further. Afterward, Rebekah told Micah and Isabel to take the pail to the creek for more water. It was immediately obvious Rebekah wanted to speak with him alone.

She sat down heavily on the bench by the table. "I'm pregnant," she said flatly.

"You are sure?" Though lame, he could think of no other response. Any enthusiasm on his part would surely have been tossed back in his face.

"Of course I am sure."

He tried to think of some way to comfort her. "Rebekah, the Word of God says that a quiver full of arrows is a blessing—"

"Don't preach to me, Benjamin Sinclair! I've had enough of your sanctimonious blatherings." She jumped up. "The only blessing will be if I die giving birth to this baby."

"Rebekah—!"

At that moment a racket outside interrupted his impending rebuke.

"Mama! Papa! Look who's here!" Micah's tone was full of a glee that had never been bestowed upon Benjamin.

The door burst open, and three figures bounded into view.

"Uncle Haden's here!" piped in Isabel, ending with a giggle as the object of her announcement caught her up in his arms and gave her a tickle.

Haden Sinclair made quite a picture standing in the doorway of Benjamin's cabin; Isabel was tucked under one arm, laughing, and Micah stood at the man's side, grinning. Benjamin swallowed back the bitter taste of gall in his throat.

"Haden." Benjamin rose and held out his hand in a formal but polite greeting.

Haden took the hand, then jerked his brother into an exuberant bear hug. "Dad burn, if you aren't all a sight!"

"Haden, please!" Benjamin said, scolding his brother's profanity.

"Oh . . . I'm sorry. Been out in the wilderness so long, I've forgotten how to act with civilized folk. But boy, have I the stories to tell."

"Tell, tell, Uncle Haden!" urged both children.

"Later, children, I'm sure Uncle Haden must be starved," Rebekah said, also offering the man a smile, which Benjamin drank in, even if it were not meant for him.

"I could eat a horse, but not before I get a hug from my favorite sister-in-law." He took Rebekah in his arms and swung her up off her feet.

Rebekah tittered. The small glow in her eye seemed not to belong to the woman who only moments before had declared she wished to die.

Haden finished off the stew and told stories for over an hour. Everyone, even Benjamin, listened avidly. Haden Sinclair had been exploring places few white men had ever seen.

"I went as far west as a place called Palo Duro Canyon. Most of the Indians there ain't never seen a white man."

"You really seen Indians?" Micah asked. His own encounter with Indians at the camp meeting must have faded from his memory.

"Comanche. And they aren't like the Indians around here. They are mean—" A sharp look from Benjamin forced Haden to rephrase his words. "They are wild and tough. They were too curious about us to fight us, but I pity the whites when the Comanche do decide to fight."

"If I recall my geography," Benjamin said, "the Palo Duro is so far west it is doubtful any white settlers will venture there."

"Don't bet on it, Ben." Haden was the only person who got away with the use of that nickname. "Soon as Texas is independent of Mexico, I don't doubt Americans will start pouring in. And they will press west. That's just the nature of men with adventure in their blood."

"Do you think independence is imminent?"

"When I passed through San Felipe and Brazoria, it was all the talk. Won't be long."

"But Austin supports conciliation and appeasement toward Mexico." Benjamin had also heard much talk on the subject as he traveled his circuit.

"Prison is likely to change his tune. But if it doesn't, there are men in the colony who will take up arms anyway. Bill Travis is a strong leader and proponent of independence. Ever hear of Sam Houston?"

"Yes, I've heard the name. Never met him."

"There's the man to watch. An Indian fighter and seasoned military man. Bureaucrats like Austin have had their day. Now it's time for them to stand aside for men like Houston and Travis. Texas is destined to be free, and it isn't going to happen on paper. Santa Anna will fight to hang on to Texas."

"For once I agree with you, Haden. Texas must be liberated from Papist tyranny."

Haden laughed. "Knew you'd find a way to put a religious bent to it, Ben!"

"Uncle Haden," put in Micah, obviously growing bored with talk of politics, "you said when you first came that you had some presents."

"That I did, boy. Why don't you run out and fetch my saddlebags?"

"Wait, Micah," Benjamin said. "Perhaps the presents can wait until morning. It is well past your bedtime."

"But Papa—"

"Don't talk back, Micah."

"Come on, Ben!" Haden countered. "Ease up a little. Presents can't wait. Especially when I have just ridden miles upon miles to bring them."

Benjamin shrugged and nodded his consent. What else could he do? He already felt like a stranger in his own house. He didn't like adding villain to that as well.

The presents were distributed. A real Comanche tomahawk for Micah. "I had to trade my canteen for that—in the middle of a desert!" A beaded Indian necklace for Isabel. "A Comanche princess gave this to me to thank me 'cause I helped her carry water. Comanche men don't ever help their women." For Rebekah, he had a pouch of thread and a new thimble. "The store clerk in San Felipe said he heard you say you were low on thread." Then he turned to Benjamin. "This is for you, bro. It's a medicine pouch I got from the tribe shaman. Thought you two had a lot in common." His grin revealed he was making sport of Benjamin.

Benjamin grimaced at the pagan item. He felt like tossing it directly into the fire. But he knew his brother would ridicule him for that as well, and he simply did not have the heart for it at the moment. So he shoved it carelessly aside and took his cup of coffee in hand.

After receiving joyful hugs from the children, Haden shooed them off to their beds in the corner of the cabin. The adults continued to talk in low tones.

"I didn't know about the new baby," Haden said, "or I would have brought her a present."

"She wouldn't be able to appreciate it now anyway," Rebekah replied. She went to the cradle and lifted Leah, who had begun to stir.

"I'll bring something next time I visit."

"Then bring something for two." Rebekah's eyes skittered toward Benjamin, then turned quickly away. She concentrated on Leah.

"Two?" Haden grinned. "You have another on the way?"

Rebekah nodded.

"Well, well, well . . ." He slanted a sly glance at Benjamin. "You don't like to waste time, do you, brother?"

Benjamin jerked to his feet. "I better bed the horses down for the night. I'll see to yours also, Haden."

Benjamin was outside only a few minutes when Haden joined him.

"Here, let me give you a hand," he said.

Benjamin was in the roughly fashioned enclosure for the horses not far from the cabin. It had three walls and a flat roof with a split rail gate across the open wall. He had led both his and Haden's horses inside and was removing the bridle from Haden's chestnut mount.

"I hope to build a proper stable soon." Benjamin laid aside the bridle and took a brush and began running it along the flank of the horse.

"I can stick around for a while. Be glad to help."

"I wouldn't want to keep you from your adventures, Haden."

"Talk about adventures!" Either Haden had not heard the ire in Benjamin's tone, or he was ignoring it. "Was I surprised to learn you had come to Texas! Didn't ever think you'd do it, Ben. Guess you've got a streak of adventurer in you, too, eh?"

"I came in response to the call of God."

"Sure, if that's how you have to put it."

"What does that mean?" Benjamin's ire was now too apparent for anyone to ignore.

With a responding sneer, Haden replied, "It makes it easier for you to justify dragging Rebekah all this way against her will."

"What do you know?" Benjamin snapped. He'd nearly had enough of wonderful Uncle Haden.

"It's plain to see she is unhappy. And then to be pregnant again so soon. What were you thinking, Ben? Do you realize what it will be like for a woman like Rebekah to give birth out here in the wilderness?"

"And you, who never made a proper commitment in your life, are such an expert on women!" The chestnut twitched restively under Benjamin's too vigorous brushing.

"Give me that brush!" Haden grabbed the brush, then cooing gently in the animal's ear, brushed with gentler strokes.

"And a horse expert to boot!" Benjamin mumbled.

"Ben . . ." Sighing, Haden stopped his work and turned toward his brother, gazing not with anger but rather with expansive benevolence. "Come down off that high horse of yours, will you? You and I used to be friends, remember? We used to raise Cain together."

Benjamin remembered well the days of his youth, and if he chanced to think of them fondly, he reminded himself that they had been days of godless frivolity. For a time he had rebelled with Haden against their father's iron hand, but at least he had finally repaired his wayward instincts. If he longed for the close relationship he'd once had with his brother, he quickly reminded himself of the scriptural adjuration not to be unequally yoked to an unbeliever.

"I remember, Haden. I remember because it makes me appreciate all the more the deliverance of God—"

"Forget God!"

"I'll not stand for blasphemy, not from you, not from—" He stopped, reddening as he recalled the painful exchange with his wife.

"From who, Ben? Not Rebekah!" Now the benevolence turned to unabashed pity. "Oh, Ben, what's happened to you?"

"Don't you dare use such a tone with me!" Benjamin ordered. "I am not the one to be pitied. What *happened* to me is wonderful, glorious—I've been saved, sanctified, and delivered. It is you who should be pitied—and Rebekah if she continues upon her road of rebellion. You are lost, Haden. And what is worse, you don't even care."

"I'd rather be lost, Ben, than steeped in the sanctimonious mire you are in."

Benjamin opened his mouth in angry retort, then suddenly realized he himself was close to falling into sin with an anger he knew was only partly righteous. He choked back the words he'd been about to utter and slowly turned and left the horse enclosure. Before he got far, he turned back.

"You are welcome to bide the night here, Haden, then I think it would be best if you left."

"I'll not bide even the night where I am not truly welcome." Haden picked up the bridle and slipped it back on the chestnut. "Tell the children and Rebekah . . . tell them whatever pleases you."

Benjamin felt the sudden weight of his guilt. Haden was a sinner and a heathen, but though Benjamin didn't like to admit it, his brother was a decent man. And once he had been Benjamin's best friend. That friendship had been Benjamin's most difficult sacrifice for his faith.

"Haden . . ." The words came hard, but Benjamin knew they had to be said. "I misspoke. I am sorry."

"Guess we both got a little hot under the collar." Haden dropped his hand from the bridle.

"I'd be pleased if you stayed on a bit."

CHAPTER 21

THE PEACE BETWEEN THE TWO brothers held for three days. Benjamin was certain it was only because he made a concerted effort to be tolerant. But it all finally collapsed when Haden interfered in a matter regarding Benjamin's parenting.

Micah was totally taken with his uncle. He dogged his every step, clung to his every word. It was the kind of unabashed admiration any father would have had a right to envy, but Benjamin told himself his subsequent actions had nothing to do with that.

They were hauling logs to finish the stable for the horses. By their good fortune, the previous occupant apparently had intended to complete the same task or perhaps to make an addition to the cabin. As a result, there was a good supply of logs cut, stripped, and ready for the job. They just needed to be brought up to the building site. It was hard work, especially for the now thirteen-year-old boy, but he proved a great help. Haden praised him frequently. Benjamin took his brother to task a couple of times for spoiling the boy. Micah was doing what was expected of him, and it would make him lazy if he thought he deserved praise each time he did a job. Haden disagreed.

But that was not the problem that finally split the brothers, though it was no doubt a catalyst.

On the third day of their labors, they had worked all day building the fourth wall to the stable, taking time out only for dinner and a few water breaks. Around three in the afternoon, all the logs were in place, thanks in large part to Haden's experience in building log structures and his valuable suggestions for the tricky process of attaching the new logs to the ones already there. The cracks needed to be grouted, the door opening cut out, and the door built. Benjamin was eager to continue. It was October, and he could feel winter pressing upon them.

He thought they could get the door built before dark. It was a simple square structure and would not need to be as sound as a cabin door.

Wiping an arm over his sweaty brow, Haden offered another suggestion. "Let's quit for the day and take a swim in the creek. I'm about all in anyway."

"Yeah!" Micah agreed heartily.

"Time is slipping away," Benjamin countered. "It looks like another rain will come soon. I would like to see the horses properly sheltered."

"We'll get an early start in the morning," Haden said.

"There's at least three or four more hours of daylight."

"Benjamin, you are a slave driver." Haden spoke only partly in jest. "We been working our tails off for two days, and by golly, I'm gonna have myself a swim."

"I've asked you before not to curse, Haden." Benjamin spoke through clenched teeth.

" 'By golly' isn't cursing. Quit being such a stickler!"

"That's a destructive philosophy. If I allow a small evil to take root, it will only breed more until I can no longer discern between right and wrong."

"You mean evils like this?" Haden then let forth with a stream of such ripe curses it made Benjamin redden with shock.

"I have been as patient with you as any would expect a man to be." Benjamin stared hard at Haden, all the more so to cover his embarrassment.

"I don't give a hang about you, Ben. I'm going for a swim."

"Me too!" piped in Micah, whom Benjamin had nearly forgotten about.

"You will stay and finish working," Benjamin shot at his son. The minute the words were out, Benjamin knew a line had been drawn, a challenge declared.

"Don't punish the boy because of me," Haden said.

"I am not. There is still work to be done, and Micah has learned to finish what he starts."

"But, Papa, please let me go swimming with Uncle Haden." Micah's tone was respectful, imploring.

"You will do as I say." Benjamin's tone was as unbending as iron.

"Come on, Micah, let's go." Haden's tone was a dare and a temptation. Benjamin thought Satan must have sounded like that in the Garden of Eden.

Poor Micah looked between the two men—the one he adored and the one he feared. Benjamin knew which man he was, and he knew that a single word of permission from him might have changed everything. But teaching discipline was more important than being liked or adored. Micah would thank him for it one day when he was a man.

"Micah, come here and help me with this log." Benjamin met the eyes of both his son and his brother with a steady gaze. It had become more than merely a case of teaching discipline. Now it was a matter of obedience.

"I'm gonna go swimming." Micah defied his father, then glanced at Haden for approbation. When Haden nodded, the boy raced off into the woods.

Benjamin started forward, but he was blocked by Haden's imposing figure, which was as tall as his own and as broad, with the added edge of years of the toughened life of an adventurer.

Benjamin's hands, clenched into fists at his sides, were shaking. He could barely speak for the fury coursing through him. "You've gone too far, Haden," he seethed.

"No, Ben, you have gone too far. Your religion has made you into a tyrant. You've become the image of our father!" It was clear his words were not meant as a compliment. He continued. "Your boy fears you, your wife despises you, your poor little girl doesn't know what to think of her papa. God only knows what will become of the baby and the one on the way."

"Don't you dare tell me how to run my family!" Benjamin's voice shook in time with his hands. "You are a selfish, miserable, godless wretch!"

"And you are a selfish, miserable, *godly* wretch!"

"I should have made you go that first night," Benjamin fumed. "Micah would never have defied me so if he hadn't believed you would back him up. At any rate, I will correct that mistake now. Get out, Haden! Don't bother coming back."

Haden was gone within an hour. Benjamin did not watch him go but rather went to the clearing in the woods that had come to be his private place of prayer. Only he didn't pray. He just sat on the stump and seethed in his anger. He imagined Rebekah and Micah and Isabel were shedding many tears over the departure of Haden. For himself, he would shed no tears, and he staunchly ignored the ache in his heart. In the most secret part of his being, he adored his brother, too. But he knew that emotion must be displeasing to God.

Shortly after he heard Haden's horse ride off, Benjamin left his place of retreat—or hiding?—and set out to deal with the problem Haden had caused.

Micah was in the cabin. His hair was wet. He had been swimming.

"Come with me, Micah," Benjamin ordered as he took the rawhide strap from the hook.

With head tucked low between his shoulders, Micah followed. He well knew the purpose of the strap, for he'd felt its sting many times. Several paces behind the cabin, Benjamin stopped and told Micah to lower his trousers and bend over a large rock there.

"Do you know why you are being punished?" Benjamin gripped the strap, dreading what he must do.

" 'Cause I went swimming," Micah replied. Was there yet a hint of defiance in his tone?

"I think you know better than that, boy." Benjamin's knuckles whitened. "Recite Proverbs one, verses seven to ten."

"I don't remember it."

"You remember it." He required Micah to quote the verses every time he was disciplined.

With trembling voice, Micah began, " 'The fear of the Lord is the beginning of knowledge: but fools despise wisdom and instruction.

My son, hear the instruction of thy father, and forsake not the law of thy mother: For they shall be an ornament of grace unto thy head, and chains about thy neck. My son, if sinners entice thee, consent thou not.' " The boy paused, then twisted his head around so as to see his father. "But Papa, Haden is my uncle. He's not a sinner."

"You know better, boy. He is Satan disguised as an angel of light, bent on enticing the innocent into destruction. Be grateful you have a father who cares enough to set you back upon the path of righteousness." Benjamin raised the strap.

The first strike was paltry indeed, and Benjamin told himself he must not care about Micah as much as he thought. His love for his son was best expressed in the passion of his discipline. Thus, he felt he proved himself when the next blow made a red welt on Micah's skin. After ten such blows, the boy's bottom was a mass of red stripes. He would have difficulty sitting for some time. Through it all, Micah did not cry. When it was over, he rose stoically and stood straight, though a bit shakily, until Benjamin excused him. Benjamin could see a hard glint in the boy's eyes, a glint that little resembled repentance. Not knowing what else to do, Benjamin let him go.

Benjamin returned to his place of prayer, fell on his knees, and prayed for his brother and his son. His heart ached for them as he cried out to God to spare them eternal oblivion. Why couldn't they see they were wrong and their rebellion destructive? He prayed that their eyes be opened, so they could see the light of Jesus and have the kind of relationship with God that Benjamin himself enjoyed.

PART THREE

MARCH 1835

CHAPTER 22

LIZ WISHED SHE WOULD HAVE attended church more when she'd had the opportunity. She had never attended when she was a girl growing up with her father, and since the Hearnes only went for appearance's sake at election time, she had not been expected to do otherwise. During the time of her marriage she had been able to find many acceptable excuses for staying away.

Now because of who she was and what she did, she would not have been received in any church. She had to satisfy herself with getting away from Maurice's cabin to a little hideaway among the rocks and brush about a quarter of a mile away. With Mae and the other girls watching Hannah, Liz was able to steal only about an hour a week to read the little New Testament Rebekah had given her.

So far she had read up to the gospel called St. John. She knew it was a gospel because it read at the beginning, *The Gospel according to St. John*. She had no idea what a gospel was, and peeking ahead, she saw only the first four sections were gospels. After that they were called epistles, whatever that was!

She understood so little, yet wanted to understand it all!

Rebekah had been right when she suggested Liz not judge Christ by people. Christ was not at all like the Hearnes or Rebekah Sinclair's husband or any of the churchgoers Liz had encountered in her life. Not that all had been bad or unkind. Rebekah Sinclair certainly wasn't. Rowena Cowley attended church, and she had been kind to Liz. Even the slave Hattie, who had spoken of Jesus as if she knew Him, had been decent to her.

Liz supposed there must be something to all the church talk about going to hell, but thus far in her reading, hell didn't seem to be a big part of religion—at least the kind that Christ seemed to practice. Love was the far bigger part, and tolerance and fairness. She was keeping a list on a piece of paper tucked into the Bible. On it she wrote questions she hoped one day to find answers to. She also wrote down her favorite parts. One was when Jesus told his followers the two greatest commandments. "Thou shalt love the Lord thy God with all thy heart . . . mind . . . soul, and thou shalt love thy neighbour as thyself."

She had also been deeply moved by the story of the son who ran away from home, but when he returned after getting into all manner of trouble, his father received him in love. She felt that perhaps God might still receive her, even though she had defiled her body and sinned in a way that she knew could not possibly please God.

This very thing was confirmed to her as she began reading that day. She came to a story about Jesus speaking to a woman of Samaria, a land that Liz surmised was not looked upon highly by the Jews. But Jesus spoke to this despised woman, knowing she had done sins having nothing to do with her place of birth. She had been with men to whom she was not married.

The story could have been Liz's own story. First, she had been despised because of the fate of her birth—her Negro blood, which she could do nothing about. Then she had been despised by the sins she supposed she could have done something about. She could have run away, accepted death, and risked the life of her child in order to remain pure.

Would Jesus speak to her, too, as He had the woman of Samaria? Was there a chance for Liz to have the peace and redemption He offered? She knew He would want her to turn from the life as one of Maurice Thomson's soiled doves. Could she take that risk? Was she strong enough? And what about Hannah?

On that last question, Liz crumbled. She simply could not risk losing her child. Yet something told her that a God of love would not require such a horrible sacrifice of her. Perhaps He would provide another way.

Liz had never prayed before. She did so now, opening her heart in the best way she knew.

"Jesus, I'm not sure I know you well enough to talk to you, but if I don't start talking, I don't suppose I will ever get to know you. I'm certain I don't know you well enough to make requests of you, but . . . I keep thinking of the lady at the well. I think you respected her because she wasn't afraid to ask something of you even though you were a stranger. So I ask you now to help me find a way of escape for my child and for myself from this life I hate. I've no one else to ask, or I wouldn't bother you. I am so alone. Please help me."

Liz returned to the cabin and found Hannah sicker than ever. She had awakened that morning feeling slightly warm, and now she was burning up. The child needed medicine, perhaps even to be seen by a doctor.

Liz was rocking Hannah when a customer came for her. Mae took the man in hand. An hour later, Maurry came storming into the cabin.

"What's this I hear about Mae taking your customers?" he yelled. He was drunk again. She could smell the alcohol from several feet away.

"Hannah has a fever. I couldn't leave her." Liz's grip tightened on the child in her arms.

"I've been too lenient with you since we've come to Texas." He stood towering over her, smugly aware that he represented a threat as ominous as his girth.

"Maurry"—she steadied her voice, not wanting to sound like she was begging, trying to be reasonable instead—"if I could get her some medicine, take her to a doctor, it would get her well once and for all. Then she'd not be a bother."

"Medicine! A doctor! Do you know what that would cost? Maybe for a good horse I might do it, but not for some worthless pickaninny."

"Please, Maurry. I'll double my load. I'll—"

"Oh, you'll double your load all right, but to make up for your slack in the past. Give me the kid."

"No!" Liz screamed. She jumped up and stumbled back away from Maurry. Was this then the answer to her prayer earlier?

"Fanny!" Maurice yelled. "Get in here!" Then to Liz he said, "I ain't going to get rid of the kid yet. I got a soft heart, I do. But Fanny is going to take her until you begin performing up to your capabilities."

"She needs doctoring. . . ."

"We'll all be better off if she just dies of natural causes."

"You animal! Then kill us both and get it over with!"

"You're much too valuable for that. Now, I can take the kid gently, or I can take her roughly. What's it to be?"

Liz had visions of Hannah being pulled and manhandled, screaming in terror, perhaps even having bones broken. And she knew her talk of death had been mere bravado. She could not stand by and watch her child's death. She held the child out, not to Maurice but, with a defiant glare, to Fanny, who had just entered the cabin.

"Good girl." Maurice sounded almost like a benevolent father. But the grin on his face held no benevolence, no warmth, only victory as he added, "Lyle will fill your time until your next customer arrives."

Liz nodded, hating herself as much as she hated Maurice. But she kept busy with her work for the rest of the day. She survived by doing what Mae had taught her months ago—by keeping her mind concentrated on other things. Only now her thoughts were filled with plans for revenge, growing fiercer when she heard cries from Hannah, who had been taken to one of the new rooms. When she grew tired of imagining shooting Maurice with his big flintlock rifle, she thought of running away. She thought of being free with Hannah, of Hannah growing up to be a fine lady.

That brought her back to the reality of Hannah as she was now. Would Hannah live long enough to fulfill Liz's fantasies—or worse, would the child grow to take Liz's place in this horrid life? The fear of that future for Hannah made Liz think more practically. She had to do something about Hannah now.

The plan that began forming in her mind was outrageous and would probably get them both killed, but at least it offered a slim chance, which was better than her present submission to Maurry that gave her no hope.

She waited three days until Maurry's confidence in her obedience was assured before carrying out her plan. After her last customer had left and all the girls had retired for the night, Liz, too, went to her bed, but she was far from sleep. She debated in her mind one facet of her scheme she still wasn't certain about. Should she take Hannah or not? If she left Hannah behind, then Maurry would know she hadn't intended on running away permanently. And indeed, she wasn't yet ready to run away for good. Hannah was too sick and would never survive. First Liz had to get her daughter well, thus her present plot. She would steal money and go to San Felipe to purchase medicine for Hannah. She knew where Maurry kept his money box hidden away. He was so cocky in his authority over his slaves that he did not fear theft and made only a small show of hiding the box.

When all was quiet in the house, she crept from her bed and put on her dress, boots, and coat, wishing she had a more practical dress to wear rather than the fancy dresses from New Orleans. When ready, she crossed the packed earth floor and stepped into the dog run. A cool breeze blew through the open corridor. The intent of the corridor was to keep the cabin cool during the miserably hot Texas summers. Now in spring, the cool air was unwelcome. It reminded Liz that the five-mile trek at night to San Felipe would not be easy. She dare not steal a horse, because Maurry valued his horses over even his money. She would have to walk to town in her threadbare coat and ill-fitting shoes, and she would have to walk quickly. If she was lucky, she could get to town, do her business as soon as the stores opened, and return home before Maurry missed her. Maurry usually did not bother the girls until the early afternoon. If her luck truly did hold and her prayers were answered, he might not even miss the two dollars she stole from him.

As Liz neared town about an hour and a half later, she began to think this was not going to be as great a risk as earlier feared. The hard part would be waiting until daylight for the store to open. She slipped into the livery stable, found a warm corner in a stall, and fell asleep.

CHAPTER 23

BENJAMIN TOOK A DETOUR FROM his circuit on that chilly day in March. He had about half his circuit finished, but he'd heard of a meeting in San Felipe he wanted to attend. He excused the extra time away from his family in the necessity of purchasing supplies.

Benjamin received a less than subsistence salary from the mission board, which expected his local flock to supply most of his needs. His family lived at a poverty level, despite the fact that the members of his circuit did indeed support him with food and supplies as opposed to money. One had given him a much needed second cow, another a bag of rare wheat, another woman had made him a quilt, and someone had even given them a rocking chair. He was seldom ever paid for his services in money, because the settlers themselves had little ready cash. However, on this recent circuit an offering was taken, and he was given five dollars.

So when Benjamin returned home at the end of the month a few days late, he knew he would be exonerated when he produced a load of items from the store, which would include a length of calico for Rebekah.

Several men had already arrived in the store, the only available gathering place, when Benjamin got there. Benjamin dreamed of one day building a church structure in Cooksburg, but he knew that dream was far from fulfillment. Even San Felipe had no church buildings of any kind.

Three of the men present Benjamin recognized from his circuit, one being John Hunter, who had become the only friend Benjamin had acquired in the area. He did not know the others but was disappointed so few had come. He had hoped to be taking part in a major political rally, one that would eventually make definite strides toward independence from Mexico. He had gathered from his parishioners that there were two opposing groups in Texas regarding the best method to use to gain independence—the "war party" and the "peace party." The peace party was more dominant, likely because it had enjoyed Austin's support over the years, but rumor had it that his months in a Mexican prison had swayed Austin more toward the war inclination.

"Morning, Reverend." Hunter welcomed Benjamin with a friendly smile.

The others Benjamin knew merely nodded and grunted vaguely in welcome. One was Amos Hawke, who had never developed a warm attitude toward Benjamin since being taken to task regarding his "marriage." The other, William Meade, had no cause against Benjamin that he knew of, but he was stiff nonetheless.

"Am I early?" Benjamin strode into the group.

"This may be it." John wrinkled his face and shrugged. "Seems most folks don't think a formal meeting will be much use until Austin returns."

"Who knows when that will be?" Benjamin said. "We can't sit on our haunches until then."

A man introduced as George said, "We ain't sitting around. I was with Bill Travis last month when a bunch of us drove off the customs inspector at the Anahauc garrison."

Among other grievances, the Texians were disgruntled over the levying by Mexico of what they considered unjust taxes that seemed to be aimed most seditiously at Texians who imported a large percentage of their goods from the United States.

"Precious good that did," Amos Hawke growled. "Travis was condemned by most of the Texians themselves for what he done. The leaders of the peace party even made a declaration of loyalty to Mexico and sent apologies to the Commandante General Cós."

"Only shows the strength of the peace party."

"Things'll change when Austin comes," Hunter said.

"One thing's certain," Meade offered sagely, "little will happen until then. Other conventions last year failed because folks don't want to act without him."

Benjamin realized he had wasted precious time for nothing. In coming he had hoped to finally meet some of the Texian leaders he'd heard so much about. Austin, for one, but also Sam Houston, Travis, and Jim Bowie. These were the men, not a group of farmers, who would push Texas toward independence. But of the leaders, only Travis was a radical war party proponent. Even Houston, it seemed, was leaning ever more toward a peaceful coexistence with Mexico.

For himself, Benjamin was a staunch supporter of independence, whether it be by war or peace. If it was to be war, he had already decided to participate. For him it was a holy war, the very purification of the denizens of evil. True, the longer he was in Texas the more he saw that the Catholic Church wasn't the pernicious evil he had feared when he first came. On paper, of course, Catholicism was indeed the only sanctioned religion in Texas, but in reality, most of the alcades turned a blind eye toward Protestant work in their regions. Benjamin had not been molested once and had even had a fairly civil encounter with a priest.

Yet the Protestant faith was still outlawed, and thus its growth would be stunted until it could operate freely. Because of the law against Protestantism, most Texians had grown complacent about any religion, practicing neither the Catholicism they professed on paper nor the faith of their birth. The Sabbath had become like any other day to them. With no churches to attend, they usually drove their cattle, cleaned their barns, or simply sat on their porches whittling. Benjamin was determined that should change.

The conversation of the men in the store turned from politics to the weather, then to farming and such. Disgusted with the failure of the political meeting and with the attitudes in general, Benjamin took his New Testament from his pocket and opened it.

"I believe it would be fitting before we part this place," he said, "that we call upon the blessing of the Lord God."

"Now, Reverend?" Meade asked.

"It ain't even Sunday," Hawke added.

"That convinces me more than ever of the need." Benjamin turned some pages in the Bible. "Hear the Word of the Lord! 'Jesus saith unto her, Woman, believe me, the hour cometh, when ye shall neither in this mountain nor yet at Jerusalem worship the Father . . . But the hour cometh, and now is, when the true worshippers shall worship the Father in spirit and in truth: for the Father seeketh such to worship him. God is a Spirit: and they that worship him must worship him in spirit and in truth.' " Benjamin snapped shut his book. "Please bow your heads." The men, glancing around rather skittishly at one another, finally complied. Benjamin prayed. "O God, our Father, we come to you as sinners, unworthy to call upon your holy name, unworthy to even touch the hem of your garment. Yet we are helpless without you, without your guidance. This land of Texas is coming to a crossroads in its destiny, and I pray no man here will embark upon that road without you going before him. We implore you to be the standard bearer of Texian independence, for you know this land cannot stand unless it is planted firmly in the Christian faith. As you did in ancient Israel, wipe the enemy of faith from the land. . . ." Upon hearing voices at the front of the store, Benjamin paused. However, never one to cut short the worship of God because of the needs of man, he was ready to dig in for one of his more lengthy prayers. "Father, purify the hearts of these men. . . ." The voices grew louder and began to capture the attention of his small congregation.

"There you are, you little vixen!" a male voice shouted.

"Maurry, don't . . . ow!" The cries of a distressed female could be plainly heard.

The attention of Benjamin's listeners was definitely lost as they began to shuffle and murmur.

"Hey, now, unhand that woman." That was the storekeeper's voice.

"Don't you tell me what to do!"

"Reverend," John Hunter said quietly, "I think you better end your prayer. Looks to be some trouble."

"Dear God," Benjamin added quickly, "whatever is now afoot, let your wisdom prevail. Amen." He looked up and was shocked at what he saw.

At the front of the store was the woman from the ship, the one whose child Rebekah had helped against his wishes. The one he'd heard was a soiled dove. He had never seen the man who now gripped her arm and was tugging harshly at her.

The storekeeper was saying, "I don't want no trouble in my store."

"Then keep outta my business," retorted the man.

John said to Benjamin, "Reverend Sinclair, what should we do?"

In the meantime, the woman had broken free of the man's grip and leaped out of his immediate reach. But when the man took an ominous step toward her, she lunged toward the nearest thing she could find for protection—a pitchfork. This she grabbed with both hands and made a stab in the air with it that forced her pursuer to step back. Benjamin thought he'd never seen a more fierce look on the face of a woman. It was more awesome than frightening though, and staunchly resolute. She was prepared to do battle. Fleetingly Benjamin thought of Joan of Arc.

"I just want to buy medicine, Maurry," retorted the woman in a voice shaking more with anger than fear.

Benjamin recalled his wife had said she was named Liz.

"Nothing wrong with that," the storekeeper said.

"Except the money she's using is stolen."

"That true?" the storekeeper asked.

"Please." Liz looked imploringly at the storekeeper, then glanced around the room as if to beg support from the other customers. "It's for my baby. She's gotta have medicine."

"She's a thief!" Maurry accused.

"Please!" she cried again, tears now welling in her eyes, and the fierce Joan of Arc began to crumble in desperation. Then those eyes once more swept the room, finally resting on Benjamin. She obviously recognized him from the ship. "You know I'm telling the truth," she said to him. "You know I have a sick child. Tell them."

"That was some time ago," Benjamin said. Then, as if he felt an explanation was necessary, he said to the room in general, "She was on the *RaeAnn* with me." To Maurry he added, "Is her child still sick?" Though he had never met Maurice Thomson, he had a feeling this man was the boss, owner, or employer of the woman.

Maurry shrugged. "Kids are always sick."

"What'll I do, Reverend?" the storekeeper asked.

There was no real law in the town. Until Austin was arrested, he had presided over much of the criminal actions. Most judicial functions were carried out by the Mexican government, which in fact was another grievance of the Texians. They did not want to have court actions deliberated in faraway Saltillo, which was now the practice. At any rate, Benjamin did not wish to be placed in this delicate position. Unlike a judicial official, he also had to consider the spiritual implications of the problem at hand. He wondered if any of the men present realized what kind of woman this was who was begging for help. If they did, they certainly would not admit to it. But *he* knew, and to exonerate her might well be the same as blessing her chosen life. Nevertheless, if an innocent child was sick, did it deserve to be punished along with the sinful mother? He thought of the Scripture that spoke about the sins of the fathers being visited upon the children to the third and forth generation.

But Maurry Thomson wasn't about to wait for any judicial deliberations, however amateur.

"Gimme my money back, girl," he sneered. "I'm losing patience." He lunged for the pitchfork, but the woman made a thrust that caught the sleeve of his shirt with one of the sharp tines. He jerked his arm back in shock. "She's gonna kill me!"

"Did you steal this man's money?" Benjamin asked as Maurry rubbed his arm, looking as if it had been torn off rather than merely scratched.

"I only took two dollars"—she bit her trembling lip—"for medicine."

"She was going to buy this." The storekeeper pushed forward some items on the counter. "Camphor, eucalyptus oil, hartshorn, and some mustard. Looks like medicines to me. She was about to pay me one dollar and fifty cents for it all."

"Did you steal the money?" Benjamin persisted.

"Yes, but . . ."

"It is wrong to steal, regardless of the reason."

For an instant, her eyes narrowed, losing all pleading. Hitching up her shoulders, she once more became Joan of Arc. Benjamin momentarily feared she would direct her pitchfork at him, but he held his ground, not flinching, not taking his eyes from her. He knew when right was on his side.

"Give the money back," he ordered.

"My daughter will die."

"The end does not justify the means. It benefits no one to live because of sin. Return the money, and you will not be prosecuted for your crime. Then trust God to provide for your needs."

She quite literally spit in his face. "Don't speak of God to me! You are no Christian!" She lowered one hand from the pitchfork, reached into her pocket, took out the money, and threw it at Thomson. This done, she continued to hold the pitchfork a moment longer, then she lowered it.

"Now, you better get on home," Maurry said, "or you'll really be in trouble."

She leaned the fork against a wall, then swung around and strode to the door.

Wiping his face with his handkerchief, Benjamin noted the extraordinary pride in her step. Part of him wanted to inform her that pride goes before a fall, but another part surged with admiration. He shook away this wayward notion as she exited the store.

Turning to the storekeeper, he said, "Wrap up those items." He then removed his wallet and withdrew one dollar and fifty cents. With the package in hand, he headed to the door. Liz was already outside. "Miss," he called, "hold up there."

She slowed but did not turn. It galled him that he had to hurry to catch up with her and that he practically had to insist on getting her attention. He thrust out the package.

"What's that?" She did not look at him, and her voice was rough.

"The medicine. I told you God would provide."

"Oh, so you are a good Christian after all?" She let the sarcasm slide from her voice like ice off a roof in winter.

"I could not with a clear conscience condone your actions."

"But it's all right now that you've taught me a lesson?"

"Have I taught you a lesson?"

Her lip curled as if she would hurl some insult, then she just shook her head. "I'm taking this only for my baby." She snatched the package from his hand.

"I am giving it only for the child," he replied pointedly. "I do not condone who you are or what you do."

"You know nothing about who I am or what I do."

She strode away, still with a step that made Benjamin gape in wonder. Who was she indeed? She was certainly like no woman he had ever seen before. Part waif, as innocent and tender as the child she cared for, but certainly part temptress as well, a she-devil in the guise of an angel.

CHAPTER 24

REBEKAH LIFTED THE EDGE OF the rawhide window covering. A draft of cold air struck her face, and she fastened down the cover once more. She must accept the dreary darkness of the cabin over the chilly spring morning. Sucking in a ragged breath, she turned back toward the room, wondering how she would face another day.

Leah was crying in her cradle, but Rebekah ignored the child and went to the hearth and tossed in another log. She would have to cook breakfast, not that she had any appetite, but the children needed to eat.

"Micah, get the pail and fetch water." The boy was playing with his tomahawk, swinging it in the way his uncle had taught him the Indians used. "I don't like you using that thing indoors, son."

"But it's cold outside, Ma."

"I know. But someone could get hurt."

Micah put down the tomahawk and headed toward the water pail. He was a good boy. Too bad his father refused to see it. Too bad Micah hardly had a father.

With a bitter sigh, Rebekah began to mix cornmeal and water to make bread. Corn and a few sweet potatoes were all they had to eat with the wild turkey and venison Benjamin had jerked. It was a sign of how bad things were when sweet potatoes became a delicacy. Benjamin earned less than fifty dollars a year, in addition to occasional gifts from his parishioners. But even if he still earned the princely two hundred dollars a year he had in Boston, it would not have mattered. Supplies were simply hard to come by here. Benjamin told her things would be better after she planted a garden in the spring. It was spring now, but she had no idea where she'd find the energy to plant a garden.

She rubbed her protruding belly. At seven months, her unborn child was large and heavy and seemed to be sapping all life from her. Not that she could or should blame her melancholy on the child. If only it were that simple. If only she had the hope that once the child was born she could be happy again. But Rebekah had come to the point of knowing she would never be happy as long as she was in Texas and, though she could barely admit it, as long as she was with Benjamin. She was miserable when her husband was gone, but she was just as miserable when he was home. He refused to understand her plight, and thus the only person she had to confide in was of no help at all.

Sighing, she wondered once again how she would survive another day. Pouring the batter into a pan, she thought how automatic were her actions. She went through all the motions of life as if she were dead rather than alive, which is how she felt in her heart and mind. Placing the pan on the rack over the fire, she returned to the sideboard, took a hunk of jerky, and began slicing it.

The knife in her hand caught a flicker of the lamp by which she worked. Not for the first time, Rebekah wondered what it would feel like to take the knife and cut herself, letting the blood flow from her veins until she was dead not only in mind but in body as well.

Only one thing kept her from such an act: her children. They would surely perish if she were not here to care for them. And she would not dream of doing anything to harm her unborn child. So for their sakes she forced herself to face each lonely, miserable day.

Oh, the loneliness! Day in, day out, no one to talk to but children. They could never understand her feelings, nor would she burden them by babbling to them. She kept it bottled up, and when Benjamin came home, it still remained corked safely inside. When she did try to reveal a little of her pain, he would only admonish her to trust God and be faithful in prayer. She was left to believe that all her troubles were from her own lack of faith. Benjamin told her she had a friend and companion in Jesus and she need not be alone. But that didn't help. It brought her no release. For the first time in her life, Jesus felt as far away as her nearest neighbor.

Only once in six months had she a visit from her neighbor, Mrs. Hunter. John Hunter looked in on her occasionally, but it wasn't the same as having a woman friend, a confidante. Mrs. Hunter, however, could have been those things. She was a kind woman but still a stranger, and Rebekah was not about to unburden herself to a stranger. Maybe if she came again . . . but who knew when that would be? She had little time to make the fifteen-mile trek very often. And Rebekah was certainly in no condition to do so. At least Mrs. Hunter had told Rebekah to come to their home when her time came near, so she could have help with the birth of the baby. But that was two months away!

Rebekah ran her finger along the sharp edge of the knife and a plan began to form in her mind—a sick, demented plan. She would wait until the baby was born and Benjamin was home. He'd be there to care for the children after the birth of the baby. He had promised. Then she'd do it. Yes, she would miss her children, but they would be better off with no mother than with the empty shell they now had.

Feeling a tug at her dress, Rebekah awoke from the near trance she had been in.

"Mama," came Isabel's plaintive voice, "can't you do something 'bout Leah? She's crying awful-like."

"Oh!" Rebekah had indeed retreated so far into herself that she had deafened her ears to the child's cries.

As she picked up Leah, she reminded herself again that her children would indeed be better off without her.

Micah was not alone when he returned with the water. But Rebekah could not even find enthusiasm within herself for the guest he brought.

"Why, Haden, this is a surprise." She did not rise from the chair she had taken as she held Leah.

Haden strode to her and kissed her forehead. "Are you not well, Rebekah?"

"I'm fine," she intoned the meaningless words.

"Don't lie to me." He sat on the bench opposite her. "Something is wrong. The children seem well. Is it Benjamin?"

For the first time in all her depressing thoughts, she faced the idea of the very real possibility of Benjamin dying out in the wilds while he rode his circuit. It sickened her to think it would make no difference to her at all if that should happen.

"How would I know about Benjamin?" she said. "He's gone like always."

Haden reached out and took her hand in his. She realized how pale and bony her hand was, but more shocking was the unsettling sensation she had from Haden's touch. The warmth, the strength, the tenderness—those were the things she wanted from her husband. She lifted her miserable eyes. Haden had always been these things, but he had been a wild one. Even when they had been children together, he'd had an adventurous spirit, constantly getting into trouble. Yes, she had been drawn to him because of this aspect of his nature, but she had been a practical girl and realized he was not the kind of man to offer a woman security. He left home at eighteen, but by then Rebekah had already chosen the older, more responsible brother, the one who had, after a fairly wild youth himself, given his life to God. She now wondered how much her choice had influenced Haden's leaving. She wondered, too, how much Benjamin's spiritual conversion had to do with Haden's decision to leave.

But Rebekah had made her choice nevertheless. She chose security and the life she knew she'd have with Benjamin as a minister's wife. But she had loved Benjamin. Back then he, too, had been tender and strong and warm. How could she have known it would all change and turn to bitter dregs?

"I could kill him for what he has done to you," Haden was saying.

"Don't talk that way," she rebuked, but with little bite.

Haden turned to Micah. "Boy, take your sister outside and play a bit. I would like to talk to your mother alone."

"Yes, Uncle Haden." Micah responded so well when he was spoken to in an understanding manner, almost like an equal. Rebekah wondered how Micah would have turned out had a man like Haden been his father. Surely he would smile more and talk, and perhaps even laugh a bit.

When the older children were gone, Haden shook his head. "I fear for you, Rebekah. I have heard of women on the frontier falling to pieces because of the harsh, lonely life. Some have—dear God! You can't be thinking of . . . of escape. Your children need you."

"And what of my needs?" she countered in a shrill, barely controlled voice. "I . . . don't know how much longer I can stand it."

Neither of them spoke the word *suicide*, but it hung clearly palatable, like a gaping, fetid wound, in the air around them.

"What can I do for you, Rebekah?"

"There is nothing to be done."

"Do you hate him? You should," Haden seethed.

Haden had loved her once, she knew. He was now rising up as if to protect her from evil. "He's my husband," she reminded herself as well as Haden.

Haden moved from the bench and dropped to his knees before Rebekah, pressing her hand to his lips. "Where is he?"

"He is doing what he believes to be right."

"How can you defend him?"

"That is the irony of it. I do hate him, or at least I no longer feel love for him. Yet I know he isn't a monster. I know all he does is from his heart—the way he believes a heart toward God should be. All he does springs from noble motives, however much I may hate those motives."

"He's a blind, dirty—"

"He's your brother and my husband."

Haden leaned closer to Rebekah. She stood up as quickly as her lumbering girth would allow and walked several paces away. He followed and, facing her, put his hands on her shoulders. She kept Leah between them.

"Put the baby down, Rebekah," he entreated.

She could feel the urgent warmth of his hands through the fabric of her dress. She looked into his eyes and realized how desperate she was to feel anything!

In the most defiant act of her life, she laid Leah in her cradle, then turned back to her brother-in-law. He took her in his arms, sending thrills through her being she had not felt in years. Yes, it had been years. Long before Texas had become the final straw in her perfunctory life. Her own arms wrapped around Haden, and she did not flinch away from his kisses. To feel passion, to feel love, uncluttered, unconditional. That was all she wanted. What did it matter that the price came so high?

Yet it did matter. She knew that when she felt the child kick inside her. Benjamin's child.

"No, Haden!"

He pulled reluctantly away. "What am I doing? Forgive me, Rebekah."

"Dear Haden, there is nothing to forgive. But we both know we cannot do this to Benjamin."

"Bah! I don't care about him. But I know it would kill you to do such a thing. And I never want to hurt you. Still, it tears me apart to see you so miserable. I wish there was something I could do."

"It just feels good to have someone here . . . besides the children. I'm so—" her voice caught on a sudden sob—"so lonely!"

"When will Benjamin return?"

"In a couple of weeks."

"I can't imagine he's very good company."

A slight smile quirked her lips. "Hardly."

Rebekah, in an attempt to release nervous energy, went to the hearth to check her corn bread. She took a hot pad from a hook and started to lift the pan from the rack. Haden hurried to her side, took the pad, and lifted the heavy pan. She hardly knew how to respond to such attentiveness.

"Thank you, Haden. Put it over on the sideboard." She followed him there, took a dish, and placed the sliced jerky on it. Noticing the knife, she gently brushed it with her fingers. "Are you hungry?"

"I suppose I could eat." But he was looking at the knife. He then raised eyes filled with fear to stare at her.

"You always had a healthy appetite," she said quickly, dismissively. She motioned toward the table. "Come and sit down." He obeyed, and she set a plate before him.

"What can I do for you, Rebekah?"

She took the coffeepot from the hearth where it had been kept warm. She wanted to say that what she must do, she must do alone. Then she realized that perhaps there was another way of escape, a way that only Haden's timely arrival could have allowed.

"Take me away from here." She said the words lightly, hardly even realizing what she was saying until they were out. Then, with the words heavy in the air, she knew that was indeed what she wanted. It was probably the only thing that would save her. She truly did not want to end her own life. She wanted to live. It was just impossible to do so where she was. She turned beseeching eyes to Haden. "Take me from here, Haden."

"But, Rebekah, we just said we couldn't do that to Ben. . . ."

"Not in that way." Absently she poured the coffee into Haden's cup. Then it became very clear to her what she wanted, what she needed. "Take me back to Boston."

"I would do anything for you, Rebekah, but what you ask is not a simple thing." He stared at his coffee a moment, then back up at her. "Perhaps if I spoke to Benjamin, told him how desperate you are, insisted that he should take you back to Boston himself."

"Do you think he would listen to you, the voice of the Devil himself? But even if he did, how could I take him from the work he believes God has called him to do? He would hate me for that as much as I hate him for bringing me here."

"So you want to just up and leave him? He'd come after you."

"If I had a two-week head start . . ." She paused and sank down on the bench next to Haden, her mind trying to sort out all the implications of this new and frightening plan. "I will write him a note, tell him not to come after me, that I will be all right. I am just going to Boston for a visit. I will leave hope that we will be reunited soon. I will adjure him to continue with God's work. That it must not suffer because of me. I think he will see the logic in that. Many men left their wives behind in the States to come here. Benjamin should have done that in the first place. He will see I am right."

"I don't know. . . ."

"Haden, if I don't leave, I know I will kill myself. I already planned to do it as soon as the baby was born." There, it was said! Even if he wanted to deny it, he had the evidence of his own eyes to confirm her earnestness.

"Oh, Rebekah . . ."

"I will, Haden. It is no empty threat. I have decided. I cannot bear another minute here. The only reason I have held off this long is because of the baby."

Haden concentrated on his coffee for a long moment, taking a thoughtful sip. "You know, even if my taking you is perfectly innocent, he will think the worst. He knows I have always loved you. He'll probably kill me."

"Benjamin would never do such an unholy act."

"He'd find a way to sanctify it."

"Leaving is my only hope." She clutched her hands together, imagining once more the feel of the knife slicing the life from her.

Perhaps he saw the cold certainty in her tone, perhaps he thought that if he did as she asked, there might yet be a chance for him to have her. Whatever his reasons, he finally said, "Can you leave in the morning?"

She nodded, a slow smile forming on her lips. She knew leaving her husband went against all she believed to be holy, but then, so did taking her own life. She had only unholy choices left.

And she could not deny that however ungodly her plan, it gave her hope and a reason to live.

CHAPTER 25

Riding his circuit, Benjamin fought the image of that proud woman in San Felipe. He tried to deny her intriguing nobility nearly as staunchly as he denied her lithe body and her dark exotic beauty. He could still see her slim shoulders hitched back, thick waves of sable hair swinging against her back, giving her rodlike strength a certain inexplicable vulnerability.

"God, forgive me!" he prayed again, as he had many times since leaving San Felipe.

He was deceived indeed to attribute nobility to such a woman. She was nothing more than a harlot. Even the term "soiled dove" was too kind to attach to a woman such as she. She was practiced in tempting innocent men such as he, especially married men who had been denied by their wives for months on end!

The more he thought of it, the more he knew this attraction he felt was an attack of Satan upon a man of God. The woman called Liz was nothing but a tool of Satan. And Benjamin refused to be used by that device.

He spurred his horse on, resisting the temptation to race over the final few miles to his home. If for no other reason, he needed a reminder of who he was. But for other reasons as well, he was actually looking forward to spending an extended period there. He had decided that with less than two months to go before the birth of their fourth child, he would remain at the cabin the entire duration and even for a couple of weeks after the birth. He would help plant the garden and perhaps put in a small crop of corn. It would be good for Micah to learn farming, since it seemed a small hope that the boy would follow his father into the ministry. Of course, the only problem with his plan was that Benjamin himself had little experience in the ways of farming. But he had brought from Boston a couple of books on the subject. That, with the help of God, should be sufficient.

Beyond this, Benjamin also anticipated spending time with Rebekah. She had grown so cold lately, and though he could barely admit it, this attitude had begun long before coming to Texas. He supposed after fourteen years of marriage such a circumstance was to be expected. But he could not remember the last time she had expressed words of love to him. And, to tell the truth, it was getting harder and harder for him to do the same. Their love seemed to have grown cold by his absences and her complaining. But he would fix that in the next few months. All a woman really needed was a little attention. He felt certain they had no problem so serious it could not be simply repaired. He would dote a bit on his wife, and she would change her attitude.

As he neared the cabin, a disturbing sight greeted him. On that chill, spring afternoon, no smoke rose from the chimney. This was too strange an occurrence to be discounted lightly. Something was wrong. Had Rebekah begun her labor early and somehow gone to one of the neighbors? But how could she have done so? He had taken the spare horse with him on this trip with the intent of getting supplies. Perhaps John Hunter had come for her.

If not that, then what? Had one of the children taken ill? Perhaps Indians had attacked—though everyone said the Indians in this area were not hostile. Yet who could really tell about such things?

"Giddyup!" he urged his mount.

In the yard of the cabin, he jumped from the horse before it had come to a full stop and raced to the door. A sudden sense of dread made him pause there. He might well find the bodies of his entire family strewn inside.

"Dear God, please don't let it be."

He gripped the latch, finding the latch string out, not knowing if this meant well or ill. Pushing open the door, he was greeted by a cold, uninhabited cabin. It reminded him of when he had first arrived here last year, except now there were disquieting signs of the recent inhabitants. Isabel's doll lay on the floor. One of Rebekah's shawls hung over the edge of a chair, and the colorful cloth Rebekah had put over the rough table was still in place. Benjamin thought it odd how much more deserted the cabin seemed now than when they had first found it occupied by wild animals. He shivered involuntarily.

Where was everyone?

Closing the door behind him, he stepped further into the eerie place and walked idly about. Dirty dishes were on the sideboard, so unlike Rebekah to leave. Then he noticed a layer of dust on various surfaces. This place had been unoccupied for some time . . . days, perhaps even a week or two.

He was trying to decide what to do—ride to the Hunters to see if his family had gone there or to the tavern in Cooksburg to see if Mr. Petty knew anything. Petty usually knew everything that went on in the area. That's when Benjamin saw the paper tucked under the china sugar bowl Rebekah kept on the table. Of course! She had left him a note. It would explain all. He picked up the paper and began to read.

Dear Benjamin,

It pains me greatly to write this letter, yet I am left with no other choice. My heart is breaking, husband. My very soul teeters on the edge of destruction. I am desperate with loneliness. I don't know how I can make you understand when I can barely do so myself. I realize only now how much I thrived on my life in Boston—my friends and especially my family. I need all that desperately. I am empty and lost without it. That is why I have decided to do what I am doing. I have left you, Benjamin. You, of course, will not believe this, but I think it was God's providence that Haden showed up at the peak of my despair. He is taking me back to Boston. You may think what you will, but I must quickly add that the situation is completely innocent between Haden and me. He is merely acting as my escort.

I ask, no, I implore you not to attempt to follow me. I will not come back if that is your intent, not now at least. I must see my family. I will have our baby in Boston. When I recover from that, perhaps I will be in a better frame of mind to return to Texas. In the meantime, Benjamin, I want you to continue with your ministry. I do not wish to be the cause of its failure. Moreover, I do not want you to end up hating me for making you quit as I hate you for making me come to Texas. Though you may now consider me to be a heathen reprobate, I believe God's work to be important. I will not stand in its way.

Forgive me, Benjamin, for not being the strong woman of God you deserve. Forgive me for . . . for everything. I guess there is nothing more to say. Perhaps someday it will be right again between us, but even you must admit it has not been so for years. Texas was only the proverbial back-breaking straw. We have had no real marriage for a long time, and right at this moment I have little hope we ever will. I can only say that time will tell. Until then, serve God. It is what you do best. God only knows what heights you will reach unencumbered by a millstone such as I.

I'll say no more, Benjamin. God be with you.

Always,
Rebekah

Before the letter tumbled from Benjamin's hand, he saw perhaps the greatest affront it held. Clearly the word *Always* at the end had been changed from another word. Rebekah had first written *Love*, then had darkly scrawled *Always* over it, as if she thought he might not be able to tell.

Taking a sharp breath, he clamped his mouth so tightly closed that it began to hurt, but the pain was oddly welcome. He stood still by the table for a while, resisting the temptation to retrieve the fallen letter and read it again. The cold began to penetrate his body and make him shake, but still he stood unmoving, his mind blank except for a white flame inside his head, which he knew was the beginning of rage.

Part of him knew he should quell that rage before it grew stronger, but another part wanted to give it full vent. Finally, it was the latter that won out.

How dare she to do this to him? The selfish, foolish vixen! And how could she write such gibberish? She'd made it sound as though their marriage was a huge disaster. All marriages had a few problems, but she had blown theirs all out of proportion. Was she demented? No, the words on that page had not been those of insanity. She had given them much thought, perhaps even agonized over them. But she was thinking only of herself—as always.

She cared neither for him nor for God, as she tried to claim. She'd always cared only for her own comforts. He could not remember a day in the last year when she had not whined about Boston. She had never given Texas a chance. She had scorned his holy call from the beginning, and now she was two-faced enough to say she believed the work of God to be important! The work of God meant nothing to her and neither did he, God's servant. She relished destroying him in this way, thrusting a knife into his heart and twisting it vilely. And the most vile twist of all was her running off with Haden! What a pitiful attempt she had made in trying to couch it in innocence.

Innocence, indeed!

His wife had run off with his brother!

Thus Benjamin raged for the next hour. He grabbed Rebekah's precious sugar bowl, the one her mother had given to her as a special going-away present. He flung it against the rough logs of the cabin wall. It shattered, spilling expensive and hard-to-come-by sugar all over the floor. Benjamin reveled in the broken china, shattered like his wife's shattered marriage vows.

And she had the nerve to think he might chase after her! Ha! He would no more do that than he would give up his ministry. Let her crawl back to him. Not that he would take her back after she had defiled herself so.

Nearly blinded by fury, he grabbed something else to throw, a piece of crockery on the sideboard. Then he saw her wedding rings lying together side by side. He knew she had never before taken them from her finger. Until now. The horrible finality of what had happened gripped him stronger than rage, stronger than fury or righteous indignation. The realization came that she was gone, his children were gone, the life he had so cherished . . . gone. It assailed him like a blow to the gut. It sent bitter, burning bile up his throat.

"Oh, God!"

His knees gave out and he crumpled to the floor, crying like a child. Great choking sobs exploded from his being. The reaction surprised him, even angered him further, but he could not quench it. The tears just kept coming. And the white flame of rage turned darkly black as his soul descended into despair.

Until the moment he found the note under the sugar bowl, he'd thought he had a perfect marriage, a perfect family. There were a few problems, as any marriage of length encountered, but he'd been so certain they needed but a small fix. Even now he found it hard to believe they could have been so serious. Could he have been that wrong? Yes, he had known Rebekah was not happy with their move. But "teetering on the edge of destruction"? Surely he was not so blind that he could have missed it. Had he known . . . had he known . . . what then? What would he have done? What could he have done? Even she had acknowledged the importance of his ministry. Did she expect him to give it all up for her happiness?

No, she did not. So she had left on her own. Did she not realize that act in itself had the potential to be just as destructive to his ministry as his leaving it? He hardly dared think of the repercussions. Yet they crowded into his distraught mind in spite of himself. How could he be accepted as a leader of his parish if he could not handle his own family?

Would he then become an object of scorn? Oh, how Rebekah would enjoy seeing that. She had on occasion pointed out what she perceived to be his arrogance, but which he defined as righteousness. Regardless of the semantics, she would love to see him shamed before his flock.

Shamed! How can I bear it, dear God?

He dropped his head into his hands as fresh tears assailed him. Then he reached out and gathered Rebekah's letter into his hand, crumpling it into a ball. With a few words, his life was ended. All that mattered was crushed as certainly as he crushed the paper in his hand.

The sound of a horse's whinny in the yard momentarily arrested his attention. Devastated as he was, the common tasks of life called. In his earlier panic he had left the horses to themselves, one still loaded with supplies.

Taking a steadying breath, he started to rise. At that moment, he heard footfall on the doorstep. He could hardly ignore the knock on the door. Whoever it was would know, with two horses roaming in the yard, that someone was home.

CHAPTER 26

BENJAMIN RUBBED HIS HANDS ACROSS his face. His first instinct was to act as if all was normal. Swallowing back the lump in his throat, he rose as a muffled knock struck his door. But even as he stepped toward the door, he wondered if he could ignore it.

But why? Should he run and hide because of a faithless wife?

A surge of renewed anger made him open the door. John Hunter faced him.

"Reverend, I'm sure glad you're here. My mother has finally passed."

"I'm sorry, John." Benjamin's voice trod roughly over the words.

"You okay, Reverend?"

What a poor actor he was! But he tried a moment longer. "Yes . . . of course. Everything is fine. It's . . . just . . . fine." His voice began to deteriorate, and he sucked in further speech.

Hunter peered over Benjamin's shoulder, and his brow wrinkled. Benjamin knew that Hunter would see at once how unusual it was for the house to be so quiet and empty of family life.

"Is it Mrs. Sinclair?" There was true concern in Hunter's voice.

"Why . . . would you ask?"

"Well, I know of her condition, an' my missus wanted her to come to our place when her time came." Hunter licked his lips as though uncomfortable. It wasn't like him to interfere in another's business, and Benjamin knew the man was even less inclined to intrude upon a minister's affairs.

"She is not here," Benjamin replied sharply. His anger, never really abated, rose again—anger at Rebekah for putting him in such an awkward position, anger at his vulnerability. "No one is here!" His voice was ragged with pain. "Do you want to know where she is?"

"Well . . . uh . . . I don't—"

"You'll find out eventually." Benjamin threw the wad of paper at his hapless visitor. "See for yourself." The letter brushed Hunter's nose, then dropped to the floor before he could react. But Benjamin could not let it go. He swept the letter from the floor and shoved it in Hunter's face until he took it in hand. "Go ahead. Read it!"

This was obviously the last thing John Hunter wanted to do, but he obediently smoothed out the paper and scanned the writing, attempting to catch the meaning without gleaning too much of a personal nature. But no matter how quickly he read, he could not avoid the basic tenets of the missive.

"Reverend, I'm sorry."

Hunter's tone made Benjamin instantly regret his impulsive act. For it was filled with pity. Benjamin spun around and strode to the fireplace, forgetting there was no fire in it to offer some distraction. He grabbed a couple of chunks of wood and tossed them inside, then reached for the tinderbox on the mantel. His hands fumbled as he tried unsuccessfully to ignite a spark.

"Reverend?" Hunter entreated gently.

"What—? This has never worked properly." He gave the flint a hard strike and the box flew from his hands.

"Let me help you, Reverend." Hunter bent down and retrieved the box. Benjamin thought his friend's words had deeper meaning, but his flock was not supposed to minister to him. He should be above their help. It was his responsibility to help them.

"Forgive me, John, I've lost track of why you came. Your mother . . ."

Hunter struck a flame, but when he bent to set it to the wood, he must have realized there was no kindling, nothing but the large pieces of wood to start the fire. Letting the little flame die, he reached for some kindling in a bucket next to the hearth.

"Don't bother with that," Benjamin said suddenly. "We need to get to your place."

"I don't expect you to come now. . . ."

"Nonsense! Your mother must have a proper burial." Anger, shame, confusion, emptiness—all retreated momentarily in a sudden sense of purpose, though it appeared more like mania as he raced outside and began unloading supplies from his horse. "As soon as I take care of these supplies, we will be off." He took an armload and strode back into the cabin with Hunter hurrying after him.

"Reverend, please. I can wait." Hunter grabbed Benjamin's arm, but Benjamin shook him off.

Benjamin piled the items on the table, but as he did so, a carefully wrapped package tore. He stared at the contents. It contained the pretty blue calico he had bought for Rebekah. Picking it up, he was about to fling it across the room when he caught Hunter's figure out of the corner of his eye. Instead, he offered the package to him.

"Your wife could use this." Benjamin's voice sounded as cold as the fireless hearth. "Rebekah will never need it."

"I can't take that, Reverend. Why don't you set it down and, while you're at it, sit down yourself. Maybe you'd just like to talk or something."

"Would you counsel me, John? What do you say to a minister whose life is ruined?"

"Now, don't talk that way." Hunter pulled out a corner of the bench by the table and motioned for Benjamin to sit. Then taking his own advice, he slipped onto the bench himself. "Come on, Reverend. Sit."

Benjamin suddenly felt once more how shaky he was. He realized he hadn't sat, much less rested, since coming home. Perhaps it would help after all. Maybe it would make his mind work and think properly, calmly. Straddling the bench so as to face Hunter, he stared at him, as if expecting the very action to somehow solve his problems.

Perhaps taking Benjamin's look as leave to speak, Hunter went on, "I'll be frank with you, Reverend. You know I don't know more than you about much of anything, 'cept maybe farming and frontier life. But even I know that no one is perfect, no matter how hard one tries to be so. Don't you think for a minute that any of your parishioners ever expected you to be perfect—or your wife. Things happen, and it don't change the man you are."

"You think no less of me for what has happened?" Benjamin wasn't certain why this should surprise him so, perhaps because he might have thought less of Hunter had the tables been turned.

"Listen here, Reverend, anyone knows this land ain't kind to women. Why do you suppose there's so few of 'em around? My wife has threatened to leave many times. After the cholera epidemic near two years ago when we lost our two youngest children, I thought she'd snap for sure."

"But she didn't."

"All folks are different."

"It is kind of you to try to comfort me in this way, John, but you and I both know more is expected of me—"

"You only expect it of yourself," Hunter cut in rather sharply for the soft-spoken man that he was.

"God expects it of me." As Benjamin said the words, it was the first time that day the full import of what had happened struck him. He hadn't let himself think of God, at least not in this context. Not in the sense that he had failed God.

"I don't know about any of that," Hunter was saying. "But as far as I can see, you haven't done nothing to let God down yet. God doesn't expect you to be perfect, does He?"

Of course He does! Benjamin wanted to shout. A father always expects his sons to be perfect. But, if only on an intellectual basis, Benjamin knew he wasn't perfect and never could be as long as he was shackled by his human frame. Yet in striving as hard as he did to be so, he had come to forget that fact. He made sure he did everything right according to the Scriptures, just so he would not have to be faced with his humanity. Perhaps that's what angered him most about what Rebekah had done. She had forced him to confront the fact that he was, after all, only a man.

"There's still a couple of hours of daylight left," Benjamin hedged. "Let's use it to make our way to your cabin."

"I wouldn't ask that of you—"

"I couldn't bear to spend the night here, John." Benjamin wondered what he would do the next night and the night after that? How long could he escape reality?

With an understanding shrug, John said, "In that case, let's finish unloading those supplies and be on our way."

CHAPTER 27

THE NEWS OF BENJAMIN'S TROUBLED marriage spread quickly through his circuit. To John Hunter's credit, it came not from him but rather from Albert Petty, the Cooksburg storekeeper. He had surmised the situation when Benjamin Sinclair's wife, brother, and brood of kids had come to the store to purchase supplies for the trail. That, together with rumors—Nell Hunter let a thing or two slip here and there—and the story was out, loaded with varying degrees of misinformation.

Not everyone received it with as much magnanimity as Hunter.

Amos Hawke had a good laugh.

"Don't that beat all!" he chuckled as he shared a glass of ale with Albert Petty. "The preacher's wife ran off with his own brother. Can't say as I blame the poor woman."

"And her several months gone with child," added Petty with a sly grin.

"You suppose the kid is even the preacher's?"

"Who knows?"

"Well, all's I can say is that self-righteous Bible-beater got what he deserved."

Because Benjamin had just completed his circuit, he used that as an excuse to stay home when he returned from reading a service over the grave of John Hunter's mother. He didn't let himself believe he was hiding out. He always took time off after completing his circuit, though occasionally a member of his flock would come to fetch him as Hunter had to perform an emergency service. Now was no different. Even a tarnished preacher was better than none at all when there was a need.

Another death forced Benjamin to ride two days to the home of Jim Wilson, whose wife had died in childbirth along with the infant. Because Wilson lived in a tiny enclave of settlers, mostly his relatives, there were about twenty-five present at the service. Benjamin had often used Wilson's cabin or one of his clan's for church services on his circuit, so he knew everyone present.

They stood around the graves in a drizzly spring rain. Benjamin quoted Scripture from memory so as not to expose his Bible to the elements.

" 'I am the resurrection, and the life: he that believeth in me, though he were dead, yet shall he live. And whosoever liveth and believeth in me shall never die.' Do you believe this, Jim Wilson?" Benjamin glanced up to see the bereaved man nod and went on. "Then I commend the spirits of Sarah Reed Wilson and Robert James Wilson into the hands of God through our Lord Jesus Christ."

Because the bodies had been laid in their graves days previously, the service ended there. The group of mourners hurried into Jim Wilson's warm, dry cabin to offer further condolences and to partake of a meal.

Benjamin was well accustomed to standing apart in such gatherings. It was a minister's lot. He was the shepherd, not one of the sheep, thus friendships among the sheep were few. At least he'd always believed his lack of friends was due to his flock's high respect for him, and that belief kept him from questioning the situation. He would not have questioned it now except he sensed innately there was a deeper chasm between him and his sheep than usual. He felt it not so much in the way they looked at him, but rather in the way they did *not* look at him. Nor was it in the words spoken, but instead in those left unspoken. No one asked, "How's the missus?" or remarked, "Them kids of yours must be getting big" or even acknowledged the situation with "Sorry to hear about your wife, Reverend. Our prayers are with you."

Perhaps it would have been better if the silence had continued. But finally Jim Wilson himself clumsily broached the touchy issue.

"Reverend Sinclair, I sure appreciate you coming all this way."

"I would not have thought to do otherwise."

"Well, considering . . . uh . . . things, I would have understood."

Benjamin could have dropped it there by nodding quietly and changing the subject. But the implication of Wilson's words ignited his defensiveness. "My ministry always takes precedence over my personal life. There is no reason for one to affect the other."

"Sure, Reverend. I never thought otherwise. . . ."

There was something in Wilson's tone that implied more, and it irritated Benjamin. "But not everyone feels as you do, is that not so, Mr. Wilson?"

"Well . . . uh . . ."

Still Benjamin could have avoided further discussion by keeping quiet. Part of him wanted nothing more than to do so. But he was by nature confrontative, whether it be disputing sin or apostasy or injustice or political issues. In winning converts to Christ or taking up a moral cause, he never backed down. And he knew if he did so now, his ministry would be over. It was time he set everyone straight and quelled the rumors he knew were spreading.

Benjamin swung around and, with a fierce glint in his eyes, called for the attention of the group.

"I have something to say to all of you." His voice was clear, as if he were intoning a sermon. "Mr. Wilson, I hope you will indulge me a moment. I will take no more because I know our purpose today is to support you." Wilson nodded, and Benjamin continued. "I am certain you are all aware of the fact that my wife has left Texas to return to her home in Boston. I am also certain that all manner of rumors have accompanied these circumstances. Let me put them to rest immediately. My wife was extremely homesick, and when an opportunity arose for her to leave, she took it—yes, without informing me, but I'm sure only because I was out on my circuit. I do not defend her actions. She broke faith with her marriage vows. But if I believed for a minute that her behavior in any way reflected upon my spiritual call and my personal soundness for the ministry, I would not now be standing before you. Her weakness does not weaken my ministry to you. I am blameless and stand with a pure heart before God. I implore you not to give place to Satan by rejecting the ministry I have begun. If you have doubts, take it to God in prayer. I know He continues to stand with me through all this, and I pray you will also."

Regardless of what anyone thought about Benjamin Sinclair, they could not attribute cowardice to him. Even if they thought his bravery was mixed with a good dose of gall, they had to admit he had pluck in standing face-to-face before them, though they did wonder about a man who considered himself blameless and pure of heart. Yet Rev. Benjamin Sinclair was the only man of the cloth they were likely to see, so they were willing to overlook his faults, just as they always had.

When the people in the cabin shook Benjamin's hand and told him not to worry about it, he took them at their word. Why would they do otherwise? He was faultless in the situation with his wife. He returned to his cabin bolstered as never before. A good portion of his daily prayers were spent on Rebekah's behalf, that God would lead her back from the path of iniquity, deliver her from Satan's wiles, and "create in her a clean heart."

He was pleased that as he prayed for his wife his own sense of anger dulled. He had often advised those in his flock plagued by anger to "pray for those who would despitefully use you." What a blessing to see this in action in his own life! In fact, he prepared an inspired sermon on this very topic, which he planned to preach when he began his circuit again.

Any sense of self-reproach he might have experienced over Rebekah's departure was thoroughly dispelled in the wave of grand benevolence that washed over him. Naturally, he knew he wasn't a perfect husband, but imperfection was not sin. It would only be sin if he had, like Rebekah, let it destroy their marriage. It would only be sin if he refused forgiveness.

And just to leave no doubt as to his spiritual righteousness, one afternoon Benjamin gathered a pen, ink, and a sheet of paper, sat at the table, and penned a letter to his wife.

Dear Rebekah,

It has been a month since your departure, and as I write this, I assume you are more than halfway home. This letter may be awaiting you when you arrive in Boston, but more likely it will follow you. In any case, I waited to respond to your actions because I feared any immediate response might have lacked godliness. Now, however, I believe my heart has healed somewhat, and I can write with a true spirit of Christian love.

In that spirit, wife, I tell you that I forgive you for what you have done. You are still my wife, and I will accept you back in my home should you seek to right the wrong you have done. Don't let a single impulsive act destroy you. Allow God to work His will in you and in your heart. Turn from your destructive ways. Turn back to God and to your husband. Return before it is too late. I will even come for you, if you write telling me of your change in heart. In the meantime, please give my love to the children. I miss them terribly.

Benjamin paused in his writing. He shouldn't have mentioned the children, for the thought of them threatened to ignite the anger he had so studiously quelled. If he was a stern father, it was only because he deeply loved his children. Rebekah knew that beyond anything else, thus her act of taking away his children was perhaps her greatest sin. Nevertheless, determined to maintain his spirit of forgiveness, he inhaled two deep breaths, and murmuring a prayer, he took up the pen once more.

I leave this final word of hope with you from the First Epistle of John: "If we confess our sins, he is faithful and just to forgive us our sins, and to cleanse us from all unrighteousness." My prayers are with you, Rebekah. I fervently hope I will hear from you soon.

Regards,
Benjamin

He thought how he, too, stumbled over the closing of his letter. He had not been able to write the word *love.* It had never been an easy word for him to say in the best of times. Now, of all the emotions he felt toward Rebekah, love was the last to come to mind. Of course he did love his wife, even if it was a love void of passion or romance. Such emotions flirted too closely with sin anyway, though he thought Rebekah looked for such things. But when she had married him fourteen years ago, she had known there was no passion between them. He had always known she had wavered between Haden and himself. When Benjamin found Christ, the scales had tipped greatly in his favor, because she had known she could not marry an ungodly man. Then when God told Benjamin that Rebekah was the woman for him, that was all there was to it—for both of them. She had married Benjamin because she knew he was the right man for her, and he had done the same. Wasn't that better than all the love and passion in the world?

Yet it left him oddly empty when he could not even sign the word *love* and mean it in the way he knew she wanted. He wondered what it would be like to love in that way—with an intense passion and starry-eyed romance, combined with the assurance of God's blessing.

He quickly banished those thoughts from his mind. It was very nearly adulterous to think that way now. His passion for God was all he needed.

Nevertheless, his hand trembled as he folded and sealed the letter. He would mail it the next time he went into Cooksburg.

CHAPTER 28

BENJAMIN GRABBED THE AX FROM its hook on the wall and headed out to the woodpile. Even now he could not admit that he desperately needed the physical exertion to release the pent-up emotions writing the letter had evoked. He was simply low on wood and wanted to bring in a supply before it rained again.

He set a chunk of oak in place on the chopping block and took up the ax in his gloved hands. The first blow split the oak cleanly. He stared, a bit surprised at his effort. He was no weakling to be sure, but physical prowess was certainly not his forte. Yet the ax had cut through the hard oak as if it were a loaf of fresh-baked bread. Could it be more than physical strength compelling his arms?

Unable to answer the question, he did the same to another piece of oak. Blow after blow, he fell upon the wood as if driving a sword into an enemy. The pile of defeated oak grew as sweat poured from Benjamin, blurring his eyes, soaking his shirt. His ears reverberated with the fierce sound of metal striking wood so that he did not hear the hoofbeats until they were well into the yard.

"Benjamin!"

He swung around at the sound of his name, ax gripped in both hands, eyes flashing as if he indeed were ready for battle. That stance did not change when he saw who had arrived.

"Haden." The name ground through gritted teeth. For a moment Benjamin saw only his brother mounted on his chestnut mare, tall and imposing in his buckskin clothes. And in that single moment, all Benjamin's practiced Christian reserve bolted, replaced by white-hot anger. It was as if no time at all had passed since that awful moment he had stood alone in his cabin and read Rebekah's letter.

But before he could actually do what his anger was telling him to do with the ax, he took in the rest of the scene. Leah was nestled on Haden's horse in front of him, and another horse carried Micah and Isabel. Still, the full import of the scene did not register.

"Are we welcome?" Haden eyed Benjamin as one might size up a wild animal.

The sight of the children had dulled Benjamin's anger, at least for the moment. Had he been able to move, he would have run to them, plucked them from the horses, and embraced them in his arms. But his feet felt like lead, and the ax felt as if it had become part of his body.

"Of course. What is the meaning of this?" His tone wasn't accusatory, rather it mirrored his complete bafflement. "Where's—" her name caught in his throat like pain, like fear, but he forced it out—"Rebekah?"

Haden motioned for Benjamin to help him with Leah, who was sound asleep. Seeing this need made Benjamin will his body into motion. First, he set the ax by the cutting block, then he walked, though still leadenly, to Haden's mount and reached up for the sleeping child. Having the child in his arms seemed to release a great tension within him, almost as much as chopping the wood had. Vaguely he thought how sad it was that he needed such an excuse to hold his own child.

Haden dismounted, and it was then that Benjamin saw he was wearing a pack on his back. The other children remained mounted. Micah looked grim, as if merely waiting for a word from his uncle in order to turn around and gallop from that place.

"Are you going to tell me what this is all about?" Benjamin was reluctant to invite Haden inside, still remembering he had once banished him from his home and knowing he now had more reason than ever to maintain that judgment.

"I . . . don't know how . . ."

"Did Rebekah decide she wanted to leave not only me but the children as well?" Benjamin simply could not help releasing some of the scathing accusations he'd repressed for so long.

"You selfish fool!" Haden yelled. "Rebekah is dead!"

Benjamin felt as though the ax had been turned upon him. He was certain Haden hoped his words would split him in two. Too stunned to speak, he shook his head. His arms felt weak and he feared he would lose Leah, yet at the same time, he clung to the child as if for life.

"It's true," Haden said, and by the tone of his voice, it appeared he had been repressing a few choice words as well. "She died giving birth to your child. How do you like that, Benjamin? Better than holding a gun to her head."

"I . . . I . . ." Words eluded Benjamin and his body was growing ever weaker. He stumbled back until he reached the cutting block, then shoving aside the ax, he sank onto the stump. "She . . . was not due for another month." It was such a foolish, idiotic thing to say, but his brain simply could not function properly.

"She should never have attempted such a journey, but she was willing to take that risk rather than die of loneliness and misery here." Haden now stood over Benjamin, glowering.

It did penetrate Benjamin's numb brain that Haden's attitude was somehow incongruent. Why did *his* words ring of accusation? Why was there murder in *his* eyes?

"What are you saying, Haden?" Benjamin finally managed. Even as he spoke, he knew it was the wrong thing to say, that somehow the question only invited more ire to be unleashed.

"She tried to tell me how completely oblivious you were to her situation." Haden shook his head. "Even knowing you, I found it hard to believe. That any man could . . ."

At last Benjamin's brain ground into motion. True, it was more like a loaded wagon lumbering uphill, but at least it began to exhibit some rationality.

"Haden! You've just told me my wife has died! How can you say such things now?"

"Because you were here, no doubt basking in righteous indignation, while I had to watch her die. I had to sit there, helpless, while the very life bled from her. I had to hold the struggling infant in my arms, knowing it was yours, and that had it not been for you, Rebekah would have lived. I had to dig a grave on the side of the trail and lay her sweet body in it. I—" His voice broke with emotion. Tears sprang into his eyes. "She did not deserve this, but I'll wager you wished her dead after she left."

"That's not true! I forgave her."

"So magnanimous of you!" Haden sneered.

"She was the one who left me—"

"Because she would have killed herself had she stayed a moment longer!" Haden stopped and gasped, then shot a glance at the two older children still seated on their horse. He obviously hadn't meant to say so much in front of them.

Benjamin was struggling with his own emotions. Had he not been holding Leah, he knew he would have physically attacked his brother. And even with the innocent baby in his arms, his hands itched for violence.

Haden spun around and strode to the mounted children. Murmuring soft words to them that Benjamin could not hear, Haden helped Micah dismount, then lifted Isabel from the horse. He gave Isabel a gentle hug and kiss before setting her upon the ground. She clung to his neck for a few seconds before letting go. Poor Isabel was nearly asleep on her feet. Micah was wearing such an impenetrable mask it was impossible to fathom what was going on in his young mind. What could he possibly think of the terrible accusations being shot back and forth between his uncle and his father?

Haden was right about one thing, as his actions indicated. The children needed tending. This impelled Benjamin to rise to his feet, and still carrying Leah, he headed into the cabin. He heard the others follow. He laid Leah on his own bed and turned to face the others.

"Come Isabel. You can sleep a bit, then we'll have supper."

She walked obediently to him. He laid a hand on her shoulder and helped her into her small bed. Could she feel his hand tremble? Did she know how he loved her and how much he wanted to protect her from harm? For the first time that day, he lifted his eyes from his own shock and grief to realize that his children had lost their mother. Perhaps they, too, had watched her die. How they must be suffering!

On impulse he reached out to take her up in his arms to comfort and love her, but then he saw she was not even looking at him. It was almost as if her eyes were purposefully averted from him, and her hands were stiffly at her side, making no move to reach out to him. He let his own impulse die. The last thing he wanted now was to have her flinch away from him.

He straightened up and turned his attention to Micah. "You can sleep, too, if you wish, son. Or, if you prefer, have something to eat. There is jerky in the crock where your mo—where it usually is."

"I'll tend the horses," Micah said coldly and left the cabin.

"So you have turned my children against me," Benjamin accused. The brief respite from their battle was ended.

"You needed no help from me, Benjamin. You did it all yourself. I doubt you care a thing for your children. You've never even asked what became of the new baby."

"I assumed . . ."

Haden, as if in response, took the pack from his back and laid it gently on the table. Reaching inside, he removed a tiny, squirming bundle.

"What?" Benjamin said roughly before his voice disintegrated once more.

"You have a son." With surprisingly deft hands, the bachelor lifted the corners of the blanket that had been tucked neatly around the baby. "He is nearly two weeks old. An old wife on the trail told me that if he has survived this long, he is likely to continue to do so." Once the child had been arranged to Haden's satisfaction, he lifted him into his arms. The infant had been asleep, but the handling woke him, and he began to make small sounds, somewhere between crying and cooing.

Benjamin continued to stare dumbly at the process. His son.

"Take him," Haden said, and it was clearly an order.

"I . . . wouldn't know what to do." Benjamin wasn't aware, but it was the first hint of contriteness he had yet exhibited.

"You've had three other children."

"Rebekah . . ."

Haden thrust the child toward him. Benjamin backed away. He had always basked so in his children and his family, but he suddenly realized he had never truly taken part in their lives, at least not in the daily aspects. He'd never diapered them, or fed them or—dear God!—seldom even held them!

What kind of man was he?

It struck him like a crushing landslide, and as though rock and dirt were literally caving in on him, he felt choked and breathless.

"What were you saying before?" he rasped to his brother.

"I said a lot of things. Maybe some were out of line." Perhaps holding the baby had softened Haden's ire.

Benjamin forced himself to remember and speak the words. He lamented his confrontative nature and that it was now about to turn on him, but he couldn't help himself. "You said . . . she . . . would have killed herself had she not left. What did you mean?"

"Forget it, Benjamin."

"What—did—you—mean?" Each word was an effort, but he had to know.

"She planned to kill herself as soon as you returned from your circuit and were here to watch the children. She was waiting only for that and the birth of the baby."

"You believed her?"

"I would not have taken her on a perilous journey in her condition if I hadn't."

"What else did she say to you?"

"Ben . . ."

"I have to know."

"Too bad you didn't have this desire to know while she lived. She was completely miserable, yet she received nothing but holy admonitions from you. Even then she was so afraid of standing in the way of your so-called call of God that she would rather take her own life than disappoint you."

Benjamin nodded silently, unable to refute his brother's words, though he desperately wanted to.

Instead he asked, "Did she love you?"

Haden quirked his head toward the baby. "This is proof of which one of us she loved."

Of all the things Haden had said, that was the most difficult to believe. "I . . . killed her then," was all Benjamin could say.

Haden said nothing but laid the baby in the cradle that Leah had used. He walked to the door and put his hand on the latch, saying not a word to refute Benjamin's statement.

"Where are you going?" Benjamin asked.

"Away."

"You can't leave me like this!"

The ironic smile that slipped across Haden's face was worse than a blow. "I feel sorry for you, Ben, but I feel no benevolence toward you. I loved Rebekah, and you killed her. I will never forgive you for that. Your contrition now comes much too late. There is no way we could dwell in peace under this roof."

"But the children—"

"I hate the thought of leaving them in your cold, heartless care, but they are your children, not mine."

"You never could take responsibility for anything—that's why Rebekah married me and not you." He had to lash out at his brother because he could take only so much self-flagellation.

"True." Haden lifted the latch.

"You selfish, miserable reprobate!"

"Good-bye, Benjamin."

"Please!" Sheer desperation collided with Benjamin's pride. "I need . . . I . . ." But pride won out.

"Even now you can't admit your weaknesses. God help you, Ben!"

Haden swung the door open and slammed it shut behind him, leaving Benjamin gaping in his wake. Alone, confused, helpless, and afraid.

CHAPTER 29

"Come back here, you teasing trollop!"

He was big and ugly and dirty. Though thankfully in the dim light of night his looks were not as discernable as his odor. He smelled of horse and sweat and cheap whiskey. But that was not as appalling as the knife he gripped in his meaty paw.

Liz wrenched from his grasp just as he lifted the shiny blade—the only clean thing about him. Trembling, she scrambled across the bed, grabbing a pillow to use as a shield, but it was too late. Drops of blood stained the pillow—her blood. In numb disbelief she saw a slice across her shoulder and the red quickly soaking her chemise. Then she saw her terror actually pleased him. He was grinning, revealing two uneven rows of yellow, rotten teeth.

He lunged with the knife. Again, she didn't move fast enough, but this time the blade only split the ticking of the pillow, spewing feathers everywhere. She tried to get around the bed to the door, but he guessed her thoughts. Clad only in long underwear, he launched himself from the bed and loomed large in her path.

"P-please! You don't need to hurt me!" She'd had men get a bit rough before, but never like this. She saw murder in this one's eyes. But she had done nothing to incur his wrath—in fact, he was not acting out of wrath at all. If he killed her, it would be out of sheer pleasure.

"I ain't gonna hurt you, girl—not permanent-like." He grinned again. "I'm just gonna make it interesting."

"Y-you can have your m-money back." Her trembling lips made her speech nearly incoherent.

"Ha! Maurry don't give refunds for nothing! Anyways, I don't want my money back."

He snatched her arm, holding her so tightly it cut off the circulation. Then he ruthlessly shoved her back onto the bed. She silently prayed he would thrust his knife straight into her heart. Why should she go on living like this? But instead of despair, sudden rage welled up in her. It had always been there, of course, lurking within her on some level, but she had been successful in keeping it under control. Now it simply overwhelmed her.

That was no surprise. The last few days had been utterly dreadful, sapping her of the strength that had aided her in the past. Hannah was sicker than ever, and Liz had been up with her constantly in the night. She'd had next to no sleep in two days. It might have been different if she had been able to spend that time rocking her sick daughter. But no, she still had to perform all her duties. The other girls, even Mae, were tiring of helping her. They had been harping a lot lately about giving Hannah to one of the town women—leaving her on a doorstep, if necessary.

Liz had been teetering on a precipice, and this mean, lumbering oaf was merely pushing her over.

"You really want to use that knife?" She gripped his hand and forced the knife down so that the tip rested just under her right breast. "Go ahead! I want to see blood, too! Real blood, not just a measly trickle from a little scratch."

"You're plumb crazy!" The oaf changed his tune as quickly as she had changed hers.

"You're all talk then!" she dared. "Come on, you lily-livered, addle-brained coward!"

"I ain't gonna hang for killing no whore!"

"Then I'll hang!"

She twisted his arm so quickly he had no time to react. His fingers spread apart, and the knife slipped easily into Liz's hand. She turned it quickly while her attacker gaped. He could have stopped her at any time, but he was too shocked to do anything. In an instant it was too late for him to make a move, for the tip of the blade now rested just below his rib cage—the soft, fleshy part, which even she could penetrate with a good jab.

"It won't kill you," she taunted, "but it'll hurt awful bad."

He licked his lips. "Easy now, sweetheart."

"Sweetheart, is it? A minute ago, you were ready to slit my throat."

"I was only playing."

"I want to kill you." She could hardly recognize her own voice, its cold, deadly tones. Her hand ached as it gripped the knife—yes, it ached to kill.

Slowly he eased away. When he saw she was not going to follow through on her threat, he scrambled even more quickly until he was off the bed. Gathering up his clothes, he backed toward the door.

"Maurry said you was a genteel plantation nigger. You ain't nothing but a—"

He didn't finish. Liz sent the knife flying, and it plunged into the door, inches from his greasy head. His retreat was quick and silent after that. He didn't even pause to retrieve his knife.

Liz fell back against the remaining pillow on the bed, her limbs shaking, her heart pounding. Fear and fury slammed against her sensibilities until tears oozed from her eyes. Yet it was neither the man's attack nor the blood drawn that made the tears erupt. As she lay there in her chemise, the tangled blankets of the bed still strong with the man's fetid odor, she felt as never before the reality of what she was. For the first time in a year, she truly *felt* like a whore—hard, dirty, but most of all, completely competent at this hideous job. The ribald battle with her customer proved she was no more a victim. She could have killed him. Maybe next time she would not hesitate. Maybe she would even kill Maurry. For an instant as she held the knife to the man's chest, she had felt strong.

Yet the tears still flowing from her eyes blatantly contradicted that.

Maybe there was hope. Maybe this incident only proved that she had more fight in her than she thought. If only it were true. One thing was certain, she might not be completely lost in this appalling life, but she was very close to being so. If the last two days had put her on the edge, she knew now exactly where she was. On one side the life of a real human being—a person, a woman of worth—was to be had. Over the edge on the other side plunged the existence of a whore. The rest of the girls were already there, even Mae, because she, too, had accepted the life Maurry forced on them all. Some of them had even convinced themselves that this life wasn't so bad. They had food and clothes and shelter, all in exchange for their virtue. They no longer thought it was an unfair exchange.

Liz swiped the back of her hand across her wet eyes. "I won't do it," she whispered. Then more firmly, "I won't do it! I won't go over that edge. Not me, or Hannah either!"

Liz knew the only way to avoid plummeting over that threatening edge was to escape. That was not a new revelation. She'd thought about it constantly for the last year. Yes, it had been a whole year since this terrible ordeal had begun. She could not face another year like it, yet none of the obstacles to her leaving had changed. If anything, leaving was even more difficult now that Hannah's condition seemed to grow worse each day.

The irony was that Liz had stayed, hoping her daughter would get better, but that obviously wasn't happening. Perhaps in trying to protect Hannah, she had in fact only made her worse.

"Hannah, I'm beginning to think we have to take the risk." She stared down at the child nestled on her lap one afternoon as she sat on her bed enjoying a rare moment of privacy.

The poor child was a little more than a year old, yet she looked more like a baby of eight months, and a small baby at that. And she still wasn't walking. She might have a sixteenth of Negro blood in her, but she was as sallow-faced as any of the blond, blue-eyed grandchildren of the Hearnes.

From that moment, the idea of escape grew more urgent in Liz's mind. Somehow she had to find a way around the barriers that kept her a prisoner of Maurry. In the quiet of her mind, she followed a path she had begun taking more and more often these days.

"Jesus, help me to find a way out of this place. I don't know *how* to do it, and I don't know *where* to go once I make the break."

The answer to the second question came quickly. She had been holding her borrowed New Testament, and all at once the leather cover practically throbbed in her hands.

Rebekah Sinclair. Of course.

Rebekah would help Liz. She would be kind to her, accept her, perhaps even protect her from pursuers. The reverend might feel differently, but Liz knew wives had ways to get around their husband's objections. Though Liz was practically a stranger, she knew Rebekah would not turn her away.

The problem of getting there was harder to solve. She knew the Sinclairs lived near Cooksburg, about forty miles north of San Felipe. The location of the Thomson place would add about ten miles to that distance, a two- or three-day hard ride on horseback. On foot, it might take several days beyond that to make the journey. At least she had feet. Supplies would be harder to come by. But she addressed that problem by pilfering scraps of food and secreting them away in her room.

The most daunting obstacle, of course, was the matter of pursuit. A woman on foot and carrying a child would be easy to overtake. And she dare not steal a horse because, though a runaway slave only risked being beaten, horse thieves were hanged in Texas.

She would just have to outsmart Maurry. For one thing, she doubted he would guess she'd go north into the wild frontier. It was suicide for a woman alone to do, especially a woman who knew little of surviving in the wilds. Smiling grimly to herself, she wondered if Maurry would guess just how insane she was. At any rate, he knew nothing about the Sinclairs, so it should not occur to him that she would head that way. No, he would first assume she'd go south to one of the ports—Matagora or Galveston. Though she had no money for passage, he'd figure she'd have no qualms about selling her favors for a few dollars.

For the next two days, Liz began to discreetly prepare for her flight. She found an old leather saddlebag that Lyle Thomson had discarded and would never miss. She also took Lyle's mackintosh. He wouldn't miss it until it rained, and by then they would know of her escape. Her plan was to wait for rain, in hope that it would cover her tracks. She had heard from some of the men that a good storm front was moving in.

"It's gonna be a drencher," one of the men had predicted. "You better see that Maurry shores up his place 'cause that creek he's near is liable to flood."

Liz dared not hope for such a disaster to befall her master. Her only stroke of luck was that the creek lay south of the Thomson place, and she would not have to cross it. The possibility of having to confront other swollen waterways was too daunting to even consider.

She avoided thinking of the many pitfalls in her plan. They were countless, she knew. In reality, she doubted she would survive. But that really was no longer an issue.

CHAPTER 30

THE STORM BROKE FOUR DAYS after Liz had first conceived her plan. No matter what became of it, she knew it must have been blessed a little by God because the storm began on Sunday, the only day Maurry did not require his girls to work. Thus, not having to entertain customers Sunday night, she would be free to leave long before dawn.

Sometimes the girls did not sleep so well on their free nights because they were accustomed to different hours. It was no different this night. Liz could hear stirrings in all the little cubicles well past midnight. Maurry and Lyle were taken up with their usual occupation of playing cards and drinking with a group of men in the main cabin. The noise of the drunken men seemed to go on forever.

Finally, around two or three in the morning, the restless throng quieted down. Some probably left despite the storm, preferring to pass the night in their own cabins. But if this was like other similar gatherings, most of the men had probably simply passed out on the cabin floor. They would sleep soundly and well into the morning.

"Well, Hannah, it's time." Liz gently brushed aside a strand of Hannah's hair from her pale face.

She filled the saddlebag with all her pilfered supplies—food, water bottle, the medicinal herbs for Hannah, and a kitchen knife, the only weapon she could get her hands on. Too bad that oaf who had attacked her came back the next day for his knife. Finally Liz lovingly tucked Rebekah Sinclair's New Testament inside. Then she snugly wrapped Hannah in a blanket from the bed. Tearing another blanket in half, she made a kind of sling in which she could place Hannah, then tie around her own body. It would help take off some of the weight, slight as it was, from Liz's arms.

For herself, Liz wore her warmest and most modest outfit, a yellow silk skirt with a heavy ruffle around the bottom and a white muslin blouse. Maurry didn't allow them practical clothes in an attempt, Liz thought, to keep them under his thumb. The yellow was bright, and the green of woods and trees would not blend with it, but it was better than the reds and purples of her other dresses. Slipping a coat over the outfit would help hide it a little.

She rejected the idea of bringing another blanket. The rain would only make it a wet and heavy burden. The clothes on her back would have to do. Placing the saddlebag by a strap around her shoulder, she completed the ensemble with the poncholike mackintosh, which was large enough to cover both her and Hannah.

At last she was ready.

She crept from her room. All was silent except for the pounding of the rain upon the roof of the cabin. In the common room that was exclusively for the girl's use, the embers of the banked fire in the hearth emanated a delicious warmth, which made going out into the cold, wet night an unpleasant thought. A fleeting notion of abandoning her crazed plan assailed Liz.

Why not accept her life as it was? Warmth, food, shelter. Who was she to think she should have more? She was no plantation belle, only a Negro slave wench.

"Stop it!" she hissed to herself.

She'd made her decision. She had considered the risks. Part of her knew she and Hannah were likely to die in this escape attempt. She was not going to debate the matter further.

She took a determined step, then suddenly froze—but this time not from indecision but rather because she saw the rocker in the sitting room by the hearth move. Someone was awake.

"Storms always keep me awake." Mae's voice was quiet, almost soothing. "You, too, Liz?"

"I . . . I . . ."

In the dark, Liz saw Mae look up. Bundled as she was, there would be no way to hide what she was about to do. But contradicting the fierce pounding of her heart, a calm stole over Liz. She could not accept that all was lost so soon.

"I guess it can be a little scary—the rain, you know." Liz spoke as if they were having a casual conversation, though in soft tones.

"Don't be scared." In the glow of the embers, Liz could see a faint smile play upon Mae's lips. "I think the rain will be your friend."

"I hope so."

Mae rose from the rocker, the old wood creaking slightly. The sound made Liz tense.

"I guess I can sleep a bit now," Mae said. "You gonna sit for a spell?"

"Maybe so. . . ."

Mae quietly approached Liz, her eyes carefully taking in the mackintosh-wrapped pair. She knew exactly what was happening. She reached up and gently patted Liz's cheek.

"You never did belong here." Mae's voice was suddenly husky.

"Neither do you, Mae."

The older woman shrugged. "I'll see you in the morning."

Liz only nodded. They both knew they might never see each other again.

The heightened energy from a midnight flight kept Liz going for some miles. When that wore off, weariness attacked her like a ferocious beast. Her arms were numb, her shoulders ached, her feet, clad in old boots that might have been made for dancing but certainly not for hiking miles over broken, slippery terrain, felt like stumps of sheer pain. The hem of her skirt was also soaked, weighing her down like lead. At least Hannah felt fairly dry.

In the dark, Liz could scarcely discern her direction, but earlier in the week she had taken a walk a short distance in the proper direction and left subtle markers. She had encountered them all, obliterating them the moment they were found. But there were no more markers now. Only instinct and a lot of prayer were left to guide her.

By the time daylight came, she judged she might have traveled five or six miles—a distance Maurry could cross in less than an hour on horseback. So despite her weariness, she pushed on, stopping only for short breathers. She kept off the trail as much as possible. Once, when she saw a rider coming from the opposite direction, she veered so far into the woods that she lost track of the trail altogether. Still she trudged on. If she discovered she was going in the wrong direction . . . well, she would deal with it when the time came.

Along about noon—though she could not tell exactly because it was still raining and there was no sun to judge by—she knew she had reached the limits of her endurance. Retreating to a part of the woods where the canopy of trees was thickest, she found a stout trunk and crumpled down, using the tree as a backrest. She made a kind of tent of the mackintosh to protect them from the moisture that found its way past the trees. Now, more than ever, she could feel rivulets of water running down her back. But she made sure none fell upon Hannah.

The baby was so quiet Liz had to bite back panic. She was still alive but her breathing was shallow. And while Liz was shivering with cold, Hannah was hot to the touch. If only it meant that the child was snug and warm, but Liz feared another fever had crept upon her.

"You need some nourishment, sweetheart," Liz murmured. Getting into the bag without soaking everything was awkward, but she finally managed to remove some jerky and bread and the water bottle. "No milk, honey, but have some water."

She touched several drops to Hannah's lips but the child made no response. "Come on, Hannah. You need this. Take it for Mama, all right?"

After a bit of coaxing, Liz got her to take in a couple sips of water and a few crumbs of bread. Only then did Liz take food for herself. She ate sparingly because she judged she had only about two days' worth of food. It would take twice that and more to get to her destination.

Though she knew it would be impossible to sleep in the rain under the poor shelter of the mackintosh, she closed her eyes. She surprised herself when she suddenly jerked awake. Had she slept a few minutes? A few hours? She could not tell but felt rested enough to continue the journey.

The rain had stopped while she slept, but the sun still made no appearance, and heavy black clouds continued to hang in the sky. Shortly after she began her trek, she struck upon the road again.

"Thank you, God!" she murmured.

A little later she passed close to a cabin. How inviting was the smoke curling from the chimney, even if it was buffeted about by wind. But she had to avoid contact with others. There was no way she could innocently explain why she was trekking through the woods with a baby on such a miserable day. And even if some benevolent soul didn't care who she was and offered her an hour of warmth and shelter, there was always the chance that word of her passing would get back to Maurry. The settler might let a word slip next time he was in town about the strange woman and baby he had helped. That could get back to Maurry, who would then know his runaway slave had gone north, not south.

No, she must avoid all contact at any cost.

However, that resolve was harder to adhere to when it began to rain again. She tried to tell herself that rain indeed was her friend, but—oh!—why did this friend have to cling so closely to her? The mackintosh was next to worthless as the wind whipped it up around her, making it more an obstruction than a help. Even Hannah was wet now.

Liz trod on through the second night and day, stopping only for a few minutes at a time to rest and eat. Late that afternoon she came to an outcropping of rock in a hilly expanse of the forest. She nearly whooped with delight when she discovered a small cave in the rocks. It went back into the rock about three or four feet and was about the same in height.

"Hannah! We've a home for the night." She didn't care that there were still a few hours of daylight good for traveling. She was going to sleep out of the elements, do or die.

Nestled in the dry cave, she slept better than she had in weeks. She was still cold and wet and stiff when she awoke, but there was no wind and rain lashing at her. If nothing else, this experience was teaching her to appreciate small blessings.

As if this signaled a celebration, she ate the last of her food after first coaxing Hannah to eat a bit. Then, with great reluctance, she started to prepare to leave their fine little hole.

The rustling of brush made her gasp and freeze. Had a stranger stumbled upon her? Had Maurry caught up with her?

At first she saw nothing. Then the creature moved, rearing up on his thick hind legs. A bear! It was about twenty feet away, but she knew the beast was looking at her, the errant intruder in his home.

Trying not to make any sudden moves, she slowly inched her hand around until it came to her bag. Just as carefully, she lifted the flap and removed the knife. What she could do against a three-hundred-pound bear with a kitchen utensil, she had no idea, but it gave her enormous comfort just to hold it in her hand.

Ready to do battle, she held her breath and waited. But all at once the beast lowered onto its four feet and, incredibly, lumbered away.

There had been many times in the days since her escape that she had felt so alone, so desperately alone, as if only her poor, frail body was all she had to fend off a thousand enemies. Yet now she knew she had never really been alone at all. She had been fair prey to countless wild animals, but none had molested her, nor had any highwaymen, whom she was certain were looking for helpless creatures such as she.

The dangers lurking in these wilds were countless, yet none had touched her. A picture sprang into her mind. As she held Hannah, protecting her from the elements and danger with her own body, Liz saw God holding her—nestled in His arm as Hannah was cuddled in hers. Perhaps God was even big enough for her to ride in the palm of His hand.

Oh yes! He was big enough!

For some reason she could not fathom, He had taken a prostitute, surely the lowest of all human creatures, and extended His watchful care over her. In the New Testament, He had spoken to the woman at the well. Later He had rebuked the men who had been about to punish another prostitute. He had gotten into trouble for consorting with people whom the more respectable citizens deemed unworthy.

Now He was doing it again. And in a strange, inexplicable way, she no longer felt like the dirty whore she had been for so long. Just the fact that He cared about her made her feel clean.

Filled with renewed strength, Liz rose from the cave and continued on her journey. An hour later the sun came out, but the warmth in her heart was only partly from that source. Most came directly from the Source of all light, of all hope.

CHAPTER 31

How a creature barely larger than his hand could make such noise, Benjamin had no clue.

The newborn had screamed until he was red in the face. And that must have reminded Leah that she was hungry also, because she started crying, too. But worst of all, Isabel, who was old enough to put words to her misery, added to the din.

"I want Mama!" she cried over and over.

Benjamin raked his hands through his hair. His head was throbbing. The incessant racket had rarely ceased since Haden had left four days ago.

"Isabel, be still!" he yelled. "You're too old to act like that!" He regretted the harsh words as soon as they came out. At least he hadn't slapped her, as he had been so close to doing.

He started toward the cradle, stumbled over something, finding, when he looked down at his feet, the dustpan. He kicked it out of the way, barely repressing an angry outburst. Besides all the noise of three miserable children, the cabin itself was in shambles. Dirty kettles and dishes were everywhere—who had time to wash up when the demands of the children were so pressing? Clothes, also, were strewn all over—very dirty clothes at that. Laundry was the least of Benjamin's concerns. Yet it was close to becoming as large a concern as the newborn's screams. With two babies in diapers, he was quickly running out. He'd seen that Rebekah sometimes dried out diapers that were only wet and reused them two or three times, but even using this method, the pile of unusable diapers was growing.

Filling the demanding stomach of a newborn quickly became his most overwhelming task. He had not the proper natural equipment, and any substitutes he tried were more often than not rejected. Micah, in one of his rare cooperative moments, told Benjamin that Haden, while on the trail, had sopped bread in water, wrapped it in cloth and dripped the resulting liquid into the baby. But the baby would be growing now and would need something more substantial than bread and water. It was only after much prodding that Micah remembered a feeding bottle his mother had in one of the cupboards. This contraption helped, but the baby often sputtered distastefully when the coned pewter spout was set to his lips.

The problem of what to feed the child was another headache. Benjamin berated himself for not paying more attention to such things in the past. Micah, again, was helpful in this, though Benjamin felt like a dentist extracting teeth to get any information from the boy. Micah had spent far more time around his mother than Benjamin liked to admit and had thus picked up a few helpful tidbits.

"Mama always boiled the milk first," he offered upon being questioned by his father. "And she put water in it and some sugar."

"How much sugar?"

"I don't know."

"Well, you must have an idea." Benjamin, desperate as he was, could not help that his tone sounded like an interrogation. "A lot? A little? A pinch? A cup? How much, boy? If I make a mistake, the baby could get sick."

The boy's recalcitrant behavior should not have surprised Benjamin. Micah had been a burr in his side from the moment Haden had ridden off. When he wasn't outright rebellious, he was silent and sullen. He helped only when threatened with physical reprisals—and even then Benjamin had to be pretty convincing. Not that Benjamin hadn't taken Micah over his knee several times in the last four days.

"Don't blame me!" Micah shot back defensively. "If you hadn't killed Mama—"

"Enough of that!"

If this altercation proved no different from the others, Benjamin would react in one of two ways. Either he would smack Micah across the face or he would grab him for a more formal spanking. Micah would escape from the cabin if he was fast enough, which was usually the case since Benjamin most often had too many other distractions to go after him.

There were times, however, when those very distractions were actually welcome. More than all the mayhem in the cabin, the absolute worst times for Benjamin were those rare hours, usually late at night, when all four children actually slept at the same time and complete quiet reigned. Facing himself proved more terrifying than the plight of starving children and dirty diapers. He seldom slept, despite sheer exhaustion. His mind simply raced far too much to give way to sleep. Pain, guilt, confusion, and yes, even terror, plagued him. Prayer grew impossible because the words caught in his throat. How could he ask for God's intercession when it became clearer each day just what a wretched soul he was? Everything Haden had told him and all the words in Rebekah's letter replayed themselves over and over in his mind, accusing him of his failure. And it didn't help that Micah chose to remind him almost every day that he was responsible for his wife's death.

Infant screams penetrated his dismal thoughts, and he glanced gratefully down into the cradle. "I guess you are good for something, little fellow."

He picked up the baby, but the screams did not cease. The child wanted food, not a father's awkward touch.

"Micah!" Benjamin yelled, though it was obvious the boy was not in the cabin. He had escaped outside in the pouring rain. Benjamin opened the door. "Micah, get in here this instant!"

Micah poked his head out through the partially opened barn door.

"Are you finally milking the cow?" demanded Benjamin.

"The cow?"

"Don't act dumb," Benjamin snapped. "I asked you to do it an hour ago."

"Why should I?" Micah retorted.

So he wasn't going to act dumb, just belligerent. "Why? Why!" Benjamin stammered, incredulous. He would never get used to such behavior. Whatever restraints had kept Micah obedient in the past were gone now.

Benjamin choked back his anger. He remembered his own father—the beatings, the scathing words. He still carried resentment toward his father for that, but now he wondered if he hadn't driven the man to it.

"Your baby brother will die if he doesn't get something to eat," Benjamin's voice shook. "Is that reason enough?"

This proved to be a good approach. At least it prodded Micah into action. He would do nothing for his father's sake, but he had no grudge against his siblings.

A few minutes later Micah returned with a pail of milk. Benjamin was helplessly holding the unhappy baby. Isabel had tried to help by tending Leah, but while trying to fetch a toy, she had accidentally knocked Leah in the head. Leah was now wailing over the minor injury and Isabel was wailing out of sympathy or guilt.

As Benjamin rubbed the small red welt on Leah's forehead, he told Micah to fix milk for the baby.

"I don't know how." Micah said, sloshing the pail onto the sideboard.

Benjamin cracked then. Spinning around from tending his crying daughters, he whipped out his free arm, grabbing Micah by the shoulder so quickly even the agile boy could not escape. With the newborn still tucked under one arm, Benjamin used the other to shake Micah soundly.

"What do you want from me, boy!" he shouted. "I admit it. I forced your mother away. I killed her! I am everything you believe me to be. I am a rotten, dirty sinner! The worst reprobate! A hypocrite, a miserable, no-good . . ." He floundered for a moment because he could think of no worse things to say. He gasped in a breath. "I deserve your hatred! But . . . I . . . I need help! I can't do it. I can't . . . dear God! I just can't."

Breathing hard, shaking all over, Benjamin stopped just short of joining all the other raving, crying beings in the cabin. Through it all, Micah stared silently. Benjamin could not tell if the boy had heard a word he'd said. The only hint that maybe something had penetrated was that Micah slowly began to prepare the milk. Slowly, methodically, with a cool deliberateness almost frightening to watch, he poured milk into a small pan, added water from the bucket, then sprinkled in a couple of teaspoons of sugar. Stirring this, he carried it to the hearth and set it over the flame. Contrary to his words, he knew quite well what to do.

Benjamin watched, as if observing a stranger, and he wondered if he had created some kind of cool, unfeeling monster.

A knock on the cabin door intruded into the scene as reality intrudes a nightmare. When the discordant sound finally registered with Benjamin, he was regaled with a new barrage of emotions. In a panic his gaze swept the cabin, which resembled a battlefield. His first thought wasn't that help had possibly arrived, but rather he lamented that an outsider was about to see his life in such shambles.

As the thought flickered into his mind, he nearly laughed. You fool! He silently berated himself. You have single-handedly destroyed your life and that of those you love, and still you worry about appearances! Benjamin Sinclair, you are the worst kind of reprobate.

The knock came again.

With an almost wicked, masochistic determination, Benjamin stalked to the door and flung it open.

What met his gaze was a creature that looked as wretched, dirty, and pathetic on the outside as he felt himself to be on the inside. And though the rain had stopped, his visitor was as soaked as the proverbial wet hen. In spite of strings of wet hair hanging in her face, which was sprinkled with splatters of mud, he recognized the countenance staring back at him. Only now the defiance and pride were gone, replaced by bone-deep weariness.

"R-Reverend S-Sinclair . . ." Her teeth were chattering with cold and her lips shook so badly she could barely speak.

"Miss . . . uh . . ." He could not think of her name. Had he ever heard it? Then it came to him—Liz—but before he could say it, she spoke.

"P-please . . . c-can I c-come in . . . ?"

"Yes, of course." He stepped aside. "You're soaking wet." He meant the statement to be sympathetic, but it came out rougher than he had intended because he was still shaking from the encounter with Micah.

"I'm s-sorry."

"That's not what I meant."

"Is M-Mrs. S-Sinclair here?" She brushed a strand of wet hair away from her eyes and glanced over Benjamin's shoulder. "I s-so want to s-see her."

"That's not possible."

"P-please! I kn-know . . ." She paused a moment, biting her lip, seemingly in an attempt to get control over the chattering. "I know I'm not good enough for her, but . . . I don't know, I just thought she was my only hope."

Touched and indicted further by this woman's words, Benjamin replied, "You don't understand. It has nothing to do with you. Mrs. Sinclair . . . is gone . . . passed away."

She stared at him, then started to sway on her feet. Benjamin wasn't certain what was happening until she reeled toward him. Only then did he realize the woman was about to faint. With only one arm free, the most he could do was break her fall a bit as she crumpled to the floor.

CHAPTER 32

THE HOUNDS WERE CHASING HER so close the high-pitched bays echoed in her ears. But Liz kept running even though her heart felt as if it would explode. Feeling the hot animal breath on her heels, she kicked furiously.

"No! Please . . . no!" She tried to cry out the words, but nothing save for mute gasps seemed to come from her lips.

"Liz."

The voice did not come from the pursuing hounds. Something touched her, but it was not rough teeth trying to tear her apart. The touch was gentle and warm.

"Liz, you are having a dream."

She opened her eyes and found herself staring up at the towering figure of Rev. Sinclair. Then she looked down at the hand still resting on her shoulder. It surprised her that his touch could be so gentle. He'd always seemed to her to be intimidating, imposing, harsh . . . but never anything close to gentle.

"I g-guess I w-was." She was shivering, partly from the nightmare, partly from the wet clothes she still wore. But despite the fact that she was now fully awake and realized she had been dreaming, she thought she had not wakened into a situation much better. She could see why she had dreamed of baying hounds, because the sound so resembled the voices of crying children that filled the cabin. "W-what h-happened to me?"

"You fainted."

Suddenly she gasped in terror as a far more pressing memory came to her. "Hannah!"

"Your child is in the bed next to you."

Liz turned, and there was Hannah, no longer in her wet bundle but dressed in a shirt and gown and wrapped in a different blanket. She was breathing, though her breaths were labored and her skin was flushed.

"She's quite sick," Rev. Sinclair said. "I tried to do the best I could with her. She would eat nothing, but that may be due more to my ineptitude than her inability."

"Th-thank you."

"You best get into some dry things now before you fall ill also." Sinclair's voice was soft, almost kind. He seemed a different man from the arrogant, self-righteous judge who had confronted her in the store only a few weeks ago. Perhaps this had something to do with his wife's death.

Liz still could hardly believe that the kind, good-hearted woman was really dead. She tried not to think what this would mean to her own quest for help and succor. Surely the reverend would not harbor a woman of ill repute in his home. No doubt she would have been booted out immediately had she not fainted.

Yet even as the bitter thought came to her, she sensed no such attitude from Sinclair now. However, with screaming children and a house that looked as if it had been struck by one of those Texas tornadoes Liz had heard about, he probably had more on his mind than rebuking a fallen woman.

"I have n-no clothes," she said, bringing her mind back to matters at hand.

Benjamin nodded toward a steamer trunk at the foot of the bed. "You may borrow something of Rebekah's."

"I c-couldn't—"

"You really have no choice," he said simply. "Micah and I will step out while you change." To the girl who looked about five or six, he added, "Isabel, mind the babies while I'm gone." Then he turned to the boy who was sitting on a small bed with an open book in his hand. He appeared to be twelve or thirteen. "Micah, come outside with me."

The boy made no response and did not even look up from his book.

"Micah!" Rev. Sinclair said more firmly. "I said come with me."

The boy did look up then, and his cold, hard eyes were a sight to behold. Liz did not think a child could be capable of such venom. She shivered. What was the story between father and son? The phrase "no love lost between them" sprang to her mind.

Very deliberately Micah closed his book and swung his legs off the bed. Sinclair watched the obviously defiant response with clenched teeth, a muscle in his jaw pulsing dangerously. Liz thought only her presence was preventing an angry scene.

When the males were gone, Liz went to the trunk.

"That's my mama's," the small voice of Isabel Sinclair piped up. A hint of challenge could be detected in the tiny quivering voice.

"Do you think she would mind if I borrowed one of her dresses?" Liz made no further move toward the trunk, instinctively knowing she tread upon delicate ground. Though she had been too young to remember losing her own mother, she had some understanding of what a motherless little girl might be feeling.

Isabel merely shrugged with uncertainty.

"I'm awfully cold because of my wet clothes." Liz gave her damp skirt a pat. "I know your mama was a kind, giving person and would not want to see anyone suffer."

"You knew my mama?"

"Yes, I did. She helped me once when my little Hannah was sick. She was such a wonderful lady."

Isabel appeared to think about this, her fine lips pursed, her brow wrinkled. In the end the kind words about her mother won out. She started toward the trunk, but as she moved, Leah, who had been sitting in the rocking chair chewing on a crust of corn bread, became restless, making very insistent noises and trying to wiggle from the chair.

Liz quickly rescued her. "Do you want to help, too, little one?" With a brief glance at the bed where Hannah was lying, Liz assured herself that her daughter was secure. She needed tending badly, but Liz saw the wisdom of caring for herself first so as not to become sick, too, and completely worthless to her daughter.

Standing Leah on the floor beside the trunk, she noted how strong the chubby baby was. Poor Hannah wobbled terribly when she tried to stand. And she was probably half the size of the Sinclair child, though, according to what Rebekah had told Liz on the ship, the child was a few months younger than Hannah.

"Why don't you choose something, Isabel?" Liz lifted the lid. "Just something plain and old. I will return it when I'm done, but I don't need anything fancy."

As Isabel rummaged carefully through the trunk, Liz noted children's clothing there as well. They were likely hand-me-downs Rebekah was saving until Leah or the new baby could fit into them. After a couple of minutes, Isabel took a dress from the trunk. It was perfect for Liz's needs. From the look of the gown, it was probably ten years old, reflecting the style of that time, with a slightly raised waist and a skirt much less full than the current modes. A brown calico printed with tiny cream and blue flowers, it had a small ecru lace collar and black buttons running down the front to the belt of black velvet.

Liz smiled her approval. "That will be perfect."

But Isabel was not finished. She must have watched her mother perform her daily toilet carefully, because she knew exactly what other items would be needed. She took out a pair of cotton drawers, a chemise and a corset, along with stockings and a pair of shoes. The shoes were rather nice, obviously Rebekah's Sunday shoes, and Liz almost refused them until she moved and felt the squish of water in her own worn boots.

Thanking Isabel, Liz took the things over to the hearth where it was warm and began dressing, laying her own wet things close to the fire to dry. They were quite dirty, in need of a good washing and some mending, but still were serviceable. Before dressing in the new clothes, Liz took a damp cloth and tried to clean the spattered mud and filth of her journey from her body. She also scrubbed her face of any rouge and eye paint that the rain had not washed off. If she had any hope of obtaining sympathy from the reverend, she'd have a far better chance if she looked as little as possible like the wanton woman he thought her to be.

Leah crawled over to Liz and began pulling at the clothes as quickly as Liz could lay them out. Squealing with mischievous glee, the baby started making a game of it, deliberately taking something that had been laid out or replaced. Not wanting to scold the child, Liz played along, though with a little frustration.

Finally Isabel interceded. "No, Leah!" Her small voice took on an incongruous motherly authority.

Leah yelled back. "Ga! Da!"

Isabel took a wet stocking from her sister. Leah screamed in protest. Then the newborn, who had been sleeping in his cradle, woke and began crying.

"Isabel, would you button me up so I can get the baby?" Liz knelt down to the girl's level. The buttoning done, Liz scooped the baby up from the cradle and sat once more on the bed. "Isabel, bring Leah over here, and I will tell you both a story."

Leah struggled and protested being picked up by Isabel, who staggered under the weight of the eleven-month-old child. But in a few moments they were all settled on the bed, and Liz had taken up Hannah in one arm while holding the newborn with the other. Leah was struggling to get off the bed, and Liz had to think quickly in order to capture her attention. Looking down at her feet, the fine shoes reminded her of a story her old nurse had told her and which she sometimes told Hannah.

"Do you know the story about the little girl who was given a fine pair of shoes?" Liz's voice arrested Leah's escape attempts, and Liz took advantage of the child's interest by freeing her arm from Hannah momentarily so as to draw Leah close to her side. "This child—her name was Goody, by the way—was so very, very poor that she had never had a *pair* of shoes, ones that actually matched, and sometimes she didn't have any shoes at all. So when she received the new shoes, she was simply ecstatic with delight. She went around telling everyone she saw about her *pair* of shoes. Everyone began calling her Goody Two-Shoes."

Liz couldn't remember all of the original story, so she made it up as she went along, describing Goody's encounters as she walked about in her new shoes. The children snuggled around Liz and quieted. Even the newborn responded to the soft drone of Liz's voice. When Liz paused a moment to think up a new encounter for Goody, she noted the silence. It was certainly the first time since she had come to the Sinclair cabin that such quiet had filled the room. She almost didn't want to disturb it by starting the story again, but then, it was the story in the first place that had encouraged it.

"Little Goody had a brother named Tommy—" Liz began but was cut off suddenly when the cabin door burst open.

CHAPTER 33

LOOKING SLIGHTLY WILD-EYED, Benjamin Sinclair stumbled inside, his gaze sweeping the room as if he expected to find mayhem. Noting the peaceful scene on the bed, his panicked expression turned quickly to bewilderment.

"I . . . thought . . . didn't know what to think," he stammered. "It was so quiet."

The sudden noise of his entry had startled the newborn, and he started to cry again.

Liz smiled weakly. "I was telling them a story."

"A story?" Benjamin gaped incredulously, as if the idea were some fabulous new invention.

"Goody Two-Shoes. Do you know it?"

"I don't know many stories." He was still staring at her.

She wondered if it was disturbing to him seeing her in his wife's clothes. Did it make him cringe to think someone like her was wearing precious Rebekah's fine dress? She could hardly blame him. If she thought about it, it disgusted her also, as if a devil were tramping on holy ground, desecrating not only a dress but the woman's children as well. Suddenly she felt uncomfortable holding Rebekah's child, and she held him out to the father.

Making no move to take the child, a new look of panic crossed Benjamin's face.

Then the cacophony of children's noise began again. "Ga! Da! Ga!" insisted Leah, tugging at Liz's sleeve.

"Finish the story," Isabel put in. "Please."

Even Hannah found the strength to join in. "Mama!"

Wanly, Liz looked imploringly at Benjamin.

"I've upset the apple cart," he finally said rather pathetically.

"They wouldn't have stayed quiet for long." She couldn't believe *she* was attempting to bolster *him*. She slipped from the bed and stood, adjusting the newborn up against her shoulder. "Sometimes they just want a change of position." The baby quieted a bit, and she smiled, relieved. She walked around the cabin, remembering that Hannah had liked movement at that age. "Reverend Sinclair," she said conversationally, "I have figured out the names of all your children except the littlest one."

He was busy getting hold of Leah who, while still yelling for attention, had wiggled off the bed and was crawling toward the hearth. Catching her and lifting her in his arms, he shook his head, a hint of apology in his eyes.

"There hasn't been time . . . to think of a name."

Watching him jiggle Leah up and down to distract her from yelling in his ear, Liz could certainly see that he had nothing to be apologetic about. Naming a child was a small matter indeed, taking into account the demands of four motherless children.

"Mama wanted to name him after Uncle Haden," offered Isabel.

That brought a look as opposite to apology as possible to Rev. Sinclair's face. For an instant he looked more like the imperious, self-righteous man she had met previously. Then the look melted into something like—could it be irony?

"I don't think that will do," he spoke with restraint through a clenched jaw.

"Neither did Uncle Haden," said Isabel.

A smile invaded his face, in no way touched by humor but by far the most pleasant expression he had displayed yet.

"I guess I'll have to think of one for him. But I have to do something about supper first."

For the first time Liz saw that light no longer came through the cracks in the rawhide-shuttered windows. She also became aware of her own hunger. The thought of staying for supper brought to mind a more delicate situation. Where would she spend the night? Certainly a minister with no wife present in the home would have serious reservations about inviting a fallen woman to bide the night in his home—especially *this* particular minister. Shoving uncertainties about her own future from her mind, she tried to focus on the present. Whatever happened in an hour would happen. After several days in the outdoors, most of which was in the pouring rain, another did not seem so daunting.

"Why don't you mind the children," he said suddenly to Liz, "while I get supper." It wasn't as if he had been reading her mind, but it was an answer at least to her most immediate problem.

She had no easy task in quieting down the brood now that supper had been mentioned, but Liz managed to keep them fairly distracted. Still holding the newborn, she got Isabel to help her tend Hannah's fever. While she laid Hannah before the hearth, she had the girl dampen with cool water a large cloth Rev. Sinclair provided. This she wrapped around Hannah's naked body, covering it with a dry blanket. Though Liz did not want to think of where she would spend this night, she did pray for Hannah's sake that it would be in the warm cabin.

Before long the meal was ready. Sinclair had managed it with no cooking, save the preparation of coffee. It consisted of dried smoked turkey and dry corn biscuits, which very likely could have been baked when Rebekah was alive, for they looked too hard to chew. However, dipped in coffee or milk they would be palatable.

Micah was called in for the meal, then everyone squeezed around the table. No formal invitation was offered to Liz, but a place was made for her. Except for the various noises of the young children, all who could talk were silent. Liz noted that Micah, especially, was silent and sullen.

There was a moment, unsettling even to Liz, of uncomfortable silence before Rev. Sinclair took a biscuit from a dish, signaling for the meal to begin. Liz herself was not accustomed to saying grace before meals, but she'd assumed a religious family such as the Sinclairs would do this by ingrained habit. She knew the omission of this was the cause of the momentary lapse.

When Rev. Sinclair spoke midway during the meal, his voice was awkward amid the chortles of babies. "I have given thought to naming the new baby." His voice was strained and formal. "When we, that is, your mother and I, named each of you, there was always some special meaning to your names. Micah, you know your name is that of a biblical prophet I had been studying at the time of your birth. The name means 'like unto the Lord.' Isabel was the name of your mother's favorite aunt. Leah means 'weary,' and though it is not the most joyous of names, Leah was one of the great matriarchs of the Bible." He paused, glancing at his youngest daughter who chose that moment to grab her spoon and pound it noisily on the table, obviously aware that she was being spoken of. Benjamin's lips quirked at the child's antics but did not quite make it all the way to a smile. "That brings me to the new baby," he continued with a brief glance at the cradle where the child in question had waked from a brief nap and was crying for his supper. "I have decided to call him Oliver. The name is Latin for olive tree, which is the traditional symbol for peace. I hope some day he will live up to his name." Sinclair paused, then added wryly, "I hope it is sooner rather than later."

Liz thought to chuckle at what she perceived to be a rare bit of humor from the dour preacher, but when no one else at the table responded, not even Sinclair himself, Liz remained silent. And there was no further fanfare to the momentous occasion of naming the child. The meal continued silently, at least as silent as it was likely to get with five children present.

Micah was the first to bolt from the table without so much as a "by your leave." Rev. Sinclair looked as if he might protest the boy's rudeness but instead clamped his mouth shut in disgruntled silence. When Isabel asked to be excused, Sinclair only nodded. He then caught hold of the very active Leah as she began clamoring to be let down.

"It's time for you children to get ready for bed," Rev. Sinclair announced.

General mayhem followed while nightclothes were found and trips to the outhouse were made. Liz made herself useful by preparing a bottle for Oliver and feeding him. The bedtime routine, if the ordeal could be called that, went on for half an hour, with each of the children finding excuses to remain awake, even Leah managing to do so without the ability to talk.

Finally Rev. Sinclair, who appeared to be rising steadily to a boiling point, exploded.

"Silence! This instant!" There was more desperation in his tone than authority, but seemingly the children sensed they had pushed him to his limit because there was indeed instant acquiescence to his order. "I am turning down the lamp. The first one who makes a sound after that will be spanked!"

He went to the table and turned down the lamp until there was just shadowy light in the cabin. Only then, as he lifted his head, did he become aware once more of Liz's presence. She had been sitting so quietly feeding the baby, he must have forgotten about her—at least he must have wanted to forget about her.

They exchanged looks filled with questions both were afraid to ask. But of course they must eventually be asked, and as Sinclair knew, the task fell to him as host.

"I'll go to the barn," he said simply.

"I appreciate your not turning me out."

"Did you truly think I would do such a thing?" He seemed both incredulous and hurt at this.

"I . . . didn't know what to think with Mrs. Sinclair gone."

He sighed. "I suppose our previous encounters might not have led you to believe otherwise, but I assure you, Liz, I am not the kind of man to put a helpless woman out in the cold."

"People might talk if I stay."

Then he did smile, but it was too cynical of a gesture to do him any good. He even chuckled, but the sound was as dry as a dead branch. "They already are talking."

"Oh." She had nothing to say to that cryptic statement and thought silence was the best approach anyway.

"In any case, I'll sleep in the barn. If tongues wish to waggle over that, then so be it. I hardly care." He quickly grabbed a couple of blankets, then headed to the door where he paused. "Your bed comes not without a price." His gaze swept the room. "You will be at the mercy of the menagerie here."

He swiftly exited, as if fearing she might choose the cold night instead. No such thought had entered Liz's mind. Rev. Sinclair could not begin to imagine the kind of quarters she had escaped from. A night with five children, even if they kept her awake all night, would be absolutely heavenly by comparison.

CHAPTER 34

BENJAMIN THOUGHT IT WAS FITTING that even in the respite of the quiet barn he found no peace. By the time the first light of dawn penetrated the cracks in the log walls, he'd only found a few hours of fitful sleep. Wide awake now, he knew he should return to the cabin and feed Oliver. But the thought of facing his unhappy children once again nearly paralyzed him. If only Liz knew how grateful he was for her in those moments.

Yet the reprieve from his children did not give him a reprieve from himself. What was he going to do? How was he going to find the will to face life each day? In the past it had been so easy. Always he could turn his burdens over to God. Prayer had been his greatest comfort. Now he could not even find the courage to utter grace before meals.

At first he questioned the use of the word *courage*, but the more he considered it the more apt it became. Courage was exactly what he needed to face God, knowing he had failed Him so miserably.

Yet as much as the weight of his failure crushed him, it also still bemused him. He had spent his life serving God, trying to please Him.

Where had he gone wrong? Some of Haden's final words returned to him.

"She was so completely miserable, and she received nothing but holy admonitions from you. . . ."

Benjamin had always thought he'd been aiding Rebekah's faith, helping her draw closer to God. Had he been wrong, then? Had he instead pushed her away from God? But everything he'd said had been right, completely scriptural. Suddenly a new slant occurred to him. Perhaps this tragedy was not a punishment of him but of Rebekah instead.

"The wages of sin is death," the Scriptures said.

Maybe it wasn't his fault after all. It was a thin hope—no, not even that. It was a *sick* hope. Rebekah had made her share of mistakes but nothing so horrible as to deserve such a terrible end. She had always been of a gentle, kindly spirit.

Then it was something else. Haden? Yes, of course. He had led her astray. He had filled her heart with discontent and hate toward her husband. Oh yes, what more could one expect from a man who was an avowed atheist! Benjamin let himself bask in this line of reasoning for several minutes before he came up against an irrefutable wall of truth.

Haden was many things, even some of the things of which Benjamin now accused him. But Haden was no liar, and he cared for his family, Rebekah included, and would never purposefully harm them. And Benjamin could not conjure up enough venom to accuse him of behavior that the man simply was not capable of. Whatever Haden had done, it had been done out of ignorance.

Then why, God? Why has all this happened? Are you toying with me as you did with Job? Even as he sought to blame God for his troubles, Haden's words came back to mind. And more convicting, Rebekah's words. Though she tried so poignantly hard not to accuse him, the indictment was there so clearly.

"I am desperate with loneliness . . . forgive me for not being the strong woman of God you deserve. . . ."

How many times had he preached at her to be stronger? To trust God more? To support him in all his endeavors? Always he had focused on her, finding fault with her, never with himself, so that in the end she had done the same. Near to taking her own life, she still refused to lay blame at Benjamin's feet.

And he had refused to accept any blame.

Until now.

The cycle of blame had come full circle. First Rebekah, then Haden, then even God himself. What kind of fool is so blind? What kind of arrogant miscreant could possibly think he was blameless in the shambles around him? Benjamin thought about the confession of guilt he had burst out to Micah. Even then he hadn't realized the truth of his words.

But it was all his fault. And he was not just being cavalier in this admission. He saw it clearly now to the very core of his worthless being. His eyes were being pried open, and what he saw made his stomach twist painfully. Like images in a heinous nightmare, his faults paraded before him, like Judgment Day, when a man's deeds were laid to his account. And Benjamin's account was spiritually and morally bankrupt. He was a failure as a husband and a father. He'd been insufferably self-righteous. No wonder he'd turned away all who should have loved him.

Still Benjamin could not pray. He didn't know what to say. It dawned on him that he had never in his life asked anyone for forgiveness. He didn't know if he could now. He knew the theological basis of forgiveness. But everything he'd learned in seminary seemed to be mere words now. Nothing had ever truly gone to the core of his heart, not of what he'd learned and not of what he'd practiced in his ministry.

Suddenly he could see it all so clearly for the sham it was. He'd wrapped himself in words and bound everyone he knew in them. But it had been . . . yes, "a whited sepulchre . . . full of dead men's bones. . . ."

"Oh, God!" he choked in agony. He knew it to be true, yet the truth was like a sword thrust through his heart. This moment of self-discovery was perhaps even worse than losing his wife and losing the love of his family because this revelation destroyed the very fabric of who he was, crumbling the only foundation upon which he could bear his losses.

He had nothing now.

"God, I want your forgiveness, even though I don't deserve it!" he cried out, not even realizing this was his first true prayer since he'd heard of Rebekah's death. Perhaps it was the first real prayer of his life.

Weeping, he found himself sprawled out on the floor of the barn, his face ground into the dirt. Yet as empty as he was, he was too afraid to complete the circle by asking God for absolution. God was a vengeful God. Benjamin preached constantly about God's wrath. And he knew, among even the worst of his congregation, he deserved far more punishment than he'd already received.

"Reverend Sinclair." A voice outside broke into his misery, but it wasn't welcome. He was far from finished with his emotional flogging.

"What do you want?" he demanded hoarsely through the closed door. Then he thought what better punishment than to bare his humiliation before a stranger, especially this stranger whom he had once so pridefully rebuked. He jumped up and flung open the door. "I said, what do you want?"

"I . . . ah . . . it isn't important." Liz backed away from the door.

"Been too long without a man?" he sneered, not knowing why his self-accusation should be turned upon her.

She blanched at his crude words.

"Get out of here!" he yelled. "Leave me alone!" It was as much to spare her as for his own sake. He slammed the door shut. He heard her retreating footsteps and fell back against the rough surface of the door, a strangled sob escaping his lips. "What have I become?" he moaned.

More important, what was he going to do about it? He knew what he wanted to do. He wanted to go on punishing himself. He wanted to draw blood, emotional if not physical. He wished Haden were here to do the job. He needed—needed!—to be hurt. But he couldn't even indulge himself in that. He had the children to care for. They might be alone right now. Liz would have every right to walk out after his unforgivable words. No matter how much he wanted to stay where he was and continue mentally attacking himself, he had to return to the cabin. If anything happened to his children now because of him . . . Dear God, he didn't even want to think of it.

He forced himself to his feet, and though he was far from finished wallowing in the mire of his wretchedness, he made himself return to the cabin.

CHAPTER 35

LIZ RETURNED TO THE CABIN thinking she would fetch Hannah and leave. She had not escaped one nightmarish situation only to be plunged into another. She was through taking abuse from anyone, especially men. And Benjamin's words had hurt as much as any physical exploitation from Maurry's customers. They had hurt because even despite Rebekah's absence, Liz had begun to feel she had found succor here.

When Liz reentered the cabin, she found the same peaceful scene she had left a few minutes before. Micah was sitting in a corner whittling on a piece of wood, chips flying everywhere. True, the cabin was in shambles, but the wood seemed to add insult to injury. Though she could not be certain, Liz thought that Micah rather reveled in the mess.

Oliver was napping after his feeding an hour ago. Leah and Hannah were playing side by side on the bed. Hannah's fever had improved, though she still had deeply congested breathing.

The only thing that appeared to be amiss in the cabin was that Isabel was sitting on her little bed weeping. When Liz went to her, the child lifted plaintive eyes to her.

"I miss my mama." Her small voice trembled over the words as huge drops of moisture fell from her sweet blue eyes.

Liz knew she should not remain in the cabin lest Sinclair come in, find her, and continue to cast rebukes at her. But she simply could not turn her back on the miserable child. Liz sat on the bed and placed an arm around Isabel's shoulder, a small gesture that the six-year-old, obviously starved for affection, took full advantage of by crawling into her lap. Liz's heart clenched. How sad that the child must seek affection from a stranger. It made her think of the man she had encountered in the barn. What kind of man was Rev. Sinclair? He seemed as hard and cold with his children as he was with the vile sinners he preached to.

"Isabel, I am so sorry about your mother," Liz said tenderly. "I know it is a hard thing to lose your mother."

"Y-you d-do?" sobbed the child.

"I lost my own mother when I was young, too. I was probably younger than Leah."

"D-did you miss her?"

"When babies are very young they aren't completely aware of what is happening." Liz ran a soothing hand through Isabel's silky yellow hair. "But then, babies can't tell anyone what they are feeling. I think they have a big empty place inside them. It wasn't until I was just about your age when I truly understood what it meant to have a mama, that I really missed her. I miss her still."

"I'll always miss her?"

"Yes, but it won't always hurt as much." Liz kissed the top of Isabel's head just as she often did to Hannah. "But you have something special that I didn't have. You have memories of your mama, and they are special gifts from God to help the pain. I'll bet if you close your eyes, you can see her face."

"Papa says it is wrong to bet," said the small voice quite innocently.

Liz smiled. "If your papa says it, it must be so."

"Can you see your mama's face if you close your eyes?"

"No, because I never knew what she looked like. I never even saw a picture of her. There is a painting, though, and I hope to find it some day and finally see what she looked like." Only as she spoke the words did Liz realize how they signified a growing seed of hope that her escape had planted within her. Before her flight she had given up thinking of the painting because of her hopeless situation. Now maybe she wouldn't be so ashamed to look upon her mother's face. She returned her attention to Isabel. "Close your eyes, Isabel, and tell me what you see."

Isabel obeyed and a few moments later said with a damp smile, "I see Mama's hair. It was so pretty and shiny and kind of red, but Papa called it brown, because he said red was not sedate for a Christian woman. And I see her eyes—everyone always said mine were like hers. She's smiling, too, but she didn't smile much since we came to Texas."

"That's good, Isabel. And you have other memories, too. Did she call you an affectionate name?"

"Sometimes she called me 'Auntie Is,' because I was named for her aunt. She mostly did it when I was acting stubborn 'cause Aunt Isabel could be very stubborn, too. But when Mama called me Auntie Is, she always did it with a little smile on her face because she loved her aunt a lot."

"It was her way of telling you she loved you even if you were a bit stubborn."

Isabel nodded. "I didn't mind when she did. It usually made me less stubborn."

"Does it help, sweetheart, to remember?"

Again the child nodded. "Once, when I was just four years old and we were still in Boston, Mama took some of her grocery money and took me out to a fancy hotel for tea. Just her and me. She said sometimes girls need a time just to themselves."

"You are awfully lucky to have such memories—" Liz stopped as she heard a creak. Looking up, she saw Benjamin standing in the doorway. She wondered how long he had been there, unnoticed. She also wondered why Isabel stiffened slightly in her arms.

From outside he'd noted the quiet inside the cabin and had entered cautiously. He was now certain that it was he alone who had stirred such chaos in the place. Still, Benjamin was surprised at the scene that greeted him, especially that of Isabel cuddled in Liz's lap. He'd heard a bit of the conversation, too, and only by great effort had he reined in his own tears. He knew it was the first time since coming home that little Isabel had received any comfort over her mother's death.

Not wanting to disturb the tranquil scene, yet in a pathetic way wanting desperately to be part of it, he took a step into the room, closing the door behind him. The door creaked.

"I . . . uh . . ." he stammered when several heads jerked up. He felt like an interloper in his own home. He *was* an interloper! But he forged ahead with his initial intention. "Liz, may I talk with you?" He tried to sound as nonthreatening as possible. He knew she had every reason to spit in his face, but amazingly, she didn't.

"Yes, of course." Gently she slid Isabel from her lap, then giving her an encouraging smile and a quick hug, she rose.

"Can we talk outside?" he asked. "It's not raining."

She turned to Micah. "Micah, would you mind keeping an eye on the children while your father and I go outside?"

Benjamin marveled at how she asked the question as if it were her responsibility. But even more astounding was Micah's response.

"Sure, Liz." No rancor, no grimace, just simple willingness.

Benjamin swallowed back the bitter bile of further self-recrimination and led the way outside.

The sun had come out, warm rays slicing between a scattering of gray clouds. It appeared as if the rain of previous days had finally played itself out. In a way Benjamin regretted that, because the rain had provided an excuse for staying homebound, not that caring for four motherless children wasn't excuse enough. But he did wonder what his future held. He couldn't devote himself forever to the tending of his children, even if he wanted to. They had to have income. The source of that income was still very much in question with him. Even vague thoughts of the future of his ministry created a sickening lump of gall in his stomach. He simply could not face that now.

It seemed almost a pleasure to face instead the problem of the woman following him outside. Repenting of his harsh words was not nearly as difficult as the prospect of facing his scattered congregation. Though words now were practically impossible.

He walked to the edge of the yard, aware of her presence a couple of steps behind him. Pausing near a clump of small, new-growth pines, he searched his mind for some way to broach the delicate subject.

"You are good with the children." Perhaps if he skirted around the thorn, approaching it from a peripheral direction, it would be easier.

"They are good children." She had come up next to him.

That comment took him by surprise, and he knew he looked it.

She added, "Don't you think so, Reverend Sinclair?"

"I've never thought of it in quite that way." He paused, considering his next words, then realized he was only trying to find a way to put himself in the best light. Old habits do indeed die hard. Somewhat harshly, he said, "I've always regarded them as more of a burden of responsibility."

"How sad—for you as much as for them."

There was real sadness in her statement and no judgment that he could discern. "I was wrong for what I said in the barn," he said suddenly.

She shrugged. He sensed she'd heard a lot worse, but he did not want to be let off so easily. "I'm in a very confused state of mind these days. I won't bore you with all the details, but . . . I . . . just . . ." His reluctance had less to do with boring her than it did with his sheer inability to bare his soul.

"Say no more, Reverend Sinclair. You have been through a terrible tragedy. I would be surprised if you were anything less than confused and hurt."

"I am the blame for my wife's death!" he blurted. He refused to accept Liz's reprieves. He jerked his head around as if daring her to exonerate him. "I am a miserable specimen of . . . of . . . anything! I lashed out at you in the barn because I did not want to confront the wretch that I am. You cannot know what I have done, how I cared only for myself, how I drove everyone away, how my wife would have sooner risked death by returning to Boston than to spend another minute with me—" With a horrified gasp he stopped. Two factions fought desperately within him—one that wanted to lay bare his miserable soul, to cut out his very heart and cast it upon the ground to be trampled upon. Yet the other wanted to cling to some vestige of the façade of holiness he once had. He turned away from her in shame, as if she had rebuffed him. If only she would!

Finally he went on, attempting to salvage the skewed conversation—as much for her sake as for his, since she surely had no desire to be sucked into the tangled mess of his life. "You came here seeking help, but look what you found—a pathetic situation, to say the least. Made even more unforgivable because since you arrived I never thought to inquire of your own difficulties—that is, what you wished help for."

A little smile invaded her lips. "Yes, my woes did rather fade by comparison."

"But surely they must have been serious for you to brave the storm? You must have been out in it for days."

"Hannah was very sick, and your wife had helped her before. I thought she, of all people, would accept me." She paused, looking down at her hands clasped in front of her. She was perhaps uncomfortable at the pointed statement, "she, of all people," but she said nothing to amend it.

"Rebekah would have helped you. Against my will, of course." A hint of levity in his tone softened the statement.

Trying to keep it in that vein, she replied, "I hoped you would not be home."

"But I was." He sighed, as if the moment of levity was too much of a strain.

"And you did accept me."

"I let you in my home." His words in the barn returned painfully. "I am not fit to accept or reject anyone."

"Well, I am grateful for what you have done." Her eyes skittered up to meet his, then jerked away again. He knew that unspoken question was rising once again.

What would he do with her now?

"Would you care to tell me something of your situation, Liz? My intent is not to pry. It is just that . . . I am not sure what I can do for you. And what you wish."

"I have left my former . . . uh . . . life. But doing so has made me a runaway slave, a fugitive. Taking me in has, I'm afraid, made you a felon."

"Bah!" Some of Benjamin's old fire momentarily returned. "I do not hold with slavery. It is an abomination. I do not consider myself bound by any laws concerning it. Besides, one of the few applaudable acts of the Mexican government was to abolish slavery."

"But you and I know that the Mexican government turns a blind eye to the issue where Texas is concerned."

"Nevertheless, I still stand by my own beliefs." It seemed to be the only belief he could stand by for the moment. "Yet regardless of how I feel, I do understand your position. Will your master be looking for you?"

"Yes, but I don't think he'll take me to be crazy enough to go deeper into the frontier."

"That was rather an insane move," he said wryly.

"I believed it was my only chance. He knows nothing of my acquaintance with you or Rebekah, so he'd have no reason to suspect I have come here. He will think I've gone to one of the ports. When he doesn't find me there, he might assume I found sea passage."

"Your plan does have merit." Indeed, he thought it was desperate and foolhardy but probably her only option. He gazed at her for a brief instant and remembered the noble pride she had worn like a battle shield that day in San Felipe. He thought of her trudging forty miles through a storm, holding a sick child, fending off the many dangers of the wilds. He had wondered before what kind of woman she was, and he did so again, but in a new light. As words like *courage* and *tenacity* sprang to his mind, admiration formed a lump in his throat. And suddenly he was embarrassed by the frank awe he knew must be dominating his expression.

She must have been embarrassed also because a bit of pink rose in her cheeks. He directed his gaze into the woods beyond the yard.

"That is my situation," she said. "My child and I are homeless unless I return to that other life. But I will tell you, Reverend Sinclair, now that I have made the break, I don't think I can go back to it. I *know* I can't go back to it. I believe I would rather die than return to it. I stayed in the first place only because Maurry threatened the life of my child, but I now see that it did not help her. She became sicker each day I was there. Finally I decided she was going to die either way."

"I am so sorry."

She mistook his words. "Of course I know I can't stay here."

"That's not what I meant."

"Well, Reverend Sinclair—"

"Before we say more, may I ask that you not call me reverend?"

"Are you no longer a reverend?"

"I don't know what I am anymore. But taking all into consideration, I cannot bear that title. Mr. Sinclair, or even Benjamin, would do fine. Though I must add, I feel it improper for me to call you by your first name."

"Are names so important, Rev—Benjamin?" Then she laughed, but he could see she was not really laughing at him. "I guess I shouldn't question you. I've done the same thing myself."

"You changed your name?"

"I took the nickname given me by one of the other girls. It better fit who I had become, or at least it helped me to forget who I once had been."

"And what of now?"

"I don't know."

"Nor do I." He paused, giving the matter some thought. He saw now that her story was not as simple as it appeared, especially not as simple as a judgmental preacher had wanted to believe it was. Ironically, it now appeared as if their stories were not all that different—or at the least they had significant similarities. "How about if I call you Miss Liz?"

She hesitated only a moment, then with dark eyes flashing in resolution, she answered, "My name is Elise Toussaint. Call me Elise. At the moment I am feeling a bit rebellious against societal formalities."

"Elise . . ." he said softly. All the terrible things he had once thought of her were oddly dispelled as he spoke the name. When God changed Jacob's name to Israel and Simon's to Peter and Saul's to Paul, there had been great significance in the change. What would the significance be now to her? As simple as a new life?

And what of him? It was not lost on him that his particular name change was in reverse of the others. He was going from a name of honor to . . . to what, he feared to guess.

"Well, Elise, I don't know if you'd consider it a boon or a burden, but you are welcome here."

"That is kind of you, but . . ."

"Let me worry about what others might think. Perhaps I am feeling a bit rebellious myself. In any case, I could not with a clear conscience let you leave while your child is ill."

"All right, then. Thank you."

CHAPTER 36

HAVING ELISE IN THE CABIN helped tremendously, but it did not immediately solve all things. Five children were still five children with all the demands and noise thereof. And though Micah was civil, even pleasant to Elise, he continued to treat his father with great disdain.

Benjamin's patience with the boy was thinning. It was bad enough to bear his own self-reproach, but to have it heaped further upon him by his son every chance the boy got made the weight upon Benjamin's shoulders nearly staggering. His precarious forbearance nearly snapped once again when he went to the barn and found the cow had not been milked. He'd reminded Micah about it over an hour ago.

Not seeing Micah anywhere about, Benjamin set about the task himself. Fuming the entire time, he was surprised the cow did not kick him soundly for his fierce tugging at the animal's teats.

As he was leaving the barn with the pail of milk, Micah chanced to be ambling up the path from the creek.

"Where have you been, boy?" Benjamin accosted him the moment he came into sight.

"Down by the creek." Micah's words were clipped, tight, as if he doled them out like precious stones, stones that could at any moment be cast in anger.

"Who gave you leave to go to the creek?" Benjamin demanded.

"I just wanted to go."

"And what of your chores?"

"You got Elise now to take Ma's place. You don't need me." Micah's sneer managed to hold meaning beyond his words.

"Don't take that tone with me!"

Micah's eyes narrowed and his lips curled. "You gonna stop me?" he dared.

"Why, you—" Benjamin jerked his hands up to grab the boy, but he forgot he was holding the pail of milk. It swung up, not only spilling the milk but sending most of it splashing into Benjamin's face.

Momentarily consumed by rage, Benjamin tossed the pail wildly into the air, not really intending to strike his son, but it did none theless, glancing off Micah's forehead. Unperturbed by Micah's stunned cry, Benjamin continued with his initial intent. He reached for the boy. Micah, not seriously injured, sidestepped to the left, out of his father's grasp. But Benjamin anticipated the maneuver and reached with his right arm, his hand catching hold of the front of Micah's shirt. Micah wrenched left and right to free himself, but Benjamin held fast. It flittered through Benjamin's mind that his thirteen-year-old son had grown several inches without his noticing and was nearly his father's height—a fair match in a fight if, God forbid, it should come to that.

But anger drove Benjamin—and Micah, too, for that matter—not practicality. He swung up his free hand to box Micah's ears. Micah blocked the blow with a surprisingly strong arm. For a brief instant it looked as if the son might do more. His fist was curled tight, and his eyes flashed with intensity. The two stood glowering at each other almost eye to eye.

Benjamin was the first to back off. Hands shaking, he loosened his fingers from their grip on Micah's shirt. He knew that in another minute one of them would have hurt the other. He knew his son wanted desperately to strike him, and he could not guess why the boy had restrained his obvious thirst for violence. Benjamin also knew he would have later regretted striking his son, but he was not so certain Micah would have regretted hurting his father. Yet neither of them *had* landed any blows. That was something.

Micah spun around and walked away. Knowing it was a mistake, Benjamin let Micah leave without insisting on an apology for the boy's insolence. He probably ought to have apologized himself for his own violent behavior. Yet he could not do it. He could not face another confrontation nor look upon the hatred in his son's eyes. But in so doing, in letting Micah go, Benjamin realized with a stunning clarity that he had lost whatever fatherly control he had had over his son. Whatever stood between them was going to have to be dealt with man to man, not father to son. The realization left an empty ache in Benjamin, an ache that coursed through him, seeming to stir up all the other barely restrained aches. The weight of loss bore down upon him, and he had no defenses left to block its ravages. A noise escaped his lips, part gasp, part agonized sob.

"Benjamin?"

He swung around and saw Elise in the doorway of the cabin.

"I've lost him," Benjamin said in a shaky, tormented voice. In the week Elise had been at the cabin, there had been far too many charged situations, mostly involving Micah but with the other children as well, for him to maintain any kind of façade, especially a holy one. Now with his emotions riding so close to the surface, it was impossible.

She crossed the yard and put her arm around his shoulders. She had never touched him before. He could not remember the last time *anyone* had touched him in kindness or comfort. The gesture had the effect of setting a hot iron to ice.

He cracked.

Tears erupted from his eyes, and a full clear sob broke through his lips. He struggled to keep it in check, but his efforts only made his shoulders heave. He hated being laid so bare, so vulnerable. Yet there was something right about it, too, though just then he could not for the life of him remember what it could be.

"There, there," she murmured.

He tried to tell her he was all right, but the barely restrained sobs seemed to paralyze his voice. Though he felt ridiculous, he was powerless to control the wayward emotion. Not thinking, except about how desperately hungry he was for a kind touch, he crumpled into Elise's arms. As he turned to her, her arms came around him as naturally as if she, too, longed for comfort.

He remained in her embrace, letting her hold him as no woman besides Rebekah had ever held him. He clenched his arms around her and let his tears dampen her dark, silky mane. The smell of simple kitchen soap touched his senses; it was hardly a beguiling aroma, yet passion began to well up within him. It took him unawares because it had been so long since he had felt anything besides pain and emptiness. He'd forgotten what the simple touch of a woman could do to a man. So many emotions were raging within he could barely tell one from the other. Thus he held her a moment longer than he knew he should have. He held her even when it was his kisses instead of his tears brushing her hair.

"Reverend Sinclair?" A male voice broke into the tender interlude. Benjamin had not heard the hoofbeats, but as his head jerked up, he saw that a man on horseback was reining his mount not twenty feet from them.

Panic replaced passion. Benjamin jumped away from Elise as if she had become a hot ember in his hands. He hated himself for the guilt he knew now marred his face. At the same time, accusatory thoughts collided in his mind. Caught in the arms of a prostitute. What would Rebekah say? How could he prove his innocence? Was he innocent?

He willed his mind to focus on the visitor. It was one of his parishioners, but he couldn't recall the man's name. He'd probably not be able to correctly give his own name if pressed.

"Ah . . . Mister . . . Mister . . ." he stammered, trying to find a way to fill in the gaping awkwardness.

"Reverend Sinclair, looks like I'm interrupting something." The man's tone was loaded with innuendo. He dismounted and came to stand nearly eye to eye with Benjamin.

Benjamin suddenly rankled, forgetting his guilt and awkwardness. He had been doing nothing wrong. And he could see nothing wrong in a bereaved man seeking comfort in the arms of a . . . a friend! But lingering guilt, a product of years of indoctrination and his own personal practice of judgment, kept his protests in check.

"You are interrupting nothing. What do you want?" Benjamin did not bother to be polite.

"I came here seeking a man of God to read over my father's grave," the man replied haughtily. "Maybe I came to the wrong place."

"Listen here." Benjamin decided he would protest. Then he became aware of Elise still by his side. Glancing at her, he saw she was both pale and flushed. Perhaps shame, anger, and surprise were waging their own battle within her. "Elise, perhaps you should go in and tend the children."

She hesitated as if debating whether she would let another fight her part of the battle.

"Go on," he prompted.

She then nodded and returned to the cabin as Benjamin returned his attention to the stranger.

"Well, Reverend, what do you expect me to think, huh?" The man said quickly, as if wishing to get his blow in first. "Last I heard you was widowed—poor wife died in childbirth. Now, I see, less than a month later you got yourself another woman."

"You don't know what you are seeing. And do you think if I was going to *have* a woman, I'd do it in the middle of my yard? How dare you come here and wag a finger at me. You've no right!"

"I figure I got every right seeing as how I help pay your wages!" The stranger clamped his lips together smugly. "And I ain't gonna pay no man of God to go cavorting—"

"I was *not* cavorting!" Benjamin's tone was defensive as he spewed out excuses. "I was grieving my wife. The woman was comforting me."

He should never have tried to defend himself. The defenses sounded lame indeed.

"Comforting? *Harrumph!*"

"You have a lot of nerve judging that which you do not know!" But as he spat out the word *judging*, he nearly choked. How many times had he judged others without truly knowing their whole circumstances? He'd done that very thing to Elise. He ran a hand through his hair, shaking his head ironically. When he spoke again, his tone was moderated with humility. "I guess I can see where you might mistake what you saw. But it is entirely innocent. Elise is . . . was a friend of my wife's. She came here last week with her sick child hoping to get help from Rebekah. She didn't know my wife had died."

"She been here a whole week?"

"I couldn't turn her out with a sick child." He forced down renewed ire.

"Well . . . I dunno."

"I don't care what you think, sir. I had no choice. Besides, Elise's poor child and my own children were in desperate need of a woman's care."

"You've said yourself, Reverend—"

"I know what I have said!" he snapped. "And now I am saying that sometimes there are extenuating circumstances."

"That's fine when they're *your* circumstances, ain't it?"

Benjamin gasped in a breath, losing his patience once more. "If that's all you have to say, sir, you may leave!"

"Oh, I'll leave all right! But you ain't heard the last of this, *Reverend*." The man let the word roll off his tongue as poison. "Folks expect their minister to be at least as holy as he expects them to be." The man strode to his horse, mounted, and gripped the reins in his hand. But before he turned to ride away, he added, "I'll say my own words over my father. Reckon that'll do as well as any false preacher's."

Benjamin didn't know whether to hurl protests at the man or to applaud his wisdom. He also wasn't certain if he would have read a funeral service if invited. His doubts had begun with his recoiling every time Elise called him *Reverend.* A revulsion grew within himself, as if the word were an imprecation. To hear it actually leveled at him in that manner by the visitor brought it painfully back to Benjamin that he was indeed the vilest of all sinners, the lowest of all men, not fit to carry the banner of God. If further proof was needed of this, all he had to do was recall the scene in the yard before the man rode up. He had topped even his penchant for selfishness by using Elise, taking her gesture of kindness and turning it into something far from her pure intentions.

He returned to the cabin. Isabel and Leah were squabbling over a toy while Oliver was crying in his cradle, reminding Benjamin he still had no milk for the child. Elise was rubbing some kind of poultice on Hannah.

She looked up, smiling wanly. "Life does go on, doesn't it?"

"Unfortunately, yes." He chewed his lip, wanting to do anything but confront his behavior, but confront it he would. "I'm sorry, Elise."

"You have nothing to be sorry about. That man was insufferable."

"But you can't argue with the fact that I deserved it."

She gave a depreciatory shrug. "I shudder to think what would happen if we all got what we deserved."

"Nevertheless, I should never have . . . touched you."

"Seems I touched you first."

"You know what I mean." He paused, thinking perhaps she had noticed nothing. After all, what were a few kisses on the head to her?

"I know that you were in great grief, Benjamin. I know what happened meant nothing beyond that." She gave a forced chuckle. "Though I am sure your visitor got an eyeful."

"It's not funny," he insisted.

But her chuckle turned into a giggle. "I know, but . . ." she couldn't seem to control her sudden mirth. "I can't help but picture the look on his pinched little face if he knew the truth about me."

"And you are laughing?"

She pursed her lips together in an unsuccessful attempt to stop another giggle. "Sometimes laughing is all one can do."

He smiled. "I suppose it would have been an interesting sight." The man's dirty little mind would have absolutely exploded if he had known. A chuckle escaped Benjamin's lips. "Had he a pillory he would have clamped me firmly within it." Another snicker erupted. It wasn't funny at all, but as his grief a half hour ago had consumed him, laughter now did the same. No, it wasn't funny, but he clung to the release of humor as he had to the comfort of a woman.

"He'll have you excommunicated, Benjamin Sinclair!"

"For a hug!"

"Even you would have forgiven a hug." Her laughter continued to bubble.

"Oh no, I wouldn't!" He howled. "I was the king of insufferable wretches."

"King, eh? I always did think you had a rather high opinion of yourself." Her eyes glittered as she waggled a finger dripping with poultice at him.

"You don't know the half of it." He wiped a sleeve at the corner of his eyes now brimming with tears of laughter.

"I think I do." She giggled again. "Why, you looked rather like your visitor when I saw you on the ship that time pointing a finger at me."

"Dear God! Was that really me?" He sobered suddenly. "I was so very wrong that day."

"No, you weren't." She, too, sobered, though her eyes still sparkled as if she didn't want to let go of the pleasant moment completely. "I *should* have been ashamed of myself. I am ashamed."

"I had no right to accuse you, especially since I could not see your heart."

She finished with the poultice, wiped off her hands, and wrapped Hannah up snugly. She lifted her eyes to him. The humor was gone now, but they held such tenderness it made his heart ache. "But God can see our hearts, Benjamin, and I don't believe He's accusing you."

"My heart is black."

"I don't believe that for a minute. But even if it were, God is ready to forgive you."

"It seems I have misjudged you in many ways," he replied, skirting the real issue of her words. "You are a Christian woman?" As he spoke, Oliver's cries became too insistent to be ignored, and Benjamin picked him up from the cradle. He had no food to offer him, but perhaps holding him would help.

"I think so, but I know so little about it all." Elise picked up Hannah as well, rubbing her back soothingly. "I can count on one hand the times I've been to church, and each of those times my mind was elsewhere. But I do know this, a person who has sinned—even more than I have sinned—can find forgiveness from God. That I read in Rebekah's New Testament."

"Rebekah's?"

"Yes. She gave it to me on the ship. I've been reading it. She told me to base my concept of God on His words, not on His fallible children."

"She must have meant me."

"I have been reading it, and I have discovered a God who is far different from the one I had imagined."

"What kind of God?"

"A God who loves. A God who forgives."

"I've read God's Word, also—many times." He paused, shaking his head. Had he even gotten that wrong? Well, he wasn't surprised, since he'd botched all else in his life.

"Maybe you should read it again now that—" She stopped, obviously reluctant to complete the thought she'd begun.

"Now that my life has fallen into shambles?" he offered, sparing her.

"Now that you are not so full of yourself . . . King Insufferable." She grinned impishly. "It is amazing how much better we can hear when our pride ceases to block our ears. At least such was the case with me. Perhaps it will be so with you."

"I don't know. . . ."

"How long will you punish yourself, Benjamin?"

"I better see if that cow has any more milk to give us." It was easy to ignore her incisive words with a baby crying in his ears.

"Let me have the baby," she said. "I can hold two at once."

He wanted to thank her for releasing him so easily, but he said nothing. He'd had enough confrontation for one day.

CHAPTER 37

ELISE GAVE THE CABIN A satisfied look. In little over a week she had finally brought some order to the Sinclair home. She thought that Rebekah Sinclair would not be ashamed to give her approval to Elise's efforts.

Certainly no housekeeper by experience, Elise discovered she had a natural knack for it. Barbara, her old nurse, had taught her a few things, and even Daphne Hearne had begun instructing her in the task of running a plantation household. Of course, what a southern plantation lady needed to know about living was far different from what a woman needed to know in a cabin on the frontier. For one thing, on a plantation there were slaves to actually *do* the work. The lady of the house merely had to keep abreast of when various tasks needed to be done. Then, it was "Hattie, churn the butter," or "Missy, time to put up preserves."

But Elise was instinctively tidy. She was an accomplished laundress, thanks to Maurry. Cooking was another matter. She had never really done much cooking. On the plantation the slaves had done it, as had Maurry's slaves, leaving his girls free for other tasks. But she thought cooking merely took good sense if one could read recipes. Isabel proved to be a great help in finding the book in which Rebekah had kept her recipes. She also found another book called *The American Frugal Housewife* by Mrs. Child. These, in fact, were the only books Rebekah owned besides her Bible, so Elise guessed they must have been invaluable for her to have brought them all the way from Boston. There were actually only about a dozen other books in the house. All except a reading primer for the children were Benjamin's theological books. But the Sinclair library probably had more books than all of Benjamin's parish combined.

Since by unspoken agreement the household chores fell to Elise, she spent as much time as she could poring over Rebekah's books. When Micah or Benjamin brought in a pail of milk rich with cream, she flipped frantically through the pages to see what to do with it. Benjamin was no help at all. He not only had never helped his wife with the household chores but also had never paid much attention.

"My mind was on a higher plane, you know," he said with biting sarcasm, "not on temporal, worldly things. I can quote you all the Scripture you want, but plant a seed, tan a hide, shoe a horse? Sorry, I did naught but read and pray in Boston."

"Didn't you say you built the barn?" She was constantly trying to bolster his morale, it seemed.

"Half of it, but don't take a level to the place. My father was something of a carpenter, so I learned a bit from him when my nose wasn't buried in a book."

He said most of what he knew about frontier life he had read in books before leaving Boston. He'd also taught himself to shoot after he had accepted the position with the missionary board. "Though," he quipped, "no one it seems can teach a man how to actually hit a target. At least it hasn't worked with me."

Elise was determined to master the role of homemaker, though she wondered if it was a part she would play for long. Certainly she could not stay in the Sinclair cabin forever. Perhaps Benjamin would help her build a cabin somewhere, and she could set up her own home with Hannah.

Now, there is a true pipe dream, Elise Toussaint, she thought. A woman alone on the frontier? It would be nothing short of scandalous. Even if she didn't practice her old profession, everyone would think she did anyway. If she survived. Many women, of course, were left alone while their husbands went hunting and such, or, as with Benjamin, rode circuits. But that was after the husband had put by a supply of meat and wood and taken care of other such needs.

What was in her future? For the last year she had been so absorbed in the misery of her *present*, she found now it was rather luxurious to even contemplate a future. She tried not to think of all the complications in her life, things that might make it impossible for her to ever have a normal life again.

Instead, she focused on the here and now. The cozy little cabin, the children who were coming to depend on her and even, she thought, care for her. But that went two ways. As the children grew close to her, she also was becoming attached to them. Oliver had no idea if she was his mother or not, he simply responded to her as if she were, quieting when she held him, cooing at the sound of her voice. She had even been the one to witness his first smile.

The pain of their mother's loss was still deep in Isabel and Leah, yet because Elise made no attempt to replace Rebekah and was careful not to force affection upon the girls, they were warming up to her. And quite surprisingly, Isabel was a great help to Elise in the house. Constantly by her mother's side, she had learned much. And Elise made sure that memories of Rebekah were included as often as possible.

Micah was a problem Elise had no idea what to do about. Though nothing had been said, she knew his pain ran deeper than merely the loss of his mother. His intense animosity toward Benjamin was heart-wrenching. Elise remained cautiously out of it. She let them deal with each other as they must while she concentrated on each as individuals. Thus Micah was polite and civil to her, even if he wasn't to his father.

In addition to the strain of caring for the Sinclair children, Elise found Hannah to be a frustrating challenge that caused her constant heartache. She began to wonder if Hannah would ever be healthy again. It saddened and frightened her to compare her daughter to the younger Leah, who was as chubby and robust as Hannah was frail and withering. Elise had heard about the cholera epidemic that had struck Texas two years earlier, killing thousands. If something like that should happen again, she knew Hannah could not survive. Yet even knowing Hannah could die at any time, Elise could not prepare herself emotionally for such a tragedy. She knew her heart would break at the loss, no matter how much she expected it.

Elise glanced out the window. The rawhide had been pushed back, and she could see it was a pleasant afternoon. She best leave off with her idle thoughts, which were growing more morose with each minute. Benjamin would be home soon and would want supper. Since it took Elise twice as long to prepare meals as it would Mrs. Child or even Rebekah, she best get busy.

Benjamin eyed the buck some one hundred and fifty yards away. For the first time that day, he had spotted an animal before it espied him. He raised his hand silently, signaling Micah to stop. For once, the boy obeyed instantly.

Actually, it had been an inspired idea to take Micah on the hunting expedition. The boy had remained cold and silent most of the time and often appeared as if he'd just as soon aim his rifle at Benjamin as at any innocent beast. But at least they had not had a single falling out since leaving early that afternoon. Benjamin *had* lost his temper the first time Micah had carelessly scared off a nice plump turkey. But other than that, the day had progressed rather tranquilly.

"Let's move a bit to the right," Benjamin whispered. "Remember, a deer standing still will turn his head from the wind so he can see danger approach. That way he smells danger coming from behind him. Our best position is across the wind from the animal."

"How do you know that?" There was a slight edge to Micah's question, but Benjamin sensed the cause might be that he begrudged admitting an interest in anything his father might say.

"I read about it."

"Humph."

Micah never did have much appreciation for scholarship. He was going to have to be convinced by action that one could learn something practical from a mere book.

"The best time to hunt deer is in the early morning or early evening when they are feeding. We are lucky the animal is feeding now. . . ."

"Lucky?" Micah cocked his eyebrow.

The boy wasn't going to give Benjamin an inch of slack. Well, I don't deserve it, Benjamin thought wryly. "Yes, lucky. It's a mere word, Micah."

"So it wasn't by *God's providence* that the deer is feeding when he normally shouldn't be?"

Even in his present spiritual state, Benjamin cringed at the way Micah slurred the reference to God. Had he destroyed not only his son's relationship with him but with God as well?

"I just don't know anymore, Micah." If the boy perceived anything at all, he would see Benjamin's statement had to do with more than deer. He added uncomfortably, "We best be still before we alert the animal."

As if to prove his caution, the deer glanced up from his grazing. Benjamin mouthed to Micah to freeze. Then they waited several moments before the animal began grazing again. With a slight motion, Benjamin signaled for them to proceed. They did so with the greatest of stealth. In three minutes they were within range.

Benjamin's pulse was pounding, his palms sweating as he gripped his musket. He'd never bagged a deer before, and he felt excitement rising at the prospect. He had read that this sensation was called "buck fever." In the past he might have rebuked the emotion as frivolous and unholy, but now he let it have full rein. He honestly could not think why he had thought such excited emotions were wrong.

Glancing at Micah, he saw his son also emanated the same kind of agitation, at least if it could be judged by his pale face and taut lips and the way his jaw muscles were dancing spasmodically. Benjamin hadn't considered his son's expectations in this hunt, and they certainly hadn't discussed it. He had assumed he'd get the first kill, then if there was another opportunity, he'd let Micah have a chance. After all, they were getting low on meat and could not afford to risk a chance to fill the larders when it came. But the day was wearing on. It would take a couple hours to get back to the cabin. This might be their only opportunity.

Suddenly Benjamin knew that a unique opportunity had been given to him. A chance to cull his son's love—well, he doubted it would go that far, but he'd be happy with merely a word of gratitude from his recalcitrant son.

"Get your gun ready, son," he breathed.

"Me?"

"You've been practicing, haven't you?"

Micah nodded, then lifted his musket.

When they had first started out, they had loaded their muskets. Benjamin had been surprised at how much Micah knew. He had exhibited an ability to measure the powder, cut the grease patch, and to tamp the ball with the ramrod. Benjamin was pleased to see he had developed good technique. He'd tried to teach Micah what little he knew about shooting, but being gone so much, he knew his instruction had been fairly inadequate. He wondered where the boy had learned to place the butt of the musket firmly against his shoulder. Had Haden given him lessons while they were on the trail together?

Somewhat morosely, Benjamin thought of his brother, who had also taught him how to shoot back in Boston. Yes, Benjamin could see Haden in Micah's stance, even in the way he pushed his tongue against the inside of his mouth as he aimed the weapon.

"Remember, gently squeeze the trigger. Don't pull. And keep your eyes on your target—"

"I know what to do," Micah broke in tersely.

Benjamin closed his eyes, took a breath . . . and remained silent.

He watched as Micah sighted the rifle, took a breath himself, and held it for one long instant. Micah was patient, not like you'd expect an eager youth to behave on the occasion of his first kill. But then, maybe this wasn't his first. Benjamin was wondering about this, regretting that he might not be the one to have shared this momentous "first" with his son, when the report of the rifle blasted in his ears.

The deer fell in instant response. Benjamin grinned and slapped Micah on the back.

"Good work, son!"

Micah flinched slightly at the touch but said nothing more than a grunt in response. Benjamin bounded forward to examine the kill and started to grab an antler.

"Shouldn't you make sure it's dead first?" Micah asked with a hint of superiority.

Benjamin felt foolish, since that was a rule even a novice should know. Remembering now what he'd been taught, he reached cautiously toward the animal with the barrel of his musket and poked the buck's eye. It was then that he saw where the ball had struck.

There was a hole clean between the buck's eyes. Benjamin's head jerked back to gape in astonishment at his son. Micah wore a look of grim satisfaction. In that moment he was not a thirteen-year-old boy who had just killed a fine buck. He was a wizened old man, hardened, stonelike.

"You *have* been practicing," Benjamin managed to say.

Micah shrugged. "Yeah, some." He then added almost as a challenge, "Do you know what to do now?"

Benjamin had watched the process before but couldn't remember everything, though he wouldn't admit that. Instead he answered, "This will be good practice for you, Micah. Why don't you take it from here?"

Micah drew his knife from its sheath and slit the buck's throat, neatly severing the jugular. He then rolled the animal on its back, slicing open the belly from the groin to the chest cavity. Reaching into the opening, he rolled out the guts. Benjamin watched in awe. Who was this stranger at his side?

"Where did you learn all this, Micah?" he couldn't keep from asking, though it galled him.

"Uncle Haden showed me. You only gotta see it done once."

Benjamin said nothing, biting back a defensive remark. He realized that when he had seen it done, he hadn't been paying close attention because he'd not thought it important. For some reason it had been very important to Micah, and he remembered all the details.

They trussed up the animal and carried it home between them. Benjamin never could shake the sense that he was walking with a stranger.

CHAPTER 38

When they returned home, Benjamin sent Micah down to the creek to wash off the blood and grime from gutting the buck. He then began the process of skinning the animal. Because Micah had asked to keep the hide, Benjamin took special care in the process. Again, this was not a task in which he was adept. He should have waited for Micah, whom he knew had a vested interest in the buck, but he still had some vestige of pride left after the humbling day of hunting. And when Micah took an inordinately long time at the creek, Benjamin lost his patience and began alone. Micah had probably had more time alone with his father than he could bear.

When John Hunter rode into the yard, Benjamin was both pleased and disappointed. He longed for a reprieve from the task, and he knew John would be happy to lend more than a hand, but Benjamin also knew he'd never learn himself if he depended on others. He was thinking much lately of his future and the fact that he well might need to support his family through farming rather than the ministry.

"Look what you got there!" John said, dismounting and striding over to the area near the woodpile that Benjamin had staked out for his work. "A fine big buck, too."

"My son bagged him." Benjamin could not help his pride. "Right between the eyes!"

"Didn't know the boy was such an accomplished shooter."

"Neither did I."

"Must be a natural."

"He surely didn't get it from me." Benjamin hefted the buck in a better position to be worked on.

"Let me give you a hand."

John squatted down next to Benjamin and held one of the buck's legs while Benjamin made careful slits and began gently working his knife under the hide. "I want to save the hide for Micah," Benjamin explained.

"Might be able to get him a nice shirt out of it," John commented.

"He'd like that, I'm sure. I think he is becoming quite the frontiersman."

John chuckled. "Kids learn fast."

"Not like their dim-witted fathers." Benjamin laughed dryly.

He thought of the afternoon and how it all had come so naturally to Micah. In the past Benjamin had expected that his son would follow him into the ministry, though that dream had quickly faded after they had come to Texas. Even when Benjamin had begun to see the futility of such an expectation for his son, he had viewed it as a flaw in Micah. Now he saw it from a different perspective. Micah was not flawed at all because his interests were different from his father's. He simply had his own way, his own path. Perhaps Benjamin's ability to see this, to allow him to follow that path, was one good thing to emerge from all the tragedy.

"What brings you out today, John?" Benjamin pulled his focus back to his guest.

John hesitated, and if Benjamin had harbored a hope that this was merely a friendly visit, he knew now to brace himself for something else.

"Well, Reverend Sinclair, I don't like what brings me here, but I figured it'd be best coming from me. Leastways, I've always thought I had a bit more friendly relationship with you than some of the others in your parish."

"You've been a good friend, as good as any I've ever had, and I appreciate it." Benjamin hoped his sincerity came through. He sensed he was going to need such a friend more than ever.

"Glad to hear that, and I wouldn't say anything except as a friend. I'm concerned with your best interests. I had a visit from Harvey Doyle, who said he was up here a couple days ago."

"So that's his name. And I suppose he told you he caught me cavorting with a woman." Benjamin barely restrained the bitterness in his tone.

"Something like that."

"You believe him?" They worked as they talked, and Benjamin added, "Could you stretch out that leg a bit more?"

"I wouldn't make no judgment until I heard your side of it." John held the buck's leg tautly. "I wouldn't even get involved at all except . . ." Pausing, he ran his free hand through his hair. He was indeed reluctant to stir matters up. "I came to Texas looking for room to breathe, land where my neighbors weren't pressing down on me. But it is amazing how small and crowded this place can be where rumors are involved. Since I saw Doyle, I've had a couple of others come to me wanting to know the truth of it. Guess they came to me instead of you directly because—"

"They're just a bunch of cowards at heart," Benjamin interjected.

"Maybe so. Well, the upshot of it was that a meeting was held yesterday by several of your parishioners, and I agreed to come talk to you and get your side of it."

"Did you agree, John, or did you insist because they would have tarred and feathered me otherwise?"

John chuckled, even though there was little humor in Benjamin's statement. "They were a bit riled up, and most were willing to believe the worst. But I know you are a man of honor, Reverend, and I knew there had to be another explanation."

"I appreciate that, and let me assure you, nothing immoral has taken place inside this cabin or out of it. Fate brought Miss Toussaint here, and circumstances kept her here." Trying to be patient, he explained to John about her coming with her sick baby to find Rebekah. "I couldn't put her out, John. But I won't deny I had a desperate need for her help with my children as well."

"I can imagine. Where is the girl from?"

Benjamin had hoped he wouldn't have to explain specifics about Elise, yet he knew they couldn't be avoided. John would no doubt immediately recognize her from the store in San Felipe, for he had witnessed the altercation when she had been accused of theft.

"Let's not get into that until you tell me what's to be done about the protests of my parishioners." Maybe he couldn't avoid the subject of Elise's past, but he saw no reason to cloud the present problem with it.

"Reverend, I can see the difficulties of your situation, and hers as well. You can't put her out, especially with a sick child. And you gotta have help with your own children. If it were just me, well, I'd sure not question how you chose to solve the problems. Like I said, I respect your honor. Yet you must also see how this could undermine your ministry."

"That is a problem in itself." He studied John Hunter's plain, solid face. He realized now that because he'd always maintained a position of authority, he had never had any real friends, never had someone to confide in and seek counsel from. Perhaps he would not have come to his present state had he humbled himself enough to be vulnerable. There had been other practical and wise men like John Hunter who could have helped him find a better path where his family was concerned. Though his present sense of self-recrimination now made him feel it was too late, it also made him believe he had nothing to lose.

"John, I'm not sure I have a ministry any longer—"

"The people aren't gonna cut you off just like that," John protested.

"That's not what I mean. I am not sure I am personally fit to minister. Since Rebekah's death my eyes have been opened, and I have been forced to look inward. I don't like what I see. I am not the man I thought I was, the man I tried so hard to make others think I was. I don't believe the man I truly am is worthy of God's ministry. You read Rebekah's letter. You know what I'm talking about."

"I said it then, and I'll say it again, you can't blame yourself. But I'll go one step further. Even if it was your fault, the fact that you now realize it means something. It'll make you a better man, a better minister, even."

Benjamin shook his head, not so much in disagreement as in defeat. If only he were a simple man who could live by simple answers.

John continued. "Sounds to me like you are mighty confused right now. And I don't think you want to do anything to burn your bridges while you're in such a state. This community needs you desperately, Reverend."

"Why don't you call me Benjamin." When John opened his mouth to protest, Benjamin added, "For no other reason except I need a friend now more than a parishioner."

"For that reason, then, I'd be glad to. There's one other thing you ought to keep in mind, and that is the honoring of your wife's memory. It ain't right to her or her children if you ruin your good reputation."

"Which of course this situation does," Benjamin conceded. "And it doesn't do much good for Miss Toussaint's reputation either. But do you have any suggestions about what I ought to do about it?"

"I have been giving it some thought."

"And?"

"The facts of the matter are clear."

Benjamin marveled at John's amazing matter-of-factness. He decided then and there he was going to sit at this man's feet—figuratively at least—and learn what he could from him.

"You need help. And this here Miss Toussaint needs help, too, it seems."

"There's more to it, John." Benjamin knew he could no longer avoid this moment. "You'll find out soon enough anyway. Do you remember when we were in the store in San Felipe and a woman was accused of stealing?"

John nodded, then a light of awareness lit his face. "Miss Toussaint?"

"Yes."

"Who was the man? Not her husband. I could tell that. But I wasn't certain."

"Not her husband. He . . . sells women—"

"You mean she is—"

"Was, John. *Was.* She was being forced into it. That despicable man used her little daughter to make Elise do his bidding. She finally escaped and came here. She wants to make a new life for herself, but if I send her away, the chances are that man will find her and force her back into . . . that life."

The men fell silent, focusing their attention on the hide, which, with a couple more motions, was severed from the animal's carcass. Benjamin had no ready answers, so it was easy for him to remain silent about Elise. He had a feeling John would want to ruminate a bit before speaking.

"I have no idea what to do with this hide now that it's off," Benjamin admitted.

"I've done a few in my time. I'll give you some pointers, if you'd like."

"Thanks a lot, John." He lifted his eyes and met John's, and in the way of men, much more was spoken in that look than their words could express.

"What you do with the skin depends on what the boy wants it for. If he wants a shirt, you're not gonna want to salt the hide. Just soak it in water till the hair slides off. Maybe add some wood ashes to speed up the process." John took an end of the hide and spread it open on the ground. "First, let's scrape as much of the fatty tissue off as we can. You can use the dull side of your fleshing knife."

"I don't have one."

"A kitchen spoon will do."

Benjamin disappeared inside the cabin and returned quickly with two large spoons. They set to work on the hide with John making suggestions as they went. "Be gentle. Don't want to gouge the hide. Leave anything too difficult—it'll come off during soaking."

The man held a wealth of information, and Benjamin could have listened to him and questioned him for hours on the many tasks involved with making the best use of the newly killed buck. But still hanging between them as distastefully as a deer carcass was the subject they both would have liked to avoid. But Benjamin knew the topic hadn't been forgotten.

Finally John inhaled a breath and paused in his work. "You know, Benjamin, I sure wish I knew as much about people as I do about simple work like this. You see, I came here today with a solution in mind to your problem, but considering what you just said about Miss Toussaint, I'm not sure what you'll think of it." John folded his arms in front of him and took a moment to appraise Benjamin. Apparently satisfied with what he saw, he continued. "I was going to suggest that you . . . well, that you consider marrying Miss Toussaint."

Those were the last words Benjamin ever expected to hear. In fact, he was thinking Hunter would offer to take Elise and Hannah into his own home. When the shock wore off at this new twist in the mounting complexities of his life, Benjamin began to babble all the reasons why such a thing was impossible.

"I hardly know her. How can I marry a stranger? I've been a widower less than a month. My children already despise me. What will they think if I so suddenly try to replace their mother? Who is to say she'll want to marry me? She knows what a terrible husband I was."

The one argument that did not occur to him was how he, a minister, could marry a prostitute. It was John who mentioned it.

"Benjamin, what about that . . . other thing? You know, about the woman's past?"

Benjamin smiled. "I hadn't thought of that. I've only known her for a week or so, John, but I can tell you with all certainty that no matter what she was before, she is no part of that now. I don't believe she ever was in her heart." He paused thoughtfully. "She is kindhearted and gentle. You should see her with the children."

"Well, I reckon God has forgiven folks of worse sins." There was a certain edge to John's voice, accompanied by a sideways look that Benjamin chose to ignore.

"I believe He has with her," Benjamin replied.

"Folks around here might have a different take on that." John looked very much as if he hadn't wanted to mention that, but it was a fact that had to be voiced.

Benjamin's answer surprised even him. "Let them try to judge her."

John eyed Benjamin with a questioning gaze and followed it with a smile. John might be wondering about Benjamin's impassioned support of a woman he claimed to be a stranger. Benjamin wondered a bit also. He decided the cause was simply that after his own fall from grace, he had greater sympathy for those in a similar place.

The two men fell silent, and Benjamin considered John's outlandish suggestion. Marriage! He knew it was a solution other men in his position had resorted to on the frontier. It was, in fact, the most practical solution he could think of. It would benefit both of them. Let that Thomson lout try to molest her while she was married to him! It made him feel he did indeed have something to offer in a marriage of convenience. And because it would be a marriage in name only, it might work far better than many conventional unions did.

Finally Benjamin came to a decision. "I suppose it wouldn't hurt to mention the idea to Elise."

CHAPTER 39

ELISE WALKED TO THE EDGE of the woods. The sun was down and bright pinpoints of stars twinkled in the sky. Light from the half moon filtered through the trees, mingling with a low-lying fog to form a glittering veil. She breathed in deeply, detecting a faint scent of honeysuckle. Somehow the air smelled so much sweeter here than it had at Maurry's place, though she was certain there had been honeysuckle there, too. Perhaps it was only that she could notice it here, now freed as she was from the horrors of her former life. Only now could she fully perceive how heavily that life had weighed her down.

And Benjamin was offering her a permanent escape from it. Only a year had passed since she had been taken into bondage, though it seemed like an eternity. Now it could be over. After her miraculous escape, she'd had no delusions that she could remain free forever. In fact, she had secretly believed her only true escape would be in death.

Benjamin offered her something else. He told her he would never let her fall into Thomson's hands again. Never. And she believed him. In exchange for that, she had only to care for his children and his home. She was already developing a fondness for the children, so that should be no difficulty. And she loved keeping house in the little cabin, basking in the exquisite sense of security it offered her. It was even more pleasant than the life of wealth she had known on the Hearne plantation.

Benjamin promised to make no more demands on her.

"This is a union of mutual convenience," he had told her that evening after John Hunter had departed. "We each have a great deal to give, but beyond protection and housekeeping and such there are no other requirements. That is to say . . . uh . . ."

"I understand," she assured him. "You expect no physical . . . favors."

Reddening, he said quickly, "None at all!"

"I still worry that I have more to gain in this than you." She voiced one of several doubts.

"Have you forgotten the state of the cabin when you first arrived?" he asked wryly. "How much worse will it be when I have to go out and pursue some manner of living, whether it be farming or hunting or . . . whatever?"

"Yes, I suppose so."

"I was doubtful at first myself, Elise. But I can see that it could work rather nicely. We have gotten on fairly well since you've been here. We have no glaring differences. You are certainly a congenial sort." Pausing, he gave a rueful sigh. "And you have no illusions about what kind of man I am. You well know I was a terrible husband, but the tragedy of the last weeks has, I think, opened my eyes a bit, and I believe I will not . . . at least I will try not to make the same mistakes."

"That's all anyone can do." Oddly, the least of her fears had to do with Benjamin himself. Though he seemed contrite now, even broken, he might well slip back into his old ways. Yet Elise believed that for all his previous flaws—arrogance, self-centeredness, and pretension, to name a few—he had never been a cruel man. Having lived for the last year with a truly brutal man and consorted with others of the same nature, she thought arrogance and such were faults she could deal with.

She had retreated from the cabin a few minutes ago to have some time alone to consider the offer and make her decision. She could have told him yes then and there. In fact, how could she refuse when it meant so much to her survival and Hannah's also?

But the word *yes* had caught in her throat.

Since leaving the Hearne plantation, Elise had thought little of her former marriage, placing it in a far corner of her mind so it could not torment her along with everything else. She had been successful in that effort because, though it had been only a year since they had been parted, it seemed far enough in the past to feel as though that ill-fated union had never existed. She certainly no longer had an emotional attachment to Kendell. What he had done to her was enough to thoroughly erase any residual feelings of affection she might have clung to. But it could never obliterate the fact that there had been a marriage, even if annulment was supposed to render the marriage as nonexistent. If nothing else, Hannah was proof it had indeed existed.

In the last year Elise had never even considered the possibility of another marriage. As a slave, she'd had no choice in the matter. As a prostitute, she'd doubted any respectable man would want her.

Now a respectable man did want her, and of all men, it was Rev. Benjamin Sinclair! That was mind-boggling enough, but that he was also willing to overlook her former life . . . well, it was unimaginable. He'd been able to see how she had been forced into that despicable life and thus could not find it in himself to hold it against her. This was the new Benjamin Sinclair, a man who had come to understand that circumstances could both rule and destroy lives. Of course, it helped her cause that there were few women on the frontier. Yes, his need was nearly as desperate at hers.

But what of her former marriage? Might that be the limit over which Benjamin could not cross? Men were peculiar. He could excuse her prostitution because she had been coerced into it, but to have willingly given herself in marriage . . . he might see that as a different matter entirely. Many men, especially those of highly religious conviction, considered divorce or even annulment illegal and remarriage unacceptable. Something told her that not long ago, Benjamin must surely have been one of this ilk.

Had he changed? Dare she take that risk? Should she tell him of her marriage?

She knew how a lie had destroyed her previous marriage. Could she deceive again? But could she risk losing this opportunity? The thought of returning to Maurice Thomson—as she knew would happen if she was set adrift once more—brought a gnawing sickness to her stomach. She would sooner be killed and watch her child be killed before returning to Maurry.

Surely if the truth ever did come out, Benjamin would understand and forgive her because of her plight. It would be better for him if he didn't know, just in case . . . if later . . . well, who could say what might happen in the future. But should the truth ever come to light, it would be best for his sake, his reputation, if he could plead complete innocence. Of course, it would be entirely different if this were a union of love. She would never do such a thing to a man she loved or who loved her. But they were both in accord that this marriage would only serve practical purposes. No love, no physical joining, no emotional bonds. Thus no one could possibly be hurt. Convincing herself of this, Elise knew she would say yes. She could do nothing else. It was the only way she and Hannah could stay safe. Hannah would surely die if cast out into the world again. Even God would understand. He would be the last to throw a helpless woman and child to the wilds.

Then a new thought came to her, bolstering her decision. Wasn't it possible that Benjamin already assumed she'd been married before, because of Hannah? The question of Hannah's origin had never arisen. He might think the child merely to be an unfortunate result of Elise's occupation. But no, she was certain she had told him she had been with Thomson for only a year. A quick calculation would indicate Hannah had been born before this.

Of course! He did realize she had been married. There was no reason to say anything. Either way, whether he knew or not, she believed she would be fully exonerated. She breathed in another draught of air, and it smelled even fresher. All would be well.

As she headed back to the cabin, her heart pounding furiously but her feet moving relentlessly, she forced from the fringes of her mind thoughts of what had happened the last time she kept a secret from a man she would marry.

Benjamin was sitting in the rocking chair feeding Oliver when Elise returned to the cabin. He looked up and, seeing her face, knew what her answer would be. He was both relieved and frightened. Part of him had thought her good sense would put an end to this foolishness.

A marriage of convenience indeed!

And he had thought his brother was a hairbrained fool! This went leaps beyond any of Haden's schemes.

Yet he still could not completely forget the dire circumstances that forced this decision upon them. If he were in closer fellowship with God right now, he'd be able to come up with a score of spiritual reasons against this marriage.

Or could he?

When one really considered the matter, there was nothing unspiritual or even unscriptural about the arrangement. Certainly nothing in the Word of God promoted the idea of romantic love as part of the marriage commitment. As far as the element that would be missing in the proposed union . . . well, becoming "one flesh" was scriptural, but he couldn't think of a law that indicated this was *necessary.*

In fact, he was certain he could find far more biblical precedents for this event than otherwise. It was a matter of honor, respect, protection, and caring. There could be no scriptural law against these. And Benjamin knew that once he made the commitment to marriage, he would treat it with no less reverence than he had the day he had married Rebekah.

But this assurance did not completely salve the gnawing fear that he would carry into this marriage the same flaws that had destroyed his first marriage. He did not love Elise, but he did not want to ever be responsible for doing to her what he had done to Rebekah.

"Benjamin," Elise said softly.

"You have come to a decision?" It was hardly the place to discuss such matters, surrounded as they were by four children. Micah, at least, was absent as usual. On the other hand, Benjamin thought there was probably no better place, since it was this very situation that had fomented the arrangement in the first place. Nevertheless, he added, "Shall we step outside?" When she nodded, he rose, laid Oliver in the cradle, and followed Elise outside.

She stopped at the edge of the yard. In the moment before Benjamin joined her, he paused and studied her solitary figure. He wondered again how he could have so harshly judged her before. As she stood there now, the moonlight falling about her slim shoulders like a veil, her beautiful face in profile, solemn yet very alive, he thought perhaps he could find his faith again. He saw her now not as a fallen woman but rather as a profound answer to a prayer he'd not even had the faith to utter.

Trembling inside like a boy about to speak his heart for the first time to a schoolgirl, Benjamin came up beside Elise.

"Benjamin, before I can make a decision, there are two things that trouble me." She spoke seriously, and he braced himself for the logic he had both desired and dreaded. Taking a breath she continued. "My Negro blood—"

"That is not a problem to me," he cut in quickly, surprising himself at how ready he was to shore up any gaps in this outlandish plan.

"But why?"

"I suppose because of the . . . uh . . . nature of this union, I have never given it a thought. Beyond that, well, I am a man to judge others upon many grounds, but race has never been one of them. I see you as who you are, and that is all that matters to me." She was staring rather incredulously at him, her mouth hanging slightly ajar. He had to prompt her by adding, "What is your other problem?" He watched her delicate throat constrict as she swallowed.

She replied, "There are some who would consider it just as heinous for you to marry a woman such as I, a fallen dove as it were, as it would for you to live in sin with me. What I am saying is that it could still ruin your reputation."

"I don't care about anyone who would hold such a thing against you. I have been there, and I will not go there again myself or abide anyone who does."

"Nevertheless—"

"Besides, it is unlikely anyone except John Hunter will ever know. Even he said that after he saw you he would not have recognized you from the girl he saw in the store. Without the face paint and fancy clothes . . ." He paused and almost unconsciously his eyes studied her again. She had changed quite dramatically. Not only was the paint gone, but the hard, bitter aspect he had noted before had disappeared, leaving a softness, even an innocence that did indeed make her seem another woman entirely. "Elise, you have changed," he breathed, his own throat constricting a bit.

"What if . . . ?"

"We will deal with that if and when it should ever happen."

They both fell silent. It seemed all major barriers had been breached. This marriage—foolish, unorthodox, but exceedingly practical—would indeed happen, though proper, formal consent had not yet been given.

As if reading his mind, she turned and said to him, "Then, Benjamin . . . Yes, I would like to accept your proposal." She seemed to be restraining a smile, perhaps deeming it inappropriate under the circumstances, but her eyes glittered like light glancing off jet.

"Thank you." He, too, practiced restraint but mostly because he wasn't sure what to do now. It seemed wrong to stand there staring at her, but an embrace would not have worked either.

"When . . . shall it take place?" Her voice trembled a bit.

"As soon as possible, don't you think?" Certainly before I find a reason to back out, he thought ruefully.

"That would be best. Will you tell the children?"

"Micah and Isabel will have to be told, though I fear they won't much like the idea." Flustered, he added, "Not because of you."

"It might help if they know I won't try to replace their mother."

"You've already shown a sensitivity toward this. They accept you quite well. I don't think anything will change much."

"No . . . nothing will change . . . much."

He didn't know what to make of her hesitant tone. Nothing *would* change. She would be a housekeeper, he would be an employer of sorts. The marriage certificate would simply remove any question of morality in the arrangement. "We will tell them tonight."

CHAPTER 40

THE PROBLEM OF WHO WOULD perform the marriage ceremony was addressed by John Hunter in his infuriatingly practical manner.

"I heard from Albert Petty that a priest was in the area. A Father Murphy."

At first Benjamin gaped at the suggestion, then he, too, became practical. "Will he marry a Protestant?"

"I've met Father Murphy, and he's been known to bend the rules a bit."

"Well, for once I can appreciate such an attribute."

But as the day drew near, Benjamin was getting shakier and shakier. He became short-tempered with the children and clumsy with his daily tasks. He spilled milk, caught the hearth rug on fire, and finally nearly lopped off his foot with the ax while chopping wood. It was at that point that Elise interceded.

"Are you all right, Benjamin?"

He hadn't realized she had come outside. When he saw her, his cheeks burned.

"Guess I'm all thumbs today," he offered with a lopsided smile.

"Would it have anything to do with what is going to take place tomorrow?"

He gave a dry snort. "You mean aside from the fact that I am a Protestant minister about to be married to a prostitute by a Catholic priest?"

"Well, if it helps, I am an *ex*-prostitute," she answered just as dryly, then smiled.

Benjamin laughed, really laughed, until his lips hurt and his eyes watered. He hadn't laughed like that since . . . well, maybe never. She joined in the mirth, even though she didn't throw herself into it with as much exuberance as he demonstrated. He saw she hadn't been offended by his words, that she understood he had not meant them in that way.

When the greater part of his amusement subsided, he said, "You are a remarkable woman, Elise. I have no qualms about that."

"No, but I can see this is all quite a leap for you to take."

"It is a leap I want to take, a leap I believe is right. It is only the vestiges of the man I was that threaten to throw me off-balance a bit." Considering his statement, he added, "I suppose it is not who I was that worries me as much as that I am not yet certain of who I will become."

"Benjamin, can I ask you something personal?"

"In a matter of hours you will become my wife. I should think you can ask what you wish."

"Do you still believe in God?"

"Of course I do!" The certainty of his response and the immediacy of it rather surprised him. "My worry is that He no longer believes in me."

"Do you think that could happen?" Her question sounded sincere, reminding Benjamin that the faith she professed was fairly new. Yet he felt peculiarly on level with her because so many new ideas and considerations, both spiritual and otherwise, were bombarding his senses.

"You don't want to get into a discussion of eternal salvation and predestination now, do you?" he asked with a hint of sarcasm.

She wrinkled her brow, perplexed at terms she no doubt had never heard.

With more sincerity, he answered, "Theologically speaking, yes, I have always believed it could happen. But to others, not to me!" He gave a wry, self-depreciating smile. "I know better now. I know in a very personal way that my faith is not so very secure."

"I know I am fairly ignorant in these matters, but I have a feeling inside me that says we would have to turn away from God before He would turn away from us." She smiled shyly. "If you want to be close to God, He will be there for you."

"If only it were so simple."

A slight smile twitching her lips, she said, "You will work it out, Benjamin, I am sure."

The next morning dawned with an overcast sky threatening rain. Benjamin thought it was quite fitting because the rain had brought Elise to his home in the first place.

By ten, John and Nell Hunter had arrived to act as witnesses. Father Murphy, whom John's eldest son had tracked down a few days earlier, arrived an hour later. He was the perfect picture of an Irish priest—short, rotund, and florid, with a faint hint of whiskey on his breath.

"I am so happy to finally be meetin' you, Reverend Benjamin Sinclair!" Murphy spoke with a thick Irish accent, but at least it wasn't Spanish. Early on, the Mexican Church had seen the expediency of importing Irish priests for the purpose of ministering to the largely English-speaking Texians. Benjamin had heard these priests were often outcasts from their native Ireland and thus tended to be rather unorthodox.

If Benjamin needed nothing else right now, he certainly needed an unorthodox priest.

"I'm surprised you knew of my existence," Benjamin replied, offering the priest a seat on the bench at his table.

Elise sat in the rocking chair with the baby. The Hunters found other makeshift seats, while the children ranged elsewhere about the house. Micah was absent because he refused to be present at the ceremony.

"Oh, sure'n! Word got around. I'm only sorry business in Mexico City prevented me from meeting you until now." Murphy lifted his cup of tea, stared at it wistfully as if trying to imagine the cup containing something stronger, then took a sip. "The few days I've had to get about the circuit have indicated ye have taken very good care of things in my absence."

Benjamin didn't know how to take the man's comment. If it were meant to be an insult, it was said in the best of good humor. "I hope you don't—"

Much to Benjamin's relief, Father Murphy broke in before he could frame a reply. He really wasn't certain how to respond anyway.

"Don't be takin' it wrong, me dear Reverend!" The priest replied with expansive good nature. "I sincerely appreciate your work here. Heaven knows these dear people were never the best of Catholics, now, were they?"

"Well . . ."

"Ah, but what am I talking of politics when there is a joyous event about to transpire?" Murphy turned a smiling face toward Elise. "Me dear, ye'll make a lovely bride. Would ye like to tell me if ye have special requests for the nuptials?"

Elise's eyebrows raised at this. "I hadn't really thought about it." Glancing at Benjamin, she added, "I suppose something traditional, don't you think, Benjamin?"

Murphy added, "Now, as to the matter of Catholic or Protestant . . ."

"I think you should do whatever you are comfortable with, Father," Benjamin put in. Then in response to the slack-jawed looks of the others in the room, he added, "Father Murphy has come out of his way to perform this ceremony. I would not want to make undue demands on him."

"Well, we can eliminate the Nuptial Mass," Murphy said. "Other than that, the vows and such are not so different from the Protestant service."

"As long as it is legal," Benjamin said.

"Oh, it will be that!" grinned Murphy. "Once I tie a knot, it seldom comes loose."

The priest's words made Elise's stomach flip like a hotcake. They made her realize in her very soul what she'd known only intellectually until then.

That which was about to transpire in an hour would be a commitment of incredible, even stunning, permanence. She intended it to be so, and she knew Benjamin also intended it. They both knew what an unstable thing permanence could be, but that did not change the intent of their hearts.

Nor did it change the way it was now wreaking havoc with Elise's insides. For the rest of her life, should God be so kind as to will it, Benjamin Sinclair would be by her side. *Only* by her side, no more. However, she couldn't deny that it would not exactly displease her if it became more. He was a handsome, desirable man. But desire was a word she had carefully avoided. There had been times since coming to the cabin that she had felt stirrings toward him, but she had pointedly disregarded them. First out of respect to Rebekah, but mostly because Elise feared any emotional attachment to a man. She convinced herself those "stirrings" were merely physical anyway, nothing to truly fear unless they became deeper.

Yet what might happen in a month? A year? Ten years? How many times had participants in arranged marriages heard the juncture, "You will grow to love each other." That could not happen to her. She would not let it.

Well, she thought wryly, perhaps he will just revert to his old ways and I will become disgusted with him again.

She welcomed the fact that for the next hour she had more places to spend her energy than in fearsome thoughts. Though Elise had given little consideration to the ceremony itself, Mrs. Hunter had no intention of letting something so wonderful as a wedding be entered into unobtrusively. As soon as she deemed Father Murphy had been properly refreshed from his journey, she shooed the men outside so preparations could be made.

Elise hadn't given thought to making the wedding an *occasion*. She had supposed it would be a simple affair, just enough of a ceremony to make it legal before man and God. Benjamin's comment earlier about it just being legal indicated he had the same line of thinking. But Mrs. Hunter's enthusiasm was contagious. Besides, even if this marriage would entail no physical joining, it was still a marriage. And . . . well, what woman, even an ex-slave prostitute, didn't want her wedding day to be special?

Elise found yet another reason for this to be made into an occasion when Mrs. Hunter asked about Elise's wedding attire. Elise merely shook her head dumbly. What she was to wear simply had not occurred to her, but Isabel had apparently given it much thought. She took an item from the trunk that was wrapped in a sheet.

"This was my mama's best dress," the child said, carefully lifting away the covering.

She held it up as high as her little arms would reach, a lovely gown of Chinese green moiré silk. Its *revers* neckline was of forest green velvet. The full sleeves tapered snugly from mid forearm and were trimmed with velvet. That same rich green velvet also belted the full skirt and made a trim around the lower skirt, a band from which velvet leaves hung regally. Though perhaps a few years behind the latest fashions, it was a gown worthy of any Elise had seen in New Orleans.

Since coming to the cabin, Elise had worn only the brown dress she had first taken from the trunk, alternating it with her own clothes, which, though shabby, had washed up and were still serviceable. She had been careful not to trespass upon the trunk again. Tears rose in her eyes as the child held the gown out as an offering.

Emotion clutching her throat, she couldn't speak. She merely shook her head.

Isabel said softly, "Please take it, Elise. When you marry Papa, you'll be my new mother. I know it is a very special occasion."

"Oh, dear Isabel! I don't ever want to take your mother's place."

"I think she would have chosen you," Isabel said with such simple confidence, it brought a lump to Elise's throat.

Tears streaming from her eyes, Elise took the dress, laid it on the trunk, then wrapped her arms around Isabel. "I do love you!" She kissed Isabel's downy soft yellow curls.

"S-so, you will wear the dress?" Isabel asked through her own tears.

"If it will make you happy."

And thus Elise realized there needed to be a celebration today for the children's sake, especially for Isabel and Micah, even if Micah showed outward disdain for the entire matter. The children had no concept of the unconventional aspect of the marriage. To them, their father was getting married to a woman who would now become part of their lives—a permanent part. They needed a point of reference by which they could know this was a solemn, serious commitment.

Perhaps for the same reason she needed it herself. Because of her sullied past, she needed it to be clear for her own sake that she was entering this marriage commitment with all earnestness.

As these things dawned upon her, Elise's concept of her wedding changed dramatically. It must be a celebration, as festive as possible. She wished she would have realized this a few days ago when she had agreed to the marriage so that better plans could have been made. She also knew that all the children had to be a part of it—especially Micah.

Elise suddenly became animated. There were a million things to do!

"Mrs. Hunter, would you mind the babies while Isabel and I tend to a few arrangements?"

"I'll be most happy to." The woman seemed to pick up on the new level of excitement. "Perhaps I can even take an iron to that dress while you're gone."

"Thank you so much. We shouldn't be long." She grabbed a basket and gave it to Isabel. "Isabel, would you gather all the wild flowers you can find? Stay close to the cabin. We haven't time to wander far."

They went outside, and as Isabel set about her assigned task, Elise turned to the three men who were standing idly talking.

"Benjamin," she said approaching the men with purpose, "there is going to be a slight delay."

"What?" He blanched, no doubt thinking she'd had a change of heart.

"I've been amiss in my casual view of this wedding," she explained, taking him aside. "No matter our reasons for marrying, we *are* getting married, and I feel it must be treated with dignity. We must stand proudly before God and our children, not slink to a makeshift altar as if we were somehow ashamed of what we are doing." When Benjamin continued to stare in dumbfounded silence, Elise added, "I know this is sudden. I just realized it myself. But I know it is the right thing."

"Well . . . uh . . . of course."

She could see his Adam's apple work spasmodically as he swallowed a couple of times.

"What should I do?"

"You need to dress in your best suit," she answered without hesitation. "Why don't you do that while I see to another matter."

She hurried away toward the creek. She had discovered that Micah had a little retreat set back from the shore amongst several large rocks. She had stumbled upon him accidentally one day, and since he had not seen her, she had remained silent about it. She hated to intrude now but was determined to talk to him. When she neared the rocks, she made noise and called his name, then turned away from the retreat so he still might not know it had been discovered. She thought a boy like Micah needed his privacy. In a few minutes, she heard him move in the brush and turned.

"Oh, there you are, Micah!"

He just scowled in response.

"Can I talk with you?" she asked.

He shrugged.

"It's about the wedding—" she began.

"I don't want to talk about it," he cut in sharply.

"I know this isn't easy for you, though I don't pretend to know all the reasons that might be in your heart. I'm sure your grief at your mother's loss is still very great. And I know that for some reason you are angry at your father." She paused and tried to walk closer, then stopped when he tensed, fearing he might bolt. "I'm not asking you to give up your pain. I know it would be too hard for you to do that right now. I have pain, too, and so does your father. This wedding doesn't mean we are going to instantly forget it all. But you are old enough to understand that life must proceed despite our pain. Your brother and sisters and my Hannah need a proper family. Please try to understand—that is why your father and I are doing this, not because we in any way want to forget your mother."

"It's easy enough to say," he muttered.

"Yes, I suppose it is. What can I do to convince you otherwise?"

Ignoring her query, he said, "I don't care if you marry my father. And I sure don't care what he does."

"Then why won't you come to the wedding?"

"No one will miss me anyway."

"That's not true!" She paused, not sure how to proceed, how to make him believe his presence was important. She uttered a silent prayer for wisdom before continuing. "Micah, I would like to invite you to my wedding as *my* friend. You may sit on the bride's side."

He cocked a wary brow at her, and she nearly smiled. He certainly hadn't expected this tactic. No doubt he thought she would try to make him attend out of love and respect for his father. To leave Benjamin out altogether—well, she could see in his eyes that it put the entire matter into a new light. Micah had nothing against her. He had even been friendly toward her in the last weeks.

"I'll think about it," he said finally.

"We'll be ready in about an hour." She turned and walked up the bank back to the cabin.

CHAPTER 41

EXACTLY ONE HOUR LATER EVERYONE gathered in the cabin. Elise had considered holding the ceremony outside, but it started to sprinkle, forcing them indoors.

John and Nell Hunter stood as best man and matron of honor. Nell held Hannah and John held a very wiggly Leah. Elise thought it quite apropos that instead of flowers, her matron of honor held a child.

Isabel, dressed in a white cambric muslin dress trimmed with pink braiding, was a sweet flower girl. She carried a nosegay of freshly picked bluebells, lilies, and Indian paintbrush. At Elise's insistence,

Oliver was also present, but it was Benjamin who held him. This, too, seemed quite fitting. Even with his tiny son in his arms, Benjamin cut a dashing figure. He surprised everyone when he appeared not in the broadcloth frock coat and trousers he wore on the circuit, but rather in a fashionable—at least ten years ago—tan linen suit, with cutaway coat and pinstripe trousers, black waistcoat, cream shirt, and black silk cravat. The suit emphasized his broad shoulders and narrow waist and nearly made Elise forget what this marriage was all about.

As the wedding party lined up, Elise glanced several times toward the door, despairing that Micah would not come. Father Murphy cleared his throat and opened his prayer book.

"Dearly beloved, we are assembled here—"

Suddenly the door creaked, and a slightly damp Micah came in. He studiously avoided his father's eyes as he maneuvered as inconspicuously as possible—though it was hardly possible at all in the small cabin—into a place very clearly on Elise's side of the room. For an instant their eyes met. She smiled, and he nodded an acknowledgment.

Benjamin glanced at his son, cut deeply that the boy would not look at him. It was obvious Micah had come for Elise, not his father. But at least he was here. Benjamin was struck anew with the assurance he had made the right decision in bringing Elise into his home. Perhaps somehow she would find a way to heal the rifts in the Sinclair family.

Father Murphy continued. "Ah-hem . . . let's see now . . . we are assembled here in the presence of God to join this man and this woman in the bonds of holy matrimony."

Benjamin could not help his sense of awe as he gazed at his bride. He had always realized she was a beautiful woman, but now she was stunning, decked out in a gown that must have been Rebekah's, though he did not recall it. But what took his breath away more than her looks was the fact that she had considered the event important enough to go to the trouble of making it an occasion for them all to remember.

Elise actually blushed at Benjamin's frank gaze of admiration. When had a man last looked at her like that? Not with lust, not with desire, but rather with tender respect. She feared more than ever that Benjamin was not going to make this strictly platonic arrangement easy for her. She felt her heart beat a wild cadence.

Father Murphy was saying " . . . which is instituted by God, regulated by His commandments, blessed by our Lord Jesus Christ, and to be held in honor among all men. Let us therefore remember that God has established and sanctified marriage."

These words are no less true now than when I myself had uttered them to others, Benjamin thought. And though I feel unworthy, I still believe them to be true. If ever I needed your blessing, Lord, it is now. Perhaps what Elise said is indeed true. If you haven't turned your back on me, then maybe it is possible you are present now, truly sanctifying this union.

I know so little of your ways, dear God, Elise thought. I don't know why marriage is so important to you. But please know, it is so very important to me also. I truly desire to make this union bring honor to you. Please help me where I am weak and inexperienced.

"For as much as these two persons have come hither to be made one in this holy estate," the priest said, "if there be any present who knows any just cause why they may not lawfully be joined in marriage, I require him now to make it known or ever after to hold his peace." Father Murphy then looked at the bride and groom. "If either of ye know any reason ye may not be lawfully joined together in marriage, now confess it. . . ."

I may think of a score of reasons against this marriage. I may have thought it foolish and hairbrained. On the other hand, I have yet to see the perfect marriage, and certainly I have seen unions far less compatible than this one appears to be. Part of me wants to shout in protest. But the larger part senses a rightness to this that goes beyond each of our mutual needs. I don't understand it. I can't define it. But I know, if only in the sense of commitment I feel, that it is there.

How can I protest when you are saving me from hell itself? Elise glanced around at each of the children, her gaze resting a moment longer on Micah. And if you, Micah, have no protests, and if Isabel believes your mother would have chosen me, then what more assurance do I need?

"Benjamin, will ye speak these vows after me?" Father Murphy asked.

Repeating the priest's words, Benjamin said, "I, Benjamin, take thee, Elise, to be my wedded wife. To have and to hold from this day forward, for better for worse, for richer for poorer, in sickness and in health, to love and to cherish till death do us part, according to God's holy ordinance. Thereto I plight thee my troth."

Benjamin wondered if he was amiss in speaking such a vow. Was he wrong in making a vow to love? Yet if he had learned nothing else lately, it was that love was a matter he knew little of. He thought he had loved Rebekah, but it turned out to be a selfish love that was not real love at all. He was no longer certain what true love was, but he thought if it were expressed in comfort and honor and protection and faithfulness, then he could indeed commit to love Elise.

"Elise Toussaint, will you repeat after me?" asked the priest.

Elise repeated, "I, Elise, take thee, Benjamin, to be my wedded husband, to have and to hold from this day forward, for better for worse, for richer for poorer, in sickness and in health, to love and to cherish till death us do part, according to God's holy ordinance. Thereto I plight thee my troth."

Elise gave the man beside her a shy side glance. A few hours ago she had expected this wedding to be simply a rote affair of legal import only. But the meaning of the words just spoken reached deeply inside her. Each one pulled at her heart, filling her with the sense that this was far more than a mere arrangement. It was a marriage.

"Have you a token of this marriage covenant?" asked the priest.

Much to Elise's surprise, Benjamin reached into his coat pocket. She tried to ignore the fleeting twinge of regret that he was about to give her Rebekah's wedding ring. He might not even have considered what one woman might feel at wearing another woman's wedding ring. Elise herself hadn't thought such a gesture would bother her the way it now did. Only when she held out her trembling hand and looked at the ring Benjamin was about to place on her finger did she see it was not a woman's ring at all.

"This is my ring from seminary," he explained. "It's large and hardly appropriate, but . . . it was all I had."

She smiled in response, not just because it wasn't another woman's ring after all but because his simply and humbly spoken words—"all I had"—bathed her in comfort and security as much as had the spoken vows.

The priest said, "Take this ring, Benjamin, and place it upon the finger of Elise's hand and let it be the seal of your mutual fidelity and affection and a memorial of this sacred service."

When Benjamin slipped the large ring on her finger and Elise closed her hand around it so it would not slip off, she felt she was grasping more than a ring of gold.

"With this ring, I thee wed," Benjamin said with quiet intensity, "and with all my worldly goods I thee endow, in the name of the Father and of the Son and of the Holy Ghost. Amen."

I have little to give you, Benjamin thought, not even a sense of who I am. My future is uncertain, and my past an indictment. The only gift I have is loyalty and commitment. But these I give freely.

"And now, having heard you make these pledges and take these vows of fidelity," Murphy decreed, "I do, by the authority of the Church of Christ and by the laws of the state of Mexico, pronounce ye husband and wife, no longer twain, but now one, in the name of the Father and of the Son and of the Holy Spirit. Amen."

I don't know what being one will mean to us, Elise. Something different perhaps than we ever expected.

I always thought love and physical joining made a husband and wife one, but I think that which will make us one is surrounding us—five sweet children. We are united in love for them. Elise smiled.

Now with a full grin on his round face, Murphy dropped his formal bearing and said, "There we have it! Those whom God hath joined together, let no man put asunder." Still grinning, he added, "Now, me boy, ye may kiss your bride!"

There was only one instant of awkwardness, then Benjamin bent down and lightly kissed Elise's forehead. She smiled to assure him he had done the right thing.

Then the room erupted into motion as the Hunters offered congratulations and the children, who had been so cooperative for the last fifteen minutes, began their usual squirming, crying, and jabbering. Elise thought it was a better recessional than any traditional wedding march.

As evening approached Benjamin expected the routine of life to continue unhampered. And indeed it seemed to do just that at first. Unimpaired by the rain, the Hunters and Father Murphy had departed shortly after a fine wedding meal prepared by Mrs. Hunter with Elise's help.

Following a supper of leftovers from the midday meal, the children were put through their going-to-bed paces. It was only as Micah blew out the candle by his bed and Benjamin turned down the lamp on the table that he fully realized this was his wedding day. He'd known all along that the usual significance of the wedding night would not be happening. He had never wanted it. The marriage had never been intended for that. Yet he could not ignore the sudden awkwardness he felt as the cabin quieted and the subtle shadows of night prevailed.

Straightening his back, he took a covert glance to where Elise stood over Oliver's cradle, tucking in the quilt around the child. The baby had been asleep for a half hour, and Benjamin had already checked the covers. But he sensed that Elise, too, was feeling a bit disconcerted. Deciding it was best to confront the matter head on, Benjamin strode to her side.

"It's been quite a day," he said softly. "It has even worn out the children."

"Yes . . ." She gently fingered one of Oliver's soft brown curls.

It surprised him how deeply her small gesture stirred him. It was as if she truly were the mother of his child. It confused and flustered him and made him want to flee from the cabin, forgetting all attempts to deal with anything. He tried to steady himself by conjuring up an image of Rebekah in his mind, but all that did was stir up angst and misery. Licking dry lips, he was about to turn and make a hasty retreat when she touched his arm.

"Benjamin, I know this is difficult for you," she said as if she had read his mind. "In marrying me, I am afraid you have given up your home."

"I don't understand."

"I just don't feel right that you should be relegated indefinitely to the barn. It is cold and drafty in there. Not fit for the man of the house."

"Are you suggesting . . . ?" he could not voice what he was thinking.

"I am suggesting that it is only right for *me* to stay in the barn."

He burst out laughing. But when Oliver stirred, he choked back his amusement to a silent snicker.

"What—?" She reddened. "Oh, dear me! You didn't think . . . ?"

"Elise, this has easily been the strangest day of my life." His laughter calmed, but he still felt an unaccountable lightness, though it was vying against all the other raging emotions warring inside him at the moment. "I don't know what to think about it, or what to do. Marriage has always been a deep and solemn matter for me. I can't just brush aside what occurred here today. I thought up until the moment we stood before the priest that that's what we would do. Then everything . . ." His mind was in such disarray he could not think of the proper words.

"Went haywire?" she supplied just the right words.

"Yes . . ."

"I felt it, too. Perhaps it was wrong to have tried to make a celebration of the wedding." She sighed. "I thought it would be good for the children. I never considered how confusing it would be to me—"

"To us."

She stared at him, and he wondered by the way she looked if she was seeing him for the first time.

"We are married, Benjamin! I, too, hold the state of marriage in high regard. We made vows today, commitments. And it was only as I uttered them that I realized I meant them. I truly intend to abide by them."

"I do, too." Benjamin walked to the table and sat on the bench. Elise joined him. "Part of me feels that I am being unfaithful to Rebekah. Our marriage was far from perfect. I'm convinced now that she did not really love me, not that I deserved her love. In fact, I doubt I loved her in the way I should. But I was always faithful to her. I never even thought about other women. Ah, but I'm sure my faithfulness was not so much in honor of her, rather it was really because I had to look good. I had to maintain the appearance of a godly man and minister of Christ. Nevertheless . . ." He idly fingered a spoon left on the table. He didn't know what he was trying to say or how to express it if he did. "It's . . . been a strange day," he repeated.

"Perhaps all will seem normal by the light of a new day."

Did she truly believe that? Nothing would ever be normal again. Benjamin's true struggle was in deciding whether that was a good thing or a bad thing. He studied her by the tiny flame in the lamp, shadows dancing about her face and occasionally flickering in her eyes, causing light to sparkle in them like moonbeams.

She was his wife, for better or worse. Instinctively he sensed it would be for *better*, that they had done a good thing today, though it scared him, confused him. Suddenly he rose.

"Thank you for listening to me." He knew he had to leave, because everything inside him was telling him to stay.

"Where are you going?"

"To the barn." When her brow knit, he added lightly, "Don't feel sorry for me. Actually, it is I who feels twinges of guilt. I am going to the child-free haven of the barn, leaving you to fend off the hordes." He smiled down at her. "I think it is an even exchange."

PART FOUR

MAY 1835

CHAPTER 42

Quiet moments were not many in the tiny cabin, thus Elise had not been free to read her New Testament for some time. Having read only the first three books and part of the fourth, she wasn't even halfway through the book. There was so much more to discover, to learn. So one spring afternoon shortly after her wedding, while Oliver and Leah—easily the two most time-consuming of the children—napped and Isabel was entertaining herself with her doll, Elise took Hannah in her lap, sat in the rocking chair, and opened the book.

She turned to chapter seven of the book of John and began reading. Much of it was confusing, but the gist she caught was that there was much disputing among the people about who Jesus was. Some people, especially the leaders, were angry at Him and wanted to kill Him. She remembered all this from the previous books and knew, of course, that they eventually did kill Him. She marveled at why they would want to harm Him. Couldn't they see what kind of man He was, so good and decent? Even if they could not see that He was God, surely they should have known He meant only good for them.

She started the eighth chapter and was immediately taken up in the account of a woman caught in adultery. She'd already noticed how Christ freely associated with people whom the general society looked down upon—beggars, tax collectors, lepers, even harlots. Now the leaders who were angry at Christ were trying to use one of these people to trick Him. The leaders wanted to stone the adulteress as their law commanded. They wanted Jesus to break the law by freeing her.

Elise's heart raced, clearly picturing the scene. The accusers with stones in hands and leering, ugly looks on their faces. The woman, alone, trembling, knowing death was but minutes away. Jesus, caught in the middle.

Elise laughed with glee when she read Christ's answer. *He that is without sin among you, let him first cast a stone at her.*

But it was what she read next that truly moved her. *Woman, where are those thine accusers? Hath no man condemned thee? She said, No man, Lord. And Jesus said unto her, Neither do I condemn thee: go, and sin no more.*

Having felt so recently the powerful presence of God's love herself, Elise knew what the woman must have felt. She knew what it was like to feel so dirty and shamed she could hardly look at herself. Then here, to have someone look past all that, to see it, to see the filth—and to love you anyway!

Elise looked at the list she had been making of favorite passages. As soon as she found a pen, she would add this to it. In the meantime, she flipped back to others she had written down. It was a long list! But touching on only a handful, she saw one thing clearly stood out: God's love. She also had written a list of questions, and there were many of these as well, for a lot of what she read was confusing. Yet the reality of God's love rang through like the most pristine chime imaginable. Yes, men like Benjamin could study the Bible their whole lives, write books, and preach countless sermons. They could debate theology forever, but all that would never change the precious truth of *love.* Nor could years of study make it any more comprehensible. It was simple enough for a child to grasp, or a fallen dove such as she. Elise understood that the love of God was at the core of this thing called Christianity. All else was . . . well, she didn't know what it was. It was perhaps like the difference between a fabulous plantation manor and this tiny cabin. The cabin provided all one needed. The rest could come or go as long as one had the solid little room for basic warmth and protection.

Jesus could have showered the woman with all the reasons why what she had done was wrong. He certainly could have pointed out all the legal ramifications. But no, He had said simply, "Neither do I condemn thee. . . ."

When He added "Go and sin no more," Elise was certain the woman did just that, not because she had learned all the reasons why she was a sinner, but rather because this man Jesus loved her, and she could do no less.

Oddly, Elise thought of Benjamin. Yet the passage was obviously intended for her, an adulterer and a fornicator. How could it relate to a man like Benjamin who had been a religious man all his life, a spiritual leader who understood the Bible perfectly and no doubt had much of it memorized?

That was it, of course! In all the depths of Benjamin's study, and in the course of living according to Christian rules, had he perhaps forgotten the simplicity of love? Could that be why he was having trouble believing now? Was it possible that all he needed was to be reminded of these things? An excitement welled up in Elise. She reread the passage, and it confirmed to her that what she had come to know about God was indeed true. And she was certain Benjamin had not yet discovered it.

Her heart fairly galloping over this discovery, she rose from the rocker.

"Isabel, would you mind Hannah while I talk to your father?" She set Hannah on the bed as Isabel came over with her doll. The two immediately engaged in a game of some sort as Elise left the cabin.

Benjamin was in the field east of the cabin trying to plant corn. He'd borrowed a plow from John Hunter, hitched it to one of the horses, and was trying to make a furrow—not too successfully. The horse was not a plow horse and apparently was intent on making that clear to its inexperienced master, the results of which produced furrows that were rather askew. Micah walked alongside the horse, his hand firmly gripping the bridle.

Elise had paused before leaving the cabin to fill a pail with jerked venison and biscuits from breakfast along with a jug of fresh water. She was glad she had done so because Benjamin looked exhausted. She paused a moment to watch his progress. It was a fine day in early May with a clear blue sky overhead. The sun was unusually warm, evidenced by the streams of sweat Elise could see pouring off Benjamin's head, unimpeded by his wide-brimmed hat. His shirt was soaked through, clinging to his chest and shoulders.

Riding a circuit was a physically demanding job, and Benjamin had always given the impression of being quite fit. But he was pushing himself harder than ever trying to plant the field with corn. It was a couple of acres in size and had already been cleared by former residents, but the field had lain fallow for some time and was now covered with weeds and brush. Benjamin and Micah had been plowing for two days, and Benjamin had hoped to finish today, but there was still some ways to go.

Elise hesitated to interrupt the work. Telling of her discoveries could have waited until evening, but her enthusiasm had overtaken good sense.

By chance Benjamin paused in his work, removed his hat, and wiped a sleeve across his damp brow. In the process, he detected Elise's presence. He raised an arm and waved.

"Is everything all right?" he called.

"Everything's fine." She hadn't thought that her appearance might raise an alarm. "I thought you might like some refreshment." She held up the pail as if in confirmation.

Signaling for Micah to take the plow handles, Benjamin hiked across the clotted earth to where she stood at the edge of the field.

"You are making good progress," she said.

"John Hunter expected his plow back yesterday." He seemed discouraged. "The earth was much harder packed than I thought. I am determined to get this done today, though."

"Then forgive me for interrupting. I'll leave the pail and get back to the house."

"It was very kind of you to come."

"You've been working so hard." Shielding her eyes from the sun with a hand, she gazed out over the field. "I've never realized what an accomplishment it is to cultivate a raw piece of land."

He chuckled dryly. "At least it is for an inept ex-preacher. I've never even so much as planted a garden."

"Ex-preacher?" She couldn't help picking up on the phrase and being concerned. He'd never stated it in such final terms before.

"For the time being."

"You've decided to be a farmer, then?" She studied him momentarily with the same scrutiny she had given the field. In a way, he was like that field—hard and raw, in need of a tender but firm hand to work out the rough places. She doubted she could be that hand, yet she felt compelled to try because like the field, he was full of potential. His yield would be richer than the sweet corn, perhaps only to his family, perhaps still to the settlers who so needed a spiritual leader. How sad it would be if he let the earth of his life lie fallow. Yet he was doing just that.

"If I don't fail at that, too," he answered as if to mock her very thoughts.

Sighing, she said nothing in response.

"I best get back to work." He took the pail from her hand. "First, I wouldn't mind some of that water." Uncorking the jug, he lifted it to his lips and took a long drink. He then set jug and pail on the ground. He headed back toward the field, paused, and called over his shoulder, "Thank you, Elise."

She watched a few minutes longer. Benjamin sent Micah to the jug, and as the boy had a drink, Elise gave him a few words of encouragement before he, too, returned to the plow. Elise headed back to the cabin, uncertain what to do. She had been so enthusiastic about sharing her Bible reading with Benjamin, yet she could not see how her words would do any good. He had to find his own way. He'd be as wary as any man to be preached at, especially by a woman who was a complete novice in such matters. Perhaps if she found a way to approach him with a question.

He returned for supper appearing more discouraged than ever. The horse had gone lame, and since he feared risking the other horse, the rest of the work would have to be done by hand until he could get into Cooksburg and have Albert Petty, who was also a blacksmith, repair the animal's shoe.

Elise had worked hard to make a good meal. Nell Hunter had shown her how to make johnnycakes, a staple here where corn was the main food. It was amazing what a little salt and water added to cornmeal could do. The pot of soup to go with the johnnycakes was culled from a recipe in one of Rebekah's books. It had called for beef, but Elise used venison since that was all she had. It also called for a cut-up lemon for flavor but, since lemons in Texas were as rare as paved roads, she substituted a variety of spices she found in Rebekah's larder—summer savory, sweet marjoram, and a dash of pepper. Several onions completed the soup and made it fill the cabin with a delightful aroma.

Elise tried not to be disappointed when Benjamin hardly noticed her culinary success and merely picked at his meal. Micah, at least, had three bowls of soup and several johnnycakes.

Shortly after supper, the process of bedtime preparation for the children began. They had by now fallen into a nice routine, but since work in the field had begun, Elise insisted that Benjamin and Micah didn't need to help to the extent they had. Elise really managed quite well on her own with some help from Isabel. However, tonight Oliver was a little fussy and needed more attention than usual. But in just over an hour, the older children were in bed, and Oliver was settling down as Elise rocked him in the rocking chair.

Benjamin rose to take his leave. Sometimes after the children were in bed he might tarry a few minutes to converse with Elise, usually about problems with the children or plans for the next day. But most often he left the cabin immediately after the children were down. They had little other opportunity to talk during the day, so Elise knew if she was going to talk to him about what she had read, she must grasp the moment or see it lost to another day.

"Benjamin," she said as he reached for his coat on the hook by the door, "might you spare a moment? I . . . wanted to ask you something."

He turned back into the room and found a seat on the bench near the rocker. "What is it?" There was some concern in his tone.

"It's nothing ominous," she said awkwardly. "It is only that I have been reading the New Testament again, and I have a question."

"Elise, I don't feel in much of a position to be giving spiritual or theological guidance." He arched an eyebrow, as if expecting an argument.

"Oh . . . well, in that case . . ." she let her words trail away, hoping she appeared sufficiently disheartened.

"If it's a simple question," he relented, "I suppose I could see what I can offer."

She smiled, trying not to look too triumphant. "I'm sure it's simple. I'm so ignorant of these things that all my questions are simple. I was wondering about the story of the woman caught in adultery."

He nodded with a peculiar look in his eye as if to say, "Ah yes, she would pick up on that bit."

With a shrug she continued. "I thought it odd that Jesus, an upright, law-abiding man, not to mention His being God and all, would let the woman off so easily. Hadn't she committed a crime?"

"Christ is simply making the point that God is the judge. The book of James says, 'There is one lawgiver, who is able to save and to destroy: who art thou that judgest another?' " He paused, his brow arched. "That's what it says." His tone was almost apologetic. "Not that we should let all criminals free. But the Scriptures further state, 'For all have sinned and come short of the glory of God; Being justified freely by his grace through the redemption that is in Christ Jesus: Whom God hath set forth to be a propitiation through faith in his blood, to declare his righteousness for the remission of sins that are past, through the forbearance of God.' "

Elise marveled at how the words rolled as easily from Benjamin's lips as the water flowed down the little creek by the cabin.

Benjamin looked a bit bemused himself. Rubbing his chin, he added dryly, "I can quote more Scriptures if you like."

"You know a great deal."

"Yes, I do," he answered simply, ironically.

"It still seems rather amazing to me"—Elise steered the conversation back to the Scripture—"that after the terrible thing she did, Jesus only said, 'Neither do I condemn thee.' I suppose I shouldn't be surprised, knowing that I have God's forgiveness for my own mistakes. But still, it seems so easy."

"I've often thought so, too." Pausing, Benjamin stretched out his hands, studying his fingers that now bore blisters from plowing. His mouth hardened as he murmured, " 'The wages of sin is death.' "

"But we are not all dead, are we?" she asked quietly. "I think Jesus saw inside the woman's heart, as He saw inside my heart. He sees inside your heart, too, Benjamin—" She stopped as she realized her slip and that her little deception was now revealed.

"So all you had was an innocent question, eh?" Except for a slight quirk of the corner of his mouth, she could not tell if he was amused, angry, or indifferent.

She gave a sheepish shrug.

"Is this your subtle way of trying to preach to me?" There was only a hint of reproach in his voice.

"Well, I suppose I should get at least one chance to do so." She gave him a wily grin. "It will make us even."

Now both corners of his lips quirked, obviously in spite of himself. "All right. Let me have it."

"I wouldn't know how to preach even if I tried." She lowered her eyes toward the baby in her arms to organize her thoughts away from the intensity of his gaze. She noted absently how this child, more than the others, resembled Benjamin even at only two months. "I have no right to preach anyway. It's just that . . . I was so excited when I saw this story, and then I saw you so clearly in it. You know this Scripture, yet you refuse to accept Christ's simply spoken words, 'Neither do I condemn you.' But if He would forgive this woman caught in the act of sin, why wouldn't He forgive you?"

Benjamin lifted his gaze from where it had been fixed on the table. If there had been a shadow of amusement in his eyes before, it was gone now, replaced with a hot intensity. "Maybe God has looked inside my heart and found it very black."

"I don't believe that."

"After what I've told you?" Abruptly he jumped up, strode to where he kept his books, rifled through one, and withdrew a piece of paper. "Perhaps if you heard it in Rebekah's words." He dropped the paper on Elise's lap.

She picked it up. It was spread smooth now but had at one time been seriously crumpled. "I . . . don't feel right reading this."

"You are my wife now," he said. "You ought to know what you might be in for."

A thrill akin to fear sizzled through Elise, almost as if she had unknowingly unleashed a repressed demon in the man before her. He'd warned her before that he had his faults, and she'd personally seen some for herself. But lately they had seemed so distant that she had nearly forgotten about the harsh, judgmental man who had driven his wife away and to her death. She realized that except for brief glimpses, she really did not know what had gone on in the home of Rebekah Sinclair.

Now as she caught a flicker of that man still lingering within, she trembled at the power it could have. It was perhaps even more powerful and dangerous now that his faith was weakened. She forced herself to remember that whatever wars raged within Benjamin Sinclair, they *were* repressed by his own hand, by his own will.

"I'll read it but only because it might help me to understand things better." She unfolded the page. When she finished reading, she looked up, tears standing in her eyes. "She never once accused you, Benjamin."

"She wouldn't, would she?"

"No, I suppose not," she answered reluctantly. It wasn't hard to read between the lines and to put that together with the man Elise had known before coming to this cabin one rainy day. No question about it, Benjamin had been a hard man. Hard as glass. And now he was a broken man, shattered like a pane on a window. "How long will you punish yourself, Benjamin? Certainly you know God doesn't want to punish you. He loves you."

"It's not that simple." He went on, his voice as harsh as brimstone. "God is an avenging god, a god of judgment and punishment. Do you think because I feel sorry for what has happened it makes it all right?"

"Yes."

"That is only for children and for women forced to do immoral things against their will." He glared at her.

She realized the bitter passion she had seen in his eyes was not directed at her but rather at himself. "God is a god of love!" She reached down and grabbed the New Testament from where she had laid it on the floor next to the rocker. "It says it here." She waved the book in his face.

He backed off, as if the book were a snake.

Her voice softened. "Benjamin, I think you've forgotten, if you ever really knew, just what kind of god you have served all your life. But maybe it was just easier for you to perform righteous acts in order to gain acceptance from God."

"Even the adulterous woman had to do something," he countered. " 'Go and sin no more,' Jesus told her."

"I don't think so." As she spoke, his brow arched as if daring her, a mere spiritual babe, to debate him, a biblical scholar. But she had come this far, had already risked his wrath, and he had done no more than glare at her. She forged ahead. "I'm no scholar. I can only figure things out by what I read in God's Book here. A lot of it is very confusing, but one thing is clear. Christ did not make people perform deeds in order to receive absolution. Christ told the woman He didn't condemn her *before* He told her to go and sin no more. He forgave her before she did anything. That's the kind of god Christ is!"

Benjamin leaned back, folding his arms across his chest. "You make a good argument," he said grudgingly. "But this never had anything to do with God's forgiveness."

"It has to do with your *accepting* His forgiveness?" Her words were part question, part statement.

"It's not that simple!" he practically growled, then lurched to his feet.

"I think it is."

"You know nothing about it," he retorted, towering over her now, seeming more ominous than ever.

"Is there a different law for you, Benjamin? For the perfect, holy, exemplary preacher who makes a mistake?" She spoke levelly, trying to ignore the strength of his formidable presence.

"You know nothing of these things!" There was an edge of warning in his tone. "Stick to the gentle little faith you have found and quit tampering with that about which you are ignorant." She could tell he was expending great effort not to shout.

"Well, it is simple. I think you have just gotten too big for your holy britches, Benjamin Sinclair!" Her voice rose, but she kept it under control when Oliver stirred.

With a loud "Harrumph!" he stalked to the door and left the cabin.

CHAPTER 43

ELISE AND BENJAMIN DID NOT speak at all the day after that, and in the days that followed, conversations were brief, to the point, and dealt only with necessities. Elise made no attempt to return to the previous conversation, nor did Benjamin give her any chance to do so.

Perhaps she meant well, but she would never understand the bitter angst in Benjamin's heart. Benjamin himself hardly understood it, and he was growing sick with grappling with it. Not that he was ready to let it go, even if some nagging little part of him knew that's all he had to do.

Instead, he threw himself into the field work with practically the same passion he'd once applied to the whitened fields of spiritual harvest. With the horse lame, he finished plowing without it. Even with Micah steering the plow, it was backbreaking, grueling labor. It took two more days to finish the job.

He had planned to send Micah back to the Hunters with the plow when they finished and have him stop in Cooksburg to get the lame horse shod. By leaving at first light and riding briskly, it was possible to make the round trip in a day. However, Benjamin changed his mind, deciding he needed to get away himself. He also decided he would set a more leisurely pace. Elise had agreed it was a good idea not to push himself, for he'd been working so hard. It rather surprised Benjamin that she made no protests at all to his being gone for two days. When Rebekah had been alive, he could not recall a time he left without her making many protests. He couldn't decide if this was good or bad. Had Rebekah cared too much and Elise not enough? Certainly the way he'd been acting lately he could well fathom that Elise did not want him around.

Benjamin left after breakfast the next day. He rode the good horse and led the lame horse, after packing the plow and a few supplies on it. The day was fine despite a chill in the air and a stiff breeze out of the west. The sky was a pristine blue, and it made him think how much wider and clearer it was in Texas than it had ever been in Boston. Sometimes he felt this new land was out to crush him—perhaps it already had. He should hate it, but he could not deny that it was a good land, open and free and full of promise. Many men had come here fleeing their pasts. Perhaps he could do so, too.

Sucking in a breath of the crisp air, pungent with the scents of grass and dust and sweet flowery fragrances, he was reminded of the first time he had ridden his circuit. What an exhilarating experience that had been! Oh, the guilt he had felt enjoying it so! He'd felt made for that job, that ministry.

That initial exhilaration was now replaced with a sharp pang of regret. But it was foolish to still long for his old ministry. It was probably only a longing after adventure and excitement he was feeling. He'd never wanted to admit how much like Haden he was, but maybe it was time he did.

He reached Cooksburg just after midday. Albert Petty fixed up the horse in no time, then gave Benjamin a meal of stew and biscuits. Benjamin turned down an offer of a bed for the night, saying he wanted to get a few more hours of travel in before night. In truth, he was looking forward to camping on the trail.

Though he feared being alone with his thoughts, he was also becoming more and more shy of people. He cringed at the looks of pity and smugness and outright contempt. Some of the people held his past ministry against him. He was certain they were thinking, *"Oh, how the mighty has fallen!"*

Others, the more self-righteous of the lot, held his present situation against him. They were still ready to expel him from the church, even if he had married the woman they believed he had been living in sin with.

If he cared at all about pleasing these people, he would have been hard-pressed to do so. A thought pierced his mind like the prick of a blade. Was that how they had felt when he had been their minister? The weight of the law he had placed upon them must have been staggering. He had criticized them if they had no Bible in their homes. If they did have a Bible in their homes, he judged them because they did not read it. If they read it, he exhorted them to read it more. Did they pray? If so, it wasn't for long enough. Did they partake of ardent spirits or tobacco? How could they and call themselves Christians? Did they use profanity? Well, *darn* was not better than *damn*. Did they make mistakes? Then repent!

Benjamin snorted derisively. What a load of guilt and judgment he had heaped upon them! He had believed faith was all in performance. He had lived it, too. "Faith without works is dead" had been his watchword. But there was another side to it. One that he had ignored. "Justified by faith without the deeds of the law." Scriptures suddenly bombarded his mind. He knew them by heart, of course. He saw now what he had never seen before. He supposed Elise was right in saying that he had needed works because they came easier for him. Now that the foundation of works had crumbled in his life, he could hardly function—not spiritually or in any other way.

The last thing he wanted now was to grapple with spiritual issues. Elise had been right about another thing—he knew far too much. He knew it all. Yet he knew *nothing* at all!

Forcing his mind from this direction, he made himself focus on his surroundings. He willed himself to drink in the keen, sharp relief of trees bursting with the pale green of new growth. John Hunter had once tried to educate Benjamin on the many species to be found here, but Benjamin had brushed aside the man's attempt as frivolous. He wished he knew some of the names now, for it would provide a marvelous distraction.

The tree with the tiny greenish flower and the gray-brown trunk was surely hickory. White hickory, John had called it. He'd said the seed of the nut was edible. Made good coffee when the real thing couldn't be found, and the wood was good for smoking hams.

That low spindly tree was mesquite. And, of course, there was oak. Benjamin saw a large one draped in a pale green veil of Spanish moss. Whether out of old habit or from some real inner sense, Benjamin felt awed by the majesty of a God who could create such wonders.

Well, he'd never denied God's existence. . . .

There you go again, Benjamin. You can't seem to escape it.

He rode on. A hawk soared overhead. Then his mount grew restive. Pausing, Benjamin peered through the trees and tall grass, concerned there might be some wild animal near. Horses usually sensed such things first. But he saw nothing. The gentle waving of the grass appeared undisturbed. The trees rustled a bit in the breeze, but that was all.

He made camp shortly before sundown at the foot of a small grove of oak trees. He could hear a creek close by bubbling over rocks, probably on its way to meet the Brazos. Though he had jerky, he decided to try to catch fresh fish for supper. But getting down to the creek proved to be tricky, having to negotiate a slippery ten-foot bank.

Even if he didn't catch a thing, the effort was well worth it just for taking in the scenery along the creek. When was the last time he had sat on the bank of a stream and done nothing more than *look*? When his stomach began growling, he took the rod he had fashioned from a hickory branch, tied a line to it, baited it with worms dug from the edge of the creek, and plunged it into the water.

The sun was fully down by the time he returned to his campsite, two good-sized trout in hand. He built a fire, and lacking the proper cooking equipment, he speared the fish on sticks and roasted them over the fire. A pot of coffee and a few of Elise's johnnycakes completed the meal. Sitting back against the trunk of an oak, he ate one fish with his fingers while it still sizzled. The other he placed between two johnnycakes. His mouth was open, poised to take a bite when one of the horses snorted and both animals moved restlessly. Putting down his meal, he rose and ensured they were hobbled securely. Again he peered into the woods and brush but saw nothing in the dark.

Oddly, he wasn't afraid. Perhaps his appreciation of nature had dulled his ability to fear that which was so beautiful. Of course, such thinking was foolishness in the wilderness. There were two sides to such beauty, just as with everything else. He took his musket and powder horn from the saddle and carried them back to camp.

He was settling down once again to his meal when he heard a twig snap. An instant later company appeared in the clearing of his campsite. Indians. Three of them.

Now fear gripped him. Meeting a handful of Indians protected by a crowd of fifty whites was far different than doing so alone in the wilds. He immediately recognized the tallest of the trio as the leader of the group that had come to the camp meeting. Again they were far from their usual home along the coast. No doubt they had come north in search of game after a sparse winter. Benjamin hoped that was the case and they would be satisfied with *game*. He couldn't forget rumors of cannibalism. And since that earlier encounter, he'd heard of other gruesome practices of the fierce and primitive Karankawas.

Shuddering, Benjamin resisted an urge to raise his rifle and start shooting. Instead, he sat very still, appearing as calm as he could.

"Good evening," he said levelly, remembering that the tall man spoke some English. Maybe they weren't as savage as he'd heard.

"You preacher man," said the tall Indian.

"Yes . . . yes . . . I suppose so." Benjamin's throat was dry. "Will you join me for supper?" Anything to get them to sit so they didn't seem so tall and ominous.

"We have meat." He held up two rabbits. One of his companions also had a rabbit.

"Then you are welcome to use my fire."

The three conferred briefly then the tall one nodded, but first they skinned and dressed their game. When they finished, they toasted the rabbit flesh with sticks as Benjamin had his fish. The smell was pleasant, rolling away images of vicious cannibal rites.

When they offered Benjamin some meat, he took it, though he was full from his own meal. He shared his coffee and johnnycakes with them. They smacked their lips over the cakes, grinning appreciatively.

"Good!" said the spokesman. "You make?"

"No, my wife made them, but she will be happy to know you liked them." Benjamin smiled as he thought of Elise's reaction when he would tell her what a hit her cakes had been. Perhaps they would even save his life.

When every scrap of food was gone—Benjamin would have nothing, not even coffee for breakfast in the morning—the Indians belched contentedly and sat back against nearby rocks. Benjamin wondered what would happen next. Were they planning to sleep in his camp? At least they must be too full to want white man for dessert.

They had spoken little during the meal. Introductions had been made, but Benjamin could not pronounce the names of his guests, and they found it no easier to say his name. The leader settled for calling Benjamin "Ben" and was not himself offended when Benjamin shortened his long name down to "Kay." The tall Kay had only a passing command of English, which did not allow for much in the way of conversation. Thus Benjamin was surprised when the man tackled a very difficult topic.

"You tell about Jesus-god," he said. "Who you talk about at big meeting."

"What?" Benjamin was more nonplussed at this than he had been by the arrival of the supposed cannibals.

"Jesus-god very powerful. Want to know more."

Benjamin stared in stunned silence. Time was he would have been ecstatic to have someone ask to know more about God. He had a grand speech made up for just such an occasion, punctuated with all the appropriate salvation Scriptures.

"Well, I . . ."

"You tell like you did before!"

By the sound of Kay's voice Benjamin wondered if he had a choice. *Wonderful!* he thought wryly. *Now that my life may depend upon it, the words stick in my throat.* He rubbed the rough stubble on his chin, wondering if Kay actually wanted him to jump up and begin shouting and exhorting the Word of God. He still remembered the sermon he preached that day. It had been one of his finest. He could belt it out now just as flawlessly, satisfying the Indians and perhaps saving his own neck.

"I . . . can't," Benjamin croaked.

"Why can't?" Kay leaned forward, his dark eyes intense under a creased brow. "This Jesus-god only for white man?"

"It's not that. . . ." Benjamin sighed. Here was a man eager, it appeared, for spiritual teaching, and Benjamin could say nothing. "Jesus is for all men, Kay."

"Karankawa too?"

"Yes, of course."

"What I do for this god?"

"Do?" Benjamin scratched his head. He wasn't going to get a reprieve. "Well, you have to believe in Him and repent of your sins."

"Sin? What that?"

"The bad things you do. You must change your ways."

"Or Jesus-god throw me in fire like you said? He cook me?"

"Something like that," Benjamin said without much conviction in his voice. It all sounded rather bizarre given Kay's simple interpretation.

"I don't want to burn," reiterated Kay.

"Then you must repent. . . ."

Suddenly Benjamin thought of his conversation with Elise and of Jesus' words to the woman caught in adultery. *"Neither do I condemn thee."* It was that simple. As simple as love. Of course there was a place for repentance, but first there is love. Simple enough for a child, simple enough for an adulteress, simple enough for a prostitute. Simple enough for a savage Indian.

"Listen here, Kay." Benjamin now fixed his own gaze, growing with intensity, on the Indian. "I'm going to tell you something I left out before. It's very important. God loves you, Kay. You don't have to do anything to have His love. It's always been there."

"No fire?"

Benjamin shook his head.

Kay added skeptically, "This love not very powerful."

"You are wrong there, Kay. It is the most powerful thing there ever was." Smiling, Benjamin went on to tell his listener about the power of God's love. " 'For God so loved the world that he gave his only begotten Son that whosoever believeth in Him should not perish but have everlasting life.' "

The Karankawas left a few minutes later. Benjamin wasn't certain Kay ever really grasped much about "Jesus-god." Maybe he'd have another chance someday to talk to the Indian, but for now Benjamin was certain the encounter had been more for his sake than for Kay's. Long after the Indians had departed, Benjamin continued to think about this God of love. Everything Elise had said was right.

" 'For thou desirest not sacrifice, else would I give it: thou delightest not in burnt offering. The sacrifices of God are a broken spirit: a broken and a contrite heart, O God, thou wilt not despise.' "

Benjamin had not thought of that psalm in a long time. But then, in the past he'd pretty much ignored most of the references of that sort. For a proud man, living by works had been far easier than being broken and contrite. "Holy britches" indeed! He smiled as he thought of Elise's impassioned words.

But he was broken now, no doubt of it. Broken as only a man can be who has watched his weaknesses destroy others. Incredibly, God did not despise him. He never had. Benjamin had once told Elise he feared God no longer believed in him, but that had never been the case. Of course he was unworthy of God's love. He *never* had been worthy, not even as a so-called flawless preacher. The only difference between now and then was that he now realized the unequivocal truth of his unworthiness. He had no more been able to earn God's love and acceptance as a devoted preacher than he was able to do so as a failed husband and father.

"Neither do I condemn you."

Dear God, it's true! You don't condemn me. The words seared his heart as never before. The truth became clear. If God didn't condemn him, then who was he to condemn himself? He had never let himself think about this before. It would have been too easy.

Simple enough for a child, an adulteress, a prostitute, a savage. Simple enough for a preacher wearing "holy britches"!

Weeping, Benjamin sat before the fading embers of his campfire and made peace with God, and then with himself.

CHAPTER 44

THE LITTLE CABIN IN ITS pleasant clearing made an inviting picture. Benjamin felt more enthusiastic about returning home than he had in months. He was anticipating sharing with Elise his discoveries out on the trail.

As if to make his homecoming perfect, Elise opened the cabin door as he rode into the yard and waved a greeting. Had she also been anticipating his return? No doubt, with a house full of demanding children. But the smile on her face was not haggard; in fact, she looked quite fresh and beautiful.

"You're back early," she said as he dismounted.

"Yes." He smiled awkwardly, realizing he was happier to see her than he had a right to be. "I'll take care of the horses and be right in."

Ten minutes later, he was ensconced in the cozy warmth of his home. Noisy children were everywhere, for which Elise apologized. It was late afternoon and naps were over and tummies were getting hungry for supper. But Benjamin took it all in with a kind of zest he'd never been able to feel before. He'd always considered his children a burden. He'd felt the heavy responsibility of rearing them to godliness. Now he experienced a side effect of his own personal release from the law. He could actually enjoy his children, knowing perfectionism was no longer required of him.

He bent down and kissed Isabel's cheek. She looked up at him shyly but with a little twinkle in her pale eyes. Leah, not wanting to be left out, crawled up to him and squawked, tugging at his leg until he picked her up and kissed her cheek also. Then, with Leah balanced on his hip, he went to the rocking chair where Hannah was sitting and kissed the top of her head. Only as he straightened did he realize Elise was watching him.

"I can probably count on one hand how many times I have kissed my children," he both explained and apologized.

"They appreciate it." She was kneading dough on a board at the table. As she spoke, a strand of her dark hair fell in her eyes. Tucking it back in place, she smudged flour on her nose.

He swallowed hard, trying not to think about how that silly smudge seemed to make his heart race. His experience on the trail showed him his need to not be imprisoned by his past any longer, but there were still some things he could not forget. He could not forget Rebekah, nor could he forget that he had made an agreement with Elise regarding their marriage, which he was bound to honor.

Still holding Leah, he went to the cradle where Oliver cooed and gurgled contentedly. "They all seem so healthy and happy."

"Even Hannah is better." Elise finished with the dough, placed it in a bowl, covered it with a cloth, and set it by the hearth. Wiping her hands, she turned back to Benjamin. "I've almost forgotten, but we have a little surprise for you."

He cocked a brow. "A pleasant one I hope." But he couldn't imagine anything else in the idyllic setting his home had become.

"I think you'll be pleased."

She came near him, and as she reached for Leah, he caught the scent of lilacs.

"Come here, Leah," she said and took the child from his arms. Moving a couple of feet away, she instructed, "Kneel down, Benjamin." When he complied, she set Leah on her feet. The child wobbled a bit and twisted around, her arms reaching for Elise's neck. "Come on, Leah, show your papa what you can do. Benjamin, why don't you call her?"

Discerning what was about to take place, Benjamin held out his arms. "Come to me, Leah." He tried to make his voice enticing and sweet, though it came out more like a rusty creak.

Leah looked back and forth between Elise and Benjamin, then suddenly seemed to realize she was the center of attention, a place she liked very much to be in.

"Come, Leah," Benjamin encouraged.

"Show your papa," Elise prompted.

For a brief moment it appeared as if Leah might not be able to propel those chubby legs, then, like a barroom drunk, she tottered forward. One step . . . two steps . . . three steps, finally careening into Benjamin's outstretched arms.

Benjamin caught her with a laughing whoop. "You did it! That is wonderful, sweetheart!"

Leah giggled. "Mo! Mo!"

Benjamin set her on her feet again, and Leah reversed the procedure until she toppled into Elise's arms. Both adults rose, Elise holding Leah and swinging her gaily.

"She took her first steps last night," Elise said. "She was sitting on the floor and just got up and started walking. She took two steps, then suddenly realized she was doing something new, lost her concentration, and tumbled to the floor. She wouldn't try again all day today, so I wasn't certain she'd do it."

"But she did." Benjamin's grin faded slightly. "I have never been on hand to watch my children's first steps—their first anything, for that matter."

"Well, there's Oliver yet to give you that experience."

"And Hannah."

Now Elise's mirth dimmed. "I hope so."

"Now that she is better, it will only be a matter of time." He knew how this weighed on Elise and glanced at the child as if to confirm his prognosis. She was breathing easier than he had ever seen her, but she was still pale. Her curly, dark brown hair framed delicate, frail features. Her brown eyes, large as a doe's, were shadowed yet with dark rings.

"I pray for that every day," Elise responded.

"I will also."

She had turned to continue supper preparations, but with his statement, she abruptly swung back. "You?" She tittered with embarrassment over how her query must have sounded. "It's just that . . ."

She gave him a frank scrutiny now that made him want to squirm, though he forced himself to remain still.

"I see it now," she added. "Something has happened, hasn't it?"

"Yes." He smiled. "But I'd like everyone to be here when I tell it." He glanced around the cabin. "Where is Micah?"

"Working in the field."

"Really?"

"Yes. He's been harrowing the dirt and doing a decent job at it, too."

"Well, I'll be . . ." He'd had to bribe and threaten Micah to work on the field earlier. Maybe it wasn't the work that had been distasteful to Micah but rather the man with whom he had been forced to work.

It was hard to wait, but Benjamin was more determined than ever that Micah hear of his father's experience. Perhaps if Benjamin confessed his mistakes and God's loving acceptance to Micah, it would be the thing to finally reach his son. Thus Benjamin held his tongue until the boy came into the cabin an hour later. He was sunburnt from working outdoors, but the work had toughened him up considerably. He was clean, his slicked-back wet hair indicating he had probably taken a dip in the creek before coming in for supper. His tall, lanky frame was filling out with sinewy muscles, which were emphasized by his shirt, which was a couple sizes too small. He'd grown so much his trousers ended at least three inches above his ankles. He looked several years past thirteen, both in size and in the cool aspect of his expression. Not for the first time, Benjamin felt daunted by his own son.

Micah acknowledged his father's greeting with a mere grunt. He then took a leftover johnnycake and sat at the table gnawing at it to tide him over until supper.

Benjamin took a breath before speaking, then lost his nerve and remained silent. He repeated this ritual three more times before finding his courage, reminding himself that he had never been one to shy away from a challenge—and Micah was becoming the greatest challenge of his life.

"I had quite an interesting trip," he said lamely, but at least it was a start.

"I'm dying to hear," Elise said gamely.

Benjamin opened his mouth, but before he could get any words out Micah lurched to his feet.

"I'm going out to . . ." Micah faltered, clearly with no immediate reason to make an exit. Then he grabbed the water bucket. "To get water." He headed toward the door.

"Micah, I want you to hear this." Benjamin's voice held a quality of desperation.

"I don't care to." Micah's voice was cold as he grasped the door latch.

"Why do you have to be so difficult?" Benjamin felt his old anger and frustration return. He wanted to strike the boy. Instead, he curled his fingers so tightly around the arm of the rocker where he sat that his hand began to cramp. "Stay, Micah, and hear me out."

"Are you gonna make me? Maybe take me behind the barn if I don't?" sneered the boy.

"I've been trying to give you a little slack, boy. The least you can do is the same for me. We've both got to live in this house. We ought to attempt to do so as peaceably as possible."

"Who says I have to live here?" Micah retorted. "I can take care of myself. Maybe I'll go find Uncle Haden—"

"If Haden had wanted you, he would have taken you before!" The words were out before Benjamin could rein them back. He regretted them the instant they had been leveled, but he couldn't apologize for them because they were true.

"I'll make it on my own then," Micah intoned coolly.

"You're a child. You'd perish out there," Benjamin shot back.

"I'd take my chances."

Benjamin jumped up. "I'm sick to death of your attitude!"

"I wish you would—" Micah stopped, perhaps sensing that actually stating his wish would be more of a risk than even he was willing to take. His jaw tightening, the muscles working furiously, he glared at his father. "I'm just gonna get water. If you wanna make me stay—"

"Never mind!" The words came through gritted teeth. Benjamin was shaking inside with fury and defeat. He hated that Micah's threat had taken hold. But if it took concession to keep Micah at home, then there seemed nothing else for it. "Get the water." He spoke with the evenness of a sharp blade.

Micah left, and Benjamin slumped back in the rocker, letting his head loll miserably in his hands. In a moment, Elise was at his side, a slim hand on his shoulder.

"I'm so sorry," she murmured.

He sliced his fingers through his hair. "Like in a battle," he grunted, "defeats must be taken with the victories."

"Would you care to tell me about your victories?"

He looked up at her, and his heart clenched. He'd seldom felt a greater need, and here she was to fill it for him and encourage him—just like a real wife. As much as he wanted to reach out and draw her to him, he also wanted to push her away. He feared needing her too much. There were just too many reasons why he couldn't, why he shouldn't. But, oh, how he ached with need!

"Believe it or not," he said dryly, with enough cynicism to counter his neediness, "while I was away, I finally made my peace with God and with myself."

She smiled sadly, seeming to truly understand his conflicted emotions. "Tell me about it."

"Not now. Maybe some other time."

She dropped to her knees before him so as to look directly at him. "Benjamin, I think now is the time you most need to talk about it. It will be good for you to remember a victory."

Taking a steadying breath, he told her everything that had happened on the trail, and as she predicted, remembering was a kind of healing balm. So was her rejoicing with him and even her tears of joy. He wept also when Isabel came close to listen to him, and when he finished, she laid her little hand on his arm and offered him a small smile, the first he had seen in a long time.

Impulsively he embraced both Isabel and Elise, his tears dampening their hair, his need receding from a stabbing ache to a whisper of hope.

CHAPTER 45

BENJAMIN GAINED GREAT SATISFACTION IN watching the corn sprout in his field. By early June it was a foot high. If all went well—there were many crop hazards along the way—he'd have enough grain come fall to feed his family for the year. Caring for the crop would keep him sufficiently occupied until then, too. That, and hunting and chopping wood and maintaining the cabin. He also thought he ought to build an addition to the cabin. Sleeping in the barn in spring and summer was bad enough—come winter it would be intolerable.

He definitely had his work cut out. One afternoon while most of the children were napping, he took the notebook in which he used to write his sermons, found a blank page and, sitting at the table, began sketching a rough drawing of a possible addition.

Yes, he could keep quite busy caring for the needs of his family. And he thought he could be fairly content doing only that. Perhaps that was what he was meant to do after all. It could well be that his ministry had failed, in part at least, because he had never truly heard the call of God in the first place. Perhaps he had only convinced himself that he had because he had desired the glory and sense of power the ministry had offered.

Now he felt he could be quite content indeed as a nondescript, obscure farmer.

Almost.

He wondered if he could ever be truly content doing anything until he was certain it was time to close the door on his ministry. The only way to know that was to step back into the waters of ministry. He supposed he wouldn't have to plunge in headfirst, though that might be in his nature, but even the thought of merely getting his toes wet was a bit frightening. It would mean facing his flock again, humbling himself before them, confessing his failures—which would make any proud man, even a broken man, cringe.

Before he did anything, though, he decided to take the problem to Elise. He was finding great succor in her gentle wisdom, her unassuming simplicity. They'd had many discussions about life since his encounter with the Indians and his personal renewal. Elise had a way of taking Scriptures that theologians had debated for years and distilling them down to their simplest truths. In matters of life in general, she had the same uncanny knack. He marveled in watching her with the children as she imparted simple truths to them in a natural, loving way.

Too bad Micah seemed not to benefit from Elise's homey teaching. He seemed too scarred from Benjamin's years of trying to hammer truth into the boy to listen to much of anything these days. If Benjamin's new humility touched the boy at all, he didn't show it.

Benjamin hadn't heard Elise approach. He smelled the lilac first. She had found a way to crush the leaves of wild lilac and mix them in her soap with quite pleasant results.

"I didn't want to disturb you," she said quietly.

"I don't mind at all. In fact, I was about to seek you out."

"Truly?"

"Please sit." He gestured toward the place next to him on the bench so they could both look at the drawing. She seldom was ever this close to him. When her shoulder brushed his and the fragrance of lilac became nearly intoxicating, he decided it wasn't such a good idea after all. But it was too late to do anything about it.

"Are you thinking about building on to the cabin?" she asked, nodding toward the drawing.

"Yes. Now that the corn is planted, I believe there will be time to get it done before winter. What do you think?" He tapped the drawing with a finger. "I've tried to make it simple. I'll cut a door into the existing north wall of the cabin. A loft would fit nicely along the rest of the wall in the main cabin. By keeping the work confined to one area we can do all the bracing and such at once." He paused, his brow quirking with skepticism at his own words. "The only thing I have ever built is part of that barn out there, and it leaks like a sieve when it rains. A stout wind—of which I've heard Texas is famous, though I've not seen a tornado yet—would doubtless blow it down."

"Perhaps John Hunter will help you," she suggested.

"He's done so much for me already, and I have so little to give him in return."

"I've never had the impression John expected anything for his help."

"You are right, of course." Leaning his elbows on the table, he propped his chin thoughtfully in his hands. "I want to make this cabin sturdy so that it will stand for a long time."

"May I ask something? It may not be any of my business, but . . ." Her voice faltered.

He sensed her awkwardness, which most often occurred when she was about to cross into the gray areas their peculiar marriage had made for them. He nodded an encouragement for her to continue.

"Do you have a claim on this land or does your church?" she asked.

He chuckled dryly. "Actually, both I and the man before me were merely squatters. Because of the Mexican laws, the Methodist Church certainly could make no claim. Nor would ministers of that church, since it would mean converting to Catholicism to receive the prescribed league and labor."

"League and labor? I've heard of that, but what exactly is it?"

"A labor amounts to 177 acres, and by the terms of the grant would be farmland. A league is about 4,500 acres of grazing land for cattle raising."

"That is a lot of land." She was clearly impressed.

"No wonder so many were willing to convert." He smiled, remembering the issue he had made of this in the past. "I used to think Catholicism was among the worst apostasies imaginable."

"Used to?"

"I talked to Father Murphy a bit on our wedding day and came to the conclusion that he was indeed a Christian man. I still disagree with many doctrines and practices of the Catholic Church, but perhaps there are some godly people among them after all. Of course, there is disagreement among the Protestant denominations also. Ah, Elise, you are fortunate to be innocent of all this sectarianism in the church. And I am fortunate to have had you to steer me toward what is truly important about faith." He turned, focusing an earnest gaze upon her. "Fortunate indeed," he breathed. Then, rather nervously, he jabbed his finger back at the sketch. "Well, I see the point you were trying to make about the wisdom of building more permanently upon land that does not belong to me. Yet . . . if I know nothing else, I know this is where I wish to put down my roots." Suddenly a new concern struck him. "But I haven't asked you . . ."

"You don't need to—"

"Yes, I do!" His eyes darkened with intensity. "I dragged Rebekah out here against her will. I never *asked*. I *told* her it was God's will, and that was that. I won't make that mistake again—at least I want to try to be better this time. We may not have a true marriage . . . in every sense, but what we have . . . well, I want it to be different from my first marriage. I want you to be happy, content. What do you think of Texas?"

"You are forgetting, Benjamin, that I was dragged here against my will as a slave. But unlike Rebekah, I had nothing in my past to long for."

"Nothing?"

She swallowed and momentarily looked away from him. "Nothing." Swinging her gaze back to him, she added, "You have given me my life back, Benjamin. You have made me happy just by taking me and my daughter in. I ask for no more."

"You deserve more."

"Don't you see? For a woman it is enough to have her home and family around her. It matters not in what place they are as long as they are with her."

"It wasn't enough for Rebekah."

"Rebekah didn't have you, did she? Not really." Elise's tone was quiet and gentle, absent of all rebuke.

"Neither do you," he murmured. "Not really."

"But I did not expect to. There's a big difference."

Feeling suddenly restless, Benjamin jumped up and strode to the window across the room. The rawhide drape was pulled back to let in the June sunshine. A slight breeze touched his face. He inhaled a deep breath. He had no right to feel so good about life. And no matter how lavish the grace of God, he would always feel his inadequacy.

Mistaking him, she said quickly, "I'm sorry, Benjamin. I didn't mean to stir up difficult issues."

He turned, confusion momentarily knitting his brow, then he realized she had misunderstood him. "You haven't. But I realize I have much to learn about women, about wives. That is why I want to include you in my decisions. It is the one thing I *have* learned."

"Then far be it for me to stand in the way of progress."

He noted by her smile and the way the corners of her eyes crinkled mischievously that she was teasing him.

He came back to the table and sat, but this time on the bench opposite her, so he could look at her more easily, he told himself. "I would like to make my home in Texas. It is a good land now, but when we break from Mexico, it will become a land full of possibilities. I want to be part of that. If this suits you, then my only ambivalence comes in just *how* I will be part of Texas. Farmer, cattleman, teacher . . . or Methodist minister." His chest tightened just saying the word *minister*. Was it because he could not let go of a lost dream, or because he feared it was a dream yet to be fulfilled? "I need help," he confessed. "The ministry was all I knew, all I wanted. It was everything to me, and I sacrificed everything for it. I am not willing to do that again. I won't do that again."

"I don't think God expects you to."

"I am not sure I know how to find a balance, and that frightens me."

"Is that the only thing keeping you from it?"

His head jerked up, taken aback. He hadn't quite thought of it like that. "Yes, I think it is. That and a complete sense of inadequacy."

"Well, if you want my opinion . . ." Pausing, she searched him with her eyes, and when he nodded she went on, but rather shyly, still with little concept of the power of her simple wisdom. "When Jesus came to earth, all logic should have led Him to the religious and political leaders for his support—you know, the priests and the Pharisees and the Saddu—oh, I can never remember that one."

"Sadducees," he offered.

"Yes, them. Anyway, He didn't go to any of the leaders. Instead He went to fishermen and such. Simple men. Simon Peter was a perfect example. I really like him. Not only was he simple and uneducated, he was also constantly making mistakes, just as we all do. But it was he, not the high priest, whatever-his-name-was, who Jesus made the head of his church."

Benjamin shook his head in awe at the clarity of the point she was making. "In the past I always dismissed Peter because I could not understand him, nor Christ's choice of him."

"He was a perfect leader because he knew what it meant to make mistakes, to be human," she suggested with quiet intensity.

A grin spread across his face. "That's it, of course! Jesus said, 'My grace is sufficient for thee: for my strength is made perfect in weakness.' "

"Yes," she said, "and that is why He chose the men He chose. And that is why I think He might choose you, Benjamin."

"I am definitely the weakest of the lot!"

"Oh . . . I didn't mean . . ." she reddened, as though realizing her words could be taken as an insult.

He took her hands reassuringly in his. "Elise . . ." Her name rolled off his tongue like a prayer. As his eyes met hers, her unlikely past flickered through his mind, and he knew she, too, had been used of God. For only God could have seen past the filth of her life to the precious jewel within. Only God would have had the patience and love to coax it to the surface. Only God could have known how profoundly she would affect Benjamin's life and those of his children. Only God would have known that this fallen angel was in fact a true angel.

"What, Benjamin?" she breathed. Her hand was trembling a little in his.

"I was just thinking about what a gift you have been to this household . . . to me."

"Oh, goodness!" she attempted a dismissive laugh, but her face still reddened, both with embarrassment and with pleasure. "So . . ." Her voice squeaked over the word, and she paused nervously to clear her throat. "Do you know what you will do, then?"

"I'm going to see if these Texians want a flawed, bruised, and rather worse-for-the-wear man to lead them."

CHAPTER 46

MICAH, I AM SURE YOUR mother would have wanted you to have lessons." Elise thrust the primer under the boy's nose. "Or else she wouldn't have brought this all the way from Boston."

"My ma wanted a lot of things she didn't get," Micah retorted.

"Don't be disrespectful of your mother!" Elise scolded firmly.

"I ain't being disrespectful of her . . . or you either," he added quickly.

He didn't have to say where his disrespect was aimed. It was clear enough he blamed only one person for the fact that Rebekah Sinclair would never realize any of her dreams or desires. But Elise was determined that, if nothing else, she was not going to allow Rebekah's children to be ignorant or illiterate. Elise was barely literate herself—education of female members of southern gentry was discouraged—but she could read, and she would expect no less from her—that is, Rebekah's—children.

"Now you open that primer, Micah," Elise ordered, "and start to read. Isabel, you follow along."

Actually Micah was quite a good reader. He'd had very good instruction before coming to Texas, where, by his and Benjamin's admission, his teaching had been neglected. Isabel, on the other hand, was completely unlearned. Now seven years old, she knew only some of the sounds of the letters and a few words by sight, but little else beyond that.

When it came Isabel's turn to read, the first word on the page stumped her.

"T-ha-e," Isabel paused. "That doesn't sound right."

Micah said with big-brother superiority, "It's *the*. 'Th' makes one sound. You should know that."

"You'll get it," Elise encouraged when she saw Isabel's lip quiver. "Why don't you look at the word and say it again. That will help you memorize it."

Isabel did so and with similar prompting, managed to finish a sentence.

"That was very good!" Elise exclaimed, perhaps with overstated enthusiasm, but she hoped her praise would be incentive for future lessons. "Your father will be pleased and proud of both of you when he comes home."

Isabel beamed, wanting nothing more than to please her father. Micah merely smirked and rolled his eyes.

Elise let out a sharp breath, frustrated as always by his attitude. This time however she couldn't let it go. "Micah, why don't you try to give your father a chance? If you'd open your eyes for a minute, you'd see he has changed."

"So what?"

"So what!" her voice made a discombobulated squeak. "You can't hold his mistakes against him forever!"

His hard stare seemed to say he could indeed do just that. "I don't care what he does now. He ruined our lives, and I'll never forgive him for that." Pushing aside the primer, he jumped up and strode to the door. "I gotta feed the animals." He opened the door, slamming it behind him as he exited.

Elise looked at Isabel as if the child might understand her frustration. She was about to voice her emotions to her, as she had become the closest thing Elise had to a friend. But she reminded herself that this was just a seven-year-old child who had her own burdens—she still awoke at night crying for her mother. She didn't need adult burdens to compound her own.

"Perhaps you should go out for some fresh air also," Elise suggested to the child.

Isabel rose. "I'll pick some flowers."

"That would be nice." Elise smiled and, giving the child a brief hug and kiss on the cheek, sent her on her way.

The cabin was quiet now. Elise had finally managed the feat of getting the younger children all to take their afternoon naps at the same time. But the quiet of the cabin and the incident of wanting to vent her emotions to Isabel made Elise realize how much she missed Benjamin.

He'd been gone on his circuit for three weeks now, although this time his aim was to see if he still had a ministry to his Texians. She had encouraged him to go, not fully realizing what that would mean to her. It wasn't that she was lonely, not in the way she imagined Rebekah had been. Elise was entirely content with her life in the little cabin. Caring for the children fulfilled her in a way that often surprised her. And she enjoyed keeping house as well. She had found a length of red gingham in the trunk and with Isabel's help and encouragement had made curtains for the windows and a cloth for the table. With other fabric, a pretty blue calico Benjamin had brought home for Rebekah shortly before her death, and old patterns stowed also in the trunk, Elise made dresses for all the females in the house, including herself. She'd also taken the hide from the deer Micah had shot and Benjamin had tanned and was in the process of making a shirt for Micah. She hoped to have it done by his birthday, which was coming up soon. From the scraps she would make a pair of booties for Oliver.

Then there was the challenge of other household tasks new to Elise, but which she was quickly mastering—churning butter, making medicines, soap, candles, and preserving the early harvest from the vegetable garden she had planted a couple of months ago. She was also working on perfecting her technique for cooking and baking in the hearth. Baking johnnycakes was one thing, but she was determined to make Micah a cake for his birthday. So far all she had produced were burnt offerings.

No, loneliness and boredom were not a problem. Neither was discontent. Still, she missed Benjamin—for himself alone. The intensity of his voice, even when he laughed or teased. The flash of his eyes when he was passionate about something, the blue that could turn so vivid at times yet also could fade to a gentle softness that took her breath away as much as the dark intensity they sometimes held.

She missed his laughter and the way it would surprise even him when it slipped out unexpectedly. At times he was like a child, discovering life for the first time. And he would make her part of those discoveries, whether it be a spiritual truth or a farming technique or an antic of one of the children. He was always seeking her out to tell her about something new he'd found, and she was doing the same with him. They were learning afresh about life—together.

All at once, as if wishing indeed could make it so, Elise heard the faint sounds of hoofbeats. Could she be imagining it? She went to the window but saw nothing. Perhaps Micah was exercising their second horse. It couldn't be Benjamin, because he'd told her it would take at least a month to cover his circuit. But Elise's thudding heart made her head for the door and step outside hopefully.

The sound drew closer, and she was certain now a horse was approaching. Unconsciously she smoothed her hands over her dress, sorry she had put on her old skirt and blouse today while laundering the better dress that had belonged to Rebekah. She patted her hair, the mass of curls escaping the pins she had put in place that morning. Nothing could be done for it now, especially as she soon saw a head bob up behind a clump of mesquite.

It was definitely Benjamin, his straw-colored hair glinting in the sunlight as if gold dust had been sprinkled in the hay. She wondered somewhat protectively why he was not wearing his hat. He would get sunstroke in the afternoon heat.

But she forgot this as his figure emerged from behind the brush and trees, tall in the saddle, almost regal, though he had exchanged the fine black frock coat he used to wear on his circuit for the simple garb he wore while working the field—a coarse white homespun shirt and brown trousers braced with suspenders over strong, sturdy shoulders. He'd said the other clothes were too pretentious. They had belonged to a different man, a man he wanted to put in his past.

Her breath caught, and her heart, which had already been thumping wildly, now skipped a beat. Was it wrong to feel this way? He was her husband. Everything within her shouted that she was no more than a housekeeper, yet the fact of the matter was that their lives had touched and intersected in such a way that it should not be surprising more might have grown between them. They had been drawn together, two souls as different as night from day . . . even adversaries of sorts at first. But mutual need had forced them to see past those differences, oblivious of where it would lead.

Then she remembered her secret. She hadn't thought about it since her wedding day. That had been a terrible mistake, because her forgetfulness had made her careless of her emotions, of the fact that she had no right to fall in love. Was it true, then? Is that what had happened? Perhaps it wasn't too late to make it go away.

She could deny it. She *should* deny it. Yet as her heart careened like a raft out of control on a wild river, it was almost impossible to hide from the truth, to repress the burgeoning fact, the terrible, the wonderful fact that she . . . loved him, her husband.

———

As Benjamin rounded the corner of the path where the cabin first came into view beyond the brush, he saw her. Standing in the yard, her slight figure appeared forlorn, like the poor waif he had once imagined her. That image was heightened by the frayed, old dress she was wearing. The garish yellow silk of the skirt and the tattered ruffles of the blouse gave her the appearance of a child playing dress-up. But that image ended with surface observation. He knew there was so much more beneath mere appearances. Like her hair, the sable black strands gleaming in the sunlight, unruly curls escaping from the restraints of the pins, there was rich complexity mixed with her tender vulnerability. He'd once equated that life with evil, but he knew now it was nothing of the sort. The life she displayed radiated light, and that light had descended upon his life in an astounding way.

In the three weeks on the trail he had thought about her more than he let himself admit, thinking often of small things, the way her eyes crinkled tellingly when she teased, the music of her laughter, the sweet smell of lilac. He dreamed about her and woke from those dreams feeling a disturbing mixture of disquiet and exhilaration, missing her as if an important part of him had been left behind.

He hadn't wanted to think how anxious he was to get home. After the first week on the circuit, he had practically raced through the rest, until his poor horse was ready to collapse with exhaustion. He had ridden hard the last two days thinking always of his home, his children, but mostly of her.

It was wrong. He knew it. Wrong because Rebekah had been gone not even six months. Wrong because he had made an agreement with Elise. He could not feel this way. He could not feel such happiness, such contentment, such stirrings that he sometimes ached with the fullness of it all. It was wrong, wasn't it? It was wrong to love this woman, his wife.

He rode into the yard and dismounted. They both stood still, facing each other. His throat was so dry, he could barely creak out a stilted "Hello." His arms ached to reach out to her, to draw her to him, to hold her and feel the warm security he knew he'd find in her arms.

She didn't know what to think of the crooked smile on his lips that did not seem to match his eyes, which smoldered like ice caught on fire.

How she ached to run into his arms like a wife should upon her husband's homecoming. Her answering "Hello" was the most inadequate word she had ever spoken.

"You look tired." She resisted the urge to brush away a drop of sweat trailing through the travel grit on his face.

"You look . . . well." He could barely get that final word past the lump in his throat, especially when it hardly began to describe just how excruciatingly wonderful she did look. To steady himself, he reached for his saddlebags.

"Let me help," she said, stepping close and reaching up her slim hand. Even the smell of trail and sweat and horseflesh did not abate the wild beating of her heart with the nearness of him.

"I've got it." But he wasn't fast enough to avoid brushing her arm nor her loose tangle of lilac-scented curls. He wanted to plunge his whole face into those curls, breathing lilac until the sweetness of it oozed from his own skin.

She giggled as he pulled one way on the saddlebag and she pulled the other. She dropped her hand when she saw he had a firm hold on the bags, but she could not seem to make herself move away from him. It was he who moved, rather quickly, she thought.

"You must be hungry," she said.

He had been hungry for three weeks, deprived of the sustenance of her presence. He had been empty and realized only now just why.

"That's a good guess" was his casual reply. "Let me get my horse settled first."

Could he possibly guess just what he was doing to her at that moment? Could he see how every fiber of her heart, even her soul, was stirred? Could he realize what she was only just now discovering? Perhaps he would despise her if he knew, resent her for ruining a perfectly good arrangement.

She forced herself to walk calmly at his side toward the barn. But as they walked, the door of the cabin flung open, and Leah appeared.

"Papa!" The child grinned, then toddled forward. She had been walking for a few weeks now but was still not completely steady. With her eyes focused on her father, she forgot about the step as she careened toward him. She tumbled down.

Elise and Benjamin both rushed to her rescue. They reached her at the same moment, their four hands thrust out. As they bent, their heads brushed.

"Sorry," they said in unison, their warm breath mingling. It was a full moment before they jerked apart and refocused on the child sprawled at their feet.

Benjamin scooped Leah into his arms. She was whimpering a bit and had a skinned knee, but otherwise she was no worse for the mishap. Her father and stepmother, however, were practically panting, as if they had been the ones to fall—not down a single step, but rather down a precarious cliff.

CHAPTER 47

YOU MIGHT SAY I RECEIVED a mixed reception," Benjamin told Elise when she asked about his circuit. "I frankly confessed my mistakes and asked their forgiveness. I wanted to tell them all about the new perspectives I've been learning, but I restrained myself for the most part."

"Why is that?" Elise asked.

They were alone in the barn. Micah had left when Elise and Benjamin entered, taking Leah with him back to the cabin. He looked anxious to leave the barn as soon as Benjamin had entered and attempted to engage him in conversation. His answers to Benjamin's questions had been short and strained. He'd noted Leah's skinned knee and volunteered to tend it.

Elise should have gone back to the cabin also to check on the children, but she simply could not pull herself away from Benjamin's side.

She asked Micah to let her know if she was needed. She wanted to hear about Benjamin's trip almost as much as she wanted to be near him.

"I didn't want it to appear as if I was just foisting a new doctrine upon them." He paused thoughtfully as he brushed his tired horse's coat. "It is all so very personal that I found it hard to properly express it. I hardly know how to preach from my heart. It would be best if they saw it in a changed life rather than in words from my mouth."

"But that's rather difficult, seeing them as you do only on the circuit."

"Yes. I wish it could be otherwise. For more reasons than one." He lifted his eyes to meet hers. His were nearly the color of sapphires now in the dim light of the barn.

"What do you mean?" As she looked into his eyes, she sensed that somehow she was involved in those reasons.

She was right.

"I realized something while I was gone," he said. "I missed being home. I missed . . . everything. The children . . . everything."

"Everything . . . ?"

"Yes, you know . . . *everything*."

As he breathed that final word, her heart began its thumping drumbeat again. She could barely steady her voice to ask, "What will you do, then?"

"Maybe I should make my parish come to me for a change!" He chuckled. "At any rate, as things now stand, I doubt very many would. I wrote a letter to the mission board in Boston and left it in Cooksburg on my way home for Mr. Petty to post. I haven't communicated with them since Rebekah's death, when I wrote to inform them of that and of my inability to maintain my circuit, what with caring for the children. This time I formally requested an extended leave of absence."

"So you aren't going to continue your circuit?" She tried to mask the hopefulness in her tone.

"I can't right now. Maybe it is just my imagination—a pathetic hope that it is so—but I feel I am needed more in my home now. I need to strengthen my bonds with the children. I cannot lose the younger ones as I have Micah. You have been wonderful with them, Elise, but they still need a father."

"I agree."

"I set out on my circuit this time mostly to discover just where I belonged, and it was never clearer to me that I belong here. Oddly, though, I made that discovery just as I have realized I have so much more now to impart to my parish than I ever did before." He shook his head. "Life is never simple, is it?"

"No, it isn't, but . . ."

"Yes?" He looked at her eagerly, as if he hung on her every word.

A bit flustered, she continued. "Nothing is truly final. Now you will bide a season with your family because that is where the need is. Another time may come when you will be free to minister again."

"Of course. I see that . . ." His voice trailed away, but his gaze lingered on her a moment longer, then he jerked away. "Everything seems so clear and simple when I am with you, when I talk it out with you." The brush hung limp in his hand, the horse seemingly forgotten. "Elise . . ."

She heard a small thud as the brush fell into the hay, then suddenly his arms were around her. The embrace was hard, even clumsy, but she felt his arms tremble with fervency. He kissed her hair, and somehow the pin came loose and the waves tumbled in his face. He murmured things she felt rather than heard.

"Benjamin . . ."

She lifted her face, her lips parted and inviting. He accepted the invitation and pressed his lips to hers. She felt the hunger of his kisses, the passion seeming to explode. There was no finesse, little gentleness, only passion and immediacy, as if something had burst within him and escaped his control. She responded at first because she had longed for him more than she realized. Then his kisses grew rougher and seemed to bruise her lips. He pressed her so tightly to him she could hardly breathe.

Panic seized her as images of other men gripped her—men filled with urgency and nothing else. Men who had had their way with her, then tossed a few coins in Maurice Thomson's cash box.

"Benj—" She tried to stop him. "P-pl—"

Suddenly he did stop, and she knew by the devastated look in his eyes that he was as appalled as she over what had happened.

"Wh-what have I done?" he gasped, horrified, his entire body shaking.

"It's all right." She tried to steady her voice.

"I didn't mean . . ." He closed his eyes. "I never wanted to make you feel as you did . . . before . . . with Thomson."

"Benjamin, listen to me. I understand." Instinctively she knew what had just happened had nothing to do with her past, with cash boxes, with cruelty.

He stumbled back against the wall of the barn, hugging his arms to his chest. "How can you understand when I don't—dear God! I have never taken a woman like that. I have never lost control. I almost—"

"But you didn't!" she was shaking, but she knew him too well to believe for an instant that he would have hurt her in any way.

"It's just that it's been a very long time, and you were so close."

If only he'd said anything but that. Yet what had she expected? Declarations of love? They had an agreement, and he was a man of honor—a man of honor who was only human. But had it meant nothing then? Nothing but the primal urges of a long-deprived male? Did he feel nothing at all for her? She thought she had sensed something from him when they were in the yard, but no doubt her own feelings had made her attempt to read something in him that just wasn't there.

Miserably she realized her love once again had been spent on a man who would not return it. At the thought of Kendell's harsh rejection combined with what now seemed another rejection, sudden tears sprang to Elise's eyes.

She tried to blink them back, hoping, praying Benjamin would not see them, but they just kept flowing, ignoring her attempts to stifle them.

"I'm so sorry," he said miserably.

"It's n-nothing." She sniffed and swiped the back of her hand across her eyes. But the tears would not cease.

"This will never happen again. I swear!" Benjamin was a man of honor, she knew, and he meant what he said.

The tears continued to flood.

"Please don't cry!" he implored.

"I c-can't help it!" Then she turned and fled.

Benjamin slammed his fist hard against the barn wall, barely grazing the hard log but drawing blood from his knuckles. He didn't even consider chasing after Elise and comforting her—well, he did consider it for a crazy, idiotic instant. But who was he to comfort anyone?

It seemed all he could do was hurt the women he cared for. And even if he couldn't admit more, he knew he cared for Elise. She had done so much for him, been so kind to him, encouraged him, supported him, loved his children, and he repaid that by treating her like the kind of woman he had once thought she was. But he knew in his heart Elise had never truly been *that kind of woman.*

What must she think of him now? How she must despise him. Yes, she said she understood, but just what did she understand? That he was like all the other men, thinking of her as merely an object with which to release his baser urges?

Was that in fact the case? He didn't know . . . he didn't think so. . . . He was so confused.

She was his wife, yet she wasn't. He had missed her so on the circuit but shouldn't have. He had yearned for her while he was gone but had never thought of her body, not in that way. Then the moment she was close, he had wanted her, body and all.

And the most confusing thing of all was that he still wanted her, yet feared losing her—not her body, but rather her sweet, dear spirit. She had run off in tears, probably wounded to the core. She would never be able to look at him again.

Perhaps that was for the best, after all. He couldn't bear to hurt her as he had hurt Rebekah. He should never have allowed himself to get close to her, to need her, to even enjoy her. Their marriage was and could only be words on a piece of paper. It had been pure folly to have let it grow into more, to have become emotionally involved. He hadn't planned for that to happen. They just seemed to have slipped into being comfortable with each other.

It wouldn't happen again.

He'd put a tight rein on himself. If need be, he wouldn't even look at her. It wouldn't be easy, what with having to interact in the care of the children. Even eating meals was going to strain him. Too bad he couldn't fall back on his circuit. But he would find enough distractions with his chores to maintain a proper distance from her.

He glanced down at his hand, blood crusting on his raw knuckles. He could still feel her, and he could still taste her lips on his. And the scent of lilac still lingered on his shirt. Like phantom pains he'd heard amputees feel, he curled his hands into fists, wincing at the pain.

He could stop looking at her and touching her, but how could he ever stop needing her?

CHAPTER 48

ELISE BENT OVER THE HEARTH, scraped away a layer of hot coals that were covering the cast-iron Dutch oven, and lifted the lid. A sweet aroma of vanilla wafted up to her nose. It smelled right. It looked right. She slipped a knife into the center of the cake. If felt right. The knife pulled out clean.

Smiling, Elise took the Dutch oven from the coals and carried it to the sideboard. "Thank you, Lord!" she murmured.

Today was Micah's birthday, and she had prayed the cake would turn out. She so wanted to make this a special day for him. In the last month he had been working hard with his father and John Hunter to build the addition. He deserved a celebration.

Unfortunately, she feared it wasn't going to be much of a party. Things had been so tense around the cabin in the weeks since that ill-conceived scene in the barn that it was going to take a Herculean effort for both her and Benjamin to lay aside their personal difficulties long enough to offer a festive atmosphere for Micah.

If Elise had harbored a distant hope that she and Benjamin might be sharing that new room, it was more than hopeless now. Benjamin did not even move into the cabin when the room was completed but steadfastly continued to sleep in the barn. He came into the cabin only for meals and to play a bit with the children, all but ignoring Elise.

She told herself it was for the best. She could not bear another rejection. And she dare not do anything to risk ruining the good life she had found for herself and for Hannah by clinging to an unrequited love. She could be distant, too, and she would be that if it was the only way to make this arrangement work. In time she would forget those stirrings she had been feeling. Why, those feelings probably had nothing to do with love at all. She'd just been lonely for companionship, that's all.

It had no doubt been the same for Benjamin.

Yes, he was wise with this new tack. The companionship that had grown between them before had been a dangerous mistake. They were both too wounded to take such risks.

After supper Elise presented her cake to Micah. He seemed pleased and surprised. For a few minutes some of the tension in the household lifted. Benjamin even acknowledged Elise by complimenting her on the success of the cake.

When Elise presented the buckskin shirt to Micah, he was actually speechless for a moment, his mouth hanging ajar as he gazed at the garment.

"It's a bit large, I know," Elise explained. "I used one of your father's shirts for a pattern, because I thought you'd be filling it out in no time."

He slipped it over his head, then fastened his leather belt at his waist, which took up enough of the excess so that it did not look ungainly at all, especially after he rolled up the sleeves. He fingered the soft, supple fabric.

"Thank you," he said, looking directly at Elise.

"Your father worked on the hide at night after you went to bed." Elise felt obliged to tell him, because Benjamin was not going to say anything to take credit for his part in the gift.

She was gratified when Micah jerked his gaze toward his father and said, "Thanks." He appeared to mean it, too.

Then the party was over, the children put to bed, and Benjamin made a hasty exit to the barn, though before leaving he announced he would be going to San Felipe in the morning for supplies. He would leave at first light, so she shouldn't expect him for breakfast.

Elise took a lighted candle and went to the new room. How cold and empty it felt now, though with the door left open during the day, the heat from the hearth penetrated the room nicely. Her shiver had little to do with the room's temperature. How she longed for things to be as they were before she had made such a fool of herself in the barn.

Climbing into her soft bed of prairie grass, she thought her silly notion of love had ruined everything, and she feared this new cool aloofness would not help matters. Wildly, irrationally, she wondered about taking the great risk and declaring her love to Benjamin. What was the worst that could happen? He could reject her more pointedly than he had in the barn. He could turn her out from his home, nullifying their marriage, which he'd have every right to do since it had never been consummated.

That was the worst. And though the prospect was horrible to Elise, she reminded herself she had experienced worse things and had survived.

But Benjamin was too decent to take such an action with her. . . . Yet hadn't she thought that of Kendell?

Benjamin is a different man, she argued silently with herself.

Could declaring her love really hurt any more than the pain she now felt? It might be all he needed to open up to her. Maybe if there had been more than physical desire in what had happened in the barn, he feared declaring himself because he didn't want her to feel any obligation. Or maybe . . .

Who knew what motivations were driving him? Her own emotions were so tangled and confused she hardly knew what was going on. Perhaps he felt the same. Perhaps all that was needed was for one of them to step out and speak their heart.

She should have gone to the barn that very moment and had it out with him. She even started to do so, swinging her feet from the bed. Then panic gripped her as she thought about actually going to him and revealing her heart.

"I love you, Benjamin! You have filled my heart and soul with such contentment and happiness that those small words can only barely express it." She murmured the words, and they rang in her ears.

Suddenly she knew the true depth of what she felt for him, and the intensity of her love frightened her more than ever. Benjamin had touched a part of her that had never been touched by any man before. The love she thought she had carried for Kendell was a childish infatuation by comparison. Kendell had never touched her very soul.

Her throat clenched with a lump of fear. What if Benjamin responded to her with pity?

"I am sorry, Elise, but I cannot return the feelings you have for me," he'd say. Kindly, of course.

If the depths of what she felt for Benjamin were so much deeper than her feelings for Kendell, then did it not stand to reason that her devastation upon being rejected would be that much greater?

She kicked her feet back into bed.

"Dear God, please help me know what to do. This is getting much too convoluted and twisted for me to fathom."

When she had thought she would never sleep that night, she dozed off ten minutes later and slept soundly. She woke in the morning to find Benjamin gone.

Elise must have made ten different decisions about what she would do when Benjamin returned. When he finally did come home five days later, she questioned the wisdom once more of introducing love into their relationship. Benjamin seemed so much like his old self that she did not want to spoil the moment.

He passed out small gifts for everyone, even bringing a new thimble for Elise. He then began chatting easily about the news from the more civilized centers of Texas.

"Austin has finally returned to Texas," he said, sipping a cup of coffee Elise had placed before him.

"He was in prison in Mexico, wasn't he?"

"Yes, and as many predicted, that experience has made him very favorable toward breaking with Mexico. Oh, he isn't as gung ho as William Travis and his War Party, but Austin is willing to talk now. There's going to be a meeting in Brazoria next month, where doubtless a vote will be taken."

"That will mean war, then, won't it?"

"Santa Anna won't just give Texas away, that's for sure."

Elise tried to keep the conversation flowing. "You used to be supportive of revolution. Do you still feel that way?"

"My feelings about the Catholic Church may have changed some, but I still believe there should be complete freedom of religion, which the Mexican government opposes. A man's rights should not be based on the faith he practices. It's just not right."

They chatted for a few more minutes about the political situation, then Elise launched into a report of the happenings about the cabin in Benjamin's absence. Oliver had started teething. Isabel had finally mastered the first primer. Micah had done an excellent job weeding the cornfield, and Leah had said her first real word—"No!"

They laughed over that, and Benjamin quipped, "Well, she's heard it directed at her enough!"

"And Hannah stood all by herself the other day."

Benjamin turned to Hannah, who was seated on the floor playing with some spoons Elise had given her. "Is that true, Hannah? You must be very proud of yourself." She flashed a smile at him. Kneeling on the floor, he reached his hands out to her. "Would you like to show me?"

She placed her tiny hands in his and let him gently tug her to her feet. She grinned at her accomplishment, but when he tried to slip away his hands, she grasped them more tightly.

"Let's see you do it all by yourself, Hannah," he encouraged. After a bit more coaxing, she let him remove his hands, and she stood, swaying to be sure, on her own. "Wonderful!" As he spoke he scooted back a bit from her. "Can you do anything else, Hannah?"

"I'm afraid I tried everything," Elise said, "but she seems determined not to—"

Elise stopped abruptly because even as she spoke, Hannah was refuting her words. She took one step, then another, right toward Benjamin's beckoning arms. Elise watched in stunned and delighted silence, fearing any sound might break Hannah's concentration. Only when the child stumbled into Benjamin's arms did Elise voice her excitement.

She dropped to her knees and with a squeal threw her arms around her daughter, forgetting that such a gesture would essentially throw her into Benjamin's arms as well. Her hair brushed his face, her arms skimmed across his chest. Then she froze.

Their eyes met in a single confused moment. Then they jerked away from each other as if one of them were a hot ember. Poor Hannah was left truly on her own, momentarily bewildered until Elise, recovering more quickly than Benjamin, took Hannah in her arms.

Elise covered up her awkwardness by chattering to Hannah. "You walked, Hannah! Wasn't it fun? You are such a strong, brave thing. I'm so proud of you."

Benjamin rose to his feet. There was a slight smile on his lips, but the turquoise of his eyes had deepened with perplexity.

"I'm glad it was Hannah," Elise found herself saying.

"Pardon?"

"I'm glad you were there for her first steps."

"Yes, it was an experience I'll not soon forget. The look on her face was priceless."

"You are the only papa she knows." Elise didn't know why she said it. Was she trying to use Hannah to hold Benjamin to her? She knew it wasn't right, but she was at a loss on what else to do. She took a breath. She'd tell him now—the timing couldn't be better.

He spoke first. "I best go out now." He strode to the door.

"Benjamin?"

"What?" Was that impatience in his voice? Perhaps he was just tired after his long trip.

It flustered her nonetheless. "I . . . I . . ." Her heart thudded, and blood throbbed in her head. She looked at him and saw the cold veil pulled once more around him. "G-good night."

With a curt nod he hurried from the cabin, almost as if he had been released from prison and feared his jailer might change her mind.

Elise stared after him, her gaze boring through the wood of the closed door.

CHAPTER 49

THE GLOWERING WEATHER SEEMED TO mirror the disintegration of Benjamin and Elise's relationship. The heavy dark sky was like a weight, and the heat was stifling. The release of rain would be a blessing.

Around noon Elise heard the sound of approaching horses. It was too early for Benjamin to have returned from hunting. He and Micah had left after breakfast and expected to be gone all day. Had something happened?

She opened the cabin door as riders came to the edge of the yard. Her palpitating heart skipping several beats, Elise quickly slammed the door shut, drawing the bar into place with trembling fingers. Leaning against the door, she sucked in a breath like someone starved of air.

Maurice Thomson!

She had nearly forgotten he existed. She had let herself think all these months that she was indeed a simple housewife, caring for her family just like any other woman on the prairie. Despite the strained relations with Benjamin, she had felt very normal and secure. The vague images of an octoroon slave, chattel to the lusts of men, had become like a bad dream she knew she'd had, but all the details were dulled by wakefulness.

That had been a mistake—she feared a costly mistake. She had seriously underestimated Maurice. But then, he had hung on to his resentment over losing her mother for twenty years. What made her think he would give up on her after only a few months?

Of course he hadn't. Somehow he had found her.

The horses came to a stop in the yard, and sounds reached her ears of men dismounting. Maurice was here with his brother, Lyle.

Elise had only seconds to decide what to do. Both guns were gone. Benjamin hadn't liked leaving her unarmed, but she had pointed out she didn't know how to shoot anyway. He'd said he had put off giving her lessons long enough and tomorrow she was going to learn.

Tomorrow. It had seemed like such a minor goal. Now she wondered if there would be a tomorrow. Even if Maurice didn't kill her, taking her back into his custody would be tantamount to death. She'd once said she would die before going back to that life, but the words seemed so glib now that she was faced with that very choice. She had something to live for now. She had a life she desperately wanted to live out. It wasn't perfect, but despite all its difficulties, it had fulfilled her and made her happy.

Footsteps approached the cabin.

She shook away her fear. "Isabel," she said softly but urgently, signaling for the child to keep quiet. "Take Oliver into the new room. Hurry." She spoke in a tone that commanded immediate obedience.

As Isabel gathered up her brother, Elise took Leah and Hannah in hand and half carried, half dragged them into the room. Leah attempted to protest in her noisy manner while Elise hushed her several times, finally clamping her hand harshly over the child's mouth.

"Isabel, keep the children in here and don't open the door," she instructed. "Try to keep them as quiet as possible, but whatever happens *stay in here*. No matter what you hear outside. Stay!"

"Is . . . it . . . Indians?" Isabel stammered.

"No, but they are bad men. You must stay here until your father comes home, so you can tell him what has happened."

"Where will you b-be, Elise?"

"I don't know. They may make me go with them. But you are not to worry. Just pray, all right? And tell your father it was Maurice Thomson."

"I . . . I'm afraid, Elise." Isabel had started crying.

"I know you can be brave." Elise bent down and kissed her. Then there was a pounding on the front door. "Don't leave this room!" Elise admonished emphatically as she shut the bedroom door and strode to the cabin door.

"I heard someone in there," came the rough familiar voice Elise had so dreaded to ever hear again. "I know you're home!"

Elise debated about not opening the door. But there was easy access to the cabin through the windows, which were covered only by rawhide. Maurry need only poke his head through to see it was her. Perhaps he would climb in and cause a struggle inside that would scare the children so much they would reveal their hiding place.

Convinced it was her only recourse, Elise gripped the bar, but it took every ounce of courage to throw it back. She opened the door only enough so she could step outside. No matter what happened, she must protect the children. She shut the door behind her.

"So it is you!" Maurice spoke in that tone that bordered on vulgarity.

"What do you want?" She willed her voice to steady, but her lips trembled over her words.

"Now, that's a dumb question." His gaze roved over her. "I come to collect my property."

She knew she could respond with either defiance or humble supplication. And though she wanted to spit in his self-satisfied face, she knew for the children's sake she had to avoid antagonizing him.

"Maurry, please don't do this!" It sounded so inadequate, so pitiful, but what else could she say? He'd consider no argument, no defense from her.

"What kind of a setup do you have here, Liz? Did you go into business for yourself?" He glanced over at his brother. "Lyle, go inside and see if there's anyone else—"

"I'm alone!" Elise cut in quickly—too quickly, for it would only raise his suspicions.

"Where's that brat of yours?"

"She died. I . . . I have a man, but he's out cutting wood."

Maurice smiled, a slanted, twisted motion full of innuendo. "You are in business, then."

"It's not like that. We are married."

"Oh, you got a respectable setup, eh?" He laughed. "Of course it isn't that respectable since you already have a husband."

"That's not true. My marriage was annulled."

"I heard differently. Your husband went addlepated. Wouldn't sign papers. Seems he just sits all day living in some fantasy world."

"When did you hear this?" Elise's mind was suddenly in a whirl of disarray. Kendell insane? No annulment? It couldn't be true! It had to be a mistake.

"My lawyer came through San Felipe a couple months ago and paid a visit. Had all kinds of information. Your pa's back in the country, too. So far he has no idea where you are."

Her father? But like before, he still could not help her. She had to find a way on her own. But first she had to clear her mind. She could not think of what Maurice had just told her, of how the small deception she had carried over Benjamin had now become a huge, disastrous one.

"Maurry, what'll it take for you to leave me alone?" Somehow the words came evenly, belying her quaking insides. There might yet be a chance to have this life she had come to love.

"A nigger woman like you don't come cheaply." His eyes scanned the pathetic-looking cabin. "Neither you or your man's got enough money."

"Please, Maurry!" She was within a heartbeat of falling on her knees in supplication.

He laughed in her agonized face. "I remember your mama begged me like that, only she got on her knees. 'Please let me go, Maurry, I met a man who loves me.' I laughed at her, too."

"And she ran away," Elise could not repress the defiance in her tone.

"And you've run, too, but I've found you—and I'm not gonna let you get away again."

"What are you going to do?" she sneered. "You don't have my baby to hold over my head." Dear God, don't let him figure out about the children. She had inched her way down the step and was moving as inconspicuously as possible away from the cabin.

"I'm gonna do what I should have done before." He went to his horse and took a whip from the saddle.

"Hey, Maurry," said Lyle, "before you get her all bloodied up, let me have a few minutes with her." He stepped close and grabbed her arm.

Elise cringed at the touch, filled as it was with all the horrible things she'd hoped she had escaped. Lyle wrenched her into his arms, his hot, foul breath singeing her cheek.

"I missed you, sweetheart." His sweaty hands held her fast.

She struggled to break free. "Please . . . don't . . ."

Then somehow she did break free, and for a wild, insane moment she forgot everything except her vow to die before a man used her like that again. She made a dash away from Lyle, but she tripped over the hem of her skirt and crumpled to her knees. Lyle dove at her and sprawled on top of her in the dirt. She screamed as the weight of him pinned her down. There was nothing to stop him, no one to save her. Desperate sobs broke from her lips, then she heard Maurry laugh.

"Lyle, at least you can have the decency to go inside the cabin," Maurry chuckled.

Shrugging, Lyle grabbed her and hauled her to her feet. Given a bit more freedom, she began to struggle again, pounding at him and sobbing as he dragged her up the step. Only then did her personal terror lift enough for her to remember the children.

"My man will be back any time now!" She screamed. It was a desperate and much too obvious ploy, but she had to keep them out of the cabin.

Maurice barked a scoffing laugh. "You must think I'm a first-class fool."

Choking back sobs and horror, she tried to sound convincing. "He really will be back . . . for his midday meal. It's that time isn't it?" She was a pathetic liar. A child would see through it. "His son is with him. They are both armed and excellent shots. They have been living in the frontier for years." She knew she was babbling, having already stepped over the line to hysteria. But the lies kept coming. "He was raised by Indians. He could creep within a foot of you, and you'd never know. He's probably already heard me and is in the brush now, waiting to attack." Maybe a huge lie would be more believable than a small one.

She wanted to howl with delight when Lyle jerked a quick glance over his shoulder.

"You're both dead men if they find you here," she went on, the words flowing almost of their own volition as she built a delusion, one she hoped and prayed would save her life and protect her children. "Benjamin has fought Indian wars back east, and I saw him with my own eyes hang a horse thief. What do you think he'll do with someone who steals his woman?"

"Funny," Maurice said, unruffled, "but I heard he was just a preacher."

Elise snorted derision, her terror finding some succor in her performance. "That's a hoot! The preacher was squatting here, and Benjamin ran him off because he wanted this parcel for himself."

"You're lying!" challenged Maurice.

And though all good sense told her she had lost, she still could not give up. "It would almost be worth it to invite you in so I can watch what he does to you when he finds you."

"Maurry, let's get out of here," said Lyle, his tone almost a whine. "I knew a fella named Ben Gutherie over in Kentucky. He's a mean critter, and I heard he was heading out to Texas. It could be the same man. I saw him shoot a man just for bumping him in a tavern."

Maurry shrugged. "Well, whether it's true or not, I reckon it makes good sense to get on our way. It's a sure bet you aren't living here alone, though I'm fully in my rights taking you. But I don't want no violence."

Elise swallowed back her relief. She let Maurry haul her up on his horse, not because she had decided that her old life was after all preferable to death, but rather to lure her captors away from the cabin and the children. When Maurice climbed into the saddle behind her, she suddenly felt an unaccountable calm. Death, or worse, still loomed in her path, but the children were safe. Nothing else mattered. She uttered a silent prayer that Isabel would be able to tend things until Benjamin returned home that evening.

As they rode off, she didn't know whether to pray for Benjamin to rescue her or for him to stay put. Poor Benjamin. Contrary to her grand lie, he was the worst shot she ever saw. He might make a mistake and shoot her instead of her captors. Or worse, get himself killed.

CHAPTER 50

ONLY A SLIVER OF MOON provided light on the dark trail. But it would have been impossible for Benjamin to do the logical thing and wait at home till morning to find Elise.

He'd gone half crazy when he had come home to find Isabel shut in the new room with the younger children. She had been hysterical, and it had taken some time to coax information from her. He had hated to leave her, especially when she had clung tearfully to him, but when he heard the name Maurice Thomson, he knew he dare not waste time. He kept remembering that Elise had said she would die before returning to her former life.

"Dear God, please don't let her do anything foolish!" he murmured as he picked his way on the shadowed trail.

But what if she believed she had nothing to live for? After the way he had treated her since that stupid encounter in the barn, she might well believe he thought he'd be better off without her.

Nothing could be further from the truth. It had only taken that instant when he realized she was gone for him to know just how much he did need her, how much he wanted her, how empty his life would be without her. Only a moment of panicked fear made him realize just how deeply she had become entwined in his life, how she held him together, gave him uncanny balance. He knew as he fought the strong urge to race his horse over the rocky path that his need for her transcended his children's demands. And it went beyond physical needs, too. He could do without a cook or a laundress, or even the fulfillment of desires he'd expressed in the barn. What he could not do without was the way she touched his heart, his spirit.

What would he do if something happened to her and he could never express his true feelings to her? What if he could never fix the way he had been treating her lately? How could he live with himself?

Please God, give me another chance. Allow me to get it right just once.

He peered into the night, hoping he was still heading south, hoping he'd guessed right that Thomson would head back to his place near San Felipe. But if Isabel had been accurate about the time they left the cabin, they had several hours' head start. They could camp for the night, and still Benjamin, forced to travel at this cautious snail's pace, might not catch up to them.

In that case he would simply go to Thomson's place, maybe even get a few men from town to accompany him. But the inadvisability of that idea struck him immediately. If he involved anyone from town, several undesirable things could happen. First, Elise's past would become public knowledge. He didn't care for himself, but he knew it brought her great shame. So far they had been able to keep it quiet because they were so isolated, and of the few people they encountered, most had no dealings with a man like Thomson. Yet a raid on Thomson's place, though long overdue, would be devastating to Elise's reputation.

But the other far more dangerous problem in involving others, especially the legal authorities, was that they might well side with Maurice's claim. She was his slave, and there was much support of slavery in Texas among the Americans. And with the issue of revolution becoming hotter each day, the Mexicans might have little to say in the matter.

No, Benjamin had to deal with this himself. But he wished there had been time to get John Hunter's help. Benjamin feared that alone he'd be pretty useless against a man like Thomson and whoever was riding with him. His rifle was loaded and ready to fire, but hitting a target was another matter. His confidence had been further diminished by the day of hunting in which Micah had killed the two turkeys they brought home. They had tracked a deer, but Benjamin had arrogantly insisted on taking the shot—and had missed.

Poor Elise. Her only rescuer was an inept fool. But if the sheer force of his determination meant anything, he would be successful.

Benjamin's horse stumbled over a tree root. "Whoa." He reined the mare to a stop.

Did he dare go on? What if his horse should become injured and he'd have no way to get to Elise at all? He debated this issue for several moments, and finally good sense prevailed; he found a place to make camp. It was several hours until dawn. He didn't expect to sleep and, indeed, lay awake for two hours fretting and agonizing until pure exhaustion finally forced him into a fitful slumber.

"You troublesome little tart!" Maurice jumped from his horse, then dragged Elise down after him. "I oughta just shoot you!"

Elise spat at him, but the momentary pleasure she received from hitting her mark was short-lived as his big hand shot up, striking her full across her face. Her hands were tied behind her, and having no way to balance herself, she stumbled back and fell to the ground.

She took a moment to glance up at the sky. It was almost dawn. She had tried to escape, and though her attempt had been unsuccessful, she had delayed her captors, hoping to give Benjamin, if he was foolish enough to come after her, time to catch up.

The thought of Benjamin made her wince with gnawing pain, not a physical pain but rather one that seared through her very heart. Her escape had brought but a brief reprieve from the inevitable. Before she had run off, her captors had been threatening to have their way with her. Lyle was driven purely by lust, but Maurry believed it to be the only way to ensure his control over Elise.

When they had stopped to make camp, she had known it was only a matter of time. And she was sickened by the realization that she was not ready to die as she had sworn to do before being shamed again by a man. She knew that when the moment of reproach came, she would surrender.

"Dear God, I am so sorry!" she had silently agonized.

But she simply could not ignore her deep longing to live and the sense that she now had so much to live for. The children needed her. Hannah, of course, but Benjamin's children, too, had come to depend on her and even love her. And she loved them and wanted to be there for them. She wanted to help Micah shed his anger. She wanted to comfort Isabel when she woke from her nightmares. She wanted to protect Leah and Oliver from facing another loss in their young lives.

And yes, she also wanted a life with Benjamin. He needed her, though he might not realize it. He needed the love she had to offer him. How ironic it was that because of her love for him she would do something that might surely destroy it. How would he be able to face her, knowing she had been so weak as to let Maurice and Lyle shame her? If Benjamin despised her before, what would he think when he found her? And she dared not let herself think about what Maurice had said about Kendell. Benjamin had learned much lately about forgiveness, but just how much mercy did he have in him?

She could not keep from clinging to a sense deep within her that there was more to what had happened between her and Benjamin that day in the barn. Something special had grown between them in the last months. For her, that something had become love. Was it possible it might be the same for him, and he would not admit it? It was the only thing that truly explained the change he exhibited lately. He was afraid of what was happening. And if that were the case, maybe, just maybe, he might be able to forgive anything.

It would hardly matter once she had placed her life above honor and virtue and all the things she knew were important to Benjamin. She would be alive—but at the expense of all she had wanted to live for. Yes, she would fight her attackers, but there were two of them, and short of death, there was no way to beat them. They would take her, shame her, defile her. She was just too weak in body to prevent them, too weak in mind to take her only other way out.

She had forgotten the truth she and Benjamin had talked about some time ago, about the peculiar beauty of weakness. But now it came back to her as she considered—no, wallowed—in her weakness. What was the verse Benjamin had quoted? "*My grace is sufficient for thee: for my strength is made perfect in weakness.*"

Even in her misery, a small smile quirked her lips. She was indeed the perfect specimen for God to use in order to show His marvelous strength. But even that did not instill her with hope. She continued to await her fate with resigned dread. She certainly did not think it was God's hand when Lyle produced a bottle of whiskey from his saddlebag after a hasty supper.

"What you got there, Lyle?" Maurry nodded at the bottle, a gleam in his eye. "You gotta have some liquid courage before you take on the little spitfire?"

Lyle snorted with disdain. "Haven't had a drink all day, that's all." He uncorked the bottle and set it to his lips.

As he pressed the cork back in place, Maurry said, "Ain't you going to share?"

"Ya need some courage yourself, Maurry?" Lyle sneered.

"Just gimme that bottle!"

Both Lyle and Maurry were hopeless drunks. Maurry had more self-control than his brother, but once he started he usually kept going until the booze ran out or he simply passed out. Lyle passed out drunk practically every night, and since coming to Texas, Maurry had been adversely influenced by his brother. Thus, they shared the bottle this night until it was empty, then Lyle produced another. He had only a couple of swigs before he stretched out on the ground.

"I jes want a few winks 'fore I have the girl. . . ." he slurred. "Ya go ahead . . . I'll be along. . . ." He was snoring before he finished.

Maurry, seeing that he would soon be going the way of his brother, staggered to his feet. "Got ya all to m'self. . . ."

He propelled himself toward her, then crumpled to his knees, finally toppling over on her. She started to fight him off, only to realize in seconds that he had passed out also. With an odd mingling of disgust and relief, she pushed his wretched body off hers and scooted away.

Instantly she knew this was a prime chance for escape. Not that she had expected to be successful. With her hands tied, she couldn't hope to get far, but at least she could try to stall what must eventually happen. She would run back in the direction they had come, closer to home. She no longer worried about the children, for Benjamin would be there by now. At any rate, she didn't expect to reach the cabin. She hoped only to buy time, perhaps give Benjamin, if he was looking for her, a chance to catch up.

It had taken three hours for Maurice to find her—three precious hours closer to Benjamin and to possible rescue. And now it was almost dawn.

Was Benjamin out there? Was he close? Would he save her? She tried not to think of anything else, of the danger he'd be in or the horror he'd feel if—when!—he found out about Kendell.

But the harsh voices of her captors forced her back to the present.

"Well, I've had it with you!" Maurice was saying. He grabbed a handful of her hair and dragged her to a nearby tree. "But you're too valuable to shoot."

With Lyle holding a rifle on her—not that she had either the strength or heart to run again—Maurice untied her hands, made her wrap her arms around the tree, then retied her hands so that she was hugging the tree.

It was almost with relief that she realized Maurry had other intentions at the moment besides rape. Yes, now she remembered he had other methods for keeping his slaves in line. Visions of little Gina's scarred back intruded into her mind.

"I should've done this long ago," he said. She heard him walk to his horse. "I'm gonna make sure you don't run again."

Though she was expecting it, that first stripe with the whip made her gasp in shock more than pain. The pain was there but did not really penetrate her senses until the second and third blows. Then all was pain. Sharp, tearing, wrenching pain. She wanted to be brave and not cry out, and she bit her lip until she drew blood. But after a while stoicism seemed a rather lame virtue, and soon she could not prevent the cries of agony from escaping.

She lost count after the first ten blows. Still, it kept going on and on as if he was indeed going to kill her. It had to be well past twenty—somewhere in the distance she could hear Lyle's voice keeping count—that she began to lose her senses. As unconsciousness finally closed in upon her, the most peculiar thoughts crossed her mind. She was wearing Rebekah's pretty brown dress and she had promised Isabel she would take care of it, but now it was surely ruined. Her last conscious thought was that despite her escape from rape, she was going to die after all. Maybe it was just as well. Who could love her now, ruined and scarred?

Then blackness engulfed her even as the snap of the whip continued.

CHAPTER 51

BENJAMIN WAS NO TRACKER, BUT he didn't have to be because Maurice was taking no pains to hide his passage. They were keeping to what passed for a trail in these parts. What Benjamin couldn't tell, however, was how long since the signs had been left. He could not judge how close he was to them.

Then the unthinkable happened. It started to rain. The water fell in thick sheets, and when it stopped an hour later, not only had it washed away any trail signs, but it slowed Benjamin's progress considerably, especially when he came to a creek he must cross. An hour earlier he could have walked across on his horse without trouble. Now the water raged in a torrent down the narrow creek bed.

There might be a better crossing, but it could be miles down the creek. For one panicked moment he considered fording the water anyway.

"What am I going to do?" He stared at the creek, as if God might part the waters for him.

But the torrent just kept on its roiling and boiling journey, unaffected by his despair, untouched by his prayers.

"Benjamin, is that you?"

It was a miracle in itself that Benjamin heard the voice over the rage of rushing water. But it was unbelievable that the voice, as if from heaven itself, was that of his friend John Hunter. Hunter was carefully directing his horse down the steep bank.

"John!" Benjamin shouted, full of glee. "It is me. I've got to get across the creek."

"I'm gonna go down a few miles and see if I can find another crossing."

"There isn't time!" Benjamin wondered if he could convince his friend to be party to a suicidal attempt.

"What's wrong?"

"It's a long story, John. Elise's in trouble. I have to find her."

Thankfully, John restrained what must have been a natural urge to question further. "Well, we won't get far here—"

"I've got to try!" Benjamin cried frantically. "Even if there is another crossing, it might be flooded, too."

John grasped his arm. "Listen to me, Benjamin, you are not going to do her any good if you get yourself killed. That river we crossed when you first came here ain't nothing compared to this. I'm not even sure the horses can swim it."

But Benjamin's wild-eyed gaze was proof enough that he was willing to take that risk.

John studied the creek for a few long moments. Then he scratched his head. "You determined to do this?"

Benjamin gaped at his friend as if he had just sprouted horns. "She's at the mercy of a man I doubt knows the meaning of the word. God only knows what he'll do to her if I don't get there."

"All right, then. You got rope?" John dismounted, taking his own coil of rope from his saddle. Benjamin handed him his rope, and John tied the two ends together, giving the knot a yank to test its soundness. "That ought to hold."

Benjamin marveled at the man's skill. In awe he watched as John made a slip knot around one of the loose ends of the rope to form a lasso. "I'm gonna try to lasso that stump over yonder." He gestured across the creek to the opposite bank. Benjamin saw the stump, and it appeared sound. The last thing they wanted was to have their lives depend on a rotten tree.

John hoisted the coil of rope over his head and gave a mighty heave. He missed. It took three more tries before the noose finally fell evenly around the stump. Benjamin let out a whoop.

John smiled but said cautiously, "That's the easy part."

After securing the other end of the rope to a sturdy tree on their side of the creek, they were ready to cross, using the rope for guidance and support. Not wanting to trust the rope entirely, Benjamin suggested they add a few silent prayers.

"I been praying all along," John said.

"Then we can do no more." Benjamin took a breath. Though the words had not come to his mind in a formal way, he knew he'd been praying since leaving his cabin yesterday.

Benjamin went first. If this makeshift pulley wasn't going to work, he'd be the first to be swept down the creek, and maybe John would have time to get back to safety. His heart was pounding both in fear and in frustration at the painstakingly slow pace he must progress. But he dare not urge his horse too much lest he spook her. She was already shy of the rushing water; in fact, it took some doing just to get her to step into it. She grew skittish in the middle of the creek where the current swirled wildly, and Benjamin had to stop completely.

He rubbed the animal's neck and murmured encouragement into her ear. "It's all right," he lied. "You're doing fine, just take one step at a time."

They started again, and as the opposite bank grew closer, Benjamin had to resist every urge to dig his heels in and hurry from that dangerous torrent of water. But even as he reached the bank and stepped onto solid ground, he knew the drama wasn't over yet. He had to watch the process all over again as John crossed.

Only when his friend came up on the bank safely did it occur to him to wonder what was John's need to be crossing the flooded creek.

"I was just going into Cooksburg to have Albert fix the blade on my scythe. Harvest will be coming along soon." He answered Benjamin's inquiry.

"You could have waited until the river went down."

"Are you trying to tell me you don't want my help?" John asked matter-of-factly.

"Well I—"

"No matter. I ain't gonna let you go off on no rescue when I'm here to help. Now, we best get going."

As they rode along, Benjamin filled John in on a few more details of what had happened. He had never told John the full circumstances of Elise's past, but he felt if John was going to place himself at risk, he ought to be informed of the whole story. It really didn't surprise Benjamin that when John heard the story, he responded with hardly a wink. He had no more thought to judge Elise than he had to decline rescuing her. He knew only that she was a good woman and Benjamin's wife, and that was enough.

They rode hard for several hours before they spotted the smoke of a campfire. It was a couple of hours before sunset, so Thomson—if it was Thomson—and his party had made camp early.

"If that's your man," John observed, "then it's pretty careless of him."

"He doesn't think he has anything to fear." Benjamin stared hard at the stream of smoke. "I mean to make him regret that."

John did a double take, both at Benjamin's words and the hard resolve of them.

Benjamin added, "I mean to kill him if I have to."

"I don't have a problem with that," John replied evenly, with just as much conviction.

They loaded their rifles, then split up, each to approach the camp from opposite directions. Benjamin would make the first move, hoping Thomson would think him alone, thus saving John as a surprise, an "ace up your sleeve," as John put it, forgetting that Benjamin knew nothing of card playing. Benjamin did know what the phrase meant. He only hoped he could maintain enough of a poker face to make the best use of the subterfuge.

CHAPTER 52

BENJAMIN TRIED TO STEP QUIETLY through the brush. He remembered how stealthily the Karankawa had come upon him that day in his camp. Unfortunately, Benjamin only got within twenty yards before he stepped carelessly on a branch, snapping it loudly. He stopped in his tracks and held his breath.

Away in the camp he heard voices.

"You hear that, Maurry?"

"We got visitors."

"Maybe it's Indians."

"Shut up a minute!"

Benjamin had to move fast then in order to beset them before they could get to their weapons, if they didn't already have them. He barreled into the camp, gun ready, breaking into the clearing just as Maurice was reaching for his pistol. The other man was busy loading his musket.

"Drop it!" Benjamin yelled, aiming at Maurice.

Thomson's fingers had just barely touched the pistol, but he instantly jerked his hand away. In that same instant, the second man, whom Benjamin had only a peripheral glimpse of, moved. Benjamin could not know for certain if the man had finished loading, but out of the corner of his eye he saw the weapon raise. He started to turn, intending to fire, but before he could take aim, another shot rang through the air.

He gaped in shock as his would-be target jerked violently, then fell back to the ground. He stared dumbfounded as a circle of blood spread on the man's shirt in the vicinity of his heart.

Then Benjamin shook away his shock, realizing he had not finished his rescue. But he didn't shake it away soon enough. He'd left enough time for Maurice to retrieve his pistol. Thomson took aim. Benjamin could not expect another reprieve from John, who needed time to reload.

As Thomson squeezed the trigger, Benjamin made a desperate lunge to the left. The shot whizzed past Benjamin, tickling his right ear. Sprawling in the dirt, Benjamin hit something solid. The form made a pitiful groaning sound. At that same moment John stepped into view, came up behind Thomson, and jabbed his rifle into the back of his head.

"Put that pistol down now," John drawled in that matter-of-fact way Benjamin was finding so admirable.

The pistol clunked into the dirt. Benjamin sat up and turned to inspect what he had struck. With trembling fingers, fearing what he would find, he lifted the corner of the blanket covering the moaning woman he was certain must be Elise.

"Elise . . ." he breathed. "What have they done to you?"

"B-Ben-jamin . . ." Her voice seemed to catch, and she could say no more.

At first he could not see what was wrong with her. There was a red welt on her cheek, but he saw no blood on the front of her dress to indicate a bullet wound. Then he lifted away more of the blanket and saw the most horrible sight he had ever seen in his life. The back of her dress was ripped to shreds, and the exposed flesh was crisscrossed with blood-encrusted welts.

Had Benjamin given it conscious thought, he would have known in that moment what white-hot fury was like. But he didn't think. Instead, he was driven by animal instincts as he leaped to his feet and flew like a crazed beast at the man who would dare inflict such dreadful harm on the woman he loved. He clamped his hands around Maurice Thomson's throat, prepared to choke the life from this evil man.

Thomson, gagging, turning red in the face, then blue, tried to fight Benjamin off, but somewhere Benjamin found the strength of ten enraged men. Thomson would have been dead in another minute had John Hunter not intervened.

"Benjamin, you sure you want to do this?" he asked calmly. "I figure you got every right, but you're gonna have to live with it when you're done."

It wasn't so much the words as it was the quiet, almost soothing manner in which they were spoken that penetrated Benjamin's inflamed senses. He stopped, his hands loosening a slight degree from their death grip. He glanced at John, who had moved, with musket aimed at the struggling Thomson, to the front of the man and about ten feet away so he would have a good advantage.

Perspiring and shaking, still feeling he wanted to kill, Benjamin forced himself to back off. He returned to Elise's side.

"Th-thank you," she murmured.

He wasn't sure why she was thanking him. For rescuing her? For not killing Thomson?

Smoothing back the damp, tangled hair from her face, he didn't know what to say except what he had been hoping he'd have a chance to say since leaving the cabin after her.

"I love you, Elise." He kissed the mass of hair.

"Ain't that sweet." Thomson's snide voice reminded Benjamin they weren't finished with him. He was sitting up again, rubbing his throat, but not looking too bad after his ordeal.

Benjamin tried to convince himself he had done the right thing in letting that miserable creature live.

"So you are a preacher after all," Maurice continued. "I almost believed her when she tried to tell us you weren't. I mean, who would of thought a preacher would take up with a common trollop, eh?"

"Shut up, Thomson, or I will kill you," Benjamin warned. "And believe me, you try to harm my wife again, and I will do it—and do it joyfully."

"Wife, you say?" Thomson's eyes glinted with amusement.

"Yes, and you have no more claim on her."

"We'll see about that. I got a legal claim, and now I got a moral claim for you killing my brother. You are gonna pay dearly for that!"

"I am sorry about your brother. But he wouldn't have come to harm if you hadn't tried to bring harm to others yourself." Benjamin glanced at Elise so that despite his regret over the death of Thomson's brother, he could be reminded about the kind of man he was dealing with. "No law will condone what you've done to my wife."

"Even if she was your legal wife, she was my property first. But last I heard, a woman can't have two husbands." He sneered. "It appears she's put a big one over on you preacher, 'cause your so-called *wife* already has a husband back in South Carolina."

Benjamin quickly brushed off the statement as a lame attempt by Thomson to force him to give up his claim on Elise.

"Give it up, Thomson," Benjamin said. "You've lost. Even if the legal authorities uphold your claim of ownership, you are going to have to come and get her—and you'll have to get past me to do so. I won't hesitate again." He then rose and glanced at John. "What'll we do with him?"

"You won't have any peace unless he's dead," John said with more logic than ire.

"Killing the other man was self-defense. It had to be done," Benjamin said. "But neither you nor I could kill a man, even a rascal like this, in cold blood."

John nodded, though he didn't look any more convinced than Benjamin felt. If Thomson lived, Elise would always live under a shadow. Yet no matter how he or John felt, Benjamin knew they could not live with murder, which killing Thomson at this point would amount to.

So with deep reluctance, Benjamin found a length of rope from among Thomson's supplies. The best he could do was to tie his hands, take his weapons and his horses, and let him fend for himself. He and Elise would find some way to live with the threat of Thomson.

"After I tie your hands, Thomson," Benjamin said, "we're going to ride off. I'll let your horses go after a few miles, and no doubt they'll find their way back to you. I'm giving you half a chance to survive. But if you ever show your face on my land or make any attempt to harm me or mine, like I said, I will kill you."

Benjamin stepped close to Thomson, who was still sitting on the ground. He was about to step behind him to bind his hands at his back when Thomson's arm shot up, a flash of metal catching a ray of the setting sun. Before Benjamin could react, Thomson's arm encircled Benjamin's neck with a viselike grip, the point of the knife pressed against Benjamin's throat.

"All right, you!" Thomson yelled at John. "Drop that gun." When John hesitated, Thomson sneered, "You're both fools. You should have killed me when you had the chance. I ain't leaving without my property, and *I* won't hesitate to kill you both." As if for emphasis, he tightened his grip on Benjamin. "Now drop the musket!"

John let the weapon slip from his hands too quickly. It struck the ground hard, discharging the loaded shot. John jumped back in surprise. The explosion took Benjamin and his captor by surprise also. With the knife at his throat, Benjamin couldn't move. Thomson only jerked slightly, but that momentary distraction was all Benjamin needed. The instant he felt the tip of the knife move, he lunged his elbow back hard into Thomson's stomach.

Thomson fell back, still gripping the knife, then quickly shook off the effects of Benjamin's blow and made a swift lunging uppercut at Benjamin's arm, slicing the fabric of his sleeve. Benjamin spun around and, in the same motion, caught Thomson's knife hand and jerked it back, forcing Thomson to the ground. Benjamin tried to smash his hand against the dirt, but Thomson held fast his weapon.

The two men grappled on the ground, first with Benjamin on top, holding back Thomson's jabs with the knife. Then Thomson gained the advantage and rolled on top, the knife hovering above Benjamin's face. Out of the corner of his eye, Benjamin could see John lying on the ground. Had he been struck by the discharged shot?

Benjamin quickly forced his concentration back to his opponent, who had once again maneuvered the knife into a good striking position. Benjamin held back the knife hand, but a sharp pain coursed up his arm. It was then he realized Thomson's earlier blow had done more than cut his sleeve. Blood dripped from the ragged fabric of his shirt.

With the strength in one arm ebbing, Benjamin made another desperate attempt to dislodge the knife from Thomson's powerful hand. Lying on his back with Thomson on top of him, he managed to wedge his knee between them. With all his strength and concentration focused on his arms and the battle to keep the knife at bay, his thrusts with his knee were not as strong as he wished. Once, twice, slowly his effort began weakening Thomson's hold. With the third thrust, Benjamin managed to get an advantage over the knife hand.

He twisted the arm back, drawing a loud, pain-filled bellow from Thomson. Another full body thrust, and Benjamin was on top once again. Thomson's arm was definitely weakening, and he offered little resistance as Benjamin attempted to smash the hand against the ground.

The knife bounced from Thomson's hand. But Benjamin made the mistake of loosening his grip in order to shove the knife out of reach. Thomson was not about to let that happen. As Benjamin loosened his hold, Thomson proved faster and smashed his fist into Benjamin's nose. Nose bloodied, head spinning, Benjamin fell back. Then Thomson grabbed the knife, jumped up, and charged Benjamin. Either Thomson thought Benjamin was still stunned from the blow, or he was simply too full of confidence, but clear shock registered on his face when Benjamin rolled in time to avoid the charge.

His momentum having a life of its own, Thomson could not pull back in time. He hit the dirt where Benjamin's form had been an instant earlier. Benjamin jumped up, expecting his adversary to do the same. But Thomson did not rise. Instead he lay there, his body jerking convulsively.

Cautiously, Benjamin approached the fallen form that had suddenly grown still. He tapped it with the toe of his boot. Nothing. He bent down and shook a shoulder, then heaved the body over and saw Thomson had impaled himself on his own knife. Blood oozed from his mouth. He was dead.

Benjamin looked around. John was sitting up now, rubbing his head.

"It's over," Benjamin said, panting, voice raw and sick.

"You all right?"

Benjamin nodded, still looking dazed. "How about you?"

"Sorry I wasn't much help," John said. "Tripped over a rock when that rifle fired and hit my head on that." He pointed to a large sharp-edged rock. One of the edges was tinged with blood.

"He's dead," Benjamin said, trying to make that awful fact penetrate his benumbed senses.

"Let me have a look at that arm of yours." John reached for Benjamin's wounded arm.

"It's all right. It doesn't hurt. I have to see to Elise." He returned to her blanket-covered form and laid a hand on her shoulder.

"Benjamin . . . I'm s-so sorry!"

"Shh, it's time to get you home, Elise."

PART FIVE

OCTOBER 1835

CHAPTER

53

For days Benjamin did not know if Elise would live or die. The wounds on her back had festered, and fever assailed her. She was never fully conscious. In her delirium she would cry out incoherently, seemingly in pain. At other times she mumbled things, often just Benjamin's name.

It frightened the children. Hannah clung to her mother, often crying herself. Benjamin thought how fearful Elise had always been of losing Hannah. No one ever considered that the loss could be reversed.

Isabel was inconsolable at first. "Papa, will she die?" Her weeping was pitiful to behold.

But Benjamin wasn't much help. He lifted his own tear-filled eyes to his daughter. "I . . . I don't know. Dear God, she can't die!" He hugged Isabel to him, and they cried in each other's arms.

They both soon found strength in tending to Elise's physical needs. Keeping her inflamed skin cool was a full-time endeavor. Nell Hunter came to help for the first three days. John's grazed head was healing nicely, but he remained at home to tend neglected chores. Nell had insisted on cleaning and bandaging Benjamin's cut arm. He'd hardly felt the wound in his concern for Elise but it was a deep cut, and Nell was worried that it would putrefy and cause lockjaw. She made a poultice of garlic and witch hazel, which she swabbed on the wound to prevent inflammation, then bound it with a rind of pork, explaining that would fight lockjaw. Benjamin accepted these ministrations impatiently.

But Nell, wise and logical like her husband, said, "What good will you be to Elise if you get sick?"

Finally, she turned her attention to Elise. Benjamin could hardly watch the process of cleaning her battered back. In fact, he'd had to leave the cabin once, sickened by her cries of pain at the mere touch of the wounds. Also sickened at the raw, angry sight of them. It was Isabel who helped Nell most. Once the stripes were cleaned, Nell put the garlic and witch hazel poultice on her patient's back. This done, she covered the back with a bandage, instructing that it must be changed frequently.

Somewhat reluctantly she turned to Benjamin, who had ventured into the sickroom again now that the worst of the work had been done.

"Reverend Sinclair, I know you don't approve of ardent spirits. Neither do I, for that matter, but"—she gazed sheepishly into Benjamin's eyes—"I have administered a little whiskey to your wife. It was all I had for pain," she added quickly, then appeared braced for rebuke.

Benjamin looked down at Elise, lying on her stomach and moaning softly. "Give her all she needs," he said firmly, "if it will take away the pain." He didn't even think to inquire how sweet, God-fearing Nell had come by whiskey. He really didn't care.

"We need not go overboard, Reverend." She smiled. "A little will go a long way in a woman of your wife's tender sensibilities."

But as the days passed, he wondered if all the care in the world would help. He agonized by Elise's bed day and night, thankful Nell was there to care for the children. Eventually Nell had to leave because her own family needed her. Then Benjamin's home returned nearly to the state in which Elise had first found it so many months ago. It was only slightly better because Oliver was older and less demanding and Isabel was able to take on more responsibility. But it was far from the pleasant, peaceful home Elise had created.

Benjamin prayed by Elise's bedside as much as he wept. He simply could not believe that God would restore his life to him only to wrench it away again. Perhaps that was his worst difficulty. He refused to say, "Thy will be done." He refused to let go of Elise. He feared if he did so it might be his undoing. He could almost hear Elise gently admonishing him that God would never require more of him than he could give. It was wisdom that came from a heart sensitive to spiritual things without theological enlightenment. Thinking of what she would say to him if she could, Benjamin was reminded of the scriptural promise. "God is faithful, who will not suffer you to be tempted above that ye are able."

He clung to this and other Scriptures in the dark days when Elise teetered on the very precipice of death. And he clung to God as he had never done before—in helpless humility. But he did not contemplate what his life would be like if Elise wasn't there. He simply could not face that.

He marveled at how his love for her had grown, washing over him like gentle waves flowing over the seashore. All doubts about it were gone, all fear that it could not be right. Only God was capable of sowing such love. And just so, God had given him Elise. He didn't even stop to wonder if she loved him in return. He merely remembered the expression on her face when he had kissed her in the barn and knew it could only be love, for Elise was capable of nothing else.

Elise awoke to crisp sunlight flooding through the window. Her first thought was that it must be morning. At her request, Benjamin had placed the window in the east wall of her room, where it looked out on a pretty little hill dotted with trees and lovely wild flowers in spring.

Then she moved, felt the pain in her back, and darker images flooded into her thoughts. She remembered Maurice Thomson and the terrible things he had done to her. But she was home now. She must be safe. Benjamin had come for her. She remembered something else, but it was so vague it seemed more a dream than reality.

"*I love you, Elise.*" It had been Benjamin's strong baritone that had uttered the words, or had she just imagined it?

Oh, if only it were true! She smiled, her face scrunched into her pillow. She could not roll over and knew instinctively she should not even attempt to rise from the bed, though she was anxious to see everyone. Where were they? How long had she been lying here? What would she say to Benjamin?

A little shiver ran through her as she thought of his dear face, the turquoise eyes dancing with intensity, the smile tentative but warm and caring. His arms so strong they would feel the closest thing to heaven wrapped protectively around her. Oh, Benjamin! Please let it not be a dream. Let it really be true that you said those words I most—

Suddenly, with a sharp, stabbing pain as if a cruel hand had scraped across her wounds, she remembered other awful images from her captivity. Shaking her head, she pressed her face deeper into her pillow, willing it to blot them out. How she wanted to forget! But she could not. She had been spared the worst abuse by her captors—Benjamin might have forgiven that as he had forgiven and looked past her old life. He would understand that she had chosen to survive, if indeed he loved her.

But how far could a man's forgiveness be tested? He'd forgiven so much already. It would be asking too much to expect him to overlook her greatest mistake—no, *deception* would be more correct, and he could not be blamed for considering it so.

As she agonized over what Maurice had told her about Kendell, she wondered if the truth had to come out. Did Benjamin know? Why put him through more torture if he didn't?

Oh, Elise, you are evil indeed! Longing for love on one hand, but in the same instant plotting even more deception. With clenched insides, she knew she had to tell him. However, a moment later when her door opened and she heard his heavy footstep, her courage fled.

He stepped close to the bed and laid a hand, so warm and secure, on her head. She tilted her head and opened her eyes.

"You . . . are awake?" He breathed the words as if he dare not believe them.

"Yes. How long has it been?"

"Ten days." He pulled the chair close to the bed and sat. "We feared you might die, but you—" his voice caught, and moisture filled his eyes. "I have you back," he said quietly. "Elise, I want to tell you something. . . ."

"First I must tell you—"

"Please, let me say this. I have feared for days now that I would never have the chance. Now that I have my opportunity, I don't want to lose it. Elise, I love you!" He bent down and kissed her forehead. "You are so cool now. There were times when the fever raged that I thought my lips would burn when they touched you."

"Then . . . I wasn't dreaming? They were really your kisses?" And she tried to convince herself again of the stupidity of spoiling what they had finally found. "I love you, too, Benjamin."

"It would have been a fine mess if you didn't!" His voice was so cheerful, so light. Why ruin it?

"A mess . . ." she mused almost to herself.

"I better not tire you." He started to rise.

She grasped his hand. "I would never tire of you! Please don't leave. Not yet."

She told herself it wasn't the proper time to tell him. Benjamin looked so pale and worn. He'd obviously spent himself caring for her. She decided to wait until they were both stronger. They had been through so much. Why not enjoy each other for just a while longer?

Maybe it would be easier later.

CHAPTER 54

IF ANYTHING, IT BECAME MORE DIFFICULT.

When Elise learned the details of the rescue, that Benjamin had been party to the deaths of two men in order to save her, she despaired of telling him the truth. She even became so desperate as to convince herself that what Maurice had said might have been a lie to taunt her.

Though physically she grew strong, emotionally she disintegrated as the deception ate away at her. Benjamin suspected nothing, thinking her melancholy was simply due to her illness. She let him think that. What was one more deception?

In two weeks she had returned to most of her household duties. Everyone helped out because she tired easily, but she was determined to return to her previous worth. Maybe if she made herself indispensable again, she might continue to hang on to her home and her life. Now that Maurice was dead, it was possible her secret could die with him.

But that thin hope fell apart one autumn day. It was the beginning of October and as warm as a summer day. Benjamin was in the yard chopping wood. He had shed his shirt, but sweat still ran in rivulets down his shoulders and back. His pale hair lay plastered to his head.

Elise brought him a jug of water.

"You didn't have to," he said as he impaled the ax into his chopping block and straightened. "You're barely on your feet. I surely don't expect you to wait on me."

"I want to, Benjamin." She offered a smile and held out the jug.

Their touching this way, then, was a rare contact, and it sent a thrill through her and made her heart trip as if he had kissed her. She did not pull away, though she knew she should.

"Thank you," he said, smiling. He, too, was aware of the energy caused by the touch. "Elise . . ."

"You best have a drink before you expire," she said as lightly and casually as she could muster.

He obeyed, taking a long swallow of water, then pouring some over his head. "Ah, that feels good."

"You've got quite a bit of wood cut," she observed.

"Yes, but not nearly enough for winter. I'll have to leave off with the cutting today because John is coming tomorrow to help me harvest the corn. Micah and I could manage on our own if we had an idea of what to do. I thought I could figure it out with my book, but that is turning out to be a joke."

"Thank God for a good friend like John."

"And a friend who knows much. I have never met a man so accomplished in practical matters." He paused to take another pull from the jug.

"You will get there, Benjamin. John didn't learn everything in a day, or even a year."

"But he wasn't thirty-five when he started!" He laughed. "I am learning the patience of Job."

"I will let you get back to your work." She turned to go, but he laid a hand on her arm.

"Elise, I've been doing some thinking while I work—that is the beauty of physical labor." He paused. "Would you sit for a minute?"

"Well, I . . ."

"Please."

She could not refuse him. He turned up a couple stumps he had yet to chop and shoved them close, then gestured her to take one. They sat quietly for a long time. Elise knew no light subject was about to be broached. A fleeting stab of fear made her wonder if Maurice had shared his secret with Benjamin. How would she know? She had been senseless during much of the rescue. But it wasn't possible—Benjamin would not have remained quiet about it this long. Would he?

Her dread building with this thinking, she was more shocked than ever at what was on Benjamin's mind.

"I've been thinking that . . . well, perhaps the time is right for us to begin living together as husband and wife." He had been looking somewhere over her left shoulder, but suddenly his gaze shifted, and his eyes met hers. The blue intensity made her throat constrict. How she loved him! How she had longed for this moment. Yet how she now dreaded it.

"I . . . I . . ." Words caught in her throat. The walls of her heart felt squeezed, as if a fist had violently grasped it. Lies and deceptions faded on her lips. It was no use. There might have been an excuse for it when she had not loved him. But now . . . two people in love did not deceive each other. Still, the truth felt like gall in her soul, bitter and rancid.

"What is it, Elise?" he asked tenderly.

It would have been easy then to plead illness and flee. But to where would she run? All she wanted, all she needed and cared about was here before her, wrapped up in this man who loved her, who wanted to share his entire being with her. Who, in spite of that, perhaps even *because* of that, would be repulsed by the truth.

The words spilled from her lips. "Benjamin, I lied to you. I deceived you! I didn't mean to. When Maurice took me he . . . he—"

"Is that what has been troubling you?" he asked, still no rebuke, only loving acceptance in his voice. "I feared such might have happened, but, Elise, I am glad you chose to live. When I was searching for you, I remembered what you said about dying before returning to that life, and I prayed you would do all you had to do to survive. I can accept the other, but it would have killed me had you died. Please don't let it bother you!"

"If only that was all!" Tears filled her eyes. "You've forgiven so much, but this—oh, it's just like with Kendell. I didn't mean to deceive him either, but my father told me on my wedding day! What was I to do? I was afraid of losing him, and I am so much more afraid of losing you. But you must believe me, Benjamin, I didn't know!"

"What didn't you know?" There was an edge now to his voice, as her words were starting to register but obviously in jumbled confusion.

She took a breath. The least she could do was to present her personal indictment rationally. "I was married before." She could not look at him but rather stared at her hands. However, her gaze saw only the ring he had given her on their wedding day. She had wrapped yarn around it so it would fit. Now it glared back at her accusingly. "Did you never wonder about Hannah's father?"

"I thought—"

She interrupted, not able to bear hearing his voice just then. "Oh yes, of course, the product of my occupation. But no, I let you think that rather than tell you the truth. I feared if you knew I'd been married before . . . well, I thought you could accept the other because you knew I had been forced into it, but marriage was a different matter. I know religious people who don't accept divorce or even annulment as legal, no matter what the law says. I didn't know what you would think, and ours was only a business arrangement. Had there been love, I would have told you. I never thought we would . . . oh, Benjamin, how was I to guess we would come to love each other?"

"So you were married before. . . ."

She could almost see his mind work, making allowances, gauging how much more he could indeed forgive. That made her next words nearly impossible to utter. "There's more."

"I was afraid of that." He nodded for her to continue. His countenance was impassive, hard like the ax blade impaled in the stump close to where he sat.

"When Maurry captured me, he told me he had heard the annulment of my marriage had never been formalized. He said my husband had become demented and refused to sign the papers. Believe me, Benjamin, when I say I truly believed the marriage had been annulled." She could have laughed at her words "believe me." How would he ever believe her again?

Benjamin was silent for a long time. She began to wonder what it would be like if he never spoke to her again. She was already beginning to feel like the vast wasteland she'd heard occupied the western half of Texas. Dry, empty, barren.

"What happened with your other marriage?" he asked methodically, like a lawyer interrogating a witness.

"He found out about my Negro blood." Shaking her head, she covered her tearstained face with her hands. "I deceived him, too. My father told me on my wedding day that my mother was an escaped slave, a quadroon. What was I to do? Why did Papa do that to me? He said his conscience was bothering him, but he would leave it to my discretion whether to tell my groom. I couldn't tell him. I let myself think the secret would be safe. It was safe for about a year. Then Kendell's father, William Hearne found out. The family disowned me, and Kendell . . . he just did not have the fortitude to face life as an outcast. I was every kind of fool possible. Because of my weakness I lost him, and now I will lose you."

"Did you love him?"

Was he trying to torture himself and her as well? But he had every right to know. It was only natural that he ask.

"Yes," she said. The time for lies was over. "But you must not think I could still love him after what he did. He turned away from me and his own daughter. He let me become a slave. Because of him, because he did not love me enough, I ended up with Maurice Thomson, losing my honor, my virtue, nearly my soul." She lifted her head and made herself look into the icy pool of Benjamin's eyes. "You gave me my life back, Benjamin, but that's not why I love you. I love you because you are a man who knows how to love enough."

For the first time, his stoic façade cracked. He snorted a dry laugh. "You can say that after Rebekah? After Micah? Perhaps you only hope I can love enough. I fear I might be just as weak as this Kendell of yours." He closed his eyes. "I fear you are asking too much."

"Benjamin, I only ask—"

"Don't ask any more of me!" He burst out angrily.

He lurched to his feet and started to walk away. His shoulders were hunched like mountains, and she feared they were unscalable mountains. She could do nothing but let him walk away. Then he paused but did not turn.

"I loved you, Elise." Then he kept walking.

"Loved . . . ?" she murmured, but he could not have heard her as he strode off.

She let out a strangled sob. She had only herself to blame. Twice she had pushed love to its limits, and twice she had learned just what a fragile thing love is.

CHAPTER 55

THE NEXT DAY JOHN CAME to help with harvesting. Benjamin was ready to throw himself into the task despite the fact that he hadn't slept all night.

Before they began their labors, John brought news.

"A rider come through Cooksburg," he told Benjamin and Micah as they were in the barn gathering the implements they would take out to the field. "He was one of many Austin has sent 'round to the settlements to call for mobilization of a militia."

"Yes, I heard about that," Benjamin said. "That was nearly two weeks ago."

"My oldest son joined up. He went down to San Felipe to see what was going on and came back yesterday with news." John picked up Benjamin's scythe, noted the handle was loose, and worked on fixing it as he spoke. "It's a real war now. They had the first skirmish in Gonzales. Seems the Mexicans wanted to repossess a cannon from the Gonzales militia, but the Gonzales men were reluctant to comply. Well, the Texians—must have been a hundred and fifty of them—formed a line with the cannon in the middle of them. Then they put a banner over the cannon that said 'Come and take it!' " John chuckled. "Took guts for them to face down a hundred armed and mounted Mexican dragoons like that."

"What happened?" This was Micah, who had stopped his work loading one of the horses to listen to John's account.

"Some shots were exchanged, but they were too far away to do much damage. The Texians advanced but didn't get far before the Mexicans retreated!"

"Were there any casualties?" asked Benjamin.

"None serious. The Mexican commander claimed he was under orders to prevent casualties. That's why he retreated." John loaded the repaired scythe on a horse, and they led the animals out of the barn. "I've been thinking of joining up," John said suddenly.

Benjamin stared at his friend. Though the man was adept at many tasks, Benjamin would never have thought him a soldier. Of course, if Texas was to mount any army at all, it must consist of men like John—farmers, hunters, storekeepers.

John laughed, perceiving what was in Benjamin's frank stare. "I know. I've never done a stitch of soldiering in my life, but I figure this is my home, and it is my duty to defend it."

"I used to feel that way myself." Benjamin sighed thoughtfully. His priorities had shifted considerably since those days when he was such a vocal proponent of revolution against Mexico. "I still do but don't see how I could join the army now."

"No one expects it, Benjamin. You can't leave Elise to care for the farm in her present state of health."

Benjamin was about to voice his appreciation for these words of encouragement, when Micah piped up. "I'll go in his place!"

Both men looked at Micah as if noticing him for the first time. And indeed, Benjamin realized afresh that there was so much more to his son than he ever imagined.

"How old are you, boy?" John asked.

"Fourteen!" Micah replied, as if this should seal the issue.

"Too young to go to war," Benjamin said firmly.

"I can shoot and ride as well as anyone! Why, I'd be worth more in a battle than you any day!" He suddenly reddened as he realized the disrespectful tone of his words. To his merit, he usually reserved his disrespect of Benjamin to when they were alone, refraining from showing it in public.

"That may be true," Benjamin rejoined, "but you are still a child, so get such outlandish ideas out of your head." Benjamin had far too much weighing on him now to add worry over his son's notions.

Micah opened his mouth to fire back a retort when he was stopped by John's more reasonable voice.

"There's no way they will take a fourteen-year-old, no matter how good he is." John looked between father and son as if he were an unwilling mediator. "We best get that crop in."

"Yes." Benjamin said.

They trooped out to the field and began to work. John showed Benjamin how to cut the stalks and taught Micah how to bind them together. The work was rather simple, not absorbing enough, Benjamin found, to keep his mind from other matters. He quickly forgot about the talk of revolution, as his mind was pressed with a far more difficult subject.

Elise.

If he had been confused over his growing love for her, this new conundrum was leagues beyond that. What would he do if the marriage that had begun as a business arrangement, grown into love, and was about to blossom into a real marriage turned out to be entirely illegal? Part of him wanted to ignore it all, forget that she might have another husband, forget that she had deceived him. Why not go on as if nothing had happened? He knew she had not meant to deceive him, at least to the extent of hiding a legal marriage. He believed she had truly thought the marriage to have been annulled, and he understood her fear in revealing even that much. The man he had once been would have refused to marry any woman who had been married before, except perhaps in the case of widowhood. He had no idea what the man he had been at the time of their marriage would have done. That man had been willing to accept the fact that she had been with other men, forced though it had been. He had accepted the fact that she had Negro blood, something even the most liberal of whites might not have done.

Yes, he had accepted much. He might even have accepted a former marriage if she had been honest about it from the beginning, if only she had not let him fall in love with her, only to have that love trampled beneath the weight of lies. She'd said she would not have done it had love existed from the beginning. Yet did that really make it all right? At best it only made what they had a sham. At worst it made it a crime. She had thought only of herself, not of what such a thing would do to him. If it got out that he was married illegally, he would be expelled from the church, and rightly so. If his path to ministry was to be closed off, he wanted it to be his choice. He did not wish to be drummed from the ministry in disgrace.

But it went so much deeper than his future occupation. He was not a man to give his love freely or easily. After Rebekah, he thought he would never have the courage to take that step again. But he had. And he had loved Elise so completely that his guilt over betraying Rebekah had dissolved. Now he must face the fact that it had been built on lies. He might never have married Elise had he known about the first marriage, had there been any doubt that it was legally over. Thus, he would not have come to know her and eventually to love her.

She had tried to tell him she had not intended to deceive him to the extent of an illegal marriage. Yet he could see by how tortured she was that she had known all along it had been a possibility.

Even now, remembering her tears of agony during her confession, he wanted to forgive her. He wanted to forget it all and go on as if it had not happened. His love had not come easily. Neither would it depart easily.

He could not erase his love, nor could he erase the fact that she had known of the possibility that her marriage had not legally ended.

His mind struggled over this a dozen times before he and his companions paused for a midmorning break from their work. As they shared water from the jug and snacked on johnnycakes, John and Micah continued the earlier conversation about the revolution. Benjamin barely noticed Micah's rapt interest. Nor did he pay attention to John's answers to Micah's questions and his imparting of the news he'd heard about the politics of it all. Benjamin's mind continued to be distracted, though he tried to pull away from the tiresome inner debates and focus on talk of war strategy and possible commanders.

"So what do you think of Sam Houston?" John asked, and it took a full moment before Benjamin realized the question had been directed at him.

"I . . . I don't know the man," Benjamin said. Then, afraid his mind might burst if he kept agonizing over Elise, he made himself join the conversation. He tried to recall all he knew about Houston. "He was once governor of Tennessee. He lives over in Nacogdoches, doesn't he? He was elected to represent that town in San Felipe for political meetings."

"And he's got the best military experience of any man in Texas," John added.

"Well, then, it's good he's here." But Benjamin didn't care about Houston or armies or battles. His life was being shattered once more, and he didn't know what to do about it.

". . . you ever hear that, Benjamin?" John's voice came as if through a fog.

"What's that?" Benjamin blinked, then made a feeble attempt to laugh off his distraction. It didn't work.

"You all right?" John asked, concerned.

"Yes . . . sure . . . fine." If Micah hadn't been there, he might have been tempted to tell his troubles to his sage friend. Yet even if he could have surmounted his shame to discuss his problems, what could John say? This was something only he could work out, or so he told himself. "We better get back to work." He lurched to his feet and headed back to the field.

The previous sleepless night had combined with the day of hard work harvesting to provide a sound night's sleep for Benjamin. But his first thought on waking at dawn was of Elise. It was ironic that John had been able to spend the night in the cabin, while Benjamin was still exiled to the barn, self-exile though it was. Would he ever be free to have a normal life with the woman he loved? Could his love survive this latest blow?

Going into the cabin for breakfast, he was again struck with the confounding circumstances of his life. The sight of Elise's lovely person tending a pot of mush over the hearth fire with a lock of her curly dark hair dangling in her achingly beautiful eyes made him long to take her in his arms in a husbandly embrace. The deceptively normal scene pricked his heart. And her skittish gaze, her unsmiling lips, tore at him further. This wasn't right. They loved each other. Yet he was as helpless to remedy the situation as Oliver was to rise from his cradle and prepare his morning milk.

When they sat down to eat, he first noted Micah's absence.

"He wasn't in the barn?" Elise answered his inquiry as to Micah's whereabouts.

"No. I didn't see him outside at all."

Though Micah was for all practical purposes emotionally detached from the family, he seldom missed a meal. But with the rest of the harvesting yet to be completed and John needing to leave by midday to get home by sunset, there was no time to delay breakfast for Micah or to go in search of him.

Benjamin did not become truly concerned until he returned to the barn after breakfast and discovered the bay gelding missing. Had it been gone when he woke that morning? He hadn't noticed. But after a more thorough investigation, he became certain that it had been missing for some time. In the cabin, Elise discovered that several johnnycakes left over from the day before were gone, along with a good supply of jerky. Micah's musket and powder horn were nowhere to be found. The final proof that Micah had slipped off during the night came when Isabel told what she had seen.

"I thought it was a dream," she said. "It was still dark, but Micah was getting down his gun, and I asked, 'Where're you going?' And he said, 'Nowhere. Now *shh* and go back to sleep.' He kissed me on the forehead, and I closed my eyes. I guess I went back to sleep."

"He kissed you?" Elise said, voicing surprise at this odd behavior from Micah.

"That's why I thought I was dreaming."

Benjamin looked at Elise. "He kissed her because he thought he wouldn't see her again."

"What do you mean, Papa?" Isabel asked, now worried.

"I think Micah is trying to run away from home," Benjamin said as lightly as he could to allay her fears. "He'll be back." Again he lifted his eyes to Elise. It was not lost on him how natural it was for him to look to her for strength. He will, won't he? his eyes silently implored.

"I wonder how long he's been gone?" asked the practical John. "I didn't hear a thing last night. But my wife always says I could sleep through a hurricane."

"Well, he got past me in the barn, too, horse and all." Benjamin shook his head. "The one time I have a good night's sleep."

"He's probably been gone for hours." John paused in thought, then added, "I'll bet that rascal took off to join the army. He seemed mighty interested in that yesterday."

"You may be right."

"I'll help you look for him, if you want."

The thought of going on another frantic search through the woods for a missing family member did not appeal to Benjamin, nor did he want to ask John to join him. His friend had done far too much for him already.

"Thanks, John, but I think I can handle this alone. It certainly isn't as desperate as the last chase."

"What about the corn?" John asked.

"That can wait another week or so, can't it? You head on home this morning, and I'll finish the crop when I get back." He wanted to add, "When Micah and I get back," but he couldn't muster the confidence. Even if he found Micah, how was *he*, of all people, going to convince him to come home? Wearily, he raked a hand through his hair. "John, you have been a good friend—the best a man could ever hope for—but you've got your own family to tend to. Sometime, we Sinclairs have to fix our problems ourselves."

"I understand," John said, gathering up his jacket and belongings. "I'll go on out and saddle my horse. I'm sure you'll want time alone with the missus. I'll see you before I ride off."

Ah yes. Benjamin needed time alone with the missus. Time to tell her . . . what?

When they were finally alone in the midst of chattering children, they stood silent, like two rocks in the middle of a churning river.

Benjamin spoke first. "Maybe this comes at a good time. I mean, maybe it is good for me to get away from here for a few days."

"Perhaps so," she said. Her tone held a quality that did not sound convinced.

"I can use the time to work things out." He was less convinced.

"I understand. . . ." her voice quavered.

"I am so sorry I can't just . . . make it all go away," he blurted in frustration. "I'm sorry I can't tell you I don't care, that we can just go on as if Kendell Hearne wasn't hanging over us like a specter. I wish I could say I could live that way. I wish I could just say, 'I forgive you' and that could be the end of it. But . . ." He shook his head.

"I know you can't. I don't ask it of you."

"I cannot share you even with a specter," he tried to explain, though she had asked for no explanation.

"I know." Her eyes filled with moisture, making them look like sable washed in rain.

"I'll be back." He forced himself to look into those eyes, though he feared he might be tempted to lose himself and all his problems in them.

"Will you?" Her lower lip trembled, and she bit it as a lone tear dripped down her cheek.

He could not give her the assurances she wanted. Though they both knew he'd be back physically, if for no other reason than for his children, he could not say if he'd return for her.

CHAPTER 56

BENJAMIN ARRIVED IN SAN FELIPE without having sighted Micah on the trail. The boy had covered his tracks amazingly well, though an occasional forgotten sign had indicated that he was heading south. The obvious place for the boy to try to join the army was San Felipe.

Once there, Benjamin spoke with a few men he knew, but none had seen Micah. The town, however, was fairly chaotic these days.

"Many men have taken off for Gonzales," the storekeeper told Benjamin. "Austin is forming an army there."

"Still seems pretty busy in town," Benjamin observed.

"Others have come here to manage the new government."

"New government!" This was astonishing news, momentarily jogging Benjamin from his personal woes. "When did that happen?"

"It ain't formal yet, I suppose," the storekeeper said. "Austin is still claiming that the rebellion is just to uphold the Constitution of 1824, which Santa Anna has been playing pretty fast and loose with lately."

Benjamin leaned against the counter and accepted a cup of water from the clerk. "I suppose Austin is trying to hedge his bets."

"Well, there's a long row to hoe yet before we get our independence and mighty big odds to beat."

"David against Goliath," remarked Benjamin.

"That's right."

"My son may be in the midst of it all if he has his way." Benjamin drained the cup, wiping a sleeve across his damp lips. "You are sure he didn't stop in here for supplies?"

"It's been a fair piece since I've see the boy, Reverend. Can't say as I'd recognize him."

Yes, Micah had sprouted considerably since first coming to Texas. "I guess he looks a lot like me. Tall for his age and rangy in size. Light hair like mine only with considerable more red in it. His eyes are blue, like mine . . ."

Benjamin let his words trail away, for they had begun to get choked in his throat. How alike he and his son were. It was both sad and ironic. They could have had so much together as father and son. But now, it seemed, they had nothing. All Benjamin's efforts to repair his past mistakes had been to no avail. He had lost his son, and not just upon the trail.

"Sorry, Reverend. All I can say is if he's bent on joining the action, he'd probably go to Gonzales."

"Thanks. I'll head that way myself."

Wearily, Benjamin headed west toward Gonzales. If there was an army being formed, he had no doubt that's where Micah would have gone.

He wondered, not for the first time in the days since leaving home, what good it would do to find Micah. The boy hadn't listened to him since he'd stopped beating him. As this occurred to Benjamin, he realized for the first time that he had indeed stopped whipping Micah, though he hadn't consciously done so. He hadn't taken him behind the barn for a couple of months, not because Micah hadn't deserved it on many occasions, but rather because Benjamin had simply lost the heart for it. The beatings hadn't done any good. The cessation of them had done no good either.

Benjamin felt completely helpless to keep his son in line and feared this present search would in the end prove futile. If he found the boy, nothing short of knocking him unconscious and binding him would probably get him to come home. Once home, nothing short of imprisonment would keep him there. Nevertheless, Benjamin felt he had to try.

Perhaps there was more to it than that. As he'd told Elise, this quest might largely be for the purpose of deciding his own future, not his son's. And again his thoughts turned to Elise.

Still, he had no clear concept of what to do. He fleetingly considered forgetting about Micah, who was bound to follow his own mind anyway, and setting out for South Carolina. He would find Kendell Hearne and force him to sign an annulment. It seemed a simple, straightforward matter. But something told Benjamin that it would be far from simple confronting the man who had once loved Elise and then cast her off to a life of the vilest shame. Benjamin had already killed or been a party to killing two men who had harmed Elise. What would he do if he came face-to-face with the man who had started the path of anguish for the woman Benjamin loved? Just thinking about the man made him tremble with rage.

What kind of monster must this man be to have allowed his wife and child to be sold into degradation and dishonor? He deserved death! Yet shouldn't Benjamin feel a small kinship with this man? Hadn't Elise deceived him also? Perhaps Benjamin could understand a bit of Hearne's pain and anger.

No. There could and should be no forbearance for what that man had done. Yet wasn't Benjamin considering doing the very same thing—turning Elise and her child out to a fairly certain fate?

But she deceived me! he silently cried.

Even as his heart swelled with hurt and anger, he was confronted with another reason for not going to find Hearne. What if Kendell Hearne had repented of his actions and desired his wife and child to be restored to him?

That thought sent paroxysms far different than fury coursing through Benjamin. What he felt now was fear—true, staggering fear. But he had to face that possibility whether he went to the Hearne plantation or not.

How could a man be so torn? Wanting her desperately, yet at the same time filled with such pain and anger he wanted to push her away. Desire warred against revulsion. Pardon against condemnation.

More than three hundred Texians had marched to Gonzales and were calling themselves "The Army of the People." Benjamin arrived in time to see the army forming ranks under the command of Austin, who himself had arrived two days before and had wrestled the ragtag force into a semblance of order.

They were planning to march within the hour on San Antonio, the locale of the most formidable Mexican presence in Texas. At the fore of their ranks was the banner emblazoned with the defiant words *COME AND TAKE IT.* Benjamin learned this was the very flag used in the Battle of Gonzales several days before. Despite his own inner conflicts, Benjamin was stirred by the sight. And he thought it quite apropos that the very cannon from Gonzales was being pulled by two yokes of Texas Longhorn steers.

In the mayhem of an army about to march, Benjamin despaired of finding his son, especially since the ranks seemed to be swelling by the minute as new recruits arrived. He saw Haden first, and only then realized he might have done better to have looked for his brother all along. Micah was mounted on the chestnut gelding right beside his uncle.

It took some courage for Benjamin to ride up to the pair. He prepared himself to eat whatever pride he had left.

"Haden," he called loud enough to be heard over the din of voices, the stomping of horses, and the rattle of arms. He had to call again before he was heard.

Haden turned in his saddle. "Benjamin!"

Benjamin maneuvered his mount close. "You look surprised to see me." He glanced briefly at Micah.

"Well, I—"

"Are you taking a fourteen-year-old boy into battle, Haden?" Benjamin could not help his deprecatory tone.

"No one's *taking* me!" retorted Micah. "I'm going on my own." He directed defiant eyes at Benjamin, echoing the battle cry of the army, "Come and take it!"

"There wasn't much I could do to stop him," Haden said reasonably enough.

One look at Micah proved the truth of Haden's words. Benjamin used the only argument he could think of. "You are too young for this, Micah. Why, you are worrying Elise half to death. You know she cares about you." As do I, but he could not say the words.

"You're gonna have to drag me back," Micah challenged.

Benjamin took off his hat and wearily combed his fingers through his damp hair. Finally, drawing upon all the humility he'd learned in the last months since Rebekah's death, he turned to Haden. "Haden, can't you reason with him?"

"I tried, Ben, I honestly did. But look around." He swept a hand toward the ranks of the army. "There's plenty of boys here. Texas needs anyone who can shoot, and Micah can shoot, better'n me if the truth were told. Let the boy go, Ben. I'll look out for him, I promise."

Like you looked out for Rebekah, Benjamin thought, eyeing his brother critically.

Haden must have understood that look and what lay behind it for he replied, "I know I'm not the most responsible man around, but I swear I love this boy as if he were my own. I'll protect him with my life.

I would have done the same for Rebekah, but I could not intercede in the very workings of nature."

Benjamin's jaw tightened, and his breath caught in his chest. Suddenly he let the breath out and relaxed his jaw. Though a small part of him still wanted to blame Haden for Rebekah's death, he reminded himself he had come beyond such accusations. He also knew mere men could indeed only do so much to protect those they loved. It was wrong to ask more.

"I know . . ." Benjamin said softly. "I know, Haden."

He thought sadly how he'd lost his brother as he'd lost his son, and he could do nothing about it. A man can change his ways, but that doesn't always mean past damage can be repaired. Sometimes the wreckage must stand as a reminder to do better in the future.

"So I can stay?" Micah asked. Did he not yet realize Benjamin had no control over him? Or was this his small way of binding up some of the damage?

"Yes, but . . ." Benjamin glanced at Micah. How he wanted to embrace him, but their horses, not to mention miles of fear, separated them. "Take care of yourself."

In that moment, Colonel Austin issued the command to march. Benjamin stood still as the sea of horses and men surged forward. He had to take a tight grip on his reins, as the mare seemed to want to join the march.

"Not now, girl. We have other battles to fight."

He stood there until the entire army passed him by. "Dear God, please protect my boy. I may have lost him, but your eye will always be on him, and you will never lose him."

Benjamin reined his mount around and headed back to San Felipe. He had no idea what he would do once there. On the way he encountered many riders going to San Antonio to join Austin. Maybe he should join the fighting after all. Elise might be weak, but she could no doubt handle the children alone. At the moment, fighting in a war seemed preferable to going home and humbling himself once again.

Dear God, how much humbling can a man take?

He camped a day's easy ride from San Felipe. He built a fire, made coffee, then with cup in hand he stared into the dancing flames of the campfire. All he could think of was the cold expanse of life apart from Elise, the void he would feel bereft of her sweet inner beauty, her dear wisdom, her tender heart. Those had been the very things that had helped guide him back to God. Without her he might still be mired in the depths of his self-abnegation, his shame, his misery. She had said he gave her back her life, but she had done the same for him.

Perhaps that's what made it so hard to forgive her now for her lies, because they threatened to tear down what he had so painfully achieved.

"Howdy, stranger!" came a voice from beyond the brush.

"Hello," Benjamin called in reply. He didn't relish the thought of company, but one could hardly be unneighborly in the wilderness.

A horse came into view, led by the visitor. In the growing twilight he could only vaguely make out the appearance of the man, but he seemed harmless enough.

"Saw the fire and smelled that coffee, and, well, I figured fightin' could wait another day," said the rider. "Mind some company?"

"No, you are welcome, of course."

The man hobbled his horse, then came forward and hunkered down in front of the fire. It was then, as the flame flared in response to Benjamin laying on another chunk of wood, that he saw clearly the face of his guest.

"Mr. Fife! Is that you?" Benjamin exclaimed.

The man blinked as his eyes adjusted to the flickering light of the fire. "Well, it sure is. And you might be—? Why, if it ain't Reverend Sinclair!"

"And they say Texas is a big land," Benjamin said wryly to the man who had guided him and his family to Natchez nearly two years ago. "Seems a rather small world now, doesn't it?" Benjamin refilled his cup and handed it to Fife. "I'm afraid I have only one cup."

"That's kind of you, Reverend, but I have a cup." Fife opened his saddlebag, which he had carried from his horse, and removed a tin cup.

Benjamin filled the cup as he spoke. "Looks like you made it to Texas after all."

"Well, I got to thinking more and more about this place after leaving you and your family," Fife replied, pausing only for occasional sips from his cup. "When I got back to my place, it just seemed so old and so familiar. I came there looking for adventure, but all the adventure was gone. Why, I had neighbors less than two miles from me! I felt ready to see what else was out there. And now I get here and find not only a new land but a war as well."

"Yes, that is most unfortunate."

"After a fashion I suppose it is, but I'm a mite ashamed to say it is exciting, too."

"You on your way to Gonzales to join Austin?"

"Thought I might see if they could use my help."

He smiled, revealing yellow, rotting teeth. Benjamin wondered how his children could have become so fond of this man. But they had no doubt seen what Benjamin had been too stupid to see back then. There was a gentle spirit behind the grime.

"How about you, Reverend? You going to fight?"

"No, actually I've just been to Gonzales. I'm on my way back home." He didn't know why he added what he did, perhaps it was because he knew the man had been fond of Micah. "I was trying to make my son give up his notion of fighting. He ran off and joined Austin."

"Your boy?" Fife's bushy eyebrows arched. "Why, he's just a kid."

"Fourteen. But he's shot up several inches since you last saw him. He's nearly as tall as me."

"Ya don't say!" Fife helped himself to more coffee. "Well, I reckon when they get that old, there ain't much you can do with 'em."

Benjamin remembered how he and Fife had locked horns so many times on the trail. Benjamin had preached at the man, berated him, condemned him to hell, and had firmly forbidden his children to speak to him. The memory seemed to open up a floodgate of more unwanted memories—of a man who was all but a stranger now. Hard, arrogant, unyielding, unforgiving.

A man he never wanted to become again. Yet since Elise had made her confession to him, he could feel the hard shell that had once imprisoned him begin to clamp back into place. He could feel that arrogant pride take him captive once again. He inhaled a strangled breath.

"You all right, Reverend?" Fife's voice penetrated Benjamin's muddled senses.

Benjamin lifted his eyes to the man before him, a man he had wronged as he had wronged so many others in his life.

"Mr. Fife, you've reminded me of a debt that is long past due—"

"You mean the money?" Fife cut in. "I told you—"

"Not the money." Pausing, Benjamin started to lift his cup to his dry lips but, finding it empty, forced himself to continue without the benefit of a distraction. "I treated you abominably when we were traveling. You saved my life and the life of my family—" When Fife opened his mouth to protest, Benjamin raised his hand to stop him. "It's true. Had you not come along when our guide stranded us at that river, I would have been pigheaded and arrogant enough to forge ahead alone, and that would have surely been death to my family."

"You are being too hard on yourself, Reverend."

"Not hard enough. At any rate, you did not deserve my judgments and my derision, but that's all I gave you. And for that, Mr. Fife, I am sorry. I'd ask your forgiveness, but I suppose you'd have to forgive me a good many times to make up for the way I treated you. So I will just say with all sincerity, I am sorry."

Fife gave a self-deprecating wave of his hand. "You are making too big a thing of it. I mean, compared to a refined man like you, a true man of God, I am crude and all. No one would blame you. Fact is, you was probably being mighty accepting as folks go."

Benjamin shook his head. "You did not deserve my poor treatment. My children saw what I did not, that you are a good man at heart. I am ashamed of what I did and do not deserve your forgiveness."

"Well, I'd be a small man indeed, if I couldn't forgive you, Reverend . . ." he paused and smiled. "Even if I thought it necessary. Don't the Bible say to forgive seven times seventy? I figure you got a few more on account at that rate."

Benjamin smiled also. He thought it was probably the first smile Fife had ever seen from him. "Thank you, Mr. Fife. I can't deny you are right about the Bible. You are—" Then it hit him as if he'd been struck by the book in question itself. "Mr. Fife, you are very, very right!"

"I am?" The thatch of Fife's brows rose again, obviously nonplussed at having a minister be enlightened by him on spiritual matters.

That night Benjamin stretched out to sleep, staring up at the night canopy of stars. He thought about the fool he had been and all he'd lost because of it. Much of those losses were gone forever, but he did not have to add Elise to that lot. All he had to do was forgive her. And he would—again and again and again. If a man like Fife could forgive *him*, how much more could Benjamin forgive the woman he loved? He only hoped she would forgive him for having even considered to do otherwise.

What would happen after that, he did not know. If her first marriage proved to be still valid, then he might have to give her up after all. The thought of losing her stabbed his heart.

Then he remembered something else. Elise had once told him something Isabel said to her on their wedding day, when Elise had assured Isabel that she didn't want to take the child's mother's place.

Isabel had said, "I think she would have chosen you."

Benjamin had thought it a sweet sentiment when he first heard it. Now he thought of the Scripture, "Out of the mouth of babes and sucklings thou hast perfected praise."

Long ago Rebekah had given Elise her New Testament. She'd not an inkling then of the part Elise would one day have in her husband's life and in the lives of their children. Yet Benjamin now knew God had even then been preparing the way—and what better person to use to accomplish His purpose than the one whose place Elise was destined to take? It was just the kind of thing God would do in His infinite knowledge and wisdom.

Finally the weight was lifted, and Benjamin could breathe the words he had been fighting for days. "Thy will be done, O Lord."

CHAPTER 57

Elise had left the cabin door open to let in what breeze there might be on that unseasonably warm day. She was going to take the children down to the creek when she finished the breakfast dishes.

Her hands steeped in soapy water, she tensed when she heard the approaching hoofbeats. It could be Indians. It could be thieves.

It could be Benjamin.

But he had been gone only a day, and she didn't expect him back this soon. She should have been glad at the prospect of his return, but fear dominated her feelings at the moment. Had he found Micah so quickly? Had he so soon decided the fate of their lives? A sinking sensation in her stomach told her that if it were so, it could not be a favorable decision. He'd been taut, confused, even angry when he left, and she could not believe he had changed so quickly.

Drying her hands on a cloth, she slowly walked to the door. Hannah tugged at her skirt.

"Mama," the child said plaintively. Had she sensed the sudden flux of tension? Surely not.

"Yes, dear." Elise lifted the child into her arms as if she could be a shield against the calamity about to descend.

"Shoe." Hannah held up her little slipper.

Elise smiled in spite of herself. She hadn't noticed the shoe in her daughter's hand, so wrapped up was she in her gloomy prognostications. "I'll get it in a minute. Let's see who our visitor is."

Hannah's little intercession seemed to make Elise feel braver. She stepped into the open doorway and saw that the approaching rider was not Benjamin at all. It took a full moment before it registered just who the visitor was. Then she set Hannah down and rushed down the step into the yard.

"Papa!"

The man sitting tall and straight in the saddle of a fine-looking roan grinned, revealing a set of straight, white teeth. He reined his mount to a stop and leaped spryly from the saddle.

"*Ma petite* Elise!" His long legs covered the distance between them in two strides.

Elise opened her arms as he threw his own arms around her. She immediately detected the familiar scents associated with her father—good cologne, fine cigars, and even better whiskey. She felt like a child again in her papa's tender embrace. Though her father had never been much of a symbol of security to her, he was still her father, and there was something quite reassuring just in that fact.

When they parted, he stood back a step to appraise her. "Ah, look at you, *ma chère*!"

She self-consciously patted her dress, the patched and mended dress she had worn when she first came to the cabin. She had the new blue calico dress to replace the one ruined by the whipping but had not felt much like wearing the gown made with fabric belonging to the woman she had suddenly begun to feel jealous of. After all, Rebekah had had what Elise was beginning to fear she would never have—Benjamin's love, devotion, and the security of his name.

"Forgive me, Papa, I look a fright. I did not expect visitors." She tried to smile, but her confidence was quickly ebbing.

Her father had always been very cognizant of fashion, and even when they were as penniless as paupers on the street, he saw to it that both she and he were garbed to the hilt of fashion. Even now, after no doubt many days on the trail, he looked quite dapper in a stylish suit—Elise had no doubt it represented the height of fashion in men's clothing—with a nattily tied silk cravat and a houndstooth checked waistcoat. Handsome at fifty, his hair was still quite black and thick, with just a few streaks of gray adding a touch of distinction. A top hat, tilted just so, was perched on his head. He was clean-shaven save for a thin mustache curled rakishly at the ends. He had always worn one whether in fashion or not.

"Oh no, ma chère! You are beautiful! A vision! Even in an old, ragged dress you are . . . ah, so like your mother!" Dorian Toussaint had always spoken with a French accent, liberally peppering his speech with French, but he was American-born, a Creole of New Orleans. Elise noted his accent seemed thicker than ever, perhaps a result of time recently spent in Europe.

"Thank you, Papa." She knew he had paid her a high compliment indeed. "Now, come in, please."

He tied his horse to a post in the yard, then followed Elise, but not before noticing her companion for the first time.

"And who is your little friend hiding behind your skirts?"

Elise took Hannah into her arms again. "This, Papa, is Hannah, your granddaughter!"

"Ah! But I should have seen it, *non?* She has her mother's eyes. But I think she has my nose, does she not? What a pretty creature!"

Hannah dipped her face shyly into her mother's shoulder, carefully leaving one eye free so she could continue to observe this stranger.

Dorian made another exclamation when he entered the cabin. Isabel was sitting on the floor playing pat-a-cake with Oliver. Leah was busy removing pans from a cupboard.

"What have you here, ma chère!" Dorian said. "A regular nursery. But they can't be yours, not all of them."

"No, they are not. But it is a long story. Come and sit down, and I will fix you coffee or tea."

"Oh, coffee, please. After being in Europe, I find Americans make simply horrid tea." With a neat flip of his coattails, Dorian seated himself on the bench at the table. "But first, chère, I must know . . . are you all right? You look wonderful, but . . . well, are you *all right*?"

She was glad that he had asked, glad for the expression of real concern on his well-chiseled face. Yet she was not eager to be reminded of her all-too-recent ordeal, especially by the man who, though innocently, had been the cause of it all.

"Yes, Papa, I am well." Forgetting the coffee for the moment, she slipped into the bench opposite him. "I admit it has not been easy, but I believe it is, at least I hope it is, behind me." She deemed it unnecessary to delve into her present uncertainties about Benjamin.

"You are a brave child." He sighed, his dark expressive eyes glinting. "When I returned to the country and learned what had happened . . . Ah, chère, can you ever forgive me?"

"It wasn't your fault," she replied, and if it was lame, it was sincere. The time for making accusations had long passed.

"Those animals! Turning you out to the slave quarters, then selling you to *him*!" He clutched his chest dramatically. "I could hardly believe it when I heard. Ah, ma chère! What you must have suffered! When I went to the plantation, I demanded satisfaction from Kendell."

"What do you mean, Papa?"

"I challenged the filthy cur to a duel!"

"Oh no, you didn't!" Elise gasped, her mind spinning at what the ramifications of such a deed might be.

"I did indeed, but that cowardly pig did not have the gumption to even show up at the appointed time. How you could have loved him, I do not know. And how I could have consented to that marriage, I am also perplexed."

Elise did not know how she could have loved Kendell either, but she did know that her father had been all too anxious for the match. He, in fact, had all but pushed her into the marriage, considering it a match of his dreams—money, position, political power. Only at the last minute had his feet become slightly chilly, probably fearing the repercussions of duping such a powerful family. But again Elise remained silent on these matters.

Instead she said, "I'm happy the duel failed. You could have been killed."

Dorian laughed. "I am the best shot on two continents!" Pausing a moment, he added, "Ma chère, I could use that coffee now."

Elise rose and went to the hearth where the perpetual pot was still warm from breakfast. She found the nicest cup in the cupboard, which had only a few chips in it, and filled it. Setting it in front of her father, she sat down. Taking a breath, she broached the subject of Kendell Hearne again.

"Papa, how did you find Kendell? I mean, I had heard he'd lost his . . . ah . . . mental faculties."

Dorian snorted. "In my opinion the man never had them. His mind was but a sponge for his mother's commands." He sipped his coffee, his little finger fastidiously raised. "But in the technical sense, at least, he seemed of sound mind when I saw him."

"I was told not long ago by Maurice Thomson—"

"Him!" Dorian exploded. "Pah! The blackguard, the scoundrel! Of him also I sought satisfaction. I came here to rescue you and to kill him. But the scum had the audacity to get himself killed before I could get to him. Woe to me! How I wanted to avenge what happened to you, but I was robbed of it all."

"I don't need to be avenged, Papa. I am all right."

He lifted a slim hand and gently touched her cheek with a manicured finger. "Tell me that Thomson did not use you."

"It is in the past."

"Oh . . ." He moaned softly. "I have failed you."

Not sure how to reply, Elise decided instead to give her father a chance to redeem himself by giving her information she desperately needed. She wrenched the conversation back in the direction she desired. "Maurice told me a few weeks ago that Kendell became addleminded after I was sent away and refused to have our marriage annulled. Papa, I have married again, and if that is the case, then my current marriage is nullified. Is what Maurice said true?"

"It is true that for a time that weak-livered fool lost his senses." When Elise gasped in dismay, Dorian hurried on, "But he came out of it fast enough when he met a woman who was willing to marry such as he."

"What are you saying? Did Kendell remarry?"

"He did. That is why I am certain his marriage to you must have been annulled. She is just a step up from white trash, believe me, but he could do no better after what happened. Even that shrew Daphne gave her blessing."

"So our marriage was annulled?" She hardly dared believe it.

"As far as I know, yes. But if you like, when I return to the States, I will procure the legal documents. So, ma chère, you say you have married. Where is your husband? What kind of man is he? I hope you have done better this time. Are all these other children his, then?"

Elise smiled, the first time she'd truly felt like doing so in days. Not everything was settled, of course. Benjamin still had every right to hold her deception against her, but if he chose not to—Dear God, please let him choose not to!—then they still had a chance to be together. She felt truly free of her past, free to give the man she loved all he had a right to desire.

"Let me tell you about my husband, Papa. First, he is a very good man. . . ."

An hour later the verbose Dorian Toussaint was stunned to silence after hearing of his daughter's most astounding odyssey in the last year and a half. He sat saying nothing for a full two minutes before finally breathing, "*C'est une vraie aubaine!*"

Elise knew enough French to understand her father was attributing her final good fortune in finding Benjamin to God.

"Yes, Papa," she said, "I feel very fortunate despite all that has happened."

"But there is still a worry he may renounce you for the deception about your former marriage?"

"Maybe, but don't you think God will work that out also?"

"Who am I to question, eh? It would seem you have a greater father than I looking over you."

Smiling warmly, Elise took her father's smooth hands in hers. "I love you, Papa. And I am glad you have found me."

"I have nearly forgotten, ma chère! I have a present for you. Wait a moment." Dorian jumped up and left the cabin. In a few moments he returned with a package. It was about the size of a painting.

CHAPTER 58

DORIAN DEPARTED THE NEXT MORNING. He had tried to put a brave face on it, but Elise could tell he had been most uncomfortable in the rustic cabin. He promised to return soon to meet Benjamin. Elise knew she could not count on his promises. But she urged him as strongly as she could not to forget his promise about the annulment papers.

Over the next days Elise wavered between dread and anticipation. She imagined a dozen different scenes of seeing Benjamin again, half of which ended blissfully. The other half ranged from her worst nightmare to . . . well, anything short of a happy reunion was a nightmare.

Late one afternoon when Benjamin had been gone a week, Elise was in her room admiring the painting her father had brought. She sat on the edge of the bed, propping the portrait against the rough log wall. What a handsome pair her father and mother made. Dorian, proving to be quite an ageless creature, looked practically the same in the painting as he did now, though without the gray in his hair. Elise thought it fitting that her father was gazing not at the artist but instead down at the woman seated in front of him. Elise had always known her father loved himself more than her, Elise, but she had never resented that. It was plain that the one bit of selfless love he had ever offered anyone had been reserved exclusively for Claire Toussaint, Elise's mother. It was, in fact, the one thing father and daughter had in common. His love was for the woman taken too early from him. Elise's love was for the mother she would never know.

Claire Toussaint. Stunningly beautiful, skin the color of café au lait, hair as black as a raven's wing. Her eyes brown as mahogany, though not clearly discernable in the painting, because they, too, were not focused at the artist. Instead, they were gazing down at the child in her arms. Elise tingled at the sight. She could almost feel her mother's arms around her now, the touch of those fine, graceful hands, the security of a nearness that seemed to transcend oils and canvas.

Like Dorian, Claire had also been a Creole, though born of a French father and a mulatto slave. And, like Elise, she had suffered much for that fluke of birth. As a child, Elise had often tried to imagine her mother, but with only her father's superficial images to guide her, Elise had never been able to find more in her mother than beauty and grace. Now studying the golden-skinned woman, Elise experienced a deep kinship with her mother. And she missed her more than ever.

Claire would understand rejection for no reason other than the color of her skin. Claire would understand the shame of selling one's virtue for the sake of survival. Claire would understand secrets and deceptions because she had lived the last year of her life in deception. But mostly she would understand the kind of love that filled one with fear and joy, anticipation and dread.

Claire Toussaint would, as no other woman could, be able to hold her grown daughter close and whisper lovingly, "It will be all right, my dear. True love will win out in the end, as it did for your father and me."

Oh, Mama, if Benjamin and I could have but half the love you and Papa had—if only for a year—I would be content!

Elise was still gazing at the painting when she heard the footfall at her door. It wasn't one of the children, for it was too heavy. It must be Benjamin. Suddenly she felt paralyzed, unable to turn. How she wished she could crawl just then into the painting and become the infant protected by her mother's embrace.

True love. Would it win out? She had but to turn to find out.

He came into the room and laid a hand on her shoulder, the warm vibrancy of his touch sending a chill through her tense frame.

"Elise . . ."

Desperately she tried to read that single, softly spoken word, her name. But her mind suddenly became dazed. Finally, stiffly, with none of the grace she should have learned from her mother, Elise rose and turned.

Benjamin gathered her into his arms.

"Will you forgive me," he implored, "that I could ever have considered for even a moment turning away from you? I have been such a fool. And I may always be so, but I am a fool who loves you, who cannot live without you."

Tears flooded her eyes and strangled her response. "Benjamin, I—" But emotion choked out her words.

"Shh . . ." He brushed his lips against hers, softly, gently. "I don't know what we'll do about . . . that other thing, but there must be a way for us to be together. God will find a way. He has brought us this far, hasn't He?"

She nodded, her head pressed against his chest, still unable to speak. For the moment she was merely content to be held by him, to feel the intensity of his love, the conviction of his heart. Seconds passed, and she knew she could have stood thus forever, but she had to speak, she had to tell him God indeed had found a way.

"Benjamin, I must tell you something. . . ." She sniffed as her emotion calmed.

"Elise . . . ?" She could feel the tense catch in his tone.

She hurried on, "Oh, Benjamin, I love you. You must never doubt that, and I will keep no more secrets from you. What I have to tell you is wonderful news. My father came while you were gone. He brought this painting of my mother. He also told me my marriage has been annulled, and Kendell has remarried. Benjamin, we are free!"

"Oh, my dear!" he breathed and sagged against her, as if he had been braced for a battle that never came. "Why should I be surprised? I knew God would take care of us." Then he laughed, a little hysteria mixed with glee. "I knew, but I didn't believe."

"Neither did I. But we'll do that much better next time."

"Next time?" He laughed again. "Don't you know we will live happily ever after?"

She joined his mirth. "Of course we will, through work and storms and hardships and . . . our God only knows what. But we will know happiness."

Suddenly Elise felt a tugging down around her knees.

"Papa?" came Hannah's small voice, still sleepy after having just risen from her nap. "Papa home."

Then Leah bounded into the room. She also had just woken from her nap but looked bright-eyed and ready for mischief.

"Up! Up!" she insisted.

Brought back to sweet reality, Elise and Benjamin suddenly heard more insistent sounds from the other room as Oliver woke with hearty cries.

Benjamin let go of Elise only to answer Leah's demands. He scooped her up in one arm, then, when Hannah also held up her arms, he took her in his other arm. The four moved into the other room in a circle of embraces, Elise still with her arm around Benjamin.

Isabel slipped from her bed. "Papa, you're home."

"Yes, my dear," he answered with a look that seemed to say, *I wish I had a third arm.*

Elise drew the seven-year-old into their warm embrace.

"Oliver is crying," Isabel said, as if anyone needed to be told with the din now echoing through the cabin.

Elise smiled. "He certainly is."

Benjamin grinned. "And all is as it should be."

HEAVEN'S ROAD

PART ONE

EARLY SUMMER 1842

CHAPTER 1

March 1836
Goliad, Texas

DEAFENING GUNSHOTS PIERCED the chill air. Cries of shock, pain, and even defiance mingled with the shattering blasts. And above it all a voice shouted, "Run, Micah! Run!"

The boy hesitated. "No, Uncle Haden."

"I said run! Your pa'll kill me if anything happens to you."

The boy looked at his beloved uncle, then beyond him to the wall of slaughtering Mexican soldiers. Micah could not have moved even if he had wanted to, frozen as he was with sudden panic. Men were falling everywhere. They were unarmed and helpless against their Mexican executioners, but many were fighting desperately against the massacre with their bare hands and with the butts of rifles seized from their attackers. Still, they fell mercilessly.

"Run!" Uncle Haden's voice wrenched Micah from his panic.

Two Mexican soldiers approached the boy and his uncle, ready to fire. Micah wanted to die with his comrades, but the voice kept screaming.

"Run . . . run . . . run!"

Haden then thrust his own body like a shield between Micah and the approaching soldiers. Only then did Micah know he must obey this man who was giving his life to save his nephew. That life could not be given in vain.

He turned and ran. A lead ball whizzed past his head. Another grazed his shoulder with searing pain, but he kept running. A thick stand of trees lay ahead, then the river. Upon reaching the cover of the trees, he paused to gasp in a breath but made the mistake of looking back at the field of slaughter. The two Mexicans were standing over Uncle Haden's body, firing into the fallen form as if he had not been killed by the first shot. Then the soldiers took off toward the woods.

After Micah!

He wanted to fight them. He wanted to kill them. But Micah had no weapon. Rage supplanted all fear and horror. All he could think of was getting revenge. And he knew now why he had obeyed his uncle. He would run now, but he would one day fight again. The Mexican murderers would pay dearly for what they had done at Goliad.

Micah turned and ran again. How he hated to run, but he now was buoyed by roiling thoughts of vengeance. He reached the steep riverbank, but as he was about to plunge over the side, another ball struck his leg. He made a desperate lunge over the edge, where he figured he would probably be dashed to bits by rocks and debris or frozen by the icy spring runoff. But miraculously he hit the water cleanly even as more shots rang above him. Gasping a deep breath, he went under. He held his breath until he thought his head would explode, and only then did he slowly rise to the surface of the water to carefully venture a look.

The soldiers had given up their chase, no doubt believing he had drowned. He swam to the opposite bank, crawled from the water, and forced his numb body to move.

"Run! Run! Run!" The words kept echoing over and over in his head. "Run . . . kill! Kill! Kill!"

1842

Micah felt a sharp pain in his side. He flailed with his arms and let out a shuddering groan.

"Hey, Micah!"

A voice penetrated the sleep-numbed fog.

"Get up 'fore you wake every Injun and greaser around."

Micah opened his eyes, panting as if he truly had been running. Sweat drenched him. He looked around. His friend Jed Wilkes was standing over him, looking perturbed. They were outdoors, and Micah was lying in his bedroll on the hard earth. Though still dark, the damp chill indicated it was the early hours of the morning.

"Can't a man sleep in peace?" Micah growled harshly to cover the shaky insides left in the wake of his fitful sleep.

"Sounded like you was havin' that nightmare again." A look of worry creased Jed's broad, simple face. "Ya looked awful scared, Micah. Ya ain't never scared 'cept when you have them dreams."

"And I ain't scared then either!"

Micah ran his hands over his face. That cursed nightmare! Six years had passed since the Goliad massacre where his Uncle Haden, along with four hundred other Texans, were brutally murdered. Yet Micah still could not get those sickening images out of his mind. He had been a boy of fourteen at the time; very impressionable, he supposed. Still, he was a man now—almost twenty-one. What must his partners think seeing him flailing around in his sleep, probably crying out like some yella' kid?

"Did I wake anyone else?" He looked around. Only Harvey was up. Joe was just starting to stir.

"It's time to get up anyway," said Jed, who then turned his attention to packing up his bedroll.

Then Micah remembered. They were supposed to be up several hours before dawn so they could start working. Smirking to himself, he thought of the euphemistic reference to work. Well, it *was* work. It kept him fed—that is, it usually it kept him fed. Sometimes the pickings were slim, and he'd get a bit slim as well. Only two weeks ago they had been unsuccessful in usurping a small herd of Longhorns. The owners had chased Micah and his partners into Mexico, where they had been living like animals since, trying to stay alive until something else came along. Running across the herd of mustangs two days ago had been better than finding water in the desert. Mustangs went for a lot more money than cattle. If they were successful this time, they should get a nice little wad of cash. The herd of about two hundred fine mustangs was grazing not far away. All they had to do was round up a few of them.

"Rounding them up" was also rather euphemistic. The better word was "rustle." Yes, Micah Sinclair, son of a preacher man, was nothing but a horse thief. He only hoped his father knew about it and it was a nagging thorn in the man's side.

Harvey Tate, the erstwhile leader of the little band of rustlers, called everyone together. Micah stowed the last of his gear on the back of his roan mount and ambled up to the group.

"I could sure use some coffee," he grumbled.

"Sure, Micah, go ahead. Build a fire and warn everyone within ten miles that we're laying in wait here," sneered Harvey.

"Maybe I'll do just that and put an end to this stupid scheme." Micah stood toe to toe and eye to eye with Harvey. Micah could shoot straighter and was probably smarter than his boss. The only thing Harvey had on any of the other men here was age—he was almost ten years older than Micah. Thus Micah figured he'd let the man lead until he himself could garner the kind of respect afforded by sheer age.

Micah's pale hair, despite the streaks of red, and his fair skin made him look like a babe. He hated it, especially in that these traits had come directly from his father. He tried hard to cover them with a smokescreen of swagger and grit. He had probably killed as many men, if not more, than all his outlaw friends combined—that is, if one included the Battle of San Jacinto. But he sure didn't look like no war hero. He didn't look like an outlaw either.

"You got a better plan for getting those horses?" Harvey was saying.

"I don't like stealing from Anglos, that's all. And I got a funny feeling about that herd."

"Ain't no time to be choosy. We ain't had a good haul in a month." Harvey spit a stream of tobacco juice into the dirt. "Besides, they're Mexican. You saw how they were dressed."

"Yeah," put in Joe Stover. "I been a whole month without whiskey or women. I'll steal from my own mother if'n I have to."

"You ain't never been without whiskey," Micah retorted. "And I'll bet you ain't got no mother either!"

Jed laughed, snorting loudly. "He got ya there, Joe. You an orphan like me, Joe? Ha, ha!"

"Why you half-witted—" Joe began, turning viciously on Jed.

Micah stepped between them with fist raised and would have planted it in Joe's face, but Harvey grabbed Micah's fist from behind.

"No arguing, ya hear?" Harvey glared at his men, and Micah had to admire a man who could look fearsome like that—not that he himself was afraid. Nevertheless, he did back down. They had more important matters to attend to. Even Joe, an *hombre* every bit as tough as Harvey, relented.

"Listen, Micah, I don't want to steal from Texans either," Harvey said. "Shoot, we could hang for that. But they're Mexicans. I'm sure of it. And we're in Mexico, so it stands to reason."

"Nah, Harvey," put in Jed. "We crossed the Rio Grande yesterday, so we're bound to be back in Texas now."

"Not according to the Mexicans," said Joe, who fancied himself not only a lady's man but also a scholar because he'd read one book in his life. "There's never been agreement on that fact. The Mexicans put the boundary at the Nueces—"

"Shut up, ya bunch of yammerin' fools!" burst Harvey. "It's gonna be daylight soon, and we ain't gonna get nothing if we keep standing here exercising our jaws. I say them horses are Mexican, and that's that!" He swung around sharply toward Micah. "You with us, or what?"

Micah shrugged. "I guess so." He had no qualms at all about stealing from Mexicans. Truth be told, he wasn't squeamish about stealing from Texans, but because the penalties were a far sight stiffer, he tended to avoid it. Texans stealing from Mexicans were simply considered resourceful. But those stealing from Texans were labeled bandits and received no quarter.

The four outlaws mounted up and headed out. They rode for about three miles, slowing a safe distance away from the herd and covering the last several hundred yards as soundlessly as Indians. Their plan was simple enough. Under cover of darkness they would cut out about fifty horses and drive them to a box canyon Harvey knew of where they would lay low for a couple of days while they changed the brands on the animals. Then they would take the small herd to Laredo and sell the mustangs to a friend of Harvey's.

The four rustlers paused on a ridge overlooking the grassy meadow where the herd had been bedded down for the night. There was only one guard on lookout. Micah had noted when they first spotted them two days ago that they were running with a skeleton crew. His best guess was that there were no more than five or six drovers, including one driving the wagon. And he was certain one of them was a female, though he was baffled why there would be a woman present in this wild country. In any case, the drovers were for the most part outfitted like *vaqueros*, wearing wide-brimmed sombreros and mounted on Spanish saddles. But what worried Micah was that a couple of the men definitely looked like gringos. Still, it wasn't unusual for Mexicans to wear a combination of duds. The presence of the gal worried him, too, but if all went well, there should be no danger to anyone. And even if there was, Micah had no problem killing Mexicans. He would never finish exacting the debt owed him after Goliad.

A small part of Micah knew he was trying to justify his own questionable actions. Honesty had been drummed into him much too hard as a kid. He didn't *like* being a thief. He had just fallen into it. After San Jacinto he had been pretty aimless. A fourteen-year-old with no one but himself to rely on. His uncle was dead, and he sure couldn't return home. A life of crime had been far more preferable than facing his father.

Tom Fife, the man who had guided his family part of the way to Texas years before, had offered to take him under his wing. But Micah had been rather cocky after the heady experience of fighting a battle as well as any grown man. He had proven his prowess in battle and thought he could take care of himself. Fife had meant well, but Micah rather liked the new taste of independence he was feeling.

He had drifted around after that, hungry most of the time but too proud to let anyone know. He fell in with various gangs or worked by himself, doing whatever he had to do to survive, but never doing more than merely keeping himself alive. He joined up with Harvey last year, and it was then that he began his formal schooling in the art of preying on others for financial gain. Harvey had done everything dishonest that was possible in the States and had fled to Texas—just one step ahead of the authorities. He was a worthy teacher. They stole mostly from Mexicans. Micah liked to call it raiding, and in truth, he never had stopped fighting the war. At any rate, he figured it didn't count if you stole from Mexicans. When he was forced to steal from whites, he managed to justify it by telling himself that he was a war hero and deserved what he could get. He didn't doubt, though, that if caught, the Texans would hang him, war hero or not. And in that sense, his lot was cast. There was no way out for him now except by bullet or by noose.

Micah glanced up at the sky. The moon was up, bright and full. "Comanche Moon," he muttered.

"What's a Comanche Moon, Micah?" Jed asked.

"Nothing," Harvey broke in. Then turning sharply toward Micah, he added, "Shut up, kid. We don't need to hear none of that."

With a shrug Micah said no more. They all knew that, unlike other tribes, the Comanche had no fear about attacking at night, especially on nights like this when the moon illuminated their prey. The rustlers knew it also illuminated *their* prey and them as well. They'd had a long discussion about the danger of rustling under a full moon, but by then everyone was thinking more of full stomachs. Game had been scarce for a week, and even Micah, notably the most cautious of the gang, was easily convinced that such an opportunity would not come along again soon.

"Micah"—Jed's voice broke into his thoughts—"how much money you think we're gonna make today?"

Micah glanced over at his friend, a freckle-faced boy of nineteen. Jed was tall and rangy, a bit awkward on his feet but good with a gun. Problem was, his mental facilities were slower than his gun hand. His mind had probably been addled after seeing his family killed in a Comanche raid nearly ten years ago. Maybe he bumped his head during the raid, or maybe he just didn't see any point in facing life as an adult. Regardless, he was a good man and a loyal friend. He and Micah had met not long after San Jacinto. Jed, orphaned, had run away from a cruel foster father who thought regular beatings and hard work were all the kid needed. Micah saw that Jed would not make it on his own, so he let the kid tag after him. They wandered around together and sometimes starved together. Micah taught Jed how to use a gun and taught him how to steal as well.

"Enough money, I reckon," Micah casually replied. The money never did appeal to him. Besides the matter of survival, he figured he did what he did in large part just for the thrill. It beat the daylights out of farming and ranching. No way did he ever want to settle down to that kind of life.

"Harvey says we'll stay in Laredo after this and raise some Cain," Jed said.

"Sounds good."

"Time to move out," Harvey ordered.

Harvey led the way, and Micah followed with the others ranging behind. They picked their way with great stealth down the ridge. Micah made sure his rifle and pistol were loaded. They weren't expecting trouble, but they'd better be ready for it.

CHAPTER 2

AT THE BOTTOM OF THE RIDGE, Micah cut away from his companions. His job would be to eliminate the guard. In two days of covertly observing the herd, Micah had discovered something of the drover's habits. Each watch was about four hours long, and by Harvey's pocket watch, it would be a little more than an hour before the new guard came on duty. They planned their move near the end of the watch, when the guard was growing weary. The guard made about three or four circles of the herd in an hour, then usually headed up to the camp for a quick cup of coffee. The camp was not far from the horses, so striking while the guard was getting his coffee would not work because the man still had a good view of them.

There was no way around it. The rustlers had to get rid of the guard, and it had to be done quietly. This job fell to Micah, who made use of the guard's coffee break by slipping among the herd and taking one horse while the man was away. He noted that the horses were unusually restive, but the little bay filly he roped came fairly easily. He led the animal away toward a tall clump of mesquite. The guard would pass this clump on his rounds and see the stray and come to fetch it. At least Micah hoped it would work that way.

The wait seemed interminable. The man must have had two cups of coffee. Finally he started his ride around the herd, and when about halfway, he noted the stray.

"Don't know why the herd's so jumpy tonight," the man muttered to himself. He was wearing a sombrero and had a Mexican serape around his shoulders, but he didn't sound Mexican.

Shrugging away his disquiet, Micah pulled his bandanna over his nose and mouth, then drew his pistol. When the guard was well within range, Micah stepped from the cover of the mesquite.

"That's far enough, *señor*," he warned.

"What the—?"

"Easy, now, and no sound from you, or I'll be forced to shoot. Get those hands up where I can see 'em." The man obeyed, and Micah lifted the fellow's pistol from his belt. "Now dismount."

Up close, Micah saw the man was definitely a gringo. This made his task a bit harder, because he knew he'd pay dearly if he killed the man. A Mexican . . . well, that would be different.

"Lie down," Micah ordered. "Face in the grass." When the man had complied, Micah quickly took the rope he'd used on the bay and tied the drover's hands behind him. With a powerful blow, he clipped the man on the head with his pistol butt. That ought to put him out of commission for a long spell, but just to be safe, Micah also gagged the man.

Returning to his partners, the four began cutting out horses. They wouldn't be greedy. They could get away with fifty head without causing too much of a stir. This was a nice-looking herd, and even fifty ought to bring each rustler a fair bankroll.

Half an hour later the job was nearly done. Harvey and Joe were already well away with at least two dozen animals. Jed was a couple of hundred feet behind leading away ten horses, and Micah was about to lead away a dozen more. That's when it all broke loose.

Micah first heard a shout. He thought it might be the guard having regained consciousness and broken free of his gag. But it was coming from the wrong direction. Then a split second after the shout, there came a shot. Now Micah knew the sounds were coming from the camp.

More shots blasted, followed by loud bloodcurdling whoops that could only be Comanche. He heard a scream. The woman traveling with the drovers? Suddenly his thoughts were distracted when the horses began milling skittishly around him. His own roan sidestepped and whinnied. Micah tried to steer his mount away from the press of the herd in case they should stampede. An instant later another shot split the air, and the mustangs took off.

Micah tried to hold back his mount, but in doing so he jerked too hard on the reins. A stupid thing to do. He knew better. The roan was a good animal but young and nervous. All the sudden commotion was just too much for him. With a wild neigh, he took off with the other horses. Micah reined him hard, and the frightened beast reared. Micah knew he should have been able to control him and would have, given another moment. But just then the horse collapsed right out from under him.

Micah jumped from the falling beast to avoid being crushed under the weight of it. He bounced over grass and rocks until his head crashed against one sharp rock, stunning him. He lay still for several heartbeats, black and white spots undulating before his eyes. He knew he was about to pass out but willed himself to stay alert. He tried to stand, but everything was spinning too much for that. Instead, he crawled toward his horse, the ground seeming to rise up beneath him as he moved. His insides quaked. Hands trembling, he reached for his rifle and powder horn. He might not be able to walk, but he sure wasn't going to just lie there defenseless. Much to his dismay, he saw an arrow through the roan's throat. The animal was dead. A good horse, and his only means of escape.

His hands had barely touched the rifle when he heard another scream. It was closer this time, and it was definitely female. Using the fallen roan for support, he pulled himself up to a sitting position. When the spinning slowed, he saw a Comanche race away from the camp carrying a captive. The woman! And they were riding in his direction.

With hardly another thought, Micah raised his rifle and took aim at the moving target. The galloping Comanche was a good hundred yards away. It was a one-in-a-hundred shot, but he'd made harder ones, only this time his vision was still blurry. His finger moved on the trigger, then he stopped. The woman was flailing against the Indian, fighting for all her worth to free herself. A heroic effort, but it hampered his purposes greatly.

"Hold still," Micah murmured, as if she could hear.

Suddenly the woman sagged. Micah was almost certain the Indian had struck her. No matter, he had a clearer shot now. He squeezed the trigger. An instant later horse, rider, and captive toppled to the ground. Then all was still.

Had Micah killed them all? Forcing himself to his feet, he laid aside his rifle and made his way to the scene with his pistol drawn. He felt steadier now. The ground only quaked a little under his feet, and his vision, though still fuzzy, no longer had those sickening spots dancing before his eyes. Within a few feet of the fallen threesome, Micah saw movement. The passengers had been thrown free of the horse, and it was the woman who was now moving. As she sat up, Micah prodded the Comanche with his toe and found him to be very dead. The horse was alive, but its leg was badly twisted.

"You shot him?" the woman said.

"Yeah."

"Who are you?"

That was a good question. Micah reached up to scratch his head in thought and realized his hat was missing. He scratched his head anyway.

"Well, I was just riding by," Micah said lamely.

"I saw . . . no one. W-where were you?" She looked mighty pale, even in the moonlight, and her voice quavered as she spoke.

"The stampede spooked my horse." Micah jerked his head toward the dead roan. "I was just coming to from being thrown when I saw you and that Comanche."

The woman stood rather shakily. Micah gave her a steadying hand. Then she looked at the fallen Comanche and gave a shudder. There was a hole in his left temple. She swayed a bit on her feet, and Micah feared she might go down again, but she hitched back her shoulders, seeming to defy gravity itself.

Her eyes wide and her lips trembling, she said, "Y-you made that shot from way over there? I-I'm g-glad you didn't miss."

"Oh, I seldom miss. I was a bit worried though 'cause my eyesight was still blurry from knocking my head against a rock."

"B-blurry . . . ?" That was all she said before her eyes rolled back in her head and she started to topple over.

Micah lurched forward and caught her in time. For a moment he stood there helplessly holding her slender form, now slack-limbed as a rag doll. He glanced around as if hoping for rescue himself. There was still fighting in the camp, but the drovers seemed to be holding off the Comanches. He brought his attention back to his burden and saw by the light of the moon that she was a pretty woman. Well, *woman* was hardly the right description, because she was probably younger than he. Still, she was comely, and the feel of her in his arms was almost as dizzying as his fall from the roan. It had been weeks since he had even seen a woman, and as for holding one this close . . . well, it had been far too long.

She moaned softly, and her eyes flickered open, then closed again.

"Miss . . . ?" Micah murmured rather helplessly, but he could not bring her around.

Getting back his wits, which had been slightly stunned by her sudden nearness, Micah laid the girl down on the grass. Tucking his pistol back into his belt, he waved his hand several times over the girl's face. The moonlight glimmered off her creamy skin and illuminated a mass of curly dark hair tangled around her face. Her closed eyes were thickly fringed with dark lashes. She was beautiful. But still very unconscious.

Micah noted that the shooting up at the camp had stopped now. Looking in that direction, he saw the Comanches were riding away, and he knew he had to do something. It was a sure bet the drovers weren't going to buy his tale that he had just been riding by.

"Miss," he said determinedly, "wake up." He gave her shoulders a shake and considered leaving her. She wasn't dead, but he couldn't leave her lying there like that. He didn't know, but maybe a woman could die of shock. In any case, with the roan dead and the Comanche's horse injured, Micah had no hope of getting far.

Finally the girl let out a little moan and lifted her head. "Wh-what happened?"

"Guess you fainted."

"I've never fainted before." She stated this so matter-of-factly that Micah actually began to wonder if he had been mistaken.

"That's what it looked like to me." Micah glanced toward the camp. The men were heading toward them.

"I thank you again, sir." She smiled and the gesture was sweet, warming her large dark eyes so that he nearly forgot his imminent danger.

He smiled back, stupidly, foolishly, like a gawk-faced schoolboy.

"Miss MacCallum!" called one of the drovers. "You okay?"

"Yes, Pete. This gentleman rescued me."

"I feared you was a goner when that Injun grabbed you." Pete turned to Micah. "Thank you for what you done."

"Weren't nothing" was all Micah could think to say.

"Sure was fortunate you happened along when you did," said another drover.

"Yeah, guess so," Micah replied vaguely.

There were now three drovers standing over Micah and the girl, both still seated on the ground. Micah saw that two of the men were indeed Mexican. One had his hand over a bloody shoulder. They were all armed. Still, he thought there might be a chance of bluffing his way out of this dicey predicament—that is, until two newcomers approached.

"Hey, look what I found!" said one.

"I got jumped," said the other.

"What're you talking about, Tandy?" the drover named Pete asked.

Tandy, whom Micah clearly recognized as the guard he had knocked out, brought a hand to his head and, as he rubbed, said with a grimace, "I say, I got knocked out and tied up."

"By Comanche?"

"No, you dim-witted fool! By a rustler. Leastways—"

Tandy's eyes suddenly took note of Micah. It had been dark back at that mesquite bush, even with the full moon, and Micah had been wearing his bandanna, but it would not take long before all the pieces fell into place right on top of Micah.

"Who're you?" the guard demanded.

Before Micah could respond, Pete spoke. "Said he was riding by when he saw the Comanche attack."

"I'd bet my boots that's one—"

But Micah did not wait to hear more. Quickly jerking his pistol from his belt, he grabbed the girl and pressed the barrel of the gun to her head. It was her gasp that drew the attention of the men.

"Drop your weapons now," Micah ordered, "or I'll have to shoot the girl."

"You ain't gonna shoot no girl," said Pete, who still appeared a bit stunned at the rapid sequence of events.

Micah cocked the hammer of his pistol. "Well, if it's her or me, I'm not gonna debate it much."

A tense moment followed. The other drovers looked to Pete, who did indeed seem to be debating in his mind just how desperate this baby-faced outlaw was. Reaching the only logical conclusion, Pete tossed his rifle into the dirt and signaled the others to do the same. That done, Micah gestured for the girl to stand. He rose with her, still holding her with one arm while with the other he held the gun on her. Only then did he really note how steady the girl was. She wasn't whimpering or crying or even shaking. His own knees were still a little mushy, but he attributed that to his fall from the horse. His head throbbed, but his vision had cleared.

Micah didn't like to leave the weapons within such easy reach of the men, but he could only handle so many details at once. He had to hope none would be fool enough to shoot at him while he held the girl. Nudging her along, Micah went up to where the saddle horses were hobbled in the remuda. Thankfully these had been unaffected by either the stampede or the Indian attack. On the way past the camp, he saw three bodies sprawled on the ground—two Comanches, one white man.

Nodding toward a nice sturdy-looking chestnut horse in the remuda, he said to the girl, "Saddle that horse up for me. Remember, I got my gun on you, and as you seen before, I don't miss."

She licked her lips, the first sign he noted of any stress.

"That's one of our best animals."

"If I'm gonna hang for stealing a horse, it may as well be a good one," he answered casually. "Go on now," he added, "and hurry up."

After she did as he asked, he said, "Now mount up."

"What!"

"The minute I ride away, your drovers are gonna start shooting. You're just gonna give me some insurance—only for a short distance. I ain't fool enough to take you far."

With a resigned shrug, she mounted. She had no difficulty at all with the large animal; in fact, she swung up into the saddle with elegant grace and sat as if she had been born to it. Micah stood for a minute staring in admiration. Then he remembered he was holding a gun on her and that she was his hostage. He mounted behind her, took the reins, and spurred the chestnut away. Again he had to remind himself that this was a desperate getaway. Yet feeling her close, her silken masses of fragrant hair blowing in his face, wreaked havoc with his sense of reality.

After a final warning to the drovers not to follow and assuring them he'd let the girl go soon, he rode about half a mile away before he stopped and let her dismount. The drovers had not followed. They were practical men and no doubt figured Micah was practical, too. He wasn't about to kill a girl if he didn't have to. And Micah figured they wouldn't waste time to go after one rustler when there was hope of still getting back their herd.

"Sorry I had to inconvenience you," he said as soon as the girl's feet touched the ground.

"I'm sorry your day was wasted, and you only got away with one horse." She smiled wryly.

"Maybe I'll do better next time." He decided to make no mention of the two or three dozen mustangs he hoped his partners had successfully made off with. The drovers might just think they had been lost in the stampede.

"Then until next time . . ."

Their eyes met and held for a long moment. It was the strangest moment Micah could ever recall experiencing. Her look made him forget who and what he was. It made him feel almost clean, like he might even deserve to have a girl like her look at him in that way.

CHAPTER 3

THE MACCALLUM RANCH WAS A large spread even in a land where everything was larger than life. Located a two-hours' ride south of San Antonio, it had been founded more than a hundred years ago by Joaquin Vasquez. The land had passed through his male Mexican scions until his grandson had only one child, a daughter. Rosalind Vasquez married an Anglo from Kentucky named Reid Maccallum, a Scotsman with red hair, towering brawny bulk, and a smile that could charm the scales off a rattlesnake.

Reid was a fine man, and his future father-in-law had no qualms about passing his ranch to his daughter to be run by the gringo. Tejas was changing, being overrun by gringos who even changed the name of the Mexican province to Texas. A gringo would better understand these changes and the irascible Americans who had brought them. Besides, Rosalind loved the Scotsman, and the Scotsman loved her. So what was a father to do, especially a father with no sons?

Lucinda Maria Bonny Maccallum, child of this union, thought about her Scottish father and Mexican mother as she rode up to the house where she had been born nineteen years earlier. She was glad to be home. How she had missed her papa, and how she wished her mother could be there to greet her as well. Mama had died two years ago of consumption, taking with her a little of the sweet life that had always infused the Maccallum place.

Lucinda, or Lucie, as most everyone called her, left her horse in the stable for one of the hands to tend. Usually she did this task herself, but she was anxious, for more reasons than one, to see her father. She wanted to get to him before their foreman did with the report of their adventures—or rather, misadventures—on the trail from Mexico.

She hurried around to the back of the house, slipping inside through the kitchen door. She always used this door but it was a mistake this time because she was immediately waylaid by Juana, their housekeeper, who would, however deservedly, require more than a cursory greeting.

"Oh, Señorita Lucie! You are home!" The woman quickly set down the basket she was carrying and threw thick, sturdy arms around the girl. Juana had been with the family for years and was practically a member. There was little, if any, servant-mistress formality between them.

Lucie kissed the woman on her plump cheek. "*Hola,* Juana."

"Look at you! I think you have grown an inch in the month you have been gone. But you have lost weight."

Lucie chuckled. To the housekeeper, anyone who weighed in at less than Juana's solid one hundred seventy pounds was a skeleton. "I am sure you will take care of that."

"Come, I have some nice sweet rolls warm by the stove." Juana tugged at Lucie's hand, urging her toward the table.

"I'm anxious to see Papa."

Juana's eyes, bright as lumps of onyx, clouded. "He is anxious to see you as well, *mi pequeña*."

"How is he, Juana?"

"Some days are better than others. But now that you are home, I think there will be mostly better days, eh?"

It was hard to believe that the large brawny Scot was not a well man. Reid Maccallum had the biggest, most loving heart in the world—at least in Lucie's world. But it was that very heart that appeared to be failing him now. It did not seem right that so soon after her mother's death, Lucie should have to face the possibility of losing another parent. She tried hard not to think that it was a very great possibility.

"Maybe I should not have gone to Mexico," she said with a sigh.

"Now you think that?" Juana said with a slight edge to her voice. She had been against the trip from the beginning. "Ah, Lucie . . ." The woman's tone softened. "Think nothing of me. Your papa no doubt would be the first to insist you live your life to its fullest. He would not want you to sacrifice it nursing him."

"It would be no sacrifice."

Juana raised a hand and gently patted Lucie's cheek. "Señor Maccallum has raised a precious child."

"It is only that he gives me so much. It would be a small thing for me to give to him in return. As it is, all I can do for him is to pray."

"That is a great deal, *pequeña*!"

"Of course it is—" Lucie stopped, momentarily distracted by the sound of footsteps in the dog run that divided the house in half, next to which the kitchen was located.

"Mr. Maccallum" came Pete Barnes' voice.

"I'm in the study," responded Lucie's father. "Come on back."

Well, it looked as if Pete had made it to her father first, after all. She hoped the foreman would be sensible enough to give a watered-down version of the troubles on the drive. Perhaps he would leave out Lucie's own close call during the Comanche attack altogether.

"I know one thing you can do for your papa," Juana said, drawing Lucie's attention back to the kitchen.

"What's that?" Lucie asked eagerly.

"Find yourself a husband so that he knows you will be taken care of."

Lucie could not hold back a responding groan. If dear Juana had one fault, it was this burning need to push Lucie into marriage.

"Oh, Juana . . ." Lucie glanced toward the door leading to the dog run as if contemplating escape.

"A girl your age should be married or at least betrothed."

"It doesn't seem to concern Papa," Lucie answered, perhaps a bit defensively. She wondered, though, if this weighed upon him now that he was ill. "Juana, I want to do what is right. But . . ." When she tried to put into words what she felt, it all seemed so silly. Juana, practical woman that she was, would not understand how Lucie wanted to find a special man to marry, one whom she would love. She wanted what her parents had had. A bond of hearts and minds and souls. Perhaps it was expecting too much, especially in view of the fact that no man had yet come along who even came close to what she was looking for. Juana would say she was too choosy, that if she found a good, honest, decent man, she would come to love him in time, and that was enough to expect.

Lucie sighed.

Juana patted the girl's shoulder. "Come, *pequeña,* sit, and I will fix tea to have with those rolls. You must be hungry after riding all day, and it is a while until supper."

"Thank you, Juana, but I really want to see my father." She forced a smile to her lips. The woman meant well. Then Lucie left the kitchen.

A nice breeze was blowing through the dog run, which was, after all, the purpose of the open-air area. It became a necessity during blistering hot Texas summers, such as the one that was now descending upon them. Lucie followed the corridor toward the back of the house where her father's study was located. She wondered, as she often did, what the old house built by her great-great-grandfather had been like. She had only a vague memory of it, but Juana had told her it had been of a hacienda style such as could be found in Mexico, with arched porticos and tile floors. But a devastating hurricane had destroyed it when Lucie had been but five, and her father had rebuilt it in the style of the American settlers, two rooms divided by the dog run. However, in the case of the Maccallum home, there were several more than two rooms. They had been quite prosperous in those days.

When she reached the study, she heard the voices of her father and Pete. She hesitated before knocking. Maybe she should wait until Pete was done. But no, she missed her father and did not want to wait another minute. She raised her slim fist and tapped on the door.

"Who is it?" her father said.

"It's me, Papa."

"Lucie, sweetheart! Come on in."

She opened the door and entered. Pete Barnes was seated before the large mahogany desk that had once belonged to Joaquin Vasquez. Behind the desk sat Reid Maccallum, his great hulk filling his chair, which was at the moment tipped back, precariously leaning against the wall. His laced fingers were propped behind his head, and he looked rather imposing, especially with his untamed red hair sticking up everywhere. But the grin on his face warmed Lucie's heart down to its core.

Reid righted his chair and quickly jumped up, striding out from behind his desk and into his daughter's outstretched arms. He wrapped his own thick logs around her in a breathtaking bear hug, lifting her several inches from the floor in the process.

"Papa!" she giggled. "Put me down. I'm not a little girl, you know!"

"And what else are you, then?"

"You'll always be his little girl, Miss Lucie," Pete said.

"Oh well, then why fight it?" Lucie kissed her father's cheek. "It is so good to see you."

Reid put her down, then held her at arm's length. "You've grown and put a bit of meat on your bones."

"Not according to Juana."

"Ha! She won't be satisfied until you are as fat as she, with three double chins besides."

They both laughed until Reid paused, taking a sudden gasp for breath.

"Papa, what is it? Are you all right?" Lucie had seen this before in recent months since his heart trouble had begun.

"Oh yeah, fine," he said with a deprecating wave of his hand. "Sometimes my breath just gets a little behind, that's all. Now sit in that other chair. I'll just be another minute here with Pete."

"We can finish later, boss." Pete rose. "Lucie deserves a chance with you before me."

"Thanks, Pete. Come on back after supper."

Lucie took Pete's vacated chair. It was larger and more comfortable. "Papa, I am never going away for that long again," she said after Pete left. "I feel like it's been forever."

"You were the one who insisted on going," Reid said.

"Yes, I suppose I did have to twist that arm of yours, but you know Uncle Ramon preferred to turn the horses over to a member of the family. He didn't know Pete or any of the men. Besides, I really did want to visit with my aunts and uncles and cousins. Goodness, there are a horde of them, too! At least a dozen more than when we last went there before the war."

"Well, they are your family, and it is good to keep up the ties." His step seemed a bit heavier as he returned to his own chair. His color was a little pale, too. "Perhaps keeping up such ties will help hasten true peace between our two countries. Still, with all the unrest it was foolhardy of me to let you have your way."

"Papa, it didn't burden you with any undue worry, did it?"

"Of course it did!" he said with a gentle smile. "I worry about you whenever you are out of my sight. Guess I'm worse than a mother hen."

"I didn't think before I left that it might make you ill." She eyed him closely. Sometimes he seemed so well that it was hard to remember his illness.

"You are back safe and sound, and that's what matters. I would have worried a long sight more if I'd known about the Comanches. And rustlers to boot!"

"So Pete told you?"

" 'Course he did, child! How else was he gonna explain the death of one of our vaqueros, not to mention the loss of seventy-five fine mustangs? And when I think how close you came—"

"Papa . . ." Lucie leaned forward and, reaching across the desk, took her father's hands in hers. "Please don't strain yourself over it. Praise our God, it all came out fine. Did Pete tell you how one of the outlaws saved my life?"

"Saved your life? What—"

"Oops!" Lucie lowered her eyes and leaned back in her chair. It seemed Pete had been more discreet than she gave him credit for. "Nothing, Papa," she added. "I forgot to tell you about the beautiful dresses I bought in Mexico City—"

"I think you better tell me about this outlaw." Reid narrowed his eyes in as stern a gaze as he was ever likely to focus on his daughter. "Out with it, Lucinda Maria Bonny Maccallum."

Lucie swallowed. When her father used her full name, he usually meant business. "Oh, it was really nothing to speak of. One of the Comanches grabbed me from our camp during the battle. He was riding off with me when a rustler shot him. I don't know how he got there—the rustler, that is. I suppose he was in the process of stealing some of our horses when the attack started. He must have been caught in the stampede. We later found his horse with an arrow in the poor beast's throat. But, Papa, you should have seen the incredible shot that man made! He hit a moving target at over a hundred yards and struck the Indian in the temple. I have never seen such shooting. And he said his vision had been blurry at the time from his fall."

As she paused to take in a breath, she noted her father was staring, or rather gaping, at her incredulously. She smiled weakly. She had probably again said more than she should have. But she was just too accustomed to telling her father everything.

When Reid finally spoke, his voice was barely a tight gasp. "Why, the fool!"

"He saved my life, Papa." She didn't know why she was defending the man. Yes, he had saved her, but he was also a thief, and he had used her as a hostage to escape. All that must negate his heroism. But somehow it didn't.

"He could have killed *you* with that shot. It was a fool, stupid thing to do."

"I guess it was." But she wasn't convinced. "Anyway, I had a feeling he knew what he was doing. But no matter—he could have stayed hidden, let the Indian carry me off, then slip away himself, unnoticed. But he even came over to make sure I was all right after the Indian's horse fell. And he caught me when I fainted and stayed with me until I came to, even though he could have been caught at any time. Eventually he was."

"What's this?" Reid leaned forward raptly. The color had returned to his face. "Did my boys get that rustler?"

"Well . . ." Her father wasn't going to be happy at all when he heard the rest of the story. But why should it matter if her father was happy about some rotten rustler?

"Come on, Lucie, all of it," prompted Reid.

"The men came over before he could get away. Then one of them identified him as a rustler because he had knocked him out—"

"Who knocked whom out?"

"The rustler . . . um . . . knocked out our guard. Well, at least he didn't kill him, now, did he?"

"You seem a bit defensive of this man."

"He saved my life."

"He also stole our horses—"

"We don't know that. They could have been lost in the stampede."

Reid ran a hand through his wild hair. "Do you realize it is not likely your rustler was working alone? Pete said he found several tracks up on a ridge overlooking your camp. Figures there was four of them. Pete decided to round up what he could of the mustangs rather than pursue the outlaws. But other tracks indicated they almost certainly got away with a good number of our horses. Moreover, Lucie, before you start glorifying those men, it was pretty heartless of them to ride off when they could have helped defend my men against the Comanches."

"They didn't all ride off."

"You said yourself that fella's horse had been shot out from under him. He had no choice."

"But he did, Papa."

"Let's not argue over the matter, child. Of course you are grateful to the man. I suppose I am a bit, too. But don't ever forget he is still a criminal. Pete is gonna ride into San Antonio tomorrow and speak to the ranger captain and see if there can be some sort of search for those men. It is likely they thought they were stealing from Mexicans. They will see what a costly mistake that was."

Lucie didn't like it when steel glinted in her father's hazel eyes. She knew that though he was as loving and gentle as a father could be, he was also a strong, tough man. He had to be to survive in this rough frontier.

"Yes, Papa," she murmured contritely.

"Oh, Lucie, I don't want you to think I am angry with you." He rose from his chair, walked around the desk, and kneeled down before her. He took her chin between two fingers and lifted it. "Come now, let me see a smile." He prodded her with his own grin.

"Papa, will those men hang if they are caught?" She just couldn't smile.

"You know the law."

"Even the one . . . ?"

Reid nodded gravely to her half-spoken question.

"He was just a boy."

"A boy, you say?" When she nodded, he added, "A handsome boy?"

"Papa!" But her blazing cheeks belied her protests.

"Handsome or not, young or not, he is still a thief. If nothing else, he stole Pete's best saddle horse. He surely knew what he was doing."

"I suppose so . . . but Papa, if he is caught, could you mention what he did for me?"

"I'll think about it, my love, but only if you give me a smile."

Lucie did smile then because he asked, and it was hard to refuse her father. But also because she knew he was a fair man and would see that justice was done in the case of the young outlaw if he were found. She still secretly hoped the handsome heroic criminal was never caught.

CHAPTER 4

LUCIE HAD WANTED TO GO to San Antonio with Pete but simply could not justify leaving her father so soon again. Besides, what did she hope to gain by giving her side of the story to the authorities? Not that they would give much heed to a woman anyway, especially a young one.

But why did she feel so compelled to defend that rustler? Over and over she tried to convince herself that he was bad, a thief, maybe even a killer. But she wasn't convinced. Instead, Lucie kept remembering the gentle way he had held her when she nearly fainted. She had been conscious enough to feel his arms around her, and she even recalled a brief glimpse of his utterly distressed expression at her plight. She had caught a flicker of something else deep in his eyes. A wounded look, perhaps? And the kindly words he had spoken. He had been truly concerned for her. What she tried not to think about was his fine-looking visage. Eyes as blue as a Texas sky, hair like a red-gold sunset descending over that sky, and dimples forming in his ruddy cheeks when he smiled. And that smile! It had only flashed momentarily, but it had not been the smile of a hardened outlaw. Maybe that's why Lucie felt so compelled to come to his defense. It seemed to her when he had knelt over her, his concerned expression softening to that smile, that he was simply a nice boy. A boy her father would probably like. And now she was almost sure it was so. He had just taken a wrong turn in life and needed to be nudged back to the right path by a caring friend.

Her?

Well, she doubted she would ever find out. More than likely she would never see him again, and that was just as well. She didn't want to see him again, not if it meant he had been caught. Besides, her father would never let her be friends with an outlaw, even an ex-outlaw.

Lucie did, however, remember one thing she could do for the young man who had saved her life, one way she could repay him even if she never saw him again. She knew someone else who cared about him.

"Dear Lord, I think it is all right to pray for outlaws, isn't it? Now that I think of it, even you prayed for the outlaw who hung on a cross next to you. Well, I pray that my outlaw never gets to that place. I suppose it is wrong to pray that he never gets caught, but I do pray that if he is, you will somehow take care of him, protect him, maybe even help him to find you. I guess it is safe to assume that since he is an outlaw, he must not know you very well. I saw good in him though, just in the few minutes of our encounter. He saved me, Lord, so I pray you will save my outlaw."

My outlaw, Lucie mused. What a silly notion. But he certainly was God's outlaw if not hers. And thus, she left the young man—she did not even know his name—in God's hands.

"Lucie, we have company," her father called from the front of the house.

Lucie had been in her room taking a rest after the midday meal. Her room was the coolest in the house on these hot summer days. She rose from her bed and patted out the wrinkles in the beige-sprigged calico of her day gown. It was not her best dress for receiving guests, but if they had come unexpectedly, they surely would understand. She glanced in the mirror of her dressing table. There was not time to give her hair the attention it needed. The unruly curls never obeyed her combs and pins, but at least the long braid at her back, carefully plaited that morning by Juana, looked presentable. She repositioned the combs, doing her best to tame the dark auburn tresses. Papa often said her riotous mane best represented the mixing of her wild Scottish blood with her beautiful Mexican heritage. She thought it was usually more wild than beautiful.

As she entered the parlor, she saw the Carltons from the neighboring ranch had come to visit—Axel, his wife, Violet, and their son, Grant.

"Good afternoon," Lucie said with a smile at her guests.

The men stood and bowed slightly, offering polite greetings. Axel kissed her hand. He was from Virginia and fancied himself a true gentleman. Grant just grinned at her. He was twenty-one and fancied *himself* Lucie's prime suitor. Lucie didn't fancy either of them. She thought both Carlton men were too full of themselves. But she had to admit that Grant did appear to be prime husband material. In a land where the men were supposed to outnumber the women by ten to one, she had found precious few decent prospects—not that she was looking.

"We were so happy to hear you had come home," Violet said. "Come, sit by me and tell me all about your trip." She patted a place beside her on the couch.

Lucie liked Violet well enough, though she could be a bit simpering at times. That Virginian breeding, Lucie supposed. But she had been a good friend of Lucie's mother and had always been kind to Lucie. Before taking a seat, Lucie offered refreshments, but her father said Juana was already seeing to them. So Lucie sat next to Violet, who immediately put her arm around Lucie's shoulders in a motherly fashion.

"Your father tells us you were in Mexico City," Violet said.

"It was my first time—my first time in any large city, actually," Lucie replied. "I have never seen such splendid buildings. The Church of Santo Domingo, which I believe is the largest church in the Americas, was breathtaking."

"We don't hold with Papist trappings," Axel said dourly. "Not anymore, since Texas is free of all that."

"Oh . . ." Lucie swallowed. She was not Catholic either—a sore point with her Mexican relatives to be sure—but beauty was beauty, and the cathedrals *were* awe-inspiring. She tried to politely counter Axel Carlton's rudeness. "Well, of course, there was much more in the city. Violet, you would have loved Alameda Park and the splendid courtship ritual that takes place every Saturday afternoon. The young girls, decked out in all their best finery, circle the fountain while the young men circle in the other direction, all hoping to meet a future mate. My *tia* Maria took me there."

"And did you join the ritual?" Violet asked breathlessly.

"Oh no. I would not want to marry a man who lived so far from home." Lucie regretted her words the minute Violet's gaze skittered toward her son. To cover her discomfiture, she quickly added, "And the shops! Papa gave me money to buy some new things, but I had the hardest time deciding. After we have refreshments, Violet, you may come to my room and see what I bought."

"That would be delightful!" Violet exclaimed.

"One day Texas will be just as prosperous as Mexico," Axel said.

"If we can ever get out of debt," Reid said.

"And curb all the lawlessness," Grant added.

"You are right there, son," Axel said. "Reid, our cattle were raided again. Those cursed Mexicans stole a hundred head—" He stopped suddenly as his wife daintily cleared her throat with a warning glance at Lucie. "Ah-hem. Well, of course, Lucie, my dear, I don't mean you. I hardly think of you as Mexican at all."

"But I am, Mr. Carlton," Lucie said softly and without apology, keeping ire from her tone as well.

"Only half," put in Grant. "And you seem as American as anyone here."

Lucie pasted a gracious smile on her face. "But I am *Texan*, Grant, both halves of me. Not American, if the truth were told."

"Of course. We're all Texan," Grant replied, "but not for long if a good portion of our citizens have their way."

"Unfortunately, we have little to give the States right now to entice them into offering statehood to us," Reid said.

Lucie knew that her father was one who would prefer for Texas to remain independent.

"And that brings me back to my lost cattle," Axel groused. "I do not mean to offend anyone present, but those Mexican banditos are wreaking havoc on local ranches. Something must be done."

"I have reason to believe there are gangs of gringo rustlers operating as well," Reid said. He paused as Juana entered the parlor with a tray of lemonade and coffee and an assortment of sweets.

"Thank you, Juana," Lucie said as the housekeeper set the tray before her.

Lucie poured coffee for Axel and her father and glasses of cool lemonade for Grant, Violet, and herself. Then she offered cookies and such to all. Juana had stood back to allow Lucie the place of hostess; however, the housekeeper did wait a moment to observe before exiting. Lucie smiled to herself. Juana was making sure Lucie had not forgotten her manners during her absence.

"So what is this about white outlaws?" Axel asked between sips of his coffee. "I know we have them, but as long as they keep clear of whites, I don't see the problem."

"I believe it is a problem no matter who they steal from," Reid answered dryly. "But they stole a good portion of the mustangs I had just purchased in Mexico. I figure they have certainly crossed the line."

"I am still more concerned about the Mexican banditos."

"Are you certain it was they and not the gringos who stole your cattle?"

"One of my men saw him. He was certain it was that blackguard Joaquin Viegas. I'm gonna personally attend his hanging when they catch him." Axel snatched up a cookie and popped it into his mouth as if this sealed the gruesome matter.

Lucie glanced at her father. His jaw was taut with repressed anger or pain, she couldn't tell exactly which. He lifted his gaze to briefly meet hers, then looked away. In that brief moment, Lucie knew it was mostly pain assailing her father, and not from his illness, but rather from a deep emotional wound. She wanted to go to him and hold him tight. She was feeling some of his pain as well. But they both sat still and politely entertained their guests, who were becoming more objectionable as the visit wore on.

"Mr. Carlton, please, this is mixed company," Violet scolded.

Dear Violet. She was an absolute saint to put up with a man like Axel Carlton, Lucie thought.

"Sorry again," the man said tightly, obviously not one bit regretful of his words but only of the fact that he might have overstepped etiquette a little.

The visit droned on, interminably it seemed to Lucie. Her only relief was when she and Violet retreated to her room, where she showed off her new gowns and trinkets from Mexico. Violet clapped gaily like a little girl, her pale ringlets bobbing around her head as Lucie paraded out each item. It was almost like having a girlfriend. Lucie hardly believed the woman was a matron of forty.

They returned to the men, and soon after the Carltons departed. As everyone was exiting the parlor, Grant Carlton contrived to detain Lucie alone in the room while the others made their way outside.

"Lucie, I must tell you I'm delighted to see you again," he said as he turned just the right way to block her exit from the parlor.

"I am glad to be home," she replied shortly. He stood within inches of her, and there was no way to escape without being rude.

"You look absolutely fetching in that gown."

She nearly replied, "This old thing?" in the coquettish manner such things were said, then remembered it *was* an old dress and looked horrid. Grant was just plying her with false flattery. And she didn't much like it.

"Grant, if I weren't around," she said mockingly, "I declare you'd make eyes at Juana."

He momentarily appeared affronted, then suddenly smiled. "There isn't that much of a dearth of women around here. There are, in fact, several young gals in San Antonio who might catch a man's eye. But you, Lucie, are the most beautiful—" He held up a hand to forestall her attempt to protest. "It is true, ask anyone. And it doesn't bother me much that you are half Mexican."

"Not much, eh?" she said sharply, then whirled away from his nearness, not caring a whit if she was rude. "If my father heard you say such things, he'd challenge you to a duel." That, of course, was not true, since Reid deplored such senseless violence as dueling, but she didn't know how else to vent her ire. She'd had just about enough backhanded slurs from the Carlton clan in one day.

"Please forgive me." Grant followed her around until he was near again, then put his hands on her shoulders. "When I am around you, I get positively senseless. You make my head spin, Lucie. I don't—"

She glanced at his hands reprovingly. "Please, Grant, you are indeed forgetting yourself."

He dropped his hands, a flash of shock in his dark eyes indicating his realization that he had indeed gone beyond his carefully honed Virginia chivalry.

"Lucie, there is to be a ball in San Antonio next week. Will you do me the honor of accompanying me there?"

"That is really too much, even for you." She attempted to affect her father's stern gaze. Failing at that, she let a slight smile slip on to her lips. "I believe my father will escort me to the ball, but I shall certainly give you a dance or two."

He smiled. "Two! More than I could have hoped for. Thank you, Lucie. I will look forward to it!"

She watched him go, bemused by the entire scene. For all of Grant's past attempts at wooing her, this was the most forward he had ever been.

Perhaps he had spent her absence fearing she would find a husband in Mexico, and now that she had returned still unattached, he decided he must take more affirmative action. It was almost enough to turn her head.

Almost.

Grant was a nice-looking man. Tall, broad-shouldered, with a trim waist, fine features on his clean-shaven face, neat brown hair. Even his teeth were straight and fairly white. But she simply felt nothing for him, except when he was boorish, as he had been this afternoon. Then she felt sheer distaste. But he wasn't always a bigoted boor. He could be charming, and he did say the sweetest things. She knew better than to be enticed by flattery, but at times he did sound so very sincere. What girl didn't like to hear she was beautiful?

Maybe Juana was right. Her choices were limited. Grant Carlton might be the best of the lot.

"Ugh!" she groaned disdainfully.

She was starting to sound like a rancher choosing horses from a herd. It was disgusting. Sound body, good teeth, gentle ride! That was no way to choose a husband, a mate for life. She refused to fall into that trap. She knew it distressed Juana, maybe even her father, but she was going to look for something else. What exactly that something else was she wasn't sure, but she hoped and prayed she would know it when it came along.

"Oh, Lord, please help me to *know*. Help me to find the right man." Then Lucie stamped her foot in frustration. She wasn't looking for a husband! So she added to her prayer, "Or better still, Lord, help everyone else just to leave me be. I only want a husband if that's what you want for me. And if you find him, I know he will be as perfect as all your wonderful gifts."

Vaguely she thought of the other recent prayer she had prayed, the one for the outlaw. Then she laughed. Even God is not that ironic, she thought ruefully. Then remembering her place as hostess, she hurried out in time to wave good-bye to her guests.

CHAPTER 5

Micah took off his hat and wiped a sleeve across his sweaty brow, then coughed when a cloud of dust caught him just as he inhaled a miscalculated breath. Who said stealing was easy money? He hadn't worked so hard in months.

When he had finally caught up to his cohorts, half a day after rustling the mustangs, he'd had to work along with the others to drive the small herd to Harvey's box canyon. After two days of swallowing dust and eating dirt on the trail, the work of changing the brands had come. There were only thirty-five head, but they were wild, not cooperative at all.

Then Harvey had the hairbrained idea of partially breaking the animals. Said they'd fetch a better price that way. All in all, it was nearly a week before they started on the way to Laredo.

"Hey, Micah!" Jed edged his mount near enough so he could be heard. "I been thinking—"

"Tell me later, Jed. This dust'll choke us if we talk." He and Jed were riding drag on the herd, and even with bandannas pulled up over their mouths, it was miserable.

"I gotta tell you now, in case something happens." Jed's voice was muffled under the red cloth. "Micah, I feel powerful bad I didn't come back for you when them Injuns attacked."

"Forget it, Jed." Jed had been apologizing for this all week. It was wearing thin in Micah's ears.

"I shoulda. But I was mighty scarit, though I'm ashamed to admit it. I was so scarit!"

"Listen here!" Micah said sharply, with impatience. "I'm telling you for the last time, you would have been a fool to come back. You hear? It would have been a dumb, stupid, crazy thing to do. And I don't ever want to hear such foolishness from you again."

"You mean you forgive me?"

Micah rolled his eyes again. "You got the thickest skull I ever seen, Jed! I want you to give me your word you'll never even think of doing something like that again."

"Well . . ."

"Do it. Now!"

"All right. I'd swear on a stack of Bibles, if I had 'em."

Micah snorted, then coughed as he inhaled grit up his nose and into the back of his throat. "If you're gonna swear, do it on something useful—like your gun."

"If it makes you feel better, Micah." Jed let go of his rein with his right hand and laid it on the butt of his pistol. "I swear by this here gun that you yourself gave me!" Jed grinned, or at least there was a gap in his bandanna where his lips were.

Micah grinned, too, then his lips tensed as Jed added, "What you got against the Bible, Micah? I remember my ma and pa set much store by it."

"Nothing," Micah answered shortly. "Now get back to work before Harvey chews you out."

He purposefully edged his mount several feet away from Jed to discourage further conversation. But Jed was obviously bored with driving horses, especially when there were so few it hardly took four men to do the job. He maneuvered within earshot again.

"Can I ask one more thing?" Jed asked.

Micah shrugged. He supposed he was bored, too. "Just as long as it ain't got nothing to do with Bibles and such truck."

"Nah, ain't nothing like that. I was wondering if you'd tell me again about that gal you rescued?"

All the men had been interested in that. They had wanted detailed descriptions, too, almost as if he'd done more with her than catch her as she fainted. Micah pitied the poor women in Laredo when these outlaws arrived.

"Well, she was a pretty little thing." Micah supposed he, too, liked remembering that soft, smiling female creature. "Even if she was dressed nigh like a man."

"Did she have on trousers?"

Though Jed well knew the answer, Micah provided it anyway. "No, course not! But she had on a leather vest and flat-brimmed sombrero, just like a vaquero. She mounted a horse like an expert."

"Astride?"

"She was a lady, you fool!" Micah surprised himself with his quick defense of the girl's honor. He knew nothing at all about her, not even her name. No, wait, someone had called her Miss Maccallum. He just realized it. She was a gringo, further establishing his fear they had raided a Texan herd. Anyway, he had no idea if she was a true lady. For all he knew she might be some camp follower.

No. Not that one. Tender innocence had glowed from her, along with a strength that even now made his breath catch in his throat. Instinctively he knew she was not the kind of woman they would be hunting in Laredo. She was the kind of woman men like him could not even dream of.

But they did. He guessed that's really where Jed and the others' interest had sprung from. They weren't just starved for women. They hungered for the kind of gentility, even civility, women represented. Good women, decent women—not the bawdy house kind. They craved the mere sight of a woman in calico stirring a pot of stew in a humble log cabin. A woman of soft-spoken delicacy, tender-eyed, just the kind of woman who would probably faint dead away at the sight of a bunch of grubby outlaws.

He smiled. The gal on the drive had fainted upon sight of him, though he figured it was more due to the ordeal of almost becoming a Comanche captive.

"I ain't so bad, am I, Jed?" Micah asked suddenly.

"What'd you mean?"

"You think a real lady might take a fancy to a man like me?"

Jed laughed his usual snorting croak, oddly dulled by the bandanna. "Thinking of settling down, Micah?" he taunted.

"No! Last thing in the world I want."

"But you gotta settle down for a lady."

"What do you know?" Micah derided his friend harshly to cover his own discomfiture at his idiotic words. "You ain't nothing but an addlepated kid. Ya ain't got the brains you was born with."

"I know that."

Jed's solemnity cut like ire through Micah.

"I know I'm stupid. Can't help it, Micah."

"Aw!" Micah gave a disgruntled shake of his head. "Don't mind me." He smacked the side of his head with his hand. "I'm the fool. I know less than you about anything, especially women."

"Naw, that ain't—"

But Jed's words were cut off by the sharp crack of a gunshot. Twisting in his saddle, Micah saw a half dozen or more riders in the distance, not within rifle range but closing the distance behind them. They weren't Mexicans either. But why would they just start shooting? Could they be rustlers?

"What'll we do, Harv?" Micah shouted up ahead.

"Outrun 'em!"

They'd lose the herd if they did that, but then again, Micah sure didn't want to die protecting a measly thirty-five mustangs. There had to be a better way. Micah dug his heels into the flanks of the big chestnut until he was abreast of Harvey.

"We can't outrun them," he shouted after tearing off his bandanna. "And they outgun us. Maybe we can parlay with 'em."

"Can't. They're rangers."

"How can you tell that?"

"Joe recognized one of the mounts. He's almost certain it's Big Foot Wallace's mule."

Micah glanced back once more. If those riders were indeed rangers, then their only choice was to try to outrun them and forget the herd. Micah slowed to allow Jed to catch up, then relayed the news to him.

"Rangers! Oh, Micah—"

"Don't worry, Jed. We'll get away."

But Micah had far less confidence than his words indicated. The riders—he could see now there were at least ten of them—were gaining fast. He spurred his mount into a full-out gallop. The chestnut was a very good animal and would have no difficulty getting away. Glancing back, he saw Jed's mount was also striding at a gallop now. The herd was running, too, and scattering.

"Hah!" Micah lashed the chestnut's flanks with the ends of his reins, his confidence growing by the minute, especially as there was no more shooting. The pursuers would not be able to shoot during the chase. That first shot must have just been a warning, as if the rangers—if they were rangers—thought that would stop the outlaws.

Harvey and Joe were well ahead. Jed was several lengths behind. Micah twisted his head. "Come on, Jed!"

At that moment Jed's horse stumbled, and Jed was thrown over the top. Micah cursed, then slowed enough to turn the chestnut. He reached the place where Jed was sprawled over a low mesquite bush and leaped from his horse before it had come to a full stop.

"Jed! Jed!"

Micah dragged Jed's body to solid ground, then dropped to his knees next to the boy and gave his shoulders a hard shake. Jed groaned, but Micah had no time to feel relief that his friend was at least alive. The riders were within gun range, and Micah quickly drew his pistol and fired, clipping one in the shoulder. Grabbing Jed's pistol from his belt, Micah fired again. He missed, but he hadn't been aiming to kill. The last thing he wanted was to kill rangers. Still, his gunfire had the hoped-for effect. It divided the force. Half continued in pursuit of Harvey and Joe, while the other half dismounted, taking cover behind rocks and brush, then returned fire. Micah also took cover behind a rock, tugging Jed along with him as best he could.

There were several volleys of shots after that, then one of the riders yelled across the distance.

"You best give it up!" The voice was vaguely familiar. "We're rangers."

"What're you shooting at us for?" Micah called back, taking the defensive. Perhaps they would believe it if he claimed he ran because he'd thought they were rustlers.

"We just wanted to get your attention. No one asked you to run."

"How were we supposed to know that?"

"Why don't you surrender, then we'll talk some 'bout it."

Micah was considering what other options he might have when Jed groaned again. His arm was twisted grotesquely, and his head was bleeding. He was hurt, maybe badly, and needed help. Micah might have decided to shoot it out if he had been alone. He figured he could pick off half of those rangers, then maybe the remaining ones would think twice about capturing him and would retreat. But what about Jed? He might die if he didn't get some doctoring. If he surrendered, the rangers would see to it that Jed got help—that is, if they didn't decide to string them both up here and now. Glancing quickly around, Micah was gratified to note there were no hanging trees nearby.

"Do you give your word you'll hear me out?" Micah asked. "And that you'll see my friend gets help?"

"You got my word. Now throw out them guns."

Micah complied, then very carefully moved to stand out in the open, his hands in the air.

"Easy, boys," warned the same man who had spoken before. An instant later he, too, stepped out from his cover.

In a few moments all the rangers had come out and were approaching Micah. Before he knew what was happening, one grabbed Micah's arms and tied them behind his back.

"I thought you was gonna hear me out!" Micah protested.

"Reckon you can still talk with your hands tied—" The speaker stopped abruptly and gasped. "Well, I'll be! Micah Sinclair! That really you?"

Micah peered more closely at his captor. That voice had been familiar. The man was sporting whiskers now, but there was no doubt just who he was.

"Yeah, it's me." For some reason Micah could not explain, he felt a twinge of shame as he made the admission.

"You remember me?"

"Yeah. Tom, ain't it?"

Micah looked the man up and down, from the top of his slightly tattered slouch hat to the tips of his worn, dusty boots. The man's teeth were just as yellow and rotten as Micah remembered. And his skin looked even more like an old boot than when Micah had last seen the man—that is, what skin could be discerned under the thick growth of brown-gray whiskers. This man, this ranger, was clearly the same fellow who had rescued Micah's family years ago. It was old Tom Fife.

Micah didn't know whether to be relieved or even more worried about this unexpected encounter.

"So you're a ranger now, Tom?" he said, cautiously feeling the man out. Was he a hard-nosed lawman now or the same easygoing character who had been so kind to Micah years ago?

"Reckon so." There was a sheepish quality in Tom's tone, as if the admission was somehow embarrassing. "And you are . . . ?" He paused, his eyes, which seemed to have a permanent squint in them, giving Micah an incisive appraisal.

"What're you up to, Micah?"

Before Micah could answer, another ranger approached, leading the chestnut by the reins. "Look here, Tom. This horse fits Pete Barnes' description. And see this—" he moved his hand to the animal's rump. "The brand's been tampered with."

"Looks that way," Tom said noncommittally.

"Besides that, this here fella fits the description—yellow hair, baby face."

"Whadd'ya got to say to that?" Tom asked, an inscrutable expression on his grizzled face.

"Nothing," Micah said, trying to affect his own inscrutable look.

"I reckon I'm gonna have to take you in," Fife said.

"Guess you gotta do what you feel is right."

Fife shook his head slowly and, Micah thought, rather regretfully. Micah felt confident that at least he'd have the benefit of a trial before they hanged him.

CHAPTER 6

MICAH LAY ON A COT in a San Antonio jail cell, his eyes scanning the ceiling for the hundredth time. He was coming to know intimately all the cracks and holes where the adobe had chipped away completely, revealing the rough, crumbling insides of the bricks. Old as this place was, he had no doubt it was solid. The oak door of the cell was several inches thick.

Escape was out of the question. He'd already tried it once on the trail when the rangers were taking him in and had received a lead ball in the thigh for his efforts. Well, it had only grazed his leg, but it hurt like the dickens. Tom, who had fired the shot, had been mighty sorry about it and hoped Micah understood he'd had no choice.

Micah rubbed the place on his leg now covered with a thick bandage. He couldn't figure out Tom Fife. Everything about the man indicated he didn't like having to arrest Micah, yet he seemed in no way disposed to looking the other way for a few moments in order to give him a bit of a break. Guess the man had indeed grown hard-nosed, taking his job as a ranger a bit too seriously.

At least he had gotten help for Jed, though it had been a grueling three-day ride to San Antonio and Jed had suffered mightily. Micah still had no idea if the doctor had been able to help the kid. He'd been in jail two days now, and there'd been no word about anything. It seemed that Fife had dumped him in jail, then forgotten about him.

Micah's gaze was diverted to the far side of his cell where a cockroach the size of a walnut was making its way across the soiled wall. Micah took off his boot and gave it a hard toss. *Thwack!* The critter fell to the floor, either stunned or dead, but it didn't move. This had been Micah's chief amusement the last couple of days. The floor was littered with carcasses of dead varmints. This complemented his mood perfectly.

Since coming to jail he'd been having frequent nightmares. He was almost afraid to sleep anymore. He was starting to wonder if all this was his comeuppance for an evil life. After six years he still could not shake all that religious prattle from his mind. He'd always sensed God was an angry God with an appetite for retribution. Well, now He would get His full measure.

Maybe I deserve it, Micah thought.

At twenty, Micah had already seen and spilled so much blood that he felt certain he deserved the nightmares as well. He thought he had lived through hell but wondered if surviving was something to brag about. He certainly had not escaped without scars and soul-deep wounds that still were not healed.

After a few early skirmishes in the war, Micah and his Uncle Haden had been sent to the presidio of La Bahia near Goliad to join General Fannin, who was rebuilding the fortress that he had renamed Fort Defiance. Eventually four hundred twenty men gathered at the fort.

Fourteen-year-old Micah had observed this fighting force with skepticism. "Uncle Haden, some of them men don't even have guns."

"Or shoes either," Haden replied. "And I hear Fannin is low on supplies himself."

Micah wanted to leave. This motley group did not represent glorious warfare as he'd imagined it. But Haden said they were bound to get in some fighting soon. Rumor had it that a call for reinforcements had come from Travis at the Alamo. Haden promised Micah that they would be the first to join up with these reinforcements. But Fannin would not release any troops to aid Travis. Some said he couldn't make up his mind what to do, others said what passed for a revolutionary government in Texas was sending Fannin a stream of contradictory orders. At any rate, Fannin's army lolled away at the fort in frustration and boredom while a war passed them by.

Finally Fannin organized a relief force, but en route supply wagons kept breaking down, delaying the army. Then news came that the Mexican General Urrea was closing in on Goliad. Fannin ordered the ill-fated force back to the fortress. Not long after, word came that the Alamo had fallen. In response to this defeat, Houston ordered Fannin to blow up the fort and retreat.

"Ain't we ever gonna fight, Uncle Haden?" Micah had complained. He hadn't gotten to shoot anyone yet and was growing bored with this whole idea of war.

At last, however, they met the enemy in battle, if the minor skirmish outside La Bahia counted as such. Fifteen hundred Mexican troops against Fannin's paltry force. Micah was in the rear and didn't get a chance to fight. But his efforts would have hardly mattered. With nine dead, sixty wounded, and overwhelming odds, Fannin surrendered, and his army was led back, captive, to the fortress. The prisoners were told they would be paroled to New Orleans. They wanted to believe that more than the rumors of vast executions of Texans by the Mexican army. When a week later they were told they would be marched out the next day and taken to ships bound for New Orleans, Micah figured his fighting days were over before they had really begun.

That last night in the fortress the men were in good spirits. Some had heard the Mexicans would allow them to stop on the way to the sea to say farewells to their families. And New Orleans wasn't such a bad place. Eventually they would make it back to Texas, hopefully before the war ended.

Micah lay back on the bare ground, using his blanket as a pillow, and gazed up at the stars. Uncle Haden was sitting beside him smoking a cheroot. They had become quite close in the last months. Though neither talked about it much, they both shared the deep pain of the loss of Micah's mother. Haden understood Micah as his father never had.

"Uncle Haden, you ever been to New Orleans?"

"Yes, a time or two. It's a beautiful city."

"I was there once on my way to Texas." Micah didn't like to think of those dreary times, but for some reason he had an urge to speak of them now. "We didn't really go into the city. Pa called it an especially godless place, the Devil's playground. So we mostly kept to the harbor some miles south."

"I forget you've done some traveling yourself, Micah. You're getting to be quite a worldly fellow." Haden smiled that grin of his that made his eyes twinkle and made anyone who saw it want to grin in return.

"Guess I got my pa to thank for that," Micah said dryly.

Haden laughed heartily. "He was good for something, then, I reckon."

Micah only replied with a loud "Harrumph!"

"Too bad you couldn't have known your pa when he and I were younger," Haden said. "He was quite a rascal, that one."

"My pa?"

"He ever tell you about the time we set the parson's barn on fire?" When Micah shook his head, Haden added ruefully, "Oh no, he wouldn't. Well, we didn't mean to do it. We had hid in the barn during a picnic in order to smoke a couple of Wilfred Miller's big stogies we had found—actually, we had found them in the pocket of the man's coat, which he had laid over a chair while he played horseshoes. Anyway, our pa came in the barn looking for us, and we knew we'd catch it if we were caught. Ben grabbed both stogies and stuck them in a pile of hay. Not too smart, your pa!" Haden laughed, not in a derogatory way, but rather as if at a pleasant memory. "You can guess what happened after that. We were lucky the house and the entire town didn't go up in flames. Our pa blistered our bottoms so bad we couldn't sit for a week." Haden sighed, then crushed out the stub of his smoke. "Religion spoiled your pa."

"That's why I'm gonna stay as far away from it as I can," Micah said firmly.

"Can't say as I blame you, boy. But I wish . . ." Pausing, Haden glanced over at Micah, sadness replacing his earlier humor. "Your pa ain't all bad. Fact is, I heard he'd changed since Rebekah's death. Fella told me he'd come before his parishioners recently real humbled and talked about how he'd been wrong in some of his notions about God. I saw something, too, Micah, when he came after you last month. Maybe . . . maybe he ought to get another chance."

"Not after what he did to Ma." Micah's tone deepened to that of a steely man, not a boy. "He don't deserve to wreck everyone's lives, then say he's changed and expect to be forgiven."

"Maybe not."

"Would you, Uncle Haden? Would you forgive him?"

Haden drew up his knees, rested his folded arms on them, and was silent for a long while before answering. "I ain't quite ready to forgive him either, but if I live through this war, I might go and talk to him at least."

But Haden did not live past the next day. In the morning the prisoners were marched out of the fortress in four separate groups, each heading in slightly different directions. When they were halted a half mile from the fort, some began to realize what was going to happen, but it was too late for anything but a defiant shout.

"Hurrah for Texas!" the doomed men cried.

Within seconds the shooting began. Micah saw his uncle gunned down before he obeyed the man's order—or was it a plea?—to run. The sight of the massacre of Haden and the others would be etched in Micah's mind forever, both waking and sleeping. Only a handful of the four hundred and twenty men, Micah among them, escaped.

Wounded, weaponless, and starving, Micah had spent a harrowing five days on the run before he caught up with Houston's army. Lying in the brush with nothing but a growling stomach for company, Micah had thought only of avenging his uncle and the others. When one of Houston's men gave him a rifle, his fingers had truly itched to use it. It had been hard not to shoot at some of the Mexicans fighting with the Texans. There was a distinction in Texas, and always would be, between good Mexicans and bad Mexicans—meaning those who fought with Texas and those who didn't. Fourteen-year-old Micah found that distinction extremely hard to fathom. He still did.

Adding to his frustration was the fact that Houston kept retreating from the Mexicans. They called the retreat of the army and the settlers from the path of Santa Anna the "runaway scrape," and it was quickly causing Houston to lose face with his army. Hundreds deserted, mostly to aid their families, who had become refugees in the face of the enemy's advance. But in the end Houston led the army to San Jacinto.

In all the time of the retreating, Micah's bloodthirst had not abated. He fought bravely, if savagely, on the battlefield of San Jacinto. He only vaguely remembered the first man he ever killed, a Mexican private. It had happened quickly, and the heat of battle did not allow him to think much about it, especially as many more fell by his hand after that. But Micah remembered too clearly the last man he had killed in the war. He still had nightmares about it.

The battle was mostly over. Victory belonged to the Texans. The Mexicans had dropped their weapons in surrender, and that's when Micah realized he was not the only one still longing for vengeance.

A yell ripped through the battlefield. "Take prisoners like the Mexicans do!"

Even Houston could not stay the hand of slaughter. The Texans fell on their prisoners, stabbing, slashing, and clubbing them mercilessly.

Cries of "Remember the Alamo!" "Remember Goliad!" mingled with the screams of the victims.

Those screams would sear Micah's memory, but he had joined in the slaughter. For once Scripture stood him well. "An eye for an eye, and a tooth for a tooth." But instead of the killing quenching his thirst for revenge, it only seemed to whet it more. Near the end, he chased a Mexican soldier, pinning him up against the bank of the bayou. The man fell on his knees before Micah, hands clasped beseechingly, tears oozing down his battle-stained face.

"Have mercy, por favor!" the man begged.

Micah stared into those pleading eyes, leveled his pistol, and fired.

Holy retribution? Yes, Micah had no doubt he was in for a strong dose of it. He could almost hear his father's voice quivering with fervent zeal.

" 'And now also the axe is laid unto the root of the trees: therefore every tree which bringeth not forth good fruit is hewn down, and cast into the fire.' "

Micah smiled as he realized he himself had spoken the oft-heard words out loud. For good measure, like a sword thrust, he added, "Matthew chapter three, verse ten."

How Micah hated that he knew all this. But it had nearly been rammed down his throat. He'd been forced to memorize half the Bible! He'd like to exorcise it from his brain, but no matter how much he tried to forget, a sneaky little verse would invade his mind at the most inopportune moment before he had a chance to do anything about it.

At any rate, Micah was headed for the fire for certain now. He wished he didn't believe in heaven and hell. Well, he wasn't so sure about heaven, but he knew without a doubt there was a hell. He'd lived in it for years now.

CHAPTER 7

SOUNDS OUT IN THE CORRIDOR captured Micah's attention. He'd just had supper, so it couldn't be that. Maybe a new tenant was arriving. The distinct sound of a key in a lock proved this was probably true. Then a door opened with a groan and a moment later creaked shut again. Footsteps thudded in the corridor again, and then there was silence.

"Micah, you there?" came Jed's voice.

Micah jumped from his cot and with a single stride, though limping slightly on his one bare foot, went to his cell door.

"Jed? You okay?" he called out the small barred opening in the door.

"Yeah. My arm pains me still, but my head feels better."

Micah hated to admit how good it was to hear a friendly voice and to know this particular friend was all right. Funny, but he hadn't given near as much thought to Harvey or Joe.

"You break your arm or something?" Micah asked, just to keep up the welcome flow of conversation.

"Don't know for certain. The doctor said he had to 'locate' it. But I could see my arm was there the entire time. Don't know what he meant."

Micah could almost picture his friend's bemused look.

"But that locating business hurt worse than that time I sat on a cactus! The doc liquored me up good but still I about passed out. Now he's got it all trussed up in a sling. Said it'd be better in a few days."

"Glad to hear that, Jed. Did you hear about anything else? Did they bring in Harvey and Joe?"

"Not as I know of."

There was a long pause. Micah tried to think of another topic for discussion but could think of nothing besides their fate, and he didn't really want to consider that at the moment.

It was Jed who brought it up. "What's gonna happen to us now, Micah?"

"I was told we'd stand before a judge soon, but they didn't say nothing else."

"What about that fella you seemed to know? Maybe he'll get us out."

Micah shook his head as if Jed could see. "Don't know."

"He came to see me at the doc's. Just to see if I was okay. Maybe he'll help us."

The hopefulness in Jed's voice was a little pathetic, even desperate. Micah cursed himself, as he had done continuously since his arrest, for getting Jed involved.

"I told him how you were a good man, and how you wouldn't have got caught 'cept that you came back for me. Maybe it'll help."

"Maybe." Micah spoke tonelessly, knowing even that much was a dream.

"Micah?"

"Yeah, Jed?"

"Why'd you do it?"

"Do what?"

"Why'd you come back for me? You told me it'd be a stupid, dumb thing to do—"

"Well, I never said I was any smarter than you!"

"You're lots smarter," Jed replied so matter-of-factly that it made Micah's stomach clench. He knew Jed practically worshiped him, and he hated it. Hated the burden of responsibility, hated knowing it was the most misplaced worship ever bestowed upon a miserable creature.

Micah returned to his cot and plopped down, making the flimsy wooden structure creak and sway. "I want to get some shut-eye," he said. "It's late."

In the morning Micah and Jed were brought before the town magistrate. Because the evidence was overwhelmingly against them, they were easily convicted of horse thieving and sentenced to hang. Jed cried. Micah stood like a stone, not even blinking at the words of the judge. When the execution was scheduled to take place in three days, Micah's stomach quivered, but no one could see that.

Back in his cell he killed a couple more cockroaches, and when the midday meal came, he ate every scrap of it, though his insides felt like a big knot. He'd give no man the satisfaction of seeing him regret anything about his life.

Jed tried to talk to him, but Micah answered tersely, then told his friend to shut up. It was cruel, because he knew Jed was scared and needed to talk about it. But Micah was scared, too, and he needed to be silent. Despite the fact that he'd always suspected his end would come in this manner, he'd believed it would wait a few years. He wasn't even going to see his twenty-first birthday in a few weeks. But he was not going to whimper about the thing. What was done was done. He'd accept it like a man, and when the moment came . . . well, he just hoped he'd be able to take that like a man, too.

He'd chosen his path a long time ago. Maybe not consciously, but he'd always known he would take whatever route was the exact opposite of his father's. He had made that decision one dark night as he sat by a campfire and watched his mother die. No one had said much to him, and certainly no one had explained why he and his sisters found themselves many miles from home with their uncle and their mother, but not with their father. No one had *said* their father had driven them away. No one had *said* his mother was dying because she had chosen to travel in a delicate condition instead of enduring another moment with that monster Micah must call "Father."

No one said anything.

But Micah was twelve years old at the time, and he perceived far more than anyone had given him credit for. He knew his mother had been a long-suffering saint while his father was demanding, harsh, self-righteous. And when his mother had breathed her last, Micah had silently sworn to himself that he would hate his father and all that he stood for as long as he lived.

He had never thought his father would outlive him. In a way, though, that was rather a sweet irony. At least it gave Micah a small satisfaction in his inglorious death. For that religious hypocrite to know his son had hung for horse-stealing, well, there was a certain beauty in that.

Footsteps in the corridor intruded into Micah's grim musings. Glancing at the small barred window high up near the ceiling on the wall opposite of where he lay, he saw it was full dark out, and he had not even noticed the growing darkness in his cell. He did not move from his cot even when he heard a key twist in the lock of his door, nor did he glance toward the door.

"Micah, you ain't asleep, are you?"

The voice belonged to Tom Fife. He was holding a lighted candle that illuminated his face in an eerie orange glow.

Micah only grunted in reply.

Fife stepped around so as to see Micah better, and probably so Micah, who remained still, could see him.

"I'd like a word with you, if I might." He set the candle on the table near the cot.

"I'm locked in here. I don't got a choice," Micah muttered.

"True . . ." Fife drew out the word as he laced his fingers through his beard. "I got a proposition for you."

Micah's eyes, almost against his will, flickered toward the ranger. He hated demonstrating even the slightest interest or curiosity. But "propositions" for a man in his position couldn't mean too many things. More'n likely they wanted him to give up Harvey and Joe in exchange for some concession. But Micah had never yet said so much as a word about the others. And he wouldn't either.

"Make it fast, Tom," Micah said as if he didn't care. "It's late, and I want some sleep."

"Well, since your sentencing today, I been talking myself blue in the face trying to get you some kind of lighter sentence. I just been two hours with Captain Hays trying to convince him you are worth saving—"

"Sorry you wasted your breath, Tom."

"It wasn't wasted."

Micah's heart did a double beat. What did that mean? Was he going to get off? No way would he turn in his friends. He said nothing, however, continuing with his stoic indifference.

"Why, you knuckleheaded, impudent, thick-skulled, addlepated, foolish little brat!" Fife suddenly raved.

This forced Micah's attention. Fife's face was turning beet red, his fists were clenched, and he looked about two breaths away from murder. In fact, in the next instant Fife's fists swung into motion and grabbed Micah's shirtfront, dragging Micah into a sitting position.

"You ornery little twit!" Fife continued to yell. "I know you got better manners than that. You look at me when I talk to you!"

Micah licked his lips. He was thirsty, that's all. But his eyes shot up to meet Fife's fiery gaze. "Calm yourself, Tom," he said in a tone barely above a squeak.

"Do you realize you are gonna die in three days, boy? Is that what you want?"

Tom's gaze bore into Micah like a knife, only this hurt far worse than a stab with any blade. Though his gaze was sharp and furious, there was no hatred in it. Though the man's voice shook, it was filled with something that finally penetrated Micah's senses. Tom Fife was scared. Scared for Micah.

"N-no." That realization made Micah's voice tremble. And, God help him, moisture rose in his eyes. He turned his face away. He didn't care if Tom smacked him. He couldn't let the man see him cry.

"Boy?" Fife said softly, loosening his grip on Micah's shirt.

"I ain't a boy no more." Micah wiped a sleeve across his face, eyes still averted from the ranger's.

"I want to help you."

"I won't give away any of my friends."

"Didn't think you would. And I never thought to ask." Fife sat on the foot of the cot. "You want to hear my proposition?"

Micah swallowed and blinked back the brimming moisture. Then he nodded. He supposed it wouldn't hurt to listen. He really didn't want to die.

"Well, I convinced Captain Hays that in view of your tender years—"

"I said I ain't no boy—"

Tom held up his hand. "I know . . . I know. But it wouldn't be so bad to be thought a kid if it'd save your life, now, would it?" Without giving Micah a chance to respond, he went on. "Besides, I think he was more impressed when I told him you was also a hero of San Jacinto. He wondered why you was stealing horses instead of working your land allotment. I wonder the same thing. What happened to your land grants? You should have got six hundred forty acres, and another six hundred forty as your uncle's heir. That could have set you up real good, Micah."

"Are you gonna lecture me, or are you gonna tell me about this all-important proposition of yours?" Micah asked, risking only a mild sneer in his voice.

"All right." Tom sighed resignedly. "Captain Hays figures that maybe you deserve another chance. He's prepared to release you into my custody for a probationary period of one year, during which you will serve the Republic of Texas as a ranger. If you conduct yourself in an honorable manner in that time, he reckons to commute your sentence."

Micah stared, disbelieving. All he could manage to say was "A ranger?"

"That's right."

"A lawman?"

"Not exactly . . ." Tom scratched his head. "But close enough."

"You mean to tell me that this here captain of yours is willing to take a thief and make him into a lawman? Don't make no sense. . . ." Micah leaned against the wall, shaking his head. "No sense at all."

"I spoke up for you, Micah."

"What'd you tell him? You don't know me." He studied the ranger more carefully. Tom was looking at him, but what did he see? A frightened kid clinging to his mother's skirts, ripped from the home he loved and forced to endure hardships of a life in a rough, strange land? Or perhaps a boy smeared with gunpowder and blood and the stench of death, fighting battles meant for men? He surely did not see the man Micah had become: at best, a thief; at worst, well, at worst a man who did deserve to hang.

"It has been a long time," Fife admitted. "But I'm willing to take that risk."

"Why?"

"I seen lots of men in my time, Micah. And I know when a man's bad to the core, and you ain't one of those. Leastways, I'm willing to stake my reputation on it. Now, are you gonna accept my proposition or not? You ain't got a lot of time."

"What about Jed?"

"Huh?"

Micah jerked his head toward the next cell. "My friend. He get the same proposition?"

"Aw, now Micah, it'd be pushing it mightily just to get it for you." Tom lurched to his feet and paced across the cell. "We can't be letting every horse thief loose."

"What about Jed's tender years? 'Sides, he's even younger than he looks. His mind ain't quite all there, you know."

"I thought maybe he was a mite slow."

"And he don't deserve to hang, even more than me."

Tom turned and faced Micah. "The captain won't go for it." He chewed his mustache and shook his head. "I'm truly sorry."

"Don't matter," Micah said imperturbably. "I wasn't gonna take your offer anyway. I don't want to be a ranger."

As Tom left the cell, Micah experienced a twinge of regret. This rangering business might not be too bad. In fact, it might offer him all the excitement and adventure he'd found riding with Harvey Tate without the constant threat of, well, of where he was right now. He'd heard of the exploits of the rangers since they had been officially recruited just after the war. They mostly fought Indians and Mexicans, protecting the borders of the new republic. Imagine that! He'd be able to fight all the Mexicans he wanted, and it would be perfectly legal.

But there was no way he'd let Jed hang alone. It was his fault Jed was in this position, and Micah might be a lot of unsavory things, but he wasn't the kind to desert his friends.

CHAPTER 8

TWO UNEXPECTED VISITORS CAME TO see Micah the day before his hanging. He was eating his midday meal when the first one arrived. He wasn't much interested in the beans on the tin plate and the hunk of bread. He and Jed had had lengthy discussions that morning about food because they had been told that for supper they'd be able to have anything they wanted since it would be their last meal. Jed couldn't decide between ham and fried chicken. He was very definite about what he wanted for dessert—pecan pie. And not just a slice, but the whole thing!

Micah moved the beans around on his plate with his spoon, the only eating implement his jailers trusted him with. He wondered if he'd have an appetite for anything when supper came. Then he heard the noise of someone approaching. With a defiant flourish he scooped up some beans and stuffed them into his mouth, following that with a huge bite of corn bread. When his cell door opened, he nearly choked on the food.

"Hello, Micah."

He just stared at the figure nearly filling the doorway, his mouth and throat working desperately to swallow the food that had suddenly become as dry as sawdust. But even without the food, he would not have known what to say. In fact, he wasn't certain he'd say anything. He'd finished talking to this man six years ago . . . no, long before that. He'd quit having anything to say to his father the day he had dragged his family from their home in Boston.

Benjamin Sinclair ducked under the door lintel and stepped fully into the cell as the jailer closed and locked the door behind him. Micah continued to stare silently. But silence wasn't going to make the man go away. His father filled the small cell with that presence he'd always had, some inner force that made people listen to him, fear him, and hate him. His preaching had often driven people to tears. His recriminations had made them tremble. Micah himself had trembled often in the man's presence. There had been a time when he was a very young boy that he had even regarded the man with awe. Micah had thought that the fiery Almighty whom Reverend Sinclair had so eloquently preached about had actually been his father and that if he worshiped his father, his father would love him, but if he fell short, that same father would condemn him to hell. Then Micah had grown older and wiser, realizing there was nothing he could do to please either father—the one in heaven or the man now standing before him.

"Say something, son," Benjamin said in a tone of soft entreaty.

It reminded Micah of how his father had claimed to have changed after his mother's death. He had behaved kind of differently then, but the changes had come too late. For Micah, at least.

"What're you doing here?" Micah could barely speak. The food was gone, but his throat still felt constricted.

"Tom got word to me about what happened. I . . . had to see you, Micah."

"Why?"

"W-why?" The man now returned the same gaping expression his son was wearing. "You're my son!"

"You figure to take one last chance to save my soul?" Micah taunted.

"I don't know what I figure to do. I haven't seen you in over six years, had no way to find you. I guess when I heard you'd finally . . . well, lighted in one place, I just came."

Benjamin continued to stand, towering over Micah. His legs were slightly apart, his hands clasped behind his back like a soldier at ease. He looked like he could and would stand there forever.

Micah resisted the urge to squirm. But he could not deny the inner sense of being an errant child awaiting deserved discipline. He knew if he stood, he'd be just as tall as his father. He knew if he wanted, he could engage in a physical battle with this man and win. Yet he wouldn't. And he had no idea why. But he would not hurt this man, at least physically. Still, he grasped his spoon as if it were a weapon.

"I don't want to talk to you," Micah said stiffly.

"I've come a long ways to see you."

"No one asked you to."

Benjamin's jaw began to work spasmodically, and a brief flicker of something like fire glinted from his eyes. Micah had seen that look before. It had usually come just before a particularly painful beating.

But Benjamin continued to stand like a statue. Finally he spoke, tightly at first, then seemingly gaining control of his ire, his tone relaxed.

"Tom Fife tells me they have offered you a way out of this mess. I guess it wouldn't help if I encouraged you to take his offer."

The corner of Micah's mouth quirked slightly into a hint of amusement.

Benjamin shook his head. "So you'll let them hang you just to spite me?"

"Don't flatter yourself, Pa. I got my reasons, and they don't have nothing to do with you." Deliberately, Micah laid down his spoon and pushed aside his tray, which was on his bed.

"Don't be so stubborn, son!"

"You ain't got no right to tell me how to be or what to do," Micah rejoined.

"No . . . I suppose I don't." He paused, his eyes blue like the summer sky, blue like Micah's, searching his son. "I know you'll never believe it, but I have changed. I've made mistakes—I still make mistakes—but I've learned that God sees only a man's heart, and I am trying to do that as well. Not always successfully, I admit. But . . ."

The fire was gone now from those incisive pools, replaced by something Micah could not read . . . or did not want to.

"Son, I know I am to blame for the parts of your heart that are dark and painful. But I know, too, that your heart is not all dark. I know that because, even more than me, your mother had a great influence upon you. Her love and her tender spirit are in you as well. And just maybe they are even stronger than my part. I think that is what Tom Fife sees, and that is why he is willing to take such a risk for you. I ask you—not for me but for your mother's sake—to stay alive."

"My mother is dead." Somehow Micah's flat monotone managed to convey volumes of scorn.

Then the statue of the man moved. Benjamin lifted a hand and raked it through his hair, blond like Micah's.

"You know what I mean." A desperate quality suffused his voice.

"Well, just remember this. If I live or die, it has nothing to do with you." Micah's voice rang clear and confident, though in his heart he feared the fate he chose would have everything to do with this man.

"I know."

The pain in those two words made Micah's stomach twist. "Now leave me alone," Micah said.

Benjamin turned toward the cell door, then paused. "Do you care to know how your sisters and brother are, and my wife?"

Micah shrugged.

Benjamin, apparently taking that for assent, continued. "You've got a half brother and half sister now. The youngest was born a few months ago. The whole family is well. Isabel is growing into a pretty young lady. She wanted to come with me and told me to tell you she misses you—"

"Do they know about me?" Micah cut in, not really understanding the sudden concern rising in him.

"They don't hear as much news as I, so I doubt it. I would never tell them."

Micah shrugged as if he didn't care, then said with the most sincerity in his tone that he'd yet used, "Well, tell Issy I miss her, too. And the other kids. And Elise." He thought briefly of his father's second wife. She'd been kind to him, and he hoped she didn't one day suffer the same fate as Rebekah Sinclair had.

"I'll do that, Micah." Benjamin put his face close to the barred opening in the door. "Guard, I'm ready."

His voice held a hesitancy, as if he truly was not ready, as if he had more to say. But he remained silent as he waited. Micah did the same.

It seemed to take forever for the guard to come. Micah did not realize he was holding his breath until the door creaked open, and he expelled a sharp burst of air.

"Good-bye, Micah," Benjamin said in a tone that seemed rough and brittle, then he paused a moment before stepping outside.

If he had been waiting for parting words from his son, Micah disappointed him, remaining silent. The door then clanked shut, and Micah was left alone.

The next visit came just before sunset. Micah thought it would be Tom with one last plea. And Micah wondered what his response would be, desperately wanting a way out but believing that would not be possible.

When the door opened, it wasn't Fife who stepped inside, but a dream. At least he wondered if he was dreaming while still wide awake. He'd had this dream several times since the Comanche attack, and it had been a welcome respite from his Goliad and San Jacinto nightmares. He'd dreamed of a beautiful, genteel girl with a smile that could melt stone or turn a dry riverbed into a rushing stream of water, dancing and sparkling in the desert sun. He'd dreamed that smile was meant for him, only him. And he'd wake with a gnawing ache, knowing he would only see such a smile in the netherworld of sleep.

That's why Micah rubbed his eyes and stared, half expecting the vision to suddenly dissolve. But she was still standing there, all feminine in cornflower blue, her dark hair escaping the confines of her lace bonnet and falling around her lovely face.

The spell was broken by Tom Fife's discordant voice. "Got a visitor for you, Micah." Then he added, "I'll be right outside here, miss."

Before Micah could say a thing or give his leave, the door shut. This time, however, Tom did not lock it.

She smiled that smile, and Micah realized he remembered it perfectly from their last meeting.

"I hope you don't mind my coming unannounced," she said.

Mind? Micah could have been ready to die that minute just with the sight of her, feeling his life had been complete.

"Naw, I don't mind," he said casually. "It gets kind of boring in here." Then remembering his manners, he jumped up. All at once he became acutely aware of himself and his surroundings.

He was still wearing the same dirty clothes he'd been wearing the day of the Comanche attack. And, of course, he hadn't had a bath in all that time either. Nothing unusual about that. Not enough water on the trail earlier, and now no one cared to waste the effort if he was just gonna die in a day. He smelled like rotten onions, and his week's growth of beard made his face look like he'd been kissing dirt. He didn't have much of a beard, but what he had was darker and ruddier than his hair. Instinctively his hand shot up to his chin, then he grimaced, and instead of welcoming this visit, he decided that before he died tomorrow, he would kill Tom Fife.

"I don't have a chair to offer you," he said, as if this admission could account for everything else.

"I don't mind standing."

The corners of her lips twitched, and he realized she was just as nervous as he. She held her hands in front of her, twisting them together.

"Didn't figure I'd ever see you again," Micah said.

"I heard you'd been arrested, and I felt so bad, I just couldn't stay away."

Her dark eyes were like lumps of obsidian, only fluid and expressive. They glittered now with what Micah dared to hope was sadness.

"I don't hold nothing against you," Micah replied with just a hint of magnanimity in his tone. He thought about holding her that day when she had fainted and decided the experience was well worth arrest, maybe even hanging. "You had to tell the law what I done."

"Please don't think that!" The obsidian now flashed with passion. "I would never have turned you in after what you did for me. I prayed they would never find you. But it was Pete's best horse you took, and, well, he was pretty upset."

"I'm sorry I did that, and not just because of . . . well, what's gonna happen tomorrow." Micah shifted nervously on his feet. In truth, he wasn't entirely sorry, but he couldn't have her know that. "I didn't know you was Texans, and . . . I wouldn't have done it if it had been his only horse." That, at least, was true. "Anyway, I am sorry."

"I came to town to tell the constable about what you did for me, how you might have escaped free and clear with no one able to identify you if you hadn't come back to see to me—"

"You shouldn't have done that," he broke in, horrified on several different levels, most of which he could barely define. But for certain he hated the thought that she had come merely out of pity.

"You rescued me at your own peril," she insisted.

"I also took you hostage—"

"Pooh!" She gave a dismissive wave of her hand. "You never would have harmed me."

"How do you know that?"

"I just do."

Completely abashed, Micah said rather helplessly, "Well, at any rate, you shouldn't have come here, because you'd likely ruin your reputation if folks believed you had any truck with a man like me."

"I don't care what people think. I owe you my life, Mr. Sinclair."

"Still . . . it ain't right."

She then bestowed upon him such a look—part smile, part admiration, part impish rebellion—that it made him suck in a breath of shock.

"My father would have a conniption if he knew I was here." A curl fell in her eyes, and that impish look had full reign for a moment before she lifted a hand and flicked the silken wave back into place.

She was the most beautiful thing Micah had ever seen.

She continued. "But I learned something about you the day you saved me, Mr. Sinclair, that no one else knows."

"Y-you did?" He silently cursed the flustered squeak in his voice.

"You are a decent man, Mr. Sinclair. I know that and . . . and I can't bear the thought of . . ." Her own voice broke with emotion. "Goodness! I didn't think I'd . . ." She fumbled with the reticule that hung from her twisting hands and withdrew a handkerchief.

"Miss! You . . ." But as much as Micah knew he should say something, he was speechless. This beautiful girl, this vision of sweet dreams, was weeping . . . for him! He didn't even think how this would be the ideal opportunity to hold her once again, just to comfort her, of course. Instead, he just stood there, gaping woodenly.

She dabbed her eyes daintily. "I'm so sorry for carrying on this way."

"You oughtn't cry, not over me," he finally said.

"But . . . but . . ." her tears kept flowing.

"Tom! Tom!" Micah yelled, not knowing what else to do.

The door flew open, and Tom leaped into the cell like an avenging knight. "What's going on?"

"It ain't my fault!" Micah declared preemptively.

"No, Mr. Fife, it isn't Mr. Sinclair's fault." She sniffed and her words trembled. "I just don't want to see him . . . I can't even say it! And I am to blame!"

"No you ain't, miss."

Tom reached out and did what Micah had been hungering to do. He put an arm around the weeping girl. But at the same time Tom made this gentle gesture, he turned blazing eyes on Micah.

"What'd you say to her, boy!" he accused more than asked.

"N-nothing!" But Micah knew in his heart he was totally the cause of her distress. Yet he was helpless to do a thing about it.

"He was a perfect gentleman," she said through her tears.

How could she defend him? He'd stolen from her, held her hostage, and put her through emotional distress.

"I'm taking you out now, miss," Tom said. "Your pa would kill me if he knew I'd let you in here. And now look at you!" He nudged her toward the door. Pausing only for a backward glance at Micah, he added threateningly, "I'll be back to talk to you later."

CHAPTER 9

TOM DID NOT RETURN FOR two hours, during which time Micah fretted as if worse could happen to him than already was going to happen tomorrow.

That girl should never have come to his cell. It had been pure foolishness! And Micah would chew Tom out good for allowing it to happen. What had the man been thinking, letting a decent girl into a depraved man's jail cell to see a condemned criminal? Even Micah would have known that a girl's delicate sensibilities could have been upset by such a thing.

Then he thought about those tears, erupting from obsidian, coursing down pure ivory, and all for him. It should have disturbed him to have a gal like that pity him so, yet as he mulled over the visit in his mind, Micah began to sense that there had not been anything like pity in her response. Maybe it was just wishful thinking on his part, but it might be true that her sorrow sprang from something else entirely.

What that might be, he dared not think about. It was no use anyway. He was going to die tomorrow.

But if there was a way to avoid the inevitable, well, he might just take it. He could stand being a ranger if it meant pleasing a gal like Miss Maccallum. If it meant he could dispel those tears and the distress in those lovely eyes.

"Hey, Micah!" Jed called.

With a jolt Micah remembered why he would never see those eyes smile again.

"What!" Micah snapped. But it really wasn't Jed's fault. Micah had gotten Jed into this mess, and he was going to stick by him till the end. That was that. A bit more gently he added, "Haven't heard much from you today, Jed. What's going on?"

"You sure have had a slug of visitors. I saw a pretty female in the hall."

"Yeah. Of all things, Jed, it was the gal from the trail drive."

"The one whose horses we stole?"

"The same. She was crying because of me."

"You don't say!" Jed gave a low whistle. "She sure was pretty."

Micah shrugged, then swung his legs off his cot and stood. Striding to the door, he added, "When do you suppose supper is gonna come? I'm starved." He didn't want to talk about Miss Maccallum. He didn't want to be reminded about all he was losing.

The outer door opened, and Tom stepped into the corridor. Micah took it as a good sign that the man seemed to have calmed since his earlier visit.

"Hey, Tom, when's supper?"

"Yeah," Jed put in. "I'm gonna get ham and fried chicken, right?"

"I got more important things to discuss than your stomachs." Tom came to Micah's cell, opened it, and stepped inside.

Micah immediately noted the door was kept unlocked and slightly ajar. But no doubt the outer office was filled with rangers armed to the teeth. Micah knew escape was impossible, but he could not prevent himself from thinking about it.

Snapping the door shut behind him, Tom ordered, "You! Sit down and listen to me!"

He took a step toward Micah, who retreated until he was at the edge of the cot and forced to sit anyway.

"Tom, you're not still mad at me, are you?" Micah hated having to look up at the ranger, again feeling like a naughty kid.

"That girl was still crying when she left here," Tom went on in a tone so even it was frightening.

"I swear I didn't do nothing to her!"

"Shut up and listen to me! You're gonna take my proposition." When Micah opened his mouth to protest, Tom added firmly, "No ifs, ands, or buts about it! I ain't gonna watch that girl's heart break over a low-down, no-account, sidewinder like you. You're gonna become a ranger. No arguments."

"I can't do it," Micah said, his own conviction floundering as he thought of the miserable girl and his own demise. "You know why . . . and I just can't."

"Aw, shoot!" Tom practically shouted. "You're both gonna have to become rangers, then."

"Both?" Micah was certain he had not heard right. "You mean Jed, too?"

"Yeah, him too. I'll live to regret this, I'm sure. You'll both likely drive me to an early grave—"

But Micah had jumped to his feet and, nearly knocking Tom over, was at the door. "Jed, you hear that? We ain't gonna hang!"

"What?" Jed said, several steps behind everyone else as usual.

"I'm telling you we ain't gonna die. Tom's made us a deal. All we have to do is become rangers."

"Huh?"

Remembering the door was unlocked, Micah flung it open and strode down the corridor to Jed's cell. "I'm telling you, do you want to be a ranger?"

"A ranger?"

"It won't be much different from what we've been doing 'cept we'll get paid for it, and"—he added this last part quickly as Tom approached—"of course we can't steal no more."

"And we don't have to hang tomorrow?" Jed asked, still bemused.

"Nope," Tom answered. "But don't think you're gonna get off easy. I'm gonna make you work your tails off. You're both gonna be the best durned rangers in this here republic, or I'll want to know the reason why. I ain't risking my own neck just to have a couple of poor malcontents hanging around my neck. Got it?"

"You don't have to worry about us," Micah said. "We won't let you down." And oddly enough, he meant it. He suddenly glanced at Tom and felt a peculiar tightening in his chest. He wanted to tell him thanks but couldn't get the words out.

"Does this mean I don't get no pecan pie?" Jed asked.

Fife rolled his eyes. "Saints preserve me! What have I gone and done!"

"Angry? That does not begin to describe what I'm feeling right now."

"But, Papa, I had to do what I felt was right." Lucie hated to have her father upset at her. She looked at him now, his face more florid than usual, and searched in her mind for something to say that would ease him. "Papa, you taught me yourself to follow my heart—"

"I did not teach you to consort with criminals, nor to defy me!" Reid gasped a breath and sat down at the table in the kitchen.

It had been a silent ride in the back of the carriage as one of the hands drove them home from San Antonio. Lucie knew her father was fuming and feared anything she might say would set off fireworks. She was still upset as well, her eyes red and puffy, and she continued to be on the verge of tears. Deciding it was best to let matters cool a bit, she had gone to the kitchen to fix some tea. She'd offered her father a cup, but declining, he had retreated to his office.

That had been two hours ago. Finally her father had come from his study, finding Lucie still in the kitchen moping over her now cold tea. She had asked him if he was still angry and learned that, though he had calmed, he indeed continued to be irritated.

"Would you like some tea? The kettle is warm." She started to rise, but he laid a restraining hand on hers.

"Forget the tea, Lucie. We need to talk this out."

"Yes, Papa, I know."

"Tell me, whatever got into your head to go into that jail?"

She sighed. "It was the right thing to do—at least speaking in the man's defense was. As far as going to see him . . . I don't know. Maybe it was not wise." She bit her lip as sudden emotion threatened her again. "Oh, Papa! He is a nice boy, I just know it! And I didn't help him after all. Tomorrow . . . tomorrow . . ." A hiccough escaped her lips.

"Now, now, Lucie, baby . . . you mustn't fret so."

As if she had intended it, her tears were softening her father. She found the effect of a woman's tears on a man to be astounding, and though she dared not use such power brazenly, it was rather comforting to know she did have some small recourse as a woman. However, it hadn't helped in the case of Micah Sinclair. Her tears had not softened the heart of that ranger captain. They would not save the young horse thief.

"Papa, it just isn't right that a man with so much life to live, so much promise, should have it all end in such a way. He is not a hardened criminal, I am certain. Surely something awful must have happened to him that set him on the wrong path. He was very kind to me. And I felt I had to let him know someone cared." She sniffed and her father handed her his handkerchief. She wiped her eyes and blew her nose. "Can you imagine having to die all alone? And, Papa, he turned down a chance to avoid his sentence. They were going to let him become a ranger—"

"I know. That is the most outlandish thing I ever heard. And I told the captain so," Reid said.

"One of the rangers cared enough to take him in hand . . ."

"There you go! He did have someone else who cared for him." A satisfied looked spread across Reid's face.

"Well, it doesn't matter anyway," Lucie said with just a hint of disrespectful ire. "Micah refused the offer because he would not let his friend hang alone."

"Sounds like pure foolishness to me."

"Oh, Papa, you can't fool me. You know as well as I that it was an act of grand courage and honor."

Reid looked down at the table, fumbling nervously with the handle of the teapot. Finally he looked up at his daughter, a smile teasing the corners of his lips. "Well, maybe it was at that."

"I think you would like him, Papa. I think you would like him a lot." For a brief moment Lucie nearly forgot her father would never meet the young man, thinking instead she might actually see that handsomely boyish face again. Then reality struck her, and a sob broke through her lips. "Papa, even prayer did not help him."

"You don't know that, sweetheart." He grasped her hand in his. "We can never know what God intends."

"It seems so hopeless!"

"Well, I kind of think it's in hopeless situations where God shines most. Now, don't fret, all right? You leave the lad in God's hands, eh?"

She nodded tearfully.

Then Reid rose. "Maybe I would like some of that tea. You just stay put. I'll get it."

She watched her father lumber to the stove and lift the kettle from the iron surface. It had been a trying day for him as well. The two-hour drive to and from San Antonio alone was taxing. In addition to that he'd had his own business to attend to. Maybe it had been selfish for Lucie to insist upon going and being allowed to speak to the ranger captain, and then to slip away and visit the jail while her father was at the bank. Maybe she should have thought before putting her father through such an unnecessary ordeal. Maybe she should have put his well-being before that of a stranger.

Yet she knew a large portion of her father's surly response was only out of concern for her. She knew he would be the first one to insist upon justice and fairness and mercy. Had she not been involved, Lucie felt certain Reid Maccallum would have been the first man to stand up for Micah Sinclair.

Juana came in just then. "Señor Maccallum, let me get that." She reached for the teakettle as he brought it to the table.

"I've got it, Juana," Reid said. "Sit and join us."

"When there is work to be done? You know me better than that, señor." She chuckled, adroitly taking possession of the kettle as she did so.

Shrugging his surrender, Reid resumed his seat and let Juana continue the task. She filled the teapot with the hot water, took the kettle back to the stove, and returned with a dish of biscuits and a pot of butter.

"So how was your trip to San Antonio?" she asked.

"Tiring," Reid said.

"Frustrating," Lucie added.

"I want you both to stay home for a good long time now. No more trips to San Antonio or anywhere." She lifted the teapot and refilled the cups.

Lucie shrugged, in no mood to argue. In truth, she felt little desire to leave home at the moment. And she had no desire to go to town for a good while, because she did not want to hear stories of what had already occurred or what would occur on the morrow.

Lucie and her father were sipping their tea in silence while Juana was mixing bread dough when a knock came at the kitchen door. Juana let in Pete.

"I just got back from town," he said. "Thought you might want to hear the news."

"Come on in and sit down," Reid said.

"Thanks, but I only got a minute. I need to see to my horse—I came right here." He glanced at Lucie. "Looks like you're gonna get your wish, miss."

Lucie could not tell from his expression if this was a good thing or bad. At least Pete did not seem to be bubbling with happiness.

"My wish?" Lucie asked.

"That kid in jail that you was so worried about? Looks like he isn't gonna hang after all."

"Pete! Really?"

Now Pete let escape a hint of his personal view in the matter. A slight grimace twisted his broad tanned face. "He got a reprieve for being so young and for being a hero of San Jacinto. Same with the other kid. I reckon now everyone who was even close to San Jacinto will take this as leave to rob this here country dry."

But Lucie heard little of the foreman's diatribe. Micah Sinclair was going to live! Maybe, just maybe, her words had done him some good after all! She wanted to jump up and dance around the room. She wanted to kiss her father and maybe even that old leathery foreman.

Suddenly she thought of something else. Maybe she would see Micah again. When she glanced up from her joyous musings, she noticed both men were staring at her. Only then was she aware of the wide grin on her face.

CHAPTER 10

TRY THIS FOR SIZE." Tom held out the pistol.

Micah turned the weapon over in his hand. He'd heard of these but had never seen one, much less held one in his hand. A Paterson Colt single-action revolving handgun. A five-shot .40 caliber affair.

"Five shots, no reloading," Micah murmured. "Hard to believe."

"Give it a try," Tom said. The gun was already loaded because Tom had demonstrated how to do it a few minutes before. He had also given a couple of pointers about using the Colt.

They were in a field near the area where a group of rangers were camped on the edge of town. A few other rangers had gathered around to have a look at the newcomers. Micah noted such luminaries as Big Foot Wallace and Sam Walker. There were also a couple Mexicans; in fact, the ranger company had several Mexicans. But these were from the good families, the ones that had fought with Houston.

Tom had set several rocks in a line on the ground in the center of the mesquite- and sagebrush-covered field. Micah positioned himself just within gun range of the rocks. With a quick glance at Tom, as if still uncertain that he might actually have this privilege, he took a breath and raised the gun. He felt oddly calm in the august presence of so many veterans. But shooting was one thing he felt confident about. Biting the inside of his lip, a habit he'd picked up from his uncle, he cocked the pistol to release the trigger, then squeezed it nice and easy. A rock skipped into the air, shattering into pieces. He repeated the process four more times, never missing.

"Mighty fine shooting," Wallace said in his Virginia drawl.

Micah shrugged at the big lumbering ranger. "Ain't nothing to shoot at rocks."

"Yeah," put in one of the other men, "just wait till he's got a dozen Comanches breathing down his neck."

"My boy could take on more than that, no sweat," bragged Tom like a proud parent.

Micah rolled his eyes, uncomfortable with the attention, yet a certain part of him basking in the praise. He handed the Colt to Jed.

"We gonna get one of these?" Jed asked in awe.

"Only if you got about forty dollars to spare," said Walker, who was the resident expert on the weapon since he had gone back East to tour Samuel Colt's New Jersey factory and had offered suggestions on making improvements in the weapon. It was, in fact, Walker's Colt they were now trying out.

"I hear tell Captain Hays is trying to work out a deal with navy ordnance to get some Colts they have and ain't gonna use since they have been decommissioned," Wallace said. "I'm thinking, though, that we do just as well with our flintlocks and percussion caps." He paused, taking his flintlock pistol from where he had tucked it into his belt. "Truth be told, that Paterson is just a bit too tender for me."

"Well, you gotta keep the grit out, or it gets touchy," Walker said, "but these Colts will take over the West one day. You just wait until Sam Colt makes his improvements."

"So, Jed, you ready to give it a try?" Tom asked. "You remember how to load it, don't you?"

"Sure, it's easy." Jed took the powder pouch and poured a measure into each chamber. Tom had told them not to put in too much powder or the recoil might, in his words, "Wrench your arm out of its socket." But Tom now looked on approvingly at Jed's technique. When the powder was in, Jed set a ball on each chamber opening, tamping them down in turn.

"You'll get faster loading as you get more practice," Tom encouraged.

Micah had jogged out to the middle of the field and put up a row of new rocks, then he stepped aside and gave Jed the go-ahead. Jed hit three out of five.

Wallace nodded at the display. "Well, Tom, your horse-thieves-turned-rangers might just work out after all."

That was high praise indeed coming from the famous Texan. Micah felt like grinning as Jed was now doing, but he was already suffering under the greenhorn, new-recruit stigma, so he merely gave the man a cool nod.

The rangers were careful not to waste powder and lead, and soon the shooting demonstration ended, the men dispersing about to their own business. Supplies and finances were a constant burr in the rangers' skin. Though theoretically each ranger was to receive a monthly stipend of around twenty-five dollars, few ever saw any money. Sometimes the government came up with the cash months after the ranger's term of service was completed, but usually not at all. Sometimes they received land for compensation—one commodity Texas had plenty of. But basically these men simply were not in it for the money. Sheer thirst for adventure or a sense of duty to their country drove them. This was not a job for any man who cared for the comforts of life. Their living quarters consisted of the sky for a roof, the dirt as a floor, and the brush for walls.

They were expected to provide their own equipment and fill their own bellies. However, when there was no pay coming, this became a serious problem, especially when they were too busy scouting and such to hunt. For some time Captain Hays had been keeping the men from his own pocket, thus far, to the tune of some three thousand dollars.

Though Micah was officially a ranger, not much had changed for him. He still had the same clothes, though he had allowed himself the luxury of a bath. He wore no badge or other insignia. But for all the poverty of the other rangers, Micah was much worse off because he lacked the most essential tool of a ranger—a good mount. Or for that matter, any mount. At least Jed had his horse and saddle, though he almost lost it when he nearly admitted to having stolen the beast a few years before. Only a sharp jab in the ribs from Micah prevented that costly error.

Rangers were required to have a horse worth at least a hundred dollars. Many had fine-blooded animals from Kentucky. Their horses were their most important piece of equipment. They often lived or died as much by the skill and stamina of their mounts as by their own. The vast open plains of Texas, often with neither road nor trail, required a good mount. And it was frivolous to even consider facing the mounted Comanches or Mexicans any other way. Micah worried over his lack of a mount, wondering also how he would afford one of those fine revolving pistols.

"You don't need much besides a horse and a good gun," Tom assured him. "Rangers travel light, living off the land when we can, starving when we can't."

"Just what we been doing for years, huh, Micah?" Jed said.

"That still don't solve my biggest problem," Micah said. Without a horse he might just as well be without a leg or an arm. And a hundred-dollar horse? That was easily four months' salary, when the impoverished republic could afford to pay salaries.

Sometimes the rangers had a small remuda of captured horses, but their supply was rather depleted at the moment. The best of the handful of beasts was a broken-down old Comanche pinto that had seen better days some twenty years ago. After the discouraging experience of examining the remuda, Micah, Jed, and Tom went to a cantina in town to slake their thirst. Both Micah and Jed were dragging a bit after a day of firing practice and the other drills Tom felt necessary to get the two new rangers up to par with the others in the company.

Micah was lifting a glass of beer to his lips when a fellow about his own age stepped inside the door that had been left open to let in what little afternoon breeze was there.

"I was told there might be a Micah Sinclair in here," he said.

Micah swallowed, glancing nervously at his companions. He supposed it would take more than a couple days to shake that apprehension at being singled out, which came naturally with criminal behavior. Tom was suppressing a grin, making Micah feel all the more foolish.

"That'd be me," Micah finally answered.

"I got something for you."

"What is it?"

"You gotta come outside."

Micah studied the young man closely. He didn't appear to be looking for trouble. With a shrug, Micah strode toward the door.

The stranger had gone to a hitching post, loosened the reins of one of the horses tied there, and was leading it toward the sidewalk in front of the cantina. "This here is yours," he said simply.

"Whadd'ya mean? I ain't got no horse."

"You do now. You're supposed to look at the note in the saddlebag." The stranger thrust the reins once more at Micah.

Instead of taking the reins, Micah walked down the step of the sidewalk and circled the animal, finally lifting the flap to the bag. Inside he found the paper, which he took out. "Who's this from?" he asked as he tore open the seal.

"I reckon the paper will tell all you need to know. I brought the horse from the Maccallum place."

Micah scanned the few lines on the page written in the fine script of a female hand.

Dear Mr. Sinclair,

I realize nothing can ever properly repay you for all I owe you in saving my life, but please take the gift of this horse as a small gesture of my appreciation.

Yours sincerely,
Miss Lucie Maccallum

Below this was an addendum: *This is an official transfer of ownership of this buckskin gelding to Micah Sinclair. R. Maccallum.*

Deliberately, Micah folded the paper and replaced it in the saddlebag. Saying nothing, he continued to stand, now on the street, and contemplate the animal. It was indeed a fine-looking buckskin with a light tan coat and silky black tail and mane. It looked powerfully built, too, though sleek as well, as if it had been built specifically for the needs of a ranger desiring both stamina and speed. And it had a good Mexican saddle on it, too, not new by any means, but broken in nicely. The whole lot was worth far more than a hundred dollars.

By now Jed and Tom had come outside. "Whadd'ya got there?" Tom asked.

"Its from that Maccallum girl," Micah replied darkly, no gratitude apparent in his tone. "She had a mind to give it to me."

"Hey! That's great!" Jed said.

"No, it ain't great at all." Suddenly Micah sprang to life. He grabbed the reins from the stranger and swung up into the saddle.

"Where you going?" asked both Jed and Tom.

"I'm taking this horse back, that's where." Micah started to urge the animal forward.

"Wait one minute!" Tom called. "Don't do anything without thinking first, Micah. You need a horse."

"Not this horse."

"What's wrong with that horse?"

"I'm not taking no gift from a woman, for one thing."

Tom rubbed his whiskered chin. "I see your point. But you still need a horse."

"I'll get me a horse myself!" Micah didn't know where his sudden ire was coming from, but he knew it was indeed anger surging through him now.

"Okay, but how you gonna get back to town once you leave off that animal?"

Micah grimaced at Tom's practicality, then quickly solved the problem. "Jed, get your horse. You're coming with me."

CHAPTER 11

THE TWO-HOUR RIDE TO THE Maccallum ranch impressed upon Micah the probable folly of returning the horse. The buckskin was a better mount than even its looks had indicated. It had taken to a new rider admirably, showing its intelligence and even temper. In fact, as they neared the ranch, Micah could not believe how comfortable he felt on the buckskin. It was almost as if they had been meant for each other.

And though Jed's sorrel was a fairly good mount, Micah found he had to check the buckskin's pace to let Jed keep up.

By the time they came within sight of the ranch buildings, Micah knew he was making a mistake giving up the horse. But he had also had time to solidify his ambiguous emotions in the matter. He knew a large part of his anger stemmed from the fact that since leaving his parents' home six years earlier, he had pretty much lived for himself, answering to no one. Yes, Harvey Tate had made demands, but Micah had always had the choice of walking out of the gang.

Now all of a sudden it seemed as if Micah's freewheeling world was closing in on him. First, he was all but owned by the rangers, at least for a year. All he had to do was mind his p's and q's. It would be like being in prison for a year, or worse, being home under the thumb of his father.

If that weren't bad enough, now Lucie Maccallum was . . . well, what *was* she trying to do? He couldn't quite put his finger on it, but the giving of that horse made him mighty jumpy. She said it was a gift for saving her life, but in his mind gifts, no matter what the reason for them, just made a body beholden to the giver. And why would she feel the need to gift him anyway? Had she forgotten he had stolen nearly thirty-five of her mustangs? Maybe it didn't count because he was no longer in possession of the animals, but they were still gone.

He couldn't explain it. But he was certain she must have some motive. One didn't give away fine animals just like that.

He rode into the yard of the ranch. A quick glance behind indicated Jed had fallen back quite a bit since Micah had spurred the buckskin into a gallop as he had neared the ranch. Now he slowed, not so much for Jed's sake as because a female figure was walking across the yard toward him.

He came to a halt a few feet from her and dismounted. "Good afternoon, miss," he said, tipping his hat politely.

"Hello, Mr. Sinclair. This is a pleasant surprise," Lucie Maccallum said. An afternoon breeze had sprung up and it was blowing wisps of her hair into her face, and she lifted a hand to push them back, revealing lips parted in a warm, welcoming smile.

He didn't want to be reminded of how pretty she was, but how could he not be when she was standing so close that he could smell her fragrance, an oddly heady mix of hay and horseflesh and rosewater. Her dark eyes, too, were sparkling in the afternoon sun. And her riding dress, a brown color that perfectly matched her eyes, seemed to emphasize the clear glow of her skin, which had the aspect of tanned ivory. His throat suddenly went dry and his anger was forgotten, as was his reason for coming to the ranch.

He stood there staring dumbly.

"Mr. Sinclair . . ." she prompted.

"Miss Maccallum . . ." He swallowed, finding no moisture in his mouth. The afternoon heat was as debilitating as this beautiful young woman's presence.

"You've no doubt had a long ride," she said. "May I invite you in and offer you a cold drink?"

It was the offer of yet another gift that snapped Micah back to himself. "No, miss." He remembered the buckskin's reins gripped in his hands. "I . . . uh . . . I've come to bring back your horse."

"I don't understand. I gave him to you." She looked truly perplexed.

"I can't accept him."

"But—"

Micah's resolve gathered back around him with each word. "I know you probably meant well, but I can't take him. I don't want, nor do I deserve, a gift for what I did."

"Are you saying my life isn't worth a gift?"

"Yes—I mean no! Confound it! That ain't what I mean at all. It's just . . ." Pausing, he saw how her eyes were searching him, seeking to understand. And all he could respond with was a jumble of half-formed emotions. "It's not right. Don't you see?" Micah tried once more to explain, yet it was difficult since he wished to avoid the issue of the stolen horses. "I did what anyone would have done in the same place.

And to take something in return . . . it doesn't set well with me. And no matter how you put it, giving me such a fine gift makes me beholden to you."

"I respect your sense of honor in the matter," she responded, "but try to look at it from my viewpoint. I am indebted to you for my very life. The gift helps me to not feel so beholden to you."

"Is that why you gave it to me?" Instinctively, he thought differently.

The way she ducked her head, glancing sheepishly at her toes, indicated his instincts had been correct. "I gave you Jose—"

"Jose?"

"The buckskin," she amplified, then at his nod to continue, she did so. "Anyway, I gave you Jose because you needed a horse, and I wanted to do that for you. It is as simple as that."

Somehow he didn't think it was that simple at all, but he knew she was telling the truth. He gave a deep sigh, then said, "And I can't take it . . . simple as that."

"I told you he wouldn't take it, Lucie," interjected a new voice.

Micah looked around to see a big redheaded man approach. Micah had never met Lucie's father, but he was certain this must be he. In addition to a certain family resemblance, the man carried himself like the owner of one of the largest ranches in Texas. Micah was six feet tall himself, but this man seemed to tower over him by several inches. He was one of the biggest men Micah had ever seen. And his size was only emphasized by his husky girth—not fat by any means, simply *big*—and by his shock of thick hair that was truly as red as a carrot.

Lucie's voice drew Micah's attention from the awesome figure. "Papa, you said if he was worth his salt, he wouldn't take the horse."

"That's right, I did." There was a touch of smugness in the man's tone. Then he turned fully toward Micah. "I'm Reid Maccallum, Lucie's father." He held out his hand.

Micah took it and, remembering a lesson from his youth, gripped the man's hand firmly. "Micah Sinclair."

"I am happy to meet the man who saved my daughter's life." For some reason Micah could not fathom, Maccallum's tone was taut, lacking the ebullience his words might have called for. No doubt he wouldn't forget the loss of his mustangs as easily as his daughter appeared to have done.

"As I was trying to tell your daughter," Micah said as he let go of the huge meaty hand, "I don't expect no payment for what I did."

"I myself did not think you deserved any," Maccallum said flatly.

These words were unexpected. Micah opened his mouth to respond to what he had expected, then snapped his lips closed, nonplussed.

A tight smile twitched upon Maccallum's lips. "My daughter forgets that the men you were with got away with a fair number of my horses."

"I expect, then, you might have preferred that I hang," Micah replied dryly.

"I have always believed hanging a bit harsh for the crime of horse stealing, especially considering the murder of human beings often goes with a far lesser punishment. But that aside, I only know my daughter would have been extremely unhappy at your demise, Mr. Sinclair."

Maccallum glanced his daughter's way, and Micah noted a hint of tenderness flicker across the man's stern visage.

"And that, sir, I could not abide," he concluded.

Micah remembered something. "Mr. Maccallum, if I recall rightly, your signature was on that transfer for the horse."

"Yes, Lucie prevailed upon me." Glancing over the heads of both his companions as if embarrassed, Reid added, "I have been told I tend to be an overly indulgent father."

"At any rate, sir," Micah said, "I won't be taking the horse."

"Yet you need a horse in order to fulfill the terms of your release from jail, do you not?"

"I'll find one somehow."

"Somehow?" The man's hazel eyes squinted with a touch of reproach.

"Not by stealing, sir!"

"You have the money to buy a horse?"

"Not exactly . . ."

"He don't have one red cent," put in Jed, who had by then rode up and, though still mounted, was listening to the exchange.

"And who might you be?" Maccallum inquired, giving Jed a careful appraisal.

"That's my friend Jed Wilkes," Micah answered. Things were getting complicated enough without the added element of Jed, who, if true to form, would only confuse matters more. "He was in jail with me."

"Ah . . . yes," Maccallum said. "My daughter mentioned him." Maccallum paused, rubbing his clean-shaven chin. "As I said, you no doubt plan to purchase a mount. But having no ready cash, you might find this difficult unless you buy on credit."

"Credit?" Micah knew what this was, of course, and didn't like the sound of it.

"I wouldn't speak so skeptically of this method, Mr. Sinclair. The entire Republic of Texas has made extensive use of credit for its survival and is no worse for it—well, at least it is surviving because of it. No doubt if the republic intends to pay you for your services as a ranger, it will do so by loans it has received from other nations and such. There is no reason, then, why you shouldn't purchase a horse—a desperately needed horse, I might add—by the same method."

"Who would give me credit? I don't have any collateral or nothing." Micah knew there would be a ready answer for his query or Maccallum wouldn't have brought up the subject.

"I'll extend credit to you for this buckskin. If it weren't for my daughter, you would be dead now and thus in no need of a horse, so I feel rather obligated to make the situation right."

Micah restrained a smile at the man's rather twisted logic. Part of Micah knew Maccallum was simply attempting to make the giving of the horse tolerable to Micah's sense of honor. Thus he still wanted to refuse the offer. But it was such a fine horse. And how else was Micah to get a horse? He'd considered going out to the open prairie and catching a wild mustang, but that would take considerable time. Credit seemed to be the only practical way. So why not arrange some credit with Maccallum? Glancing at Lucie, Micah could think of many reasons against an arrangement that would tie him yet closer to her, but he could also think of a few good reasons for doing so. One of which was that her feelings would be terribly hurt if he didn't. And the last thing he wanted to do was hurt her.

"I guess since you put it that way . . ." Micah said thoughtfully. "I suppose we could work out a deal."

"Come on into my study," Maccallum said, "and we will discuss it further."

Micah glanced up at the lowering sun. He didn't want to refuse the man's invitation, but as it was, it would be nearly dark by the time they returned to town.

"I don't mean to be unsociable, sir, but I'd like to get back to town before it gets dark."

Maccallum nodded, understanding. "Of course. Well, the matter is simple enough. Let's say the horse and saddle is worth one hundred fifty dollars. You can pay me in monthly installments of say, five dollars."

Micah did some quick ciphering in his head. "That would take nearly two and a half years, sir!"

"If you should come by a windfall and would like to pay the debt sooner, I would have no problem with that."

"I might not get a salary for months on end," Micah said practically.

"I will take that into account, since it would be through no fault of your own."

"What about interest?" Micah might be giving in to his better judgment, but at least he wanted to be businesslike about it.

"I do not hold with the setting of usury." Maccallum appeared firm about this, so Micah made no argument.

"All right, then," Micah agreed. "If you make up a contract, I will sign it."

"I believe a man's handshake is better than any piece of paper." Maccallum thrust out his hand.

A bit bemused, Micah took it. They shook firmly. He glanced at the buckskin as if to remind himself again what this was all about.

"He is yours now, Mr. Sinclair," Lucie said. Micah had almost forgotten her presence, caught as he had been in the wake of Reid Maccallum's *presence.*

"I thank you kindly," he said rather dumbly. He had made a business deal with Maccallum, yet he still felt beholden to these people. He shook away the vague sense of unrest over this. He needed that horse. Well, he needed a horse. He *wanted* that horse. "We best be on our way." He swung up into the saddle of the buckskin named Jose.

"Good-bye, Mr. Sinclair," Lucie said.

Glancing back at her, something strange happened inside him. His heart felt like a fist had grabbed it and shoved it up into his throat. He couldn't speak. He could only lift a hand and wave in response. It was all he could do to ride away at an easy canter, when what he really wanted to do was ride like the Devil himself was nipping at his heels. He was more scared now than when he used to hear his father's sermons about hell and brimstone. Lucie Maccallum was more frightening than that.

"You are looking quite smug, Lucinda Maria Bonny Maccallum," Reid said, thick arms crossed in front of him as he gazed quizzically down at his daughter.

"We have done a good thing just now, Papa." She gazed off into the distance at the rapidly disappearing riders. "We have helped set a man upon a path of . . . good, or even righteousness."

"Lucie, it is a mistake to try to change men."

"Don't you think men can change? That God can change men?"

"Let's get in out of this heat," Reid said and started walking toward the house. Lucie caught up as he continued. "Men change, but it is folly to try to effect changes, especially for women to try to change men they have an eye for—"

"Papa! Really, I have no—"

"I hope and pray you don't, sweetheart." They reached the kitchen door, and Reid opened it, stepping back to allow Lucie to enter first.

It was hardly any cooler in the kitchen with the stove going in preparation of supper. After a brief greeting to Juana, the pair exited the room and continued back to Reid's study. Inside, they found their favorite seats. Reid, the big leather chair behind the desk, and Lucie, the big upholstered chair opposite. By silent agreement, they both seemed to realize their conversation was not finished.

Staring into her lap and toying with the tassel at the end of her belt, Lucie spoke reluctantly. "Why do you pray not, Papa?"

He knew what she meant without further elaboration. "He's a wild one."

"But weren't you impressed by his returning the buckskin?" Her tone reflected her hopefulness at having her father's approval.

"I'm not saying he's a bad sort, even though we came into his acquaintance through his criminal behavior." He smiled. "Half the men in Texas are horse and cattle thieves. That's how many of the ranchers around here got their starts."

"You, Papa?"

"Harrumph." Reid made the characteristic rumbling sound deep in his throat that usually indicated he was rattled or slightly abashed. "No men are perfect, no matter how much you want them to be, Lucie," he hedged. "I expect from what you've said and from what I've heard that this Sinclair fellow has some good solid values and just fell into thieving as a means of survival."

"I am almost certain of it, Papa!"

"But some men just got wild hearts, even if they aren't basically bad. And I am afraid you'll end up hurt if you try to tame this fellow."

Chewing rather disconsolately on her lower lip, Lucie lifted her eyes to meet her father's gaze. "I'll try not to, Papa."

"I think you already have," he replied gently without rebuke. "That's what the horse was all about, wasn't it? You figured if he had a horse, he'd stick with this rangering job and keep away from crime."

A shaky sigh escaped her lips as emotion sprang into her chest. “You helped him, too, didn't you?”

“A foolish thing for me to do, but . . . if your heart's going to be lost to such a wild one, I at least hope to keep him on the straight and narrow.”

Reid leaned forward, his eyes turned to pools, and Lucie felt certain he was feeling a bit of emotion himself.

“Lucie, can you try not to fall in love with him?”

“I . . . I'll try.” Her voice was small and uncertain. What was this young man she hardly knew doing to her? She was not in love with Micah Sinclair, was she? But what did she know of love? Did it have anything at all to do with the way her insides trembled when he was near? Or with how her thoughts were never far from him? Or how he figured into many of her dreams, both waking and sleeping?

No, she was not in love with Micah.

But her father was smiling a rather peculiar smile, wise and sad and full of resolve but with little humor.

When she spoke again, she forced a firmness she didn't quite feel into her tone. “Don't worry, Papa.”

But his smile looked worried.

PART TWO

LATE SUMMER 1842

CHAPTER 12

Micah's first assignment as a ranger came within days of receiving the buckskin. The company, usually consisting of around two dozen men when Captain Hays could recruit that many, was sent to patrol along the Nueces, where increased Comanche activity had been reported. After a week with no enemy sightings, half the company returned to town while the remaining half was to make one more sweep of the area and then also return to San Antonio.

Micah was with this half, and he wasn't the only one getting itchy for some action. But it looked like any Comanches previously sighted had cleared out long ago. There weren't any fresh signs. Tired, mostly from boredom, the men made camp late one afternoon, an hour earlier than usual. A hunting expedition brought back two plump turkeys to feast upon for supper.

While a couple of men cooked up the meat, Micah set about cleaning his rifle, wondering if he was ever going to get the chance to use it. The last thing he expected as he began taking apart the weapon was to look up and see a woman standing like an apparition in the late afternoon light. He blinked once, but when she was still standing there, he laid aside his gun and jumped up.

"Hello, ma'am," he said softly. He noted now that she was ragged and battered and looked as skittish as a colt eyeing a rattler.

"It . . . can't be . . ." she rasped.

Seeing that she was about to collapse, Micah rushed forward, catching her as she crumpled. "Tom! Come quick!" Micah yelled to his friend, who happened to be nearby.

Tom came running as Micah was laying the woman down on the grass. Several others joined him.

"What you got there, Micah?" Tom asked.

"She just appeared out of the brush . . . just like that."

"She looks half dead," Bill McBroome said.

"Jed, get some water," Micah ordered. Then he said to the woman, "Ma'am, what's happened to you?"

"Indians!" she said. "They have my baby—" Her voice rose shrilly, then disintegrated into a wracking cough.

Just then Jed returned with a canteen, and Micah set it to her swollen and parched lips. As the water touched them, her tongue flicked out, catching some of the drips. Micah let a bit more drip from the canteen, and she lapped this up eagerly.

"Easy now," Micah said.

The water seemed to revive her a bit, at least giving her strength to speak again, though still with great difficulty. "I thought if I could escape, I could get help. Please . . . save my baby!"

She poured out her story in fits and starts, often incoherently. Micah tried to get her to stop and rest, but she seemed to have a need to tell it. Her name was Martha Hornsby. Apparently she, her husband, her ten-year-old son, and her infant son were traveling by wagon to their new homestead south of Austin when they were attacked. The husband and ten-year-old were killed, and she and the baby were taken captive. That had been, by her best guess, some four days ago, though she had been unconscious some of that time, so her estimation of time passage was not completely reliable.

She was in bad shape. Dehydration and malnutrition were the least of her problems. The worst was a wound in her head and one in her leg from which she had lost much blood.

As one of the men who had some skill with doctoring tried to clean her up and tend her wounds, Micah tried to get details from her that would aid them in tracking the Indians. Yet it seemed it might be a hopeless pursuit. The woman had managed to escape from her captors two days ago, giving the Indians a good head start.

"Find my baby!" Martha Hornsby gasped again, nearly spent now. "They had him wrapped in hides and tied to a gray mule. That's . . . what you . . . should look for. . . ."

"We'll find him, Mrs. Hornsby," Micah said with confidence. Only a quick glance at Tom indicated he wasn't as confident as his words sounded.

Leaving four men behind to stay with the woman and guard the camp, the rest, eight in all, departed without waiting for supper. They didn't want to waste the daylight left to them. Jed was told to stay behind, and Micah was certain he also would be one of the unlucky ones to be stuck in camp. But the others felt that since he had found the woman, so to speak, he should have the privilege of joining the search for the child. He was thrilled and excited as he hurriedly put his rifle back together, loaded it and his brace of pistols, and mounted the buckskin.

It wasn't until the next afternoon that they located fresh tracks. Apparently the Indians had spent some time trying to find their missing captive. They also did not appear to be in a great hurry, nor were they exercising much caution, which no doubt explained how the woman had escaped. Perhaps they felt enough time had passed that they were safe from pursuit. Or they might simply feel confident in their numbers, which Big Foot estimated at about twenty. Nevertheless, Micah was frustrated when the rangers had to halt for the night so as not to destroy the signs in the darkness.

Two hours after sunrise the next morning, the rangers located the Comanche camp on the edge of a dense cedar break. The Indians were only beginning to break camp. Indeed, they seemed as relaxed and unconcerned as if they were on a Sunday picnic. Only when they heard the approach of the rangers did they spring into action, grabbing weapons and horses, leaving all else behind, and dashing for the cedar. The Comanches weren't about to make a stand against the obviously better armed and better mounted rangers.

Micah dug his heels into the buckskin's flanks. They would lose their prey if they reached the trees. Before realizing it, he was several lengths ahead of his comrades. In another minute, he was in the midst of the

Comanche camp where the braves were still running helter-skelter in a frenzied escape attempt. Several had already reached the trees. They were on foot, since horses would be of little use in the dense wood. One Indian paused and fired at Micah. The ball from the Indian's ancient musket tore Micah's hat from his head. Micah jumped from his mount and fired back but only grazed a tree as the Indian took off running.

Micah fired again at the retreating Comanche with his second pistol, bringing him down. He quickly reloaded and was about to continue pursuit when someone yelled his name.

"Micah!"

He spun around in time to see a warrior bearing down on him with a drawn knife. Micah pulled the trigger, but his pistol jammed. The Comanche leaped for a final attack, but a shot from behind stopped him. Micah saw it was Bill McBroome who had come to his aid. He didn't have time for more than a nod of thanks because the Comanche Bill shot was only wounded and was now dashing for cover. Micah also raced toward the trees.

But he was too late. The Comanches were quickly disappearing into the cover of the break. It would be useless to attempt to engage them in the thick woods, but it was a hard reality to accept. Only one dead Indian for the rangers' efforts. And no baby. Discouraged, Micah joined the others in search for booty, mostly horses that the retreating Indians had not had a chance to take. Four horses and two mules.

"A gray mule!" Micah yelled.

He found his reward carefully wrapped in several layers of hides. The squirming, wailing baby was definitely white and seemed no worse for his ordeal.

A few minutes later Big Foot Wallace came up to Micah with another unexpected reward. "Reckon you got the only kill of the day, so you earned this." He held out a bloody swath of black hair.

It wasn't the first scalp Micah had ever seen and would surely not be his last, but he'd never get used to them, to the blood, the gore, and the gruesome kind of victory they represented. He only took the thing and tied it to his saddle because he thought it might give Mrs. Hornsby some comfort knowing at least a small price had been exacted for her loss.

But the screaming child made him quickly forget all this. Tom was holding the baby, but completely bewildered, he handed it off to Bill, who grimaced as if he'd just been handed a rattler. He held the child out at arm's length, looking desperately around for rescue.

Micah took the baby almost instinctively, though it had been years since he'd been around children. "He's wet," Micah announced. "Anyone got a spare shirt in their saddlebag? I don't have a spare, or I'd use it."

Tom found a shirt and gave it to Micah. "What'd you need that for?"

"You'll see. In the meantime, someone get a fire going and boil up some water with a couple pieces of jerky in it." Almost in spite of himself, Micah began warming to the task. It brought back many memories. Most were unwelcome, but not everything about his growing up had been unpleasant. Like any normal boy, he hadn't liked helping his mother care for his siblings, yet there had been something nice about the companionship of his mother and sisters. These tasks had formed a bond among them. A bond that had excluded his father.

Micah stripped off the baby's diaper, a mere rag that looked as if it hadn't been changed for days. The smell caused tears to sting his eyes. The other men stepped back with various noises of disgust. Micah cleaned the boy, who appeared to be about eight months old, with the damp ends of the old diaper, which he then laid aside.

As he positioned Tom's shirt under the squirming child who was fully exercising his healthy lungs, Tom leaned in closer to see what was to become of his shirt. At just that moment, the baby decided to release more than tears. A stream of urine struck poor Tom right between the eyes.

"What the—" he sputtered, then jumped away, looking like he'd have rather been shot.

The other men howled.

Bill was nearly doubled over with laughter. "That kid's got a better aim than Micah!"

Then, as if Tom's humiliation wasn't complete, he began to perceive exactly to what use his shirt was being put when Micah wrapped the main part of the shirt around the baby's bottom, circling the sleeves around his middle to fasten it all together.

"That's my best shirt!" Tom protested.

"It'll wash up fine," Micah assured him.

"I ain't wearin' no shirt that's been fouled by a kid's innards!"

"You'll smell better'n ya do now," taunted Bill.

Tom was sputtering, trying to think of a retort, when Micah picked up the old diaper and thrust it out. "Here, Bill, go wash this out in the stream."

Bill jumped back, hands raised, obviously appalled. "I ain't touching that!"

Micah marveled that men who thought nothing of lifting a human scalp were so repulsed at a little child's mess.

"Do I gotta do everything?" he railed. "This baby has to eat. Now one of you sorry varmints take care of this rag. We'll need a spare, unless someone has another shirt . . ."

With a curse, Bill picked up the offensive item and marched off to the stream. Micah lifted the child against his shoulder, and at last the baby's wails began to subside a little. He walked around the camp patting the boy's back and cooing softly. Soon the broth was ready. After it had cooled some, he took off his bandanna, loosely knotting one end, and dipped it into the broth. He brought the sodden knot to the infant's lips and the baby sucked hungrily at it.

"Well, I'll be!" said Big Foot. "Looks like our horse-thieving ranger is also a baby's nurse. Wonders will never cease!"

"Where'd you learn all this stuff?" one of the other men asked.

"I was the oldest of four," Micah replied casually. "I've changed my share of diapers and such."

"Well, I was from a big family, too," said one of the men, "and I never learned all that. My pa made sure women's work was done by the women."

My pa didn't give a hang, Micah thought but said nothing out loud because he didn't care to open his personal life to everyone. He did allow himself a private grin when he remembered those days his father had suffered so, right after his mother had died. Benjamin had been in way over his head trying to care for the newborn, in addition to the other children. Micah had taken special pleasure in making the task as hard on his father as he could, never volunteering information and helping only when it seemed that to do otherwise might be harmful to the children.

"Well, Micah," said Big Foot, "I'd start to wonder about you if'n you wasn't so good with a gun."

Micah responded with a disgruntled snort, then gave the baby another taste of broth.

When they returned to the camp where they had left the child's mother, they learned that Mrs. Hornsby had died hours earlier.

"Well, boy," Micah said gently to his little charge, "I'm sorry for you. You poor kid." He ran a finger over the child's downy soft yellow curls. "You don't even have a name," he murmured. "Ain't right that you have no family and no name either." He smiled into the limpid brown eyes. "When my brother was born, I wanted to name him for my uncle, but my pa would have none of that. I think I'll call you Haden . . . just so I don't have to keep calling you kid."

He held the child a little closer, rocking him gently. He'd had sole responsibility for the baby on the ride back, and now it looked as if he'd have to continue to do so until they got to San Antonio. He'd gotten a couple of the others, Tom included, to help some, but it seemed the baby was most content when Micah had him. Sometimes as he rocked the baby, humming little snippets of tunes he remembered from his childhood, he'd find his thoughts wandering to Lucie Maccallum. That amazed him more than anything. It gave him a kind of warmth all over, a sensation he hadn't felt in many years. But he knew it was a dangerous sensation to feel, much less enjoy.

They arrived in San Antonio four days later on a Sunday afternoon. As the rangers rode past the new Protestant church, Micah decided the service must have just recently concluded because the members were still milling around outside visiting. He saw the big redheaded figure of Reid Maccallum, then quickly jerked his head away before his eyes made contact with Lucie, who he knew would be somewhere near her father. He wanted to see her, to talk to her again. But he knew it wouldn't be a good idea.

He and Tom took the baby to the constable's office so they could discuss what was to be done about the boy. Once apprised of the situation, the constable sent his deputy over to the church to see if any of the women could help out. In the meantime one of the other men found some milk to feed the child. Micah warmed the milk and fed the boy while the child's future was being decided.

"I'm pretty sure Martha and Ned Hornsby had family up around Austin," the constable said.

"Then they'll take him," Micah said hopefully. He himself was growing much too attached to this kid. The sooner he was rid of him, the sooner he could get back to an existence he understood.

"It'll take time to reach them, of course."

"Well, surely one of the women here will take him until then."

"No doubt."

About fifteen minutes later, a woman did come to the constable's office. Lucie Maccallum. Micah was alone with the baby. Tom and the constable had gone to see how the deputy was doing finding a temporary home for the child.

"I heard about what happened," she said softly, lowering her voice even more when she saw the baby was asleep.

"Poor fella," Micah said. "It's a rotten thing to happen to an innocent kid."

"Yes. To lose his mother like that . . . it makes me sick." She gingerly lifted the corner of the blanket, Micah's trail blanket he'd torn in half to use for the child. "But he seems awfully content now."

She lifted her eyes from the baby, focusing fully on Micah. He felt like squirming under her gaze but willed himself to keep still. So as not to disturb the boy, he told himself. He didn't know why his heart seemed to stop moving as well.

"Th-the constable says he's got other family up north, so that's good." Micah's voice squeaked nervously over the words.

"Mrs. Wendell at church said she'd take the boy until his family can be found."

"Well, where is she?"

"Are you going to be able to let him go?" She smiled, her eyes twinkling, but not in a taunting way. "Tom explained how you've cared for the baby since he was found. He said you had a special knack—"

"That fool Tom!" Micah exclaimed, his raised voice causing little Haden to move and whimper in his arms.

"What's wrong with that?"

"I just did what had to be done."

"Like when you rescued me?" Her smile broadened and now contained a trace of smugness.

"Oh, that's—" But Micah was cut off as the door opened.

Mr. and Mrs. Wendell, accompanied by the constable and his deputy, entered. Micah was never so relieved and so unhappy about seeing anyone. Micah told himself the child needed a woman's care. As for himself, he had Indians to hunt and Mexicans to kill. He had a job to do that held no room in it for babies and such.

Yet when it came time to relinquish the boy, Micah found it difficult to release him. But he wasn't about to let it show. With a grunt and loud sigh of relief, he deposited Haden into the woman's outstretched arms.

"Thank goodness you finally got here," he said. "This kid was about to drive me crazy."

Micah hurried from the office the first chance he could, choosing a moment when Lucie was occupied in conversation with Mrs. Wendell. He raced outside, gasping in air as soon as he'd exited. His throat felt constricted, and his eyes were burning.

He gulped deep breaths. How could he have let that kid get to him so?

Then Lucie was there at his side. She'd gotten to him, too! And it scared him.

But he couldn't resist looking at her. Now that his arms felt so achingly empty from the departure of the child, he thought it would be so easy to fill them with Lucie's soft, inviting form.

"I must see to my father," she said, her words not quite breaking the spell but at least keeping him from doing something very foolish.

"Give him my regards."

"I will." She gave him a parting smile, turned, then paused and turned back. "Mr. Sinclair, I was wondering if you knew about the ball to be held here in town next weekend? You might enjoy it, and if you attended, I would love to save a dance for you."

"Well, I . . ." He stared at her, incredulous. He had never been to a dance in his life, and he certainly had never been promised a dance with a beautiful, genteel lady such as she. It smacked of civilization, and coming as it did on the heels of the unsettling experience with the baby, it frightened the life out of him. But in an odd way, it enticed him, too. He knew he should tell her "no thanks."

Babies and dances and genteel ladies were not for men like him.

"I'll see if I can make it," he heard himself say.

CHAPTER 13

MICAH DECIDED NOT TO GO to the dance. He didn't know why. It just seemed like a good idea to avoid such vestiges of civilization. He had gone out on another patrol with several rangers, and he had hoped that would have kept him away, but as ill-luck would have it, they returned to town Saturday morning.

"Plenty of time to get yourself spruced up for that dance," Tom suggested as they tended their horses.

"And how am I supposed to do that, Tom?" Micah groused. He was tired and ill tempered. The patrol had not gone well. He had been sent off to investigate some tracks leading to a ravine and had gotten turned around and lost his way back to the main force. When he finally did catch up to the company, the men had ridiculed him unmercifully, all in good nature, of course, for days after.

"A bath would be in order first," Tom replied, wrinkling his nose.

"You smell like a coyote yourself, Tom, so don't go making fun of me!"

But Micah did smell, and his beard was stubbly and itchy, and his hair was plastered down against his scalp with sweat and grime. However, these drawbacks could be easily repaired. What he could do nothing about was his clothing. He had no change of clothes, and there was no way he'd take more charity. Even if he was of a mind to go to the dance, he could not do so in dusty, worn dungarees and a matching shirt. The worst of it was, if he attempted to launder these items one more time, they would probably fall apart.

"Anyway, how'd you know about that dance?" Micah asked.

"Jed mentioned it."

Micah glared at Jed, whose lips were curved into a smirk. "I ain't never seen no one with a bigger mouth!" Micah rebuked his friend.

"He also told me as how that pretty little Maccallum gal wanted to dance with you," Tom added.

"So what?"

"You're at an age where you ought to be thinking of settling down." This seemed a peculiar statement coming from the grizzled bachelor.

"What are you? My mother?" Micah sneered.

Tom grunted a couple of unkind remarks, then returned his attention to his horse, loosening the bindings and removing the saddle.

They were in the field near the edge of town where the rangers had staked out their camp while off duty. One of the men had built a fire and was cooking a late breakfast. Others were grooming their mounts after the stint on the trail and others were heading to the river for baths in what little water there was so late in summer.

"If I had a gal like that who wanted me," Jed declared, "I sure wouldn't refuse."

"Then take her," Micah muttered.

Jed only snickered and snorted in response. "But, Micah, you got things turned around, don't ya? First you got the baby, then you got the gal, and you ain't even got married yet." He laughed even harder at his humor.

Cursing at his friend, Micah turned to tending his buckskin. Even if he had botched this most recent mission, Jose had performed admirably. As Micah unhitched the saddle, his thoughts turned to the woman who had given him the horse, though he truly wanted *not* to think of her. He wondered what it would be like to dance with her, to take her dainty little hand in his, to see her smile and glow with the exertion of the rousing music. He'd heard of a dance called a waltz where couples actually held each other. It wouldn't be as close as he'd held her when she had fainted, but close enough, he supposed.

What was he thinking? He couldn't even dance, for heaven's sake! He would trip over his own feet and hers as well. Was civilized dancing the same as he'd done in cantinas and bawdy houses? He'd learned a few things about dancing from those gals. But it couldn't be the same, could it?

"Hey, Tom," Micah said, "you think they dance the same at a respectable ball as they do in a saloon?"

"Ain't as much holding on to the gals as you might do in a saloon," Tom answered thoughtfully.

"So you've been to a ball like the one tonight?"

"Once or twice," Tom replied rather shortly, then turned his back to Micah.

Micah had the feeling Tom was holding back. Not that he was the most ebullient of men, but it seemed as if he was leaving something very important unsaid. Micah also sensed from Tom's suddenly solemn demeanor that it was best not to probe further.

Jed, not as sensitive to subtle changes in temperament, started laughing once again. "You, Tom?" He snorted. "Show us, Tom! Show us how they dance respectable like."

"Micah's right!" Tom growled, "you got a mouth bigger than the Palo Duro Canyon. Now shut it up!"

Still laughing, Jed urged, "Come on, Tom, you're supposed to be our teacher. Teach Micah to dance!"

In a mere blink of Jed's eyes, Tom snatched his Bowie knife from its scabbard and held it threateningly before Jed's face, which had paled a shade or two in response to the sudden action.

"Shut up, or I'll ram this down your throat!" Tom growled.

Jed backed up a step. It was clear the usually mild-mannered ranger had a dangerous side that Jed had seriously stirred.

"All right, all right," Jed muttered, "I was just funning. Can't no one have no fun!" He stalked away with his head jutted forward, still muttering as he went.

Tom sheathed his knife, tied his horse, then said, "I'm going to the river."

Securing Jose, Micah followed Tom. He still saw no way he could attend the dance, but he needed a bath nonetheless. On the way they met a couple dripping rangers.

"Reckon you got the water all muddy for the rest of us," Tom grumbled.

"What's got into you?" asked one of the men.

"None of your business!"

The rangers just rolled their eyes and continued on. Micah caught up to Tom. He knew it was risky, but he asked, "What'd Jed do to set you off, Tom?"

"Nothing."

They reached the water's edge and stripped down to their long johns. There were already two or three men splashing around in the water. Micah and Tom joined them. The water was muddy but cool in the summer heat. One of the other swimmers offered the use of a hunk of lye soap. Micah lathered up his hair, and as he ducked under the water to rinse he thought he would smell like lye, but at least he'd be clean. But why did it matter? He wasn't going anywhere.

A few minutes later he sloshed out of the water and onto the shore to dry in the sun before donning his clothes. Tom came up the bank a couple minutes later.

"Can't go to no dance in these," Micah said, picking up his shirt with two fingers and giving it a shake, sending a cloud of dust all around.

"Yeah, they do look pretty sorry," Tom offered.

"Maybe they can stand one more wash."

"Won't help." Tom gave his shaggy wet hair a shake, sending a spray of water to join the dust. "I'm sorry 'bout what I said to Jed," he added.

"Don't tell me. Tell him."

"I'm also sorry for needling you about going to that dance." Tom sat down on a rock, stretching his legs out before him. "I nearly forgot something that happened to me a long time ago. When it come to my mind, Jed's words were just like rubbing a raw nerve."

"What happened?"

"I been to only one dance, so I ain't that much of an expert. It was just before I come to Texas." He scraped a hand over his chin. "Actually, it was kind of your fault I went. I was pretty content hunting and trapping and living on my own, but when I seen your family and especially you and your little sister when I guided y'all to Natches . . . well, it just put a hankering in me to have a family of my own. I was only thirty years old, so I figured I wasn't over the hill yet."

Micah gaped openmouthed at his friend. "You was only thirty years old! I remember thinking you was an old man."

Tom snorted a laugh. "Thirty looks a lot older when you are twelve than when you are twenty-one, I suppose. Anyway, I figured to find myself a wife. I didn't fancy a squaw or a hurdy-gurdy woman, so when I heard about a respectable dance in town, I gussied myself up and went down from the hills to attend. There was a gal there who gave me a sweet smile, and I thought for sure she might take a shine to me." Pausing, his eyes glassed over momentarily, as if it were no longer Micah's grubby face before him but rather that of a pretty freckle-faced, blue-eyed dream. "I asked her to dance, and we did okay while the music was slow and easy. I didn't know the steps but could keep up, just tramping on her toes once or twice. Then the band struck up a fast reel. I got overconfident, forgetting I was just a clumsy mountain man. Somehow my feet got tangled up, and I went flying to the ground. Out of pure reflex I grabbed on to her, and we both went stumbling and tripping. I tore her dress in a most immodest way. She screamed and cried and started hitting me. Then her pa got in the act and began beating me up. I barely got out of there with my life. Swore I'd never go to another dance again."

The two men fell silent. The hot sun felt good baking on Micah's face and wet body. His underwear was drying out quickly. His hair was also dry, and to keep the glare of the sun from his eyes, he grabbed his hat from his pile of clothes and pressed it on his head. In the moody quiet that hovered over him and Tom, Micah considered the older man's sad story. His friend's experience seemed as good a reason as any to keep away from places where one did not belong, and Micah instinctively knew he would be as out of place at the dance tonight as Tom had been at his. Micah had lived wild for too many years to consider mixing with decent folks now.

"I'm glad you told me that story," he said at length. "You probably kept me from making a first-class fool of myself."

"That's not why I told you about my experience," Tom said. "I just thought you ought to know why I was acting the way I was. Just 'cause I made an ignoramus of myself don't mean you'd do the same."

"I don't get it. You still saying I should go to that dance?"

"I ain't saying nothing, you dunderhead!" Tom snapped. "Make up your own mind."

"Well, maybe I would go if I had decent clothes."

Tom jumped up and strode to the pile of clothes. He picked up an item between two fingers as if it were diseased. "It'll take another wash. And you won't look half bad once it's clean."

"I don't want no wife," Micah suddenly declared.

Tom stared at him, then laughed. "First things first, boy." He dropped the garment back into the dusty heap. "Who knows? Maybe she don't want no husband."

"Isn't that what all respectable women want?"

Tom shrugged. "Going to a dance isn't a marriage proposal. But I'm thinking a man ought to go to at least one dance in his life. I figure it has more in the way of making a man out of you than killing Comanches."

"Maybe. If it turns out the way your dance did." Micah smiled as he thought again of Tom's story. When Tom allowed himself a smile, Micah knew the tension was dispersed. "Give me a Comanche attack any day!"

"Go wash these duds of yours." Tom picked up the pile and tossed them in Micah's face.

Laughing, Micah gathered the clothing in his arms, rose, and marched resignedly to the river. He didn't know what he was doing or why. Even as he knelt by the water and began scrubbing his shirt, he still hadn't made up his mind about the dance.

CHAPTER 14

BILL MCBROOME HAD A BOTTLE of toilet water stashed among his belongings. In a moment of extreme stupidity, Micah let the man convince him to splash some on himself. Now as he strode toward the hall where the dance was to be held, Micah was certain he smelled like a bordello.

Music emanated through the open doors and windows of the place. Inside, it looked very festive, with garlands hanging from the ceilings and candles and lanterns lit all around the room. The hall was crowded with at least a hundred people. It was hard not to be self-conscious of his shabby appearance, since almost everyone was dressed in their Sunday best. There were a few other rangers present, and some of them looked no better than Micah. A couple of them were sharing a suit jacket between them, taking it in turns to dance when they had the jacket.

At least Micah had shaved, and one of the Mexican rangers who had been a barber before joining up had trimmed his shaggy hair. He was also wearing his buckskin coat, the one made for him by his stepmother shortly before he left home. It was probably the only reminder he had kept of his home, and he told himself he only kept it because good coats were hard to come by. It was stifling hot, but it was the nicest thing he owned, and it somewhat camouflaged his other worn garments.

He headed toward the punch table, where a couple of rangers were standing. He tried not to scan the crowd for the face of Lucie Maccallum. In fact, he was trying so hard to keep his eyes fixed on the punch bowl ahead as he skirted the edge of the dance floor that he failed to maneuver around a dancing couple. It was a reel, and they were moving fast. The woman slammed forcefully into him.

"Ugh!" he grunted.

"Oh, I am so sorry," she said.

"Watch where you are going, fellow!" her partner said.

"I'm sorry. It was my fault," Micah said when he gathered his wits about him.

Only then did he see he had bumped into Lucie. Visions of Tom's debacle jumped into his head.

"Why, Mr. Sinclair, you did come!" She seemed not in the least disturbed by his clumsiness.

"Yeah, I did," he said obviously enough.

"Who might this be?" asked the gentleman a bit unsociably.

"This is Micah Sinclair. He's a ranger." Then to Micah, "This is Grant Carlton, a local rancher."

The two men nodded, and Micah sensed immediate hostility from Carlton. They did not shake hands.

"Come, Lucie, let's finish the reel." Carlton put an arm around Lucie and nudged her back to the disrupted reel.

Micah thought Carlton acted rather possessive toward Lucie. Fleetingly he thought about leaving right then. But with a dogged determination he could not explain, he instead headed to the punch table. So Lucie had a beau. Well, that pretty much let him off the hook. Why didn't he feel relieved, then?

He ladled himself a glass of punch and frowned when he realized the sweet concoction had not even a drop of wine in it. He could use something a little stronger right now. But he gulped the punch, realizing as the liquid slid down his throat that his mouth was as dry as sand—from nerves, not exertion. He casually watched the dancers and, he thought just as casually, let his gaze rest upon Lucie. She was wearing a frock of a deep red wine color, and now that he had let himself observe her, she was all that he could see except for her partner, whom he was forced to take note of as well.

He was a handsome man, Micah supposed, in his fancy suit and black cutaway coat with its velvet collar and his striped silk vest. He complemented the lovely Miss Maccallum quite nicely. And they danced well together, too. Lucie was smiling and laughing while Carlton's hand took every opportunity it could to rest upon her trim waist. Micah's throat got even dryer as he watched. He gulped another swallow of punch.

Bill McBroome sidled up to him. "Ya want a little fortification in that punch?"

"I'd like more than a little," Micah said wistfully.

McBroome took a flask from his pocket and poured a measure into Micah's glass. Micah never expected his wish to be fulfilled, but he grinned his appreciation. Several glasses of Bill's punch later, Micah was emboldened to stride onto the dance floor, right up to Lucie and her partner.

"Ahem!" he said politely, tapping a finger on the fine fabric stretched over Carlton's shoulders, for indeed it was Carlton dancing again with Lucie.

Carlton ignored him, but much to Micah's pleasure, Lucie didn't. "Mr. Sinclair, are you ready for that dance I promised you?"

"I reckon so."

Carlton glared at him as Lucie stepped between the two men. "You have been monopolizing me, Grant."

So *Grant*, was it?

"People will talk, you know," she added.

"I wouldn't mind that, Lucie, *my dear*."

The way Carlton emphasized "my dear" set Micah's teeth on edge.

Lucie gave Grant a rather coquettish smile, then grabbed Micah's hand. "Come, they are starting up a new reel."

As they moved deeper onto the dance floor, Micah drawled quietly, "I ain't the best dancer."

"Just follow my lead and watch the other men. You'll catch on."

He did as she instructed and managed quite well. All the while, though, he kept track of his own feet. No way would he trip and tear her pretty dress.

Lucie was glad to be rid of Grant Carlton, but she knew that accounted for only part of her joy at the moment. Micah had decided to come to the ball! And he had mustered the courage to ask her to dance. She well appreciated it must indeed have taken some courage to break in on another man and risk refusal. But he had done it, and now they were hand-in-hand, stepping to a lively Virginia reel. He was a bit awkward on his feet and had stepped on her slipper more than once, but she supposed he had not been to many balls such as this. At any rate he was picking up the rhythm and the steps well. He seemed to be enjoying himself if the smile on his face was any indication.

Too soon the music stopped, but the leader of the musicians had an announcement to make. "We're gonna try something new. A waltz. I heard several of you know the steps. Everyone else can watch and learn."

"Shall we give it a try, Micah?"

"Sure."

Glancing around, she saw Grant heading toward them. Quickly she placed a hand on Micah's shoulder, drawing him close. Then the music began, and it was too late for Grant.

"Put your hand here." She took his hand and placed it on her waist.

"Whoa!" Micah breathed. "They allow this sort of thing?"

Lucie giggled. "It is currently very popular. Now listen to the beat of the music. One, two, three . . . one, two, three." She moved her free hand in an approximation of the rhythm. "Let me have your other hand."

Free hands clasped, she nudged him into step with the music. His boot nicked her slipper once or twice, but she bit back a cry of pain even though it did hurt some. It was easy to overlook pain when she concentrated on his nearness. His hand on her waist was warm and oddly secure. The touch of his other hand in hers sent a tingle through her entire body.

"D-do you like it?" she asked, her voice cracking a little as she looked up at him. They were barely an arm's length apart.

"Yes," he replied.

Lucie sensed he wasn't talking only about the dance. The way he was looking at her made her knees rather weak. He was so handsome, but not in the polished, slick way of Grant Carlton. She could tell he had spruced himself up for the dance, but there was still something very rough-cut about him. And thinking in those terms, she thought of an uncut gem. That's what Micah Sinclair was. Wild, her father had said, but even he had to admit there was something solid beneath the untamed exterior. Remembering his tenderness with that orphaned baby only reinforced her conclusion. And that was the difference between Micah and Grant. Grant was a diamond, cut in all its glory. But what shined on the surface was all there was to him. She thought of the quote she'd read in *The Merchant of Venice*: "All that glitters is not gold." How true in this case. Lucie was certain the real gold dwelt beneath worn cotton and denim, not serge wool and silk.

"I'm glad you came to the dance," she murmured.

"So am I." There was a very slight tremor to his voice. But his gaze was so steady, almost boring into her like a shaft of blue light. His hand tightened on her waist, and she thought he had eased her ever so slightly closer to him.

Neither of them noticed when the music had stopped. Lucie was certain it was several heartbeats before that fact penetrated. He dropped his hand first and stepped back, obviously flustered.

"That was nice," she said dreamily.

"I gotta go now."

"What?"

He turned and all but fled the dance floor. In another moment he had disappeared among the crowd. She strained to see over the heads of those pressing in about her and thought she caught a glimpse of him exiting the building. She would have gone after him, but Grant came up to her.

"That was rude of him to leave you standing here like that," he sneered.

"He . . . he . . ." She didn't know what to say or what to make of Micah's surprising behavior.

"What more can you expect from trash like that," Grant droned on. "As I waited for the dance to finish, I was told by one of the gentlemen that he was a horse thief who barely escaped hanging by joining up with the rangers. Had I known that, I would never have let you in his company."

"I . . . I think I need to freshen up." She was feeling a trifle flushed and warm, but it wasn't really the seclusion of the ladies' parlor that she wanted.

Without waiting for a response, she headed across the room in the direction of the parlor, passing her father on the way. She smiled at him—at least she offered a thin disguise of a smile—then continued on her way. She stepped into the corridor that ran at the rear of the ballroom and, seeing a woman exit a door, noted the location of the parlor. But Lucie went down the corridor, past the parlor door to the end, where she found another door she knew led to the outside. This she opened and plunged into the cool night air.

Indeed it was a warm evening, but the air was fresh and pleasant after the crowded, stuffy atmosphere indoors. It seemed Micah felt the same way. He was leaning against the sidewalk rail in front of the building next door. His hands gripped the rough wood of the rail, and he was gulping in air as if he had just risen from being buried alive.

Lucie had never chased after a man in her life. Her father's words came back to her with alarming clarity. "Lucie, can you try not to fall in love with him?" Perhaps it was too late.

"Micah," she said, coming up behind him.

He jerked around, truly startled. "What're you doing out here?" he asked sharply.

"I . . . I was afraid you might be ill. You left so suddenly."

"Go on back inside. It's not right for you to be here all alone."

"I don't like people telling me what to do."

He rolled his eyes with just a hint of humor. "I surely feel sorry for your pa, then."

"Yes, I am a sore trial to him." Her lips twitched with uncertainty at how her attempt at humor might be received.

"You ain't worried about your reputation at all?"

"I suppose I am a little." She moved up beside him and leaned her back against the rail so as to face him. He turned back to the way he had been standing before, hands on the rail, looking into the now quiet street instead of her probing eyes. "I was having a nice time dancing with you and didn't want you to leave," she added.

"Well, it ain't right, that's all!"

She gazed at him. He could have meant so many things with that statement, and perhaps he meant them all.

"Why did you leave?"

"If I'd have stayed . . ." He loosened his grip on the rail long enough to run a hand through his thick pale hair. It hung in waves to the top of his collar and curled slightly around his ears. He wasn't wearing his hat. Maybe he had planned to return to the dance after all.

"I was afraid I might have . . . kissed you!" He swung around now, facing her full on. "Right there in front of everyone."

"Oh . . ." She hadn't expected that response, but now that he'd said it, she understood that the feelings she had been experiencing on the dance floor had been mutual. It pleased her, though she knew it ought to frighten her as well.

"I still want to."

His eyes were riveted upon her and her heart nearly stopped with anticipation. But he made no move toward her.

"Oh my." She could think of absolutely nothing else to say.

"Go back inside, Lucie, before—"

"Before what?"

His eyes, now pools of confusion and something else she could not quite define, raked over her in a manner that caused her to wince.

"You don't belong with me, and I don't belong with you. Simple as that," he said.

"That's the most ridiculous thing I have ever heard!" she replied crisply to hide her quelling insides.

"You are a God-fearing woman, aren't you? Churchgoing and such?"

Perplexed, she answered, "Yes."

"There you go!" There was a triumph in his tone, as if that settled everything. "You ain't supposed to be unequally yoked."

"Are you a heathen?"

"Look at me!" he practically yelled. "What do you think?"

"I do not judge people on surfaces. Neither does God."

"Don't tell me what God does. I know all about it. And believe me, God turned His back on me long ago. I'm a reprobate, a sinner—"

"We are all sinners, Micah."

He cursed under his breath, almost with humor. "Oh yeah. I forgot that. But you know as well as I that churchgoing sinners smell a mite sweeter than horse-thieving, gun-toting, carousing sinners like me."

She laughed in spite of herself. "Where'd you get ideas like that?"

"My pa is a preacher." He ground out the words, leaving no doubt that he believed this was a heinous admission indeed.

"You?"

Now he laughed. Bitterly, this time. "A real shocker, huh?"

It was, but Lucie didn't want to admit it, so she said casually, "And your pa told you these things?"

"More like he bludgeoned them into my head."

A silence fell between them. Again he had left her speechless. Part of her knew that at least some of what he had said was true. She did not wish to be "yoked" to a heathen. But now she was more certain than ever that Micah was far from a heathen. He had grown up in a religious home and no doubt knew the Bible better than she. That didn't necessarily make him a Christian man, of course, but she knew now why she had sensed there was so much more to Micah than the surface presented. He had an intimate knowledge of God, no doubt, and for some reason was deeply bitter—toward God perhaps, but most especially toward his father. She wanted to know why. She wanted to know what lay in the deepest parts of Micah's heart. And because of that, she could not let go. And probably because of that, as well, she did not *want* to let go. There was a diamond beneath that rough, tarnished exterior. She was certain of it now. And she had to see it chipped and polished into being.

"Maybe some of those things are true," she said quietly. "I don't know everything. I only know how I feel, Micah. And I feel something toward you."

"Don't say that!"

"It's too late."

"I'll bring you nothing but grief."

She nodded, feeling the sting of tears rise to her eyes. "I know."

"You are a foolish woman."

"And you are a wild man. What a pair we make—" she began glibly.

But he broke in fiercely. "We are not a pair!" Then, as if to belie his words, he grabbed her.

She gasped as his arms violently encircled her, tightly, nearly choking the air from her. Then his lips pressed down upon hers, hard, savagely as his arms drew tighter and tighter about her. She didn't fight him and even tilted her head ever so slightly to better accommodate him. She'd never been kissed before and anticipated the sweet sensation of tender lips touching. But this wasn't like that at all. This was rough, aggressive, punishing. She tensed in his arms, feeling the power of his strength, the awesomeness of her helplessness. She was lost, and the worst of it was that part of her *wanted* to be lost forever in that embrace.

But not like this.

Her resistance increased. She wrenched her head around, knowing all the while that her paltry strength was no match for his had he chosen to press home his assault. But the vicelike grip of his arms loosened. He was breathing hard as he let go, but no harder than she was herself.

He mastered his wits first. "Don't ever get involved with a man who would kiss you like that," he said.

Then he walked away.

"Micah!"

He didn't turn back.

He had hurt her. Not so much physically, though her lips burned and throbbed, but he had hurt her by not giving her credit for having a brain. Didn't he realize she'd see through his puny attempt to frighten her? Oh, she was frightened, to be sure, but not in the way he had intended. His very attempt to do so had only made her see another facet of Micah Sinclair. He was a good man. She knew it.

CHAPTER 15

MICAH AND ABOUT A DOZEN men of Hays' ranger company were patrolling along Cutter Creek where they'd received word that Joaquin Viegas, with at least two dozen of his banditos, had been spotted.

Since the invasion of Texas by Mexico in March and the subsequent occupation of San Antonio, the rangers were being especially vigilant.

The occupation by Santa Anna's army lasted only a few days, but it was nevertheless harrowing for the residents. They did not want a repeat. In the months that followed, rumors flew rampant in the area, the most persistent being that the gangs of banditos threatening Texan borders were actually in the pay of the Mexican government, and their purpose was to disrupt Texan life enough to give Mexico another chance to invade.

The rangers had been tracking Viegas's gang for two days before finally coming upon the outlaws' camp. Unfortunately, the Mexicans saw the rangers approach and opened fire.

The rangers quickly dismounted and returned fire. Micah killed two bandits in the opening volley of shots and only then realized the Mexican shooters in the front line were providing cover while the main force was escaping.

"Hey, they're getting away!" Micah shouted.

By then the others saw the ploy. They also saw there were far more than a mere twenty-four bandits—more like fifty! Hays ordered pursuit but emphasized caution because of the disparity of numbers. More shots were exchanged, then Micah detected the pungent odor of smoke in the air. The Mexicans had fired the grass, and the wind, as well as the smoke, was heading directly for the rangers.

Cursing rose from the ranks of the rangers to join the blinding smoke. Micah pulled a bandanna over his nose, but it didn't help much.

"Sneaky greasers!" he muttered.

The rangers had to pull back.

"Take defensive positions!" ordered Hays. The captain feared the fire was merely a cover for a full-scale attack.

Coughing and grumbling, the men obeyed, gripping their rifles. Eyes burning and watering, throats on fire, they waited. Micah tried to peer through the smoke, but it was too dense to make out anything. He hated just sitting there when Mexicans were so close he could smell them. Well, he could have if the acrid stench of smoke wasn't numbing his nose! He'd only killed two, and he knew he could get more if given half a chance.

But when the smoke finally dissipated, Micah saw he'd lost his opportunity. The banditos were gone.

Determining that the Mexicans couldn't have gone far, Hays decided to track them. Micah welcomed not only the chance for vindication but also the opportunity to hone his tracking skills. He didn't think about what might happen if the rangers actually did catch up to the banditos. A dozen against fifty could be a bloodbath. But he'd seen these rangers in action now for some time, and he had every confidence in them. He also had no little confidence in his own prowess, despite a few mistakes he'd made in the beginning. Even Tom had told him he was coming along fine.

Lucie was happy to be back home in familiar surroundings. The time in San Antonio, especially after the events of the ball, had been trying. To make it worse, her father had grown ill after church the Sunday following the ball, forcing them to remain in town with friends for a few extra days. He was better now, at least not so frightfully sallow and breathless, but the doctor had strongly admonished him to keep indoors and to his bed whenever possible.

Lucie had nursed him faithfully, though he accepted her ministrations grudgingly. Until this morning, that is. Then he had lost his patience completely and told her to quit hovering about him like a fly on raw meat. He ordered her to go out and get some fresh air. So she did, leaving Juana in charge of the recalcitrant patient.

She saddled her piebald mare and rode away. The men had long since ceased arguing with her about riding alone, and she was glad of that because she especially needed to be alone now. She had hardly had a moment since the ball to mull over all that had occurred.

But first, she just wanted to appreciate the wide outdoors. Since her return from Mexico, she had been out riding only a few times, and then not far from the ranch for fear of her father needing her. She didn't know what was different about today, but she wanted, perhaps even needed, to feel the open, empty vastness of the prairie around her. She sucked in a breath of the air, pungent with the scents of grass and earth and cow dung. Even in the summer heat there was a crispness in the atmosphere carried by the dry prairie wind.

She loved this land, hot and alive, dangerous and inviting. Not unlike the man who had been haunting her dreams and thoughts. The man whose kiss still burned upon her lips. The man who sought to push her away with actions that only made her desire him more. Both he and her father had warned her she would be hurt, but wasn't that always a risk where the heart was involved? She knew so little of love, perhaps she should listen to them. To what purpose, then? To be safe and marry the likes of Grant Carlton?

If the Texas settlers had thought that way, they would have been denied the exquisite joy and yes, also the pain, of this wonderful magical land.

She rode south for about two hours and knew she was on the farthest reaches of her father's ranch. She really should begin to think about turning back toward home. The sun had passed its zenith, the time further evidenced by the growling of Lucie's stomach. She had brought a bit of food in her saddlebags and was looking about for a pleasant place to stop for a snack when she heard the gunshots.

She paused her mount's easy canter and listened. They could not be more than a mile away. Sound traveled oddly on the prairie, but the shots seemed to be coming from north of her. Was it just vaqueros and ranch hands showing off? Or banditos? Or Comanches? If it was either of the latter two and they were involved in a skirmish of some kind, they might well soon be heading south toward the border. Right past her!

It was definitely unwise to head for home now. Nor could she hope to outrun them. Perhaps her best course would be to find some cover and wait it out. The stream, a branch of Cutter Creek that bordered the ranch, was not far. She had smelled the moist, muddy proximity of water. There would be shelter there.

"Come on, Belle," she said to the mare, speaking mostly for the comfort of hearing something besides her pounding heart.

The shots had ceased by the time she reached the creek. It had probably been nothing after all. But just as she had begun to be successful in convincing herself of this, she saw a plume of smoke rise toward the sky from the direction of the gunshots. Now what? Did this have something to do with the shots?

No matter what it was, whether a mere prairie fire caused by careless travelers or an attack, the creek was still her safest refuge. Easing down the creek bank among a stand of cottonwoods, she forced her racing heart to calm.

"It's nothing," she murmured.

Where the trees stood thickest, she dismounted. She tied Belle to a low branch, took her saddlebag of food, the musket she always brought when riding alone, and found a place to sit where she was as secluded as possible. It was an outcropping of rock set into the bank with a few boulders around it for good measure. Convinced now that she had blown the disturbance out of proportion, she relaxed, opened the bag, and took out a cloth in which some jerky and a biscuit were carefully wrapped.

She had barely finished the meal and settled back for a bit of a nap when the sound of pounding hooves shattered her solace. She froze. They were coming near, almost certainly heading for the creek. Scooting farther back behind the cover of the rocks, she clutched her rifle and held her breath. Quickly she loaded the weapon.

Her heart began thumping wildly when she heard the scramble of horses descending the creek bank.

"*Alto, amigos!*" came a man's voice. "I think we have lost them." He spoke in Spanish, which Lucie understood as well as English.

"That was close, Joaquin."

Joaquin? Now Lucie's heart skipped a beat. Could it be he? Joaquin Viegas, he called himself. The famous bandito. She had to find out. She had to know. Gripping her rifle, she crept as stealthily as possible from her hiding place to the edge of the farthest boulder. She could see forty or fifty riders, all Mexican, all heavily armed. Her gaze focused on one in particular, mounted on a fine black stallion with one white sock. This man was taller than his companions, swarthy skinned, broad shouldered, lean and strong. He wore a sombrero, but she knew the crop of hair beneath the hat would be brown, not black, and much lighter than her own.

She studied him closely, forgetting all else. He sported a thick mustache now, something that had been absent the last time she had seen him. Other than that, he was not much changed.

"Why did we run, Joaquin?" asked one of the men. "We outnumbered them."

"There is no point in taking unnecessary risks, especially when we have nothing to show for it." Joaquin answered. "Besides, they were rangers, Gustavo."

The tall bandito lifted a canteen from his saddle, took a long swig, then inclined his head, apparently listening. Lucie could not take her eyes from him. She took in his every movement as if she were imbibing a drop of water on a desert and it would be many miles till the next watering hole. She had forgotten the musket in her hand, and when her arm went slack, the weapon clanked against the rock.

"*¿Qué es?*" one of the banditos said.

Before she could do anything about it, her presence was revealed. Only vaguely did she realize that she had probably wanted to be seen.

Joaquin's eyes met hers. Though his gaze flashed, the rest of his features remained passive. "What is this?" he said.

"Señor Viegas," she quietly acknowledged him.

"Come out from behind that rock. Let me see you," he ordered.

Licking her dry lips, she obeyed.

"Drop the rifle," Viegas said.

She did so. Then they stared at each other for such a long time the horses grew restive, snorting, twitching, prancing.

"Joaquin, we must go," urged the bandito named Gustavo.

"I must go," Joaquin said to her in a soft, almost apologetic manner.

"I know," Lucie replied.

"Can we leave her?" Gustavo asked. "She will give us away."

Joaquin's mustache twitched, and though it was hard to discern beneath the thick growth, he might have been smiling.

"Can we leave you, señorita?"

"*Sí,* Joaquin, you can."

"I thought so." To his men Joaquin added, "*Vaquamos los hombres!*"

The banditos needed no more command than this and in a few moments were heading toward the creek. But Viegas paused and looked back.

"Joaquin," Lucie called, "Papa has not been well."

The bandito leader nodded. "I am sorry to hear that."

"He would like to see you."

"Would he?"

"Yes, he would." It was a small lie, Lucie knew, but she could not help herself.

"I must go now," the bandito said, then urged his mount across the creek.

Lucie watched his retreat. He rode with such assurance as he caught up with his men, tall in the saddle, shoulders square, completely in command. He had shown no sense of panic over the fact that the law was breathing down his neck. Nevertheless, the pace of the banditos increased considerably after they ascended the far bank and reached more level ground. They were out of sight in a matter of minutes.

Several minutes later the noise of riders coming from the other direction pulled Lucie from her reverie. That would be the rangers. In a mere moment Lucie decided what she must do. Quickly she scooped up a handful of dirt, which she smeared on her clothes and swiped across her face, and knocked her hat to the ground as well. A kind of calm stealing over her despite her thudding heart, she sat down on the ground, arranging herself in as much disarray as she could.

Her heart had calmed by the time the rangers crested the bank, but it flipped again when she saw that one of the men was Micah. In that moment she feared she could not proceed with her plan. But she had to. She must help the banditos get as much distance between them and the rangers as possible.

"Lucie!" Micah called when he saw her lying in the dirt. He was off his horse the instant it finished scrambling down the bank. "What happened?" The clear distress in his tone made her nearly quell again at her deception.

There were half a dozen rangers with Micah. Tom Fife, Jed, and three others Lucie did not know. She laid the back of her hand against her forehead and shook her head as if faint.

"You okay?" Micah knelt down beside her. "Was it the banditos?" The look in his eyes as he spoke made Lucie shiver. It contained far more than mere distress. For a brief instant, there was pure murder in his eyes.

"No . . . I'm all right. . . ." The lies did not come easily, but she was too motivated to fail now. "I fell and twisted my ankle."

"Did them banditos hurt you?" Tom asked, a look of consternation on his face also but far less intense than Micah's.

"No, it wasn't them," she said firmly. She did not want to make it worse for the outlaws. Suddenly she almost smiled as she thought of the irony of her being in yet another situation in which she must defend an outlaw. "I saw them and was running in the opposite direction so they wouldn't see me when I tripped. They hardly even noticed me as they rode by."

"Which way did they go, miss?" Tom asked.

"I was so dizzy . . ." What an awful lie! She hated sounding like a simpering female. But she went on, stuck now with her resolve. "I . . . I hardly noticed. Maybe that way." She lifted a limp hand and pointed vaguely in the right direction. These were rangers, after all. They would easily pick up the trail, so lying would hardly help.

"How long?"

"I've lost track of time. Seems like forever, but perhaps fifteen or twenty minutes."

"We best get moving," urged one of the other rangers.

"Hold on, Bill," Tom said. "We can't just leave Miss Maccallum." Tom took off his hat and scratched his head, then said, "Micah, you see the lady home. The rest of us will continue the pursuit."

"But Tom—" Micah protested.

"Ain't nothing else for it."

Lucie was more than a little disappointed that Micah appeared less than eager to be with her. Yet she had come between him and his work, his duty, and thus she ought to consider it a good sign that he had such a sense of responsibility toward this new job of his. She hoped that was the cause, at least.

"We'll be going, then," Tom said. "Micah, you may as well head on back to San Antonio when you're finished. I don't reckon we'll keep tracking them hombres if they cross the border."

"Mr. Fife," Lucie said quickly, searching in her mind for something else that might delay the pursuit, "I don't mean to interrupt your work, but if you brought me my horse and helped me to mount, I am certain I could get home on my own."

"Not in a million years!" declared Tom. "Anyway, what you doing out here alone?"

Oh, this was good! It always took time for men to browbeat her for her independence. The banditos would easily get across the border now.

"Well, Mr. Fife," she began thoughtfully *and* slowly, "I just hate to impose. . . ."

"Shouldn't you get going, Tom?" Micah urged.

Lucie restrained a smirk at his untimely intercession.

"Yeah, of course. Miss, if you'll pardon us . . ." Tom tipped his hat then gave his mount a crisp "Geeup!" The others followed.

Well, she had done the best she could. Joaquin Viegas would have to do the rest. She relaxed and blew out a deep sigh.

"Something wrong?" Micah asked, concerned.

"No, it has just been a trying day."

"I'll get you home right away."

"Could you let me have a drink of water first?" Now that she no longer had to worry over the banditos, she was in no particular hurry to go home, especially since she had Micah Sinclair all to herself.

CHAPTER 16

LUCIE WATCHED MICAH AS HE went to his horse, removed his canteen, and brought it to her.

"Where's your horse?" he asked as he returned. Kneeling beside her, he handed her the canteen.

She jerked her head toward the trees. "In the shade." She uncorked the waterskin and took a long swallow.

"You sure had a close call with those banditos," he said. "We're pretty sure that was Joaquin Viegas himself we were chasing."

"Really! Oh my!" She swayed, raising her hand to her head again. She better not drop her ruse too quickly, or it might arouse suspicions. To her surprise and delight, Micah's arms went quickly around her. He grabbed the canteen from her hands and splashed a dollop in her face. "Bah!" she sputtered. She hadn't expected that.

"I thought you was gonna faint," he said in obvious distress.

"I assure you, I wasn't." She gave her head a shake, sending a spray of water in his direction. Then she smiled. "That was kind of you . . . holding me, protecting me."

He glanced down and seemed to fully realize that she was indeed in his arms. He wrenched them from her so quickly she nearly fell into the dirt. But she caught herself, remaining in a sitting position. He scooted away from her.

"You don't make it easy . . ." he said. "Protecting you, that is. You might have been in serious trouble if them banditos had taken a mind to hurt you."

"I don't think they would have harmed me. They weren't even interested."

"You are mighty thickheaded, ain't you?"

She shrugged, then changed the topic. "Do you think the rangers will catch the bandits?"

"I doubt it. They got too much of a head start. But we'll get them eventually." Micah's tone was as hard edged as the rocks surrounding them.

"What will happen to Viegas if he's caught?"

"I wouldn't think even you'd have to ask that."

No, she didn't have to ask, but there was still a naïve part of her that hoped for justice. "I suspect he will be tried and . . . punished."

"Tried?" Micah snorted derisively. "Ain't no way he'd make it back to San Antonio alive. If the rangers don't hang him on the spot, he'll likely get shot while *escaping*." He spoke that final word with relish.

Lucie was certain Micah hoped to be the one to bring down the famous bandito. This was definitely a side of Micah she hadn't glimpsed before, and she didn't much like it. She wondered how deep the hidden diamond inside him was.

"Every man deserves a fair trial," she replied.

"You ever seen four hundred unarmed men gunned down without benefit of a trial, fair or otherwise?"

Beneath his harsh gaze she saw a flicker of pain.

"No, Lucie. You won't find me giving no Mexican a fair trial."

"All Mexicans, Micah?"

He shrugged, obviously uncomfortable with the direction of the discussion. "Soon as you're feeling up to it, we'll be on our way." His initial concern had faded, and now he spoke woodenly, like a man hiding something behind a flimsy facade.

"Micah?" Lucie reached out to touch the hand he had resting in the dirt to support himself as he sat.

He inched a bit farther away from her.

"We haven't talked since the dance."

"Nothing to talk about, is there?"

"Are you afraid of me?" She glanced down at his hand so near hers, though she had restrained from actually touching him after his reaction.

"Tarnation, lady! I'm scared to death of you!" He jumped up and spoke as if ranting, or at the very least, flustered. "You're dangerous, you hear? Very dangerous! Sitting there looking so helpless, yet I think you could take on Santa Anna's entire army if you wanted to with just a flap of those eyelashes of yours or a shake of hair that looks every bit like an earthy mountain full of copper when it catches the light of the sun. I've faced vicious enemies and wild animals, and I've looked death in the face more than once, but none of it compares to the bone-chilling fear you put in me." Micah paused, breathing hard, and she thought perhaps she did note fear in his remarkable blue eyes.

"What is it you fear most?" she asked quietly, in sharp contrast to his own frenzied response.

He snatched off his hat and ran a hand through his red-flecked hair. "I told you at the dance."

"And you tried to make me afraid, but it didn't work." She gazed up at him, and the flutters in her heart grew more pronounced.

"You're a stubborn woman," he said.

She nodded.

"You should be very afraid, Lucie." His tone was steady now, so serious it made her tremble as nothing else had.

"When I see you talk about your enemies," she said, "it does scare me a little. But something in me says there is much more to you than that."

"I keep trying to tell you—"

"Sit down, Micah, and tell me about yourself."

He gaped at her sudden change of tact, and she knew she sounded like she was inviting him to tea. Here they were in the middle of the wild, empty prairie, outlaws in the near vicinity, and she had the audacity to request a social conversation. It was rather outlandish, if not downright ridiculous.

She giggled lightly. "We do manage to meet in the oddest places. But I always say to seize opportunity when it knocks. Who knows when I will see you again? And even if everyone may be right about our being mismatched, couldn't we at least be friends?"

He shook his head, still nonplussed about the oddity of the situation. Then he plopped down beside her, however at a safe distance.

"So what'd you want to know?" He was serious, yet he had allowed a small hint of amusement to trifle with the cool blue of his eyes.

She scratched her chin thoughtfully. "How did you come to be an outlaw?"

"Now, there's a nice neutral subject to start with," he said dryly. "Anyway, there isn't much to tell about it. After the war I was kind of aimless. I was fourteen. I needed to survive somehow, and I just took the easy way."

"You fought in the war?"

"Yeah."

"What was that like?"

"Next question," he said flatly.

She did not press, for she didn't want to spoil this time. It occurred to her that after all they had been through together in such a short time, this was the first chance they'd had to really talk. She was liking it very much.

"Were you born in Texas?" she asked. This was a nice safe query.

But he scowled in response, the blue of his eyes darkening like a cloud passing over a sparkling stream.

"No," he said evenly.

She could tell it took effort to talk about his past.

"I was born in Boston. Came here when I was twelve."

"Do your parents still live here?"

"I don't want to talk about my parents."

"Is there anything you do want to talk about, Micah?" she asked, unable to completely hide her frustration. Altering her tone a bit, she added, "Maybe you should just tell me what you want me to know."

He was silent for a long time, and she feared the conversation had ended before it had had much of a chance. Finally he spoke.

"My ma died about seven years ago. My pa . . . is still here."

He turned upon her intently, the blue in his eyes still dark, but not shadowed. Just very, very dark.

"Okay. I'll tell you about my pa." It was almost as if he were answering a challenge. "He killed my ma—not directly, of course. He killed her by dragging her out here from Boston, then leaving her high and dry while he went about God's work. He rode a circuit up north near Cooksburg that was more important to him than anything, especially his family. After a while Ma just couldn't take the loneliness anymore—leastways, that's how I see it, though I was just a kid then, and no one really told me anything. One day while my pa was gone, my uncle came to visit, and she got him to take her and us kids back to Boston. She was in a family way, and we didn't get too far before she gave birth and died."

"And you blame your father?" Lucie asked softly. She had sensed he was a man who had known pain, but to have it laid before her like this so clearly, so coolly, almost like it wasn't a deep wound in his heart, was disconcerting. She sensed Micah was a man who had grown quite expert at shielding his true feelings.

He snorted a sharp, hard laugh. "Who else should I blame? He has even admitted to it."

"He admits it?"

"Yeah. After my ma died, he acted like it grieved him terribly. He said it changed him."

"People do change." The hopefulness in her tone sprang from more than just trying to convince *him.*

"I don't care. Even if he did, it was too late. He killed her. He ruined our lives. A person just can't do that and expect forgiveness."

"Maybe you are being a bit hard on him," she ventured.

"Oh yeah!" he retorted. "Guess all you religious fanatics got to stick together."

She blinked, shocked at the venom in his response.

He added a little more gently, "You didn't deserve that, I guess."

"I didn't mean to defend your father, Micah. But I think all the hate you seem to be storing inside is hurting you more than it's hurting him. Hate is a double-edged blade."

"What do you know about hate?"

He was studying her closely. Then, to her amazement, a small smile played upon the corners of his lips.

"You've never hated a soul in your life, have you, Lucie?"

"I don't think so. I have never had reason to, I suppose."

"I fear you'll one day come to hate me," he said, no humor now in his aspect.

"My mother and father had a little pact between them," she replied. "They said they would never let the sun set upon their anger. I think hatred comes from anger that is allowed to fester."

"Many suns have set on my anger," he said grimly.

"My parents would give their anger to God."

"I think . . . I hate God as well."

"Oh, Micah!" She wanted to weep for him.

"I wish I could be like my Uncle Haden. He didn't even believe in God. But unfortunately, I believe."

"Who is the God you believe in?"

"He looks a lot like my father."

Her barely checked tears now erupted at the vast emptiness in his tone. She reached out to touch his hand because she simply could not leave him there so alone, so empty. Her hand brushed his, and scarcely had contact been made when his arms came up and gathered her to him. He held her fiercely, but not like he had at the dance. Now there was a desperation in him, as if he might crumble without her to keep him intact. She felt the grate of his day's growth of beard in her hair as he pressed his cheek hard to her head. She thought he was trembling a bit, but perhaps it was her own quaking she felt.

This was different than before, not a physical need, but a need that went to the heart, the very soul.

"It's been so long," he murmured. "So long . . ."

Lucie wasn't certain what he meant, but she had a feeling he had not held a woman out of sheer emotional need since the death of his mother so many years ago. She wondered if anyone had held him, loved him since then. She encircled him with her own arms, patting his back, cooing comforting words.

Still holding her, he moved his head and looked into her eyes. "I knew you were dangerous. You are so decent, so sweet. . . . Oh, God . . ."

"I love you, Micah!"

"Don't say that."

"Why won't you let yourself love a little?" she entreated. "Maybe it will chase away some of the hatred."

"I'm not sure I'd know how. It's been a long time." He ran his finger along her cheek. All the shadows had fled from his eyes. They were the purest of blue now. "I could love you, Lucie."

"That's enough for now, then." She smiled, though she knew she was lying. She would never be satisfied until his love was as complete as hers. "I won't ask for more." She was telling herself as much as him.

He bent closer and his lips touched hers. The kiss was as gentle and tender as the last kiss had been heated and passionate. He knew as well as she that what was happening now far surpassed anything physical.

"We better go back," he said, his grip on her loosening.

She nodded. She did not know what would happen now. She only knew a line had been crossed, one she couldn't turn back from. She loved this man. She prayed God would understand.

He rose, but she did not see the hand he had extended to help her as she jumped to her feet.

"Looks like your ankle is better," he said matter-of-factly.

"Oh . . . uh . . . yes, it is." She remembered her deception and felt all the worse for it after what they had just shared.

CHAPTER 17

THE SUN WAS LOWERING IN the west as they rode up to the ranch. The sky was a dusky shade of orange and red with a deeper purple near the horizon. Micah and Lucie had been silent for most of the two-hour ride. There was so much more to be said, yet already they each had as much as they could handle to consider.

Micah could hardly fathom what had passed between them. Lucie had said she loved him. Even now, to remember her profound declaration made his chest constrict. He had not realized until that moment sitting there on the creek bank how desperately empty of things like love he had been. Until Lucie had come along, it had been easy to shrug off this need, and he knew it was indeed a need.

She had said maybe a little love would help wash away some of the hate. But he had lived with hate for so long that maybe it was too deeply a part of him. Maybe hate had made him the man he was. If he gave it up, it might be relinquishing too much. Yet that little touch of love he'd felt from her had been so sweet. And as he'd felt it, he realized just how much he'd missed it.

He glanced over at her. The lowering sun was shimmering in her dark hair like flames. She was so beautiful he could hardly believe she had reached inside him and touched something that had so very little to do with physical attraction. If he believed in God, or rather, if he acknowledged the God he knew was there, he'd feel certain she could be the answer to a man's prayers.

She smiled, catching his open appraisal of her. "We're almost at the ranch. Won't you stay for supper?"

He could see the house and outbuildings on the horizon. He wondered what it would be like to sit to supper with these decent folks. That scared him as much as anything.

"I don't know," he hedged. "It's getting late."

"When was the last time you had a home-cooked meal?"

"A coon's age, I reckon. You doing the cooking?"

She laughed. "Not tonight. But I do cook, if that's what you're getting at."

He didn't know at all if that's what he'd meant. He was afraid of her thinking of him as a man evaluating the qualifications of a prospective wife. He shook away the thought. What was he thinking? He knew she was a dangerous woman.

They rode into the yard, and as they brought their horses into the stable, several of the men offered Lucie friendly greetings. For Micah they only offered cautious stares. Instead of being offended, he was glad these men felt a protectiveness toward her. He wanted her protected, cared for. He just didn't know if he was the man for the job.

Once in the house, Lucie ushered him into a parlor. "Why don't you make yourself comfortable while I tell Juana there will be one more for dinner?"

He didn't recall actually telling her he'd stay, but he made no protests. Micah wanted this as much as he feared it. He simply could not remember the last time he'd been in a family home. Once or twice when he and Jed had been youngsters and wandering around, a couple of folks had kindly taken them into their homes and given them meals. But for the most part he lived under the sky, with occasional visits to bawdy houses or maybe even a hotel when he had some money in his pockets. He'd never been in a simple cabin with a family, a woman in calico, children toddling about, the fragrance of bread in the air.

Not since his own home. And oddly, when he thought of home, it was the dingy Texas cabin that came to mind, not the fine frame house in Boston. For all the misery he'd known there, that cabin had represented something he now sorely missed. A certain cohesiveness, even security. Especially after his stepmother had come and brought a bit of happiness to the place. Not that Micah had ever been able to embrace that happiness. But if he had . . .

Micah shut out such thoughts. They were confusing, and the last thing he needed was more confusion. Instead, he wandered around the Maccallum parlor. It was a nice room, tastefully but expensively furnished. A far cry from the simple Sinclair cabin. The furnishings were made of dark-stained wood of Spanish design. Micah imagined they were old. No doubt Reid Maccallum had purchased them from former residents. Though of course he could have had them shipped from Spain or Mexico City, but the man did not appear the type to indulge in such tastes. In fact, Micah was rather surprised to find such fancy things in his home at all. Lucie had said her ma had died two years ago, so this might well be her influence. Still, most frontier women tended to ship household items from the States, not Mexico.

Micah ambled aimlessly over to the fireplace. This was made of good Texas stone. No fire burned on this warm summer day. Above the hearth was a large portrait of a woman, a beautiful woman. A Mexican woman. She was dressed in a deep red gown, stylishly designed and obviously expensive. On her head was a veil of the kind Mexican women wore for special occasions, which Micah had heard called a *mantilla*. It was of black lace and blended with her dark hair, piled fetchingly under the mantilla. She was probably thirty years old, but her creamy tan skin was flawless, and Micah thought this was more her natural appearance than the strokes of a skillful artist.

He stepped back from the portrait to get a better look. He didn't know why it captured him so. Probably because out on the frontier one seldom saw fine works of art. Yet there was something else about this particular painting. Something vaguely familiar. Something—

"It's beautiful, isn't it?" came Lucie's soft, almost reverent, voice from over his shoulder.

"Who is it?" His voice held a bit of reverence as well, though at the same time a small knot began to form in his stomach.

"My mother."

His mouth went suddenly dry, and he could not speak. Perhaps he should have known all along. Her rich dark hair and eyes, her skin tanned—he'd thought from the sun. But maybe he hadn't wanted to see, to know what now was so unavoidably true. Lucie was Mexican.

"Y-you never said anything," he said hoarsely, with some accusation.

"I didn't think it mattered."

He spun around to face her. What he saw was the absolute truth of her heritage. He also knew she was lying. She had known it might matter. She must have faced prejudices from whites before. And he knew without doubt he was prejudiced. Unlike some, he could not separate loyal Texan Mexicans from those who had murdered his uncle.

"I don't know what to say," he breathed, hardly able to speak the words because he knew they would cut him off from what his heart desired.

"I'm disappointed in you, Micah."

"Me? How about you?" his voice rose with both defensiveness and accusation. "Why did you hide it, Lucie? Are you ashamed?"

"I am proud of who I am!"

With her chin jutted out and her eyes flashing, he had to believe her.

"I said nothing because it never occurred to me that there was any reason to stand and shout, 'I am Mexican!' And I didn't believe you could be so petty until this afternoon when we were talking about the banditos. I glimpsed a bit of it then. Maybe I should have run when I saw it."

"Maybe you should have."

"I wanted to believe there was more to you, that the hate was only a small part that could be eased away with enough love. I see now it is bigger than I thought." Her voice shook, but it was cold, too, especially as she spoke those last words. "You are just a bigoted fool!" She spat her final words.

"And I've got every right to be!" he spat back. "And it's not just bigotry. It's founded in solid facts. I watched while your people slaughtered hundreds of men, my uncle among them. Slaughtered them! Gunned them down when they were unarmed and couldn't fight back. And then when they were dead, them Mexicans just kept shooting and shooting. I swore I'd hate and kill as many as I could. That ain't being a bigot. It's pure revenge."

"It is bigotry," Lucie retorted. "I wasn't one of those murderers, and neither were many others. Yet you lump us all together."

"It ain't that simple."

"Like hating your father isn't simple?"

He could tell she knew her words would hurt.

"I think you just thrive on hatred, any way you can get it," she added.

"I ain't listening to this! You lied to me. You deceived me. So you don't have any cause to get righteous with me!"

"Leave this house immediately!" she practically screamed.

"Oh, I'm leaving all right! I'm leaving right now!"

As he quickly saddled his horse and rode away, Micah didn't know why he kept thinking she would come after him. And he certainly didn't know why he actually *wanted* her to. She represented everything he hated. He didn't go around gunning down every Mexican he encountered in the streets, though part of him wanted to. Maybe not women and children, 'cause he wasn't an animal. But he held no great affection even for them. In San Antonio, ninety percent of the population was Mexican, so it was hard to avoid them. But he tried.

Even he had to admit, however, that it was wrong to lump them all together. He rode with a couple of Mexicans in Hays' company of rangers. And there was an entire company of Mexican rangers run by Antonio Perez. They were good men. They had covered his back on numerous occasions. But he knew he consciously tried not to think of them as Mexican. Contrary to what Lucie had implied, he didn't walk around with hate just oozing from him. He could be tolerant. But that didn't mean he'd be squeamish about killing Mexicans when they deserved it.

Micah could be tolerant of Lucie as well. Question was, did he want more than a relationship of mere tolerance? And no matter what he felt, she had told him she loved him. He had repaid those extraordinary words by accusing her of deception and defaming her heritage. Being Mexican didn't really change who she was, and it shouldn't change what he thought of her. Maybe if he could find it in himself to accept this about her, it might go toward diffusing some of the hate inside him, just like she'd said.

He truly didn't want to be so wrought up with hate, especially if it was going to prevent him from having any good come into his life. He was due for some good, wasn't he?

"I reckon I can be man enough to let go of some of it. . . ." he murmured into the wind. "Just a little for now, then see what happens. Maybe I'll die without it to sustain me. But just maybe I'll actually like it."

He reached out a hand, smoothing it over the buckskin's dark mane. "What do you say, Jose? Do ya think I should give it a try?" He smiled. "You're Mexican, ain't you, boy? You've done all right by me."

Shrugging, he nudged the buckskin to turn around and headed back to the Maccallum ranch.

Lucie was shaking as she sat on the velvet divan in the parlor. At first her gaze remained fixed on the place where Micah had been standing, as if he might reappear and the entire scene could be replayed and maybe changed. But as much as she wished the fiasco hadn't happened, she was still angry. The things he'd said angered her, but even more, she was furious at the fact that she'd been so wrong about Micah.

Perhaps it was a good thing all this had taken place now, before she'd become any more entangled with the man. She could deal with their differences in faith because she'd felt so certain God could and would change him. She could accept his wild nature because she'd known there was a gentle side to him as well. But add bigotry to the mess, and it was too much. Too many barriers to overcome. Too many differences.

Lucie, some things just aren't meant to be, she told herself, trying to feel pragmatic about it, even though she felt her heart was being ripped from her chest. She had told him she loved him, and she had meant it. But now she feared what her father, and even Micah, had said. Love wasn't enough. But neither could love be turned off so easily. She knew she would hurt for a long time, but it was still better this way. She could not be with a man who disdained the very blood that coursed through her body. The one thing that could never be changed.

It was better this way.

Wasn't it?

"God, I fear I have imposed too much of my own desire in this situation. I had hoped you were in it, but I didn't wait to see. I blinded myself to good advice and blundered ahead, thinking I could perform miracles. I could not have been more foolish. I think I know better now. Miracles are your business, not mine. But is it wrong to still hope? I cannot help myself. I still believe Micah Sinclair is worth hoping for. And I believe you think so, too. I guess I just must be patient and wait to see what you will do with him."

She smiled. Patience was not her best virtue. Yet she was indeed willing to wait on God. She only prayed He would let her know when to stop waiting and move on with her life.

Feeling a bit restored, she rose and went down the hall to look in on her father. As she passed the kitchen, she saw Juana busy with supper preparations. She should tell her their guest had left, but she couldn't face that just yet. She continued on to the back. Quietly she turned the latch on her father's door and opened it. He was snoring peacefully. She was glad the heated conversation earlier in the parlor hadn't disturbed him.

Lucie returned to the kitchen and was about to tell Juana about their absent guest when she heard a tapping at the front door. Her heart jumped, thinking it might be Micah. Well, she wasn't going to change overnight, she thought ruefully.

"I'll get it, Juana," she said and retraced her steps down the hall, trying to walk in a deliberate, sedate fashion, ignoring the urge within her to run.

She opened the door to find one of the stableboys. "Señorita Lucie," the lad said, "I have a message for you."

"Who is it from?" Again her heart raced.

"I was out a ways from the stable walking the newly shod mare when a man came up out of the shadows and called to me. He was a stranger."

"What did he want?"

"He said I must tell you, and only you, to meet with him out by the mesquite tree, the big one that was split by lightning some years ago. Do you know this place, señorita?"

"It happened before you were born, Pedro, but I think I know the place." What Lucie did not know was how Micah knew about it. "Is that all he said?"

"Only that you should come alone and as soon as possible."

Why was Micah acting so mysteriously? He certainly couldn't be afraid to come directly to the house. And she just did not see him as trying to entice her into some romantic rendezvous.

"Thank you, Pedro."

"I will go with you, Señorita." The lad squared his shoulders in a sweet attempt to look older than his twelve years.

"I'll be fine." She smiled confidently. "It's just a friend of mine playing games. Now run along and don't worry."

She saddled Belle as she fended off inquiries from the men in the stable. She told them she and her friend were just going on a moonlight ride. Questions of being properly chaperoned were broached, but she handily ignored them. Anyway, it was just sundown, hardly midnight. There was nothing improper about riding with a *friend*.

It was about a quarter of a mile to the tree on mostly level ground. She knew the way. As she went, she continued to puzzle over the oddity of Micah's behavior. She also tried *not* to puzzle over her own swift response to his request. But she couldn't ignore him, could she? Just because she had decided to give God full reign in the situation didn't mean she was to cut herself off from Micah completely. Did it? What if he did apologize and recant all his harsh words? She simply did not know how she would or should respond to that.

Then she remembered something her mother had always said: "When in doubt, pray."

So Lucie did just that as she drew close to the rangy old mesquite tree. Though the sun was down, there was still enough light for the tangled, gnarled branches to stand out a stark black against the faintly lighted sky. The tree looked quite pretty, even if most residents considered mesquite more a pest than a marvel.

"Lucinda!" came a soft call.

She gasped, the sound taking her by surprise. Only then did she wonder why Micah was using her given name. She did not think he knew it.

CHAPTER 18

LUCIE GASPED AS A MAN stepped out of the shadows. A man, tall and lean, but not Micah.

"Joaquin!" Lucie breathed. "Oh, Joaquin, you came."

"Hola, Lucinda. I wondered if you would remember the tree." He spoke in Spanish.

"How could I not?" She also replied in Spanish as she dismounted. She knew he had his reasons for not speaking English, and she did not wish to offend him, at least this soon in the meeting. "I remember many races to this tree."

"I always won," he replied, his tone as soft as the gathering dusk.

"Yes."

"But you never stopped racing me."

"I loved you all the more, Joaquin, because you never pandered to my inexperience and femininity." She smiled at the thought of those long-ago memories. "You were my friend as well as my brother."

"Sometimes I could weep at the crazy hand life has dealt us."

His face was drawn and hard, in no way indicating a man given to tears. Yet she remembered when she had seen him slip in unobtrusively among the crowd gathered at their mother's graveside two years ago. Tears had erupted from the hard black surface of his eyes then. Tears only she had seen, for he had disappeared before even Reid had noticed his presence.

"I am so glad you have come," she said.

"I could not stay away. I am a fool for doing so, but . . ." He shrugged as if to complete his sentence.

"But what, Joaquin?" she pressed. "Are you a fool for wanting to see your father before he dies? Are you a fool for not wanting to be cheated like you were two years ago?"

"I did not say I would see our father." He shifted on his feet and chewed on his mustache. "But the few minutes today just was not enough."

"You won't see Papa?" Lucie's voice rose. "Then why come at all?"

"At least I can see you—"

"I'm not dying," she cut in fiercely. "I am not lying in bed aching inside because I fear I will not have one last chance to see my son before I die. You are so selfish! I thought you were better than that."

"I am a bandit!" He retorted, his eyes flashing now. "I am better than nothing! I prey on others, especially you Texans. I have a price on my head—a large price. If I am ever caught, I will be executed on the spot. Is it selfish to guard my skin? I would like to live to a ripe old age, but I doubt I will. Yet, still I come . . ." He shook his head harshly. "No, you are right. I am selfish *because* I have come."

"I don't understand."

"I hoped at least Papa would."

"Tell me why you don't come, Joaquin," she implored, more gently now.

"Think about it," he said. "If your association with me is discovered, it could bring you and Papa both down. Papa could lose everything if he is thought to be a spy for the Mexicans. I have seen it happen to others. You have also, I know. And it could happen to a gringo as well as a Mexican. Don't fool yourself. Things are happening now, politically, that would make such an association even more dangerous. It is far too risky for me to come any closer than this to the ranch."

"But why even come this close? It is Papa you need to see."

"How bad is he?"

"He had a bad spell a few days ago and has been confined to his bed. We won't be able to keep him down much longer." Her lips twitched as she thought of the big Scot chomping at the bit like a racehorse hitched to a freight wagon. "It is hard for him to accept his illness."

"I can well imagine."

Joaquin's gaze shifted up toward the dark sky. Lucie recognized the ploy as a way to hide emotion.

"Does he hate me much for not coming?"

"He loves you, Joaquin!" she said emphatically. "As you well know, at first he resented the fact that you sided with . . . the enemy."

"Mexico was never my enemy," he replied ironically.

Yes, she and her brother had always been caught in the middle. She was younger and more sheltered by her parents, so it was easier for her, Lucie supposed. And even though she had darker hair, Joaquin looked far more Mexican, aided by the fact that he maintained a more Mexican persona. He dressed in Mexican clothes, spoke Spanish almost exclusively, and he practiced the Catholic faith. As a boy he'd been frequently mocked for his heritage by neighboring Texans, even when he tried to look as American as they did. Then in his adolescence, he reacted by rebelling. He took on Mexican ways in open defiance of those arrogant Texans who, in his mind, thought they could come swaggering into the land of Mexico and rudely denigrate all the traditions of that land.

When the war broke out Reid had not been surprised, though it had sickened him, when his son joined Santa Anna. Lucie remembered finding her father in tears the day after Joaquin had left. Reid's disappointment only deepened when after the war Joaquin had turned to outlawry in defiance of the new republic. At least he had protected his father's name and even that of his Mexican grandfather by taking an alias for a surname. Nevertheless, Lucie hadn't fully understood it all. She had never felt anything but Texan. Maybe, she thought bitterly, she would have thought differently if she'd encountered more people like Micah. Maybe that would have stripped away her loyalty. But she didn't want to think of Micah now, for she was confused enough being confronted by her brother after so long.

"I cannot stay much longer," Joaquin said suddenly.

In desperation, Lucie grasped his arm. "Don't let Papa die like Mama did without seeing you one last time."

"Do you think I wanted her to go that way?" He turned away from her, sighing, the tension almost visible in his broad, strong shoulders. "I tried to get back, but I was spotted as I crossed the border. Two of my men were killed."

When he turned back to face her, she saw the pain he had suffered, both then and now. She knew he had wanted her to see it, and only for that reason had he revealed it.

"All I could do in the end was to creep like an interloper at my own mother's grave! It is one more score against the gringos who have forced such a life upon me."

For an instant he sounded far too much like Micah. Had her heart not been wrenched by the similarities and the irony, she might have smiled.

"You can make up for it now," she suggested.

"It is a bad time now. More dangerous than ever." He paused, seeming to carefully consider his next words. "Lucinda, things will soon be happening . . . and you will want to distance yourself more than ever from me."

"What things?"

"Ah, you never could just accept things, could you, dear one?"

His mustache twitched, and she wanted to believe he had allowed himself the luxury of a smile. She remembered that even when they were children, her brother had seldom smiled.

"At any rate, I cannot tell you more. Only that you should keep away from San Antonio for a while."

She asked no further questions. She didn't want to know more. How she hated being in the middle. She always had.

Joaquin continued, "Tell Papa I love him and explain why I could not come to see him. Tell him I hope he understands. Tell him also that I have taken a wife and have a child on the way—"

"A wife! A child!" Lucie exclaimed. Then impulsively she threw her arms around her big brother. She was tired of conceding to his reserve. "When?"

"The child should come by Christmas. My wife is in Mexico, of course, near Saltillo."

"What's her name?"

"Pilar."

For a moment his features softened, and Lucie was comforted to know her brother had found love.

"She is a gentle, sweet woman. But she doesn't like me to be away so much."

"I shouldn't wonder!" Lucie smiled, already feeling a kinship to the sister-in-law she might never meet.

"Someday I will stay home with her for good. When all the trouble ends, when there is peace between our two countries."

"Let us pray for peace, then."

"I must go," he said reluctantly.

"Try to find a way to tell us when your baby is born. Papa will be a grandpa, and I will be an aunt. We want to know when that happens." And though she had wanted to be brave, she could not prevent the tears from spilling out of her eyes. She threw her arms around him again.

She felt a deep fervency in his returned embrace. He kissed the top of her head.

"*Adios!*" he said finally, letting go of her reluctantly.

He retreated to the far side of the tree where Lucie now saw he had carefully concealed his horse. *Adios*! She tried to reply but could not get words past her constricted throat. She lifted a hand instead in mute farewell.

Oh, God, let him come back! Please let him come back.

Micah had seen Lucie ride out to the big misshapen mesquite tree. He would have called to her, but he didn't know why he kept silent. She had been riding with such purpose that he was reticent to stop her. He didn't know what to make of her riding out like that so near dark and all alone. Is that what she did when she was angry? Then all the more reason not to approach her, even to apologize. He didn't want to face her anger again. It had hurt him more than he cared to admit. It had hurt to have such a wedge driven through the sweet things that had happened between them such a short time before.

He decided to just keep an eye on her for a few minutes to gauge if it was safe to go to her. He reined his buckskin up sharply when she dismounted at the tree and a man stepped out. Micah pulled his pistol, ready to kill the man if he tried to harm Lucie, but it quickly became obvious this was no chance meeting.

Micah dismounted Jose, tied him to a branch of one of the few other trees nearby, then crept in closer to the pair. He wanted to make certain Lucie was not in trouble, but if she wasn't, if this was some friendly meeting, well, he wanted to know about that, too!

Circling the mesquite tree, Micah found the man's mount. It looked vaguely familiar. Where had he seen such a horse? It had been recently. A sleek black stallion with one white sock.

He made his way back to where he had a view of Lucie and her . . . friend? He was still too far to hear their conversation, though he could discern it was in Spanish. And it was obvious that, though it was impassioned at times, it was not hostile. Who was this man? One of the vaqueros? Surely he was Mexican. Then Micah remembered. It had only been this morning, though so much had happened since to cloud his memory, that he had chased just such a stallion.

Joaquin Viegas rode a black mount with one white sock.

Then Micah's breath caught painfully as Lucie threw her arms around this man, not once, but twice! And that embrace had been filled with passion. What was she up to? What kind of game was she playing? What kind of fool was she playing Micah for? Here he had come back ready to apologize for his harsh words, ready to accept her heritage or at least to tolerate it. And what was she doing? Having some kind of romantic rendezvous, not only with a man, but with a notorious Mexican outlaw!

Sweet Lucie? It couldn't be.

But there was the proof before his eyes.

Then Viegas—it had to be him!—rode away. He headed south, so Micah was not in danger of being discovered. But he knew he was, nevertheless, in very great danger. And he had worried about hurting *her*! He had to be the worst kind of fool. And like the fool he surely was, he was not about to just slither away, leaving her to her machinations. She was not going to get away with it. So intent was he on confronting Lucie, it didn't occur to him he was missing a prime opportunity to catch the outlaw.

He jumped up from his hiding place and fairly charged into the clearing by the deformed tree. He saw her race to her horse and was afraid she was going to get away. But he quickly saw escape was not on her mind. He screeched to a halt, looking down the barrel of the rifle she had suddenly drawn from her saddle scabbard.

"Stop there or I'll shoot!" she cried.

"Lucie, it's me."

"Micah?"

"Yeah. Put that rifle down!"

She lowered the weapon but did not replace it in its scabbard. "What are you doing here?"

"Maybe I could ask you the same question," he accused. "I came back to apologize, only to find you in the arms of another man."

"What are you talking about?"

Even in the deepening darkness he could see the bewilderment on her face. "I saw, Lucie. I saw him." It surprised him how wounded he felt. Ever since he met her, he had been trying to push her away. He should be glad she wasn't interested in him. But the white-hot anger he now felt proved otherwise. And the fury was even greater than when he'd seen her with that Carlton fellow. Probably because since then she had made empty confessions of love to Micah. It certainly wasn't because the man was a Mexican, an enemy.

Lucie sighed. "You have it all wrong, Micah."

"I saw you two embrace."

"And what should that matter to you, anyway?" she said, her temper flaring. "A little while ago you walked out on me—"

"You told me to leave."

"Only because you insulted me."

Micah cursed in his frustration.

"And don't you curse at me either!" she warned.

Micah sucked in a steadying breath. "Who was that man?"

"I don't have to tell you anything!"

"He was Joaquin Viegas, wasn't he?"

She drew her lips taut, as if she feared what might escape them. Then she, too, took a breath. "Go away," she said tightly, "before we . . . before things get out of hand."

"What were you doing having a secret rendezvous with a low-down, traitorous outlaw?"

"Who said it was secret?"

He rolled his eyes. "Come on!"

"I am not saying another word!"

"Lucie, this is serious." Only then did the full import of the situation truly strike him. "If it wasn't a romantic tryst . . ." Please let it not be that, he silently prayed! "If not that, then the only other conclusion that can be drawn is that you are somehow in league with Viegas's band."

"That's ridiculous."

Micah tried to rein in his anger. This was serious, more so than he at first thought. It went far beyond his bruised feelings.

"Listen," he said with forced control, "you are courting disaster here. You better consider yourself lucky it was me who found you—"

"What? And not some narrow-minded bigot?" she rejoined snidely. Then she gasped, obviously sorry about what she had said.

They both fell silent, a silence filled with tension and confusion. Staring at each other, Micah knew she was probably thinking the same as he. How could they get out of the corner they had backed into? How could their harsh words be retracted? And more importantly, who would make the first move toward conciliation?

It wasn't going to be him. He still wasn't certain he'd done anything wrong. Well, maybe not now, but he had been wrong before, back at her house when he had accused her of deception. Or had he been wrong after all? He had just found her with a Mexican bandit.

"Ah, Lucie . . ." he breathed, not even realizing he'd voiced his dismay. But now that he'd started, it was easier to continue. "We've made a real mess, haven't we?"

"I guess so," she replied tightly.

"It's my fault." At first he'd thought to be magnanimous by taking the blame, but as he said the words, he knew the full truth of them. "It was wrong of me to accuse you of deception before. You have the purest heart of anyone I know. I, of all people, had no right. As for what happened now . . . I have no hold on you. For heaven's sake, I have done all I could to discourage you. I'm a real jackass for making accusations. I—"

She raised a finger and set it against his lips. "Joaquin Viegas is my brother," she said quietly.

"Your what?" he gasped. This was more stunning than any surprise he'd had thus far.

"I hope you can understand why my family has kept this secret. I didn't mean to deceive you."

"How can this be?" He had been thrown seriously off balance by this and was trying desperately to make sense of it. One of the worst enemies of the Republic of Texas was Lucie Maccallum's brother. The man whom it was Micah's sworn duty to hunt down, capture, and most likely kill was Lucie's brother. It suddenly seemed this was the final blow to fantasies he'd only barely let himself have about this sweet, decent gal.

"Joaquin had his reasons to throw in with Mexico," she said.

"No one knows about this?"

"Papa has one or two loyal friends who may know, but for the most part, it has been a fairly well-kept secret. Most folk think my brother just went to live in Mexico or the States or perhaps even died." She paused.

He now noticed her lip was trembling. He wanted to hold her and comfort her, but that would only compound all the mistakes he'd made that day.

"Lucie, today by the creek bank—"

"Yes, I tried to distract you and the other rangers to give him time to get away. What else could I do? He's my brother!" Tears welled in her eyes.

He thought he could handle her anger better than her misery, though he'd made a poor job of that as well. "Folks might not see it that way," he said lamely as he tried to figure out what *he* thought about it. She wasn't going to give him a break, though.

"What do you think?" she asked incisively.

"It don't matter what I think—"

"Yes, it does! It matters to me! Do you think I am in league with the notorious outlaw? That perhaps I am his spy?"

"Shoot!" He kicked at the dirt. He hated being in this position. Maybe he could lie. But she was too smart to fall for lies. "I don't know what to think. Your loyalties are torn. I can see that."

"I love Texas. I am not a traitor."

"Maybe without even realizing it—"

"No!" she shouted. "I am not a traitor."

"Your pa—"

"Don't even say it, Micah!" Her eyes flashed like a lion protecting her young. "My father is a hero of San Jacinto. He fought against Santa Anna when he knew his only son was in the army of the enemy. No one had better *ever* question his loyalty!"

"People will talk."

"Not if they never find out." Her words were a clear challenge.

"Unless I find any clear evidence against you, I won't say anything, Lucie. I swear to God."

"To God, Micah?"

"I guess that's a pretty empty oath coming from me, but what else would convince you I mean it?"

"I'll just take your word for it." Her tone had grown cold.

He hated himself for asking, "Is everything spoiled now, Lucie?"

The smile that slanted upon her lips was as cold as her voice, and her eyes—her beautiful, warm, dear eyes—stared at him now like a chill frost. And he knew he had lost something he'd not even had the courage to grasp.

"I'd like to be left alone now," she said.

He nodded. "Sure . . . I . . . uh . . . will go, then." He paused, not knowing why, just hoping. But she did not stop him. "I'll see you."

"I don't think so. You were right, Micah. We are too different."

When he didn't move, she turned and walked to her horse, mounted, and rode away.

Micah watched. He remembered only one other time he'd felt emptier. The day his mother had died.

Young Pedro waited until the gringo rode off before making his own way back to the ranch. He knew it was wrong to eavesdrop, but who could blame him for being too afraid to make his presence known? Señorita Lucie had just been talking to two very dangerous-looking men. One, the gringo, Pedro had seen before at the ranch and knew to be a ranger. But the other, could it be possible he was really Joaquin Viegas?

Pedro had been near enough to hear much of the conversation except when the wind carried away the sound before it reached his ears. Hearing was one thing, however. Understanding was a different matter. One thing was clear, the *patrón*'s daughter was closely related to Joaquin Viegas.

What to do about this matter now plagued Pedro as he returned to the ranch, running all the way. Only as he saw Pete Barnes walking from the stable to the bunkhouse did he decide.

"Señor Pete!" he called, jogging up to the foreman.

"What is it, Pedro? You look all in a lather."

"Señor, I have seen something." Pedro paused and glanced nervously around. "I must talk to you alone." There was no one in the yard at the moment, but it might not remain so.

"Let's go to the springhouse," Pete said.

Once at the springhouse, Pedro launched into his recent experience. "Pete, I saw him! She was talking to him, not a quarter of a mile from here—"

"Saw who, boy?"

"The bandito—I am certain it was him. Joaquin Viegas himself!"

"What's this?" Pete leveled narrow, incisive eyes at the boy.

Pedro would have trembled at the foreman's look had he not just survived being a stone's throw away from a notorious outlaw. Besides, though Pete could be tough, he had always been good to Pedro. Trying to remain calm and speak clearly, Pedro related what he had seen and heard of the conversation between Lucie and Joaquin. Pedro did not mention the gringo, only because it did not seem important beside the incredible encounter with Viegas.

"That's a mighty tall tale," Pete said when the boy was finished.

"I swear it is the truth!"

"Well, seeing as how you and I share the same name, and you have always been a good boy, I'm gonna take you at your word."

Pedro sighed with relief, not only that his story was believed, but also because he did not like carrying something like this alone. "What should we do?"

"You think a lot of the *patrón* and his daughter, don't you, Pedro?" When the boy nodded emphatically, Pete continued, "Well, then, the best we can do for them is to forget all about this. Don't sound like the *patrón* is involved at all, and with him ailing and all, it just wouldn't do to worry him over this."

"*Sí,* Señor Pete!" The last thing Pedro wanted was to bring more grief on the family that had been so kind to him over the years.

"So you won't say a word to anyone, right?"

Again the boy nodded.

He really didn't think it counted when a few days later he was bragging to that bully stableboy over at the Carlton place and let slip about having seen the infamous bandito.

CHAPTER 19

Tensions were mounting in San Antonio, rumors flying as thickly as Texas dust. It was believed that the Mexican general Adrian Woll had a force camped on the left bank of the Rio Grande and was poised to invade Texas.

Over the summer Congress had approved the raising of new ranger companies to defend against such encroachment. President Houston, a major proponent of statehood for Texas, knew that as long as Mexico was such a threat to the republic, the United States would drag their feet regarding admission. But little had come of the recruitment efforts.

"I can barely keep the men I have," Hays complained one hot morning at the beginning of September.

"It ain't that you haven't tried," offered Tom.

They were seated in a cantina trying to fight the heat with a tall beer. But Hays' rising frustration wasn't helping to dissipate the effects of the temperature.

"The men are practically destitute." Hays shook his head dismally. "How many who have lost horses in battle have been able to replace them? Precious few."

"Or they are forced to ride them rangy, sickly Indian ponies we capture. It's pathetic. We all live in fear of getting our horses shot out from under us—maybe even more than getting killed ourselves."

"It's a sad state of affairs."

Micah, Jed, and Big Foot Wallace walked in just then and joined the two men.

"Well, how did that inventory of supplies go?" Hays asked, though the look on his face indicated he already knew it wasn't going to be good news.

"Pathetic," said Wallace, who pulled out a chair and sat straddling it. "Jed, get us some beer. I'm parched."

Jed, always eager to serve his ranger companions and never taking offense at his status as "kid," went to the bar. In a couple of moments he returned juggling three glasses of beer.

"The barkeeper still giving us credit?" Big Foot asked.

"He wasn't too happy about it," said Jed, "but he did . . . 'this time,' he said."

Micah brought the conversation back to the earlier topic. "Captain, I hate to mention this, but any word yet on when we're gonna get some pay? Look at this—" He held out his leg, displaying the knee of his trousers where even the patch was worn through. "And you should see my backside. It's getting indecent."

"I'm sorry, boy," Hays said.

Micah had to smile at the captain's words, since he was only a handful of years older than Micah himself.

"What about the other supplies?" Hays continued.

"In a terrible state," said Wallace, taking a gulp of his drink. "Powder and lead are so low we couldn't fight a passel of Sunday school teachers. And there's something else—" Wallace glanced around, then leaned forward. "I been in these parts long enough to know just about every face and name there is. Well, I been seeing a lot of strange Mexicans in town lately. I don't like the look of it."

"All right, Wallace, I'm going to have to send you up to Austin to try and scare us up some powder and lead and whatever other supplies you can lay your hands on. Take Jed here with you. I got a little money in the budget you can have. Use credit if you have to."

After finishing their drinks, the men dispersed. Micah and Tom walked with Wallace and Jed to the livery stable and helped them get off on their journey to Austin. Jed was obviously quite pleased with himself, going off on his own with the redoubtable Big Foot Wallace on a vitally important mission.

"Just don't get yourself killed," Tom admonished Jed.

"Better yet, don't get *me* killed!" put in Wallace.

"I'm gonna do good," Jed assured, his grin taking some of the edge off his earnestness. "Just you see!"

Micah slapped his friend on the shoulder. "While you're at it, see if you can scare me up some new trousers."

"I won't leave that town without some," Jed promised.

"Let's move!" Wallace ordered.

Micah watched the two ride off with a sense of despair he couldn't quite identify. He supposed it had to do with the probable futility of the Wallace mission. The chances were quite slim they would find enough powder to hold off the Mexican army. And if they did, would they get back in time? Though it was all still speculation, Micah had a funny feeling in his gut that trouble was near. He thought about what Wallace had said about all the strange Mexicans in town. He thought about Lucie's covert meeting with Viegas. Her brother? He hoped that was all it was. But it was just too coincidental that the impending trouble had come so close on the heels of that meeting. If it had been anyone else but Viegas, he might have let the matter drop. Yet he had given his word to her to keep quiet about the meeting. She would truly despise him if the matter became known and she discovered it was he who had turned her in.

And as rocky as their relationship had been lately, the last thing he wanted was her ire upon him. Even if it turned out that she was indeed a spy . . . well, he didn't know what he'd do about that.

"Tom," Micah asked as casually as possible, "you think Joaquin Viegas is really working for the Mexicans?"

"No doubt about it. Why do you ask?"

"Just wondering. Guess that's why he's been spotted so much lately in the area."

"True," said Tom. "If there's gonna be an invasion, you can bet Viegas has been laying the groundwork by keeping these parts in turmoil."

"You think he's working alone? I mean, could he have some locals spying for him?"

"I wouldn't be surprised." Tom paused, then gave Micah a careful appraisal. "You know something, boy?"

"No," he answered, probably too quickly. "I'm just curious, is all."

Just then Hays approached, cutting off any response Tom might have made. "I can't believe the people around here," he said without preamble. "The town leaders are afraid of panic among the citizens, so they are trying to go about business as usual. I just pray that all we are looking at are rumors. God help us if there's anything to them."

Indeed, for the next few days nothing unusual happened, and life settled once more into a dull routine. Then Antonio Perez, captain of a Mexican ranger company, confided to the mayor of San Antonio that a force of fifteen hundred Mexican troops had crossed the border. A meeting was held that included a hundred native citizens and not quite that many Anglos. When one of the men reported seeing a hundred mounted riders in the vicinity, everyone seemed content to believe the invasion rumors had overblown the danger, and the townsfolk felt confident in their ability to hold off such marauders. Nevertheless, Hays was commissioned to take his men and patrol the area.

Micah was glad to do something. He'd be happy to prove once and for all that there was no threat of invasion. If it should be proved otherwise, he would be just as happy to fight. He felt he was going soft lately, thinking too much of romance and such nonsense, too little of settling old scores and righting old wrongs. Lucie had said he ought to let a little love disperse some of his hate, but he wasn't ready for that, and he needed a good fight to remind him of that fact.

The rangers patrolled south along the Laredo road, the most likely approach of a Mexican army. They turned up nothing, and two days later returned to San Antonio. Upon reaching the outskirts of town, they were astonished to find it was occupied by General Woll's army. Apparently while the rangers were scouting to the south, Woll, with well over a thousand soldiers, had slipped around to the north and invaded from that direction.

Hays took his men and retreated to Seguin, about thirty miles northeast of San Antonio. There, several days later, they met with Wallace and Jed, who luckily had stopped there to get feed for their horses before going on to San Antonio. Wallace had a keg of powder, and Jed had a box of lead balls and some percussion caps.

"We ran into Comanches," Jed said.

They were seated around a campfire on the edge of town eating stewed rabbit Micah had shot and exchanging news.

"Jed killed one," added Wallace.

"Good thing they didn't get either of you," Hays said. "We're gonna need every man we can get now."

"I still can't believe that old varmint Woll slipped into San Antonio like that," Wallace said.

"I wouldn't be surprised if someone didn't let him know just when we'd be gone on patrol," Tom said.

Micah squirmed uncomfortably. Lucie could not have had anything to do with that, but still, sitting on his secret was wearing away at him.

"I don't reckon it would have done any good if we'd been there," Micah said. "A couple dozen against a thousand?"

"Only took a hundred twenty-five men to take San Antonio from the Mexicans back in '35," Tom said. "Caldwell down in Gonzales has at least that many mobilized and will march when he doubles that number."

"I've sent couriers all over," said Hays. "We'll raise an army now that Woll has made his move." He didn't add that it was too bad it took an invasion to rally an army, though all were thinking it.

Then Jed jumped up. "I nearly forgot!" He went to his saddlebag and took out a small bundle that he then held out to Micah.

"What's this?" Micah asked.

"What you asked for."

Micah unfolded the brown bundle, revealing a pair of trousers, slightly used, but still in fairly good condition.

"Where'd you get them?" asked Wallace. "I didn't see you buy nothing in the store."

"I bought them from a woman who was hanging out her laundry." Jed's reply was edged with defensiveness.

"Where'd you get the money?" asked Tom. It was understandable the man would be concerned, since Jed was his responsibility and still on probation.

"Well . . . I . . . didn't—"

Jed, suddenly flustered at the negative attention, glanced at Micah as if asking his friend to get him out of this mess as he usually did. But this was a rare time when the two had been apart, and Micah didn't know what to say in Jed's defense.

But he couldn't remain silent. "Hey, you got no right accusing Jed like that!"

Tom softened his tone. "It's just that . . . well, Jed, we know you meant well. But what else are we supposed to think? You ain't got no money, and you wouldn't be the first man to lift an item from some housewife's clothesline."

"I didn't! Honest!" Jed exclaimed.

"Least you can do is believe one of your own men," Micah said, growing more and more perturbed, especially since this had all been started because of him. "Jed's covered your behind more than once, Tom."

"We all get tempted occasionally," Hays said in a placating tone. "But I expect my men to be above reproach."

Micah snorted snidely, but a sharp look from Tom made him think again about showing disrespect toward his captain. "Well," his own tone altered slightly, "I ain't met a ranger yet who could pass for an angel."

"That may be true," Hays said.

"I'm thinking it's more important that we stick together," Micah added, and if he would have listened closely to himself, he would have noted a self-righteousness in his tone that sounded hauntingly like his father. "We ought to back each other up instead of thinking the worst and accusing—"

"All right, Micah," Tom cut in. He obviously was not happy about the way the matter had disintegrated. They had bigger problems to solve. "Jed, I apologize for what I said and what I thought."

"I reckon I do, too," said Big Foot.

"Thank you kindly," Jed said sincerely. "Just so's you know," he added, "I helped that woman carry a couple of tubs of water up from the creek—that was while you was in the cantina, Big Foot. Remember, I went for a walk around town. Well, that lady said she wished she could pay me for my help, but she didn't have no extra money. I asked if she had a spare pair of trousers her husband might not miss. That's how I got 'em."

"Let's see how they fit," Micah said, glad for an opportunity to further disperse the tension in the air. Quickly, and with Jed's help, he tugged off his boots. Then he slipped off his old pants and put on the new ones. They were a pretty good fit. A bit short, but otherwise could have been made for him.

He looked at Jed. "It's been a long time since I had a new pair of pants."

"They ain't new," Jed said almost apologetically.

"New enough." Micah ran a hand along the slightly worn fabric, feeling a touch of emotion. He didn't appreciate Jed's friendship enough and was going to have to find a way to make it up to him.

The other men, mostly for Jed's sake, added their own compliments. Captain Hays even commended Jed on his resourcefulness, saying that was a prime ranger attribute and proved Jed was coming into his own as a ranger. That made Jed forget all about the previous altercation.

CHAPTER 20

THE SOUND OF HORSES CLAMORING into the yard drew Lucie to the front door. Opening it and stepping outside, she saw several riders, perhaps a half dozen. They were familiar faces, her neighbors. The lowering late afternoon sun set them into a shadowed relief, making dark expressions seem even darker.

"Your pa around?" asked Axel Carlton without so much as a howdy-do.

"He's not well," she replied. "What can I do for you?" There was not a friendly face among the lot of them.

"If your pa can walk, he best come out here and see us," Carlton ordered.

"I'm sorry." She wasn't sorry at all and made that clear in her tone. Lucie didn't like his attitude. "My father isn't leaving his sickbed, so you best tell me what the matter is."

"Never you mind, Lucie," Reid said from just over her shoulder.

"Papa, I'll take care of this—"

"Maccallum!" Carlton broke in harshly. "You got some explaining to do."

"Yeah, Reid," said one of the other men, the foreman out at the Samson ranch. "We been hearing things—"

"And we want to know just what is going on!" Axel finished, with a sneer on his face. He had obviously wanted to be the spokesman in the group. "We hear your daughter's been meeting secretly with Joaquin Viegas."

Reid had come up beside Lucie, and now he gave her a quick unreadable glance before facing Axel. "What are you implying, Carlton?"

"It's pretty obvious!"

"Of all the nerve!" Lucie piped up, desperate to shoulder the load of these accusations for her father. "Where have you heard such lies?"

"Don't matter where I heard them," said Carlton, with no intention of backing down. "You sure they are lies?"

"If my daughter says they are, Carlton, then that's all anyone needs to hear." Reid put a protective arm around Lucie.

It felt so good, and she needed his support so much. She hated lying, but what else could she do?

"We got a witness who says she met with Viegas just a few nights before the Mexicans took San Antonio," Carlton said. "This witness says Viegas is her brother, and there's just no reason he'd make this up. What do you say to that?"

"We have been your neighbors for years, Mr. Carlton," Lucie began.

But Reid stopped her, laying a hand on her shoulder. "I am a loyal Texan, Axel." His tone was weary but somehow managed to be forceful as well. "As is my daughter. I fought with Houston, and I'll not listen to anyone who calls our loyalty into question. But I will not lie to you—I am tired of secrets and lies. Joaquin Viegas is my son—"

Startled gasps from the group of still-mounted riders interrupted Reid. Lucie noted an ugly look of triumph on Carlton's face. She was a little gratified to see that Grant Carlton, mounted next to his father, wore an expression of supreme discomfort. Maybe he had a redeeming quality after all, but she would still have a hard time forgiving him for even being present at this obvious witch-hunt.

"So you have been lying," Axel said.

"When my son went off to fight with the Mexican army in '36, I wasn't proud, to be sure. I disowned him." Reid's lips trembled slightly over the words, and Lucie knew he was barely keeping his emotions in check. For six years he'd swallowed his pain over his son's actions, and he was not about to reveal any of it now, especially not in front of the hostile men who used to be his friends. "When folks got the idea he'd returned instead to my relatives in the States, I let them think it. None of you people had accepted him much anyway, and you sure didn't miss him. Soon he was forgotten. I let it happen. But *I* never forgot him. When I heard what he was doing and who he was . . . what was I supposed to do? What would any of you do?" Lucie felt her father lean more heavily upon her. Now she placed a supportive arm around him.

"Papa, let me take you in."

"Not yet, Lucie. It's time these things were said." He took a labored breath. "I am a dying man," he said, and no one could deny that at the moment, "and God help me, but I want to see my son once before I die. I don't care what he's done or who he is. I haven't seen him in six years, but if he should come, I will see him."

"What about your daughter?" Lloyd Samson asked.

"No one will say anything against my daughter!" Reid growled, momentarily gaining some of his old vigor. "You try that and there *will* be trouble here."

"You need some help, boss?" called Pete Barnes.

Lucie glanced beyond the riders and now saw all the Maccallum ranch hands had taken defensive positions, encircling the riders. They were on foot, but each man carried a rifle. She wanted to cheer but only let a small smirk tilt her lips.

"Thanks, Pete, but I got it under control," Reid said. "These gents were about to leave."

The riders, too, had noted their precarious position.

Carlton still refused to act defeated. "Because you are a gringo, Maccallum, I'm going to give you the benefit of the doubt. But I don't know about . . . anybody else. If Viegas comes here, it is your duty to report it."

"Don't you dare tell me my duty, Carlton. Now get off my land!"

There followed a tense moment when it was unclear if the riders would obey. The Maccallum ranch hands raised their rifles as if to add emphasis to Reid's words. Then Carlton turned his horse and rode away. The other riders followed suit. Grant was the last to leave. Just before he caught up with the others, he threw a look back at Lucie. She didn't know what to make of it. Maybe it was regret, but she didn't care.

She turned her attention to her father. He was practically hanging onto her, barely keeping to his feet.

"Pete!" she called.

The foreman hurried forward to give a hand. It showed the extent of Reid's fatigue in that he did not protest such assistance, especially within sight of his men. He let them help him to his room and to a seat on the edge of his bed. Even then, however, he refused to lie down like an invalid in the presence of his foreman.

"Thanks, Pete," Reid said, "I mean for what you did out there. Tell the men, too. I just thank God it didn't erupt into something ugly."

"They had no right saying the things they did," Pete said.

"Even if they were true? At least about Viegas being my . . . son."

"They had no call to question your loyalty."

"I appreciate *your* loyalty. To me." Reid clasped his foreman's hand. "You're a good man. Now I think I want some rest."

"All right, boss. I'll go talk to the men."

When Pete left, Reid lifted his feet onto the bed. As he lay back on it, he said to his daughter, "We're alone now, Lucie. . . . You got something to tell me?"

"Don't you think you should rest, Papa?"

"Ain't no way I'll rest proper until you tell me. Did you see my son?"

Lucie tried to stall by fussing over her father. She drew a blanket up over him and straightened his pillows. She poured him a glass of water from the pitcher at his bedside.

"Lucie . . . ?"

Sighing, she plopped down with defeat into the chair at his bedside. "Papa, I didn't tell you because I thought it would only cause you more anguish . . . knowing he was so close but had not tried to see you. He had his reasons."

"Does he still believe I want nothing to do with him?"

"No, I am sure he doesn't. He understands. He only stays away because he wanted to prevent just what happened today."

"Bah!" Reid shifted in his bed, which creaked with his weight. "I don't give a hang what those people think any longer. That they would turn on us so quickly at the word of—I wonder who it was anyway, informing on us like that."

Lucie played with the lace on her shawl. "I think I know." She didn't let her eyes meet her father's for fear he'd see the anguish this caused in her.

"Who is the rascal?"

"It doesn't matter, Papa." Then she hurried on to shift the direction of the conversation. "Papa, Joaquin told me he is married now and has a child on the way."

"A child . . ." Reid smiled for the first time that day. "I'll be a grandfather . . . though I'll never see the child."

"Who knows, Papa? They live near Saltillo. It is not a horribly long journey."

"Even if I live that long, he is still an outlaw, and he would be taking too much of a risk to come see me. And I could never make such a trip. With the trouble now between our two countries, I couldn't make it even if I were healthy." He reached out a hand, and Lucie took it. "Ah, Lucie, it is a lost cause. But I am happy you saw him. Tell me some more about him. What does he look like? What does he sound like . . . ?"

Lucie spent the next hour, until her father drifted off into sleep, telling him every detail she could about Joaquin . . . Maccallum.

She left his room and ate a quiet supper with Juana, neither having the heart to wake Reid for the meal. Juana was more silent than usual. She was the only one outside of family who had known about Joaquin, so all that had transpired came as no surprise to her. She made it clear that her silence had more to do with grief over the family's plight than with disapproval. She may as well have been a member of the family, for all her deep bond with them.

Lucie went to her room right after supper. It was dark by then, and there seemed nothing else to do but get some sleep. However, sleep eluded her. All she could think about was how Micah had broken his promise. She tried to defend him, thinking that it was too much to ask, especially of a lawman, to keep such a secret about an outlaw. Yet she had believed him. She had trusted him. She had wanted to trust him.

And he had betrayed her.

It always came back to that. And she could not prevent her rising anger and hurt. It wouldn't have killed him to keep silent. He knew she could not have had anything to do with the invasion. But even if he had believed her to be a spy, why not face her himself rather than take such a cowardly way out?

She had thought better of him, and perhaps that's what hurt the most.

But wasn't it best she discover all this now before she did something really stupid? It was bad enough she had declared her love. How much more foolish could she be!

Lucie squeezed her eyes shut. She wanted sleep. She wanted to force all thoughts of Micah Sinclair from her mind. She wanted the impossible.

CHAPTER 21

THE RANGERS HAD BEEN KEEPING busy since Woll's invasion, making frequent sweeps around San Antonio, watching the Mexicans' movements to ensure they did not go farther east. There was no time to hunt, and they had little other food supplies, so the men were all but starving. When it was decided to make a more determined strike against the Mexicans, Micah was the first to volunteer. Hays only wanted the men with the best horses, and Micah's buckskin, even on low rations, was just that.

Micah tried not to think about whether Hays' plan was a good one. It might be foolhardy, but at least it was doing something. Thirty-eight of the best mounted men of the two hundred now gathered near San Antonio were to approach the Alamo fortress near the town where the main force of Mexicans was encamped. There Hays and his men would act as a decoy to draw out the Mexican army. For the most part they hoped to use the enemy for a bit of target practice. If they could get some away from the fort, they'd lead them into an ambush Hays set up near the banks of the Salado. If they could get at least part of the enemy there, they might well knock down the formidable odds of eight to one against the Texans.

Gesturing and taunting loudly, the Texans challenged the Mexicans to come out and fight. The ploy worked. But instead of a mere forty or fifty soldiers emerging from the fort as they had expected, six hundred mounted Mexicans poured from the gates of the Alamo.

"Retreat!" Hays screamed, and it almost seemed as if he were truly in a panic and not merely feigning as the plan required.

The Texans took off at a full gallop. Micah's buckskin performed admirably. Under a barrage of Mexican fire, the Texans led a merry four-mile chase. But the Mexicans were too well trained to be lured into the ambush. Still, Hays' scouts were able to hold off the enemy until Caldwell's two hundred arrived to reinforce them.

The Texans had good cover and knew the terrain. The enemy sustained heavy casualties, while the Texans had one dead and several wounded. The skirmish forced Woll to send four hundred more of his men from the town to aid the army in the field.

The next morning Micah was sent to scout out the town. He returned with good news.

"The Mexicans are definitely leaving town," he said.

"What about prisoners?" Hays asked.

"I'm pretty sure I saw some gringo captives."

"Then we'll maintain pursuit."

Micah knew for a fact there were a handful of rangers among the captives in town, those who had been left to aid in the defense of San Antonio when Hays had made that first scout just before the invasion. He was now determined to get his men back.

An opportunity arose at the Hondo River. Hays encouraged the other commanders to strike the Mexicans before they crossed the river, but they were reluctant to face Woll's cannons. Hays responded that if he had a hundred men on good horses, he'd capture the artillery first. By then the ranks of the Texans had swelled by a few more hundred, and the commanders were then emboldened to commit two hundred to reinforce Hays once the cannon was taken.

At sunrise the next day, Hays, his rangers, and almost a hundred Texans charged Woll's front line. The Mexican artillery fired wildly, overshooting Hays' men and giving them the chance to draw close enough to make lethal use of their rifles and pistols. McBroome's horse was killed and several men were wounded, but they broke through the Mexican artillery. However, when Hays looked about for the promised reinforcements, he saw nothing.

"Micah," Hays yelled, "ride back and see what's keeping those reinforcements. Tell 'em to get their sorry behinds up here pronto!" Hays' eyes flashed darkly. He was a mild-mannered type until riled, then he well earned the name the Indians had for him, Devil Jack.

Micah wheeled around and, flanking the artillery that was quickly regrouping, made it down the hill to the camp. Caldwell's men were nowhere near to being ready for an attack. Micah set upon the first man he saw.

"Where's Caldwell?" he barked. Micah had escaped the charge unscathed, but his buckskin had been grazed in the neck and, though not hurt mortally, was suffering more than Micah cared to see. He was furious to find that no one was even making an attempt to aid Hays.

The man whirled around. "How am I supposed—" But he stopped abruptly as both men locked eyes and recognized each other.

The man whose gaze was now just as sharp as it had been on the dance floor back in San Antonio was Lucie's escort that evening. Grant . . . someone. Micah had seen him before during the last weeks with the army but had managed to avoid him. He thought it odd that there should be such antagonism between them, but there was no denying it. It had been there the night of the dance, and it was no less present now.

But there was no time to consider personal affairs. His comrades would not be able to stand for long against Woll's army if help did not soon arrive.

"Why aren't you men preparing to advance?" Micah demanded. "Captain Hays is gonna be slaughtered up there."

"We have received no orders," Grant said.

"Well, I'm ordering you to mount up and move it."

A sardonic grin slipped across Grant's finely chiseled face. "You and who else?"

Micah knew he had little authority, but he put as much bluff and bravado as he could behind that little he had. "I'm authorized by Captain Hays, and his orders are for you to move."

By now many of the men had gathered around. Grant's eyes swept the group. "Anyone here see Hays?" Of course no one did, and none of them were going to take orders from anyone lesser. "We ain't taking orders from you, Sinclair."

Micah wanted to leap from his horse and strangle the man, not only for his personal agenda but because Grant's blatant unconcern for his endangered comrades inflamed him beyond reason. Then he made the mistake of glancing again at Grant's sneering, superior face, and reason left him completely.

"You low-down snake!" Micah growled as he vaulted from his mount.

He smashed into Grant with enough force to practically knock the air from both of them. He backed up the force of his body with a well-aimed fist, and Micah could not remember anything feeling so good as the sound of the crunching cartilage of that smug face.

Blood spurted from Grant's patrician nose. He touched his face, then looked with horror at his bloodied hand. Grant was about to make a counterattack when a gruff voice stopped him short.

"What's going on here?" It was Caldwell himself.

Micah pulled his attention from Grant, for though his hands itched to do more damage, he knew he had larger things to consider.

"Where's the reinforcements?" Micah asked, his voice shaking. He didn't care if this was the commander of the Texan army. He'd pound him, too, if he tried to wheedle out of his responsibility.

"You're one of Hays' rangers, aren't you?"

"That's right. We broke through the artillery, but it was no use because there was no one to back us up. We're getting torn to pieces!" Micah didn't even try to curb his accusing tone.

"The ground is too boggy, and our mounts are simply too exhausted to make a go of it," Caldwell replied, somewhat defensively. "It'll be in my report."

"Hang your report!" railed Micah. "What about Captain Hays?"

But Caldwell was spared, for the moment at least, as Big Foot Wallace on his stout mule galloped into camp with the news that Hays was in retreat.

"Anyone killed?" Micah asked.

"None that I know of."

Micah shot a glance at Grant as if he would have been held personally responsible had any of Micah's comrades been dead.

"You want to finish what you started," dared Grant, "I'm ready."

Micah advanced, but Wallace, who had dismounted, sized up the situation and stepped between the two.

"Hold on there," he said. "We have too many problems without adding fighting among ourselves to 'em."

Micah swallowed his rage. He knew it was unfounded. This man was nothing to him, certainly not a rival for the affections of a girl he could never have. And as far as Hays' failed attack, Grant could not even be fairly blamed for that. He was just following orders.

"I guess I overreacted," Micah admitted, though through gritted teeth.

Grant touched his nose again. Blood was beginning to congeal and crust, and the skin was turning an ugly shade of black. "Wallace is right. There's more important things to see to right now. But I owe you, Sinclair—for a lot."

"What'd you mean by that?"

"No one takes what's mine. That's what I mean. Not that you *could* take what belongs to me, but I'm not forgiving you for trying."

Micah snorted derisively. "That's ridiculous. If you're talking about Lucie Maccallum, I don't believe she belongs to anyone—me or you. She's her own woman. But aside from that, unless you've a mind to marry her, I got just as much right to pay her attention as you."

"I'm merely protecting her from scum—"

Micah made another menacing move, but Big Foot intervened again. "Carlton, this is the last time I'm gonna stop my friend. Next unsavory remark from your mouth, and I'm gonna let him at you—and believe me, you don't want that. I've seen Comanches fall before his fists, and I don't reckon you're anywhere near as tough as a Comanche."

Grant's inner debate was obvious on his face. Finally he took a breath and spoke. "You can't blame a man for desiring to protect a woman's honor."

"Well, go do it someplace else," Wallace said.

Grant stalked away, very obviously not in defeat but mollified for the time being. There were other battles to be fought. They both knew that.

When they were alone, Micah turned to Wallace. "Big Foot, I ain't never fought a Comanche with my fists."

"Never?"

Micah shook his head.

"Well," Wallace said, an easy grin bending his lips, "I reckon you'd be pretty fierce if you ever did."

"Thanks, Big Foot."

"Now let's go see to our men."

Hays' company had by now ridden into camp. Thankfully, they had but one horse killed and five men wounded. But they were as ready as Micah had been to vent their fury upon Caldwell's army. Hays barely held them in check. Tensions, however, rode high in camp that night and weren't helped when they woke in the morning to find that Woll's army had slipped away during the night.

Reinforcements from Bastrop and La Grange brought the numbers of Texans to nearly five hundred. After several more successful engagements, Woll's army fell into a full retreat. When the Mexicans reached the border, the Texan commanders argued to end the pursuit. There was a small contingent of dissenters, but the majority won out. There were too many practical considerations. The army was worn out from long marches and little food, and most of the horses had reached their physical limits. Ammunition supplies were also low.

Micah's first taste of real battle since San Jacinto proved not to be as satisfying as he would have hoped. Most of the time he was off scouting, and the encounters he did participate in were far too few and too brief. He hated letting Woll escape across the border and was hardly mollified at the promise that the Texans would regroup in a month, after men and supplies were bolstered, to continue the pursuit.

Regardless of how disgruntled he was, he had to admit that at least this battle had not left a legacy of nightmares. He decided he had finally grown out of all that.

CHAPTER 22

SEVERAL WEEKS AFTER THE DUST of battle settled, as November made its appearance, Lucie made a point to go into town. Even her father did not protest. He knew as well as she the importance of being seen standing proud among their neighbors.

Manuel Ruiz, the shopkeeper, kept his eyes averted as he spoke to Lucie. "You have a long list, Señorita Lucie."

She nodded, trying with her own eyes to get him to look at her, but he kept staring at the paper she'd written on. "We ran low on many things during the fighting," she said to the bald spot on the top of Ruiz's head.

"Supplies are low here as well, but merchandise has started coming in. Flour, yes," he said referring to the list. "But no sugar. And I can give you a pound of coffee, no more. I may have a few buttons—white, not black."

"That will have to do, then."

Ruiz hurried to the back storeroom as if fleeing the Evil One himself. Ruiz had been a family friend, drawn closer because he and Lucie were among the few Mexican Protestants in the area. He attended her church, a small assembly that had sprung up since the revolution. But she tried not to blame him for his reticence now. He had himself to protect.

Some Mexican citizens of San Antonio had departed the town with General Woll. Among them were Juan Seguin and Antonio Perez, two prominent citizens. Those who left would never be trusted again. Those who remained were not officially reprimanded in any way, yet a pall of suspicion would hang perpetually over them, perhaps forever. They would have to work harder than ever to prove their loyalty. They would have to studiously avoid suspicious associations, such as with the sister of a notorious Mexican outlaw. Lucie understood this. She understood that the only reason she was able to remain north of the Rio Grande at all was because her father was an Anglo, and no one who knew him could honestly reproach his loyalty.

Many white males had taken Mexican wives and could thus be held suspect, and in fact, many were. But this alone could not condemn a man. Reid was probably the only one who also had for a son a man who was an outlaw and most assuredly an agent for Santa Anna. Yet Reid had many friends, including Sam Houston himself. It would take more than the likes of Axel Carlton and his handful of cohorts to discredit Reid.

Lucie wandered idly around the store as she waited for Ruiz to fill her order. She was looking through a small crate of books, the only books to be found in the store, when the front door creaked open. Glancing up from the volume she held open in her hand, she saw Micah Sinclair.

Framed in the open door with the glaring afternoon sun behind him, he looked as if he were some kind of ethereal creature, illuminated by a hallowed glow. For a moment Lucie forgot all about her animosity toward this man who had betrayed her. She saw only the handsome boyish face of the man who had saved her life, tenderly holding her, risking his freedom for her. She remembered how vulnerable and dear he had been with the orphaned baby, and how hard he had tried to camouflage the soft core of his heart.

Micah took off his hat as he entered the store, perhaps out of habit in the presence of a lady. His hair, seeming more golden than ever with the sun glancing off its tangled strands, had grown since she had last seen him, curling about his collar, the long side strands tucked haphazardly behind his ears. His complexion was quite ruddy from long hours in the sun, and his chin and jaw were covered with reddish stubble.

"Ma'am," he began casually, then he took more than casual note of the woman in the store. "Lucie!" he said with soft intensity. For a moment his eyes glittered with blue warmth, and a smile invaded his lips.

Lucie tried not to think of the touch of those lips upon hers, or that even now, in spite of everything, she longed to be held by him again. But even as her heart skipped a beat or two, even as her body reacted hungrily to the sight of him, she remembered his betrayal. And she steeled herself against her own betraying body and heart.

"Mr. Sinclair," she said stiffly, formally.

"How you been doing?" He stepped fully into the store, letting the door slam closed behind him. Though his tone was casual, she sensed a forced quality to it. From guilt?

"Fine." She snapped shut the book in her hands. "Just waiting while Señor Ruiz fills my order."

"I'm here to pick up a few supplies as well." He shifted uncomfortably on his feet. "Won't be long before the army invades Mexico."

"Are you sure you should be telling me that?" she asked coldly.

"It's common knowledge."

"Good. I wouldn't want you to reveal any state secrets. I may tell Santa Anna, you know."

He squinted at her, perplexed, then shook his head. "I know you ain't gonna do that."

"Do you?"

"Of course I do!"

The certainty of his tone made Lucie momentarily doubt herself. Yet no one else had known of her meeting that night with her brother.

How desperately she wanted to believe that Micah was innocent, but the facts of the matter were too clear to be denied.

"Then why did you inform on me, Micah?"

"What're you talking about?"

"The whole county knows about Joaquin being my brother!"

"Well, they didn't hear from me!"

"Who else?"

"Never mind, Lucie," he cut in sharply. "You believe what you want to believe."

He turned away from her and wandered over to a barrel of apples. He gave these his attention, pawing through the contents, lifting out one apple, then another, as if searching for the perfect one. He finally found a likely candidate, plucked it out, and wiped it against the sleeve of his shirt, a peculiar action since his sleeve had to be dirtier than any apple skin.

Thoughtfully, as if he'd gained some wisdom in the apple search, he said, "Listen, if it got out about Viegas, I reckon it's only natural you'd think I was the one who told. I didn't, but I'll allow the way it must look."

"Well . . ." she tried hard to be as magnanimous as he, "I shouldn't really blame you for doing your duty as a ranger. It was wrong of me to place you in such a compromising position."

"Except I didn't do it." A tense silence fell between them. Micah continued to rub the apple against his sleeve as if polishing silver. Finally he spoke again. "We just can't cut a break, can we?" The regret was clear in his tone, clearer in the darkly blue surface of his eyes. "I won't deny there is something powerful between us, something I can't explain. But whatever it is, even you've got to admit it has been doomed from the beginning."

"It hasn't been given much of a chance," she allowed.

"*Doomed*, Lucie," Micah said with more emphasis. "You said it that last night. We are too different, and there are just too many things going against us. You made the right decision when you said we shouldn't see each other again."

"I know I did," she softly, reluctantly admitted. "I was right, but—"

He gave his head a dismissive shake. "But nothing, Lucie! A polecat and a prairie flower ain't never gonna mix."

"A polecat and a prairie flower?" She permitted a touch of amusement into her voice. "Who is the polecat, Micah?"

"This ain't no time to jest."

"If only there had been more jesting between us, more fun. Have I ever seen you smile, Micah, really smile? Dear me, how I would have liked that."

"I never smile much," he said flatly.

She had a sudden urge, despite the pain of the words spoken between them, to do something outrageous—a flying somersault, or perhaps take that mop rag and perch it upon her head—anything to draw one raucous belly laugh from her solemn ranger. But it wouldn't happen. Not now. It was too late.

"You see it, too, don't you?" he said dismally.

"Yes, but I don't have to like it."

"I hope then we can part on good terms—that is, with you not thinking I would betray you."

She sighed with the hopelessness of it all. "Even if you had betrayed me, Micah, I don't think I would have stayed mad at you long."

"And I would not have cared about you being Mexican—" he broke off with an apologetic bent to his mouth. "I don't mean that in any demeaning way. I guess I just mean that there are some things that can be accepted and others than can't."

"We have too many that can't."

"That's the problem."

Sighing, she replaced the book in the crate and turned toward the front counter. "I wonder what's keeping the shopkeeper?"

"I'll be on my way, Lucie."

"What about your supplies?"

"I'll come back later. Ruiz is busy now anyway." He turned to go, opened the door, then paused.

The light again glinted in his hair, and the sight caused a lump in Lucie's throat.

"Like I said before, the army will be departing soon. Can't say how long we'll be gone or what will come of it—" he stopped, a rueful, humorless twist to his lips. "Guess that don't matter, though. I mean, you and I . . . we won't be seeing each other again anyway."

"Maybe occasionally, in the store like this," she said, unable to mask the longing in her tone.

"Maybe. But . . . well, good-bye, Lucie."

"Good-bye, Micah."

When he left, closing the door behind him, it was truly as if light, glorious, sweet light, had been cut off. Lucie wondered about what fools they both were. Fools for loving the unattainable. Fools for succumbing so easily to barriers. Fools for setting themselves up in the first place for what had been destined to fail.

But how could she be a fool if she had done the right thing, the only thing possible in ending this relationship with Micah?

Why did she feel such loss now, not only for what they'd had but also for what she had once been so certain they could have had? She had loved the man Micah was, but perhaps even more, she had loved the man she had believed him destined to become. Maybe that had been wrong, as her father warned her. And for that reason, she had said that "good-bye" a few moments ago. Yet it did not wipe out the love she still felt, and it did not make her believe in Micah any less.

"Dear God, I just don't know what is right or wrong anymore. I only know I still love him. I am willing to let him go—" she snorted a dry laugh—"well, I hardly had a choice." But even as she murmured the words, she realized she indeed had very much of a choice. She knew Micah felt something for her, and thus it would have been quite easy to use her feminine wiles to bend him to her will.

But it wasn't her will she wanted.

"God, I can't turn off my feelings for Micah. I'm not completely sure if some of them, at least, aren't from you. But I am willing to place those feelings into your hands. Take them away from me, Lord, if it is your will. But if you would have us together, then change the situation between us—his prejudices about my blood, my fears about his life-style, his fears about losing his freedom, but most especially, his bitterness toward you. Bridge the gaps between us, Lord. If you can do that, then I will know it is a match made in heaven."

CHAPTER 23

RAIN DRIPPED DOWN MICAH'S NECK. His hat sat like a pathetic, wilted flower on his head. Even his buckskin coat was soaked, weighing down on his shoulders like the burden of a failed life.

"This can't go on much longer," he muttered to no one in particular.

"I seen bogs like this go on for miles," Tom said. "We could be mucking through here for days."

"Days!" groaned Jed. He was afoot, leading his lame mount.

"We got Somervell to thank for this," Tom said.

"I heard he decided to abandon the Laredo Road and go cross-country in order to flank Laredo," Micah said, wiping fresh drips of rain from his eyes.

"Hogwash! He says that now to cover up the fact that he don't know squat 'bout what he's doing." Tom hocked and spit his disdain into the wet air.

He was not the only disgruntled member of the hapless Texan army. It was now nearly the end of November. The army had sat idle for weeks, waiting for orders to begin an invasion of Mexico. In that time, the army that had swelled to a thousand was now down to less than eight hundred. Men had simply grown tired of waiting. Most were not soldiers and had left farms and families to join the army.

But even this might not have stood in the way had there been better leadership. Somervell, commander of the militia, was perhaps the essence of incompetence. He wasted time with frivolous training and never indicated if he had a plan in mind for an invasion of Mexico. No wonder few believed it when he said this stumbling into a bog had not been entirely by accident.

"I gotta admit I had my doubts," Micah said, "when we waited for that cannon to arrive—"

"Two weeks! Two whole weeks we waited for that cursed cannon," Tom erupted. "And then the blaggard decided not to take it!"

"We ever gonna fight, Tom?" Jed asked.

"There's been plenty of fighting among ourselves," Micah answered.

"And Somervell could prevent that, too, if he'd take a stand one way or another."

Tom was no doubt referring to a confusion of command between Captain Hays' ranger unit and Captain Bogart and his sixty Washington County men. The two small units had been combined to form a company, but there was no agreement as to who should be in command. Somervell had come up with a cockeyed plan for splitting the duties.

"Any stupid idiot knows you can't have two chiefs," Tom declared.

"What if it's Bogart that leads instead of Hays?"

"Why, that would be pure nonsense. Hays is the best man!"

And so the friction within the company continued, but that was only a small picture of what was plaguing the entire army.

For three days the men slogged through the bog, rain, and cold, chilled to the bone. Tom's horse broke his leg and had to be shot. Micah, seeking to spare his buckskin, took to walking ankle-deep and sometimes knee-deep in mud.

By December snow and sleet dogged the army, but they had finally come within sight of Laredo. Desperately needed supplies were requisitioned from the town, which, though Mexican, was not overly hostile toward the Texans. Then about sixty Texans decided the supplies received weren't enough, and on their own volition, they raided the Mexican town, plundering and looting what supplies were left. Though these men were severely reprimanded by Somervell, their actions turned the heretofore cooperative Mexicans against the invaders. And it gave more proof than ever that the commander had little control over his army.

When an order was issued by the adjutant general, on December 19, for the army to return to Gonzales and disband, it was enough to further split the disintegrating army. Half the army was ready to go home, while the remaining force wanted to ignore the order and continue with the invasion of Mexico.

Several of the rangers discussed the matter as they sat around a campfire, barely flickering a small flame because only damp wood could be found with which to build a fire. Even the rangers were divided over the issue raised by the general's order.

"We came to fight," Big Foot Wallace said. "So far all we've done is scare the dickens out of a couple of Mexican villages."

"What's the point anymore?" Tom mused. "We ran Woll's army out of San Antonio and out of Texas. And it's pretty clear they had no intention of really taking Texas in the first place. They were just gauging our forces. What tactical purpose would there be in invading Mexico?"

"A show of force," said Bill McBroome. "If we don't hit back hard, they will just make further attempts until they succeed."

"Well, we don't have enough of an army to hit anything hard," argued Tom. "Why, if the political situation weren't so shaky and disorganized in Mexico City, I doubt we'd have gotten this far."

"Ain't like you, Tom, to give up like this," observed Micah.

"I'm cold and wet. My shoes got holes in 'em big enough to drive a wagon through. I ain't giving up. I'm just being practical. We can't fight with an army that's half dead already."

"Does that mean you ain't gonna stay?" Jed asked.

Instead of answering directly, Tom turned to his captain. "What're you gonna do, Jack?" he asked Hays. "I'll go along with whatever you decide."

Hays held his hands over the paltry flame and gave them a thoughtful rub before responding. "First off, I give you men leave to decide for yourself. But let me tell you what I told Fisher, who plans to lead the new invasion enterprise. I was scouting down Mier way, and I heard the Mexican army was gathering a large force to oppose us. I recommended to Fisher that he abandon his plan because we do not have the resources to meet such a force. I don't like turning back, but I believe it is the prudent thing to do."

"Even if it means following Somervell?" asked Wallace.

"I don't like following that man," Tom said, "but I don't like a lost cause either."

"Some would have said Texas back in '36 was a lost cause."

The debate continued for some time. But in the end the majority of rangers, including Tom, decided to follow Hays and return to Texas. Wallace, McBroome, and a handful of others would remain with Fisher.

"What about you, Micah?" Tom asked after most of the men had abandoned the sickly fire for their damp bedrolls, leaving only Tom, Micah, and Jed to siphon off the last bit of heat from the dying flames.

"I came to fight Mexicans," Micah replied.

"Yeah. That still a burning desire of yours?"

"Of course it is." But Micah sensed that his friend had probably guessed before even he realized it that his vendetta against his old enemies had dulled in the last weeks. Maybe Tom had also guessed that the reason for this was a certain half-Mexican gal, a gal Micah could not get out from under his skin even after such a firm good-bye.

But the Mexicans were still the enemy, even if Micah was coming to see for the first time in years that the enmity he held did not have to extend to an entire people. Maybe he could actually accept that there were good Mexicans and bad Mexicans. Yet what good was such a conclusion now, now that he'd lost the whole reason for coming to it in the first place? It seemed all he had left were his old enmities. At least continuing with the invasion would give him some purpose and would keep his mind from plaguing thoughts of what he'd lost.

"I reckon I'll go on with Fisher," he said finally. "I been wanting to fight Mexicans for years, and it would be pure stupidity to give up the chance just for . . . for something that don't exist anyway."

"Then I guess we'll be parting company in the morning," Tom said.

"What about our probation?"

"Aw, that ain't necessary no more. You proved yourself many times over. I'm sure Hays would agree."

Micah grabbed a twig and tossed it on the last ember of the fire. Avoiding the sudden discomfort he felt at the prospect of parting from his friend, Micah turned to Jed, "What about you? You gonna stay or leave?"

"I'm doing whatever you do, Micah. We always stick together, don't we?"

Micah scowled, not liking the sudden burden this seemed to place upon him. He didn't like the uneasiness he felt even more. Maybe he should follow Jed's lead and stick with his friend and mentor, Tom. Yet it was hard to let go of a passion that had driven him for so long, even if that passion seemed not to fit very well anymore.

Micah did not let himself nurse regrets in the disastrous days that followed. He'd made his decision, chosen his path. But it was a path paved with blood.

The first and only engagement of the Texan invasion force occurred near the Mexican town of Mier. Numbering only three hundred, the Texans managed to prevail, causing the blood of their enemies to practically flow in the streets of the town. The rampaging Texans looked too much like images from Micah's nightmares. Yet this was what he wanted. This was what he'd sought. Wasn't it?

When the fortunes of war turned against the Texans, Micah refused to philosophize about it. It began when Fisher was wounded, leaving a serious gap in command. Sick and unsure of himself, Fisher listened to rumors that Mexican reinforcements were on the way. Short on supplies, as usual, and barely maintaining order, he believed his army would not withstand another battle. He surrendered to the Mexicans after receiving a guarantee that his men would be treated as prisoners of war and kept near the northern border.

Instead they were marched inland to Monterrey. Micah and his comrades were tossed into a Mexican prison, where Micah would come to entertain new nightmares.

CHAPTER 24

TOM FIFE LOOKED AS OUT of place in the Maccallum parlor as another younger ranger had so many months ago. Tom twisted his battered hat in his hands as he sat on the edge of the upholstered divan. At least he'd bathed for this visit, his hair was slicked back, and his clothes were clean. He hadn't groomed his beard, and the tangled mass, streaked with gray—salt and pepper, Lucie's father would have called it—was bristly and made his face appear grimy despite his scrubbing.

But Lucie was less concerned with his appearance than she was with the news he bore. Micah had been captured in battle.

"But he is alive?" she asked hopefully.

"I believe so, miss. But—" he stopped, scraped a hand against his chin, then continued with resolve. "He is! I know it. I feel it here."

He thumped himself, and Lucie could not tell if he'd intended to indicate his heart or his gut, maybe both.

"But it is not certain?"

"Miss, nothing's ever certain in battle. Reports are confused and such. We just gotta hope."

She nodded but could say no more.

"President Houston is trying to get to the bottom of the matter," Tom added. "We'll soon have a list of all the prisoners."

"What will . . ." She tried to force the words out. She had said good-bye to Micah. They had both realized the futility of their relationship. Why, then, did she still feel as if she'd been kicked in the stomach? As if Micah had been something to her? She made herself speak. "What will become of the prisoners?"

"It's hard to say. I imagine Houston will negotiate for their release."

"I know about Mexican prisons."

"Don't think about that, miss." He licked his lips and turned his hat. "I ain't a churchgoing man, Miss Lucie. Why, I don't even pray regular-like. But I do believe in God, and I believe He kind of has His eye out for us all down here. I figure He's got His eye out for Micah, too, even if that boy tries to talk disrespectful 'bout God."

Lucie could not repress a small sad smile at the tenderness in the man's voice.

Tom went on. "I get the impression you have a strong faith, stronger than mine, for certain! Anyway, I think your prayers'll be mighty powerful right now."

"Thank you for reminding me, Mr. Fife."

"He's a good boy, Miss Lucie." Tom's lip trembled a bit beneath his whiskers. "He's been like a son to me these past months."

Lucie reached out and patted Tom's rough, gnarled hand. "I am so happy he has a friend like you."

"You been a good friend to him, too."

She shook her head. "I'm afraid I have only caused him grief—"

"Don't say that!" Tom laid his other hand on top of Lucie's in a mutual gesture of comfort. "I think you saved him. If you hadn't come visit him way back when he was in jail, I doubt he'd of ever listened to me. Miss Lucie, you have shown him that life can be good, real sweetlike, you know. Oh, he's got a hard head and may fight it longer than is good for him, but I don't think he'll fight forever because he knows now, because of you, there is something better out there."

"I pray that is true." She looked down into her lap, a bit ashamed of her last meeting with Micah. "I am afraid we said good-bye to each other just before he left with the army. Good-bye forever."

"You young people got no idea about that word *forever.*" Tom's whiskered lip twitched with amusement. "When you get old like me, you realize nothing's forever. Things happen. Things change. They just have to be given a bit of time. Patience, ya know?"

"I was never much good with patience."

"Most young folk aren't. But take it from an old codger, you and Micah have plenty of time." He gave her hand a final squeeze, then rose. "I best not be keeping you any longer, miss. Thank you for seeing me."

"It was my pleasure, Mr. Fife, despite your awful news." She made herself smile, imbuing the gesture with all the warmth she felt for Micah's friend. "Come and visit anytime. Perhaps next time my father will feel up to receiving you."

"That'd be nice. Now you take care, and I'll keep you informed about Micah."

Lucie walked him to the door and watched him ride away. It was surprisingly hard to let the man go. He was a part of Micah, and she wanted to keep him there to talk more about him, to get him to tell her all he knew about the man. She expected they had spent many hours together as they ranged the countryside. They probably talked about many things. Oh, the things Tom Fife must know about Micah! The little things—what he liked to eat, his favorite color, his birthday. Goodness! Lucie thought dismally, she did not even know Micah's birthday.

But with even more dismay, she wondered if she would ever learn those things. Even if it was true what Tom had said about nothing being forever, Micah was gone now. Would he return?

"Dear God, please protect him! Bring him back. Not just for me, but because I feel so certain you still have special things to do with Micah."

Not relishing the idea of being alone just then, Lucie wandered into her father's room. His eyes were closed as he lay in bed, so Lucie turned to leave, not wishing to disturb his sleep.

"That you, Lucie?" he called softly from his bed.

"I didn't mean to wake you, Papa."

"I can sleep anytime, sweetheart, and these days it seems to be *all* the time. Come sit with me." He patted the edge of the bed.

There was a chair at Reid's bedside, but Lucie sat on the bed itself, and needing only the further encouragement of her father's outstretched arm, she bent down and hugged him. His arms went firmly around her, and he kissed the top of her head.

"What is it, Lucie? What's wrong?" It took only those tenderly spoken words to bring Lucie's emotion fully to the surface.

"Tom Fife, the ranger was here. . . ." She paused, interrupted by a sob. "The . . . the army that went into Mexico surrendered and was taken captive. There's no word yet which men survived the battle." Sobs and tears prevented her from saying more.

"There . . . there . . ." soothed Reid, patting her head.

He held her thus for several minutes, just cooing words of comfort and gently caressing her. How good it felt. How desperately she needed her papa! What would she do if she lost him on top of Micah? She would not be able to bear it.

"The last time I saw Micah," she said at length, her words muffled because her face was still buried in her father's chest, "I told him good-bye, that I couldn't see him again."

"I'm sorry," Reid said.

"Are you, Papa?"

She lifted her head just enough to see his face and see him sadly shake his head.

"I'm sorry it hurt you so," he went on, his voice husky with the difficult truth. "But you know how I felt about the boy. It could not have worked."

"Yes . . . I saw that, but . . . oh, Papa! Why does it still hurt so? Why do I still care?"

"You are a caring young woman. You don't give your affections recklessly." He paused for a long while, then added, "Lucie, don't confuse caring with pity."

"Is that all I felt? Pity?" She didn't want to think so, yet maybe that was the answer. Maybe it hadn't been love at all she'd felt. Maybe it wasn't love now tearing her heart wide open.

"You mentioned that he was all alone," Reid said. "He has no family?"

"His father is alive."

"Is he . . . ?"

"They are estranged."

Reid nodded grimly. He knew all about that kind of thing, of course.

"So I pitied Micah." She let the words roll around in her mouth, as if trying them out. They didn't ring true.

"It is possible."

Her father wanted her to believe it as much as she wanted to. He gave her hand a gentle squeeze.

"All I want is for you to be happy, Lucie. When I die, which I fear will not be too far in the future, I want to know you will go on living a full and contented life."

"I want you to have peace about these things, too, Papa." She hated thinking about him being gone, but it was no use denying that possibility would be sooner rather than later. She could tell he needed to talk about it, and she had to admit she needed to prepare herself. "What can I do?" she asked plaintively. "How can I help you have peace? If I were safely married, you'd feel better, wouldn't you?"

His slight hesitation told her more than his words. "Only if you were happy."

"Yes . . . of course."

"We can't second-guess the future, my dear." His pale lips curved into a gentle smile. "Only God knows what is best for either of us. So let's just wait on Him."

"That's not always easy."

"You know, Lucie, there is something you can do. Not so much for me, but for another father . . . Micah's father. Perhaps you can write him about his son. If they are estranged, he probably knows nothing of his son's plight. If I were in his position, I would want to know."

She wondered only a moment at his sudden change in the direction of their conversation. Maybe he also didn't want to think about the realities his illness was forcing upon them. They would both have to eventually, perhaps even soon, but she was happy he hadn't pressed it just yet.

"That's a good idea, Papa. I think I will go do that now, so it will be ready for Pete to post next time he goes to town." She bent down and kissed her father's forehead. "I feel so much better talking to you." He probably knew as well as she that it wasn't the entire truth, but it wasn't a complete lie either. She did feel a bit better now that she had at least a small thing to do.

She went into her father's study, took paper and pen, and composed a letter to Reverend Sinclair. She kept it simple, trying to convey her concern for Micah while toning it down at the same time. No need to open her full heart to this man, a stranger. Besides, for all she knew, the Reverend Sinclair might burn the letter the moment he saw it was regarding his son. Micah had indicated how he felt about his father, but he had never said much about how his father felt about him. The minister might have disowned his son to the point of complete animosity. He was a man of the cloth, and Micah had lived a wild and sinful life. Thus, such a reaction would not be surprising.

Lucie sealed the letter, addressed it to the town where Micah had mentioned his father lived, and took it to the kitchen. Juana was busy as usual. Lucie set the letter on the table, then took up a dish towel in order to help out by drying and putting away the breakfast dishes.

"Juana, if Pete comes by, would you let him know I have a letter to post next time he goes to town?"

"Sí, Lucie." Juana paused in kneading bread dough and glanced over at the folded paper. "Who do you know in Cooksburg? That's quite a ways north of here, isn't it?"

"The letter is to Micah Sinclair's father, informing him of what has happened."

"Micah is the ranger who came calling a while back, isn't he?" Juana picked up the dough, which was still a bit sticky, and sprinkled a handful of flour on the board. "What has happened to the boy?" There was real concern in her tone, though she had shown disapproval of Micah in the past.

"He was captured by the Mexicans."

"That is too bad."

Lucie carried a stack of dried crockery to a cupboard. "Do you truly think so?"

Juana looked hurt at the words. "I did not approve of him as a suitor for you, Lucie, but he seemed a good boy, and he was trying to defend Texas."

"I'm sorry, Juana." Lucie sighed. "It's just that . . ." She picked up her papa's coffee cup and absently began drying it. "I had a talk with Papa. He won't come right out and say it, but I know he wants me to marry soon. He says he wants me happy, but I don't think I can have both."

"Because the young ranger is in a Mexican prison?"

"Even if he weren't in prison, I don't think we could have a future together." As she set down the cup and picked up another, she saw a flicker of relief in Juana's eyes. It made an anger flare within Lucie that she did not realize was in her. "Well, maybe you have a better marriage choice for me!" she snapped. "You keep nagging me about getting married. Perhaps you would have me choose Grant Carlton."

"Him!" Juana snorted derisively. "I can't believe I once thought him a suitable match. But after what he and the other ranchers did . . ." She pounded a fist into her dough, leaving no doubt as to what she thought of the actions of those men.

"Then that eliminates half the men in the county and their sons as possible suitors," Lucie said.

"It doesn't mean you have to settle for that wild ranger."

"Settle . . ." Lucie shook her head. She knew that was definitely not the case with Micah. But how could she explain what she felt, when she was not even certain herself? How could she get Juana and her father to see Micah through her eyes, eyes that saw to the heart of the man? But it didn't matter if she could. No matter what was in Micah's heart, there were still too many marks against both of them for a match to succeed.

"There is Levi Jessup's son," Juana was saying. "What's his name? No matter. He is your age, and the Jessups did not turn against your father."

Lucie didn't want to point out that Darnel Jessup was six inches shorter than she and weighed a good hundred and fifty pounds more. She didn't want to believe she was that concerned with physical appearances, but she'd tried having a conversation with Darnel once. He could neither read nor write and could only talk about cows and crops.

She looked askance at the housekeeper, then said snidely, "Why don't you just line up all the prospects, and I'll go, 'eenie, meenie, miney, moe,' and choose one. If I don't marry for love, it really doesn't matter."

"Don't get smart with me, miss!" Juana's tone was as hurt as it was miffed. "I may be only the housekeeper, but I love you just the same and want only the best for you."

Knowing full well she deserved the rebuke, Lucie wrung the dish towel in her hands. "I'm sorry, Juana." Abandoning her task, Lucie plopped down in a chair by the table where Juana worked. "I'm just so confused and afraid."

Juana lifted a hand to gently caress Lucie, then drew it back when she appeared to remember it was covered with flour. She smiled sadly instead.

"I am also sorry, Lucie dear. I am worried and afraid as well—for both you and your papa. You should marry for love, but your papa should also be able to die in the peace of knowing you will be well cared for. I fear that neither will be possible."

"Juana, I don't think I need to marry in order to be happy or well cared for." Lucie looked at the housekeeper, expecting to see shock at her unorthodox statement.

Juana's smile only broadened. "Oh yes. I forgot what an independent soul you are. And I half believe you could find contentment without marriage. You could probably run this ranch better than any man. I've no doubt you could do whatever you set your mind to."

"But?"

"But, *mi pequeña,* is that truly what your mind is set upon? To be alone, to never have babies of your own to love and care for?"

"I think I'd rather have that than be bound to a man I didn't love."

Juana sighed. "And you love this wild ranger of yours?"

Lucie's cheeks burned at the directness of the question. She opened her mouth to respond, though she had no idea what she would say. She was spared by the sound of booted footsteps on the front porch, followed by a knocking at the door.

"I'll get it," she said, relieved the uncomfortable conversation had been interrupted.

CHAPTER 25

LUCIE'S RELIEF FLED ENTIRELY WHEN she saw the caller was Grant Carlton. She fought an urge to slam the door in his face.

"Good afternoon, Mr. Carlton." Her polite words came through gritted teeth.

"Miss Lucie." He doffed his hat and gave a polite bow.

"What can I do for you?" she asked coldly.

"I've just come calling."

"Well, you do have nerve, Grant Carlton!" she said. "Seems the last time you called, it was with a gang of others ready to all but tar and feather us."

"Now, Lucie—"

"*Miss* Lucie, if you please. Or better still, Miss Maccallum!"

"All right, *Miss* Lucie. I can explain myself, if you'd let me."

Lucie crossed her arms and nodded. "Go on."

"Right here on your doorstep?"

"I'm certainly not inviting you in until I am assured your intentions are friendly."

He shifted uncomfortably on his feet with his eyes focused on the hat in his hands. It was a hat of black felt, the brim new and crisp-edged still. Lucie found herself contrasting it with the grubby hat of Tom Fife earlier. And that made her think of Micah, who had probably never owned a new crisp hat. Micah, who, despite what Tom had said, was lost to her forever. Micah, who she feared still owned her heart.

"Won't you give me a chance?" Grant finally said. His tone was contrite, but when he lifted his eyes to meet hers, there was something lacking in them. They weren't burning with blue passion. They weren't blue at all.

"Come in, then," Lucie said. Despite everything, she had to think of her father.

True, Reid would probably have a fit if he knew she was letting a Carlton into their home, but if Grant could answer for himself. . . . Lucie had sensed before that he hadn't been fully behind Axel Carlton. She supposed he deserved one chance. If he couldn't satisfactorily defend himself, she'd happily toss him out on his ear.

She led him to the parlor and motioned for him to sit on the divan. She took an adjacent chair. She did not offer refreshment.

"Lu—I mean, Miss Lucie," Grant began. "First off, I have to say I never supported the other ranchers."

"What kind of person are you, then, Mr. Carlton," Lucie said harshly, "that you would silently stand by while innocent folks are abused?"

"What could I do? It was my father, after all!"

"And why has it taken you this long to answer for yourself? It has been three months."

"I was fighting with the army, don't you know."

"I didn't know that." But instead of being impressed, Lucie could only wonder if he had fought with Micah. And would he be able to tell her anything of the ranger? But she couldn't ask, of course.

"We had a rough time of it, and I came down with the ague and have been recuperating since returning to the ranch."

What must Micah have suffered? And knowing him, he had probably been at the forefront of the most dangerous battles. Her lip quivered as she thought of him wounded and suffering.

"I'm all right now," Grant said tenderly.

Lucie realized he had noted her flicker of emotion and taken it quite wrong. "I'm glad to hear that." She couldn't very well tell him what was really in her thoughts.

"And this is the first chance I've had to come tell you how wrong I was about what happened a while back."

He seemed sincere.

"We should never have questioned yours or your father's loyalty. But you know how these things get out of hand. And you've got to admit how it looks, Joaquin Viegas being your close relation and all."

"Have the other ranchers changed their minds as well?"

"I can't speak for them. It wouldn't be right. Just as it wasn't right for me to let them speak for me before."

It sounded reasonable enough. Lucie could easily see how a young man could be so torn in his loyalties. It was no easy thing to stand against one's own father. Again she thought of Micah. For good or ill, he *had* stood against his father. Instead of submitting to the man's beliefs, Micah had left home. It was probably more complex than that, but still, in comparison with Grant, it was clear that Micah was the more principled of the two.

But she had to stop comparing them! It served no purpose. She'd said good-bye to Micah. She must accept that. And perhaps she also had to accept the reality that she must go on with her life. For her father's sake, she must!

"I suppose so," she said halfheartedly.

"Confound it, Lucie!" Grant blurted, then jerked to his feet. "How long you going to make me suffer for one mistake?" He strode across the room, agitated.

"It was a serious matter, Grant."

In three strides, he returned to her, grabbed her arm, and tugged her to her feet. "What I feel is a serious matter, too!" He pulled her into his arms.

She struggled, but his hold was firm. "Mr. Carlton!"

"I've about lost patience with your teasing and your fickle behavior," he said. "It's time you accepted what is bound to happen."

"Bound—?" she gasped hotly, but he cut her off.

"Yes! I'm willing to accept plenty about you," he said.

"No one has asked you to accept anything!"

"You are not going to find better than me." He dodged her remark. "I'll be able to give you all you need and deserve. And together our two ranches will make us the most powerful family in Texas—"

"What? I thought it was me you wanted."

"Of course I do. But it doesn't hurt that land and power will be thrown into the deal."

She made the mistake of looking into his eyes just then. Now there was passion in them, but she sensed it came less from her than from the prospect of riches and power.

She pulled away from him. "I don't consider marriage some kind of *deal*."

"Everything is a deal, Lucie. But have no fear. I want you just for you. I want you so much I am, as I have said, willing to overlook the fact that you are half Mexican and that your brother is a notorious bandit. I want you so much I am willing to defy my father to have you. I should think for that some recompense is due me."

Her mouth fell open. "Due you?"

"Be reasonable," he said. "You shall have security, protection, and the love of a good man. Your father will have peace of mind. I will gain a beautiful wife who is the heir of a fine ranch. We shall both benefit mutually. That's what makes this such a perfect match."

Aside from the fact that his words made her skin prickle, she had to admit the truth of them. Hadn't she said as much to Juana just a few minutes ago? She would never marry for love. So why not consider all the other beneficial elements? Grant was a cool, calculating man but he wasn't vicious. He wouldn't hurt her. He might even love her to some extent, probably more than she would ever love him in return. He had much to offer her—why shouldn't he expect something in return?

She must be calculating as well, and there was more to think of than her own desires. Still, she could not make herself capitulate entirely to necessity.

"I don't know, Grant," she hedged. "I suppose it all does make sense."

"Of course it does!" He drew her once again into his arms.

She tensed but not because of the forwardness of his actions. It was hard to accept the fact that she felt nothing in his arms, or that, if Grant had been captured by the enemy and she did not know whether he was alive or dead, she would be alarmed but would not feel the wrenching loss she'd felt when Tom Fife had given her the news about Micah.

"I must have time to think, Grant," she said.

"I'm willing to allow you some time." His arms tightened about her. "But not too much."

"Ow! That hurts, Grant."

"I'm so sorry. I just got carried away with my affection." He grinned. "I've waited a long time for you, Lucie. I can wait a little longer for you to be mine."

Lucie wasn't sure she liked the way he intoned that final word, "mine." It made her already shaky resolve even shakier.

"It doesn't bother you that I don't love you?" she asked, not knowing why she felt the need for such destructive honesty. Yet she knew exactly why. For her father's sake, she would consider Grant. But if he withdrew his interest, she would be freed of responsibility.

"It is not as if you love another," he said tightly.

She did not refute him. What was the use?

Then he grinned again. "You will come to love me. I have no doubt of it." His fingers pinched her arm possessively. "I will see to it," he added.

She backed away. "When my father is feeling better, I will speak to him."

"I think I should speak to him."

"All in good time." She tried to smile in a coquettish manner but could only manage a glib twist of her lips.

"I will consider that we now have an understanding, Lucie."

"I only said I would think about it."

He dropped his hand from her arm and plucked up his hat from where he had set it on the divan. "I must go. Why don't I come to dinner tomorrow night? Make sure your father is there."

He then strode from the parlor, leaving Lucie with her mouth gaping, her head practically spinning. What had she done? An understanding? What did that mean? And whatever it meant, could she go through with it? Could she marry a man in a cold, calculating manner for "mutual benefits"? Could she marry one man while she loved another? Did her father expect it?

Of one thing Lucie was certain, her father must never know of her sacrifice. If she did this thing, no one would ever know how she really felt.

If . . . ?

Then all of her doubts and questions and fears spilled over her like a summer downpour. And the imagined wetness turned real as tears once again coursed from her eyes. Tears for what her life was suddenly becoming—out of control like a spooked stallion careening wildly across the prairie. Would only crashing over the beckoning cliff stop it? Or was there some other way?

She sank down on the divan, wringing her hands and looking helplessly about for a handkerchief. But she had none with her. She caught the flow of tears with the back of her hand, then simply covered her face with her hands.

That's how Juana found her.

"Lucie, what is the matter?" The housekeeper sat beside Lucie and put an arm about her heaving shoulders.

Lucie succumbed to the embrace and cried into the woman's shoulder. "Everything is so confusing."

"I saw Señor Carlton leave. Did he do something . . . ?"

"He wants to marry me."

"But you do not cry tears of happiness, do you?" cooed the housekeeper.

"Oh, Mama—I mean, Juana!"

"I wish your mama was here for you now, sweetheart." Juana gently stroked Lucie's hair.

"I do, too, but you are almost as good—I mean—oh, you know what I mean, don't you? I am so thankful for you, Juana!" Lucie sniffed but still could not stop the tears.

"There, there. Somehow we will work out your problems." Lucie felt Juana shrug. "I don't know how, but we will."

Lucie didn't know how either, and at the moment she had little hope that the solution would make her or anyone happy.

CHAPTER 26

A FEW DAYS LATER LUCIE WAS doing her chores in the stable. She'd always had her share of work to do on the ranch because neither she nor her father believed anything was gained by her learning to be a pampered belle. But since the trouble with Mexico, with all but a few of their hands going off to join the army, her labors had been more than a matter of principle. Neither Pete nor her father had permitted her to go beyond the immediate ranch compound during the worst of the trouble, so she, with the help of young Pedro, had almost complete responsibility for the stables. Though the trouble was over and the men had returned, she kept up most of her duties. She was still needed and, in truth, needed the distraction of work.

She was forking fresh hay into the stalls when Pedro called her. "Señorita Lucie, there is a stranger in the yard asking for you."

"A stranger? For me?" She straightened her back in time to see the object of her query appear at Pedro's back.

"I thought he wanted me to follow him," the man explained with an apologetic smile.

He was a tall, sturdily built man with pale hair and striking blue eyes. He appeared to be in his early forties. He was handsome and vaguely familiar, though Lucie was almost certain she'd never met him.

"I don't usually receive visitors in our stable," Lucie said. "Please excuse me."

Though the man was dressed simply in twill work trousers and a brown cotton shirt with a homemade leather coat, there was something rather formal in his bearing that made Lucie acutely aware of her coarse woolen work skirt and smudged muslin blouse. She had no doubt her face was smudged as well, and her hair had escaped the confines of her chignon and was trailing in her eyes. She brushed a strand away with her gloved hand, and then noticed the stained leather glove. She probably smelled like horses, too.

"Forgive me for coming unannounced," he said. His eyes, so blue, so vivid, emanated a warmth that immediately put her at ease. "Let me introduce myself. Benjamin Sinclair."

"Oh my!" She couldn't help gaping. If she had ever imagined meeting Micah's father, she was certain she would have come face-to-face with a monster. This man was hardly that. But perhaps looks could be deceiving. Perhaps she was deluded by his now obvious striking similarities to Micah.

"I see you never expected your letter to prompt a personal visit."

"I . . . I don't know what I expected." Then remembering herself, she added, "I am pleased to meet you, Reverend Sinclair." She held out her hand, saw the glove, and quickly removed it.

He took her hand politely and bowed with a formality that conveyed at least one thing that set him apart from his son.

"I am very happy to meet you," he said.

His deep resonant voice was full of earnestness. She caught hints of Micah in the timbre of his voice, but Reverend Sinclair's was far more practiced and refined. He was either a born preacher, or he had spent much effort honing his voice to reflect that calling.

"And I you, Reverend." She meant her words, too, with all sincerity. No, she hadn't expected her letter would have brought the man himself to her doorstep, yet now she was pleased that this had been the result, if for no other reason than that his presence seemed to bring her closer to Micah. That is, she would be pleased if his visit didn't indicate something was wrong. "I must know, Reverend Sinclair, is . . . is Micah all right?"

"As far as I know, yes. I spoke with President Houston two days ago. I thought you might be interested in my news."

"I am!" She tried to subdue her relief, but it was difficult when she only now realized what a burden she had been carrying in her fear for Micah. She set the pitchfork she had been holding in her other hand against the wall, then removed her second glove, laying both on the ledge of the stall.

"Please, won't you come to the house," she said. "I'll fix something to drink. I'm sure you have had a long ride to get here."

"I'd like that," he said. "I am rather parched."

She led him to the house and bid him to settle in the parlor while she excused herself to get refreshments, to clean up a bit, and to see if her father felt up to joining them. Juana took care of refreshments while Lucie went to her room and quickly changed her clothes and repaired her unruly hair. Then she spoke to her father, who seemed to perk up more than usual when he heard about the visitor.

"Yes, I want to meet that man!" he said enthusiastically.

Lucie laid out his clothes for him, then left while he dressed. These days he usually only rose from his bed for meals, insisting that he'd rue the day when he had to eat in bed. Two or three times a week he'd go to his office to do paper work, and on rare occasions he would venture to the stables to check on his favorite horse and simply inhale what he felt was the best perfume around. He seldom received visitors—not that there had been many since the trouble with Mexico. He had reluctantly joined Lucie and Grant for dinner the other evening and just as reluctantly let go of his animosity to give Grant permission to court his daughter, and that only because Lucie didn't protest.

There was no reluctance now as he prepared to meet Reverend Sinclair. He was just as curious as Lucie had been.

Lucie was pouring tea for her guest when Reid came to the parlor. Lucie introduced the two men, and as they clasped hands, she noted how they appeared to size each other up, not in a hostile manner, but in the way of men gauging another's merits and faults. She couldn't tell for certain, but when they dropped hands, they both seemed satisfied with what they saw. At least they both relaxed and spoke in a friendly manner to each other.

"I hope your visit doesn't indicate bad tidings, Reverend Sinclair," Reid said as he took a seat in a chair opposite Benjamin.

"Not entirely," answered Benjamin. "I was able to set your daughter's mind at ease about that. I saw the official list of prisoners, and Micah's name was on it. However, Micah and the other prisoners aren't out of the woods yet, I'm afraid. They were initially marched to Matamoros, then to Monterrey. Now word has come that they are being marched once again to Saltillo, deeper into Mexico and further out of reach of help."

"Not that Texas can mount a rescue expedition anytime soon," Reid added.

"I am afraid not. President Houston is trying to use diplomatic channels. The United States and Britain have both made attempts to reason with Santa Anna."

"They can't keep them in prison forever, can they?" Lucie asked.

Reid and Reverend Sinclair exchanged looks. Lucie had seen such expressions often, though seldom from her father. They seemed to say, "This isn't a matter for feminine sensibilities." It must be ominous if even her father was reluctant to discuss it in her presence.

"What will they do with the prisoners?" she persisted.

"We must pray for their release," Reid said.

"I have been praying." Lucie didn't much like being put off, but she relented because she suddenly was afraid to know more.

"Then you are doing the best thing possible for Micah and the others," said Reverend Sinclair, who paused, though obviously he had more to say and was wondering how to proceed. After a few moments he spoke. "I want to say, Miss Maccallum, that I was most heartened when I received your letter. Over the years I have worried considerably about my son, so I was most pleased to see he had such a caring friend—a friend I now see is also a fine woman of faith. I want to thank you for reaching out to him."

Lucie's cheeks flushed but not so much at the compliment as because she knew her involvement with Micah went so much deeper than his father could imagine.

"Reverend Sinclair," she replied, "it was no difficulty at all for me to . . . befriend Micah. He's . . ." she paused, her cheeks heating even more. "He is a fine man. A good man. A . . . a . . ."

"Micah?" Benjamin's brow arched.

It suddenly struck Lucie that both father and son must have perceptions of each other completely differing from reality. Micah saw his father as an unbending fanatic, a hard, unfeeling monster, while Reverend Sinclair seemed to see his son as a bad seed, an amoral rebel. The irony of it made Lucie's heart ache for both of them.

Forgetting her previous embarrassment at her barely concealed feelings for Micah, Lucie lifted her eyes to meet the reverend's gaze. "Micah is a man with a tender heart, Reverend, a gentle soul. That's what I see, what I know is there despite how he tries to hide it under his swaggering, uncouth demeanor. Do you know he saved my life once? That is how we met. He was in the process of stealing my father's horses, but he risked his escape to safety in order to rescue me from attacking Comanches. He was always kind to me and gentle and honorable." She paused as a lump rose in her throat. And she was courting another because she'd lost her faith in him, perhaps even lost faith in the belief that God could and would claim him.

A long silence followed. The only sound was of the clock on the mantel ticking and Reid shifting in his chair. Lucie and Reverend Sinclair were both as still as a windless day. Lucie dropped her gaze to focus on the safer territory of her hands folded in her lap. She could not face Micah's father. She did not want to confront his denial of her words. She did not want to think he had given up on his son. As she had?

"Miss Maccallum," Benjamin said finally. "I can't . . . that is . . ."

Lucie could not help risking a look at the man. His expression was a confusion of emotions. The muscles of his jaw twitched along with his lips, helpless, it appeared, to form the words he wanted to say. He released a ragged sigh.

"Dear God! I always knew in my heart Micah could not be lost completely. But I . . . I have seen Micah once in the six years since he left home, and that was only a few months ago when he was in jail—I believe it was for stealing your father's horses. Over the years I have heard things, distressing things. I could never know how deeply his unsavory actions went to his heart. I tried never to give up hope, but I could never *know.* I suppose in six years I should have made a more concerted effort to find him and bring him to his senses. But a large part of me was afraid to find him, afraid that my worst fears would be realized, that my son was beyond help. When he was home, he was filled with such anger. I just did not know if that anger had finally consumed him."

Benjamin stretched out his hands in front of him, gazing thoughtfully at his fingers. They were large hands, brown and work worn, with nails broken and perpetually stained with earth. They seemed to conflict with the refined formality of the man's bearing, just as the man himself conflicted with all Lucie had heard about him from Micah.

Shaking his head, Reverend Sinclair continued. "I am afraid part of me gave up on him. Oh, I prayed for him and hoped he would turn around, but I was too afraid to believe. Yet here you are, a mere friend, and you have faith in Micah—"

"Please, Reverend Sinclair, I . . ." Lucie forced herself to look into the man's eyes. "I gave up on him, too. Before he went to fight, I told him I could not see him again."

"But you saw to the core of him and found him to be a good person?"

"Yes, I did. I still do. I don't know what happened. I suppose I gave up on God as well."

Benjamin returned a sympathetic look. He seemed to know exactly how she felt.

"It must not have been easy for you to maintain a friendship with one of differing beliefs"—he gave a dry chuckle—"with little or no beliefs at all, if I have a clear perception of my son's spiritual values."

"I was uncertain if I should," Lucie said. "But I feel strongly that Micah has not completely abandoned God. It's just that—" she stopped. How could she tell the truth, that Micah's faith had been trampled by his own father?

Sinclair shook his head, a sad smile on his lips. "I know, Miss Maccallum. I know I destroyed my son's faith." The man's pain was palpable, despite the fact that Lucie sensed this was not a man to bear his inner soul to strangers. It spoke more than anything else about the true nature of this man, Micah's father.

"I'm so sorry," Lucie said gently.

"As am I."

Reid shifted once again in his chair. Sensing he wished to speak, Lucie turned toward him.

"I, too, have had difficulty with my son," Reid said, catching Benjamin's gaze and holding it. "Fathers and sons are such strange animals. Fathers tend to invest their hearts and souls in their sons, perhaps more so than with daughters, because they feel so much more is required of them. Sons, for their part, want to worship their fathers. Both are doomed to fail in attaining the other's expectations. Accepting or laying blame is pretty futile in such a situation. It helps neither party." He paused and took a breath.

Lucie could tell such a long speech was taxing him. But he continued.

"I have come to believe it is the heart of a man that matters. Certainly it is only the heart that God himself sees. How many times do we want only good for our children, and yet our actions to achieve this blow up in our faces like a touchy musket? And the worst of it is that our children are the last to credit our good intentions."

"My father used to tell me, 'Boy, the road to nowhere is paved with good intentions,' " Benjamin said.

"Ah yes . . ." Reid smiled. "But the road to perdition is paved with evil intentions. I would choose the former. And I would keep hoping that one of those good intentions would get me on a path to *somewhere.* Life, and especially child rearing, is essentially a guessing game. Just when you think you have the rules figured out, they change, or your children change on you. If we do the best we can, how can we do more?"

"I only wish I would have known these things when my son was young," Benjamin said. "Unfortunately, I made rules for my children and my family, and the rules were like iron—no bending at all. Of course, something had to break if the rules would not. What broke was my son's heart, his spirit, I suppose. He has every right to resent me, even if I have changed now." Pausing, he glanced back and forth between Reid and Lucie. "I do not expect I will be the one to reach my son. Yet my faith has been greatly renewed by you folks. God has clearly shown that He is faithful to my prayers and to my son. He has brought you good people into Micah's life, and that restores my hope."

Lucie smiled. "My hope has also been restored, Reverend—by you! From all Micah has told me of you, I fully expected to meet a . . . uh . . ."

"A monster, Miss Maccallum?" Benjamin's tone revealed a hint of wry amusement.

Lucie's smile relaxed. "Yes, if you'll forgive me for thinking such a thing. But I find that is not true at all. I doubt it ever was, even if you might have been a strict parent. I know now you always loved Micah, though he might not have perceived it. And because of that, I know with more certainty than ever that there is indeed hope for Micah."

An hour later while Reverend Sinclair was washing up, Lucie went to the kitchen to help with supper preparations. Sinclair would sup with them and bide the night at Reid's invitation. As Lucie cut up vegetables for Juana's delectable rosemary stew, she felt absolutely buoyant. As never before, she had an assurance that Micah would be all right, spiritually at least. With a man like Benjamin Sinclair for a father and with friends like her and her father, Micah must eventually come to see the love of God.

There was still much uncertainty about her own relationship with Micah. But she knew she could not give up quite yet. How she would break the news to Grant, she did not know. But she did know she would not marry him now or ever. The visit with Reverend Sinclair had helped her understand her own father a bit better, and Lucie was now sure he would never ask or expect her to make such a sacrifice.

Still, Micah's captivity created a pall over Lucie's renewed spirit. Anything could happen to him in Mexico. Reverend Sinclair had not said as much, but Lucie had heard rumors that Santa Anna wanted to execute all the prisoners. That could not happen. She would not accept the possibility. God had plans for Micah. She knew it. Plans that did not include an early death in a Mexican prison.

CHAPTER 27

THE LAND BETWEEN SALTILLO AND the Rio Grande was a desert so barren, so desolate, it might have been forsaken by God as well as man.

The captives had known that much, but none had ever traversed it, so they imagined it could not be any worse than other deserts they had seen. At any rate, they had chosen to risk the unknown rather than suffer further at the hands of their Mexican captors. When the opportunity for escape had arisen, they had taken it. That chance had come in the spring of 1843 when they were to be moved from Monterey to Saltillo. They managed to overpower their guards on the road, capture some weapons and ammunition stores, and make a break. They had lost five men in the process, and only God knew how many more they would lose before they set eyes upon Texas again.

Jed stumbled over a rock and crumpled to his knees. Instead of pulling himself back up, he just sat on the dry, crusted ground, letting his head drop into his hands.

"That's it for me," he mumbled thickly.

Micah shuffled to a stop beside him. "What you talking about?" he said a bit gruffly, but who could tell with his throat parched and raw and his tongue so thick he could not keep his mouth shut.

"I tell ya, I ain't moving. I've had it!"

Micah sank down beside him. "All right, you said we're sticking together, so guess I've had it, too."

"Get out of here! I don't know how ya do it, but you got miles left in you."

Micah shook his head. "What difference does it make if I die here or in a couple of miles?"

They had already spent days in this desert. They had abandoned the road, hoping to elude pursuit, but had become hopelessly lost instead. No one had any idea, not even Big Foot, how far it was to the Rio Grande. They had no food and had long since tossed aside their weapons to spare the weight, so they couldn't hunt, not that they'd have the strength to do so anyway. They had tried eating insects and snakes when they could be caught with their knives. But there had been no way to cook anything. Micah had become violently ill trying to choke down a grasshopper.

There hadn't been a watering hole in two days, and the last one, if the moist hole in the ground could be called that, had provided enough only for the men to dampen their tongues. Some had tried drinking their own urine, but the results had been disastrous. Several men had been lost thus far on the desperate trek. There were now fewer than two hundred prisoners left. A look at the ragged line of stumbling men stretching out over the desert said there would be fewer than that by tomorrow.

"You gotta keep going, Micah," Jed was saying. "You got your gal waiting for you back home."

"I ain't got no gal," Micah insisted with as much force as he could muster. "Lucie and I . . . well, she ain't my gal, that's all. But don't you have no reason to live, Jed?"

Jed shrugged. "Sometimes . . . I don't know . . . I get tired of it all."

Suddenly he looked old and even wise, not at all like the boy Micah knew.

"Sometimes I get a strong hankering to see my ma and pa again."

Some of the other men had come up and dropped to the ground as well, this seeming as good a time as any to take a rest.

"There you go," Bill McBroome said. "You got your folks to go home to." McBroome was faring better than many of the men. He'd lived on insects and wet dirt before, years ago when he'd been a captive of the Comanches. He'd survived once before and knew he could again.

"Jed's parents are dead," Micah said.

"Oh, didn't know that," McBroome said.

"Guess I'd have to go to heaven to be with them."

"That what you want, Jed?" Micah asked.

"No, but I don't want to get up neither!" Jed took off his hat and wiped a hand across his face. He was so dehydrated he was no longer even sweating. "I might if I had a pretty gal like Miss Lucie to get to."

"Who is this Lucie?" Big Foot asked.

"Micah's gal."

"No, she ain't," Micah said.

"Tell us about her, Micah," Big Foot said.

Micah would have refused because the last thing he wanted to think of then was Lucie Maccallum and all he'd never have with her. Even if he made it back to Texas, she would never be his. Why, he wouldn't be surprised if by now she was married off to that Grant Carlton. But as he looked around at his companions, he realized they needed to be reminded of home. They needed to be reminded about why they were suffering so to get back.

"She's the prettiest gal there ever was," Micah began. He closed his eyes, and it wasn't hard at all to conjure an image of the sweet and beautiful Lucie Maccallum. He almost thought he caught a whiff of rosewater instead of the stink of filthy men. "She's got hair like black silk caught on fire—"

"Silk caught on fire?" questioned McBroome. "That don't sound pleasant at all."

Jed amended, "That's his way of saying her hair is dark, nearly black, but with lots of red in it."

Micah rolled his eyes. "You want me to tell y'all about her? Or maybe you could do a better job of telling me."

"You're doing a fine job," encouraged Big Foot. "Go on."

"Well, there ain't much more to tell. She's just pretty, that's all. And sweet. And when she laughs . . ." Micah's chest clenched as the memories were released. He should never have gotten started. "Hey, Charlie," he said to one of the other men, "you got a sweetheart, don't ya? Tell about her."

Dreamily, Charlie complied. "She's pretty, too, of course. 'Cept her hair's yella', like gold. No fire, just shining gold. . . ."

Soon everyone was telling about someone special back home, and in a half hour they all found the strength to rise to their feet and trod on.

Into the heat, into the blinding sun, into the stinging wind. They ate sand and grit when they longed for an apple pie baked by a sweet woman of their dreams. They swallowed thick saliva when their mouths ached for a cup of springwater from a slim, smooth hand.

Time slipped away until even the rising and setting of the sun meant little to them. When the Mexican army finally caught up with them, they could not have fought them even if they'd had weapons. As it was, some considered it more rescue than capture.

Santa Anna had enough of his own problems just trying to stay in power, without dealing with those pesky Texans. He was fed up with them and prepared to execute the lot of the prisoners. But when the ministers from both America and Britain learned of his decree, they raised such a protest that Santa Anna had to back down. He could never win a war against both Britain and America.

Instead, the Mexican president decided to deal with the prisoners in the Latino way. Every tenth one would be shot, to be decided by a simple lottery. The commander of the prison would place one hundred fifty-nine white beans and seventeen black beans, representing the number of the remaining prisoners, into a jar. Each prisoner would then draw a bean. Those drawing a black bean would die.

Word of the decision reached the prisoners, causing varying degrees of dismay, disbelief, and anger. But practical men that they were, they realized seventeen dead was far better than nearly two hundred. So they awaited their fate with stoicism mixed with enough fear to prove they were only human.

Micah was certain he would draw a black bean. He'd cheated death too many times lately to have any confidence he'd do so again. He was scared of the prospect, to be sure, but there was also a kind of comfort in his certainty about his fate.

A few sheets of paper were passed among the men along with a pen and ink. Those who could write were permitted to leave notes. Micah took some paper, and when he had a turn at the pen, he chewed on the tip and wondered what he would write. But what perplexed him more was who he would write to. He thought of Lucie, but there seemed no sense in that. They'd made a break. It was over. Best for her if it stayed that way.

He thought of writing to his father or, if not him, perhaps his stepmother or his sisters and brother. Oddly enough, the thought of writing, even to his father, did not bother him as much as it should. Perhaps the desert had burned some of the hatred from him. Perhaps the nearness of death was making him more pragmatic. Or maybe, just maybe, his problems with his father had been to some extent his own fault. At the very least, it might well be that Benjamin Sinclair was as much a victim of circumstance as anyone. The man had made some mistakes, some very serious ones, but then, hadn't everyone made mistakes? In the last months, Micah had seen more clearly than ever how easy it was to blunder even with the best intentions.

This revelation came as an enormous surprise to Micah. Until just a few moments before he would have been certain his hatred for the man was fully entrenched in his heart. Now he didn't know what to think. He dipped the pen in the ink jar, then set the tip to the paper.

Dear Pa, he wrote. *I guess I'm finally gonna die. Don't figure it would do any good to go to my grave filled with hate. . . .* The pen paused. He tried to write the words "I forgive you," but simply could not make his hand do it. It was one thing not to hate but something else entirely to put it all behind you by forgiveness. He knew about forgiveness, and he knew what his father's perception was of forgiveness. It was an act of sublime acceptance, and Micah could not do it.

Perturbed with himself, he drew an *X* through the words. He thought a moment, then decided upon another, far easier and more comfortable, path.

To Whom It May Concern,

I have some land coming to me from my service at San Jacinto and from an inheritance left to me by my Uncle Haden Sinclair. I hereby will all that land to one Jed Wilkes. He's a mite slow in the brain, but I know he will do right by the land. Anyhow, since I have served the Republic of Texas honorably and am now about to give my life for Texas, I figure you are bound to follow my last wish.

He signed the letter and got two men who could write to witness it, then he turned to Jed, who was curled up on the ground in their crowded cell trying to sleep.

"Hey, Jed." He gave his friend's arm a push.

Jed grunted and rolled over. "Micah? I was dreaming. I saw my ma. I was powerful happy to see her." He gave his body a stretch. "What'd you want?"

"I want to give you my last will and testament."

"Huh? You want to give me a test? Aw, Micah, you know I ain't good with schooling. Can't read or write. You know that."

"No, Jed." Micah thrust the paper at his friend. "This is my will. It says what to do with my possessions after I die—"

"What you talking 'bout?" Jed sat up and became fully alert. "You ain't gonna die."

"How can you say that? Seventeen of us are going to die tomorrow. I am certain I'll be one of them. I got a premonition."

"A prema—what?"

"Never mind," Micah said impatiently. "This paper says you are to get my land allotments. Put it in your pocket and keep it safe. I won't be around to take care of you no more, Jed. It will be important for you to have this land so's you can make a living. You can't go back to stealing and such, or even rangering."

"I can't be no farmer. I don't know nothing about it."

"You can, Jed. I know you can. I know lots of men without learning who make good farmers. You gotta take this land and make a life for yourself." Micah stuffed the paper into Jed's pocket. "Maybe Tom will help you. I had the feeling when we last saw him that he was ready to settle down."

"Maybe you should give the land to him."

"I want you to have it."

Tom had land, and if not, he had the wits to fend for himself. Jed would need all the help he could get. Even with the land, Micah was afraid of what would become of Jed when he was left all alone. He couldn't do anything about it now. He hoped the land would be enough.

It would sure do more good than some lame letter to his father with foolish words of forgiveness.

The next morning the prisoners were gathered in the courtyard of the prison. Each man stepped forward and dipped into the jar. Bill McBroome drew the first black bean. A grim smirk twisted his lips as he defiantly flicked the damning bean in the direction of the commander.

As Big Foot's turn came he commented to Micah and Jed, who would draw after him, "Them black beans are on top, so dig deep." He drew a white bean.

Micah's turn came and he hardly gave it a thought as he thrust his hand into the jar. He didn't even look at the bean he drew but simply headed to where the unlucky black bean holders had gathered.

"Look at what you got!" Big Foot yelled.

Micah glanced at his hand and was shocked to see he held a white bean. He wanted to whoop but didn't because there were still men who were going to die that day.

Jed came next. He dipped into the jar. Micah watched casually. Then he felt as if the hard earth of the prison yard had been suddenly yanked out from under him. His knees trembled, but he remained on his feet. He rubbed his eyes, but that did not change what he saw. Jed drew a black bean. Jed was no less shocked as he glanced at his death warrant. He looked at Micah beseeching, as if asking his friend to get him out of this mess. Micah wanted to run forward and exchange beans with his friend. He would have, too. He made the move, but Big Foot's big hand stopped him.

"Micah, they won't allow it," the ranger said, as if reading Micah's thoughts.

"They can't! He—"

"He took his chances with the rest of us. He's smarter than we give him credit for."

"But . . . but . . ." How could Micah make them understand? It was supposed to be him. He was supposed to die that day, not Jed. What had gone wrong?

"You let him die like a man," Big Foot said. "That's all you can do for him now."

Micah thought of the worthless paper in Jed's pocket, his lame attempt to help his friend. But Micah had been so preoccupied with himself, his stupid fears, he had not even thought to give Jed a chance to talk about his own fears. What had Jed been going through last night? What was he going through now? Micah would never know. He opened his hand and looked disdainfully at the white bean still clutched in his fist. He dropped it to the ground and smashed it with the heel of his boot.

"Jed . . . I'm sorry . . . I . . . can't help you," he intoned miserably.

"It's all right, Micah," Jed said, the shock beginning to clear from his face. "You done good by me, Micah. I wouldn't have made it this long without you." His lip trembled a little, but he bit down on it firmly.

Bill McBroome stepped from the growing group of doomed men. He put an arm around Jed and nudged him into the group. "Jed, you are gonna see your ma and pa soon."

Jed visibly brightened. "That's right! Ya hear that, Micah? It's what I been wanting. Remember? I dreamed it. Don't worry 'bout me no more. My ma will look after me now."

If Micah had not been forced to watch the executions, he probably would have hid in his cell, burrowing into the deepest, darkest corner he could find. That is exactly what he did afterward—figuratively, since it was not always possible to do so literally. For weeks he retreated within himself, becoming dark and glum. And the nightmares he thought he had finally escaped returned in full force. There was not a night that passed undisturbed by visions of death and violence.

PART THREE

SPRING 1844

CHAPTER 28

It had been a long trail from Mexico City. A hungry trail, a thirsty trail, a lonely trail.

Most of the time Micah wondered if he'd ever see Texas again. Sometimes he thought it might be best if he never went back. Too much water under the bridge, as it's said. Life had been too hard and grim in the last year since his capture. The filth and privations of prison, the struggle to survive were enough to change any man. Add to that the last couple of months since he and a handful of others had finally made good an escape.

This time they had hoped to increase their chances of getting home by splitting up. But it had been hard going trekking alone on foot through wild lands where, if there were people, he was the enemy. And because he was a fugitive, he often had to hide from danger or fight his way from place to place.

He didn't make directly for home because at first he hadn't been certain if he wanted to return to Texas at all. He had nothing there, nothing but failure and sour memories. So Micah wandered aimlessly about the Mexican countryside, and if he appeared to be heading north, it was only unconsciously, until finally the loneliness became more crushing than his fears about home. Tom was there, and the rangers. They had been like a family to him and could be again. They would accept what he had become. Many of them had suffered similarly.

Funny, though, when he thought of going home and what he would do there, it never occurred to him to return to his former life of crime.

Well, the idea might have flickered across his mind briefly, but he'd never risk seeing the inside of a prison again if he could help it.

Yet even with a purpose, it was difficult getting to the Rio Grande. He had no money and no weapons, except a knife he had stolen along the way. If he had to justify that act, he reminded himself that he was in enemy territory, and anything he took to survive was merely contraband. He became quite adept at stalking animals and killing them with only a knife. He also had been without a horse for much of the time. Only in Laredo was he accepted enough to be able to find a steady job sweeping and cleaning up in a cantina. He stayed only until he had earned enough to buy a few supplies. He got some clothes, used but in far better shape than the rags he'd been wearing since prison. They were mostly Mexican, including a sombrero and a striped serape. But more importantly he was able to purchase a cheap pistol and a mount and tack.

Micah let a bitter smile slip across his brown weathered face. It wasn't rightly a horse he ended up with, but rather a mule, and a poor excuse for one at that. He was the color of the blasted desert earth, and Micah called the beast Stew, because once when the animal was being particularly obstinate, Micah had yelled, "You mangy, no-good churn-head. Ya ain't good for nothing but a pot of stew!"

It indicated the extremity of Micah's solitary condition when he began to converse with Stew often and even started to take a liking to the creature. At least when he didn't want to kill the mule. Micah figured they deserved each other, and if there was a God, He was surely feeling mighty pleased at the circumstances.

The blast of a gunshot interrupted Micah's thoughts. Instinct alone made him dig his heels into Stew's flanks. He forgot about the tender place in Stew's stomach where the beast had once, before Micah's ownership, been mauled by a cougar. The crazy animal reared, and Micah fought to get him under control as another shot split the air several feet away. If he could get to some cover, he could dismount and make use of his pistol. But the land surrounding him was pretty open, tall grass and nary a tree in sight. As the mule sprang into a very reluctant gallop,

Micah ventured a quick glance back. There were three riders, and they appeared to be gringos. They might be rangers, but why would they be shooting at him without cause? Then he remembered his appearance. If they were looking for banditos, he certainly looked the part.

"Hah, Stew!" he yelled over the heavy beating of the mule's hooves. Though the animal was stubborn and mean spirited at times, he could be fast when he wanted, and with shots blasting in his ears, he definitely wanted to now!

Micah led a good chase. He broadened the distance between himself and his pursuers so that they no longer took shots at him. A dry riverbed spread out before him, and he scrambled down its moderately steep bank. He quickly jumped from the mule and took up a position near some rocks, the only cover to be found. When the riders crested the rise, he fired over their heads.

He'd chosen his spot well for making his stand, because the lowering sun was in the pursuers' eyes at the top of the bank, and by the time they oriented themselves as to the direction of the shot, Micah had reloaded. As he took aim, he got a better look at the three riders.

"My pistol's aimed right for your heart, Tom Fife!" Micah shouted. "I sure don't want to kill you the first time I seen you in over a year."

"Mercy me! I sure recognize that voice," Tom said.

"It's me, you dunderhead! Micah Sinclair. Promise ya won't shoot, and I'll give ya a look."

"Go ahead," agreed Tom.

Cautiously Micah stepped out into the open, flicking off his sombrero as he did so. Tom's grin made him drop all further cautions. He strode up to the three. Jack Hays and Ben McCulloch were riding with Tom. They all dismounted. Tom crushed Micah into a breath-stealing bear hug. The others slapped his shoulder until he was sure he'd be bruised. But if he'd had doubts before about returning home, they were gone now. He did indeed have friends.

"What you doing traipsing around looking like a bandito?" Tom asked.

"Don't be too hard on him," Hays said. "If he was a bandito, we'd be done for now. I'm glad to see prison hasn't dulled your edge, Micah."

"I got plenty of edges. And as for the clothes, I had to take what I could get."

"You coming back to San Antonio?" Tom asked.

"That was in my mind."

"Well, we can use you," said Ben. He glanced at Hays. "That right, Jack?"

"No doubt about it," Hays concurred. "Say, I think we have earned a bit of a rest. Let's sit a spell and talk."

There were cottonwoods on the other side of the riverbed that provided some shade, so the men let their horses graze while they sat beneath the boughs of the trees. Stew wandered back and joined the horses.

The men broke out jerked venison and hardtack from their packs, sharing what they had with Micah, whose supplies had run low since Laredo. As they ate, Micah related briefly about his escape and trek across Mexico. He omitted much detail, and the others seemed to understand because they asked few questions. On the other hand, he freely quizzed them on their activities in the last year, and they were just as free to talk.

"Had quite a time keeping the rangers together all year," Hays said. "Funds, as usual, were low. Sometimes there was as few as fifteen of us to patrol the entire Nueces-Rio Grande region. As much as Houston wants to make the borders safe from raids by Mexicans, he also wants to keep a lid on us raiding them. He wants peace so as to help his efforts to join up with the United States."

"Things did quiet down a mite last year," Tom said. "A few Indian raids and some harassing by banditos, but it could've been worse. The final two months of last year we were out of action completely."

"Jack even took a vacation," McCulloch said.

"He went a-courting, is what he did!" Tom added with a grin.

Steely-eyed Jack Hays, "Devil Jack" as the Comanches called him, looked about as close to blushing as he ever would. "Well, a man's got a right to a vacation once in a while, now, don't he?" he sputtered gruffly to hide his embarrassment.

Everyone laughed, even Jack. And Micah realized what these men meant to him. He was laughing, really laughing, for the first time in a year. He was truly with amigos, and he had forgotten what that meant.

When the joke had played itself out, Micah asked, "Well, since you are out on patrol again, are things better?"

"In February Congress authorized the formation of another ranger company," Hays said.

"And for the first time ever, they did it right!" added Tom. "They specifically designated Jack to be the commander, not that we wouldn't have voted for him anyway, but they finally are giving credit where credit is due. We voted for Ben here to be lieutenant. They allowed for forty rangers in the company. We up to that yet, Jack?"

"Nearly, but we got room for you, Micah."

"Count me in, Captain. I'd be honored to serve." In one sense Micah was growing tired of fighting and violence, but stronger than this was the sense that he didn't know what he'd do without the rangers right now. He needed them, if only because he had nothing else to turn to.

"Pay's fairly regular, too. Thirty dollars a month, paid every two months." Hays glanced at the grazing horses. "Looks like you got a good mount."

Micah shrugged. "He's learning, if mules *can* learn. But he did outrun you fellows." Then he remembered another important piece of equipment he was lacking. "I only got this here beat-up old flintlock pistol."

"We'll fix you up," Hays said.

"We have finally been issued Colt revolvers," Tom said with a gleam of delight in his squinty eyes. "I know it don't matter much to a crack shot like you, Micah, but for the rest of us, them revolvers are pure heaven."

The men talked for a few more minutes, then mounted up. After three hours they joined up with the rest of the company, then Hays told Micah to go on back to San Antonio so he could get his equipment squared away before officially joining the company. Tom was to go with him.

It was a two-day ride back to town. Neither he nor Tom were great talkers, but it was hard to avoid all conversation. Not that Micah wanted to, but he knew that with Tom alone, talk might get more personal. He was right.

"I still can't believe it about Jed," Tom said as they rode the next morning. "It was hard on you, wasn't it, Micah?"

"It was a heck of a lot harder on him," Micah said glibly.

"You know what I mean. You two was close, like brothers."

Micah nodded. His chest tightened. He still could not think about Jed without deep emotion, much less talk about him.

"I liked that boy, annoying laugh, slow wits, and all!" Tom said. "Wish there was some way to make them Mexicans pay."

"I reckon it won't bring Jed or the others back."

Tom's brow arched. "Don't sound like you, Micah." He peered more closely at his friend. "You've changed some, haven't you?"

Micah sighed heavily. "I guess I have, but mostly . . . I don't know . . . mostly I'm just too tired to hate right now. Maybe later it'll come back to me."

"Maybe it won't, and that'd be good. The hate was eating you up."

Micah thought of the last person who had expressed a similar sentiment to him. It wasn't the first time this past year he had thought of her, though he had tried mighty hard not to. But Lucie Maccallum had always been the sweetest, most pure thing in his life, and it had been especially true in the last year. Thinking of her had been both agony and delight. Sometimes he had needed delight so badly he had been willing to risk pain and agony to find it.

"So, Tom . . ." he tried to sound casual, but he could think of no way to broach the subject that was on his heart in an offhand or casual way. "You ever catch that Joaquin Viegas?"

Tom gave Micah a skeptical glance, then a slow smile inched across his whiskered face. "No, but it was him we was chasing yesterday when we ran into you. But I don't reckon you want to know about him as much as about his sister."

Micah shrugged. "How is she?"

"Last I heard she is fine. Her pa is still ailing, hardly leaves his bed is what I've heard."

"He's no doubt glad she is securely married."

"Married? Where you hear that?"

Micah took off his hat and wiped a sleeve across his sweaty brow. "I assumed she would have married that young Carlton fellow by now."

"Ha!" Tom spit into the dirt. "She'd have nothing to do with him. Why, it was his pa that fired up the ranchers against them after the invasion."

"That so?" Micah tried not to think anything of this news, yet his thumping heart betrayed him. Lucie was free! But he harshly reminded himself that free or not, they had said good-bye over a year ago, and for very good reasons—reasons that he clearly knew had not changed. He was wilder than ever and far less fit for a woman like that.

"You ought to go see her," Tom said.

Micah almost laughed at that. "Look at me, Tom! You said I'd changed, and I have, but not all for the good—very little, in fact. I've got scars inside me that a gal like that just should never have to look at."

"I'll bet that gal has a real knack at fixing wounds and such."

"Not mine. They're too deep. I'm just too far gone and wild."

The conversation waned, much to Micah's relief, as they came to a stream and had to concentrate on crossing it. The water was deep with spring runoff, and Stew was in no mind for a swim that day. A distaste for water was another of the critter's faults and now he fairly screeched to a stop and refused to move. Finally Micah was forced to blindfold the creature before he'd test the water. Once they reached the other side, as the sun beat down upon their wet bodies, warming and drying them, Tom spoke again.

"Micah, you don't know much about women," he said as he removed his bandanna and squeezed the water from it.

"And I suppose you are gonna teach me? You, who's been a confirmed bachelor all your life!"

"I know a sight more'n you give me credit for! I know that women were made for taming men. It is the natural way of things. The men come west to fight, to hunt, to raise Cain. And the women come with the cookstoves and the china and the pretty calico to make curtains on the log cabin windows. And we're glad they do, too, even if we complain about getting tied down, because down deep, part of us wants peace as much as them. We want it, but we only know the way of violence to get it unless the womenfolk show us another way. Oh, I reckon it ain't as simple as all that 'cause I ain't one of them philosophers. But it is still the basic truth that women want to tame men, and men want to be tamed—by women at least."

Micah looked away, but there was only grass ahead, and it was a poor distraction.

"I don't know, Tom," he said finally.

"If I could find a woman that'd have me, I'd jump at it." Tom looked ahead as well, but there was a dreamy quality to his voice. "Yes . . . I wouldn't mind it at all. A by-the-hearth kind of life. Do a little farming, raise a few young'uns."

"Ain't you too old to have kids, Tom?" Micah asked in an attempt to redirect the conversation.

"That ain't the point!" Tom answered crisply, not to be deterred.

"I know . . ."

"You won't regret letting her tame you, Micah."

"I know, but I'm afraid she'd regret trying."

CHAPTER

YOU GO BACK FOR THE OTHERS. I'll keep on the trail." Micah gazed ahead. There was no sign of riders, but they could not have passed that way more than a couple of hours ago.

"There's a half dozen of them," Tom said. "Ain't worth the risk. Besides"—Tom peered up into the darkening sky—"there's a storm coming. We don't want to get caught in it."

"The storm's a long way off," Micah countered. "And Viegas could be one of them bandits. It's worth the risk."

Micah had been back at the job a couple of weeks and was now on patrol tracking the banditos responsible for raiding a couple of ranches. An hour ago, Tom and Micah had picked up the trail of two riders. They were definitely not Indian, and by the look of the tracks, could well be Mexican. These tracks were the first bit of luck any of the rangers had come across. Now those tracks had met up with several more. There was no way Micah intended to lose them.

"All right," Tom said, "you go back. I'll keep—"

"Uh-uh!" Micah said firmly. "I saw the tracks first. You know my eyes are better than yours, and I got a better chance of sticking with them."

"But it's me giving the orders!"

Micah glanced up at the sky. The sun, when clouds weren't obscuring it, was directly overhead. The day was slipping away. "Be reasonable, Tom. I am the better tracker."

"I taught you all you know."

"Then you know I am good."

Tom cursed under his breath. "I knew I'd regret taking you in."

"Let's get moving. Time's a-wasting."

"You leave clear sign of where you're heading."

"I will. I will!"

Micah watched Tom turn around and head back in the direction from which they had come, then he urged his mount forward.

An hour later, he felt he was gaining on the bandits. The tracks were fresher, but he still saw no riders, which was just as well because neither did he wish to be seen by them. He just hoped Tom and the others caught up to him soon, or he'd have to give up the chase. The wind was steadily increasing, and Stew was getting restive. The temperature was dropping so Micah took his buckskin coat from his saddlebag and slipped it on.

He wondered if it was Viegas's gang he was following. What would he do if he caught up with the outlaw, Lucie's brother? He had no doubt

Viegas would rather die than be caught, and Micah also had little doubt that he himself would kill the man if given cause. He hoped he wasn't placed in such a position, but Viegas was the enemy, and he, as much as any Mexican national, was responsible for Jed's death.

No, he'd have no qualms about killing Lucie's brother. But then, it shouldn't matter where he and Lucie were concerned because there was no "he and Lucie." Why he kept thinking of her he didn't know. It wasn't healthy, that was for sure, not the way his guts twisted every time thoughts of her came into his mind.

Squinting ahead, he forced his mind back to business. He thought he spotted a small stirring of dust. Maybe it was just the wind, or maybe he was getting too close to his quarry. Then he felt a prickly sensation on the back of his neck. He jerked his head around. Small black spots on the horizon behind him were definitely approaching riders. Could they be the rangers? The cloud of dust surrounding them indicated they were gaining fast on Micah. There were three riders. The mounts did not look familiar. Tom's gray was definitely not among them. In another couple of minutes they would be within rifle range.

"Hah, Stew!" Micah slapped the mule's flanks with his reins. The mule skittered, then started at a reluctant trot. "Hah, you stupid beast!" Micah yelled. This time he purposefully dug his heels into Stew's middle, knowing it always made the mule mad and probably hurt like the dickens, but sometimes it was the only way to get him moving. Stew skittered again, bucked a little, snorted, then shot into motion. Micah made no apology to his less-than-faithful mount, for just then the riders started shooting. The shots made on horseback were not very accurate, but they were close enough to worry Micah.

In the flurry of his escape, Micah forgot about that cloud of dust he'd seen in front of him earlier. But now his error was deadly plain. The cloud was three more riders coming right at him. He thought of his bravado with Tom before. A better tracker! Ha! The banditos had no doubt spotted him an hour ago, then split up to catch him in a trap. And he had accommodated them beautifully.

His only chance now was to surrender and hope they were more interested in taking a prisoner than in killing one. That at least would give him time to think of another way out of this mess or give the other rangers a chance to catch up to him. He reined in Stew, then tossed his rifle to the ground and thrust his hands high into the air. Then he waited for the inevitable slug of lead to his heart.

Though he hoped to be spared, he was no less shocked when the bandits rode up to him and did not shoot.

"Your other weapons," one of the bandits ordered.

There were six banditos, all with weapons trained on Micah. He quickly obeyed the order, tossing down his brace of pistols and, with just a slight hesitation, also throwing down his new Colt .44 revolver. He had only had the weapon for a week, and he had come to like it a lot. He doubted Hays would issue him another one soon.

"The Bowie knife, too, eh?" said the bandit.

Micah complied. He was now completely disarmed except for the small knife he kept in his boot, not that it would do him any good in this situation. It was as he dropped the Bowie knife that he saw the rattler coiled up near a rock. Its head was raised as it contemplated this disturbance of its afternoon nap. Micah's captors had not seen the snake, and Micah wondered how he could use it to his advantage.

"So . . . I think we have found ourselves a ranger," the bandit said.

Micah said nothing.

Another bandit spoke in Spanish, "Gustavo, he must have *compadres* close. Kill him and let's go."

Micah had learned enough Spanish in Mexico to understand what was said.

The one called Gustavo said in English to Micah, "Where are the other rangers? You surely did not come after us all alone."

Again in Spanish the second bandit said, "I know this one. He is dangerous. We must kill him."

Micah knew his time was running out. Yet any escape he could think of would be suicidal. Still, even a futile attempt would be better than being gunned down like a sitting duck. Then it occurred to him how he could use the rattler. Ornery as his mule was, Micah didn't like endangering Stew, yet there seemed no other way.

Surreptitiously Micah pressed his heel into the tender place on the mule's midriff, not hard, but enough to cause discomfort. The mule, already nervous, snorted and skittered. Micah, appearing to rein him, instead edged him closer to the snake.

"Keep that mule under control," ordered Gustavo. Then to one of the other bandits he added, "Rodrigo, get those weapons and tie his hands."

The rattler, now in the mule's line of sight, moved. Stew saw and reacted predictably. He neighed shrilly and gave a panicked buck, encouraged by another prodigious jab in the stomach by Micah. Stew reared, causing a frenzied chain of events.

Rodrigo's mount, which was closest to Micah, was spooked either by Stew's behavior or by the snake. It also reared, and Rodrigo, who had been in the process of dismounting, spilled to the ground with a sickening thud. He lay still on the ground, but Micah could not pause to wonder about him. Micah could barely keep Stew under control as the rattler lurched. When he was thrown from the mule, it was only partly by design, however, he hit the ground fully prepared and made sure he rolled toward his discarded weapons.

"The ranger!" someone yelled.

By now all the horses were spooked, and their riders were having their own problems keeping them under control. One—Micah hoped it wasn't Stew—screamed as only a panicked horse can, and Micah was almost certain it must have been struck by the rattler. But he did not let himself dwell on this either. His full concentration was on the pile of weapons. His hand grasped one as a gunshot zinged past his ear. He rolled to the left toward the only cover he could find, a rock no larger than a tree stump. Flattening out behind it, he took quick aim and fired. A yell told him he had hit his mark before he saw the dead bandit with his own eyes.

Another slug whizzed over Micah's head, taking off his hat. He fired again, thankful his desperate plunge into the pile of weapons had been rewarded with the Colt. It had been fully loaded. His second shot took down another bandit. He had three shots left and there were three bandits remaining, not counting the one who had been thrown from his horse and was still unconscious. All Micah's spare ammunition and his powder horn were in his saddlebag, but even if he could have reached it, Stew had bolted.

The bandits had dismounted and taken cover behind the fallen horse, which must have been injured by snakebite or some other cause. The bandits might have made an attempt to ride off, even though they risked getting shot down in the attempt. They probably figured they had a better chance in a standoff. The odds were in their favor. He was only one man with three shots. But he had already killed two of them and caused another to be injured. This was his first real gunfight since coming back from Mexico. His first chance to avenge Jed and the others.

Another shot from the bandits grazed Micah's rock, sending a stinging spray of rock fragments into his face. Eyes burning, he fired back, but the shot only struck the dead horse. He cursed his foolishness. He couldn't afford any wild shots. Patience. And for the first time in a long time, he thought of when his Uncle Haden had taught him to shoot.

"Patience, boy, is the first and most important rule," he'd said often. "And always take time to sight your target."

Micah took a steadying breath and waited. There were three bandits behind that horse, and one was going to make a mistake sooner or later, hopefully before Micah did so himself.

"Listen to me, hombre," said the bandit called Gustavo, "you have two shots left. You don't have a chance. Give up."

"So you can kill me?"

"I would take you to see *mi jefe.* Perhaps he'll make a deal with you—information for your life, eh?"

"I'll take my chances with my two shots."

"You are a fool. There are three of us."

"And only one of you is gonna come out alive, so I'd suggest you discuss which of you it will be."

Micah knew his words were mere bravado, yet he had already made it further than he could have expected. Maybe the thirst for vengeance had finally returned to him.

The scraping sound behind him was so faint he might have mistaken it for the wind, yet something made him turn. He fired practically in the same instant he saw the figure approaching from behind. Micah did not pause to watch the man fall, nor to ascertain if his shot had been fatal. He knew it had been. He also knew the man had circled behind him in order to create a diversion. And in the next instant, Micah spun around.

A lead ball grazed his right shoulder before he could get his shot off; another shot blasted within an inch of his ear. But that was the bandits' mistake. They were not carrying revolvers. He noted that one now had to pause to reload. The other lifted his second pistol to fire, but Micah was faster. He fired and the man—Micah noted it was the one named Gustavo—fell forward, blood splurting from his head. Now only one bandit remained. But Micah's Colt was empty.

He and the last bandit exchanged looks of desperation. In that exchange, he saw in the bandit's eyes that there was no possibility of a truce. This was the same man who had wanted to kill him in the first place. But Micah had killed four of them. Four! Vengeance is mine, he thought. If he died now, he could do so vindicated. But why didn't it feel better? Why were his insides suddenly quaking? He'd killed four men. Mexicans. The enemy. For Jed.

But this was no time for thinking!

Micah knew he had only a moment before the remaining bandit reloaded. Swallowing rising bile in his throat, he made a dive for his discarded weapons still lying on the ground in the middle of the small battlefield. Ignoring the throbbing ache in his gun hand from his wounded shoulder, ignoring the wrenching of his guts, Micah laid his hand on the butt of one of his pistols.

He was too late. The bandit had reloaded.

The man fired and, amazingly, missed! But the shot struck the earth close to where Micah was lying on the ground, and it sent more dirt and grit into his eyes. Though momentarily blinded, he knew if he didn't do something quickly, the bandit would reload and finish him off. This was survival, not vengeance, he told himself. He raised his pistol, but his eyes were blurred.

"Always take time to sight your target . . ." his uncle's words echoed in his benumbed mind.

Why hadn't he asked his uncle what to do if you were blind?

The enemy's weapon should be loaded by now. He'd be taking aim. Micah raised his pistol, not aiming, not thinking, allowing pure instinct to guide him. He fired. He felt like an animal attacking an enemy, acting and reacting instinctively. What would the animal do now that all his options were used up? Micah groped around for the other weapons, all the while waiting for that final fatal shot, the one that would at last end his miserable life. But nothing came. He heard no more shots. He lifted himself up. Through the blur of his vision he saw that the last bandit was sprawled over the carcass of the dead horse. Were they all dead, then?

Micah sat there for some time, too spent to feel even relief. He just sat listening to himself breathe, amazed that he *was* breathing. Then he heard the sound of stirring. He vaguely realized it must be the unconscious bandit finally coming to. A sudden fear, a kind of dread, washed over Micah. He knew he wasn't afraid of dying. But what was it?

"*¡Madre de Dios!*" exclaimed the bandit as he struggled to his knees and surveyed the battlefield. He then focused wild eyes upon Micah, as if he were looking upon evil incarnate.

Only then was Micah fully aware of the scene surrounding him. A dead horse. Five bodies. Blood. Death. And there must still be more death. He knew then that this was the cause of his dread. He would have to kill yet again. But his body seemed to be functioning completely apart from his appalled mind. In a flash, before he had even given conscious impetus to the action, Micah had the other pistol in his hand. There was a single split second when the thought flickered on the edge of Micah's mind that he didn't have to kill this man. The bandit was reaching for his pistol, but there could not be time for him to draw it. Yet it all transpired in the space of a single heartbeat—the stray thought and Micah's trigger finger twitching faster than his mental ability to grasp the thought. His gun blasted, and the last bandit fell.

Suddenly Micah's hand began trembling so badly that the gun fell to the ground. His stomach roiled and heaved, and before he could even turn his head aside, he vomited all over himself. His legs had turned to mush, and he could not stand. He sat and stared, but everywhere he looked there were bodies.

What had he done?

The sound of galloping horses thundered through the afternoon air, heavy with the silence of death. Within five minutes Micah was surrounded by his friends.

"You all right?" Tom asked with concern. It seemed a silly question to Micah. He was alive. There were six dead men. How could he be all right?

"You done well, Micah," Hays said.

Micah stared at him, uncomprehending. "They're all dead," he said. He tried to force himself to stand, but the ground seemed to be buckling underneath him, and he had to stay put. He looked at Tom. "They . . . are . . . dead. . . ."

"You did what you had to do," Tom said, as he kneeled next to Micah and made an attempt to tend his wounds.

"What shooting!" exclaimed Bert Long. "How many weapons did you have?"

Micah gaped at the unabashed awe in the man's voice. Then his stomach betrayed him again. This time he turned aside and emptied its contents onto the dirt. But his insides kept heaving.

"This ain't the first time you've killed, Micah," Tom said. "What's wrong, boy?" His eyes carefully scanned Micah's body again, looking for hidden wounds.

"N-nothing," Micah rasped, his voice as thin and empty as his stomach.

Micah remembered the first time he killed a man. San Jacinto. He hadn't been sick at all. He'd been fourteen and had not felt even a twinge. He'd joined the slaughter with relish. Now he was a man who had been in many battles, killed many times. What was happening to him?

"H-help me up, Tom," he said. He saw Tom and Hays exchange worried looks. "I gotta get out of here!"

"Soon as we find that mule of yours."

Micah struggled on his own to gain his feet. Tom, apparently seeing the futility of trying to get him to stay put, gave him a hand. His knees were shaky, but he willed himself to be steady.

"Let me take your horse, Tom."

"We'll all be heading back together soon enough," Tom argued.

Micah leveled a look at his friend that he knew was filled with desperation. He didn't know where the feeling was coming from. He did not understand any of it. All he knew was he had to get away from this place of blood and death. The men would want to do something about the bodies. But he could not stay.

"Tom!" Micah came as close to pleading as he ever had in his life.

Hays stepped forward. "Let him go, Tom. He just needs some time to himself."

"Take my horse," Tom said. "But take this as well." He held out his revolver.

Micah recoiled from the weapon, shaking his head. "Don't you see, Tom?"

"No, I don't see at all!"

Dismally, Micah said, "Neither do I."

He mounted Tom's gray gelding and rode away. Just *away.* He had no place to go *to.*

CHAPTER 30

THE RAIN CAME AS IT only can on the Texas prairie, hard and heavy. The wind from the south drove the rain, mixed liberally with hail, into Micah's face. Lightning flashed, ragged and blinding in the night sky, followed by cracks of ear-splitting thunder. Tom's gray winced occasionally. Stew would have bolted and run for it by now.

Micah was soaked to the skin, all the blood and dirt and stomach contents washed away. But he still felt dirty. He'd killed six men. And was Jed truly avenged? Had any amount of killing ever given him peace about his uncle's death? Would he have to keep killing forever and ever?

Would he never feel clean and at peace?

Through the rain and darkness, he saw a light ahead. He steered toward it. He wasn't surprised by the light, though why he expected lamps to still be burning this late, he didn't know. He only knew that an hour ago he had begun to veer toward the Maccallum ranch. In a way, his direction had been as involuntary as that last shot in the gunfight had been. Some reflex had driven him to kill. Another reflex was driving him toward the exact opposite. The only thing Micah knew for certain was that just then he needed to find for himself, killer that he was, something completely pure and good. And Lucie was the only thing like that he'd ever known.

No one stirred at the ranch. The light he'd seen was coming from the bunkhouse. A dog barked. He rode toward the house, dismounted, and climbed the step to the porch. It took almost as much courage, or audacity, to raise his hand and knock on the door of the darkened house as it had to gun down six bandits.

For a few moments there was no response, then the light of a lantern shone through the front window.

"Who is it?" came Lucie's voice.

Just that sound made his heart do such strange things. How he needed her!

"Me," he said, foolishly thinking that she'd recognize his voice after more than a year. But his lips were trembling with cold and fear and such a longing ache that he could say no more.

He heard the metal latch being thrown back. Then the door opened, and there she was. Lucie. Real flesh and blood. Not a dream. His throat was too tight and dry to speak.

"Micah!" She was dressed in a long white nightgown with a wool shawl drawn closely around her. Her hair hung loose about her shoulders.

He'd never seen it loose before. He wanted desperately to plunge his face into the mass of dark curls.

He tried to speak instead. "L-Lucie, I . . . I . . . I killed six banditos." The words spilled out before he could stop them. He wanted comfort, but part of him must have wanted punishment as well.

Her hand went to her lips. "Joaquin!" she gasped.

"No."

She sagged visibly with relief.

"Lucie," called Reid Maccallum's voice from the back of the house, "is something wrong?"

"No, Papa." Her eyes scanned Micah, pausing briefly where the buckskin of his jacket was rent and his wound gaped through. "It's nothing, Papa. Go back to sleep." She reached a hand toward Micah's shoulder. Quietly, she said, "You're hurt."

"I had to see you."

"Just a moment." She turned back into the house, closing the door. In five minutes she returned, wearing a hooded cloak over her nightgown and carrying a basket. "Let's go to the stable. I can't see you in the house. Papa has such a hard time sleeping."

He followed her, pausing only to take the gray's reins and lead him also. "It's Tom's horse," he mumbled. "Can't let anything happen to it. I don't have good luck with horses. I . . . I lost the buckskin in the war."

In the stable Lucie lit a lantern while Micah put the gray in an empty stall that Lucie directed him to. As he unsaddled the horse, Lucie gave the animal some fresh straw.

Then she said, "Now for you, Micah." She took his hand and led him to a stool. "Sit and take off your jacket and shirt. I've got some medicine here and some bandages." He sat and she kneeled on the hay-strewn floor at his feet.

He shrugged out of his jacket, then noticed the hole. "Look . . ." He fingered the tattered hole, stained with blood and gunpowder. "I . . . can't have nothing fine," he mumbled.

"Your shirt, Micah? So I can see your wound," she prompted.

"I don't care about that," he said. "It doesn't bother me."

"The rain has probably cleaned it out pretty well, but it could fester. Let me have a look at it."

Because he wanted only to hold her, to smell the fragrance of her hair, feel her lips on his, he obeyed her command. He couldn't touch her. He shouldn't touch her. He wouldn't touch her.

Lucie still could hardly believe that after more than a year, Micah had turned up on her doorstep. Wet, disheveled, and obviously distraught, but there he was, the reality of her dreams. Forbidden dreams, but ones she could not prevent in sleep.

Unable to put her thoughts in a proper frame, she clung to the practical. "The wound is deep, but the lead did not penetrate."

"It grazed me, is all."

His voice was distracted, almost dull, yet there was an intensity in his eyes that made the cool of the blue seem almost on fire.

She poured a couple drops of liquid from a brown bottle onto a cloth, a concoction of balm of Gilead buds mixed with rum that Juana swore by for open wounds. Micah winced as she dabbed it on his shoulder. "The alcohol burns a little."

A whole year and all she could talk about was his wound. No, there was much she wanted to say, but they had said good-bye. Yet he had just told her he had to see her. What had he meant? More to the point, what had it meant when her heart had leaped upon seeing him and she had wanted only to throw herself into his arms?

"How long have you been back?" she asked as she placed a clean bandage on his wound.

"A couple of weeks." His eyes briefly flickered toward her, then he jerked them away. He was afraid to look at her, yet there was yearning in his eyes. "I know I shouldn't have come. We said good-bye."

"Micah, what happened?" She, too, focused her eyes elsewhere, on her work. She wrapped the bandage under his arm and back over the wound. "You said you've been in a . . . a gunfight?"

He nodded, still staring somewhere over the top of her head. "Six banditos took me prisoner, but I got away."

"You killed them all? By yourself?"

"It was them or me," he said defensively.

"Oh, Micah!"

"I didn't want to!"

She lifted her eyes, but still he looked away.

"Jed was executed in Mexico, you know that? He and sixteen others were shot down, and for what?" He shook his head, the muscles in his jaw and neck twitching violently.

"So you got your revenge." She could not help the words.

Micah started to jump up, but she laid a restraining hand on his other shoulder so she could finish the bandage. He glanced down at her hand, and only then did she realize she was touching his bare chest. She jerked her hand away as if from a hot iron, and he jerked to his feet. He paced a few steps away from her, then turned. She could not read the expression on his face.

"It made me sick, and I don't know why," he said plaintively.

"You killed six men, Micah!" It seemed so obvious to her.

"I've killed before."

"Vengeance wasn't as sweet as you hoped it would be."

"Lucie, I'm scared!"

She could tell he had never admitted such a thing before.

Rising, she went to him and took his hands into hers. They were rough, coarse hands, hands that had just taken six lives. Lethal hands, deadly hands. She brought them to her lips.

"Don't be frightened," she said as she kissed his palms. "Your reaction is a good thing. You are not a killer in your heart. Maybe at last your heart is trying to tell you that."

"Being a ranger is the only life I have," he said miserably. "If I can't . . . use my gun, I don't have nothing."

"Micah, are you afraid because you might not be able to kill anymore?" She could not prevent the slight rancor in her tone. She dropped his hands.

"What else have I?"

"Micah!" she exclaimed in frustration. Then she turned her back to him and walked to a nearby stall. Looking over the top of the low wall, she saw the gray gelding munching placidly on hay. She felt Micah come up behind her and stop when he was so close she could feel the heat of his body nearly sear into her back.

He spoke softly. "I knew when that last bandit fell today that it wasn't gonna help cure my anger. Maybe that's what made me sick. All the Mexicans I've killed over the years trying to heal the wounds from Goliad, and now with Jed, too—suddenly I saw no matter how many I killed, it wouldn't help. It had never helped, but maybe I'd hoped there'd be a magic number that would finally clean my filthy soul. But there isn't. The hate is there, the loss is there, the hurt is there, and nothing will stop it."

"That's not true, Micah. There is one thing that will stop it."

"I don't want to hear it."

"But it's God you are really afraid of. And so to avoid Him, you will let yourself continue to wallow in your hate and pain."

He sighed, the puff of breath stirring the top of her head. "Yes, I think you may be right. But I won't hear of God."

She turned sharply, finding herself within an inch of him. She leveled her gaze at him, forcing him to return the look. "This isn't about your uncle or Jed and their killers. It is about your father. Why don't you kill him? He killed your mother, didn't he?"

"He's my father!"

"But you want to kill him, don't you?"

"No!"

"Instead you kill Mexicans."

"You are getting this all twisted up, Lucie."

"Maybe I am." She slipped past him. He had been way too close. She couldn't think straight. Her thoughts were all jumbled. Yet she knew all the hate in Micah stemmed from his father. She knew that was the key to everything. She sat on the stool. Maybe he wouldn't get so close to her then.

"All I came here for was—"

"What *did* you come here for?" she shot back accusingly. "Did you want some kind of absolution for what you did?"

"I just needed . . ." He dropped down in front of her, taking her shoulders in his hands. "You are the only good thing in my life. I thought if I was with you, it might make me forget who and what I am. Lucie . . . please . . ."

She remembered how in the past she'd felt his desperate need for love. It was there now. He needed so to be loved. And she did love him, but though she could not deny it to herself, she must deny her feelings to him.

His hands were trembling as they gripped her. She tried to ease from him, but he held her firm. Then his hands suddenly moved until he had pulled her fully into his arms. Plying her with kisses, he half carried, half dragged her to the floor, loosening her cape and casting it away.

"No, Micah!" She fought him, but he was heavy and too wrought to respond.

His kisses grew more and more intense, painfully intense.

"I need you so," he murmured. "I need your love."

"This isn't love—"

"No more preaching. No more talk. Hold me, Lucie. Please!" But he wasn't really asking, nor did he wait for a reply.

"Will you drag me down into that pit of hatred with you? Is that it?" She fought him even harder, especially as her own body began to betray her. How easily she could let herself succumb to him, for she loved him so. Yet she could not capitulate to her desires. It would hurt them both too deeply. Still, it was clear she couldn't fight him except with words. "Admit it, Micah, I am only another Mexican you will hurt today." She tried to spit the words out forcefully but could barely get them out because of his nearness.

"What? No! It's not—" Suddenly he stopped what he was doing. He pulled away, a look of utter horror on his face.

She thought he might be sick again, as he said he had been after his gunfight when he viewed the death in its wake.

He lurched to his feet and, saying nothing, grabbed his wet jacket and shirt. Slipping into the shirt, he went to the stall and saddled the gray.

"Micah, it's raining." He had nearly forced himself upon her, yet still she cared. She knew he had not acted out of spite or malice or evil.

He led the gray from the stall. "I'm sorry, Lucie. You don't have to worry about me bothering you ever again."

He walked out, and through the open door she watched him mount and ride away, rain and wind pelting him, darkness swallowing him.

CHAPTER 31

THE PERSISTENT THREAT OF INVASION from Mexico continued to hang over Texas. Internal political problems in Mexico spared the republic from a major confrontation, but there was still raiding along the border, and Hays had to take seriously any rumors of danger. One such rumor arrived while he and several other rangers were sick with fever. With forces low, he sent only four to scout it out: Tom, Micah, and two new men, Baker and Lowe.

In the weeks after Micah's shoot-out with the bandits, he had continued on as a ranger. He had no place else to go, and truth be told, he liked the work for the most part. He liked being needed and useful, although it irked him to no end when the men held him up as some kind of hero for that gunfight. It was worse when regular citizens did the same as tales of his feat spread.

At least in all that time he had yet to be in another gunfight. Mercifully, Hays had mostly used Micah as a courier to carry government dispatches to Washington-on-the-Brazos, the new capital of the republic since Austin had been abandoned during the invasion of 1842. Micah received extra pay for this and practically had the buckskin paid off. He made the payments by depositing them directly into Reid Maccallum's account at the bank. There was no need for any personal contact. No need at all.

Except where his heart was concerned. But he did not let himself think of that. If there had ever been a chance to win Lucie, he had destroyed it that night of the shoot-out. How could he have been so stupid? He'd been blinded, he supposed, by his own aching need. She'd been so right. It had nothing to do with love. Or so he told himself whenever a thought of Lucie would creep past his defenses and haunt his mind.

Bandits had been reported along Carrow Creek near the Nueces. And that's where the four rangers were headed. Micah dreaded the prospect of encountering more bandits. He hadn't killed Joaquin Viegas that last time, but he felt he was doomed to confront and kill the bandit sooner or later. In a life filled with irony and disaster, that would surely be the greatest of all.

Toward the end of the day the rangers made camp. Tom wanted to stop on high ground so they could have a better vantage, but the others convinced him to camp by the creek. It had been a blistering hot day for the end of May, and they wanted a swim.

Baker and Lowe stripped and were in the water while Micah was bringing the horses down to the creek to water them. Tom was up on the bank getting a fire going. A dozen Comanches were upon the rangers almost before they heard the war cries. Tom had grabbed his revolver and was firing, but an arrow struck him and he fell. The last Micah saw him, he was crawling toward the cover of a bush. Micah heard splashing in the water but did not have time to turn to see what Baker and Lowe were doing.

Snatching his revolver from his belt, he managed to get off a round and wound one of the Indians. Then an arrow penetrated his right arm, jolting his weapon from his hand. The arrow went out the other side, but the pain nearly took his breath away. He grabbed his pistol, also in his belt, then took a shot with his left hand that went wild. Another arrow struck him in the side, and while he managed to pull the arrow out through his back, the pain and sudden loss of blood brought him to his knees. He tried to see what had become of Tom, but he could not see his friend and could only hope he had managed to reach the cover of a nearby mesquite bush. Baker and Lowe were also nowhere to be seen.

Micah tried to reload his pistol, but his hand was shaking too much, and his powder horn fell to the ground. As he fumbled around for it, swaying on his knees, a final arrow struck him in the head, and he fell back into the dirt. He thought about finishing himself off before the Comanches got to him. He drew his Bowie knife and brought it to the vicinity of his heart, heedless of the obvious fact that at the moment he didn't have enough strength to plunge it into his chest. But before he could make the attempt, blackness engulfed him.

When he came to, all was quiet except for some low voices not far away.

"Them Comanches are gonna come back. Let's get out of here!" That was Lowe.

"We can't just leave them," Baker replied.

"They're dead, I tell you!"

"But—"

"Lowe . . . Baker . . ." Micah rasped from where he lay. He tried to move to give some sign that he was still alive.

"You ain't dead?" said Lowe.

Micah couldn't tell if that was surprise or disappointment in the man's voice.

"Tom?" Micah breathed, barely able to form words.

"Dead," Baker said.

Micah's vision was blurred by blood and pain, but he saw that Lowe and Baker were both dressed now and appeared fairly unscathed. They had probably managed to find cover during the battle.

"Those Indians will be back," Lowe said. "We gotta go."

"Horses . . . ?" Micah said.

"Only one left. The rest run off or the Indians got them."

"We ain't all gonna make it," Baker added, and to his credit, he seemed miserable about it.

"Sinclair, I think you know you are a goner. If we try to take you, we'll all get killed," Lowe said. He looked more afraid for himself than concerned about Micah.

Micah didn't blame him. It was just the practicality of the frontier. He was mortally wounded. He could feel the life drain from him as the blood flowed from his wounds. Words stuck in his throat, and he could only shake his head. Let them make of that what they wanted. He wasn't going to beg for his life.

They carried him to the other side of the creek and left him with a rifle. They mounted the horse and rode off, but Micah did not watch them. He couldn't keep his eyes open. He had cheated death way too often and knew his time had finally come.

When he didn't die immediately, however, Micah knew he couldn't just lie there and wait for it to happen. He crawled to the water's edge and took a couple handfuls of mud and leaves and packed his wounds in an attempt to staunch the flow of blood.

About a half hour later, the Indians returned. Micah had covered himself with branches and other debris, and the Comanches either did not see him or did not think him worth the effort of even scalping. They rode away.

Though the day had been hot, the night was freezing, at least it felt so to Micah, whose blood loss left little to insulate him from the cold. He dozed off a couple of times but knew he could not sleep or he'd never wake. When dawn came he took the rifle and, using it as a crutch, rose and started walking.He hated the thought of leaving Tom's body to the vultures, but he had no strength to do anything about it. Half the time he merely crawled, but he kept on the move without sleep or food except for a few mesquite beans and cactus apples. He was fortunate enough to encounter occasional watering holes to sustain him on the way.

Micah headed north. San Antonio was a hundred miles away, and he was certain he didn't have a chance of ever getting that far. He had resigned himself to the fact that he would soon die. He just knew he could not lie still and wait for that to happen. He could only travel a few miles at a time, then usually collapsed before he could decide for himself when to stop. A couple of times he merely passed out.

He kept this up for four days. When he had the capacity to think, which wasn't often, he wondered why he was doing this at all. He had no reason to go on. Lucie was lost to him. His friends were dead. Tom! Even Tom. The thought sliced through him worse than the pain of his wounds. Tom had been the only one left whom Micah cared about, and more to the point, the only one who Micah believed cared about him. Now there was no one. He was alone.

Why then was he struggling so to live?

Thankfully he blacked out once more, preventing further rumination. When he came to, the sun was beating down relentlessly upon him, and all he could think of was finding a drink of water. He crawled over miles of rocky earth and was so thoroughly scratched and cut, he appeared to be one large wound. He envisioned a swim in a cool, wet river, the water washing over every part of his scorched and bleeding body. He imagined the prickles of icy moisture getting into his mouth—cool, refreshing drops. He worked his thick, dry tongue over his lips but found only a cracked and swollen surface. No water.

Why wasn't he dead?

They're all dead. Jed, Tom. Uncle Haden. Mama . . .

Why not me? I killed them all.

"The wages of sin is death . . ."

Yes . . . I am a sinner . . . rotten . . . dirty . . .

"What do you want from me, boy! I admit I killed your mother. I am everything you believe me to be. I am a rotten, dirty sinner! I am the worst reprobate . . . a hypocrite. I deserve your hatred. But I need help. . . ."

I won't help you, Pa, but I can't kill you either. I can't . . . kill . . .

"Don't be frightened, Micah. This is a good thing. You are not a killer in your heart."

You are not a killer . . . Pa, you are not a killer.

Micah shut his eyes against the image of his father's agonized face, as he always had. But behind his closed eyes that image would not fade.

Instead, the face changed subtly into his own! Tears oozed from the eyes—his father's tears, his own eyes. Or were they his own tears also? He could no longer tell.

"You're going loco, Micah, plumb loco!" he rasped, shocked that any sound at all could come from his dry, constricted throat.

Using the rifle once more as a crutch, he distracted himself by trying to rise and walk. He took a couple of steps, but the world spun around, and he crumpled back to the ground.

"Die, you ornery critter!" he groaned.

But he dragged himself several feet more. He didn't know why.

Another night passed. He still did not let himself sleep if he could help it. But sleeping and waking had become blurred. Dreams or reality, he could no longer tell. He spoke to his mother, and he thought he truly had finally died. But something told him his wounds would not hurt as they did if he were dead. His father's face came often, but Micah shut it out when he could, yet too often he simply had no control over it.

The best times were when Lucie came to him. Sometimes he was able to forget that he had no right to dream of her. Sometimes he imagined they had a little farm and children and love, so much love.

On the sixth day, Micah found a watering hole. It was small and muddy, but he buried his face in it and drank as if it were a crisp mountain spring. Then he passed out.

He awoke to an odd sensation, like a feather gently brushing his face.

"Mama," he murmured, not knowing why he thought of his mother just then except that the feather was soft and comforting.

His eyes were swollen and stuck shut with discharge so that he could barely open them. But he struggled to do so, because if he was finally dead, if this was the comfort he'd sought for so many years, he wanted to look upon it. He parted his eyelids just enough to see a vague image hovering over him. Not his mother, but he still figured he must be dreaming.

"Stew!"

The mule nudged Micah's cheek with his nose.

"Ya ol' churnhead," Micah croaked. "Ya ain't as worthless as I thought."

Maybe it was a dream, but what did it matter? This was a dream to be grasped. Yet the struggle he had to mount the mule was proof it was real enough. He began to think it would have been easier to continue crawling on hands and knees. He passed out twice during the excruciating process, but each time that mule prodded him back to consciousness. Finally, making one concerted effort that nearly was the death of him, Micah straddled the animal. He tried to sit straight, but everything spun so horribly that he nearly fell off again. Leaning forward, he circled his arms around Stew's neck and laid his head against the animal's head. In that way, with occasional direction from Micah, the mule carried Micah back to San Antonio, less than a two-day ride. Incredibly, Micah had already traversed over fifty miles of the journey on foot.

When he came to the outskirts of the town, he tried to sit upright in the saddle. Some crazy pride made him not wish to ride into his town pitifully half dead. But the exercise was misplaced. The world spun, and Micah slipped from the saddle as the ground careened up to meet him.

"Pride goeth before a fall. . . ."

The words came to him as he hit the dirt.

CHAPTER 32

Death was more pleasant than Micah had imagined it would be, especially when he'd always been fairly certain he'd end up in hell. But here he was lying on something soft as a cloud, clean and white, too. Just as he'd imagined heaven to be.

He opened one eye, a little afraid at what he'd find. If this wasn't heaven, if he wasn't dead, then he'd have to keep on facing life, and he just didn't feel strong enough to do that. But his vision was blurry, and he could not tell much with only one eye, so he opened the other. What he saw were the rough wood beams of a ceiling. There was a cobweb in one corner. He'd bet money there were no cobwebs in heaven. He tried to move, and the sharp pain from several different places in his body quickly proved his fears.

He was alive.

"Hey!" he called, but he could not get his voice to rise above a whisper.

In a moment the door, which the bed faced, opened, and he thought if he wasn't dead he must still be dreaming, for the figure stepping into the room was garbed in checkered green calico and had hair like the night caught on fire.

"Lucie . . ." he breathed.

"You're awake," she said, her voice causing an ache inside him that had nothing to do with his wounds.

"What are you doing here?"

"I live here. This is my house."

"Then . . . what am I doing here?"

She smiled and drew closer to the bed. He noticed now that she was holding a small basin and a towel. She set these on the bedside table.

"I had them bring you here," she said. "The trip was risky from town, but Mr. Paschel had his hands full with so many down with fever. And he's not a doctor. He'd given you up for dead. And . . ." She lowered her eyes to gaze directly into his.

Her expression was not one of revulsion, which he knew she had every right to feel after what he'd tried to do to her that night in the stable. A lump formed in his throat.

"I told him I would nurse you, and you would not die."

"Why . . . ?"

Ignoring his question, she opened a drawer and removed a few items. "I was about to change your bandages. Let me just lift the blanket."

"How long have I been here?" he asked, unable to recall anything since riding into San Antonio, clinging to Stew's neck.

"You've been back for four days now and in my house for nearly all of it. I happened to be in town the day you got there, and that's when I heard what had happened. Now let me get to work and clean your wounds. There's still a chance of them festering, and you have been feverish, so you aren't out of the woods yet." She put her hands on her hips and directed a stern don't-argue-with-me gaze at him.

"Why can't Juana do it?" he asked, not sure he wanted Lucie doing that unpleasant job.

"Well, if you'd rather she care for you—"

"No!" he said quickly. He couldn't believe he had nearly rejected her again. But what good could come of it? Nevertheless, he was simply too weak—and not just physically weak—to give up the prospect of her tender care. And he knew it would be tender despite who or what he was. "I . . . I haven't said thank you yet . . . for taking me in. I expect I'd be dead now if you hadn't."

"We're even, then." She smiled.

Micah knew he was powerless against that smile, and he might have been afraid for both of them if he didn't feel so downright good just then.

"Let me have a look at your wounds," she added.

He lifted his arm from under the covers. It was quite weak, and he had difficulty moving it. He wondered if he'd ever be able to shoot again. He forgot all about that when Lucie took his arm and helped him. There was a bandage wrapped around the fleshy part of the upper arm where the arrow had penetrated. Lucie removed the bandage, swabbed some creamy concoction over the wound, then put on a new bandage. She did the same to his head. Luckily, the arrow hadn't penetrated his skull, but it had made a deep gash four inches long over his left ear.

"Juana stitched up your head wound," Lucie said. "I think she did a nice job. It'll scar, but your hair will cover it eventually. Thank goodness you've got a hard head."

Then she lifted the lower part of the blanket to reveal his right side. Her mouth puckered in concentration as she worked. Her eyes were grave.

"Is it bad?" he asked.

"It's getting a bit purulent. At least the arrow went all the way through and didn't break off inside."

"I pulled it through," he said.

"Oh my!" Lucie's eyes flickered to his face, then back to her work. "You have much courage, Micah. Not just because of the arrow, but in making that journey back to San Antonio."

"I didn't have much choice. It was either lie still and die or try to make it back," he answered matter-of-factly, but inside he was pleased she still thought highly of him. "Lucie . . . is it true about Tom? Is he dead?"

She nodded, keeping eyes intent on her work. "I'm afraid so."

"I'm beginning to think I'm just plain bad luck to anyone I get close to."

"Don't you even think such a thing!" she exclaimed, and in her emotion she pressed too hard on his wound.

"Ouch!"

"I'm sorry." She paused a moment, then added, "Micah, people die and that's that. I'm very sorry about Tom. He was a good man, but his death has nothing to do with you."

Micah shrugged, not convinced. Desiring to change the subject he asked, "Do you know what happened to Baker and Lowe?"

"Who?"

"The fellows that left me for dead."

"Oh, them!" her voice rose indignantly. "Captain Hays gave them a severe tongue-lashing. But if you ask me, it wasn't enough."

"I would have slowed them down, gotten them both killed. And me too."

"But you didn't die and neither did they."

"Well, I ain't gonna defend them. I thought about killing them both when I was crawling across the prairie." He sighed. It was very hard to be angry at anyone with Lucie's slim, soft hands caressing him. "Most anyone would have done the same."

"Not you."

He could not fathom how she could say such kind things about him. He just shook his head in disbelief. "Lucie, I don't know how you can say that when you know the kind of man I am. I am still completely befuddled that you took me in after what I did. Nothing I ever did was out of courage. You hinted at it the last time we saw each other. Anything I've done was from pure orneriness and hate, too. Honor, courage—they just have nothing to do with me."

"I'll agree you are ornery, and you have more than your share of hate in you, but it's only part of you. You have good in you, Micah. You'll never convince me otherwise." She finished her work and tugged the blanket back in place.

Micah smiled at her. He just didn't feel like doing any soul-searching at the moment. "You bring it out of me, if it's there."

"And don't you forget it!" she said with a tart smile, then gathered up her things and moved to the door. "I'll bring you some broth if you feel up to eating it."

"Yes, thank you." He didn't know if he could eat, but he'd take any excuse to have her return.

The fever hit hard in the night. Micah faded in and out of consciousness for two days. Nightmares assailed him. Goliad, San Jacinto, battle, slaughter, death. And, as nightmares will, his made no sense at all. The victims were not always soldiers, Mexican or Texan. Sometimes his father was one of the victims, sometimes even Micah was cut down. But the worst nightmare was the one in which Lucie was hewn down on the battlefield.

Yet woven into and around the horror were moments that did not fit. He realized later that these were the moments when he came out of the nightmares into reality, a reality that seemed even less real than the nightmares. For they were moments of sweetness and peace. In them

Lucie figured strongly, sitting at his bedside with her head bowed and her dear voice murmuring over him.

"Dear Lord, spare Micah that he might know you, that he might truly see you for the loving, merciful God that you are. . . ."

Micah never thought prayer could be so good. He never thought he might actually desire to reach out for it. It was like an island of calm in the midst of a hurricane. Was it just Lucie, or was it the words she was saying?

Finally the fever passed, and he woke again with a clear mind. Lucie was there at his bedside, and he wondered if she'd ever left. She wiped a cool damp cloth across his forehead.

"You were praying for me," he breathed.

"I have been praying for two days. I couldn't help it."

He smiled at the hint of apology in her tone. "Thank you."

"Really?"

"I just remembered something. . . ." He spoke dreamily, his eyes half-closed so as not to break the wonderful spell of the moment. "When I was a boy, before I came to Texas, I caught a bad fever. My mother sat by my bed as you are doing now, and she wiped me with a cool cloth and . . . and she prayed over me. I had forgotten how many times she . . ." He turned his head away as sudden tears sprang to his eyes. "I had forgotten . . ." he murmured, then he closed his eyes, his speech exhausting him. In a moment sleep engulfed him. A sleep without dreams, without nightmares.

He awoke a while later, and Lucie was still there. He gave her a weak smile but could not speak. He slept again, and when he awoke, she was still there. He continued thus for two more days, waking for a few moments, then sleeping. He had never slept so much in his life, nor had he ever lain still for so long, especially without a gun at his side, ever alert to danger. Yet he never grew restless, and he was never afraid. The sleep was delicious. And when he was awake he often did not talk, nor did Lucie talk much to him. They were simply quietly aware of each other. Sometimes she held his hand. But she required nothing more of him.

When he finally woke and felt truly rested, Lucie was gone. His disappointment went deep to his core, but he chided himself for his selfishness. It was probably the first time in days she'd left his side. He told himself this was for the best because he feared he was becoming far too dependent on her, on seeing her dear face each moment on waking. He could easily desire a lifetime of that.

She returned a few minutes later and seemed to immediately perceive that this waking was different from the others.

"So you have decided to join us for a while," she said.

"How long did I sleep?"

"Two days."

"And no nightmares," he said, amazed.

"Not after the fever passed."

"You knew—about the nightmares, I mean?"

"You talked a lot. They must have been terrible." She reached out and adjusted his pillow behind him. "Are you hungry?"

His stomach rumbled as if in response. Surprised, he said, "I am . . . mighty hungry."

"Juana has been dying to fatten you up. I'll tell her you are ready. Though we should start slowly. Some broth and a glass of milk, perhaps." She turned to go.

Micah laid a hand on her arm. "I wasn't dreaming, was I, about you praying for me?"

"No."

"I guess you have a captive audience now," he said.

"What do you mean by that, Micah?"

"Only that . . . well, I ain't going nowhere if you get the urge to talk religion to me, that's all." He smiled, abashed at his own words.

"I do declare, Micah! Maybe you are still delirious after all!"

Then she grinned, and he smiled, too, with abandon. And it felt good.

CHAPTER 33

LUCIE DID NOT TAKE FULL advantage of Micah's offer. Oh, she had thought about doing just that at first. In fact, when he had first regained consciousness, she had even thought that now God had him where He could knock some sense into him—a captive audience, as Micah had put it. And then when he had actually given her leave to talk about God, well, she nearly attacked him with her zeal. But she remembered what he'd said once, that he knew a lot about religion. He had many Scriptures memorized and probably knew the Bible even better than he would admit to. She knew Micah did not need to be told anything about faith.

However, Lucie wasn't exactly sure what he did need or how to go about directing him. She prayed about it and realized that the best approach was to leave it in Micah's hands, let him do the reaching out.

And he did so, but slowly. A question here or there woven into a conversation. Often it was nothing deep or earth shattering. It seemed right now that Micah needed most of all to relax, to enjoy the moment, to rest from all intensity. God seemed to sense this as well. The talk was casual and even fun. They told each other stories of their adventures. Of course Micah had more exciting adventures. Lucie just had little tales of her growing up, but Micah listened as if hearing *The Arabian Nights.* They learned much about each other during this time, the kinds of things Lucie always wanted to know about Micah. And often matters of faith just flowed naturally from this.

Once Lucie brought Micah his supper and watched his eyes widen with wonder at the contents of the tray.

"Is that pecan pie?" he asked, indicating the dish next to his stew.

"Yes, and I made it myself."

"I thought Juana did all the cooking."

"Well, I confess I don't enjoy cooking." Lucie blushed at having to make such an admission to the man she loved, but she had to be truthful. "However, Juana has insisted I learn. Still, the men shouldn't be made to suffer more than once or twice a week."

"You can't be all that bad," he said.

"I'll cook for you tomorrow, and you can judge. But I do have one specialty—pecan pie. I love it and Juana hates it, so if I want it, I must make it, or so she says. Knowing Juana, she would make it if I pouted a bit."

Lifting his eyes from his tray, Micah gave her a sidelong perusal. "Somehow I just don't think you are the pouting type."

Blushing a bit, she shrugged. "I guess I've been known to use such methods to get my way. But in this case, I don't have to. I hate to cook, but I like to bake pies and cookies and pastries. I suppose it is my sweet tooth that drives me."

"Now, a sweet tooth, I can believe." He picked up his fork and impaled the pie, bringing a chunk to his mouth. He ate the pie with a look of deep scrutiny on his face.

She watched with breath more bated than she cared to admit.

Swallowing, he finally said, "I've had pecan pie only one other time in my life. My neighbor up in Cooksburg made it, and I fell in love with pecan pie. I asked my ma to make it, but she never got around to it. Those days she was feeling so poorly that we were lucky to have the basics to eat." He grew momentarily melancholy, then shaking it off, continued. "Well, I'm in love again! Lucie, this pie is even better than Mrs. Hunter's."

Lucie grinned. Micah liked pecan pie. He liked *her* pecan pie! There was something so wonderfully ordinary about it that it nearly made her weep.

Micah was attacking the rest of the pie.

"Micah," she scolded halfheartedly, "you need to eat your stew first."

"Who says?"

She screwed up her lips in thought about this. "It is just the right thing to do."

"It was only yesterday you were telling me that some things were just opposite of what we think they should be," he countered.

"We were talking about how the Bible says that with God our weaknesses can be our strengths, and how God's ways are often the exact opposite of the way people think things should be."

"Yes, and the order of my meal tonight is a perfect way to illustrate how I've learned that spiritual truth," he replied smugly.

Lucie picked up the napkin lying next to his plate and tossed it into his face. With incredibly quick reflexes for a man recuperating from near mortal injuries, Micah snatched the napkin and tossed it back at her.

Giggling, she said, "I think you are much too strong to fully grasp that notion."

"No," he said more solemnly, "I'm not." He lifted his gaze, smiling faintly. "When I was strong physically, I was very weak in my soul, my heart. Now I can't even walk. I guess I am not much stronger spiritually or emotionally, but I can see it now. My eyes are so much more open."

"That is a good place to be." Tenderly, she laid the napkin across his shirtfront.

"I don't know where I'm going," he confessed.

"It will come to you, Micah," she encouraged. "I'm sure it will."

Not long after that, Lucie began helping Micah get up. His wounds, the loss of blood, and the fever had taken a hard toll on him. He became exhausted walking just a few steps to the chair next to his bed. But within a week he was strong enough to venture outside. He asked Lucie to take him to the stable to see Stew.

"I just gotta make sure he's all right, with my own eyes, you know?" he said.

"I understand. But I have made sure that mule has been treated like a king. I personally give him a lump of sugar every day." She took Micah's arm as they walked outside. He probably did not need such assistance, but he didn't protest.

"How do you do it all, Lucie? You've been caring for me day and night, but I know your father needs help also. Then you have your chores. And still you take time for my old mule. You amaze me!"

"I don't consider a minute of it work," she explained simply. How could she tell him that every moment caring for him was sheer pleasure?

He was out of breath when they reached the stable, but he doggedly continued to the stall Lucie indicated was Stew's. He unlatched the door and went inside. Running a hand along the animal's flanks, he murmured affectionate words to the mule.

"You know," he said to Lucie, "I hate to admit it, but this ornery beast saved my life. It ain't nothing short of a miracle that he showed up when he did out there."

"I didn't know you believed in miracles," she said lightly.

"Don't think it doesn't make me angry that I just might have to change my perspective." He spoke with mock affront, then grinned. "A man can change, you know."

"I suppose anything is possible," she replied noncommittally.

Micah was sure he'd never been happier in his life. Sometimes he felt a little guilty about this, considering the loss of his two dearest friends. But he also thought that perhaps they, more than anyone, would understand. This was the first time in years that Micah was so completely removed from violence and strife. He didn't have to sleep lightly with a gun near at hand. He didn't have to move through the day in a constant vigil for danger. When he dressed for the first time—in some spares of the ranch hands because his own clothes had been tattered to shreds during his trek—he had momentarily felt naked without pistols tucked into his belt.

Yes, he had grieved the death of Tom, but it had simply not wrenched at the core of him as Jed's death had. Lucie said it was God's peace. Maybe so. Or maybe he just did not want to face the questions and deep down anger Tom's death would surely bring if he thought too intensely about it. Maybe it was hard to accept Tom being dead because he hadn't seen it for himself. That's what Reid Maccallum thought.

Micah smiled as he sat in the chair by the window in what had once been Juana's room. The housekeeper had vacated and was now sharing Lucie's room. Anyway, the thought of Reid was a pleasant one. The two men suddenly had much in common. Both were once strapping, strong men who were now invalids. Once Reid realized he was welcome, he often came and passed the time with Micah. And Micah enjoyed the visits almost as much as he enjoyed Lucie's visits.

Not a naturally verbose man, Reid could talk at great length if given encouragement. And he was knowledgeable about many varied subjects. Not a formally educated man, he still was well-read, interesting, and wise. It wasn't long before they became comfortable enough to talk about personal things. Reid talked about his son one day. This was another area Micah and Reid had in common, but from different perspectives.

"It wasn't easy for the boy," Reid said, "growing up as he did caught between two cultures. Unfortunately, I didn't see the depth of the problem until it was too late."

"Lucie doesn't seem to have problems in that area," Micah said.

"I can't exactly say why that is." Reid gazed a moment out the window. Lucie had moved another chair into Micah's room and placed it adjacent to Micah's. There was even a small table between the two chairs so the two convalescents could take refreshment together. "Maybe it was my doing. Fathers are different with sons than they are with daughters. I love them both to the depths of my soul, but I think a man expects more of a son. A son is an extension of a man far more than a daughter is. He has the potential to be everything the father could not be. It is a heavy burden to be laid on a boy. On the other hand, a son expects more from a father than a daughter does."

"A son wants to worship his father," interjected Micah. "I guess a daughter does, too, but only a son can hope to take that worship to the obvious conclusion of true imitation."

"Is that what you wanted to do? Imitate your father?"

Micah laughed dryly. "If I did, I failed miserably!"

"I guess that's really what I'm trying to say. All those high expectations fathers and sons have for one another—well, we are all doomed to fail. And it's probably just as well that we do!" He shook his head and, steepling his fingers, tapped them thoughtfully against his lips. "Joaquin did not feel he could ever be a respectable rancher, so he did just the opposite—became an outlaw, and worse, a bandit politically opposed to all I and the other ranchers stood for. I know it isn't quite that simple, and there were other factors involved, but the end was the same. My son and I were driven further and further apart. We, who loved each other very deeply, became enemies of a sort. It tears me apart inside. I don't doubt it has been part of the cause of my heart going bad."

"Do you . . ." Micah paused, his eyes flickering to the window. Outside, the sky was a clean blue and the sun was glaring. The stableboy was chasing a couple of dogs around in the yard. Again, Micah felt life was too sweet now to sully with deep introspection, especially of painful topics. Yet he was curious about Reid and his son. Clearly there were many parallels between them and Micah and his father. Micah knew that sooner or later he must confront his own difficulties in this area or relinquish all the peace he was now experiencing.

He took a breath and went on. "Mr. Maccallum, do you still love Joaquin?"

"Of course!" the man said simply without hesitation.

"Why? He defied you during the war by fighting on the other side. He defies you every day by harassing the borders of your land. Surely his actions are a shame to both you and Lucie."

"I love him because he is part of me, Micah. Just as I am sure he loves me for the same reason. That kind of love does not die easily. It would be like hating yourself."

"Sometimes I do hate myself," Micah said flatly.

"And sometimes you love yourself. Life is not black and white."

"I've often wondered if my father loves me," Micah mused, only realizing he said the words out loud when they were spoken.

"I'm sure he loves you."

"How can you know that?"

"It was clear when I met him."

Micah blinked with surprise. "You met him?"

"He came last year after Lucie wrote to him about your being in prison in Mexico."

"Lucie wrote him?"

Reid smiled. "What do you and my daughter talk about all those hours I've heard your voices from my room?"

"Everything and nothing," Micah answered. "But that never came up."

"I expect Lucie is reticent about broaching such a tender subject."

"Probably." Micah considered Reid's astounding words again. "He came here?"

"Yes, and he spent time with President Houston as well, no doubt badgering the man about your disposition."

"He did all that?"

"Sounds like a man who loves his son."

Micah rose from his chair and walked around it so he could stand facing the window. It was hard to let Reid see the sudden quandary of emotion his statement had stirred in Micah. Though part of him wanted to believe Reid's words, a part still sought to fight against them. Yet he knew that any peace he hoped to attain hinged on his coming to terms with both his father and his father's God. Having had a small taste of peace, he now knew he desperately wanted it. But could he sacrifice the hate that had sustained him for so many years? It seemed a twisted question. Who would choose hate? Micah didn't want it. But he feared the unknown more.

CHAPTER 34

THREE WEEKS FROM THE DAY Micah showed up half dead in San Antonio, Lucie deemed him fit enough to ride a bit. He still felt stiff and weak in the knees, but he was not going to argue. The restlessness that had been at bay during his recovery was beginning to creep up on him. This worried him a little, and he had confided it to Reid.

"I was beginning to think I was ready to settle down," he said. He didn't say that in his mind settling down almost certainly involved Lucie. Maybe Reid understood this, but nevertheless, Micah was not ready to approach the man about marrying his daughter no matter how congenial they had become. "I'm starting to feel itchy now—in my feet, you know."

"I sometimes get mighty restless myself," Reid said. "Might be you are just experiencing what is natural to most men. You've never had to lie on your back for long periods, have you?"

"In prison, but I guess that was different because I could still get around even if I was confined. But there were days when I wanted to scream from boredom."

"A man can only take so much," Reid agreed.

Micah hoped that was it. He hoped that the wild streak in him was finally getting tamed. He hoped so because Lucie Maccallum deserved a man at her side, not one roaming all over creation.

Regardless, he quickly dressed and met Lucie in the kitchen. She was placing some items in a basket. He peeked inside and found dishes of food—cold chicken left over from last night's supper, a loaf of bread, apples, and two slabs of spice cake, which was another of Lucie's specialties.

"What's all this?" he asked.

"A picnic."

"A real picnic?" He smiled. "I don't think I have ever been on a picnic. Not that I can remember. My stepmother took the young kids on a picnic once, but I wouldn't go. I was pretty ornery back then."

"Well, I am honored, then, to take you on your first *real* picnic." Lucie gave Micah a quick appraisal as she spoke. "But no guns on a picnic." She reached to remove the pistol he had in his belt.

Captain Hays had come to visit him a few days before and had brought him his weapons, which Baker and Lowe had brought from the battle site. Good weapons were hard to come by, and Micah was glad to have his back. He hadn't even thought about it when he had tucked the revolver into his belt upon dressing.

"But, Lucie, if we're riding any distance from the ranch, we gotta have some protection," he argued. "Against snakes or varmints, if nothing else."

"I decree there will be no varmints on this outing!"

He shook his head. "Ya just can't—"

"He's right," said Reid, who had just come into the kitchen. "That would be purely irresponsible, Lucie, and you well know it."

"But I don't want him troubled by such things today," she said.

"He'll be more troubled if you have no protection. As will I. One moment." Reid left the kitchen and returned with a rifle in hand. "Leave the pistol, but take this," he offered.

"That's fine by me," said Micah, looking to Lucie for final approval of the plan.

When she nodded reluctantly, Micah took the revolver from his belt and laid it on the table. It was with this very weapon that he had killed most of the Mexican bandits that awful day, the memory of which still burned painfully in his mind. He, more than anyone, wanted no reminders of that day just now. He was going on a picnic with Lucie. He wanted nothing to cloud the moment.

They rode about a mile from the house. The wind in Micah's face was as pleasant as the company he was with. He almost forgot the pain each jostle of the mule brought. The air of the early summer day grew warmer as the sun traveled high in the sky. And the wind was a dry Texas wind that bent the tops of the high grass and whistled through the cottonwoods on the edge of a little creek. Seldom did Micah take the opportunity to truly appreciate this country, but now as he did, he realized he loved it. His father had once told him, when he was pining for his Boston home, that Texas would eventually become home to him. Micah supposed it had, in spite of himself or his father.

He also thought of a conversation he'd had with Reid the other day, a rather cryptic conversation at that. They had been talking about the growth of Texas in general terms, about the appeal of wide open lands and such. Reid mentioned to Micah that there was some fine unclaimed land adjacent to the Maccallum ranch on the other side of

Cutter Creek. He'd said no more, and Micah was afraid to make more of the words than their surface meaning.

He didn't know why he thought of that just now. They were far from the borders of Maccallum land. Yet Micah had been thinking more and more about his unclaimed land allotments. But it must be the height of arrogance—or at the very least, outlandish fantasy—to think that there might be more to claiming land on the borders of Maccallum land than simply being neighbors.

He glanced at Lucie, and an ache replaced the peaceful joy he had been feeling. He could never be fit for a woman such as she. There was simply too much blood on his hands.

They stopped on the shallow banks of the creek under the shade of a cottonwood. Micah secured Stew and Lucie's piebald in a place where there was good sweet grass, then he carried the basket to a place where Lucie had spread a quilt over the grass.

Micah eased down on the quilt. "I didn't think a man could get tired riding, especially after just an hour." He shook his head. "I wonder if I'll ever be good as new." He flexed his right arm. "There ain't much pain in my arm anymore. Guess that's something."

"You have come a long way, Micah, considering you nearly died." She visibly shuddered. "I can't imagine life without you around."

"Like I couldn't imagine life without Jed or Tom," Micah mused. "But life has a way of getting on one way or another."

"Yes, I know that. And God would have healed me. But I am glad I didn't have to find out." She opened the basket. "Come, let's eat."

Micah agreed heartily with that. He ate from hunger, for indeed his appetite was voracious these days, but he also ate by way of distraction. He'd tried to brush off Lucie's words about missing him, but they continued to echo in his mind, reminding him that once she had declared her love for him. Yet much had passed between them since then. Surely all she must feel now was friendship.

Micah ate more than his fair share of the food. When Lucie said she'd had her fill of chicken, Micah finished it off. Same with the bread. He ate two apples and one huge piece of the spice cake. He then eyed

Lucie's half-eaten piece, which he thought had been sitting untended for long enough.

"If you ain't gonna finish that . . ." he asked subtly.

She laughed and pushed the cake toward him. "At this rate you will be fattened up far beyond even Juana's tastes!"

He ate the cake and, licking his fingers contentedly, lay back on the quilt. The sun burned down pleasantly upon him even as the wind wafted over him. This must indeed be the "good life" he'd heard others speak of.

Suddenly something snapped in the brush. Micah tensed and shot up, grabbing the rifle that he'd laid next to the quilt. Cocking the weapon, he made ready to do battle. In a bush about ten feet away, two beady eyes peered from between the branches. Soon the head appeared. Masked like a raccoon, it had a long white muzzle.

"A raccoon?" Lucie breathed.

"No." He held his fingers to his lips and they both fell silent.

In another moment the critter scurried out from its cover.

"A coatimundi," Micah said when he saw the long, faintly ringed tail, which was easily half the size and weight of the animal.

"I've heard of them, but I have never seen one," Lucie said.

"Though they're not nocturnal like coons, they are shy enough."

The animal suddenly seemed to take note of its observers and, with incredible speed, retreated back to its hiding place in the brush.

"I'm glad you didn't shoot it," Lucie said.

"I wouldn't have. I usually look before I shoot." He gently released the cocking mechanism and laid aside the rifle. "But that could have been anything. I'm glad I had the rifle."

"Yet it wasn't."

"It isn't good to get too complacent in this land. It ain't tame."

Micah lay back again and tried to recapture the moment before the interruption. It was hard. His heart was still pounding, not from fear of danger, but rather because he might have been forced to kill again. In this wild country it was a delusion to think you would never have to kill to defend yourself, your land, or your loved ones. But Micah shuddered at the thought of having to do so in front of Lucie, of soiling her with violence.

"I haven't had any more nightmares," he said suddenly. "Not since the fever broke."

"That's good." She paused and looked down at him.

His heart clenched, for such was her expression that it almost gave him cause to hope.

"Would you like to talk about them?" she asked.

"Why wake sleeping dogs, as they say?"

"Because sleeping dogs do wake. I remember I used to have nightmares right after my mother died, and my father once told me that the best way to rid myself of such darkness was to shine light on it. Bring my fears into the light is what he meant. Talking about fearful things seems to have a way of shrinking them down to proper size."

"No doubt you and your father are right." He wondered how much to say to her. Then he decided he'd never had anyone he could say everything to, and because of that he'd squashed a lot down inside him. Maybe it would help to get it out. And maybe she could be that one person whom he could trust enough to tell.

He rolled over on his side and gazed at her. "I don't want to talk to you about it because the last thing I want is to drag you into the violence of my life."

"Micah, I washed the blood off your hands when you killed those bandits. I have just nursed you from wounds that nearly caused your death. I am part of your life—violence and all. You need not protect me. This is my choice. Besides, I am not as pure as you may think. I have seen violence and strife."

"Yet still you are pure. Somehow it has not touched you. Your mother's death, your father's illness, your brother's life, the rejection of the ranchers. Your purity and your faith have remained intact. How is that, Lucie?"

"I still think you have placed me on far too high a pedestal," she replied with a small tinge of pink on her cheeks. "But I will tell you this. My faith has not remained intact in spite of adversity. Instead it is the other way around. Adversity has strengthened my faith, and the reason, I believe, is because I don't call God into question for all the ill in my life."

"Why not? He is God, after all."

"I think you know the answer to that."

"Oh yes," Micah replied a bit too glibly. "Free will, as it is called in religious circles."

"Micah, I can't argue religious doctrine with you. You probably know much more than I, and I'll bet you are a far better debater than I. So rather than debate, I will tell you one thing from my heart. What sustains my faith is love, pure and simple. God's love for me. I feel it always, and it gives me assurance that He will always treat me well."

Micah closed his eyes. Yes, it would have been so much easier to bat around doctrines and such. But love? How does one argue with something that is not a concrete issue but fairly glows from Lucie's heart? He sensed that from the first moment he saw Lucie. It was that very love that had drawn him. Not specifically a love for him, but her simple capacity for love. And he could not now debate it. He didn't want to.

He kept his eyes closed, for it was hard to look at her and confess the deepest pain of his soul. "Lucie, I haven't known much love in my life, so . . . it's hard to see, really see, these things you say about God. You talk about a loving God. I know the Scriptures tell of these things, but to me . . . He is a stranger. I have feared God, but love? I just don't know."

"I won't say there is nothing to fearing God," she replied. "He is *God,* after all. But I believe it should be more of an awe-inspiring fear, not a shake-in-your-boots fear. The most awesome thing about God is His love."

"But how can I possibly understand that love?" Micah rolled onto his back and stared up into the sky, as if the very heavens might open up and answer him.

"I think I came to understand it because of my parents," Lucie said. "I always felt their love, even when I was naughty. And I came to see how God was like that. It was easy to understand what Christ did on the cross. There's a verse in the Bible that says that God showed His love toward us in that while we were still in sin, Christ died for us."

"I never had such examples," Micah said. "Maybe from my mother, but it is so dim in my memory now. I probably would have been better off if I had dwelt more on remembering the things my mother taught me than on hating my father."

"I wish you had."

He heard the sadness in her voice. He still did not have the courage to look at her.

"I wish you had some way to see love," she added softly.

He wanted so to open his eyes and look at her, but he was afraid to. He thought she spoke of more than God's love.

"If only I could," he breathed, barely above a whisper. "I think I'd know better how to give love as well."

They were silent awhile. A fly buzzed around Micah's face, and he brushed it away. It seemed to him there must be a way for even one such as he to solve the puzzle of God's love. He knew that all had access to that love, that a man wasn't left out of the club, as it were, just because his experience was so limited. The God that Lucie spoke of—the God Micah wanted so to believe in—would not hold out a gift that was limited to only a few lucky ones. There must be a way.

Now he did venture a glance toward Lucie. She had plucked a bluebell from the grass and was studying its pretty purple petals. Her face in profile was pensive, yet at peace as well. She did not have the look of one who feared her friend might be denied what she had found. She was so certain of God. Then he thought of a matter that had nagged at him since he realized Lucie had taken him in to nurse him.

"Lucie," he said, "I have been wondering and wondering why you took me in after what I tried to do to you that night in the stable. And after all the other things I have said and done. I couldn't figure it out because I couldn't understand the reason for it. You did it out of love, didn't you? You couldn't turn me away because you love me. I wouldn't be so presumptuous as to say it was more than a Christian love, but that's what it was, wasn't it?"

"Yes . . ." she murmured, her eyes still focused on the bluebell. "But it can't be so simple."

"Why not, Micah!" Her voice rose with intensity as her eyes lifted and met his. "Even Jesus said we must become as children to enter the kingdom of God."

Micah jumped up and paced to the edge of the clearing. He knew she'd tell him how simple it was, but it was too difficult to accept that. He turned.

"Lucie, I have never been a child," he said dismally. He came back to the quilt and dropped to his knees before her. "My father certainly never let me be a child. I was constantly made to be some kind of symbol of his religious perfection. I was full grown at thirteen when I watched my mother bleed to death on the trail after having run away from my father. I was an old man when less than a year later I stood at Goliad and watched my uncle and four hundred others massacred. Those nightmares, Lucie . . . they aren't just crazy visions of ghosts and goblins. They were the reality of my life haunting my dreams. Hardly a night went by that I did not relive horror after horror. Blood! It's all over me, not just on my hands. I am steeped in it. And it is not all innocent blood like at Goliad. I exacted much vengeance for that day. At San Jacinto I shot armed and unarmed men. That's what I dream about—a boy with hands raised, begging me with his eyes not to shoot. And feeling joy at pulling the trigger."

He stopped abruptly, shocked and dismayed at what he had revealed. But it was pity, not revulsion, he saw in Lucie's eyes.

"You were fourteen, Micah," she said. "Confused, hurt, and caught in the horror of war."

"Those banditos . . ." he began, and now he dared not stop. Let her know it all. "The last one . . . I . . . think there was a moment when, had I allowed myself, I could have let him live. But I didn't think. I acted on instinct—the instinct of a killer."

"You are not a killer!" she insisted passionately. "But even if you were, do you think you'd be beyond God's power to heal?"

"I don't know."

"He has healed your nightmares."

"For the time being."

"Oh, Micah!" she exclaimed in frustration, throwing down the flower in her hand. "You are as obstinate as that mule of yours!"

"I have always said we deserve each other—me and Stew, that is." He let a smile play upon the corners of his lips. This was supposed to be an enjoyable afternoon picnic. He was desperate to bring it back to that. Tenderly he picked up the bluebell. "I'll keep this, if you don't mind. A memento of my first picnic." His eyes searched hers, imploring that she accept a truce of sorts from the previous intensity.

A smile on her lips, slightly reluctant, but offered nonetheless, she said, "I'll pick you a bouquet, if you'd like."

"One is all I need." He looked at the flower, then back up at her. "Not that I'll soon forget this day."

CHAPTER 35

It was late afternoon when they reached the house. A strange horse was tied at the post in front. And a rangy-looking animal it was. A charcoal with many flecks of white or gray, but most likely gray, because it appeared to be an ancient beast. The coat was matted and dull, either from ill care or simple age. Its head hung low and its body was bony.

"You know anyone with a mount like that?" Micah asked.

"I should hope not!" Lucie replied. "Why, he makes your Stew look like a stallion!"

They took their mounts to the stable, tending them quickly, then walked to the house. Micah hoped the visitor had nothing to do with him because he was exhausted and could only think of stretching out on his bed for a while before supper.

Lucie entered first. Micah heard her gasp just before he ran into her back as she stopped abruptly before the open parlor door. Micah was about to apologize when he glanced over her head into the parlor. Then he, too, gasped.

Unable to speak, he glanced at Lucie to ensure he was not imagining the sight that greeted him. Then he looked back at the guest in the parlor.

"Well, say something, boy, or I'm gonna think maybe I am a ghost!" Tom Fife stood, a grin plastered across his whiskered face.

"I—" Micah began, then shook his head. "You real, then, Tom?"

"Of course he is!" said Reid, also seated in the parlor. "Now come on in and give the man a proper greeting."

Lucie and Micah both came fully into the parlor, but Micah stopped just short of his friend, just short of throwing his arms around the man.

Lucie took Tom's hand and smiled. "This is so wonderful, Mr. Fife!" Tears welled in her eyes.

Tom graciously gave Lucie's hand a squeeze, then turned toward Micah. "Come here, ya ornery cuss!" He grabbed Micah and fairly crushed him in a mighty bear hug.

Micah just bit his lip. Shoot, if he wasn't gonna cry! But he blinked back the moisture as quickly as it rose. "Ya ain't dead" was all he could say.

Tom stepped back. "Not yet. And neither are you. Why, up until yesterday, I'd given you up for dead, too. Guess only the good die young."

"Like Jed," Micah murmured.

"Yeah," Tom said solemnly, then added more lightly, "You and I will probably live forever!"

"No doubt," said Micah. He grinned and gave Tom a more careful perusal. "You're scrawnier than a motherless polecat! Near as bad as that critter outside passing for a horse."

"I ain't had it near as good as you, all pampered and cozy in this fine house with the prettiest nurse in Texas."

"Micah didn't look quite so good when he first came," Lucie said.

"I know." Again Tom was serious. "I heard some in town about what happened to you. I still can't believe you walked near fifty miles. But even more amazing was what that mule of yours did. There's a story that will go down with the legends."

"What happened to you, Tom?" asked Micah.

Lucie interjected, "Why don't we all make ourselves comfortable, then Mr. Fife can tell us at his leisure."

"Yes," said Reid, "I want to hear as well. Tom's been here for an hour, but we put off his story so he wouldn't have to tell it twice. Would anyone like refreshment first?"

"No," said Micah. "I want to hear what happened to you, Tom—how you came back from the dead."

"It ain't much of a story," Tom said as he resumed his seat.

Micah noted that his friend was limping, but he said nothing and, after seeing Lucie to a chair, took a chair next to her and nodded for Tom to continue.

"I reckon those two varmints, Baker and Lowe, thought I was dead. I must've been out cold when they looked me over—anyway, I'll give them that much. But what still sticks in my craw is that they left you knowing you was alive. They should've found a way. But what's done . . . and all that."

He sighed, shaking his head, and Micah glimpsed some of what Tom must have suffered thinking Micah was dead. It fairly stunned him.

Tom went on, "So Baker and Lowe left me where I was behind a mesquite bush. I guess they took you across the river, so's you'd have more protection if the Comanches came back. Well, that's the irony of it, ain't it? We was that close, no more'n a stone's throw from each other, and we didn't even know it! I lay where I was all that day and most of the next, bleeding and dying of thirst. I couldn't move. My leg was shot up too bad. Finally I couldn't bear the thought of dying of thirst with a creek a few feet away. Maybe some of my strength had returned—I don't really know—but I crawled down to the bank. The water sustained me for two more days. I covered myself with some nearby branches and such, so when the Indians came back they didn't see me."

"I had already taken off by then," Micah said. "If I'd been in my right mind, I would have known better than to believe them varmints Baker and Lowe. But there was nary a sound or a movement from where you fell."

"Like I said, a real irony," Tom said. "I was unconscious most of the time, but when I came to, I didn't dare move too much, even if I could, for fear of the Comanches. But if you had seen me, I'll wager you'd have died for certain then because you would not have taken off without me, and I couldn't walk an inch. So it all worked out for the best."

"But if you couldn't walk, Mr. Fife," Lucie asked, "how did you finally get away?"

"Some traders happened by. They saw my body and was gonna bury me. Luckily, I had just enough life left in me to make 'em stop. Instead, they loaded me in their wagon and took me to Laredo. I tried to tell them to get me to San Antonio, but they were heading to Laredo, and it would have been out of their way. At any rate I wasn't in much of a position to be insistent. Leastways there was a doc in Laredo. But that varmint was gonna cut my leg off. I told him if he did that I'd come back and cut his heart out. I was half out of my head at the time and couldn't have been too awfully fearsome, but bless that doctor's heart, he saved my leg." Pausing, Tom stiffly moved his right leg. "For what it's worth. I reckon it'll never be the same, but at least it's still hooked on."

Micah stared at his friend in amazement.

Tom laughed. "It is a pure miracle, ain't it? I mean, you and me both coming back from the dead."

"You could call it that," Micah replied noncommittally.

"You mean to tell me, Micah, that you're still being ornery about God?" Tom turned to Lucie. "Ain't you talked no sense into him yet?"

Lucie smiled wanly. "He has a rather thick head."

"Yeah, I do remember seeing a Comanche arrow bounce off his head before I blacked out," Tom said.

Micah fingered the scar above his ear. It was still raw and tender. "It hardly bounced," he said with mock defensiveness. He looked around at the three people who had become, perhaps, the most important people in his life just then. They deserved more than a recalcitrant attitude. "I guess I've got to allow for the possibility of a miracle—well, more than a possibility!" But he couldn't say more than that, and he grew uncomfortable. "I'm sure parched, Lucie. If you'd like, I'll go ask Juana to get us some tea or something."

"I'll go," Lucie said, rising. "You and Tom can visit."

Tom stayed for supper and, in fact, was invited to stay the night in a spare bed in the bunkhouse. After the meal, Micah walked with Tom outside—or rather, Tom limped and Micah hobbled, for his wound in his side was giving him a painful stitch. Tom said he wanted to see the famous mule, Stew. Lucie gave them some sugar.

"That gal always spoiling your mule like that?" Tom asked as they came to Stew's stall.

"I guess so."

Tom reached in and rubbed the white patch on the mule's sandy face. "It's pretty clear she's mighty glad this beast saved your hide."

"Maybe . . ."

"You been here three weeks now recuperating. That all you got to say?"

"Tom, when did you get to be so talkative?" Micah asked, just a bit peeved.

"Near dying does that to a fellow. Makes you realize you better get your licks in while ya can." Tom held out his hand to Stew, a lump of sugar in his palm. The mule nearly nipped off his hand going for the treat. "Ouch!" Tom yanked back his empty hand. "And here I thought your heroic deeds might have made a decent creature of you!" He scolded the mule. Then he turned to Micah. "And same to you, boy! Didn't your experience teach you nothing?"

"Yeah. Never camp on a creek bank when there's high ground around!" Micah retorted, then his expression twisted in shame. "I'm sorry, Tom. I'm about going crazy with all the soul-searching I've been doing lately. And now to have you preaching at me—"

"The Maccallums been preaching at you a lot?"

"Nah, not really. Not even after I gave Lucie leave to preach all she wanted. It's not them. It's me. Wondering about it all, what it means." Micah went to a nearby stool and plopped down rather dejectedly. "I know something's gonna give soon, and I know it's gonna be me. And it scares me worse than dying did. Tom, what do you think about all this religion business?"

"You're asking a man who's just been hauled from the bowels of death. That ought to make a believer out of anyone." Tom turned and leaned against the wall, facing Micah. "But then again, you are also asking a man who never attended much church and such." He smiled suddenly. "Your pa once thought me a pure and simple heathen. Guess he wouldn't take too kindly to me giving you religious advice. I wish I would have gone to church more, and I just might do it now. But I always have had a mighty high opinion of God. I believe in Him, Micah, because living out in the wilds as I have, it's impossible not to. And I know it was His doing that you and I survived. Why us and not Jed? Can't say, except maybe Jed was more ready than us. And maybe God has something more He wants us for. That's a fearsome prospect."

Micah nodded. "It's all fearsome." He paused, hesitant. He picked up a bit of straw from the ground and rolled it thoughtfully between his fingers. Finally he looked up. "You ever worry, Tom, about what God thinks of all the killing we've done?"

"I ain't never shot at anything that wasn't shooting back," Tom answered.

"I have, Tom," Micah confessed. The admission did not get easier with repetition. "At San Jacinto."

Tom limped over to Micah and laid a hand on his shoulder. "That was a terrible, terrible time, boy. I should have kept you away from that slaughter, but I lost track of you. It was a confused time. Everyone's pain and anger ran so deep for what had been done in the past. I ain't excusing it, but . . . somehow I think God would understand the heart of a fourteen-year-old boy caught in that horror."

"Lucie says God loves me in spite of what I've done," Micah said. "But I just don't think that's enough. I don't know how I can ever make up for what I've done, but there ought to be something to *do*."

"Seems like it, don't it?" Tom shifted uncomfortably.

Micah jumped up. "Sit here, Tom. You oughtn't to stand on that leg for so long."

"Thanks, Micah." Tom eased down on the stool. "I guess they'll be putting ol' Tom out to pasture now."

"Ya ever think about ranching?"

"I got my land allotments up near Austin. I always thought I'd retire there one day. Don't know a blessed thing about ranching, though. I wonder if it's true about old dogs and new tricks. And an old dog with a bum leg to boot!"

"I might give it a try. Reid Maccallum said he'd teach me what I need to know."

"You could do worse for a teacher—or for a father-in-law."

"We'll see about that. I'm a long way from being deserving of a gal like Lucie."

Silence fell between them as the evening shadows lengthened, and it grew dark in the stable.

With a groan, Tom lumbered to his feet. "Best get on before it's too dark to find my way to that bunkhouse." He started toward the door, then paused. "Micah, about that other matter, you know, about religion and all. I'm sorry I couldn't be more help to you."

Smiling, Micah strode up next to his friend. "Just seeing you today helped stir something like faith in me. I'm not ashamed to admit that when I saw you, Tom, I like to have cried."

"You don't say?" Tom was clearly astonished.

"Last time I cried was when my ma died, and I swore then I'd hate too much to ever cry again. Maybe . . ." he mused half to himself, "maybe something is changing in me. God must love me some to give me a gift like you coming back from the dead."

Side by side they hobbled from the stable, one leaning on the other. Micah was exhausted in his body, but there was indeed a stirring in him that seemed a lot like hope.

CHAPTER 36

MICAH WATCHED JACK HAYS RIDE AWAY. They had just finished making a survey of a plot of land by Cutter Creek. Besides being a ranger, Hays was also a surveyor by trade. Micah was not making any commitments, but . . . well, he was bored and needed something to do. It wouldn't come to anything, but thinking about it merely filled time. He certainly had made no mention of the outing to Lucie.

Micah remained in the area, taking another ride around the place. It was a good stretch of land, with abundant grass to graze a decent herd. True, cattle ranching was not going to make a man wealthy, but who could tell what the future might hold? Anyway, Micah was not looking for wealth. Just peace. Would that be found on a ranch? Or was rangering still what Micah wanted to do? Jack had spent most of their day together encouraging Micah to return to the unit now that he was pretty much recovered.

Micah simply did not know what he would do. One thing was certain, he had to move on from the Maccallum place. He no longer needed nursing, and he and Lucie were, well, just getting way too close. The last thing he wanted to do was hurt her. And right now he wasn't certain what would hurt her more, marrying her or leaving her. He knew what would hurt him. The thought of leaving her tore him up inside. Yet he could not think of himself and his own desires in this.

Though he'd had few nightmares in the last weeks, that gunfight with the banditos still haunted him. He still shuddered at the thought of how instinct and pure reflex had caused him to kill those men, especially that last man. He knew it wasn't exactly murder, because in such a position a man did not have the luxury to pause and debate his actions. Survival had propelled him, he hoped. Yet doubt nagged at him.

Regardless, if he was a man whose first instincts were kill or be killed, he was not the kind of man for a genteel woman like Lucie.

He thought of that day on the picnic when he had grabbed his rifle at a mere sound. He'd been ready to kill. There was such a fine line between simple survival and being a killer at heart. Especially in this untamed country where dangers were very real. On which side of the line did he stand? He did not know.

Micah rode up to an oak and reined his mount. He'd seen this tree from a distance while with Hays and wanted a better look. It was old and gnarled with twisted branches, and even with its summer foliage, its long sprawling limbs made it appear barren. It was standing in the middle of a grassy meadow, the only tree for quite a distance. He liked the look of it and was glad it was on his land. He felt akin to it in many ways. But this oak must have strength and deep roots for it to remain green and sturdy so far from water.

Suddenly Micah realized what he had just thought. *His land?* Could he make roots like the oak? Strong enough, deep enough to offer shade and shelter to the woman he knew he loved? Shelter and not strife. They had already had far too much strife.

Shots in the distance grabbed Micah's attention. Riders were galloping in his direction. He saw four Mexicans being chased by three gringos. Micah jumped off Stew and slapped the mule's rump, making him race off away from the chase. Then Micah took cover behind the oak. He could not outrun the Mexicans and he saw no reason to become embroiled in a situation until he knew more. The Mexicans were probably bandits, and the gringos might well be rangers. But the Mexicans *could* be locals, and the gringos could be mere troublemakers.

Not far from Micah, the Mexicans split up, two racing off south while the other two headed north toward Micah's position. The gringos were closer now, and Micah thought he recognized Big Foot Wallace's mule and Bert Long's chestnut. Wallace and one of the rangers took off after the bandits heading south. Bert Long raced north.

Long fired, striking one of the two bandits he was chasing. The Mexican hit the dirt. The remaining bandit took aim. He had a revolver, but Micah saw Long had only used his percussion cap pistol and was going for his second pistol. He could not possibly draw it before the Mexican fired. He'd be dead if Micah didn't do something.

Having no choice, Micah drew his revolver, but in the split second before he fired, he saw the bandit's face. He hesitated, and the bandit got off his shot anyway, and Long fell. Micah fired just as the bandit wheeled his mount around. His shot struck the bandit's horse and the animal reared, throwing his rider into the dirt. The bandit rolled once and, amazingly, as he gained a squatting position, still had his gun in hand and was aiming at Micah, who also hit the dirt. The bandit's shot went astray.

In the next instant both men poised to fire again and at the same moment saw they'd both end up dead if they followed through.

A grim smile twisted the bandit's face. "I think you gringos call this a Mexican standoff."

"It appears to be just that," Micah agreed.

Carefully, each eyeing the other, both men drew to their feet. The bandit cocked a brow, arrogance and disdain marking his features. "I recognize you. Sinclair, isn't it? The man who killed six of my best men in one bloody battle."

"And you are Joaquin Viegas," Micah said coolly. "You've killed a few of my friends as well."

"So now what?"

Suddenly Micah threw his gun into the grass. Viegas could have killed him instantly then but was obviously too stunned to react to the unexpected gesture.

"I ain't gonna kill you, Viegas, so no sense drawing this out any longer." Micah hadn't realized until the instant he tossed down his gun that he was going to do it, but now he realized it was all he could do. All he would do.

"¿Qué es?" mumbled Viegas. "Why?"

"I'm plain tired of killing. Besides, killing you would hurt too many folks I care about."

"What do you mean by this? Speak clearly or I will shoot. I have every reason to kill you for what you did to my men."

Viegas's eyes were hard and steely, but Micah saw something else in them. More than a hint of Lucie's eyes were there. And around Viegas's nose and chin there was Reid Maccallum. But how could Micah explain all he was feeling to his adversary when he didn't understand half of it himself? He could have killed Viegas five minutes ago while he was mounted and aiming at Bert. But he hadn't, and he knew his skill well enough to know when he had fired, he'd missed on purpose, even if at the time he had not pointedly told himself to miss. Had it been instinct? To miss? To spare a life instead of take it?

"Speak, gringo!" hissed Viegas. "My patience wanes."

"I'm acquainted with your family."

"A mere acquaintance would not cause a man to do what you have done, risked what you have risked. Perhaps I have been lured into some trap."

Micah shook his head. Why would this man, this enemy, believe him? Yet if Micah didn't become more convincing, he was going to die. "I happen to be in love with your sister," he admitted. It was the first time he'd ever ventured such words of love, but Micah knew they were true. He wished it could be Lucie hearing this remarkable confession and not a bandit poised to kill him. "I'd marry her if I thought I was good enough for her," he added, feeling suddenly rather cocky.

"You?" exclaimed the bandit.

Micah could not tell if it was shock or fury in the man's tone. Micah snorted dryly. "Guess you'll kill me for sure now. But if it's gotta be that way, then so be it. I'd rather that than risk hurting her."

"And does my sister feel the same toward you?"

"Maybe, but I wouldn't want to speak for her."

"But if she does, would not your death hurt her as well?"

Micah hadn't thought of that. "I only know if you die, especially by my hand, it could destroy her."

Viegas eyed Micah somewhat dubiously but also with a perplexed crease in his brow. His gun hand, however, was still taut and ready.

"I think you speak truly, gringo," Viegas said slowly and thoughtfully. "But I have never known a ranger to be squeamish about killing an enemy—for any reason. And knowing who you are, I realize you could have killed me before. Stories of your abilities have spread, and I doubt you would have shot my horse if you hadn't been aiming at him."

"Well," Micah said, "it's true I wasn't aiming at you, but neither was I aiming at your horse. He turned and got the round that was supposed to go over his head."

"Still, you did not aim at me."

"You and I, Viegas . . . maybe neither of us are killers deep down. Lucie believes in us, anyway. I don't know about you, but I realize there ain't nothing I want more than to live up to her faith in me."

For the first time, Viegas's expression softened. He lowered his gun. "Find your mount and be on your way, Sinclair, before I decide I prefer a different future brother-in-law."

"Gladly, Viegas." Micah whistled, and Stew, who had not wandered far, trotted up to him. Micah mounted.

"Before you leave, Sinclair, I have one piece of advice for you," Viegas said somewhat wryly but also with a note of earnestness. "Get out of the rangering business. I do not want to see my sister made a widow."

"I'll give it serious consideration, amigo." Then Micah added, "And here's some advice for you. Go see your father. He ain't gonna live forever, and it breaks his heart more every day thinking he might never see you again. He loves you, and he don't deserve the pain you've been giving him."

"I, too, will consider—" Viegas stopped suddenly and smiled. "No, I will do it. Very soon."

Micah rode up to where Bert Long lay. He was still alive. Micah hauled him up with him on the mule. Glancing back before he rode away, Micah saw that Viegas had mounted his dead comrade's horse with the man's body secured behind. Viegas then rode away toward the south. Would he go to the Maccallum ranch? Perhaps he was just going south to take care of his fallen comrade's body and then to tie up loose ends, get his affairs in order. It would be a risky prospect for the bandit to go to the Maccallum ranch. It might be his death warrant. Yet Micah felt certain Viegas would go. Viegas did not hate his father.

Micah took Bert to the Maccallum ranch to get patched up. It was the closest destination, and besides, Micah wanted to see Lucie.

"You two gals ought to hang out a shingle," he said to Lucie and Juana as they followed him to his old room. He had Bert Long slung over his shoulder.

"Imagine that!" Juana laughed. "Dr. Juana Herrera . . . hmm, I like the sound of it."

Micah deposited Bert on the bed. The ranger groaned. "Hey, Micah! I ain't no sack of potatoes. Watch it!"

"I don't reckon he's hurt too bad if he can complain like that," Micah said with a chuckle.

Bert had taken a shot in his calf, but the lead had gone cleanly through. There was little bleeding. His worst wound was a nasty gash on his head, which had struck a rock when he fell from his horse. Assured that his friend indeed was not too badly off, Micah beckoned Lucie out into the hall.

"Lucie, I saw your brother today," he said.

"Joaquin!" Fear and excitement collided in her face.

Micah told her about their meeting. "Ain't that the most amazing thing you ever heard?"

"I . . . I simply don't know what to say!" Then, seeming to come to herself, she threw her arms around Micah. "Thank you, Micah!"

"It felt good, Lucie. I know sparing one man don't make up for all the others, but then again, in a funny way that I can't explain, it does. Inside me, it does. But I don't want to analyze it. It was a good thing. That's all that matters."

She lightly kissed his cheek before dropping her embrace and stepping away. "Yes, Micah." She was fairly beaming. "I am so proud of you!"

"I just wanted to let you know I'll be going away for a while," he said. And when the light dramatically faded from her eyes, he quickly added, "Just a few days is all! I'm heading north. I figure its time I took the same advice I gave your brother."

CHAPTER 37

IN NINE YEARS THE PLACE had not changed much. Well, that wasn't exactly true. There were some bright flowers blooming in a small garden by the front steps. And cheery curtains in the windows. There was an altogether inviting look to the place. But still Micah feared that invitation might not be extended to him.

At the edge of the yard he dismounted and walked the mule the rest of the way. He'd barely gotten to the middle of the yard when a squealing little girl came racing toward him from the woods by the house. She fairly screeched to a halt upon seeing him, and all her merry squealing ceased. She appeared to be about ten years old, chubby and rosy cheeked with a mop of golden curls on her head.

Before Micah could address her, another girl jogged into the yard.

"Leah, you give that back to me! I found it—"

Then this girl stopped abruptly as well. Slender and pale with hair the color of strawberries streaked with sunshine, Micah knew her immediately. And she, incredibly, recognized him.

"Micah!" Isabel cried, racing past her sister and throwing her arms around him.

"Yeah, it's me, but I can't believe you recognized me," he said. He felt he surely must have aged a hundred years in nine.

"Of course I do!" She stepped back and smiled up at him. Micah's heart clenched. She looked so much like their mother. Then she held a hand out to her sister. "Leah, this is our brother Micah. You were too little to remember him."

Leah bent her head back to get a good look but still said nothing.

"I have never seen her so quiet," Isabel said.

As if to defy that remark, Leah finally said, "You can't be our brother. You're taller than Papa."

Micah shrugged, not quite knowing how to answer that. "Well, I am your brother, and I am glad to meet you, Leah. You were nothing but a slip of a thing when I last saw you. And you, Issy!" He gave her an astonished look. "You're nearly a full-grown woman. How old are you?"

"Sixteen."

"Well, you've grown into a beautiful young lady, that's for sure." It warmed him that she blushed with pleasure at his compliment. He remembered when she used to look up to him as a big brother. It appeared as if she still might, though he knew he didn't deserve it.

Isabel took his hand. "Come on into the cabin and see everyone else."

"Everyone . . . ?" His throat turned dry as the real reason for his visit suddenly reared before him.

"Except Papa," piped up Leah, appearing to warm to the stranger who was her brother. "He's down to the Hunter place, but he'll be back by supper."

Relief washed over Micah. He knew he was going to have to face the man eventually, but he just couldn't feel disappointed about a delay.

"Lead the way," he said, tying Stew to a post before following the girls up the cabin step.

Inside he was greeted with a buzz of activity, though not chaotic as he remembered when his father had been caring for household matters. Rather, it was a pleasant sound of children's voices, the sizzling of some good-smelling thing on the stove, and the gentle purr of a woman's voice.

"It's all right, Oliver, don't worry, there's more milk." Elise, Micah's stepmother, was bent over the table, her back to the door, a cloth in her hand mopping up obviously spilt milk.

"Mama," Isabel said, "we have a visitor."

Micah was both touched and inexplicably disturbed by his sister's casual reference to Elise as "Mama."

Elise turned, and a look of surprise was immediately replaced by a warm, welcoming grin.

"Micah! Oh, my goodness . . . Micah!" Sudden tears welled in her dark eyes.

" 'Pears I haven't changed much at all in nine years," Micah said dryly.

Elise came up to him, took his hands in hers, and gave him a close appraisal. "Well, you've grown a foot at least. And my"—she let go of one of his hands and fingered the fringe on his buckskin coat—"you certainly have filled out the coat, haven't you?" Her eyes briefly rested on the place on his shoulder where one of the bandito's shots had penetrated and which he had clumsily patched.

"It's served me well," he said, suddenly wanting to turn away so she would not question the damage. But he forced himself to keep on facing her.

"I remember how you had to hitch a belt around you so it wouldn't billow out like a tent," she remarked.

"Yeah." He tried to smile and not remember the life of violence his coat had seen since then.

"Well, you've met Isabel and Leah, now let me introduce you to the rest of the family." She turned to the boy at the table. "This is your baby brother, Oliver."

"Mama, I ain't no baby!" Oliver said.

He was, by Micah's reckoning, nine years old. His hair was light brown and straight except where it curled around his ears and collar.

His eyes were blue-green and remarkably like their father's. He now looked up at Micah with what might well be awe in those eyes.

"Papa says you are a ranger, that you've fought in wars with Mexico and against Comanches."

"I've done some fighting," Micah said uncomfortably.

"That a revolver?" Oliver's eyes focused on the Colt tucked in Micah's belt.

Micah now realized his oversight in not leaving the gun in his saddlebag. It had been wrong to come into this cabin armed. "Yes, it is," Micah said.

"Can I hold it?"

"Not now . . . maybe later." The boy's eagerness disturbed Micah. Did the child with the name that meant peace take more after his brother than his father?

By now three other children had come into the circle, and though they were staring with unabashed curiosity at Micah, they were clinging to Elise.

Elise placed an arm around the oldest of the three. "This is Hannah."

Hannah smiled, gave a little curtsey, but said nothing. She would be ten now, and she was even more pale and frail-appearing than Isabel. Micah returned the smile, and because the girl suddenly began to blush, he thought better of saying anything.

"And these two little darlings are your half brother and half sister," Elise said. "Joseph is four, and Beth is two."

They also smiled shyly but said nothing.

"I'm pleased to meet all of you." Micah looked around the room. "You got any more hiding in the corners?" he asked lightly.

Elise laughed. "Well . . . one where you can't see it yet."

Then Micah noted that Elise was in the family way. Her apron camouflaged it pretty well, but it was plain there was a slight bulge in her midriff. He quickly shifted his eyes away, cursing the heat he felt rising about his ears. He hadn't been so young when his mother had gotten into such a condition not to notice how miserable she had been, especially with Leah and Oliver. But Elise was glowing. The new baby would make seven children for her to care for, even if they weren't all hers. Yet she was still young-looking, even beautiful. It actually seemed as if she was thriving on her circumstance. Part of Micah resented this, yet another part for the first time in his life wondered if his mother had not somehow brought some of her misery upon herself.

No, it couldn't be! His father had been a monster. He had heaped burdens and expectations upon his family that none could bear. Yet why did he sense none of that oppression now in this family?

"Micah," Elise was saying, "we'll be having supper in a couple hours, but would you like something to tide you over? I'm sure you've had a bit of a journey today."

"I did skip lunch," he replied.

Elise had him sit at the table, then she set a plate of cookies and a glass of cool milk before him. As he ate every cookie on the plate and had another glass of milk besides, they visited. Isabel joined them, but the younger children, except Oliver, who remained at the table as well, grew restless and were distracted by other activities.

In less than an hour Micah had heard all the news of neighbors he had known. He shared what little political information and news he'd heard. But the conversation waned, mostly, he realized, because he kept avoiding anything to do with his personal life. Finally he could bear it no longer and lurched to his feet.

"I better see to my mount," he said. "He's been on a long road today, too."

"Oliver can take care of that," Elise offered.

"No," Micah answered quickly. "I mean, my mule is kind of temperamental, so I better do it myself." He headed for the door. Whether Elise, who he recalled as being rather intuitive, understood his need to get away or not, she made no further protest.

She did ask as he reached the door, "You will be staying on for a few days, won't you?"

"If . . . I'd be welcome."

One did not require any special mental abilities to know exactly what he meant.

"I know you will be, Micah."

He knew what she meant, and he hoped it was true.

CHAPTER 38

MORE MEMORIES FLOODED OVER MICAH as he walked Stew to the little stable. He remembered when he and his father and Uncle Haden had built it. He remembered the huge fight that the two men had over him. Haden had left that very day, not to return until the day he took Micah, his mother, and sisters away—away from Benjamin Sinclair.

Now that Micah thought of it, Uncle Haden had never said why he had returned. Benjamin had told him never to come back. But Haden had. And during all the time Haden and Micah had spent together afterward during the war, the subject had never come up. Now Micah wondered. Had Haden come to reconcile with his brother? Had he had a change of heart? One thing Micah did recall of the time spent with his uncle was that he had not once bad-mouthed Benjamin. He had even gently rebuked Micah when he would denigrate the man.

At the time Micah was far too filled with hatred for his father to hear any defense of the man. But now Micah didn't know. He'd come home because he felt he had to, yet he had not consciously decided to forgive his father. He wasn't certain he would, though he had no idea what he would do. Perhaps that was the place Haden had been in when he had returned. He didn't know exactly why he was doing so, only that he had to do it.

Micah took his time with Stew. He removed his saddle and set it on a rack, then he found a brush and meticulously brushed the animal's coat. When he finished, he tied Stew to a post. There was a horse, a different one from any Micah remembered, in one of the two stalls, and Micah figured the other stall would be for Benjamin's mount. He was filling a bucket with some oats when he heard a sharp creak. His hand shot to the pistol still in his belt. Then he remembered there were no dangers in this place, none at least that need be faced with a gun.

"Micah" came Benjamin's resonate voice.

Slowly Micah turned. "Pa."

The two men eyed each other, both wearing impenetrable masks that were hauntingly similar. Micah had thought of a lot of things to say to his father on the journey up from San Antonio, but speech fled him now. Accusations, apologies, venom, sorrow, regret. It all seemed so empty and futile in the face of the man who must surely be Micah's greatest enemy—and his greatest salvation.

It felt as if the silence would crack right down the middle. Then Benjamin spoke.

"I'm glad to see you, son."

"Guess it's time I came back." Micah was yanking words, it seemed, from his very guts, past a lump in his throat as large as a boulder. "I'm glad I'm welcome."

"You were always welcome. No one made you leave."

"Didn't you, Pa?"

Sudden tension sparked like flint striking rock. Then Benjamin smiled, a gesture both ironic and sad but devoid of ire.

"I guess there are ways of pushing a person away without actually doing so. I did make you leave, and I have never stopped being sorry for it."

Micah did not know how to respond to that. He wanted to reach inside himself and find that anger and hatred that had sustained him for so long. But now he knew, if he hadn't before, that he had not come home to stir old flames. God only knew, he could. He wouldn't have to reach down too far to find them and fan them into a mighty conflagration. This man had hurt him—even Benjamin himself did not deny it. The wounds were deep and some even as tender as the arrow wound in his side. The past could not disappear in a word or a gesture. Yet if Micah had learned nothing else from Lucie and from the painful realities of life, he knew it did no good to cling to the destructive forces of hate. He'd come home to make a start at least of quenching flames, not fanning them.

"We've both made mistakes, I reckon," Micah said.

"You were but a child, and I made you learn to hate—" Benjamin's voice broke with emotion. His eyes glistened.

"Don't, Pa!" Micah softly entreated. "We don't need to dwell on the past. Why don't we just start over?"

"The past will always be between us, son. We can't hide from it. Perhaps we don't have to talk about it right now, but we will need to sooner or later. Nevertheless, Micah, I want you to know I love you. Did I ever tell you that . . . except when I was beating you into submission? May God forgive me for that! I love you and always have."

Sudden moisture rose in Micah's eyes. He blinked hard to push it away. Was this new path of his going to turn him into a blubbering idiot? He turned his attention to the bucket of oats, placing it where Stew could easily get to it. He rubbed the mule's face.

In another moment, confident of his control, he said, "I guess we're part of each other, Pa. We can't change that or what it means, for good or ill. I'm sorry I refused to see the love that was always there. I'm sorry I never told you the same." He looked at his father. Still, the words "I love you" were difficult to speak.

Benjamin seemed to understand that. He approached the mule and laid a hand on its flank. "So is this the famous mule that saved your life?"

"You heard about that?"

"Quite a bit after the fact, or I might have come to see you while you were ill. But by the time I heard about the exploit, you were on your feet, and I didn't want to upset you by showing up." He looked over the animal's neck at his son. "You've become fodder for legends, Micah."

"How much have you heard?"

"Enough."

"I ain't proud of any of it."

"I don't judge you, son. Honestly, I don't." They were silent for a few moments, then Benjamin added, "I think supper is nearly ready. Why don't we get back to the cabin?"

In the next three days it was fairly easy for Micah to keep interactions with his father on a safe, light level. Six children offered ample distractions, and all wanted a piece of Micah's time. And he was quite willing to give it. He wanted to get to know his brothers and sisters. He went on walks with them, swam in the creek, and joined them in their daily chores. Oliver, especially, wanted to dog Micah's every move. He nagged Micah about his guns until Micah finally relented and let the boy handle them. That wasn't quite enough, and he got Micah to take him hunting.

The boy's fascination about these things disturbed Micah. Finally one evening after all the children had gone to sleep and he was sharing a quiet cup of coffee with his father and Elise, Micah broached the topic.

He tried to speak casually and lightly. "That Oliver sure has a powerful attachment to my revolver. I found him playing with it the other day, so I hid it up on a high rafter in the barn. It wasn't loaded, but still . . ." His voice trailed away, for he didn't quite know how to verbalize his disquiet.

"Thank you, Micah," Elise said. "He is a bit young for such things."

"I've tried to teach him a bit about guns," Benjamin added. "But, if you remember, I am practically hopeless at shooting, or at least hitting a target. I manage to keep us in meat, but it isn't easy."

"You are better off that way," Micah said grimly. "Sometimes I wish—" He stopped and shook his head. "It ain't no use wishing for what'll never be. I just wouldn't want Oliver to follow in my footsteps."

"I think it might only be that he is enamored with you," Elise said. "He's never had a big brother. And well, with three older sisters, I am sure he is simply in heaven to be around you. He's heard about you. You are kind of a hero to him."

Micah gaped at her with incredulity. "That's terrible!" He jerked his gaze around to meet his father's. His eyes were filled with sudden fire. "You can't have told him about the things I've done! And I can't believe you would have held them up as heroic! I've lost count of the people I've killed, and I certainly can't say now if them or me was on the right side. And even if I thought I was right, no one—no one!—should be as proficient as I am at killing. I'm not a hero! Please tell him I am not a hero!"

"No matter what we tell him, he hears things," Benjamin said. "I've tried to impart to him a sense of right and wrong. But, Micah, I am proud of you, of what you have become in the last few years, especially. It is good to hear that you don't enjoy the taking of life, but you have been a protector of this republic. You have sacrificed greatly to keep this land safe for folks like me and my family here. Perhaps you have crossed some lines and had to deal with matters that were not always black or white, and I see clearly the toll it has taken on you. But because men like you faced these demons, men like me can live in peace. I thank you for that, and that is why you are a hero."

"You don't know everything about me, Pa," Micah murmured, shame still nagging at him.

"I don't need to know," Benjamin replied with intense confidence.

Micah was silent for several minutes as these profound words sunk into his head and his heart. He thought about the things Lucie had told him about God's mercy. He'd been wrestling so with wondering if he could really be accepted by God, if he could ever deserve peace and the genteel life Lucie offered. Then it suddenly occurred to him that his father, if anyone, would know. Micah understood now a little more about how Benjamin had suffered when Rebekah had died and how he'd finally been humbled and changed. If Micah could accept the change in his father, then perhaps it was indeed possible for him to change as well.

"Pa," he said, knowing that the time had finally come to impart to this man what lay on his heart, "Lucie told me that God loves me no matter what I've done. I know she doesn't lie and that she truly believes what she says. But . . . I've done some bad things. It just can't be that easy."

"We punish ourselves far more than God would ever think of doing," Benjamin answered. "And the worst way we punish ourselves is by our inability to accept the simplicity of faith. There is only one requirement to embrace God's love, and that is to believe in it."

"But ain't there some things that are even too much for God?"

Benjamin and Elise exchanged an odd expression, then Elise reached out and laid her hand on Micah's.

"I know for a fact there isn't," she said.

He shook his head, his skepticism obvious that this near saintly woman could not possibly have even a hint of what he meant.

She went on. "Micah, I don't think you know anything of my life before I came to this house."

All he knew, he admitted to himself, was that she showed up one rainy day with a half-dead child in her arms. He knew there were some unsavory men after her at one point, and they had kidnapped her. He'd heard the word "slave" mentioned in undertones, and at fourteen he had come to the conclusion it had something to do with that. But he'd been far too wrapped up in his own misery at the time to take much interest in anyone else's.

He continued to eye her skeptically, almost daring her to shock him. She did.

"I was a prostitute before I came to your home," she said quietly, with a hint of shame in her tone.

Micah's mouth fell open, and he quickly snapped it shut. Then he said, "I thought I'd seen and done it all, that there was nothing out there that could discombobulate me." And he didn't know what stunned him more, the fact that God had accepted Elise or that his father had.

Amusement twitched at her lips, but her eyes remained solemn. "I did not think even God could wipe clean the filth of my life, my very body. But look at me now, Micah. I am clean! Not perfect by any means, but clean. And if that wasn't enough, God also gave me happiness. Have you heard that God's love covers a multitude of sins? Well, I am proof those are more than mere words."

Micah glanced back and forth between his father and Elise. He did not doubt that what she said was true. But for him? Lucie had said so, too. It must be so.

He focused on his father. "Pa, you are sure, then? All I got to do is want that love, that peace, and believe?"

"I am positive, son."

"Then I want it."

Micah stayed on at his father's house for two more days, then felt he was ready to go back south. He saddled Stew and led him out into the yard where the family was gathered to see him off. He hugged his brothers and sisters and promised he'd come back to visit more often. Elise gave him a packet of food, then encircled him with a fond embrace. He put the food in his saddlebag and turned toward his father. There was still a reticence between them. It could hardly be helped after so many years, but Micah was certain he'd be back often now and the healing between them would continue.

He held out his hand, and Benjamin shook it stoically.

"I'll be back," Micah said. He paused, then added, "And you can come south anytime to visit me. In fact, it might be in a few months"—heat began to rise in his neck, but he went on—"well, I might be getting married, and I'd like it if you came. Maybe even . . . you could perform the ceremony."

By the look of joy on Benjamin's face, Micah's halting, awkward words might have been a boon from a king.

"I'd be proud and honored to do so, Micah!"

"I guess I'll be going, then." Micah started to mount the mule, then stopped. He jerked around to face his father once again. "Pa! I do love you!"

Now Benjamin's jaw went slack, but he recovered quickly. "Forgive me, but I've got to hug you, son!" And he did so.

Micah had never felt such a thing in his life. There was power and fierceness in that embrace, but a tenderness, too, as can rarely be found except between two men who are part of one another, bone, blood, heart, and soul.

CHAPTER 39

MICAH WATCHED LUCIE RIDE AHEAD. She had challenged him to a race, but he had slowed so he could take a moment to observe her gallop across the grass. He remembered the time he had first seen her riding with the herd of horses he had been intent on stealing. So much had passed between them since then, but Lucie had not changed. She had been the gentle constant over the years, the light beckoning him through the abyss.

She slowed to a trot and, turning in her saddle, called to him, "What are you doing, slow coach! Don't you dare try to humor me! I can win you in a fair race."

He smiled and spurred his mule up alongside her. "You have won, Lucie! You've won my heart, fair and square."

"Have I? Well, it is the first time you have admitted to it." Her eyes held an impish glint.

"I thought you knew."

"You have been acting mighty peculiar since you came back from your folks' house. But you know me. I never want to be pushy."

He laughed outright, unable to contain his mirth.

She stared at him, a look of utter astonishment on her face. "Micah, I have never seen you laugh before, not like this."

He tried to control himself. When he spoke, just a few bubbles of amusement escaped. "And at your expense, no less. I am sorry."

"Don't be sorry. You must know I love it." Her eyes swept over his features, seeming to see him for the first time. "For a minute there you looked like a boy."

"Maybe I ain't a twenty-three-year-old wizened old man after all. Leastways, I don't feel like it anymore." He stretched his arms out wide and gave a whoop. Stew, misinterpreting the sound, reared, then lurched off at a run. Micah had to fight the reins to get him under control. "Why, you addlebrained, no-account, poor excuse—"

"Micah!" Lucie interrupted in a scolding tone as she rode up next to him. "Don't you say another unkind thing to this dear mule! I won't hear of it!"

"Harrumph!" Micah snorted. "And she says she ain't pushy!" Then he grinned, and his eyes filled with the overwhelming love that was filling his heart. "Lucie, let's ride over to those trees and get off for a spell. I want to talk to you."

They dismounted, tied their mounts, and found a level place in the grass to sit. Lucie brought her saddlebag. Micah brought nothing—no gun in his belt, no rifle in his hand.

The afternoon was warm with a light breeze carrying a fragrance of prairie grass. A flock of white-winged doves flew overhead.

"A feeding flight," Micah said. "We used to hunt them by firing into the swarm. They make good eating if you are hungry enough."

"I like better 'La Paloma,' " Lucie said. "The old Mexican ballad about the doves." She hummed a tune, then in Spanish softly sang a verse.

Micah gazed at her and was reminded of her other heritage. How naturally the Spanish language flowed from her tongue. He had come to have a fair understanding of the language of his old enemies as well. But he felt no enmity for them now. That had all seemed to die with his other old hatreds. He felt no hesitation at all in reaching out to this woman. She represented only love and life and peace to him.

"Micah," she said softly as he continued to stare after she had finished the song, "you look like you have swallowed one of those birds whole."

"I feel a bit like I have, too. Not since I told my father I loved him has there been such a lump in my throat."

"Why is that?"

Her impish grin indicated she must already know the answer to her question. But she had a right to hear it with her own ears, just as his father had.

"Words like that don't come easy to me, Lucie."

"I well know!"

"Anyway, I been wanting to tell you since I came back yesterday. But there was so much else to talk about regarding those amazing days I spent with my family. I still can't believe it went so well." He caught a new glint in her eyes. "You needn't look so smug, even if you knew all the while it would be so. Though I do think you are the wisest, smartest woman—no, person!—I know. I probably won't always listen to you even when I should."

"You probably won't."

"It's already been established how thick-skulled I am."

"Yes . . ."

"You don't have to agree so quickly!" He shook his head and laughed. "All right. See if you agree with this. I love you, Lucinda Maria Bonny Maccallum! Ya hear?" He paused long enough to gasp in a breath as the full import of his own words struck him. "I do love you!"

"And I love you, Micah!"

"But you always have, haven't you?"

"When I wasn't angry at you or confused about you."

"Same here. I've loved you from that instant you fainted in my arms."

"I didn't faint!"

"Oh, maybe you was just faking so I'd hold you." He reached toward her, gathering her into his arms. "Like this . . ."

"Very likely!"

She melted into his embrace, and he marveled at how well they seemed to fit together.

"Only now there is no confusion," she added.

He nodded his agreement.

"Do you want to hear when I first knew I loved you, though I was afraid to admit it?"

Micah nodded his head, his cheek still pressed against her soft hair.

"It was when you gave that little Hornsby baby to Mrs. Wendell. She thought you ran out because you were so glad to get rid of a little nuisance. But I knew better. When you rescued me, I thought there was more to you than a rough horse thief. But in that moment with the child, I was certain. It's funny, but in spite of all the confusion you have caused me in the last couple of years, I was always certain of your tender heart, Micah. You tried so hard to hide it, but you were never very successful."

"That's one thing I'm glad I failed at, then." Reluctantly, he let his arms drop and moved a safe distance from her. "I wish I was better—" Stopping suddenly, he shook his head. "No, I won't go down that road again. I know now I'll never ever be deserving of what God gives me. I'm just gonna accept it."

"That's good to hear."

"Lucie, I want to marry you. You know that?"

"That's also good to hear," she replied just a bit dryly. "Especially since I want to marry you as well."

"I would have been back sooner from Cooksburg, but I made a little side trip. I went by the capital to file some papers. I made claim to a parcel of land."

"You did!" She beamed, then tried to temper it as she added, "I wouldn't have required it of you. I mean, if you felt as if you should continue to be a ranger—"

"What! And be off roaming all over the republic when I got the prettiest, sweetest woman in the world sitting at home? Never!" His expression saddened briefly. "I know it wasn't the whole problem with my parents, but I do know my father's circuit riding took an awful toll on their marriage. I won't make that mistake. But there is more to it. You see, Lucie, I *want* to settle down. I want to be with you and with the family we'll someday have. I'm so tired of roaming. I look back at the long road I've been on, and it no longer has any draw for me, not when looking ahead I can see the light of your smile at the end."

"My goodness! And I thought you were a man of few words!"

"There's one thing, though. . . ." He hesitated over his next words. They were difficult but had to be spoken. He jumped up and paced a bit, wondering if he could find a way to avoid what he meant to say. But he loved her too much to avoid something so important. He turned and faced her with resolve. "Well, I think we should wait a bit before we get married. For your sake, Lucie, because so much has happened to me that I just want to be sure it's all gonna take. Do you understand?"

"Yes, I do, and I love you all the more for saying it. But let's not wait too long. I want my father to walk me down the aisle." She rose, walked to him, and took his hands into hers. "But to be honest, Papa has been so greatly restored since his reunion with my brother, I think he may live forever!"

"Well, don't you worry, Lucie, I don't intend on waiting that long!" He brought her hands to his lips and gently kissed them. "I just don't know how I'm gonna be able to handle all these good things, Lucie!"

"We'll find a way, as we always have."

CHAPTER 40

December 29, 1845

MICAH WAS NERVOUS, SCARED, and exhilarated—all at the same nerve-wracking time. He tried to sit on the couch in the Maccallum parlor, then nearly jumped out of his skin at the sound of a sharp knock at the front door.

Both Micah's father and Reid Maccallum were with Micah. Benjamin volunteered to get the door, telling Reid to rest easy. Benjamin rose, strode to the door, and answered it. Micah heard the voices in the entry.

"Why, hello, Tom," Benjamin said.

"Afternoon, Reverend Sinclair. I heard you was visiting for the Christmas holidays, and I hoped I'd get back from patrol in time to see you."

"So you are still a ranger?"

"Captain Hays talked me into it. How could I refuse when he said he'd rather have me with a bum leg than some green new recruit? But I'm only signed on till the end of the year, then I'm gonna try my hand at ranching."

"Well, come on in. I'm not the host, but I am sure you are welcome."

"How is Mr. Maccallum?"

"Come see for yourself."

In another moment Benjamin and Tom Fife came into the parlor.

"Looks like everyone's here—the menfolk, at least," Tom said. When Reid Maccallum rose and extended a hand, Tom shook it heartily. "You're looking fine, sir."

"I should be. Everyone is waiting on me as if I were a king [illegible] replied.

Tom turned to Micah. "But you look awful, boy—like maybe [illegible] swallowed a cactus whole."

"Well, how do you expect a fellow to feel who's about to become [illegible] father?" Micah snapped.

"Well, sure, I expect—" Tom stopped suddenly and gasped. "Ya mean now? It's happening right now?"

Micah jerked his head toward the back of the house. "Back there."

Now Tom turned pale. "Sakes alive! I didn't mean to intrude—"

But a cry from the back cut him off. Micah jumped up and, pushing past his companions, headed toward the sound. Benjamin caught him.

"Micah, now you can't go rushing in every time there's a sound. You've got to give your wife time to do what she has to do. Elise and Juana are with her and will let you know when to come."

"But she's in pain!" Micah said miserably. "I can't just sit here and listen to her cries." He turned desperate eyes toward Tom. "Tom, she's been at it all night. How much longer can a man stand such a thing?"

Benjamin chuckled. "It's a bit hard on her as well."

"You can do it, boy," Tom said. "Why, I've seen you survive a lot worse."

"Nothing like this. Every time she cries out, I like to die inside." Micah started pacing.

"Let's have some coffee," Reid said helplessly.

But Micah had already consumed several pots of coffee. If he had more, he'd jump down someone's throat, maybe his own. A year ago on Christmas Eve when he and Lucie had married, it had been so wonderful, and each day since had been more wonderful than the last. They'd built a little cabin on their land, an hour's ride from the Maccallum place. They'd even planned on the arrival of their first child. Micah had been lulled into believing life would just be a peaceful Sunday afternoon ride. He'd never imagined that now that he and Lucie were together, he'd ever feel so torn up inside.

"We ain't having no more after this," Micah declared suddenly.

Benjamin and Reid laughed.

"You'll change your mind once it's over," Reid said. "I'll wager Lucie will want more, and she's the one doing the real suffering."

"So, Tom, what brings you out today?" Benjamin asked.

Micah knew it was an attempt to distract him, and he was glad for it.

"I got news, that's what. Texas has been voted in as a state in the Union!"

"That is wonderful!" Benjamin said.

"I was never in favor of statehood," Reid said, "but even I can see that economically we could not have made it alone. And to show my support, I offer a toast." He poured coffee for everyone, and they lifted their cups. "To the twenty-eighth state in the Union. The biggest state and always the best!"

"Here, here!" They all chimed in, even Micah.

"Ya know, Pa," Micah said, "I ain't never told you this, but I'm glad you dragged me here. I love this place, and I am truly glad that my child's gonna be born on this auspicious day." Another cry from the bedroom turned his smile into a grimace. "It will be today, won't it?" he asked shakily.

Suddenly they heard a very different cry. No one stopped Micah now when he nearly dropped his cup and raced toward the room. They all followed instead.

The door opened, and Elise poked her head out. "There you are, Micah—oh goodness, and everyone else, too!"

"Lucie!" Micah said anxiously. "Is she all right?"

"Yes, she is, and she has brought a wonderful, healthy child into the world." She held up the bundle in her arms for all to see.

All the blood in Micah's body rushed right to his head, and suddenly Elise, the door, and everything began to spin. He swayed back. Luckily, the wall of his three friends behind him kept him from falling.

"Are you all right, Micah?" Elise said.

"I think he was about to faint," Tom said, alarm and amusement vying in his voice.

"I-I'm fine. Just fine. . . ." Micah stammered. He made himself stand firm, like a man. Like a . . . father. The thought made his head light again, but he remained stable on his feet.

"Micah, you can come in now," Elise said. "I hope the rest of you gentlemen don't mind waiting a bit so the new family can have some time alone."

Micah did not need another invitation. Brushing past Elise with hardly a glance at the bundle, he strode quickly to Lucie's bedside. She was pale and obviously worn. Her dark eyes seemed larger than usual and were ringed with circles. Her hair lay in damp strands about her face. Yet for all her fatigue, she seemed to glow. Her smile, as always, was like cool, fresh water on a hot summer day. Micah drank it in, reveling in her beauty and in the deeper beauty of the love on the wings of that smile. The love for him! That would never cease to amaze him.

Taking her hand, he sat in the chair by the bed. "You are truly all right, Lucie?"

"Oh yes! Micah, we have a son! I didn't think I could be happier than I was on the day we married, but I am."

"Same here," he said, then her words sank in. "A son?"

"And our Lucie was very brave," Juana said, wiping a cloth across Lucie's forehead. "Now we will leave you two—I mean you three—alone."

Elise brought the baby to the couple. "Would you like to hold him, Micah?"

"Me?" he squeaked, all his fears flooding over him again.

"I happen to know you are quite proficient with babies."

"But this one's different. . . ." His eyes skittered to Lucie. "This one is mine . . . ours. I'm . . . a father."

"Come on, then," Elise prompted. And before Micah could say another word, the bundle was tucked in the crook of his arm.

The two older women then left, and Micah gazed at the child. Impulsively he lifted the blanket wrapped snugly around the infant. A tiny hand popped out. Micah touched the fingers, then looked at the other hand. Then he loosed the feet and counted ten toes.

"He's perfect, isn't he?" Lucie said.

Micah nodded. "It doesn't surprise me at all that anything that is part of you would be perfect. But, Lucie, I can hardly believe I am part of this as well. Something so perfect has come from me! It is far too amazing to even ponder."

"It doesn't surprise me at all, Micah, my love. I always knew there was more to you than met the eye. And in addition to that, our God is the giver of perfect gifts."

"Yes. I among all men should know that!"

"We will name him Jed, like we agreed."

Micah nodded again. And for the first time since that terrible time in Mexico, he was able to smile when he thought about his friend. "I'll bet he is grinning ear to ear over this. Thank you for letting me have this way, this joyous way, to remember my friend." He paused, then added, "But if you recall, what we really agreed on was Jed Joaquin Sinclair. A child of two proud cultures. Oh, and Lucie, there is more yet. Tom just came to celebrate the fact that today Texas has officially joined the Union."

"How wonderful!" said Lucie. "I love the symbolism it all represents. Our little Jed will be a special child, Micah. I know it."

"He *is* a special child!" Micah tucked the blanket securely back around the baby. Out of the corner of his eye he saw Lucie gazing at them. "What is it, Lucie?"

"Oh, I was just wondering what we will name our next special child."

"Next child! Then it's true what everyone said, that you quickly forget all the pain?"

"I forgot the moment I laid eyes on him."

"I kind of did, too." Micah bent down and kissed the babe's forehead. And he meant it in the broadest sense. The past could never be changed, yet God had found a way to heal many of the wounds.

"Well, if you can handle so much happiness, so can I!" Micah said, brushing her smiling lips with his.

Looking for More Good Books to Read?

You can find out what is new and exciting with previews, descriptions, and reviews by signing up for Bethany House newsletters at

www.bethanynewsletters.com

We will send you updates for as many authors or categories as you desire so you get only the information you really want.

Sign up today!